GEORGE P. PELECANOS
Three Great Novels

George P. Pelecanos

A Firing Offense
Nick's Trip
Down by the River
where the
Dead Men Go

ORION

A Firing Offense Copyright © 1992 George P. Pelecanos
Nick's Trip Copyright © 1993 George P. Pelecanos
Down by the River Where the Dead Men Go
Copyright © 1995 George P. Pelecanos

This omnibus edition first published in Great Britain in 2002 by
Orion
An imprint of Orion Books Ltd
Orion House, 5 Upper St Martin's Lane, London WC2H 9EA

ISBN: 0 75285 108 X (Cased)
ISBN: 0 75285 109 8 (Trade paperback)

A CIP catalogue record for this book is
available from the British Library

Typeset at The Spartan Press Ltd,
Lymington, Hants

Printed and bound in Great Britain by
Clays Ltd, St Ives plc

Contents

A Firing Offense

For Emily Hawk

1

Torn lottery tickets and hot dog wrappers – the remnants of Georgia Avenue Day – blew across the strip. At the district line a snaggle-toothed row of winos sat on the ledge of a coffee shop. A poster of the mayor, a smiling portrait in debauchery, was taped to the window behind them. The coke sweat had been dutifully airbrushed from the mayor's forehead; only a contaminated grin remained. My Dart plodded south under a low gray cover of clouds.

I settled my car into a space a couple of blocks down and killed the engine. Several strip joints had closed on this part of the avenue in the past year, ostensibly a reaction to pressure from local citizens' groups. The reality was that frequent, serious ass-beatings and one biker murder had closed down the clubs by way of revoked liquor licenses. Now the street was irreparably lifeless, a sodden butt drowning in the rot of a shot glass. A bathhouse and the Good Times Lunch had survived.

In the Good Times Lunch an industrial upright fan stood in the rear, blowing warm air towards the door. Malt liquor posters hung on the walls, showing busty, light-skinned women held by mustachioed black movie stars. Of the eight stools at the counter, three were occupied by graying men drinking beer from cans, and a fourth by a route salesman in a cheap suit.

Behind the counter were a sandwich block, grill, four baskets hung in a large deep-fryer, and a stocky little Korean named Kim, who walked with his feet wide apart and had forearms that appeared to be made out of brick. I took a seat at one of the remaining stools.

Kim acknowledged me with a slight tilt of his head. I ordered a fish sandwich, fries, and a can of beer. He brought the beer, and I tossed a quarter of it down as I watched him dump the frozen fish and potatoes into the same fryer basket. For the next five minutes I took long sips of beer and occasionally glanced out the window at the mounting north-bound rush-hour traffic on Georgia Avenue.

The only sounds in the carryout were that of the fan and the barely intelligible music coming from Kim's radio, the dial of which was set on WOL. I thought of work, my reprimand, and my indifference to the subject. No one spoke to me.

I guess that was the day everything began to come apart. The day of my reprimand. The day the old man phoned me about the boy.

A rock gets pushed at the top of a hill, and it begins to roll, and then it doesn't matter who did the pushing. What matters is that nothing can stop it. What matters is the damage done. So how it started, I suppose, is insignificant. Because what sticks now is how it ended: with the sudden blast and smoke of automatic weapons, and the low manic moan of those who were about to die.

Earlier in the day, the name 'Ric Brandon' had printed out across the screen of my desk phone, indicating an interoffice call. I had sipped my coffee and let the phone ring several times until the process reversed itself. His name disappeared letter by letter, from right to left. The call was then forwarded up to Marsha, our receptionist. Presently my phone rang again. It was Marsha.

'Nicky?' she said.

'Yes?'

'Ric Brandon's looking for you,' she said tiredly. 'He'd like to see you in his office as soon as you have a minute.' Her words hung in the receiver apologetically.

'Thanks, Marsha.' I picked up my coffee and headed for the john. The sound of printers, typewriters, and distaff voices swirled around me as I stepped down the hall. Passing Marsha's desk, I smiled and tapped the 'Elvis Country' plaque that she had proudly set next to the switchboard.

I pushed open the door to the men's room and moved to the sink to wash up. In the mirror I saw the scuffed-up heel boxes on a pair of wing tips beneath the stall door. They belonged to Seaton, the controller. His trousers were around his ankles as he stood urinating into the toilet. I splashed some water on my face and looked in the mirror: I was thirty years old, and had drunk several beers backed with bourbon the night before.

I had figured out, incorrectly as it turned out, the reason for Brandon's summons. One day earlier he and I and an executive from one of the local factory wholesalers had gotten together for lunch. The executive was one of those corn-fed, brighteyed men who seem to be hired by corporate giants like General Electric specifically for their slack-jawed lack of intellectual curiosity.

4

Our lunch began to deteriorate when the dapper little fellow had bragged about his company's impending contract on, as he put it, 'that Star Wars thing.' Despite a deadly stare and a nudge in the ribs from the equally vacuous Brandon, I plunged head on into a political discussion on the subject, though my enthusiasm was admittedly rooted more in my disgust for the man across the table than in my limited knowledge of the somewhat ridiculous, juvenile image of War in Space. At any rate, the executive's smile, that of a game-show host, faded, as he nervously touched the knot of his yellow tie. Our business lunch had gone immediately to hell.

Now I was about to receive what business people call, without irony, a 'slap on the wrist.'

On my way to Brandon's office I chewed a Lifesaver and passed by the switchboard once again. Over Marsha's desk was a huge, colorful bar graph titled 'Nutty Nathan's Sales Leaders!' I noted with pleasure that Johnny McGinnes' bar was far above the pack.

Ric Brandon's office was rather spartan, with only a calendar hung on the bare walls around his metal desk. The bookshelves behind him housed software and two slim volumes, *A Passion for Excellence* and *See You at the Top*. On the computer table next to his desk was a keyboard, printer, and amber screen displaying the previous day's sales report sorted by store location, salesman, model number, sell price, unit cost, and profit margin.

Brandon smiled his toothy, equine grin as I entered. He was a big-boned Swede from Minnesota, a former high-school athlete who, at twenty-five, had already become soft and fleshy. He wore his navy suits and Johnston and Murphys proudly, and always had an unread copy of the *Wall Street Journal* on his desk. (Once, on a business trip, I had watched him stare glassy-eyed at the front page of the *Journal* for the duration of the flight.) Like many ambitious, recently graduated business majors on their first professional job in the D.C. area, he had a little boy's notion of how a businessman should look and act.

'Close the door and have a seat, Nick,' he said.

I did both. Though he was already taller and broader than me, he had raised his chair higher than the others in his office to gain the psychological advantage, undoubtedly a tip he had eagerly extracted from one of his ladder-climbing guidebooks. He pulled out the bottom drawer of his desk, parked the soles of his wing tips on the edge of it, and leaned back.

'I've got an ad deadline for this afternoon,' I offered, hoping to get it over with quickly.

5

'This won't take long,' he said, segueing into a dramatic pause. I could hear the ventilator blowing and the murmur of the all-news radio station he listened to in his office. 'As the sales manager of this company, I have to do certain things I really don't enjoy doing, but that are necessary in order to establish a continuity of discipline. One of those things is terminating those who consistently and deliberately fail to follow company policy.'

I nodded that I understood, and he continued.

'Yesterday I told you that George Adgerson in our Marlow Heights store was getting to be a real problem – blowing customers out the door, smoking on the floor, not wearing his nametag, things like that – and I gave him several warnings. First thing this morning I walk into his store to let him go, he says to me, "If you plan on firing me, Brandon, you should know that I've spoken to my lawyer, who advised me that if you *do* fire me, you had better be firing all the Caucasian salesmen who break your rules as well."'

'What'd you do?' I asked, forcing down a smirk as I thought of Adgerson, up in Brandon's face.

'Oh, I fired him,' he said casually, with an obligatory and false trace of regret. 'Personnel can deal with his attorney, if he has one. The point is, Nick, he was ready for me. And you tipped him off.'

I stared at my shoes for a while in what I thought would be a fairly reasonable display of humility, then looked up to see Brandon's facial muscles twitching as he awaited my admission. 'Adgerson was a good man,' I said slowly, 'and he wrote a lot of business over the years for Nathan's. When we worked the floor together over on Connecticut Avenue, he had a huge customer following. To let go of a valuable employee just like that, because, I don't know, he blew smoke in somebody's face, or whatever – I just thought the guy deserved to know what was coming down.'

'It's not your job to think of anything when it comes to salesmen and managers. I'll do the thinking in that department, understand?' I nodded, his features softened, and he continued. 'If I didn't like you, Nick, I'd start looking for a new advertising director. I've discussed this with Rosen. He feels that your actions are a serious infraction. I've convinced him, however, that you're salvageable.'

He hadn't, of course, spoken to Jerry Rosen, the company's general manager. He was merely trying to throw a scare into me while at the same time taking credit for being a regular Joe.

'Nick,' he said, 'all I want for you to do is get with the program.' His thumb and forefinger met to form an 'O' as he talked, a peculiarly delicate gesture for such a large man. 'This is a very tough year for us. Margins have eroded to the point where we're working on ten dollar bills. Overhead is way up. And the power retailers are coming to town to put independents like us out of business. What I'm saying is, I need your experience on the team. I'm putting the ball in your court, Nick. What do you think?'

'I think you're overheating the sports metaphors,' I said. Then I shrugged sheepishly and grinned like Stan Laurel.

'I'm serious,' he said. 'I really believe in this company. I want us all to move forward, and I want you to be a part of it.'

Coming from a sales background, I had a natural distrust for managers. I didn't really dislike Brandon; I guess it was something closer to pity. I wanted to tell him to loosen up his windsor knot, sleep with some strange women, and generally act in an irresponsible manner for the next five years. But like many men my age, I was only mourning the passing of my twenties.

'I'll make the effort,' I said. He showed me some teeth, put his hand in the shape of a pistol, pointed it in my direction, and squeezed off an imaginary round. I smiled back weakly and left his office.

I picked up a stack of messages from the front desk, where Marsha had fanned them out in a decorative pattern. On the way back to my own desk I passed a girl from our service department who had an unusually tight and beautifully formed ass. We looked each other over, and I got a smile. As she slid past, I smelled dime-store perfume laced with nicotine.

I looked over the messages at my desk. Two were from radio reps and a third was from a salesman from one of the local papers. My rep at the *Post*, Patti Dawson, had called. I threw all of these messages away but made a mental note to return Patti's call. The last message was from a Mr Pence, a name I didn't recognize. I slipped that piece of paper beneath my phone.

For the remainder of the afternoon I traded retail clichés ('Katie, Bar the Door,' 'Passin' Them Out Like Popcorn') with Fisher, the company merch manager, and finished laying out my weekend ad for the *Post*.

A breathy intern answered the phone when I called the *Post* looking for Patti Dawson. She said that Patti was on the road and that I should try her car phone.

After four tapping sounds and two rings, Patti answered. There was some sort of light pop in the background, Luther Vandross or one of his imitators. Patti kept her car stereo cemented on WHUR.

'What's your schedule like today?' she asked, her voice sounding remote on the speakerphone but characteristically musical.

'I've just finished my Ninth Symphony,' I said. 'Later I'm performing brain surgery on the President.'

'You got any time in your busy day to give me an ad?'

'It's done. I'm gonna cut out early. I'll leave the ad on my desk. You can just drop Saturday's proof here and I'll correct it tomorrow.'

'I'll also drop our new rate card by.'

'Courtesy of those philanthropists at the *Washington Post*?'

'You got it,' she said, her voice beginning to break apart. I said I'd talk to her later, and she said something I couldn't make out, though somewhere in there she used the word *lover*.

I switched off the crane-necked lamp over my drawing table, considered calling Mr Pence, but decided to take his number with me and leave before any more assignments came my way. En route to the stairwell I passed the glass-enclosed office of Nathan Plavin. He was sitting in a high-backed swivel chair with his chin resting on his chest, watching his fingers drum the bare surface of his oak desktop. Over him stood his top man, Jerry Rosen, who was pointing his finger very close to Plavin's chest. Nathan Plavin, the owner of a thirty-million-a-year retail operation, looked very much at that moment like a little boy being scolded.

I looked away, oddly embarrassed for him, and passed by Marsha's desk. Reaching the stairwell, I hollered back to her that I was gone for the day. Marsha yelled to me that Karen had called, but I continued down the steps.

A nearly lifesize cutout caricature of Nathan Plavin dangled from the ceiling at the bottom of the stairwell. I had designed it two years earlier and since then used it in the head of all our print ads and mailers. The caricature depicted Nathan with an enlarged head topped by a crooked crown, overflowing with stereos, televisions, and VCRs. There were dollar bills in his clenched fists, and a wide smile across his fat face. One of his teeth was golden.

Kim brought my food and set it down. The fish had no taste and the fries tasted faintly of fish. I quickly finished my early dinner and brooded some more over another beer. Kim took my money and nodded as I headed out the door.

My apartment was the bottom floor of a colonial in the Shepherd Park area of Northwest. I walked around to the side entrance, where my black cat hurried out from behind some bushes and tapped me on the back of my calf with her nose. I turned the key and entered.

She followed me in, jumped up on the radiator, and let out an abbreviated meow. I scratched the top of her head and tickled the scar tissue on the socket that had once housed her right eye. She shut her left eye and pushed her head into my hand as I did this.

In my bedroom I undid my tie as I pushed the power button on my receiver. The tuner was set on WHFS, and I moved the antenna around on the back of the set to better the reception. Weasel was ending his show, predictably, with some NRBQ from the *Yankee Stadium* LP. I switched over to phono and laid Martha and the Muffin's 'This Is the Ice Age' on the platter.

I walked through my tiny living room to the kitchen. Behind me I heard the four paws of my cat hit the hardwood floor simultaneously with a mild thud. She followed me into the kitchen, jumped up on the chair that held her dish, and sat down. I found a foil-covered can of salmon in the refrigerator, mixed a bit of it into some dry food, and put it in her dish. She went at it after the obligatory bored look and a slow blink of her left eye.

The phone rang. I walked back into the living room and picked up the receiver.

'Hello.'

'Is Nick Stefanos in?'

'Speaking.'

'My name is James Pence,' an old voice said on the other end of the line. I fished his message from my shirt pocket. 'I'm sorry to bother you at home.'

'I received your message at work,' I said. 'Forgive me for not returning your call – I get a load of people calling me all day, trying to sell me advertising space or services. If I called them all back, I'd never get anything done.'

'I'm not selling anything,' he said, though there was a hurried, desperate edge to his voice.

'What can I do for you then?'

'I'm Jimmy Broda's grandfather.'

After some initial confusion I brought Broda up in my mind. He was a kid, late teens, who had worked briefly in the warehouse of Nutty Nathan's. We had struck up a mild sort of friendship after discovering that we had similar interests in music, though his tastes ran towards speed metal and mine to the more melodic. I had chalked that up to the difference in our ages. Broda had apparently quit a couple of weeks earlier. I had not heard from him, assuming he had joined the ranks of

9

other young, low-level employees who tended to drift from one meaningless job to the next.

'How is Jimmy?' I asked.

'Your personnel girl called a couple of weeks ago and said he had not reported to work for two days straight. Asked me if I knew where he was. Of course I didn't know. It wasn't unusual for him not to come home for stretches at a time – the crowd he ran around with and all that.'

I had no idea what he was talking about or what he wanted. I had the urge to excuse myself and hang up the phone right then.

'Two days later,' he continued, 'personnel calls again. She says to inform Jimmy, when I see him, that he's been terminated. Job abandonment, I think she called it.'

'Listen, Mr Pence. I'm sorry Jimmy lost his job—'

'He liked you, Mr Stefanos. He mentioned you at home more than once.'

'I liked him too. But Jimmy probably had a bigger idea of what I am than what's reality. Those guys in the warehouse, they think anybody who works upstairs and wears a tie has a piece of the action. I'm just a guy who lays out ads and buys time on the airwaves. I don't even talk to the people who make hiring and firing decisions. What I'm saying is, I don't have the influence to get Jimmy his job back.'

'I don't need you to you get his job back, Mr Stefanos,' he said. 'I need you to help me find him.'

A long silence followed. He made a swallowing sound, then cleared his throat.

'Why are you calling *me*?' I asked.

'I bought a TV years ago from John McGinnes in your store on Connecticut Avenue. This year I bought a toaster oven from him. He's my man there,' he said with that peculiarly elderly notion of salesman ownership. 'I talked with him yesterday morning. Said he didn't know anything but you might. Said you're pretty good at finding people when you put your mind to it.' I made a mental note to slam McGinnes for that.

'Mr Pence, if you're worried about your grandson you should call the police,' I said with what I hoped was an air of finality.

'Please. Please come see me, only for a few minutes. I have something to give you, anyway. A cassette tape you made for Jimmy.' I remembered it, the usual soft punk and hard pop. Though it was no big deal, the Broda kid had seemed mildly touched when I gave it to him.

10

'I have somewhere to go tonight,' I said, 'But maybe I could stop by for a minute. I mean, if it's on my way. Where do you live?'

'I'm on Connecticut, the first apartment building northeast of Albemarle. Apartment ten-ten. Do you know it?'

'Yes.' It was right up from the store.

'I'll meet you in the lobby then,' he said excitedly.

'Right. Twenty minutes.'

2

My gym bag was in the trunk as I headed down Thirteenth Street. Bob 'Here' was the DJ on HFS and spinning some post-patchuli oil nonsense. I pushed a Long Ryders tape into the deck. The first song, 'Sweet Mental Revenge,' had a guitar break reminiscent of the Eagles, the difference being that the Ryders had testicles. I turned up the volume.

I made a right on Military Road, passed under Sixteenth, and neared the Oregon Avenue intersection where I hung a left into a severely sloped, winding entrance to Rock Creek Park. As kids we had as a rule driven this stretch of the park with our headlights off, navigating by the moonlight that cut a path through the treeline above. God or the dumb luck of youth had always brought us safely through; tonight, even with my hi-beams on, the darkness seemed to envelop me.

At the bottom of the hill I crossed a small bridge and turned left onto Beach Drive. Soon after that I made a right on Brandywine and cut over to Albemarle, cruising by million dollar Tudor houses with dark German and British automobiles parked, like hearses, in their driveways.

At Connecticut and Albemarle I looked across the street to the left. Though there was no foot traffic at this hour, Nutty Nathan's was open. I decided against dropping in on McGinnes. By this time of day the effect of malt liquor and marijuana would have rendered him incoherent.

I parked on Connecticut, an after-rush-hour privilege, and walked across a brownish lawn to a tall, tan-brick building. As a salesman at Nathan's on the Avenue, I had often delivered and installed air conditioners here for the elderly residents of these rent-controlled apartments.

When I entered the first set of glass doors, a guy in the lobby who looked to be on the green side of seventy caught my eye. He motioned to a bored-looking young woman behind the switchboard and a buzzer sounded. I pulled on the second set of doors and entered the lobby.

The old man strode towards me quickly and with deliberate posture, though he looked as if it pained him some to do so. His handshake was firm.

'I'm Nick Stefanos.'

'I knew when I saw you,' he said in a self-congratulatory manner, then looked me over. Either Pence liked what he saw or felt he had little choice; he pointed a slim hand towards the elevators.

We passed an obese young security guard with a seventies Afro who was talking to the woman at the switchboard and ignoring us and all the old people sitting around the bland lobby. The lobby had the still, medicinal smell of a nursing home.

Pence took me to a metal door that led to the elevators and attempted to pull it open. A look of mild panic appeared on his face as the weight of the door knocked him off balance. The security guard said something behind us about the old man forgetting to take his Geritol. We heard the laughter of the guard and the woman at the switchboard as we entered an elevator.

The old man was silent as we rode to the tenth floor, though his lips were moving and there was a slight scowl across his face. He was wearing workpants pulled high above his waist, a white cotton T-shirt, and oxford Hush Puppies that he wore laceless like loafers. The thick leather belt drawn tightly around his abdomen looked water-damaged and was permanently bent in several spots. Time had eaten him like a patient scavenger.

The elevator bounced to a stop, causing Pence to grab the handrail with reluctance. The doors opened, he bolted out and I followed. He stopped at 1010 and with no trouble at all this time negotiated the lock and door.

We entered as he flipped on a master light. The apartment, with its florid, cushiony sofa and armchairs and a curio cabinet filled with delicate porcelain figures, had obviously been decorated by a woman. But a glass caked with milk on the table and the general disarray of the place told me that his wife or companion was gone.

'Have a seat,' he said. I chose one, noticing as I sat that its cushion contained a rogue spring. I remained seated, as none of the other chairs showed better promise. Though it was rather cool, I had the desire to crack a window. His apartment had the smell of outdated dairy products.

'Goddamn security guard,' he muttered, unable to forget the fat rent-a-cop in the lobby. He quit pacing and lit on a seat next to an end table, on which sat a crystal lamp, a TV directory, an ashtray, and a pack of smokes. Pence shook one from the deck directly to his mouth, looked up at me, and said, 'You mind?'

'Not at all.' He lit it with a Zippo and let out a long stream of smoke that continued to pour out erratically as he began to talk.

'You always have to ask now, before you smoke. It seems like every time I light up, in the Hot Shoppes cafeteria, or wherever, some young guy in a suit tells me the smoke's bothering him. I've got to laugh at your generation sometimes. You guys spend all your time in health clubs in front of mirrors, you're repelled by smokers, you drink light this and light that – and with all your health and muscles you're basically a bunch of powderpuffs. Forty years ago I could have kicked your collective asses – with a cigarette hanging out the side of my mouth.'

I looked at my watch and said, 'I don't mean to be rude.'

'Of course. I apologize. I bring you up here and then I ramble like some bitter old man.'

'Don't worry about it. What's on your mind?'

Pence's veined hands clutched the arms of his chair. Some ash from his cigarette fell to his lap. He glanced down to make sure it wasn't live, then looked back at me, making no effort to brush the ash away.

'I don't know how much you really know about Jimmy,' he said. 'His parents were killed when he was eleven, in a wreck on the Beltway, near what they used to call the Cabin John Bridge. He was their only child, and my only grandson.' He stopped to stub out the butt of his smoke.

'Is your wife still alive, Mr Pence?'

He shook his head. 'Janey died a year after we took Jimmy in. I guess you can imagine how hard it was. A man gets set to retire with his woman, all of a sudden he loses her and has to raise a son.' I had a quick, painful image of my own grandfather, a fisherman's cap resting on his huge pinkish ears.

'How did it go for the two of you?'

'Fairly well, from my side of things. Jimmy was an easy boy to raise, easier than my own daughter.'

'Has he ever gone away before without telling you?'

'He's nineteen years old,' he said by way of an affirmative.

'So what makes you think this is any different?'

'I'm not naïve, Mr Stefanos. The kid goes out with his friends, has a few beers, they wind up down at the shore, or Atlantic City maybe, if one of 'em has a few bucks in his pockets. But he always called me the next day, let me know where he was.'

14

I shifted in my seat. 'I'm not a detective, Mr Pence. What Johnny McGinnes was talking about, we did some process serving together a couple of summers ago, for extra cash. It was for kicks mainly, we made a game of it. But I'm not licensed for anything like this. And I told you before that I thought this was a cop job. Unless there's something you're not telling, some reason you can't or won't go to the police.'

He lowered his eyes and lit another smoke. The sound of the Zippo slamming shut echoed in the room. He was squinting through the smoke when he looked back up at me.

'Jimmy has been hanging out with some tough customers,' he said. 'The last couple of months, the guys who came to pick him up, they weren't just kids out to get a little drunk and have a good time. They were different somehow.'

'How so?'

'I don't know exactly. They wore a lot of leather. None of them ever smiled. And the music he started listening to in his room since he met those guys – it was, you know, more violent than what he used to listen to.'

'Go on.' So far, nothing he had described was all that disturbing, and the music probably wasn't much different from the music I used to listen to in the clubs downtown almost ten years earlier.

'He's been staying out all night, listening to music in bars supposedly. The way he looks when he walks in, I don't know. I've done some drinking in my day. He just doesn't look like he's been on a bender. So I can only guess, maybe the boy is mixed up with drugs.'

'Do you know the names of any of his friends?'

'No, I'm sorry. They looked alike to me. All of these guys had crew-cuts, shaved even closer than the kids wore them in the fifties.'

If they were skinheads, they either hung out at the Snake Pit on F Street or at the Corps, which was near National Place. I figured the old man had the kid pegged on his drug use, though there was no way to tell how far he was gone.

'I don't mean to make light of Jimmy's situation, Mr Pence. But I frequented the same clubs and listened to the same kind of music myself. I still do, occasionally. As for drugs, I've used plenty and I came out of it more or less intact.' His eyes seemed to widen, but only for a moment. He was obviously more interested in finding his grandson than in my lapses of morality.

'You *are* making light of this situation. You most certainly are. Because you don't want to take any responsibility here. I *know* this boy. Even if he were on drugs, he would have called. He's in some sort of trouble. If you don't want to get involved, then fine. But don't tell me there's nothing wrong.'

'I admit there could be some problem,' I said. 'And I see your angle for going private. If he's just underground because of drugs, a private cop could get him home and to some help without a possession or intent to distribute rap on his record. But I'm not that person. I paste down pictures of television sets for a living.'

'You *are* the person.' He was on his feet now and close to me. I could smell cigarettes on him and, for the first time, a trace of whiskey. 'Why do you think Jimmy talked to you so much at work?'

'What do you mean?'

'Your background and Jimmy's background – they were very similar. Jimmy told me that you were born overseas. Your parents sent you to the States to live with your grandfather when you were very young, until they could afford to join you. For some reason or another they never made it, and you were raised by your grandfather. Is this correct?'

'Roughly,' I said.

'Jimmy was at that age – he needed someone to relate to. I think he found that a little bit in you.'

'My grandfather died last April,' I said, though I was no longer talking to Pence. The moment his life ended I was doing lines off the bar in an after-hours club on upper Wisconsin Avenue.

I rose from the chair and walked to the window. The traffic had thinned out on Connecticut, the northbound headlights approaching at a relaxed pace.

'I don't know if I'm up for it,' I said. He was silent behind me and I turned to face him. 'I'll ask around downtown. Maybe somebody knows where he is. But that's all, understand?'

'Thank you,' he said, moving towards me and gripping my hand. 'I'll make it worth your while.'

I backed away. 'We don't need to discuss that now. I have somewhere to go. I'll phone you tomorrow.'

I walked out quickly. He was shouting his phone number as I closed the door behind me.

I let the cat in as I stepped into my apartment. I put some dry food in her dish and drank some ice water from a bottle in the refrigerator. Then I took two cold cans of beer with me into the shower.

After leaving Pence, I had driven to a junior-high gym in Northwest to meet Rodney White, a friend of mine who had the curious distinction of being both a physician and black belt. Though I knew next to nothing about tae kwon do, I had done a fair amount of Boys Club boxing, and enjoyed hooking up with White every couple of weeks to spar, provided he showed me some mercy.

We warmed up with some stretching and light movement. Gradually we began making contact and our sparring intensified. After punishing me for a while with hand and foot combinations, he motioned me to stop. We tapped gloves and removed our mouthguards.

'What were you just doing?' he asked. 'You let me back you all the way across this gym. You accepted all of my forward energy.'

'I was letting you kick yourself out. Anyway, I tagged you pretty good at the end.'

He shook his head. 'You had already lost. You start backing up, you're defeated, believe me.'

'I thought I'd use a little strategy.'

'Don't get too wrapped up in strategy. Technicians lose in the street. The winner in a fight is usually determined before the first punch is thrown.'

'Too mystical for me,' I said, adding, 'I'll stick to boxing.'

'Stick to whatever you want, Homeboy. But step on over here and let me show you a little something.'

In the shower I drank the first beer while washing. A bruise had formed on my bicep from a Rodney White side kick, and there was a scratch on my cheek from the nylon tie of his footgear.

After rinsing, I popped the second beer and leaned against the tile wall, shutting the cold spigot off completely. I drank deeply of the icy beer and closed my eyes, as the burning hot water rolled down my back.

3

The next morning I called the office at nine A.M. from a payphone located in the side parking lot of the Connecticut Avenue store. Ric Brandon picked up his extension.

'Hello, Ric?'

'Yes.'

'Nick Stefanos here.'

'Where are you?' In his typically tight-assed manner he was asking why I was late for work.

'I'm on my way to Connecticut Avenue,' I lied, not wanting to get the boys in trouble. None of them had arrived yet to open the store.

'What for?'

'Listen, Ric. All of last night I thought about our discussion yesterday in your office. I think one of the reasons I don't have that team spirit is that I've lost touch with what's going on out in the stores, out on the firing line.' I stopped speaking so as not to make myself sick.

'I understand.' Since he had never been on the 'firing line,' that imaginary, danger-filled zone that lowly salesmen are so keen on referring to, he could not have understood. But I had counted on that.

'What I figure is, I'll get back on the floor for a few weeks, see what's going on again, talk to some customers and find out what they do and don't respond to in our ads.'

'What about your regular duties?'

'What I can't do here, I'll finish up at night. I have a key to the office, and my *Post* contacts can do pickups here at the store. As for any important meetings or appointments, you call me here, I can be back in the office in fifteen minutes.'

'I can see the merit in this,' he said, adding, 'if you apply yourself. Understand that I'd like you to report to Gary Fisher every day as to the merchandising and advertising plans.'

'Sure, Ric. Transfer me over to Fisher then, will you?'

The phone rang several times, then Fisher picked up. In contrast to the dead calm of Brandon's office, I could hear people laughing, typewriters clacking, and unanswered phones ringing in the background. I imagined a cigarette lodged above Fisher's ear.

'Fish, it's Nick.'

'Where the fuck are you?'

'The Avenue. I'm going to be working out of here for a while. I had to get away from the office, man. You know what I mean?'

'Not really. You worked your way up from stockboy to sales to management, now you want to go backwards. Besides, I need you here.'

'I'll still do my job, only I'll do it from the store.'

'You see Electro-World's ad today?' he asked, changing the subject as if to ignore it.

'I haven't seen the paper yet.'

'They ran a TP400 for two ninety-nine, the lousy giveaway artists. Tell the fellas not to match that price, hear? If we have to take a bath, we can wait till Black Friday.'

'You're going to wait till the Friday after Thanksgiving to run a piece that everyone's in the paper with now?'

'I'm not worried,' he said. 'There's gonna be a shortage of low-end goods this Christmas. The Japs and the Koreans are holding back, trying to drive up the costs to the distributors. My guess is, the longer we hold back on the bait, we'll be the only ones in town with the plunder come D-Day. We bring 'em through the door, pass a few out, lose our asses – we'll make it up on add-ons and service policies.'

Fisher was a typical merch manager, a sloppy, chain-smoking, audio-philic pot-smoking salesman who had grudgingly been promoted to management. He was built low to the ground, had an unfashionably long Prince Valiant haircut, and motored around the office pitched forward, his fists clenched like some driven cartoon villain. He would never advance beyond his current position – the image wasn't there, and neither was the will – but he was unequalled at Nathan's in his knowledge of retail.

'What else?'

'That bitch Fein called again from Montgomery County Consumer Affairs,' he said. 'Said we've got to stop using the word *sale* in the head of our ads if we're not lowering our everyday prices.'

'So I'll call this next ad a *blowout*.'

'Perfect.'

'Do me one favor, Fish. Keep Brandon away from me as much as you can, will you?'

'Yeah, sure. But, Nick, why does the guy spell his name R-i-c?'

'I guess R-o-c-k was already taken.'

'Talk to you later.' He hung up.

I walked around the building to the front of the store and looked in the plate-glass display window. Louie Bates, the store manager, had arrived. He ambled along the left wall, switching on television sets.

I pushed on the door and entered. The layout of the floor had changed very little. Up front was a glass case that surrounded a desk and register and contained small electronics and accessories. This was also the cashiers' station and the area where the salesman closed, TO'd to the manager, and wrote deals.

The left half of the store contained televisions of all varieties, portable to widescreen. An aisle in the middle of the store was wide enough to handtruck merchandise from the stockroom to the front door. The right half of the store contained low-end rack stereos, boom boxes, clock radios, auto sound, microwave ovens, small appliances, and other low-commission goods. The entire rear of the showroom housed high-end audio, a 'room' that was simply a thinly carpeted part of the store where the lights had been dimmed. A banner hung across its entrance, grandly announcing this area as 'The Sound Explosion.'

Gold and red, Nutty Nathan's official colors, dominated in the form of signage, tags, and 'accent striping.' Salesmen were at one time required to wear gold sportcoats with a red coat-of-arms sewn across the breast pocket, consisting of a triumvirate depicting a television, stereo, and microwave oven. Salesforce rebellion in the form of filthy jackets forced management to end this dress code. The day this requirement was lifted McGinnes and I had poured lighter fluid on ours and burned them ceremoniously in the parking lot.

The outright tackiness and near-vulgar ambience of Nathan Plavin's stores were intentional. Plavin had picked the colors, as well as the jackets. On slow Saturdays he'd call managers and instruct them to scatter empty cartons in the aisles, to make it appear as if the salesmen were too busy writing up bargains to bother with keeping the place clean. But that had been in the past, when Nathan was more on top of the day-to-day operations of his company.

Louie was surprised to see me in his store. He was a short, barrel-chested guy in his fifties with a wide, flat nose that appeared to have been smashed in by a shovel. As he walked towards me, I noticed that his gut had swelled, his neck had all but disappeared, and there was much more gray salted into his hair. He looked somewhat like a cinderblock with legs.

'You lost, Youngblood?' he asked.

'Could be,' I said, shaking his hand. 'I'll be working here for a couple of weeks. Management wants me to get back in touch with the business.'

'You wouldn't be spying on your old boss, would you, buddy?'

I didn't answer that but said, 'I'll stay out of your way, Louie.'

'Whatever.' He threw up his arms in a gesture of surrender. 'Listen, your boys are late as usual, and I got to get this place open. I'll talk to you later, hear?'

Louie returned to the television section. As the manager of the highest volume store, he knew what his priorities were: to put out fires and to protect his salesmen from the main office. In turn, he was covered by his employees during his daily afternoon visits to his girlfriend across the street in the Van Ness apartments, and on those mornings when his hangovers kept him paralysed with his head on the desk in the 'employee lounge' at the rear of the store.

A small bell sounded as the front door opened, and I turned to see Andre Malone flowing towards me. He was tall, reedy, and elegant in his no-vent sportcoat, silk shirt and tie, reverse pleated trousers, and Italian loafers. Though he'd come out of one of the most hopelessly dangerous sections of the city, there was something of the aristocrat in his bearing and in the way he held his head. He saw me and widened his eyes in mock amazement.

'What's goin' on, Country?' he said. I touched the sharp crease on his trousers and pulled my hand away quickly as if I had been cut.

'You may be the prettiest person I've ever known.'

He smiled and revealed a perfect row of teeth below his Wyatt Earp mustache. 'I see you're doin' all right yourself. Finally wearin' some cotton. Used to be I was afraid to light a match around your polyester ass.'

'I'm on the fast track, Andrew. I *had* to upgrade.'

'What you doin' here, man?' His forehead wrinkled as he found a Newport in his breast pocket and lit it in one fluid movement.

'I'll be working here for a while,' I said vaguely. 'Whatever deals I write, I'll throw to you or Johnny. I might need you to protect me every so often from the office, in case I'm not here.'

'Uh-huh,' he said suspiciously, then jerked his head towards the door as the small bell rang. 'Here comes your boy now.'

Johnny McGinnes blew through the front door and goose-stepped towards the back. There was neither surprise nor delight on his face when he saw me. In acknowledgment he pulled two sixteen-ounce cans of Colt 45 from each of his stretched-out pockets and wiggled his eyebrows in my direction, then continued by.

21

A young woman entered just behind him and hurried around the glass case, stowing her books and purse somewhere below the counter. I caught her eye and she straightened her posture.

Malone was walking alongside Louie now, pleading with him to call an irate customer and iron things out. Louie would eventually do it, but at the moment was torturing Malone with silence. I made my way across the worn gold-and-red carpet squares of the Sound Explosion and entered the back room.

I walked through a short hallway that contained Louie's desk. The hallway led to the 'radio room,' the toilet, and the entrance to the stockroom in the basement. I stepped into the radio room. McGinnes was finishing a swallow of malt liquor and hiding the can behind some stock.

He was not especially tall, though his perfect posture gave the illusion of presence. His clothing was invariably a polyester blend and always clean. He had lost more of his straight black hair since I had last seen him and had begun combing it forward, out and across his forehead in an almost Hitleresque fashion. His tiny nose was set on his flat Mick face like a blemish.

I looked at the top of the Colt can showing from behind a clock radio box. 'It's a little early, isn't it, Johnny?'

'Early as hell. But if they get too warm, I can't drink 'em.' He frowned. 'Fuck are you, my mother?'

'Let's go downstairs, man. I need to talk to you.'

I followed him down the noisy wooden steps to the stockroom. The musty odor of damp cardboard met me as I descended the stairs. Naked bulbs dimly lit erratic rows of cartons. We walked to the far corner of the basement. McGinnes pulled a film canister and a small brass pipe out of his pocket and shook some pot out of the vial.

As a stockboy, I'd spent a good portion of my first two years at Nathan's in this room getting high with McGinnes. I was skinny but cockstrong then, usually wearing some kind of rock-and-roll T-shirt, tight Levi's cuffed cigarette style, Sears workboots on my feet. My stance was straight up, cigarette between the first two fingers with the occasional thumb flick on the filter and a shake of my shoulder-length hair for punctuation. McGinnes had slightly longer hair in those days, and mutton-chop sideburns pointing in towards a Fu Manchu that he wore proudly. As we were always stoned, I considered his every word in that basement to be prophetic, and he played the role of sales sage to the hilt.

Somewhere along the line I became a salesman, worked on commission as I put myself through college, cut my hair, was promoted into management, got married and divorced, and generally lost the notion that life was a series of adventures and opportunities waiting to happen. One day a stockboy in one of the stores called me 'sir,' and I was alarmed by that panicky, universal moment when we realize that aging is real and for all of us, not just for watery-eyed relatives and quiet old men on the bus.

'So,' he said, folding his arms and cocking his hip, 'you're back.'

'I'm on a sabbatical.'

'You're no professor. And you sure as hell ain't no priest, Jim.' McGinnes' speech patterns were peppered with his idea of black slang, which he picked up not from 'the street' but from the pimp sidekick characters on seventies cop shows. Though I had lived in D.C. all my life, I had never once heard a black person use the expression 'jive turkey.' Yet McGinnes used it all the time.

'You remember a guy named Pence?' I asked.

McGinnes smiled nervously. 'Yeah, I know the old cocker. Lives across the Avenue, in those apartments. I sold him a TV set a long time ago, something else this year.'

'Toaster oven.'

'That's right. He came over the other day, wanted to bullshit about his grandson or something.'

'You gave him my name?'

'Yeah, I figured it couldn't hurt. You worked with the kid, maybe you knew something.'

'It's not like you to help somebody out for nothing.'

'He's a good customer, that's all.' McGinnes shrugged, pulled a plastic tube of eyedrops from his pocket, and tilted his head back for a double shot. When he brought his head back down, a tear of eyewash was rolling down his cheek. 'So what are you gonna do, look for the kid?'

I nodded. 'I only told him I'd ask around a little. The old man's afraid the kid's in with the wrong crowd. Drugs, who knows what else. If the cops find him first, he may end up busted. A mistake like that can blow your life before you get out of the gate. Maybe I find him, talk him back home, whatever.'

'So what do *you* get out of this?'

'I knew the kid and the old man's desperate. I can't just blow it off.'

McGinnes glanced over his shoulder at the stairs, tapped another hit into his pipe, fired it up, and tapped out the ashes into his palm. This one he blew towards my face. 'Well, it will be a helluva lot easier to work on that out of here than in the office. You know Louie won't bother you. Besides, you'll be back on the sales floor, which is where you belong.'

'I might have to remind you how it's done.'

'You'd just be reminding me of what I taught you in the first place, son.'

'Remember that day I sold a sandbox to an Arab?'

McGinnes said, 'That ain't shit. What about the time I sold a blind man tickets to a silent movie?'

Louie called down that there were customers on the floor. We approached the stairs, and McGinnes elbowed me in the chest and moved ahead, gunning up two steps at a time. He was giggling like a schoolgirl as he hit the landing.

4

McGinnes chewed on a mint and checked out the floor as we walked down the showroom's center aisle. Malone stood in the Sound Explosion talking to a light-skinned woman in a leather jacket. He had a Frankie Beverly ballad playing through the stereo, and was close up in her face as he made a slow and awkward attempt at moving to the music.

A guy in a hundred dollar suit with disheveled graying hair stood with his hands in his pockets, blinking absently at the confusingly long line of TV screens lit against the wall. He unfolded my *Post* ad from his jacket, stared at it, then returned his gaze to the wall.

'Malone's back there talking himself out of another deal,' McGinnes said. 'I'll take that *yom* over there by the TVs.'

McGinnes walked over to the customer, staying loose but erect. 'How are you today?' he said, extending his hand. The customer shook it limply, without looking McGinnes in the eye.

'Fine. Thank you.'

'Something special for you today?'

'Yes.' The customer jabbed a finger at a spot on my ad. 'I'm interested in the nineteen-inch Zenith for one ninety-nine. Do you have it to look at?'

'Oh yes, it's right over here,' McGinnes said, pointing at the far left section of the wall and gesturing for the man to step ahead of him. McGinnes turned his head back to me, crossed his eyes and hung his tongue out of the side of his mouth. Following the customer, he dragged one leg like a cripple, recovering his posture just as the customer turned to face him.

'What can you tell me about this set?'

'It's a fine set,' McGinnes said, 'and a good value.' The picture on the set was lousy. McGinnes had attached the faulty antenna lead, the one he switched each week to the advertised piece, onto the Zenith.

By comparison the nineteen-inch Hitachi, which sat next to the Zenith, had a beautiful picture. The customer became distracted by this, his head moving back and forth between the two sets.

'Why does that set have a better picture than the Zenith?'

'Oh, they have a high-contrast tube in the Hitachi,' McGinnes said offhandedly.

'What is that?'

'Here, I'll show you.' In his shirt pocket McGinnes had clipped two pens, a jeweler's screwdriver, and a small folding magnifying glass, which he pulled out. He placed it over the tube of the Zenith. The color dots were dull against a pale gray background. McGinnes looked back at the customer for effect, then switched the glass to the tube of the Hitachi. The dots were brilliantly illuminated against a black field.

'Interesting,' the customer said. 'How much is the Hitachi?'

'Two forty-nine.'

The customer frowned, then pushed his glasses up over the bridge of his nose. 'That's more than I wanted to spend.'

'Well, if you think about it, you'd actually be *saving* money by buying this set.'

'How's that?'

'Electronic tuner. The Hitachi's got an electronic tuner, no moving parts in the tuner whatsoever. The Zenith, which is a fine set, don't get me wrong, has an old-style click tuner, the first part to go bad on any TV set.' McGinnes spun the dial on the Zenith harshly. 'You do that every day, it's going to wear out. And when it wears out, it's going to cost you more than the extra fifty bucks you're going to spend initially on the Hitachi. Not to mention, of course, the Hitachi's got a much better picture, which you can see for yourself. With a TV set, when you get it home you're not going to remember what you paid for it. You're only going to know whether you like the picture or not.'

'Well . . .'

'Plus the fact that we're an authorized Hitachi service center for this area. In-home service. And for a small charge, which most customers recognize the value in, you can have a maintenance agreement with Nutty Nathan's to extend that in-home service.'

'I don't think I'd be interested in that. Besides, if the set's as good as you say it is, I won't be needing any service.' The customer smiled smugly.

'Oh, it's a gamble, I know,' McGinnes said quickly. 'And chances are pretty good you'll never need the service. But you know what they're charging now just to walk through your front door? Fifty bucks! Just to step in your house, before they even touch the set! I can give you the names of ten people who've called to thank me personally for suggesting a maintenance agreement. Anyway, I'm not trying to labor the point. You *do* want the Hitachi, though, don't you?' McGinnes was nodding his head rapidly, a trick he used to make the customer do the same.

'Yes, I'm pretty sure I do.' Though McGinnes had closed, the customer's fists were balled defensively in his pockets.

'Where are you from?' McGinnes asked, and smiled.

'From up around Lancaster, P-A.'

'No kidding. I'm from the Allentown area.' The customer seemed to relax as he unhunched his shoulders. McGinnes, an army brat, was from many places, but Pennsylvania wasn't one of them. 'This city's fine, but I tell you, there's a lot to be said for my hometown. I miss the slower life, don't you?'

'Yes, I do.'

'Let's just step up to the counter and get you written up.' They walked to the front of the store, McGinnes' hand gently on the customer's arm.

The young woman who had walked in earlier carrying her books tapped me on the shoulder and I turned. She was half a foot shorter than me and had a brown speck in one of her very green eyes.

'Hi,' she said cheerfully and smiled. Her front tooth was chipped, just a little. She had on short, black, buckled boots, black patterned stockings, and a jean skirt. Her white oxford was open four buttons down, revealing the beginnings of strong, smallish breasts.

'Hi,' I said.

'You working here now?'

"Yeah. For a little while, anyway. My name's Nick.'

'I'm Lee. I work the register and sell add-ons up front. Can you take a sales call?'

I looked around. Malone was still in the Sound Explosion and appeared to be chewing his customer's ear off, literally. McGinnes was up front, writing the deal.

'Where's Louie?' I asked.

'Out making a deposit.'

'I thought he made his "deposit" in the afternoon.'

Lee chuckled. 'This one's monetary, not seminal.'

'What line?'

'Pick it up on two,' she said, jerking her thumb behind her towards the small appliance wall. 'Over there.'

I found the phone and punched in the extension. 'How can I help you?'

'To whom am I speaking?' said an effeminate voice, lowered purposely to affect masculinity.

'Nick Stefanos.'

'And your title?'

'I'm in management,' I said emptily.

'Well, then, maybe you can help me. I have a complaint.'

'What can I do for you?'

'My name is Evan Walters. Last summer your company ran a promotion where you gave away an ice bucket with any major purchase. I came in and purchased a VCR, which I'm very happy with, incidentally. The clerk explained at the time that they were out of ice buckets. Frankly, I was warned by friends beforehand that Nutty Nathan's never lived up to their advertised promises, but I was willing to give you people a try.'

'Who was your salesman, Mr Walters?'

'A Mr McGinnes. He promised me he'd get me my ice bucket. At first when I called he repeatedly said the ice bucket was on its way. Then he stopped returning my calls altogether. I know it's a small matter, but I want what was promised me. And I resent the rather cavalier attitude of your salesman. I don't want to take this any further. I *am* a lawyer,' he growled.

Of course. Announcing one's profession unsolicited was one of the more irritating affectations of eighties Washington.

'I apologize for the delay,' I said. 'Mr McGinnes may have run into some red tape in getting your ice bucket. I happen to know that they *are* in now. I'll call the warehouse manager and have him put one on the transfer truck. You can pick it up tonight.'

'Thank you,' he said curtly, and hung up.

I dialed the main office and punched in the extension of Joe Dane, the warehouse manager. I asked him to find an ice bucket and throw it on the truck that day to the Avenue.

I walked over to the cashier's station where Lee was wiping off the shelves with glass cleaner. McGinnes was handing the customer his receipts.

'Here is a copy of your paid invoice,' he said, 'and this is a copy of your extended maintenance agreement. I've stapled my card to your receipt in case you need anything. You're really going to love your set. It's got the highest IS rating of any set we sell.'

'What *is* the IS rating on this set?' I interrupted. IS stood for 'internal

28

spiff,' a Nutty Nathan's incentive to step off the advertised product onto profit pieces.

'This one's rated at twenty,' McGinnes said coolly, then turned back to the customer. 'If you'd drive around to the back door, I'll load you up.'

Lee touched my arm lightly to move me out of the way. I caught a whiff of her as she slipped by. Malone walked his customer to the front door, his arm around her waist, his hand just brushing her jeans above her crotch. They talked softly for a few minutes, then he held the door open for her, giving her his model's grin.

McGinnes, knocking the dirt off his shirtsleeves, moved quickly up the aisle towards the cashier's station. Malone arrived at the same time. McGinnes folded his arms and stood straight.

'Yeah,' he said. 'Twenty dollar spiff. Another ten bucks commission at four percent. And a fifteen dollar pop for the service policy. Forty-five bucks for fifteen minutes' work.' He paused to rock back on his heels. 'I love this business.'

'I'd love it too,' Malone said, 'if I could get an up.'

'You had an up,' McGinnes said.

'That wasn't no up,' Malone said. 'That was just a freak.'

McGinnes said, 'If you hadn't been dickdancing around with her in the back, you could have had my customer up front.'

'That's all right. I got a date with that redbone tonight. And I'm *still* gonna smoke your ass this month, Mick.'

'Listen, you guys,' I said, 'this is fascinating. But I've got to run across the street for about an hour. Tell Louie when you see him, hear?'

The old man's apartment was in the same disarray as the night before. Sunlight came through the window in a block, spotting the layer of dust that had settled on the cherrywood furniture.

Pence was wearing what appeared to be his only outfit. His hair was slicked down, and he had begun a part on the left side of his head but apparently had given up on the idea halfway through. He smelled of whiskey and Old Spice.

'You want some coffee?' he asked. 'I reheated it when you buzzed me from downstairs.'

'Black, thanks.' He marched into the kitchen with short, quick steps.

I avoided my old chair and found another seat. Near the dining room table, on a two-tiered stand, was the color set McGinnes had sold the old man, a middle-of-the-line profit model. Below it was a videocassette recorder that I didn't recognize. I got up and walked over to the unit to examine it more closely. The nameplate read 'Kotekna,' which I gathered to be a Korean brand. Stamped across a metal plate on the back were the model and serial numbers, the model number being KV100. Following industry logic, 'KV' stood for 'Kotekna Video' and the '100' series indicated that this particular unit resided in the lower end of the line. The recorder was not hooked up to the television.

'Professional curiosity?' Pence asked, returning with two mugs of coffee and setting one down on the small table next to my chair. I got off my knees, crossed the room, and took a seat. Pence sat in his chair, lit a smoke and leaned forward.

'A bad habit of mine, from being in the business too long. My hosts always catch me inspecting their equipment.'

'My grandson bought that recorder for me,' he offered. 'Some kind of employee purchase deal he worked out with your company.'

'That's a new brand for us, then. I didn't even know we sold Kotekna.'

'You sell it, son. It came from your warehouse. Still have the box.' He dragged on his cigarette.

'When's the last time you saw Jimmy, Mr Pence?'

The old man waved some smoke away from his face to get a better look at me. I sipped from the mug of coffee. 'It was the last Monday in September. He left for work at the usual time, near eight.'

'And you haven't heard from him since?'

'No. Your personnel lady called two days later, on a Wednesday.'

'And you made no effort to contact anyone about this until you reached me, two weeks later?'

'That's right.'

'You must have been worried.'

'You're damn right I was worried,' he said, agitated. He butted his cigarette. 'Let's go on.'

'When he said goodbye to you that morning, was there anything unusual about the way he acted, something that may have made you suspicious in any way?'

'I've thought about that a lot since he's been gone, as you can imagine. Jimmy wasn't one to show his affection. But on that last morning he kissed me good-bye and squeezed my hand.'

'Like he knew he wouldn't be seeing you for a while?'

'That maybe. Or he was in trouble and asking for help.'

'Was he carrying anything with him that morning? A suitcase?'

Pence laughed sharply. 'I'm old, Mr Stefanos, not senile. He only had a small knapsack, and he carried that with him every day. Kept a radio in it with earphones.'

'Is his suitcase gone?'

'No.'

'Mind if I have a look in his room?'

'Of course not.'

I followed him down a short hallway. We passed Pence's room on the way. The shades were drawn and the air was stale with cigarette smoke. Pictures of his dead wife and daughter sat on his nightstand, facing an unmade bed. I walked on.

Jimmy's room was brighter than the old man's. The single bed had been made up neatly and clean underwear had been folded and placed upon it. Posters of postpunk bands like the Minutemen and Husker Du were crookedly tacked to the wall. A bulletin board hung over his dresser, on which were tacked ticket stubs from concerts. Many of the stubs were from larger halls, like Lisner and DAR. A few were from the Warner. But the majority of them were small red tickets with black stenciled lettering, reading 'The Snake Pit.'

'You see anything?' Pence asked.

I shook my head and admitted, 'I don't know what I'm looking for. I'll head downtown tonight and ask around. I could use a photograph of Jimmy if you have one.'

'I thought you might,' he said and produced two folded pictures from his back pocket. 'One of him's his graduation picture from Wilson High last year. The other one I found in his drawer. Looks like him at a party or something.'

I took them both. The graduation picture was typically waxen and told me little about the boy, though there was a small skull and cross-bones pinned to his lapel which suggested a touch of insolence, not unusual for someone his age. I thought his eyes drooped rather sadly at the corners.

The second photo said more about the boy. He stood erect, facing the camera, while his companions danced around him. He was unsmiling, had a cigarette cupped in his hand, and wore black motorcycle boots, jeans, and a T-shirt. A shock of hair hung down over his left eye.

I felt a faintly painful blade of recognition slide into my stomach. Though the T-shirt had changed from Led Zeppelin to Minor Threat, this was me, over a dozen years ago.

'This is how he looks now?' I asked.

'Everything but the hair. He shaved it off a couple of days before he disappeared.'

I put the photos in my jacket as we left the room and walked towards the front door of the apartment. The old man grabbed my arm to slow me down.

'I took the liberty of calling some private detective agencies this morning,' he said. 'The average going rate seems to be two hundred a day plus expenses. That will be my offer to you.'

'I'm not a private detective,' I said. 'And anyway, I could run into him tonight. We'll settle later.'

'Yes, of course,' he said halfheartedly. He looked small standing in front of me. My sight lit again on the VCR wires lying unconnected on the floor.

'You want me to hook up that recorder for you before I go?'

'No, thank you,' he said. 'Jimmy brought that to me, and he can hook it up, Mr Stefanos. When you bring him home.'

The old man's eyes were still on me as I closed the door and stepped out into the hall.

5

Malone said, 'Where you been, Country? I done closed two deals while you were gone.'

'I had to see a friend.'

McGinnes was nearby, waiting on a compact stereo customer. He turned to me, cupped his hand around his tie, and began stroking it feverishly, his eyes closed and face contorted.

Louie was moving slowly down the center aisle, his short arms propelling him forward as they swung across his barrel chest. I could hear his labored breathing as he approached.

'Call your girl from the *Post*,' he said.

'You mean Patti?'

'Yeah. She sound nice. She look good too?'

'Too young for you, Louie. You'd stroke out.'

'Never too old to gyrate,' he said, and demonstrated briefly with his hips. 'Matter of fact, I'll be headin' over to Van Ness in a little while to take care of business. Might take the evening off.'

'Fine with me. Who's on the schedule tonight?'

'Lloyd just came in. He's on till six. Malone's on till six too. Lee takes afternoon classes, but she'll be back to work on through. That means you, her, and McGinnes will close tonight. That okay?'

'Yeah.'

'Hey, Nick,' Malone said. 'Check out our boy Void today. He lookin' good.'

Lloyd was absently bumping into displays as he attempted to light his pipe while making his way to the front of the store. The pipe was a Holmesian prop, an Anglophilic symbol that he believed suggested intelligence, but Lloyd was a pale, painfully thin man with a frighteningly deathlike grin, whose appearance more accurately reflected the high school outcast who hears voices from beyond as he clutches his hall locker. Today his woodgrain crucifix hung on a rawhide string over a lime green polyester shirt, hooked up with forest green bell-bottoms.

The boys used Lloyd to run errands and as the butt of their practical jokes, while Louie kept him around to fill in odd hours on the schedule. As a stockboy I had been continually demeaned by him in the presence of customers, when he wasn't critiquing my heathen lifestyle or trying to convince me of his close personal relationship with Jesus. His full name was Lloyd Danker, though all of us, Louie included, called him Void Wanker.

Lloyd looked me over in that way of his that always expressed superiority. The corners of his mouth spread into a sickly smile, and he yanked his pipe out to reveal a cockeyed row of yellow teeth.

'I see management's been good to you, Nick. You've come a long way.'

McGinnes' customer, who was walking, reached the front door, turned his head back, and said, 'Thanks.' McGinnes, waving to the customer, said, 'Thank *you.*' And then, still waving and in a quickly lowered voice, added, 'You piece of shit.'

The customer smiled, waved back, and disappeared down the Avenue.

'Good close, Johnny,' Louie said.

McGinnes shook his head and said, '*Putz.*'

McGinnes, Malone, Louie, Lloyd, and I were standing in a circle near the counter. McGinnes had his arms folded. Louie leaned against a 'stack and sell' microwave oven display with his hands in his pockets. Malone had just lit a Newport and was blowing the first heavy drag towards Lloyd, who stood awkwardly in forced casualness with his hip cocked, the pipe hanging from the side of his mouth like some comic-strip hillbilly.

'Yeah,' Malone said slowly, 'looks like I might be top dog around here this month.' He gave McGinnes a sidelong glance and held it there rather theatrically.

McGinnes said, 'The month ain't over yet, Jim.'

Lloyd jumped in with, 'I'm having a pretty good month myself.'

'Yeah,' McGinnes said, 'for a guy who couldn't sell a lifeboat on the *Titanic,* you're having a good month.'

Lloyd blinked hard and pulled the crucifix out and away from his chest, holding it gently as if Christ himself were still upon it. 'I wouldn't really expect you guys to understand, but there's more to life than closing deals and spasmating your genitals.'

Malone ran an open hand across his own crotch and said, 'Maybe so, but I plan on spasmatin' these motherfuckers tonight, Jack.' He and McGinnes gave each other skin and chuckled. Louie snorted but didn't look up.

Lloyd smiled hopelessly and shook his head. 'Anyone want coffee?'

'Yeah, get me some java while you're out,' McGinnes said, then fanned away Lloyd's outstretched hand. 'I'll get you tomorrow, hear?' Lloyd left the store, looking something like a human scarecrow.

'Thank you, Jeeesus,' McGinnes said.

'Now that Numbnuts is gone,' Louie said, 'maybe we can talk a little business. You girls don't mind, do you?'

McGinnes looked my way and smiled impishly. His eyes were slightly glazed, undoubtedly the result of several more trips to the stockroom.

'I got a call from the office today,' Louie continued. 'The Boy Wonder's been looking at his computer again. "Profit margins have eroded, competition's fierce," blah, blah, blah. Bottom line is, we've got to start selling more service policies, and I mean now. Anything you guys have to do to get the job done, you do it. If a customer refuses the policy, reduce the product price on our copy of the ticket, then add the service policy back into it to bring the total up to its original amount – *after* they've left the store, understand?'

'What if the customer finds out later they "bought" a policy they didn't want?' McGinnes said.

'I'll handle the complaints,' Louie said with a hard stare at McGinnes, 'like I always do.' He glanced out the window. 'Now you all have a nice day, and write some business. In case the office calls, I'm out for the rest of the day, shopping the competition.' Then he was gone, out onto the sidewalk and heading south with his short-man's swagger.

McGinnes and Malone split up. Malone heading back to the relative darkness of the Sound Explosion. McGinnes had picked up a sales call and was gesturing with his hands as he talked into the phone. I went around the counter and dialed Patti Dawson's number on another line.

'Pat Dawson's desk,' her assistant said.

'Is Patti in?'

'She's away from her desk.'

'When you see her, tell her Nick Stefanos called.'

A pause, then, 'She's back at her desk now. Hold please.'

I held for at least a minute and listened to New Age whale music. Finally Patti picked up.

'Where you at, lover?' she said.

'In hell.'

'Back on the Avenue, huh? What's going on?'

'Some free-lance work I couldn't get away with in the main office. I figure I can get the job done from here, with your help.'

'What do you need?'

'You got a pen?'

'Shoot.'

'The ad I mocked up for the weekend,' I said. 'Have ad services run the proofs over to me here at the store. For next weekend I want to pick up an old ad.'

'Which one?'

'Take the ad I did the second week of September, I think the head was "September Savings." Change the head to "October Values."'

'How do you keep coming up with these zingers?' she asked.

'It's pretty scary, isn't it?'

'Yes.'

'Have you got any camera-ready art down there of a horn-of-plenty?'

'I'm sure we do,' she said.

'Good. Put that in the head too, and paste down some art of televisions and radios spilling out of the horn. Got all that?'

'Yeah. It's absolutely brilliant, Nicky. I'm sure it will create a feeding frenzy. Anything else you want, while I'm doing your job for you?'

'That ought to do it.'

'They know in the office that you're just picking up old ads?'

'Patti, Nathan Plavin comes to work every day to be taken out to lunch. I doubt he's even cognizant of the advertising. The GM, Jerry Rosen, he spends more time out of the office than in. I can't even tell you what it is he does. Ric Brandon's just a boy in a suit. Only Gary Fisher keeps an eye on those things, and I'm tight enough with him.'

'Just want to make sure you know what you're doing, lover.'

'Thanks, Patti. Talk to you later.' We hung up.

Lloyd was waiting on a small appliance customer from whom the others had hidden when she walked in. McGinnes was going down the row of televisions, writing something on the tags. I dialed the office, got Marsha, and asked for Gary Fisher.

'Fisher,' he said, catching his breath.

'Fish, it's Nick.'

'Nick! What's happening?'

'Nothing much. Just wanted to keep you apprised of the ad situation.'

'Apprise me,' he said. 'And trim the fat.'

'We're running the "blowout" ad this weekend. Next week we're doing an "October Values" ad very similar to the "September Savings" promotion we ran last month.'

'So you're rerunning the same ad with a different head, right?'

'That's right.'

'As long as it pulls. I don't give a shit what you call it. Sometimes I think the public doesn't read the ads anyway. They see something's going on, they come in and spend money.' He said this almost sadly.

'Well, if you want to make any changes, let me know. By the way, when did we start buying Korean goods?'

'You talking about that Kotekna *dreck*?'

'Yeah.'

'Rosen saw those at the CES show in Vegas and brought in a hundred. One of those "show specials." Every time I'm in the barn, I see them sitting there, I get a pain in my fucking gut.'

'They're not going to turn if they're not out on the floors. They don't even have one on display here in the store.'

'Whatever. It's Rosen's problem. Later, Nick.' He hung up.

Lloyd was still with his customer, an older woman who seemed to be edging away from him in fear. I walked over to McGinnes, who was scribbling unrelated letters and numbers onto the sales tags.

'You remember the system?' he asked, continuing his markings.

'Refresh my memory.'

'The first two letters in the row are meaningless. The next set of numbers is the commission amount, written backwards. The final letter is the spiff code, if there is a spiff. *A* is five, *B* is ten, *C* is fifteen and so on. So, for example, the figure on this tag, *XP5732B* means twenty three seventy-five commission with a ten dollar spiff. That way, you're pitching the bait that doesn't pay dick, you look right beside it on the next model, you see what you get if you make the step, in black and white.' He stepped back to admire his handiwork.

'Just in case one of these customers asks, so we keep our stories straight, what do we tell *them* the numbers mean?'

'Inventory control codes,' he said with a shrug.

'By the way, Johnny. I talked to a buddy of yours today, an Evan Walters. Something about an ice bucket.'

He shook his head and chuckled. 'Yeah, I know him. A flaming asshole. I could have had that fifty-nine cent ice bucket over here months ago, but I thought I'd let his droopy ass stew about it for a while.'

'I've got it coming over on the truck today. He'll be in tonight to get it.'

'Thanks, Nick. You always did like to pick up those loose ends around me.'

'There's an awful lot of them,' I said.

He pinched my cheek, looked at his watch, and smiled. 'Time for my medicine,' he said. Then he turned and headed for the back room.

That afternoon we waited on customers and put out some fires. I closed two deals, though one of them was a write-up, an advertised piece that I was unable to get off of. The boys informed me that the next time I sold the plunder, I would follow it out the door.

On one occasion I TO'd to McGinnes, introducing him as my manager. He held the line by throwing in a TV cart, which retailed for thirty bucks but cost Nathan's nothing.

For another tough customer I excused myself to call the main office for permission to drop a price. I dialed the weather report, listened to the recording, and nodded my head repeatedly, the oldest ruse in a very old book. I returned to the customer with 'permission' to cut the price only ten dollars, and wrote the deal.

I observed the other salesmen and noticed that Lloyd was still awful. The boys were obviously feeding him just enough sales to keep his job for him and thereby keep another hotshot off their floor.

Malone's specialty was audio. His technical knowledge was extensive, though that was also his biggest weakness. He often talked himself out of deals, talked much further than the point at which the customer was giving off buying signals. But his rap was strong and especially impressive to the white clientele. To them he was the ice-cool jazz enthusiast, on a mission to turn the average Joe on to the music via fine audio equipment.

McGinnes, however, worked the floor with the care of a craftsman. He could pick up two or three customers at once, sometimes keeping their attention in groups. All of the tricks were there, and the lies, though these were vague enough to be open-ended in a confrontation. With McGinnes, the customers rarely left the store with what they had intended to buy, but they were satisfied they had made the right decision.

By four o'clock, traffic had heavied up northbound on the Avenue. Most potential customers would be focusing now on maneuvering home through the rush hour. I found the store's Polaroid up front beneath the register. I took it into the back room, had a seat at Louie's desk, and opened his junk drawer. In it I located an Exacto knife and glue.

I brought out the party picture of Jimmy Broda and laid it on Louie's white blotter. Then I swung his desk lamp over the picture and switched on the light.

Carefully, I cut the hair off Broda's head with the Exacto. After that I etched around his body, as I would cut out clip art, and pulled him out of the picture. I shot a Polaroid of the naked wall behind the desk. When it developed, I pasted the bald cutout of Jimmy Broda onto that. It looked a bit as if he were floating in a pale room.

McGinnes walked out of the radio room, belched, and bent over the desk. He popped the top on a tall Colt 45 and placed the can in front of me.

'You need to start drinking,' he said. I had a pull. It was cold and had some bite.

'You just get these?'

'I've got a twelve-pack chilling in a compact in the back. I use it when I close without Louie. You here for the duration?'

'Yeah.'

'Good.' He bent further over the desk and squinted. 'Who's that?'

'Pence's grandson, Jimmy Broda. Or my version of him, the way I think he looks now.'

'Skinny little fucker. Where you gonna start?'

'I'm heading down to the Corps after work. You come along?'

'Sure, why not? But it's a long time before we close this place up.'

'So?'

'So, shit,' he said, pulling the pipe and film canister from his pocket. 'Let's get our heads up.'

6

Lee returned to the store somewhere around five and parked her books beneath the counter. When she had straightened up, she waved to me briefly and smiled, then turned her head away in mock embarrassment. Her hair was uncombed, and I imagined it matted and spread out upon a pillow. My blood pressure jumped a bit, and I kept my stare on her until she felt it enough to look once more in my direction.

When the transfer truck pulled around back, the sales crew typically scattered. McGinnes bolted for the back room, and Lloyd gathered up his things and left for the evening.

As I went to the back door, I noticed Malone and a younger guy talking in the Sound Explosion. The man was wearing a velvet maroon jogging suit and a thick, braided gold chain around his neck. They shook hands for an artificially long time, then Malone buried his fist and its contents into his pocket.

I unloaded the truck with the help of a driver I recognized from the warehouse, a wiry, hard-looking young man who wore his Nathan's cap backwards and had a cigarette lodged above his ear. We worked without speaking until he departed with a tough nod.

I managed the merchandise onto the conveyer belt, which ran parallel to the stairs leading down to the stockroom. I walked alongside the crated goods until they hit a flat, rollered surface at the foot of the stairs, then pulled the power lever back from 'forward' to the 'off' position.

I heard the crush of an empty can and looked up to see McGinnes stepping out of the shadows of the stockroom's far corner. A fresh malt liquor filled one hand, his brass pipe the other. He handed me the can while he filled the pipe.

I drank deeply from the can. He lit the pipe thoroughly and then we traded. The pot was smooth passing my throat but singed my lungs. I made it through half an exhale before coughing out the rest and reaching back for the malt liquor. McGinnes pulled another can out from the inside of his sportjacket, popped the tab, and tapped my can with his. We tipped our heads back and drank.

We stood in a fairly thick blanket of smoke. McGinnes knocked the ash from the pipe onto his palm and filled another bowl. He lit it evenly with a circular motion of the disposable lighter flame he held above it. We smoked that while downing our Colts. I thought of how good a cigarette would taste, then thought of something else. I looked at McGinnes' face and laughed. He thought that was funny, and both of us laughed.

'Evan Walters' bucket came in,' I said. 'You want it?'

'Yeah,' he said, and a wedge of black hair fell across his forehead. 'Give it to me.'

I found it on the conveyer belt, a green cylinder wrapped in plastic and secured with a twist tie. I took a four-point stance, centered the bucket to myself, stepped back, and passed it to him with a surprising spiral. He caught and ran with it halfway across the stockroom, where he stopped and did some weird end-zone strut.

Walking back my way, he let out a short, mean burst of laughter. His jaws were tight and his eyes looked directionless, and I realized, in a sudden rush of alcohol and marijuana, that the way I felt just then was the way *he* felt all the time.

'Evan Walters,' he said, 'deserves a little extra something for all the trouble he's been through.' Mimicking Walters, he lowered his voice to an effete growl, and said, 'I've been calling you for months, Mr McGinnes, and frankly I don't appreciate . . .'

He continued the speech as he unraveled the plastic, removed the top, lowered the bucket beneath his crotch, and unzipped his fly. He looked at me glumly, shut his eyes, found his pecker, and let fly a hard piss-stream into the mouth of the bucket.

'Come on, man . . .'

'I'm a lawyer,' he whined, 'and I want my ice bucket!' McGinnes washed the urine around with a circular motion, then flung it out and across the room where it crackled as some of it hit a hot, naked bulb. He reaffixed the plastic and secured it onto the bucket using the tie.

McGinnes handed me a mint, popped one in his own mouth, and raced up the stairs. I followed him up and out into the showroom. He seemed to be skipping down the aisle, swinging the bucket at his side as if it were a picnic basket. At the front counter he handed the bucket to Lee, who gave us both a disapproving look.

'Give this to a Mr Walters when he comes in tonight,' he dead-panned, then walked away.

I had accumulated some dirt on my sleeves while unloading the transfer truck. Lee knocked it off, then brushed a hand across my chest to finish the job. I noticed that brown speck again in her eye.

'What have you boys been up to?' she asked, her smile twisting to one side.

'Science experiment in the basement.'

'Who's closing tonight?'

'You, me, and Johnny.' She laughed, rather evilly I thought, and walked back behind the counter.

Malone stopped to tuck a silk scarf into his jacket before leaving. He patted his breast pocket, felt the deck of Newports, and showed a look of relief.

'All right, darling,' he said to Lee by way of goodnight, then turned to me. 'All right, Country.'

'What about tonight, Andre? You meet us down at the Corps?'

He shook his head and pursed his lips in an exaggerated manner. 'Uh-uh. I got that redbone freak, uh, young lady, coming over to my joint tonight for dinner, some cognac, you know what I'm saying?'

'Yeah.'

McGinnes yelled from across the floor. 'You gonna get your face wet tonight, Jim?'

Malone said, 'I don't eat nuthin' you can't buy at Safeway.' He looked at Lee and said, "*Pardon* me, darling.' Then he turned and left the store.

The evening progressed with McGinnes and me hammering malt liquors one for one in the back room at an alarming rate. I was through smoking pot for the night, though the damage had been done during our earlier basement sessions. I lost count of our alcohol consumption, but I remember McGinnes racing next door to Mr Liquor (in my opinion, *the* classic name for a spirit shoppe) and coming back with a tall brown bag in his arms, his eyebrows wiggling excitedly like the kid with the fake ID returning to the party.

Lee was reading a textbook up front and pretending to ignore us, thought I caught her looking up often. By seven she had cracked a Colt and had begun nursing it in the back.

We had some traffic that night and initially handled it well. The early customers seemed oblivious to the fact that I was on a tear. I went through a good bit of eyewash and quite a few breathmints.

McGinnes, as was his fashion, became more aggressive and quicker with customers as his sobriety deteriorated, though this did not affect his closing rate. If anything, the alcohol made his rebuttals more certain, less open for debate.

I luckily hit upon several open, friendly customers who were intelligent enough to have an idea of what they wanted when they came through the door and not afraid to spend some money on it if it was offered at a fair price. Consequently, the pressure to perform impossible switches in front of McGinnes was taken off me. The confidence gained after my first sale of the evening spilled over into my rap with subsequent customers, and I was suddenly on a roll.

McGinnes became troubled by my momentum. At one point, when I moved to take an up, he stepped in front of me and threw an elbow into my stomach, keeping a wide smile plastered on his face as he greeted the customers. They turned out to be bait-snatchers who demanded to be sold the plunder, which only served to shake him further.

After he had written them up, he signaled me to the back. I followed him into the radio room, where he cracked two Colts. He handed me one and we both had long pulls.

'What's on your mind?' I asked.

'Nothing,' he said defensively, and reached into his pocket. He unraveled his fist to reveal two orange hexagonal pills, then jabbed that hand in my direction. 'Eat one of these.'

'What is it?'

'Like a 'lude, only not as heavy.' He became impatient. 'It's just a painkiller.'

'Huh?'

'Eat it, you pussy.'

I took the pill and washed it down with a healthy dose of malt liquor. He popped his dry with the flat of his palm.

'So,' I said, wiping something wet off my chin, 'what else did you bring me back here for?'

He finished another swallow. 'I just wanted to tell you that you looked good out there tonight. You haven't lost it, man, you *belong* on a sales floor. That guy in the red jacket, I saw you step him into that Mitsubishi, that was *clean*.'

'He stepped himself.'

'That's the point. You saw where he was going, you kept your mouth shut and let him roll, right into it.' He paused. 'Most of the good ones are dead or selling mattresses, Nick. There aren't many left like you or me.' He winked and tapped my can with his.

'Is this "The Closing of the Sales Frontier" speech?' I asked.

'I'm just telling you that you need to be back on the floor.'

'I don't think that's what I need.'

'You'll be back,' he said smugly. I could only hope that for once the silly bastard would be wrong.

Our small evening rush came and went without major incident. We did walk most of our customers, however, as our pitches and counter-objections increasingly consisted of alcohol logic.

At one point McGinnes nudged me and walked up to the backs of a man and, judging from her magnificent, showcase ass, his extremely attractive companion.

'Fuck your wife for you today, sir?' McGinnes asked cheerfully, running the words together rapidly as if they were one.

'No thanks,' the man said, turning and smiling. 'We're just looking around.'

I had hoped that McGinnes would someday be caught in the act of this, his oldest and stupidest trick. It was his contention that people never listened to the salesman's opening line, so anything could be said, so long as it had the proper speed and inflection. Often he'd pinch the cheek of a toddler and say to his proud parents, 'Cute little cocksucker!' or wipe his brow on a summer day and to sympathetic customers tiredly proclaim, 'Sure is cock today.' And always get away with it.

By eight o'clock the down had kicked in and brought to the fore-front all the alcohol that had preceded it. McGinnes, who had begun bumping into displays and cackling at me from across the showroom, had fallen off what was for him a very wide ledge. It was plain now that both of us were on a violently twisted binge.

When it became obvious that a Japanese-American woman who had wandered in was not going to buy, McGinnes began substituting the *r*'s in his words with *l*'s, and the outraged woman, who probably had more class in her pinky finger than he had in his entirely moronic body, walked out in disbelief. We'd get a letter on that one in the office, and she'd get an apology, most likely from Louie.

A little later, an elderly woman came in and asked for McGinnes. I broke away from Lee up front and found him in the basement. He was walking down a row of stock, jamming his forefinger through the card-board cartons with a scream, before stepping up to the next box and repeating the act. There was blood on the tip of his finger.

I left him in the basement and returned to the floor to help the woman. The false confidence gained from eyedrops and mints had equalized me, and I was doing quite well with her, explaining the features and benefits of a blender as if they were earth-shattering.

I *was* doing well, until I looked over her shoulder. Sporting an utterly absurd smile, McGinnes stood casually behind her, one arm leaning on the display rack, one foot crossed over the other like some cologne cowboy against a split-rail fence. His freckled dick drooped lazily out of his unzipped fly.

In the course of a few seconds, as she turned around to see what I was smirking at, the zipped-up McGinnes stepped forward to greet her. She walked out ten minutes later, receipt and blender in hand.

McGinnes followed me to the Sound Explosion and tried to slap me five. I pulled my hand away.

'There's no way I'm going back on that floor with you tonight.'

'Easy, Jim,' he said and pointed to the front door. A skinny man in an L.L. Bean costume and his very plain, pregnant wife entered the store and approached the counter. He said something to Lee, she handed him the ice bucket, he nodded curtly, and he and his wife exited the store.

Evan Walters ran across Connecticut Avenue to beat the onrushing traffic and left his pregnant wife stranded on the median strip. From the east side of the street he impatiently waved her across.

'Piss-bucket,' McGinnes mumbled.

In the last hour of work few customers came in. Those who did left quickly, undoubtedly recognizing the smell of marijuana that McGinnes was now smoking openly on the sales floor. More letters, apologies, denials.

Just before closing time, McGinnes, who had been ranting about management for the last fifteen minutes ('Fuck Brandon . . . Fuck him!'), emerged from the back room with a Crossman pellet gun that would have exactly replicated a Magnun if not for the CO_2 thumbscrew beneath the grip.

'This is for you, Nutty,' he yelled, and began firing into the cardboard caricature of Nathan Plavin that hung suspended from the ceiling in the middle of the store. McGinnes, who had spent a few troublesome years in the army but had escaped combat duty, was a fair shot, and the pellets tore right through Plavin's ample middle and below to his vitals.

Lee immediately shut down the showroom lights and locked the front door. I took the gun away from McGinnes and instructed him to wait for me up front. Lee walked by with the paperwork, said she'd be a minute, and disappeared into the back room. I followed her back.

She was finishing her Colt and stashing it in a plastic trashbag filled with empties when I walked in. I stood and watched her file the papers. She looked at me and at the gun, which I held at my side.

'What are you going to do with that?' she asked. 'BB me to death?'

'Thought I might bring home a bag of sparrows. For my cat.'

'Sounds yummy. But why don't you put that thing away. He keeps it in the radio room, where he keeps his beer.'

I entered the small room, had trouble finding the light switch, and groped along the wall for the spot of boxes where he usually stashed his paraphernalia. I looked to my left and saw that Lee was behind me, silhouetted against the low-wattage bulb of the office. I clumsily stashed the gun behind the nearest box.

'Where are we going?' she asked. She was near me, and her hand touched mine.

'The Corps,' I said.

'I like that place.'

'Good.' I moved closer and felt her warm breath near my face. 'Thanks for helping tonight. Things got a little out of hand towards the end.'

'You're welcome,' she said.

I cupped the back of her head and kissed her. Her tongue slid over my teeth and along the roof of my mouth. She pulled her mouth away and arched her back. I moved my hand inside the top of her shirt, reached into her loose bra, and lightly skimmed her swollen nipple. She kissed me harder this time and made a guttural sound. I reached down with my right hand and tugged on the back of her upper thigh below her buttocks, pulling her lower body up as she ground it into mine. We broke apart, and she pushed some hair away from her face.

'Well, then,' she said, and exhaled. 'Let's get going.'

7

The three of us were in the front seat of my Dodge and heading downtown. McGinnes had slithered into Mr Liquor and had emerged, mercifully, with only a six of domestic that we were now trying to kill before we reached the club.

'Drink up,' McGinnes explained, as Lee elbowed my ribs. 'The way the prices are in these places now, you've got to catch a buzz *before* you go in.'

I started to push a tape into the deck, but Tom T. was on HFS and launching into a propulsive set that was kicked off by Camper Van Beethoven's reggae-fueled 'One of These Days.' I let that ride.

We cut down Cathedral into the park, then took Pennsylvania Avenue across town. As we passed the White House, McGinnes reached across Lee and blasted the horn on the steering wheel, raising his beer to toast the protesters squatting in Lafayette Park.

In the area of the National Theater I hung a left and drove around the block a couple of times looking for a space. Between the revitalized Willard and the Shops there was plenty of nighttime congestion in this area now. I ignored McGinnes' repeated shouts, over the wailing sax solo in the Cure's 'A Night Like This,' to park illegally, and eventually found a spot.

Lee and I crossed the street and looked back to see McGinnes standing in the middle of the road, his head fully tilted back, his small belly protruding, as he shotgunned the remainder of his beer. A carload of kids honked as they drove by, and McGinnes held out his empty so that they could see the label, then met us on the sidewalk.

There was no midweek line on the polished stone steps of the Corps. A pumped-up guy in a muscle shirt with a blond mass of hair that had been plastered up to resemble a slab of cake opened the door and blocked our way. The thud of heavy bass came out with him.

'Five dollars,' he said coldly, with a fashionably down-under accent. I had loosened my tie and was wearing black pleated trousers with a blue oxford. Lee, of course, looked fine, but when the doorman got a look at McGinnes, polyestered to the nines and swaying on the steps with unfocused eyes, he seemed to regret asking us in.

'We're with the band, mate,' McGinnes said.

'There is no band, *mate*. Five dollars.'

We paid the cover and entered. I noticed the doorman signal another muscleboy next to the bar, pointing in particular to McGinnes, who was already pushing through the crowd to get to one of the several bars around the dance floor. The DJ was blasting some anonymous House music, and the air was very warm and damp.

Little had been done to the club since it had been converted from an old bank, a stately blend of marble and brass. As a child, I had come here with my grandfather, stepping on the shiny floor with deliberate force to produce a cavernous echo that would raise the heads of the elderly, wool-suited tellers. Now it was one of those trendy 'new wave' clubs that had sprouted up in this part of town, and in Adams Morgan and around Dupont Circle, but was in fact less new wave than seventies disco.

We had seen this coming in the early eighties, when Devo had a Top Forty novelty hit with 'Whip It,' when major labels began scrambling to sign any groups wearing skinny ties and funny haircuts. About this time the Angry Young Men, originals like Costello and Graham Parker, were eclipsed by no-talent fops like Duran Duran and Frankie Goes To Holly-wood. We began to realize that those early years, of the punk and new wave emergence, of rediscovering ska and dance music, of separation and alienation from all the youth movements that came before us, were over.

The result was clubs like the Corps (an utterly false play on the term *hardcore*), where Reagan youth, wealthy AU and GW students, and gold-chained, coke-carrying sons of diplomats came to party. These 'struggling' students got their forty dollar 'punk' haircuts, paid the seven dollar cover, drank five dollar, sugar-filled, lime-necked beers, and danced to the new wave beat.

I looked at them on the dance floor, enshrouded by the smoke of dry ice, while New Order pumped through the speakers. They were perfectly coiffed, with their predominately black with-a-touch-of-white uni-forms, fashionably bored looks on their blankly androgynous faces. I turned to the bar for a beer.

When I caught her eye, a woman stepped into a light that was spotted up, which accentuated her thick, white makeup and black hair. She had a tight cocaine smile and lifeless eyes. It seemed a struggle for her to unglue her lips.

'What can I get you?' she asked, wiping in front of me with a bar rag.

'I'll take a Bud.'

She produced one and uncapped it with an opener that was attached to the cooler with fishing line. She reached for a glass but replaced it as I waved it away. I grabbed the beer by the neck, had a long pull, and bent over the bar. She leaned her ear in towards my mouth.

'Joe Martinson still work here?' I asked.

'He's working the upstairs bar,' she said, too loudly.

'How much for the beer?'

She held up three fingers. I tossed four on the bar and made my way around the dance floor to the regally wide marble staircase leading to a balcony that surrounded the entire club. Young coeds with loose coat-of-arms sweaters passed me as I walked up, descending the stairs slowly and unemotionally like drugged debutantes.

I found Martinson behind a barely lit bar in the corner, doing what was probably a placebo shooter with three cute college-age girls. They laid down a ten and walked away. I stepped up to the bar.

I'd got to know Joe Martinson when he was a bartender at a wild, short-lived, tiny dance bar near Chinatown aptly called the Crawlspace. At the time his trademark was cotton oxford shirts, the sleeves of which he tore off and fashioned as headbands. The bar was always sweat-soaked and to capacity with drunks, and opened at about the time that slam-dancing had a brief run of popularity in D.C. The slamming eventually closed it down, when some Potomac preppies came in for 'the experience,' walked out with bloody noses, and sued the owners. But for one hot, lunatic summer, that had been the place to go.

'Nick,' he said, and shook my hand. He was wearing black pants with a tuxedo shirt and a black bow tie. Though working out had heavied him up in the chest and shoulder department, he looked less tough than in his earlier, wiry incarnation. 'What are *you* doing here?'

'I should be asking you that, Joe.'

'A bar is a bar,' he said, 'and anyway, that scene is over with. I wouldn't fit in if it *were* happening.'

'Yeah, but *this* place?'

'If I remember right, you were some kind of art major in college, Nick. I've seen your ads in the *Post*, and let me tell you, you cut out pictures of television sets very artistically.' We laughed uneasily.

'How about a shot,' I said, 'and pour one for yourself.'

'Sure, Nick,' he said, and looked at me as if I didn't need one. I looked over the railing to one of the bars near the dance floor. McGinnes was standing very close to a girl twenty years his junior, talking to her with his mouth very nearly on her ear. Her companion, a

49

pretty young blond boy with a wedge haircut wearing a white mock turtleneck, was standing on the other side of her gripping a beer bottle, angry but timid nonetheless.

Joe Martinson pushed a shot glass towards me and picked up his own. I looked in my glass and then up at him.

'Bourbon,' he said.

'Rail?'

He frowned an of-course-not and said, 'Grand-Dad.'

We did the shots, and I finished my beer before placing the glass back on the bar. A couple walked by me, whispered to each other, and chuckled. Martinson slid a fresh Bud in front of me and I took it by the neck.

They were playing some Pet Shop Boys now and the dance floor was packing up. Lee was with a group of friends at one corner of the floor, pointing up at me and smiling. I raised my beer to them, and one of them laughed and said something to Lee, who winked at me, then turned back to her friends.

I fished the photographs out of my jacket pocket and put the graduation picture on the bar, pushing it towards Joe Martinson.

'You recognize this guy?' I asked.

'No,' he said without thought.

'How about this one?' I placed the doctored, bald-pated photo of Jimmy Broda on the bar. He looked it over and shook his head.

'I don't know him. What's his story?'

'A runaway I'm trying to locate. I think he's hanging with skinheads. Thought you might have seen him.'

'Not in this place. They don't even let those guys through the door anymore, after they came in one night and pushed some gays around. That was one time I took the side of the bouncers here.'

'Where would they hang out?'

'Depending on who's playing, either the Snake Pit or maybe the Knight's Work on Eleventh, in Southeast. But they've pretty much stopped going to the Knight's Work – the Marines down there were kicking the living shit out of those guys on a regular basis.'

'You know any names, people I should be talking to?'

'Not a one, Nick.'

I put the photos in my jacket and looked back over the railing at the floor below. I noticed some movement from the right side of the room. A bouncer was pushing through the crowd, heading for the main bar. The DJ had begun spinning the twelve-inch version of Big Audio Dynamite's 'Hollywood Boulevard.'

50

I looked to the center of the bar. McGinnes had his hands on the blond boy's chest, bunching up his turtleneck and breathing right up in the kid's face. Martinson yelled something to my back as I moved towards the steps.

The stairs were a blur. I was on the dance floor, the strobe light stylizing the rapidly scattering partners as it syncronized its patterns with the song's drum machine.

I was vaguely aware of large bodies converging from the left and right, and as the crowd parted, I saw the redfaced blond boy, unhurt and on his ass. McGinnes had turned back to the bar to resume his drinking.

A big guy with something like an ax handle in his upraised fist brushed by me and moved for McGinnes' back. I swept him with my right foot, and he went down to his knees, dropping the weapon as he fell.

I was grabbed almost immediately from behind in a bear hug. McGinnes had turned and realized what was happening, an apologetic look on his drunken face, accompanied by a slightly sad grin that told me what was inevitably going to go down next. Nevertheless, even as he sensed another bouncer approaching him from behind, McGinnes futilely lunged for the steroid boy whose arms were around me.

McGinnes was dropped with a kidney-shot before he could get near me. The one I had tripped was up and walking towards me, a tight sneer on his chiseled, Aryan face.

I thought, as he took a wide stance and drew back his fist, how easy it would have been to drop him with a front kick square in the balls. But in those few protracted seconds I had decided that there was no way out of the club that night without being pummeled, that I might as well take it, and that McGinnes and me, we had it coming.

The lousy prick went for my nose, but I turned my head and went with the punch, catching it high on the cheekbone. The sound of the blow must have sickened the man holding me, and I was released. Then I was pushed from behind with the momentum of a wave, pushed as if my feet were off the floor. McGinnes was being moved similarly, covering his sides and face with his arms from the potshots that the bouncers were taking as they pushed him forward. Many in the crowd were yelling and laughing, the first sign of spontaneous joy on their faces that I had seen all night.

McGinnes was shoved out the door first. He tripped down the steps and fell to one knee on the sidewalk. I kept my balance as someone gave me a final push, walked down the steps, and helped McGinnes up. He mumbled, 'I'm sorry, man,' and I could see that he really was, and that he was in some pain.

51

His pants were ripped at the knee, exposing a clean scrape beginning to redden with blood. I said calmly, 'Let's just walk,' and we did, crossing the street like two gentlemen to the occasional jeers of the spilled-out bar crowd behind us.

Lee was leaning against my car, fist up to her mouth and tears in her eyes as we approached her. 'I can drive,' I said, and indeed the events of the last few minutes and the cool night air had made me feel somewhere near sober. We slid into the front seat with Lee in the middle. I turned the ignition key and drove slowly down the block.

I headed east. McGinnes found a beer under the seat, cracked it, muttered 'Jesus Christ,' drank, and passed the can. Lee handed me the can after having some herself. We drove in silence for a few blocks. McGinnes, whose right ear appeared to be larger than his left, chuckled as he turned his head my way.

'Well,' he said, 'we showed 'em.'

'That we did, Johnny.'

'Yeah,' Lee said, 'you sonofabitches really showed them.'

She was laughing through her tears and we joined her, a release that had McGinnes alternately coughing, spitting out the window, and laughing some more. He cried, 'Irish bar!' as if there were no other choice.

Lee kissed him on the cheek and then me on my mouth. I continued driving east.

We parked on the corner of North Capitol and F, in front of Kildare's, McGinnes' favorite pub. He almost exclusively drank there now, though at one time his bar had been Matt Kane's on Thirteenth and Mass, until Kane died and McGinnes began complaining about the place being full of 'wine drinkers and ghosts.'

We entered and crossed a crowded room where a tenor was singing, passed the main bar, and arrived in the back room, where a few tables were empty. A waitress directed us to a four-top. We must have looked like accident victims, though no one here seemed to take notice.

The place was all muted greens and mahogany. A geezer with a long gray beard, his cane hung over the back of his chair, drank dark beer methodically, closing his eyes with each sip. A couple of young Scots sat near us, discussing rugby as they washed down their ham sandwiches with mugs of ale.

'Now *this* is a bar,' McGinnes said, winking at Lee and smiling to expose some blood seeping from the top of his gums. He signaled a waitress who arrived with a bartray at her side.

'How you doin', Johnny?' she asked pleasantly with a shockingly thick Irish accent. She was plump with thick calves, but had a lovely, pale freckled face topped by thick, wavy black hair.

'Meg,' he said, gesturing around the table, 'I want you to meet my friends, Nick and Lee.'

She pulled out a wet bar rag and lightly dabbed around my eye. 'You boys had some fun tonight. Better wash that up in the WC.'

'Thanks, Meg,' I said.

'What will you be having, then?'

McGinnes said, 'Is Carmelita in the kitchen tonight?'

'She's just got off. Getting changed now.'

'Tell her I'm out here, Megan. And give us four Harps and four "Jamies."'

'Carmelita's already drinkin' a shift beer.'

'Then send out three Harps,' McGinnes said, 'and four whiskeys.'

I got up and made my way to the stairs that led to the toilets. At the sink I ran some cold water into my cupped hands. Someone in the stall behind me expelled unashamedly as I splashed water onto my face. In the mirror I saw that I had been slightly marked and was a little swollen, but it had all been relatively bloodless. My hair was wild and I dampened it, moving it around into some semblance of uniformity.

When I returned to the party, Carmelita, a girlfriend of McGinnes', with whom I had partied once before, was seated at the table. She smiled when I kissed her on the cheek.

Carmelita was wearing a plaid skirt, pumps, and a crisp white blouse, though she had worked in the kitchen all evening. Her hair, highlighted by a reddish rinse, was set off by her deep red lipstick. Like many other working immigrants in this city, she had an admirably fierce pride in how she looked when not on shift.

She and Lee were talking when McGinnes interrupted, and we raised our glasses without a toast, drinking down the smooth Jamison's whiskey. The amber lager was a fine complement, and we had another round of both.

We left Megan five on twenty and exited Kildare's. McGinnes told us to wait on the sidewalk, entered a smaller bar next door that had off-sale, and emerged with two sixes of longnecks under his arm. He smiled obtusely as he goose-stepped towards us and said, 'Let's get going.'

He and Carmelita climbed into the backseat of my car, cracked some beers, and handed one up to Lee, whose leg was against mine.

'Where we going?' I asked into the rearview.

'Head on up to Mount Pleasant,' McGinnes slurred. 'Carmelita lives that way. And we can drop in on Mr Malone, see how his date's going.'

'Come on, Johnny . . .'

'Do it, Jim,' he ordered, 'and put on some Irish.'

I slid some Pogues into the deck, *Boys from County Hell*, and turned up the volume. McGinnes was trying to sing along to the group's wild, punked-up bastardization of Irish music, but mostly he and Carmelita were fitfully laughing and making out.

Lee passed me the bottle and told me what a great night she was having. I laughed at that but agreed and gave her a long kiss, mightily struggling to stay within the lines of my lane, as Shane McGowan shouted at an ear-numbing volume through my ravaged speakers.

We pulled up to Malone's rowhouse on Harvard Street, a darkish block dimly lit by old-style D.C. lampposts. This was a real neighborhood, a mix of Latins, blacks, and pioneer whites. There was just enough of a violent undercurrent here to keep the aspiring-to-hipness young professionals away and on the fridge of their beloved Adams Morgan, which had become an artificially eclectic mess of condos, 'interesting' ethnic restaurants, Eurotrash discos, and parking lots.

When Malone opened the door of his basement apartment and saw the four of us on his steps, beers in hand with swollen faces and ripped clothing, like some escaped group of mentally ill Christmas carolers, a look of exasperation clouded his face. McGinnes put a shoulder to the door and a beer in Malone's hand, and we all stepped in.

In my Connecticut Avenue days I would often pick Malone up here on my way to work. We'd sit in his living room, trading bong hits and listening to Miles or Weather Report until it was time to go in. Though he'd upgraded his audio and video equipment since then, the apartment was still decorated primarily in variations of red.

Malone wore a silk kimono over pressed jeans and soft leather slippers. His date, who had changed her hairstyle since the afternoon, was standing by the kitchen door and staring in disbelief. McGinnes was already by the stereo, moving the dial off WDCU and undoubtedly searching for something more offensive.

'Just make yourself at home, Mick,' Malone said sarcastically, and McGinnes thanked him.

Carmelita was trying to talk to Malone's date, who was answering in Spanish but not encouraging the conversation. Malone had a cognac in one hand and now a beer in the other. He shrugged, tapped my bottle with his, and drank.

'Thank you *so* much for dropping by tonight,' he said. 'Will you be staying long?'

'We weren't interrupting anything,' I said, 'were we?'

'Bitch has some big red titties,' he whispered, then looked at me more closely. 'Looks like you motherfuckers got into some *shit* tonight, boy.'

I rolled my eyes, took a swig, and stumbled backwards. Lee stopped me with a hand on my shoulder. McGinnes had lost patience locating a radio station and was rifling through Carmelita's purse, finally finding a cassette and slipping it into Malone's deck.

Latin music blared out of the speakers. Carmelita broke away from Malone's date, excitedly crossing the room to McGinnes, who was dragging the center table away from the couch and moving it to a corner of the room. Malone mumbled something and followed his date, who now appeared to be spitting mad, into the kitchen.

The four of us began to dance. McGinnes was spinning and dipping Carmelita. Lee touched my cheek, and we kissed as we moved. Malone raised his voice in the kitchen. McGinnes cackled and turned up the volume.

Malone walked back into the room, moving to the beat, and started dancing with Lee and me, a fresh bottle of beer in his hand.

'Where's your friend?' I shouted.

'She says I "did her dog" by lettin' you in,' he said, and continued dancing.

Another song began that was harder, faster, and courtesy of McGinnes, louder. This was one of those horn-driven salsa numbers that stop periodically on the beat for two seconds of silence, then begin again. The repetition was hypnotic.

Carmelita had one palm on her stomach, the other upraised, shaking her shoulders, sliding her feet four steps, then turning ninety degrees and repeating. We all followed, freezing when the music stopped, then yelling out and continuing our line dance as it began again.

Malone's tongue was out the side of his mouth, concentrating on getting the steps down, then smiling broadly when he had it, yelling, 'No wonder you Latins are so happy. The music be so *festive* and shit!' Carmelita slapped him on the shoulder. Malone explained to McGinnes, 'Carmelita be sayin', "Right on time," ' and he rolled his *r* in imitation of her accent.

The music ended. McGinnes yanked the cassette from the deck, put it in his pocket, and said, 'Let's go.' We gathered our things and stood by the door.

Malone's date was staring contemptuously from the safety of the kitchen doorway. Malone, who looked genuinely disappointed, said, 'Where you goin'? We just beginnin' to throw down!'

McGinnes and I walked over to Malone and poured the remainders of our beers over the top of his head. His date spun furiously and strode back into the kitchen.

I caught one last look at him before we booked. Beer streamed down the front of his face, falling onto his silk kimono. He still had a bottle in his hand, and he wasn't moving, just staring at us and trying to look hard. But he was fighting a smile, the deep dimples of his smooth face betraying him, threatening to implode. The four of us left him just like that, and fell like sailors out Malone's front door.

We dropped McGinnes and Carmelita a couple of blocks from Malone's, on Seventeenth Street. I watched them walk away beneath the light of a streetlamp, his arm around her shoulder, hers around his waist, until they faded into early morning fog.

That is the last I remember of being in my car. Lee drove us to her place, where she undressed me and got me into her shower, then followed me in.

She washed my back, then reached around and soaped beneath my balls. I took the bar from her and noticed with some relief that I was getting a strong hard-on. I began soaping her entire body, lingering on her hard breasts and the insides of her muscular little thighs. I slipped two, then three fingers inside her with ease. She bit my lip and sucked on my tongue with a deft roll of her own. We moved each other around the shower for several minutes, our bodies sliding together, until she put her hands on my shoulders, her back to the tiles, locked her legs around my waist, and pulled me in, arching her lower back to take it all.

When her breathing became more rapid, and her lips turned cold, I hooked a soapy finger into her asshole and she straightened against the wall, eyes toward the ceiling. She yelped, then shuddered, and buried her teeth into my shoulder, while I shot off with a spasm that traveled down my legs.

We held each other until the hot water began to expire. She put on her bathrobe and dried me with a large blue towel.

Sitting on the warm radiator, I watched her in the bathroom mirror as she carefully combed my wet hair. Then I was in a deep, dreamless sleep.

8

I wouldn't have minded dying but that would have taken too much energy. I had dry-mouth and my stomach had less stability than an African government. My hands smelled like a woman and my hair hurt. The part about the smell didn't bother me much.

Lee roused me, handed me a glass of Alka-Seltzer, dropped two aspirin in my hand, and said that breakfast and coffee awaited me in the kitchen. I sat up and washed down the pills with the seltzer.

She had folded my clothes for me, and I began to dress, pausing often to sigh and rub my forehead meaninglessly. She was not wearing my shirt, a morning-after ritual that I find neither cute nor practical, and I suddenly liked her even more for that.

I made it into the kitchen and sat with her at a small table. She looked fresh and was dressed for school in jeans and a gray sweatshirt. I took a sip of the black coffee.

'So,' I said, 'did you take advantage of me last night?'

'Repeatedly.'

'And where am I?'

'Tenleytown,' she said, and after watching my expression as I looked around the nicely appointed apartment, added, 'Yes, Mommy and Daddy take care of the bills.'

'You're from where? New York? Jersey?'

'Long Island. And I'm Jewish. And I go to AU. Do I fit the profile?'

'Yes,' I said, gamely forking in a mouthful of runny eggs. 'I usually don't go out with Jewish girls.'

'Why's that?'

'Generally,' I said, 'they turn me down.'

She chuckled and gave me the once-over. 'I doubt that. Though I wouldn't try asking *anybody* out for a few days.'

'My eye, you mean? Is it that bad?'

'It's not pretty. But it's not terrible.' I got up to pour another cup of coffee, and she asked, 'Anybody going to miss you from last night?'

'Only my cat.'

'Johnny told me about your one-eyed cat.'

'I guess he told you I've been married, too.'

'Yes, he mentioned it. But I would have known anyway. By the way you held me last night when we were sleeping.'

'Forget about the sleeping part,' I said. 'Was I a gentle lover?'

'Yes,' she said. 'Well, sort of. Like a gentle freight train.'

'Sleeping with my wife – I mean, literally sleeping with her – was probably the best part of being married.'

'You must miss it. Even the bad parts must seem pretty good now.'

'Time heals all wounds? Bullshit. I miss some things. But I don't think I miss the bad parts.'

I stewed about that for a while, and she let me. After she finished her coffee, she put on her jean jacket and hung her knapsack over her shoulder. 'Your keys are on the counter and your car is on the street behind this building. I called Louie and told him you'd be late. Do me a favor and wash the dishes, and lock up on your way out.'

'Sure, Lee.'

'I had fun,' she said, in a way that both explained and negated the entire evening. She kissed me on the side of my mouth and exited the apartment.

It was near noon by the time I finished my third cup of coffee, read the *Post*, and did Lee's dishes. I phoned Gary Fisher in the office.

'Fisher,' he said, short of breath.

'Fisher, it's Nick.'

'What's up?'

'I need a favor. How about we meet for lunch today, at Good Times, say a half hour from now?'

'Lunch is fine. What's the favor?'

'Before you leave, go into my desk, top drawer. Collect all the business cards from the media, I've got them all grouped in rubber bands. Bring them with you to lunch, okay?'

'Why can't you come in?'

'I was out last night, things got a little crazy. I got my eye dotted in a bar.'

'Okay, Nick. Half hour.'

*

58

A line at the bank machine made me late. When I walked into the Good Times Lunch, Gary Fisher was already seated at the counter, drinking coffee and hot-boxing a Marlboro. A couple of beer alkies sat near him and stared straight ahead.

I sat on Fisher's right. His hair was pulled back in a ponytail. He was wearing brown corduroys with a tan poly shirt and a brown knit tie squared off at the end. He checked his cigarette, determined there was some paper left over the filter, took a final drag, mashed it, exhaled, and patted the pack in his shirt pocket.

'What's going on, Nick?'

'Nothing much,' I said, removing my sunglasses. He checked me over and shook his head.

Kim walked over with a green checkpad in his hand to take our order and gave me his usual blank nod. In the mirror above the register I noticed the poster of Billy Dee Williams, smiling over my shoulder. Public Enemy's 'Black Steel in the Hour of Chaos' was blaring from the tinny speaker of the store radio. Fisher ordered a burger and fries. I asked for the fish and a bowl of soup.

'Mr Personality,' Fisher said as Kim walked away.

'He's the Korean Charles Bronson. It's a big responsibility.'

'Here,' he said, handing me a paper bag filled with business cards.

'Thanks.' I placed the bag on the counter to my right. 'So, what's happening in the world of electronics retailing?'

He shrugged. 'The manufacturers are trying to soften the blow of price increases by policing "minimum advertised prices" in the newspaper. In other words, they're trying to fix retails by controlling the giveaway artists. It's a good idea, but the FTC will stop that shit real fast once they get enough consumer complaints. If everybody's in the paper with the same price, all the business will go to the house with the biggest advertising budget, the power retailers. Let's face it, the days are numbered for the independents and the "mom and pops."'

Fisher had been predicting gloom and doom since I'd met him. For him it was just an excuse to work longer hours and smoke more cigarettes.

'How's our business been?'

'We're up from last October.'

'What about our turns?'

'We're at about eight turns. But our "open to buy" status shows us at a hundred grand in the hole. I'm telling you Nick, the barn is so full it's ready to burst.'

We had our lunch. Fisher ate his quickly, as if it were a barrier standing in the way of his next cigarette. My fish was tasteless, as usual, but the soup was thick with beef stock and fresh vegetables, and I began to feel human.

'How's McGinnes?' he asked, pushing his plate away and lighting up.

'He's good.'

'Best retail man I've ever seen,' he said almost dreamily. 'Sonofabitch could sell an icemaker to an Eskimo.'

'They miss me at the office?'

'Nobody's throwing themselves out the window. Marsha asks about you.'

'How's my desk look?'

'A ton of messages.'

'Throw them all away when you get back, will you?'

'That's very professional of you.'

'And one more thing.'

'Another favor?'

'No, just a question. You remember that kid used to work in the warehouse, Jimmy Broda?'

'Yeah?'

'When I got back from vacation, he was gone. I borrowed a tape from him, I want to give it back. I heard he didn't show up for work a few days in a row, they let him go.'

'I know who you're talking about,' he said, 'but that's not why they aced him.'

'What do you mean?'

'He was a gonif. They caught him with his hand in the fuckin' cookie jar.'

I thought that over. 'What did he steal?'

'A third world briefcase, what else? Same thing you would have hooked if you were nineteen. He lost his job for a boogie box.'

I turned the check over, which came to seven and change, and left ten bucks on the counter. Kim watched me pay up. There was a gleam in his eye as he stared at my shiner.

My cat, trying to act bored as I approached her on the stoop of my apartment, blinked her eye and looked away. I sat next to her on the stone step and scratched behind her ear. She lay on her side and stretched. It was a fine, warm October day.

I changed into sweatpants, throwing my dirty clothes into a mounting pile next to my dresser. I boiled some water, made coffee, took the mug along with a pen and pad of paper, and sat down next to the phone. In the white pages I found the numbers for the bureaus of licensing in Maryland and D.C.

I dialed the Maryland number and inquired about the requirements for a private investigator's license in that state. A cool, efficient voice explained that one must have had at least five years' experience as a police officer or served under a licensed investigator in an apprenticeship arrangement. I thanked her and hung up.

The woman who answered the phone at the D.C. bureau reluctantly ran down the requirements. 'Basically,' she said, 'you come into our office and pick up a private detective agency package. There are several forms to fill out, and a blank application for a surety bond. You'll need four full-face wallet-sized photos of yourself when you come in. They can't be more than three months old. And you'll need to be fingerprinted down on Indiana Avenue. After that we do a background check as to any felonies or misdemeanors you might have. That takes at least a couple of weeks. If you check out, you get a license.'

'What does the license give me? The right to carry a gun?'

'No, you *cannot* carry a weapon, by law. The license and certificate that comes with it merely legitimizes you.'

'Where's your office and what's it going to cost me?'

'Two Thousand, Fourteenth Street. Third floor. The application fee is one hundred and fifty-eight dollars. Fingerprinting fee is sixteen-fifty.'

I thanked her and replaced the receiver. Then I dialed Pence's number. The old man answered on the second ring.

'What's the dope, Mr Stefanos?' he asked anxiously.

'I may have gotten a lead last night,' I lied. 'I'm going to follow it up this evening. Have you heard from Jimmy?'

'No.'

'Mr Pence, has Jimmy ever been in trouble with the law? Vandalism, shoplifting, anything minor like that?'

It took him a while to answer. 'Not to my knowledge, Mr Stefanos.'

'Good. I'll call you tomorrow.'

'Tomorrow, then,' he said, and hung up.

I dumped the rest of my coffee and walked into my bedroom, the largest single area of my apartment. In my gym bag I located my rope.

I moved my rocking chair from the center of the room, put Tommy Keene's EP, 'Places That Are Gone,' on the turntable, cranked up the volume, and began to jump rope. After twenty minutes my T-shirt was soaked through.

I had a shot shower, shaved, put on clean jeans, a deep blue shirt, and a gray, light wool Rupert Hall sportjacket I had picked up at the thrift shop for twenty bucks. On my way out I carried the cat in one hand and her dish in the other and placed both of them on the stoop. I climbed into my car and headed towards Connecticut Avenue.

The store was strangely quiet when I entered. Lee was behind the counter reading a textbook. Lloyd was sitting on a console watching the soaps. He turned his head, looked me over, and returned his gaze to the television.

Lee looked up from her book and smiled. I walked around the counter and touched her arm, leaned into her and said, 'Do you mind?'

'Not at all,' she said. I kissed her. 'You look better. Do you feel better?'

'Yes.'

'What are you up to?'

'I came in to correct the proofs for the weekend. Then I've got an appointment downtown.'

'The courier delivered this an hour ago,' she said, handing me a thin white bag filled with tear sheets and proofs.

The art department at the *Washington Post* was a sweatshop, and showed it by the manner in which eighty percent of my proofs were returned to me. In this particular proof, several different type styles were inexplicably set, art was shot upside down, key words were misspelled, and most of the phone numbers for the stores were incorrect. For this and other services my company paid a major account 'discount rate' somewhere over $120 per column inch.

I corrected the proof, using the standard editing symbols, then called ad services to tell them where to pick it up. McGinnes arrived at the counter as I hung up the phone. His eyes were watery and he was very pale. He took my jaw in his hand and turned my face to the right.

'Not too bad,' he said.

'No. It will be gone in a couple of days.'

'I wish I could say the same. The guy who dropped me *knew* what he was doing.'

'You hurting?'

'Some,' he said. 'I pissed a little blood this morning.'

'You should have a doctor check it out.'

'I'm on medication right now.'

'I know,' I said. 'I can smell it on you.'

I shook his hand and said good-bye to Lee. Lloyd kept his eyes on the television, his mouth piped and jaw ajut, like an emaciated Douglas MacArthur.

*

I spent the remainder of the afternoon running between offices down-town, standing in lines, being fingerprinted, and filling out forms in triplicate. By the time I was finished my hangover was gone, and the previous night's activities had become a romantic memory. Which is to say that I was ready, once again, for a drink.

But first I had to make another stop, to see a guy McGinnes and I knew, a whale of a man who went by the alliterative name of Fat Fred.

9

Souvenir City was a small shop on Ninth between F and G run by Fat Fred, whose real name was the somehow even less appealing Fred Bort. Fat Fred had worked with McGinnes and me on the Avenue for a brief period in the late seventies, until the company got hip to the fact that he was fencing goods stolen from the store. He stayed in the fencing business, opening this store as a thinly veiled front. McGinnes called the place, which sold an indescribably garish inventory of useless trinkets, 'Souvenir Shitty.'

Fat Fred had been a fair retail salesman, though he lost more than a few deals due to his appearance and lack of hygiene. Besides hovering at an indelicate two eighty, quite a load for a man who stood five feet seven, he smelled like an ashtray and apparently showered only on a novelty basis.

Fat Fred was in the rear of the shop when I entered, a lit weed in his hand. He took a deep drag from it and blew a cloud my way as I walked up to greet him. He was still buying his clothes from the 'Work 'n' Leisure' department at Sears, and his hair, which was plastered to his scalp in topographic sections, resembled black spinach.

'Nick,' he said.

'Freddie. What's happening?'

'You're looking at it.' He waved his club of a hand the width of the store. 'Slow tourist season. Must be the murder rate thing.'

'What about your other business?'

He grinned, then wheezed. 'What can I do for you, Nick?'

'You still do licenses?'

'Sure. What did you have in mind?'

'I need a relatively authentic private investigator's license, D. C. style. Can you swing it?'

'Sure, not a problem.'

'How much?'

'Say, thirty.'

'Say twenty, Freddie. And when you take my picture, take four extra for the real thing.'

He shrugged and motioned me to the side of the shop, seating me in front of an old-fashioned box camera. 'Turn your head to the left some,' he said, looking down into the viewfinder. 'You don't want that black eye showing up on your license. Good.' He took the shots.

'How long will this take?'

'Not long. Spell the name and address you want to use on the card.'

I did that on a piece of scrap paper and asked, 'Will this thing pass?'

His jowls shook with his nod. 'I wouldn't go flashing it in front of D.C.'s finest. But, yeah, it'll pass.'

I walked around the shop. Sweatshirts and T-shirts seemed to be Freddie's big number, the cheap Indonesian variety that begin to fray before the tourists reach the Pennsylvania Turnpike. Likenesses of President Bush and his first lady were decaled on some of these, stars haloed around their heads. I noted with some pleasure that, even when it was the artist's job to make Mr Bush seem strong, he still came off as the seventh-grade music teacher whose ass was kicked at least once a year by that particularly gene-deficient brand of student who always seemed to disappear or enter the Marines by high school.

In the center of the store were souvenir racks full of salt and pepper shakers and paperweights, all in the shape of monuments. One of these racks held dinner plates and mugs, on which were enameled the 'sights of Washington.' I picked up a plastic sphere half-filled with water containing a tiny Washington Monument, and shook it. Snow fell over the Elipse.

Fat Fred emerged from the back room about fifteen minutes later with my card. It certainly looked official enough, though I had no basis for judgment. What in the hell did I think I was doing?

'I laminated it,' he said proudly.

'You do good work,' I said, and gave him the original thirty he had asked for.

'Why do you always gotta fuck with me, Nicky?'

' 'Cause I like you, Freddie.' I slapped his arm, which should have been on a meathook. 'Thanks, buddy.' I put the ID and extra photos in my wallet and left the store.

Two doors down was a combination lunch counter, bar, and arts house called the District Seen, where one could get a decent sandwich, listen to some music, and hear anything from readings by modernist beat poets to *a capella* new wave. Though the acts more often than not were sophomoric, there was that sad and noble quality in them of the intrepid amateur.

I picked up the latest copy of *City Paper* at the door and had a seat at the black and white tiled bar. At this early hour the bartender was the only employee in the front of the house, though there was the sound of prep work coming from the kitchen.

The bartender was a burly, balding, redheaded guy I had seen working in several clubs through the years. Gregory Isaacs, the 'cool ruler' of reggae, was pouring through the Advents on either side of the bar.

I ordered a club, a cup of split pea soup, and coffee, and opened the tabloid to the arts section, skipping over the paper's customarily unfocused cover story. Joel E. Siegel, the most intelligent film critic in town, who made waste of the *Post*'s hapless duo (the gushing Hal Hinson and the unreadable Rita Kempley), had reviewed a couple of interesting documentaries. And Mark Jenkins, who on the plus side was a Smiths fetishist but on the minus side a Costello basher, had done an enthusiastic review of the neo-psychedelic Stone Roses.

After my dinner I ordered a dark beer and drank it as I finished reading the paper. I nursed a second as the place began to fill up and become noisier. When the bartender switched over to Pere Ubu on the stereo, I settled up and left.

It was dark now, between eight and nine o'clock. Working Washington was safe in the suburbs, leaving this part of the city virtually deserted. The storefronts, mostly shoe shops displaying the latest Bamaish styles, were closed and secured with drawn iron gates. This section of town had its own smell in the early evening, of dried spit and alley dirt in the wedges of cracked concrete.

Pigeons fluttered as I turned right off of Ninth and moved down F. Some punks were hanging outside the entrance of the Snake Pit, smoking cigarettes and looking patently sullen. The all-black dress and hairstyles had changed very little in ten years.

I maneuvered around them and entered a long hallway postered with announcements of shows around town. As I neared the doorway, humid, smoky air rushed towards me, along with the sound of a chainsaw electric guitar.

I paid for a ticket through a box office window and handed it to the doorman, a slight kid in black jeans and an army green T-shirt, with a bleached blond brush cut on his pale head. He ripped the ticket in half and returned the stub with his soft hand.

The main room was half-filled with young people dressed in dark clothing, blending in against the black walls of the club. They were an odd mixture here of artsy college students, punks, black hipsters, geeks, and even a few rednecks who dug the music. An overweight computer-science major who haunted used record stores could fit in just as well at the Snake Pit as the latest trendy.

I moved past the main bar and stage and headed for the back bar, which was located at the end of another long hall. The DJ was blasting through a set of garage rock, segueing from early Slickee Boys to the Hoodoo Gurus. The volume lessened as I entered the back room.

I removed my jacket, hung it on a peg, and took a seat on the wall stool at the far end of the bar. Cocktail napkins were fanned out on the bar like white flowers blooming randomly from the dark wood.

Bartenders at the Snake Pit generally had the look of the undead. The one who placed a coaster in front of me had thin, druggy arms and was sloppily dressed in purple on black. Her face was bloodless and set off by eggplant-colored lipstick, though not entirely unpleasant.

'What can I get you?'

'A Bud bottle,' I said, 'and an Old Grand-Dad. Neat.'

She hooked me up with a quick and professionally deft handling of the bottles. I thanked her and suggested she pour one for herself. She opted for Johnnie Walker Black in a rocks glass. I like scotch drinkers, when it's a woman doing the drinking. We tapped glasses and drank slowly.

'Who's playing tonight?' I asked.

'The Primitives,' she said coolly. 'Blondie via the Jesus and Mary Chain.'

'A lot of feedback?'

'Yeah,' she said. 'Feedback and angst.'

'Who's opening?'

'The Deaf Pedestrians. *Pedestrian* describes 'em.'

'I'm looking for the little brother of a friend,' I said, pulling out the shaven picture of Broda and sliding it in front of her. 'I think he hangs out with some of the skins here.'

'Fuckin' skinheads,' she said viciously and looked at the photo. 'I don't know him. But you might ask those assholes.' She pointed out the entranceway towards the stairwell, where two head-shaven boys were leaning against the wall smoking cigarettes. 'They're always here.'

'Maybe later. How about another shot?'

She poured one for me and moved down the bar to take an order. The place was getting denser and smokier. I had a warm, even buzz.

The DJ was playing something hard and fast. The bartender saun-

67

tered in my direction and leaned in towards me, her forearms resting on the mahogany bar. There was color now on her cheeks.

'Anything else?'

'No, thanks. Cash me out.' She pulled my tab from between two rum bottles on the call rack.

'Nine dollars,' she said.

I put thirteen down on the bar. 'See you later, hear?'

'Sure. I've seen you around.'

I grabbed my jacket off the wall and walked out into the hallway. The two skins were heading down into the narrow stairwell that led to the john and cloakroom. They were of average size and both wearing black jeans and black, steel-toed workboots. One had on a flannel shirt, the other a black T-shirt. I followed them into the stairwell. The DJ had kicked in Sonic Youth's 'Teenage Riot.'

I said, 'Hey,' and they turned, four steps down, to face me.

They looked smaller and more vulnerable now. The one wearing the flannel shirt had eyelids at half-mast and his mouth hung open. The other had pale, girlishly veinless arms that hung like strings from the sleeves of his T-shirt. Both were trying to look tough, but I recognized them for what they were – pussies with crewcuts.

'You guys mind if I ask you a couple of questions?' I used the friendliest tone I could stomach.

'You a cop?' the one closest to me asked, but before I could answer his friend spoke up.

'He's no cop. Cops don't get black eyes.' They both laughed drunkenly.

'I'm looking for my little brother,' I said, pulling a twenty from my pocket along with the photo of Jimmy Broda. I kept the bill and handed them the picture. They stared at it rather stupidly for a long time.

'What's this dude's name?' flannel-shirt finally asked.

'Jimmy Broda.'

'The picture's not too good,' he said, quickly adding, 'but I seen him around.'

'Recently?' He looked at his friend, then at the jacket pocket where I had replaced the Jackson.

'All this talk is making me thirsty, big brother.'

'You're covered on the twenty,' I said. 'Go ahead.'

'I think I know who the dude is, if it's the one I'm thinking of. He runs with a guy they call Redman, you know, this redheaded motherfucker.'

'Yeah?'

'And sometimes I seen him with this good lookin' older bitch. But it might be that she hangs out with Redman.'

'This Redman got a real name, or the girl?'

'I don't know his name or hers,' he said, disappointed but still hungry.

'When's the last time you saw him or his friends?'

'It's been awhile. I don't know, a few weeks maybe.'

'Would they hang out anywhere else?'

'No, man,' he said, 'this is it now. This place is happenin', even though there's too many niggers come in here for my taste.' His friend chuckled uneasily.

'Who else would know more?' I asked, revealing the twenty once again.

'We know *all* the skins, man,' he said defensively. 'You know that graffiti – you can see it on the Red Line near Fort Totten – says "United Skinheads" over an American flag?' I nodded that I had seen it. '*I* did that.'

'That's a nice piece of work. But there must be somebody else I can talk to who might know a little more.'

He looked at his friend, then at me. 'It will cost you another ten.'

I pulled out the bill and slapped it together with the twenty.

'There's a rowhouse on Ninth and G, Southeast, got a red awning over the porch. The dude you want to talk to is John Heidel. But don't tell him we turned you on to the address.' I handed him the thirty, and he eyed me suspiciously. 'You sure you're no cop?'

I looked him over and said, 'If I was, I would have called for backup by now.'

'Damn straight,' he said, missing the irony and walking, with his friend, down the stairs to hang out in the cloakroom.

I followed them down but veered off into the men's toilet. I stood at the urinal and drained, reading the names of bands and slogans etched into the black walls.

Below an anarchy symbol, two words were dug deep into the heart of the plaster: 'No Future.' I buttoned up my fly and flushed the head.

10

The red-awninged rowhouse stood in the middle of G between Ninth and Tenth, just as flannel-shirt had said. I parked in front of it the next morning somewhere around eleven o'clock.

Real estate salesmen pitched this area as Capitol Hill, and it was, though a far cry from the connotations that such a prestigious name would suggest. There were residential homes here, struggling group houses, neighborhood bars and shops, and a few marginally upscale businesses that quickly came and went.

I opened a chain-link gate and stepped along a concrete walkway split and overgrown with weeds and clover. A mongrel shepherd in the adjacent yard was on the end of its tether, up on its hind legs and growling viciously.

I stepped up onto a small porch with brown brick columns and knocked on a thin wooden door. A dirgelike bass insinuated itself through the walls of the house.

I knocked again. The door swung open and a girl stood before me. She was taller than me, even allowing for the fact that she was up a step. Her legs were long and her hips immaturely narrow. Through the sides of her green tank top I could see the curvature and bottom-fold of narrow, sausagelike breasts. Her tired eyes bore the mark of experience, though her childlike bone structure put her at around seventeen.

'I'm looking for John,' I said. 'Is he in?'

Leaning in the doorframe, she looked behind her, then back at me, and said, 'Which one?'

'I'm sorry. I didn't know there was more than one. John Heidel.'

'There's a lot of people live here, man, on and off. Johnny's in his room, upstairs and through the second door on the left.'

I thanked her, but she was already walking away. The sound of several loud male voices came from the kitchen, where she was heading. From the mismatched, worn furniture in the living room to the requisite black and white television with foil antenna, the place resembled a student group house without the books.

I grabbed the loose wooden banister and took the steps slowly. At the top of the stairs I passed a room where a kid sat in the window box smoking. He didn't return my nod.

My knock on the second door was hard enough to open it halfway. A young man lay on his back on an unmade bed, reading a paperback. Smoke rose slowly from behind the book. An emotionless voice told me to 'come on in.'

He lowered the book and, squinting from the smoke of the cigarette that was planted in his mouth, cocked one eyebrow as he sized me up. He sat up on the edge of the bed and butted the weed in an overflowing ashtray set next to a radial alarm clock. From the looks of his wrinkled jeans, this would be the first time he had risen from the bed that day. His shirtless upper body was thick and naturally strong, without the artificial bulk obtained from weight machines, and there was a crescent scar half-framing his right eye.

'What is it?' he asked, slowly rubbing the top of his shaven head.

'John Heidel?'

'Yeah.'

'I'm Kevin DeGarcey from the *Washington Times*.' I flashed him a card imprinted with the *Times* logo, not giving him time to read DeGarcey's title of advertising account executive. I extended my hand and received a grip weak with suspicion.

'What do you want?'

'The *Post* ran an article several weeks ago about the local skinhead movement that in my opinion was very negative. My editor feels they only captured, or chose to print, one side of the story.'

'I would agree with *that*.'

'He's assigned me a different type of story on you guys. I've been working on it awhile now, doing interviews, talking to different people.'

'Why did you want to talk to *me*?'

'I heard you knew most of your peers on the local level.'

'From who?'

'Two younger guys I met at the Snake Pit last night. I didn't get their names. One of them wore a flannel shirt, the other one was a little guy. They looked like they could have been in your group, but I have to admit, they were very eager to sell information.'

'They're "wanna-bes," not skins. I'll have to speak to those two about giving out my name.'

'What are you reading?' He seemed to warm to the question as I

71

pulled a wooden chair next to his bed and had a seat. I took a pad and pen from my jacket.

'*The Territorial Imperative*,' he said, 'by Robert Ardrey.' He spelled the author's name for me as I wrote.

'Any good?'

'Interesting ideas. The man doesn't judge violence. Violence just *is*.'

'What do you think about violence?'

'In what sense?' He smirked. He was probably smarter than the majority of his friends, but it was a relative intelligence. There was something stupid in his dead eyes and slack jaw.

'Skinhead violence, specifically,' I said. 'The *Post* said your group beats up gays, the occasional black who gets in your way. Is that true?'

'You and me, they call us human, but we're really animals, right? And even though we're animals, we're supposed to suppress our natural instincts to preserve and protect our turf.' He paused to rub his head. 'It just boggles my mind that there isn't *more* violence out there, that people aren't wasting each other wholesale in the street. I'm saying that since violence is a natural instinct, it's amazing that there's so little of it happening.'

'Why gays, though? Why blacks? The *Post* article said that the recent P Street Beach beatings were done by the skinheads.'

'Look,' he said, leaning in, 'here's the thing. We don't care what people do in their own homes. We really don't. But take that part of the park – P Street Beach – that's *my* park too. I should be able to walk through it without stumbling on some freak faggots. So they get stomped once or twice, maybe they'll take that shit back indoors where it belongs. As for the blacks, we send them a message every so often to remind them that we live here too. Fuckin' bootheads act like they own this town.'

'Do you personally approve of these acts?'

'I'm not even saying we do the violence ourselves. But it *is* understandable. It's a matter of protecting your turf.'

'I interviewed a guy they call Redman,' I said abruptly.

'You mean Eddie Shultz?' Heidel looked surprised and a little sad.

'That's him.' I wrote the name. 'He made some interesting connections between the music you guys listen to and the violence. Any thoughts on that?'

'Yeah. My thought is that anything Eddie Shultz says is bullshit.' He looked at me sourly and flipped open the top of his hardpack, put a smoke in his mouth and lit it, then absently threw the blown-out match onto the nightstand.

'I thought he was one of you guys.'

'He ain't shit. Eddie was okay once, but he fucked up.'

'How so?'

He looked at me warily. 'You writing a story about Eddie or the skins?'

'The skins. But that's the point. If I find out why someone falls out of favor in your group, I find out more about the group itself. Maybe the article will be more sympathetic.'

He dragged hard on his cigarette. 'Eddie started hanging with the wrong kinds of people. I mean, we just don't get into the drug thing here, as an unwritten rule. We do consume some alcohol, though.' He smiled for the first time, revealing chipped and dirty teeth.

'The times I interviewed him, he was with a younger boy and a good-looking woman.'

His smile faded. 'That's what I'm talking about, man. He started running with this kid, and they were using a shitload of coke, and flashing it around like there was quantity. Then the chick starts hanging out with the two of them, and Eddie falls for her. I told him that the bitch had no interest in him or his friend, she just wanted to be around the drugs. It was so obvious.'

'What was her name again?'

'I have no clue, man. Never wanted to know.'

'The boy?'

'Uh-uh.'

I was losing him. 'You don't know where I can reach any of them now, verify my facts?'

He snorted. 'You ain't verifyin' nuthin' with Eddie. He left town with those two a couple of weeks ago. Headed south is what he said, whatever that means. I don't know where he is.'

I didn't bother to try and shake his hand. Heidel was staring out the window as I left, smoking and squinting, as if straining to see his friend Redman walking down the street.

At the foot of the stairs I noticed the girl who had answered the door, sitting with her legs draped over the arm of a shredded easy chair. She was watching a game show on TV while listening to Joy Division on the stereo. I walked in and turned the amplifier's volume knob down. She looked over at me, only mildly bothered.

'Hi,' I said.

'Hey.'

'John said it was all right to ask you a couple of questions.'

'Who are you?'

'I'm a reporter.' An image of Jimmy Olsen came to mind.

'What do you want to know?'

'I need to talk to Eddie Shultz and the girl he was going around with.'

'Eddie left town,' she said, looking out the corner of her eye at the interchangeable horse-toothed host on the television screen.

'I know. You wouldn't happen to know where they went?'

'Uh-uh. He and Kimmy just split, with that Jimmy kid. A couple of weeks ago.'

'Kimmy.'

'Yeah. Kim Lazarus.'

'She a local?'

'I don't know,' she said, anxiously shifting her gaze to the screen. 'Why don't you ask Redman's old lady. They live in Prince Georges County someplace. I was there with him once.'

'You remember the address? The street?'

'Something "wood." Edgewood, Ledgewood, some shit like that.'

'Thanks,' I said. 'Eddie and John were pretty tight, weren't they?'

'They were, until this Kimmy chick came around.'

I readjusted the volume on the stereo, walked to the front door, and stepped out. I breathed cool, fresh air as the funereal bass trailed behind.

11

Marsha picked up and responded in her usual cheerful manner when I phoned her from my apartment.

'Nutty Nathan's,' she nearly sang.

'Hi, Marsha. It's Nick.'

'Nicky! Where are you?'

'Home. Taking the day off.'

'That's nice,' she said.

'Marsha, I need a favor.'

'Sure, Nicky.'

'Go to service dispatch and borrow their *Hanes Directory*, you know, the "crisscross." '

'Okay.'

'Now write down this name.' I spelled *Shultz* for her. 'In P. G. County, locate all the Shultzes for me who live on streets that end with the word *wood*, like Dogwood Terrace or Edgewood Road. Know what I mean?'

'Yeah?'

'That's it.'

'Okay, Nicky. Want me to call you back?'

'Please. You've got my number?'

'Yup. I won't be long,' she promised, and hung up.

I pulled the metro phone books from the hall closet and laid them out on my desk. There were about forty total listings for the last name of Lazarus, and I began calling.

It was early afternoon and many people weren't in, though I left messages on their machines. Those that were home generally muttered the 'wrong number' response and hung up quickly; a couple of elderly folks were eager to talk, but these too were not the homes of Kim Lazarus.

Two hours later I dialed the final listing and received the same treatment. I called Marsha back.

'It's Nick, Marsha.'

'I've been trying to get you for over an hour,' she scolded.

'What have you got?'

'I found a Joseph Shultz on Briarwood Terrace in Oxen Hill,' she said. 'And there's a Thomas and Maureen Shultz on Inglewood in Riverdale.'

'Give me both phone numbers and the addresses.' She read me the information. 'I owe you lunch, Marsha. Thanks a million.'

When I dialed the second number and asked for Eddie, Maureen Shultz told me he wasn't in. I identified myself as DeGarcey from the *Washington Times* and explained the sympathetic portrait of Eddie and his friends that I was struggling to finish on deadline. Could I come over to the Shultz residence to get those last few details? Sure, she said.

I drove north over the district line into Maryland, then made a right on 410, which wound, primarily as East–West Highway, through Takoma Park, Chillum, Hyattsville, and Riverdale. Inglewood was on my detail map. It was a street of Cape Cods with large, treeless front lawns. A row of oaks ran down the government strip the length of the street.

Judging by the number of nonrecreational pickups parked in the driveways, this part of the neighborhood was largely blue-collar and middle-income at best. But the properties and houses had been functionally kept with that quiet pride peculiar to the working class.

I knocked on the door of the address Marsha had given me and a heavy-hipped woman answered. Her worn housedress and graying, closely cropped hair made her appear older than I would have guessed from her phone voice. She let me into a house that was visibly free of dirt but smelled of dogs. One of them, an old setter, moved his eyes and nothing else as I passed with his mistress into the kitchen.

I sat at a table that had a marbleized formica top. She made instant coffee while I looked around the room. The appliances were avocado green and the refrigerator had no kickplate.

Maureen Shultz was an outwardly pleasant woman with whom it was fairly comfortable to sit and share coffee and conversation. But she seemed to get more anxious as we talked. Soon it became clear that she was interviewing *me*, and had apparently agreed to my visit for that purpose. She was worried about her son.

'When was the last time *you* saw him?' she asked.

'About two weeks ago,' I lied. 'He was with an attractive woman and a younger boy.'

'An attractive woman,' she sniffed. 'I suppose she was, on the outside.' She took a sip of coffee, visibly embarrassed by her display of judgment or jealousy. 'I'm sorry. I really didn't think much about her. It was just a feeling I had.'

'I got the feeling they didn't belong together, if you don't mind my saying so.'

'He brought her over here once. Eddie's friends were always welcome here. But you're right. She might not have come from money, but she had done some high living. Eddie hadn't, not yet.'

'What gave you that impression?'

'Small things,' she said, sipping her coffee. 'She was older, for one, and the etiquette she used at dinner. She commented on my china, which isn't actually very good at all. But the point is, Eddie wouldn't know china from paper plates.'

'What about her background?'

'She never said, exactly. Neither did Eddie. She had a slight Southern accent that became more pronounced as her guard began to drop, if you know what I mean.'

'Yes.'

'She mentioned that she had a little college and worked in stores and restaurants before she moved up here. She said that she liked to go to the seashore back home.'

All of that information was meaningless. Kim Lazarus could have been from any coastal state south of the Mason–Dixon line.

'I talked to John Heidel today,' I said, dropping a name that perked her up a bit. 'I got the impression he might know more about the girl, but he wasn't eager to talk.'

'He knew the girl too,' she said vaguely, straightening her posture and wringing her hands.

'What do you think about the crowd Eddie and John were in, the group they call the skinheads?'

'Eddie and John went to high school together. Grades wise, they weren't the brightest boys. I know they drank beer, raced their cars a little too fast. But that's all a part of growing up. What they do now, that's a phase too.'

'Mrs Shultz, you must be aware of the allegations against their group. The violence against minorities.'

'Yes,' she said bitterly. 'I've read the articles. And I'm not blind to the ways of my son. His father put that hatred into him. He's an insecure man, and it passes from the father to the son. But Eddie wouldn't beat up anybody if there wasn't a reason.'

'I'd like to explore his side of things. But I need to talk to him again to do it.'

'How can I help you?'

'You've known John Heidel for quite a long time. Give him a call and see if he has any idea where they were headed. I'll be at this number.' I handed her the number to my answering machine that I had written on my pad.

She began walking me to the front door but stopped in the living room to take a framed photograph off the fireplace mantel. She faced it towards me.

'That's Eddie's high school picture. He looks an awful lot better with all that hair. It's funny,' she chuckled. 'At the time, I gave him hell about it being too long.'

I could see why they called the boy Redman. His hair, long in the picture in some sort of shag, was bright orange, as were his eyebrows and the hopelessly weak mustache above his thin lips. Eddie's eyes were narrow and rather cruel, a trait I found completely absent in his mother.

'Talk to John and give me a call later,' I said.

She nodded. I hurried to the door and turned to say good-bye. I watched her replace Eddie's picture on the mantel, feeling vaguely intrusive as I saw her lightly run her finger around the edge of the frame.

Sitting in my car in front of the Shultz residence, I found myself watching a young mother a few houses down who was watching her child crawl upon a white blanket that had been spread upon the lawn.

I studied them until the mother noticed me and appeared to become uncomfortable at my presence. I cranked the ignition, and the engine turned over with some reluctance. Then I pulled off Inglewood and headed west on the highway, towards the office headquarters of Nutty Nathan's.

12

The Nutty Nathan's warehouse was adjacent to the offices and occupied about eighteen thousand square feet of the entire building. Since the bruise below my eye was still healing, I avoided the office altogether and went in through the service entrance.

It was late Friday afternoon, and the women in service dispatch sat in a semicircle discussing the weekend. I walked by them quickly and with my head down, but not quickly enough to escape a whistle and then some laughter.

I took some concrete steps up to a locked door that opened onto the warehouse loft. Upon my promotion to upper-level management I had been given a skeleton key that fit all the locks in the building, necessitated by my frequent trips to the warehouse to check inventory while writing the copy ('Only 10 to Sell!') of the ads. I used the key in this lock as I turned the knob and stepped into the loft.

The warehousemen called this area 'the zoo' because of the cages along its wall that contained the heistable goods: small appliances, boom boxes, tapes, accessories, and anything else that could be stashed underneath an employee's jacket. A large sign in red lettering hung on the wall near the first cage, and read, 'Lock all cages. Don't tempt an honest man.'

One could look down from the loft and survey the entire warehouse. It was arranged in five long parallel rows that ran the length of the building. Between each row was twelve feet of space, an allowance for the swing of forklifts that would then have a straight shot to the truck bays located directly beneath the loft.

There was a twenty-five foot drop to the warehouse floor. A three-tiered railing ran along the edge of the loft, broken only at one point to allow entrance to a caged lift that was used to move stock from one level to the next.

This time of year, as Fisher had overemphasized, the 'barn' was full to

79

capacity because of the annual fourth quarter load-in. Boxes rose from the floor and approached the legal limit, which was gauged by their proximity to the ceiling sprinklers. In several spots one could step off the loft directly onto the top of a row of stock.

I pulled open the metal gate, entered the lift, and hit the lower button on an electrical box hung over the railing. The crate lowered me in spasms.

I stepped out and walked past the bays where returning drivers were checking their manifests with the assistant warehouse managers. It was payday. Several of the drivers looked as if they had cashed their checks earlier at the liquor store. I could hear the deliberate farting of young warehousemen, and, after that, commentary and laughter as to the degree of looseness of their respective sphincters. By the time I reached Dane's office this had degenerated into a discussion of an activity called 'jamming,' which involved gerbils and then other progressively larger mammals.

The glass-enclosed office of Joe Dane, the warehouse manager, bordered the last bay. I looked in and saw the delivery manager talking on the phone. I rapped on the glass. She looked up, smiled, gave me a shrug and an exasperated look, and waved me in.

Their office smelled like cigarettes and fast food. Dane was an unashamed slob, but his female coworkers had tried to humanize the place with remnant carpeting, Redskins pennants, and stick-up Garfield cats, one of the strangest fads to come to D.C. since the Carl Lewis haircut.

Jerry Chase hung up the phone, mouthed the word *asshole*, slumped back in her chair, and dragged on her cigarette. The cherry from the last one was still smoking in the ashtray. I perched on the edge of her desk and butted it out.

'A good one?' I asked, looking at the phone.

'Oh, yeah,' she said, the smoke breaking around her mouth as she talked. 'We miss a delivery, and the customer starts about how he makes two hundred dollars an hour, he can't afford to sit another afternoon off and wait for a delivery. I wonder if he knows how many important people like him I talk to every day. I'm so tired of hearing that. If a guy really makes that kind of dough, then he wouldn't get hurt missing a couple hours of work. To top it off, these problems always come on Friday afternoon payday.' She chin-nodded through the glass towards the drivers. 'You think I can get any of these guys to go back out on a delivery now? They've been half in the bag since this morning.'

'Well, the day's almost over,' I said, hoping to slow her down, though admittedly she had the worst job in the company.

'And people want to know why I drink,' she said, giving me a knowing look. 'So what brings you down to the underworld?'

'I'm looking for Dane.'

'He got wise and split early. The "my baby's sick" routine.'

'Yeah, well. Maybe his kid really is sick.'

'Maybe,' she said, tossing her cigarette in the ashtray. I crushed it for her.

'Why don't you ever put those things out?'

'That's the man's job,' she said, and shook her hair in what she thought was a sexy manner. She had a P.G. County haircut that had gone out of style at about the time that 'Charlie's Angels' was entering its third season.

'Take care, Jerry.' I walked out and closed the door behind me.

The warehouse had the same musty odor as the stockroom, though its rows were perfectly aligned, the floors relatively dirt-free. Except for the true summer months, it always seemed cold in here, and the combination of naked steel girders, unfinished concrete, and bleak lighting heightened that chill. The young men in here worked a hard day every day, beneath insulated flannel shirts and gloves. Their occasional laughter almost always came at the expense of each other, and the turnover was tremendous.

I walked down the center aisle, dwarfed by the cardboard walls at my side. A kid I knew gave me a short horn-blast of recognition as he motored by on his forklift.

The barn *was* loaded. I took note of what we were heavy on as I walked. I would have to start dumping some of these goods, or, more likely, advertise the bait that would lead into the overstocks.

At the end of the aisle I turned left to the far corner of the warehouse, the section entirely occupied by videocassette recorders. I noticed the Kotekna VCRs that Rosen had purchased at the electronics show. Virtually none of them had moved. I made a mental note to remind Fisher that these 'dogs' would have to be shipped out to the floors.

Aware of someone behind me, I turned to face two warehousemen I had never met. They were standing four feet apart and looking at me with solid stares. I nodded but got no response.

The man on the left was leaning on a pushbroom. He was of average height, with a dark, bony face and a careless goatee. His nose was narrow and flat, his eyes almost Oriental in shape. A red knit cap was cocked on his head, filled high with dreadlocks. He wore a vest over a thermal shirt, and had the loose-limbed stance of a fighter.

His partner was a black albino with mustard skin and eyes the color of a bad scrape. There was one small braid coming from the back of his shaved head. He wore striped baggies, a faded denim shirt, and leather gloves. He was so tall that his posture and bone structure suggested deformity. There was a dead, soulless look in their eyes that I had seen increasingly on the faces of men in Washington's streets as the eighties dragged murderously on.

I walked towards them. When it was clear that they weren't going to move, I walked around them. I felt an inexplicable humiliation, like a child who later regrets walking away from a certain ass-kicking at the hands of the schoolyard bully.

I heard them chuckle behind me, and I turned. The dark one with the pushbroom blew me a kiss. Then they both laughed.

I walked out of the warehouse. In the parking lot I noticed that my fists were balled and shoved deeply in my pockets. Climbing behind the wheel of my car, I felt weak and very small.

Joe Dane lived in old Silver Spring, on a street where the houses were built very close to the kerb and had large, open porches and deep backyards. I parked my heap in front of his place and was up on his porch in six short steps.

I knocked on the door, behind which I could hear children laughing and playing and falling harmlessly to the floor. After that came a woman's voice, raised halfheartedly to attempt sternness, then foot-steps.

The door opened and Sarah Dane stood in the frame, wiping her hands dry with a dishrag. The lines around her eyes deepened as she smiled up at my face.

'Hi, Nick.'

'Sarah.' I leaned in and kissed her on the cheek.

Her baggy pants were frumpy and her sweatshirt featured a circular medallion of vomit centered between her breasts. Four kids and the raising of them had widened her hips and prematurely aged her face. But she had the relaxed beauty of contentment.

'Is Joe around?' I asked.

'He's in the backyard,' she said, tugging gently on my jacket and pulling me through the doorway. 'Come on in.'

I followed her into the living room as she made a path through the toys scattered on the throwrug. The arms of the sofa had been shredded by cats. As we walked, she touched the heads of two children orbiting her legs.

We moved into the warm kitchen where a cat was haunched down, its face buried in a small yellow dish. Water boiled in a tall pot on the gas stove. Next to it sat an open box of pasta.

I looked through the screen of the dark back porch. Joe Dane was walking slowly through their garden, his hands in his pockets. Sarah folded her arms and leaned against the refrigerator.

'You look good, Nick,' she said, focusing on the fading purplish area below my eye. 'But I see you're not really staying out of trouble.'

'I don't go looking for it,' I said. 'You look good too, Sarah.'

'Don't bullshit me, Nicky. I look like hell.' She grabbed some hair off her face and wound it behind an ear. It was fairly useless to tell her that I was being sincere.

'What have you all been up to?' I asked.

A small towhead, wearing fatigues and carrying a plastic machine gun, ran by. I tapped him on the shoulder. He ran back, socked me on the knee, and disappeared into another room.

'You're looking at it,' she said, without a trace of regret.

'You're awfully lucky to have all this.'

'All this,' she laughed. 'The funny thing is, I do feel lucky. This is what I want.'

'How about him?' I asked, jerking my head in the direction of the backyard.

'Joe's the worrier of the family. Of course, he's out in the world every day, he sees other people with more than we've got. More money, that is. And this town can influence you, make you feel like if you're not wearing the four hundred dollar suit or driving the right import, you're lower than dirt. I'm insulated from all that crap, here with the kids.' She looked me over. 'How about you? You seeing anyone?'

'Not really.'

'Talk to Karen?'

'No.' The four of us had spent many evenings together in the early days of our marriages.

'Here,' she said, handing me two cans of beer from the refrigerator. 'Go talk to him. He could use it.'

'Thanks, Sarah.'

I stepped out onto the porch, which creaked beneath my feet, and pushed open the screen door. As I walked across the yard, I noticed the kids' Big Wheels had worn a semicircular track in the grass.

Joe Dane was a broad, bearlike guy whose gut had begun to creep unapologetically over his belt. Though he was only a few years my senior, his graying beard made him look much older. There was a look nearing relief on his creased face as I approached.

We had befriended each other early on at Nathan's. He came to me for advice on record purchases, and I to him on the latest films to catch. My opinions on music were solely based on taste, but his movie knowledge came from advanced studies and a Master's in Film Theory, a degree he had earned but never used professionally.

'Nick,' he said tiredly. 'What brings you out here to "Pottersville"?'

I let that slide and said, 'Just wanted to say hi. Your kid sick?'

'No, I just bugged out a little early.'

I cracked both beers and handed him one. He winked and had a long swallow. I pulled on his shirtsleeve and brought him out of the garden to two ripped beach chairs that faced back towards the house. A calico cat slunk across the yard, brushed my shins, and settled into a ball beneath my chair.

'So, what's happening in music?' he asked, though he appeared uninterested. 'I've been out of touch.'

'You haven't missed much. This year it's the neo-folk movement, though there's nothing "neo" about it. Tracy Chapman comes out doing the same shit Joan Armatrading was doing ten years ago, only Tracy's younger and has a funkier haircut, and she walks away with all the press and the awards.'

'It's the same in film,' he said. 'There's very little in the way of originality right now. The film schools are cranking out mimics and technicians, but there isn't any soul.'

'What about your boys, Scorsese and De Palma?'

'Scorsese's still a true visionary, a genius. *Good Fellas*, man, that was a piece of work. The first time I ever *saw* a cocaine high, visualized, up on the screen. And the violence was real, not stylized. Real. But De Palma?' Dane snorted and dismissed the director with a wave of his hand. 'De Palma used to have that crippling Hitchcock fixation, and the critics hated him. I got a kick out of him, though. I mean, I had the sense, when I was watching his films, that I was witnessing the work of a madman. Then he does *The Untouchables*, and the critics love it. But it was pretty much just a straight narrative thing, don't you think? And the centerpiece of the film, the shootout at the train station – he managed to rip off both Eisenstein's Odessa steps sequence and himself at the same time.'

'Rip-off?' I said. 'You used to call that "homage."'

'Whatever. De Palma used that one hundred percent slow motion sequence once before, in *The Fury*, a much better film in my opinion, what with its theme of patricide and its dark humor. Godard called that the most honest use of slow motion he had ever seen on film.' Dane rubbed his forehead and swallowed more beer, then said, 'It's all bullshit anyway.'

With that remark we sat in silence for several minutes. The calico emerged from under my seat, and with a low crawl slowly crept up on a group of sparrows that had lit in the middle of the yard. I watched as they scattered and flew away.

'I heard Jimmy Broda got it while I was on vacation,' I said, a careful indifference in my voice.

'Yeah,' he said, closing his eyes as he killed his beer.

'It surprised me, the fact that he was a gonif.'

'Well, he was.'

'You have to fire him yourself?'

'Yeah.'

'You got a soft heart, Joe.'

'What the hell are you talking about?'

I finished my beer and crushed the can. 'I talked to our lady in personnel. She has his reason for termination down as "job abandonment." You told her that, so theft wouldn't be on the kid's record. Am I right?'

His face tightened. 'Sure. He was clean, up until the time he tried to boost that box. No reason to have that on his permanent record.'

A strong, stocky little boy ran from the side of the house and slowed to a walk as he neared us. He had his old man's pug nose and his mother's round eyes. Dane turned him around and locked him gently between his knees. He rubbed the kid's shoulders with his big hands.

'There's one thing I can't figure out about that whole deal,' I said. 'The kid's grandfather phoned me after the boy was fired. So I went to their apartment, and his grandfather shows me this VCR that the kid had bought for him.'

'So?'

'So why would a kid lift an eighty dollar piece, then turn around and pay for a VCR worth two bills? Why not steal the more expensive item, if you're going to steal?'

Dane brought his child up into his arms and hugged him rather roughly. His eyes were closed and I wondered if he'd heard me. Then he opened his eyes and spoke.

'You're talking about a nineteen-year-old kid, Nick, and you expect him to do something rational.' He put down his child. 'You think too damn much.'

'And you brood too much,' I said, rising from my chair. 'Why don't you go on inside. I've got to get going.'

'Don't tell me not to brood. The hole is just getting deeper and deeper around here.'

I looked at his beautiful kid, then at him, and said, 'You're right. A single guy like me just can't understand your "problems." ' I shook his hand. 'So long, Joe. Thanks for the beer.'

I walked across the yard and looked through the screen door. Sarah was stirring the pot of pasta, the child in the fatigues sitting at her feet. I went around the side of their house and to my car without saying good-bye.

When I entered my apartment, the top light was blinking on my answering machine. I pushed the bar. The tape rewound, then the unit made several noises that sounded like locks being turned.

The message began: 'Mr DeGarcey, this is Maureen Shultz. I reached John Heidel. He's not sure exactly where Eddie and his friends went, only he knows they went south . . . He did give me some more information on the girl. Her parents are from Elizabeth City, in North Carolina . . . anyway, that's where she grew up. That's all I got out of John, I hope it helps . . . If you talk to Eddie, tell him his father and me . . . tell him we said hello.'

13

The day after Maureen Shultz left a message on my machine was the last Saturday I worked for Nutty Nathan's.

I woke that morning after a troubled night of sleep, a night in which I rose several times to wander around my apartment, sitting in different chairs and on my couch for long stretches at a time.

Sometime around dawn I lay awake in bed and watched my room begin to lighten, and the jagged, irregular lines of rainwater slide down my bedroom window. My cat stayed on top of the radiator, staring at the wall and listening to the rain.

At eight I got up, made coffee, and sat on the couch to read the *Post*. Two more people had been killed, execution style, in Northeast. The mayor denied allegations that he was a drug user, charged his accusers with racism, and said that all of this negative publicity was interfering with his 'agenda' for running the city. There was a lengthy feature in Style on the outspoken and rather cartoonish wife of a freshman Southern senator (didn't they all come to town vowing to turn 'buttoned-down' Washington on its ear?), and the main head in Sports dealt with the upcoming Skins–Giants clash, complete with the media-generated quarterback controversy.

When I was finished devouring the last section, I showered, shaved, and dressed. I put on light wool, faintly patterned teal slacks, a cream cotton oxford, a blue and beige Italian silk tie, and my twenty dollar sports jacket. I changed the litter box and filled the food and water dishes. My cat blinked at me from the radiator as I walked out the door.

The deep gray sky heightened the slowly emerging October oranges of Rock Creek Park as I drove west on Military Road. I was listening to Billy Bragg's 'Talking with the Taxman about Poetry' on the box, and I turned the volume up enough to overtake the sound of my fraying wipers as they dragged themselves across the windshield.

When I entered the store and knocked the rain off my shoulders, the crew was in and standing around the front counter. They were drinking coffee from 7-Eleven go-cups and picking from a box of doughnuts iced in peculiarly unnatural colors.

McGinnes leaned against the counter with his arms crossed. Malone lounged beside him, coffee in one hand, Newport in the other. Lloyd was holding a doughnut up near his face, examining it as he chewed in slow, exaggerated chomps. Louie was spreading out newspaper ads on the counter.

'Black?' Lee asked, handing me a cup.

'You wish,' I said, and took the coffee.

'All right, everybody,' Louie ordered, 'listen up,' and we moved around him in a semicircle. McGinnes nudged me and pointed at the folds of fat at the back of Louie's head, which seemed to be fused onto his thick shoulders.

'Did you lose your neck, boss?' McGinnes asked.

'Shut up and look here, McGinnes.' Louie pointed to the ads he had torn from the paper and spread on the counter. 'Electric Town is running with the top-rated Sharp CD player for one nineteen. You boys know that that model has been discontinued – we don't have it and we can't get it. But they have a very sharp price on that Sharp.' Louie looked back at us for recognition of his pun.

'We get it,' Malone said. 'You sharp, Louie.'

Louie cleared his throat and turned back to the ads. McGinnes closed his eyes, dropped his chin to his chest, and began softly snoring.

'Anyway,' Louie continued, ignoring McGinnes, 'I called them up first thing this morning, and they don't have but one or two in stock. So now you know what to tell the consumers.'

'Okay, Louie,' McGinnes and Malone said robotically and in unison.

'Now,' Louie said, 'this one's tough,' and he pointed to a Stereo Godfather's ('Our Competition Sleeps with the Fishes!') ad. 'They're runnin' a TV290 for three ninety-nine. That's damn near cost. We can't meet the deal at that price. We've got to figure some way to get off of it.'

'No problem,' McGinnes said. 'Isn't that the same model that caught fire in the customer's house last year?'

'Yeah,' Malone said. 'Killed a couple kids, too. Little itty-bitty motherfuckers.'

'And we absolutely refuse to sell that model,' McGinnes said, 'until the manufacturer corrects the problem. It's a matter of principle.'

'You know what the problem with that piece was,' Malone said.

'What's that?' McGinnes asked.

'Fire in the wire.'

'Really?' McGinnes said. 'I thought it was shrinkage in the linkage.'

'All right, girls,' Louie said. 'I don't care what you tell the customers. Just don't give the damn thing away. And we need some volume today. I figure we're about twenty-five grand down in pace for the month. On the for-real side, provided we get some traffic in here, I'd like to make up fifteen of it today.'

'Shit, Louie,' Malone said, 'I'll write fifteen myself.'

'Sellin' woof tickets, maybe,' Louie said. 'There's a case of beer for the top dog today. And five percent of your volume has to be in service contracts. Any questions?'

'Just one,' I said. 'What is the meaning of life?'

Lee laughed charitably but the others ignored me. Louie was already headed for the back room.

Lloyd said, 'Did anyone see "Mr Belvedere" last night?'

'Too busy gyratin', Lloyd,' Malone said. 'How about you? You been doin' "the nasty"?'

Lloyd gave Malone an awkward wink and raised his pipe to his mouth, hitting his teeth with the stem in a botched aristocratic gesture. Splotches of pink began to form on his pasty face.

'Well, Andre,' McGinnes said happily. 'I can almost taste that case of beer right now.'

'Go on and taste it,' Malone said, pointing to the front door as the first customer of the day walked in, 'while I take this motherfucker to the bridge.'

The morning was evenly paced with customers, mostly young couples with the type of money that affords residence in upper Northwest. Malone and McGinnes handled the floor nicely and closed most of their deals, as did Louie, whose strength on the floor I had forgotten.

The boys had instructed Lee to tell any customers who phoned, inquiring about small appliances, to 'please ask for Lloyd' when they came in. This would keep him tied up in the low-commission department, and also keep him from blowing any major deals.

I took the overflow when the floor traffic became heavy and picked up my first customer of the day. She was an attractive woman in the last leg of her thirties, wearing colorful, gauzy clothing that attempted to conceal her shapeliness, but failed.

After my greeting she immediately pulled from her tote bag a copy of *Consumer Reports*, a legal pad on which she had neatly charted competitive prices, and a pen. She asked for the price of the top-rated

VCR. I explained to her that, as is often the case, the top-rated model had been discontinued one week before the article was published; that top-rated models were usually a poor buy anyway, since manufacturers, upon receiving the rating, jacked up the cost of that particular model to their distributors, who passed it on to the retailers, who passed it on to the customers; and that the intelligent model to purchase would be one of the same brand and similar features but with a different model number and hence a lesser retail.

She wanted the model number that was printed in the magazine. Further, she thought *Consumer Reports* was *just great*, a protection against sleazy retailers who take advantage of unsuspecting customers. A smug smile appeared on her face. She looked me up and down, and her implication became clear.

I wanted to ask her why any person of even limited intelligence would choose to believe an article in a faceless magazine whose writers had looked at a product for a few days, over professionals who spent years working hands on, learning all the strengths and weaknesses of every model. I wanted to show her, through back issues, how *Consumer Reports* routinely top-rated a model one year, then turned around and gave the *identical model* a low rating the next.

I wanted to, but I didn't. This truly misanthropic breed of salesmen-baiters, who spend entire sunny weekends on retail floors with their magazines and pads, imagining themselves as crusaders in some made-up battle that is significant only to them, truly lie beyond conversion to humanity. And there is nothing more indignant than a salesman who is called a liar on those rare occasions when he is struggling heroically to tell the truth.

'I'm sorry,' I said. 'We simply don't have that model. It's been discontinued.'

'I hardly have time,' she said, 'to bandy about on this matter with a *clerk*.' Then she walked quickly from the store.

Louie finished up with his customer and swaggered my way. He looked down at his shoes and scraped a fleck of dead skin off the bridge of his nose.

'That was pretty smooth, Nick. You didn't call her any names before you blew her out the door, did you, just so I know?'

'Nothing like that.'

'Yeah, well. You been off the floor too long. Half the people come in here be actin' all superior – you can't let that bust on your groove. It's part of the job, man, it's what they payin' us for.'

I looked at his sagging, tired face, and then at McGinnes and Malone, who were talking to each other in the Sound Explosion. The twelve-hour shifts, the standing on one's feet all day long on concrete floors and the varicose veins that resulted from that, the constant degradation from customers and management alike, the absence of praise or compliment, the cycle of work and drink and drugs and back again – it was taking its toll on all of them. The money became insignificant; ultimately the only reward was to get the deal, a small victory for its own sake that led inevitably to some suburban funeral parlor, where small groups of old men in stubbornly plaided polyesters stood in circles and said things like, 'I remember the time Johnny stepped a customer off a giveaway RCA to a no-name piece of *dreck* that had a fifty dollar bill on it.'

'I'm going to take a break, Louie.'

'Go ahead,' he said.

The rain was not abating. I crossed the Avenue and jogged south two blocks to an Amoco station, as the wet tires of slow-moving vehicles hissed past. I bought road maps of Virginia and the Carolinas in the office of the station and fitted them in the dry inside pocket of my jacket.

By the time I had run back up the block and entered the Golden Temple, I was heavy with rainwater. The matriarch of the family-owned restaurant seated me at a warm deuce in the rearmost corner. She set down a cup of tea and left the pot.

Her husband came out of the kitchen shortly thereafter, rubbing his hands with a rag. He was wearing a white uniform and had a white paper hat on his head. Straight gray hair shot out from underneath the hat in several directions. He clapped me on the shoulder. I said hello as he pulled the menu from my hands.

'You don't need,' he said, and walked back to the kitchen after tossing the menu behind the register.

He returned five minutes later with steamed dumplings and some combination noodles that were mixed with thin slices of pork, shrimp, spring onions, and ginger. I ate while I studied the road maps I had spread out on the table.

Mama-san handed me the check when I was finished. I left fourteen on nine and walked to the entranceway, where I dropped a quarter into a payphone and dialed. Pence picked up on the second ring.

'This is Nick Stefanos.'

'Mr Stefanos,' he said, bringing some phlegm up from his throat. 'What's the word on your progress?'

I told him nearly everything I had learned in the last few days, soft-pedaling the character of Broda's companions and omitting entirely the theft and drug angles.

'Frankly,' I said, 'I think your grandson is just on a long joyride. He'll be back as soon as the money runs out.'

'And you plan on leaving it at that?'

'Not entirely. But I believe he's safe right now.' The old man picked up the doubt in my voice.

He sighed, said in a sarcastic manner, 'You do what you can,' and hung up.

I replaced the receiver and stood looking through the window at the rain, which was slicing at the road diagonally now, powered by a fierce wind. I pushed open the heavy door of The Golden Temple, stepped out onto the sidewalk, and let the stinging water hit my face.

14

The floor was dense with customers when I returned. Louie, who was hopelessly tied up with an elderly man, raised his arm over the man's head and pointed to a couple of live ones in the TV department.

I made my way towards them, ignoring a guy in a down jacket who was carrying a clipboard and demanding, for anyone who would listen, to see some 'literature.' McGinnes approached me in the aisle, doing his clipped goosestep and obviously in a hurry to get by. I grabbed his arm and stopped him.

'That guy over there needs some literature,' I said, jerking my head in the direction of the professional stroker in the down jacket.

'I sell electronics,' McGinnes said, loud enough for the customer to hear. 'If he wants literature, tell him to go to the library.' Then he rapped me on the dick with his fist and walked away.

The pain had subsided by the time I greeted my first customers. Louie had been on the mark by signaling me, as they bought within five minutes.

The rush was unusually long and steady, even for a Saturday, and continued unbroken for the next three hours. McGinnes and Malone did battle all afternoon. From the wide smile on Malone's face and from his energy level (at one point I saw him leap over a console to greet a customer), it was clear that he thought he was trouncing McGinnes.

But McGinnes was quietly writing some business that day. I knew he was booking from the way he rushed customers to the front counter as he closed and from the look of thought and determination on his face as he prioritized the floor. Louie basically handled the be-backs and took TOs from Lloyd. Between the two of them they probably popped five grand.

As for me, I found my rhythm. During one pitch I felt the adrenalin rush at that point where I realized I had succeeded in stepping a customer into a four-piece, high-profit, high-commission deal, though ultimately Malone's sales number would go on the ticket. And the day peaked for me when I attracted the audience of three separate couples during my pitch to one of them on a twenty-seven-inch stereo monitor set. Two of the three couples stepped up and bought. From across the room McGinnes smiled, crossed his arms, cocked his hip, and gave me a broad wink.

By four-thirty the crowd had dwindled to a few customers. My voice was nearly shot. Louie and Lloyd were waiting on the last people, while McGinnes, Malone, and I stood in the shadows of the Sound Explosion and popped three malt liquors. Lee came to us with several strands of adding machine tape in her fist. I handed her my can and she had a swig.

'So what's the total, darling?' Malone asked.

'We did twenty-five,' she said. 'Louie's going to be happy.'

'Damn good Saturday,' McGinnes said.

'What I do?' Malone said.

'Okay,' Lee said. 'Here it is. Louie and Lloyd wrote almost six between them. Nick wrote six, and gave you guys three each out of that.'

'What I do?' Malone said again.

'You wrote ninety-two hundred, Andre. And Johnny did just over ten thousand.'

'Got*damn*,' Malone said, jumping up and half-spinning. 'That last motherfucker was the only customer I had all day that walked on my ass. I would've had you too.'

'You had a *day*, Andre,' McGinnes said, and slapped Malone's hand. 'You too, Nick. We all did.'

Lloyd, wearing a nylon windbreaker and galoshes, waved good-bye to us, and left the store with Louie, who locked the door behind him. minutes later he was back from Mr Liquor and marching down the aisle with a case of Tuborg cradled in his arms.

'Here,' he said, breaking the cans off the plastic rings and passing them around. 'I don't care who the top man was today. *Everybody* smoked.'

For the next hour we sat there, our ties loose at the collar, and killed the case of beer. Malone's cigarette smoke hovered around us as we told war stories of the day that became increasingly more dramatic with every beer. When the last empty hit the trash can, McGinnes suggested we shut down and walk up the Avenue to La Fortresse, a bar that he childishly insisted on calling 'La FurPiece.'

The wind and rain were against us as we crossed the street and headed up the east side of the block. Louie and Malone were ahead, trying to keep up with McGinnes as he motored up the slight incline. Lee huddled in as I turned up the collar of my jacket and put my arm around her shoulder.

La Fortresse was an alky bar with a French name and medieval decor that was owned and run by a Turk. It was one of the few bars in town that served a rocks glass full of liquor with a miniature mixer on the side. There was only one reason to come here, and that was to crawl deep into the bag.

A few old heads turned when Lee and I walked in, then returned to their drinks and the welterweight bout on the tube. We walked along the bar to the back room, which housed a piano, and where McGinnes, Malone, and Louie were already seated. The antique farm implements that hung on the wall resembled torture devices circa the Inquisition.

An easel holding an art card stood at the entranceway to the room, announcing the 'Piano Interpretations of the Fabulous Buddy Floyd.' Around Mr Floyd's name were glitter drawings of a champagne bottle, bow tie, and several musical notes. We entered and sat with the others at a large corner table with a curved leatherette seat molded into the wall.

Presently a woman with an intoxicatingly crooked smile arrived to take our order. She had beautifully textured dark skin and spoke with a Caribbean accent.

Lee ordered an Absolut and tonic with a twist; I had an Old Grand-Dad, Malone took Courvoisier with a side of coke, and McGinnes asked for rail scotch with water. Louie ordered a draught.

'Make mine a double, honey,' McGinnes said to the waitress as she began to walk away.

'They're all doubles,' she said patiently.

'I know that, sweetheart. Just joking.'

The drinks came and we toasted the day. The liquor was filled to the top of the heavy tumblers. I took a deep pull off the bourbon, one that ironed the dampness from my shirt.

McGinnes and Malone were building something with matches and straws on the table. Louie sat to my right and we listened to Lee tell us about the courses she was taking at AU and her plans for after college. Her arm was through mine, and she was refreshingly unconcerned about Louie's awareness of our relationship.

The waitress returned and we all ordered another round. McGinnes had not used any of his water to cut the scotch. Lee excused herself to go to the ladies' room.

'She's all right, you know?' Louie said, leaning in towards me as if we were conspirators.

'Yeah, I know. She's cool.'

'Don't mess her up, man. When you have a young lady like that,' he said, his hand cupped as if he were holding her in his palm, 'you don't mess with it.'

'Shit, Louie, give me more credit than that. Anyway, she already told me what was what.'

'I bet she did,' he said, smiling. 'Her shit is more together than yours, man. And she's ten years younger.'

The waitress brought our round. I took a sip and watched Louie down half his mug in one gulp.

'I'm a product of my generation, Louie. I guess it was all those Thoreau posters my junior-high hippie English teachers used to hang on the wall. "March to a different drummer," and all that. How many guys my age you read about, they're making a shitload of money, they decide to quit because they're not "happy."'

'I don't know whose product it is,' Louie said, 'but you're right. Now the kids coming up, Lee's age, they *know* what they want.'

'Like Ric Brandon?'

'Brandon's an asshole,' he said, waving his hand. 'You know what I mean. For instance, man, you don't mind my saying so, I been knowing you a long time. And you did a helluva job today. But, Nick, you fuckin' up.'

'How so?'

'You sweat your ass off moving stock, you come up through the ranks in sales, you put yourself through college to get to that management position you're in, now you act like it don't mean nuthin'.' He got right up in my face. 'What's goin' on with you, man?'

'I don't know, Louie. I just can't convince myself anymore that what I do is important.'

'Important? Come on, man, wake up. Where in the world did you get the idea that the work you do in life has to be important?' He took a swig of beer. 'Let me tell you something, man. When I was young – you don't even remember the D.C. I'm talkin' about – this town was split black and white for real. I couldn't sit with you like this in a bar and have a beer. In the early sixties I went to work in the old Kann's department store downtown, and when the riots went down, they had no choice but to make me department manager.'

Lee came back and sat next to me. We all had some of our drinks, and Louie continued.

'Well, you know they went out of business like everybody else down there. But I got hired as a manager at Moe's on New York Avenue. A couple of years later Moe died, his kids took over the business, and they went belly-up too. Then Nathan's put me on as assistant manager over in Arlington. It was rough for a while, but I hung with it and eventually they give me this store.' He finished his draught and put it loudly on the table. 'So I come a long way from the Colored Only section of this town to where I'm at. I don't just work here. I'm the *manager* of a store on Connecticut Avenue, understand what I'm sayin'? I own a house and every three years I buy a new ride. I got me a kid at Maryland, one at UDC.' He paused and stared me down. 'You want to know what's important.'

A small man with a heavily veined nose wearing a tuxedo that fit like an afterthought walked into the room. He sat at the piano and placed his highball glass filled with straight liquor on a coaster.

'Welcome,' he said into the mike, 'to La Fortresse.'

'It's La FurPiece,' McGinnes shouted, and Lee jabbed me in the ribs.

'My name is Buddy Floyd,' the man said, and began indelicately playing the piano intro to 'Tie a Yellow Ribbon.' With each chorus he turned his head in our direction and nodded in encouragement for us to sing along.

Mercifully, others began filing into the room, older couples over-dressed for this joint and out of their idea of a night on the town. Most of them were half-lit, and some of the women were elderly enough to be losing their hair, their pink scalps visible through their bouffants. For some reason I felt a tinge of sadness and kissed Lee on the cheek. Buddy Floyd was singing 'They Call the Wind Maria.'

'I'm pretty buzzed,' Lee admitted, finishing her second vodka.

'So am I. You want to go?'

'Yes,' she said. 'Can we stay together tonight?'

'Sure. But let's go to my crib, okay?'

'Okay,' she laughed. 'But aren't you a little big for a crib?'

We settled up by leaving a twenty on the table. Lee kissed Louie good-bye. Malone, who was whispering something to our waitress, looked up long enough to give us a wink.

McGinnes was behind the piano, one arm around an older woman with raven black hair in the shape of a football helmet, his other hand clutching a precariously tilted tumbler of scotch. He and the others grouped around the piano were laughing and singing along loudly to the Fabulous Buddy Floyd's interpretation of 'Hello, Dolly.'

At the district line I stopped for a bottle of red wine, then headed towards my apartment. We sat in the car in front of my place, talking and listening to some old Van Morrison. When that was over, we went inside.

A half bottle of wine later our clothes were thrown about the living room and Lee and I were writhing all over my couch. We ended it loudly and in a sweat, with Lee inclined in the corner, the tops of her calves locked beneath my ears, the soles of her feet pointing at the ceiling.

Afterwards, I slid a pillow under her ass to catch the wetness, and watched the sweat roll onto her chest and break apart as it reached her large, brown nipples.

My apartment resembled a bombed-out laundromat. The cat had Lee's underwear on her head and was bumping into furniture. Lee pulled my face down and kissed me on the mouth for a long time.

'I had a good Saturday,' she said sweetly.

'Yeah,' I said. 'Me too.' Then I pulled a white blanket up from the back of the couch and spread it over us, and we slept, holding each other until morning.

15

Lee asked, 'Where are we going?'

After a slow morning of breakfast and the Sunday *Post* at my place, we were heading south on Thirteenth Street, passing large detached homes with expansive porches. Ahead stood three-story rowhouses crowned with incongruously grand turrets.

'We're going to visit someone,' I said. 'A friend of my grandfather's.'

I turned right on Randolph and parked halfway down the block of boxy brick houses. There was little color in the trimwork or shutters here. Dogs barked angrily from alleys. Even on bright and sunny days, this street seemed to remain dark.

'This is my Uncle Costa's place,' I said. 'He worked for my grandfather when he was a young man. When he wanted to start his own business, my grandfather helped him out.'

'Let's go in.'

'I just wanted to explain to you first, before you meet him. Let's just say that some of these guys didn't really assimilate themselves too well into the American culture.'

'You're not ashamed of him, are you?'

'Not at all.'

'Fine,' she said, tugging at my arm. 'Let's just go in.'

As we walked up the steps, I waved to a man coming out of the next house who I knew to be a reverend. Behind us two gangly but tough-looking kids walked down the sidewalk, one wearing a Fila sweatsuit, the other with an Eddie Murphy 'Golden Child' leather cap on his head.

A rusted metal rocker with moldy cushions sat on the concrete porch. Black iron bars filled the windows. I knocked on the door and waited, counting three locks being undone. Costa opened the door, looked at me, and smiled.

'Niko,' he said.

'*Theo* Costa.' I gripped his hand and kissed him on the cheek.

He was short and solid, with thick wavy black hair that was gray at the temples and slicked back, and a thin black mustache below his bumpy nose. Though it was Sunday, he wore a short-sleeved white shirt with two pens clipped in the breast pocket.

'Come on,' he said, waving us in with both hands. As Lee passed him, he looked back at me and said in Greek, 'Your girl? Very nice.'

'A friend,' I answered, but he winked anyway.

I introduced her and they shook hands. A couple of cats ran by us and into the kitchen. The curtains were drawn throughout the house. Costa switched on lights as we followed him through the living room and into the dining room. The air was dry and very still.

We sat at a large table in ornate chairs with yellowed cushions. On one wall was a mirror covered with a blanket; on the other hung a sepia-tinted photograph of a man and woman that had been taken in the early part of the century. The woman, even shorter than the short man and wearing a long black dress, was unsmiling. The man wore a baggy suit, a very thick mustache, and a watchchain from vest to pocket.

'You want coffee, *gleeka*?' Costa asked.

'Thanks, Costa. Nescafe for Lee.'

'One minute,' he said in Greek, jabbing a finger in the air and stepping quickly into the kitchen.

'He's nice,' Lee said. I nodded and she pointed to the wall. 'What's with the mirrors? I noticed the one in the living room is covered too.'

'His wife died last year,' I said. 'He covered the mirrors so he won't see her reflection.' She raised her eyebrows. 'I told you.'

'It's just that it's so dark in here, and sad. He must be very depressed.'

'I'm sure he's a little lonely and misses his wife. But this house was always closed up and dark, even when she was alive. They're old-timers, that's all.'

Costa returned with a tray of two Turkish coffees, a cup of instant, and a small platter of sweets, which he set in the center of the table. On the platter were *koulourakia, kourabiedes, galactoboureko,* and *baklava.* He pushed the whole thing in front of Lee.

'Don't be shy,' he said, moving his hands in small circles. 'Eat!'

'I like baklava,' she admitted, emphasizing the second syllable as most Americans do, and chose a slice. I took a *kourabiede* for myself.

We sat and talked for the next half hour, mostly about what we had been doing in the time since I'd seen him last. The tiny cup of coffee had given me quite a jolt. Lee eventually drifted away from the table and began to wander around the house. We heard her steps on the wooden staircase that led down to the basement.

She called upstairs excitedly, 'Hey, Nicky, there must be twenty cats down here!'

'Twenty cats, Costa?' I said, and smiled.

'Maybe a dozen,' he said sourly. 'Lousy *gatas*.'

'If you'd quit feeding them . . .'

'Aah,' he said, dismissing me with a wave of his hand.

Now that Lee was gone we spoke in Greek. Though I understood everything he said, I kept my own sentences simple so as not to embarrass myself with my marginal command of the language.

Costa reached behind him and opened the door of an old wall cabinet. He pulled out a bottle of Metaxa and two shot glasses.

'Too early for you, Niko?'

'No.' He poured a couple of slugs with efficiency and we knocked glasses. He sipped and watched as I threw mine back in one quick motion, returning the little glass to the table with a hollow thud.

'You drink like a Spartan,' he said.

'Like my *papou*.'

'Your *papou* could drink. But he gave it up when your parents sent you to him.'

'I miss him,' I said.

'He would be proud of you,' Costa said. Like most immigrants he equated my white collar with success.

'I'm doing fine,' I said.

'It's time you found another woman.'

'I'm not against the idea.'

'The girl you're with. She's Jewish?'

'Yes. She's my friend, like I told you.'

'Friends, okay. And the Jews are good people, very smart in business. But it's not good to mix, you found that out. Marry a Greek girl.'

He finished his drink and poured two more shots. A gray cat with green eyes did a figure eight around my feet then jumped up onto my lap. Costa reached across the table and picked it off me, tossing it to the other side of the room.

'How is it here in the neighborhood, now *Theo*?'

'Not too bad,' he said, and shrugged. 'When Toula was alive, I worried more. They took her purse once, when she was walking home with groceries.' His eyes were a faded brown and watery, more from long afternoons of drinking than from bitterness.

'It's not the said town it was,' I said.

'You don't even remember how good it was,' he said, suddenly animated. He pointed a finger at my chest. 'When I first came here, your *papou* and me swam in the Potomac on hot summer afternoons. Now it's so dirty, I wouldn't even throw a photograph of myself into that river.'

I laughed as he finished his shot. I turned the bottle around on the table and read the label.

'Five star, Costa?'

'Yes. Very good.'

'Do you think you'll go back to Greece?' I asked, wondering why anyone would remain a prisoner in a house like this, in a city where the only common community interest was to get safely through another day.

'No, I plan on dying here. Believe me, Niko,' he said, without a trace of irony, 'there is no place in the world like America.'

Later that day Lee and I drove down to Southwest and walked along the water, checking out the yachts in the marina. Continuing west, we ended up at the fish market on Maine Avenue.

Most of the good fish had been picked over by that time of day. I bought some squid, at one forty-nine a pound, from a cross-eyed salt who was attempting to stare at Lee. We took it back to my apartment.

After removing the ink sacks and the center bone, I sliced the squid laterally into thin rings, and shook them in a bag with a mixture of bread crumbs, garlic, and oregano. Then I fried them in olive oil in a hot skillet.

We ate these with lemon and a couple of beers as we watched the first half of the Skins game. For the second half we napped together on the couch in roughly the same arrangement as the night before. We woke as the afternoon light was fading. I drove her back to her car at the store and kissed her good-bye.

Back in my apartment I warmed some soup on the stove. From the television in the living room I heard the stopwatch intro to '60 Minutes' and felt that familiar rush of anxiety, announcing that my weekend was ticking away.

Two hours later I dialed the international operator and reached Greece. For the next ten minutes I was shuttled around to various women who worked the switchboards. Finally I reached my mother at her home in a village near Sparta. I had last spoken to my parents on the day my grandfather died.

We spoke superficially about our lives. She ended most of her sentences with, 'my boy' or 'my son.' I tried not to confuse the ethnic inflection in her voice with concern or, especially, love. As our conversation pared down to awkward silences between pleasantries, I began to wonder, as I always did, why I had called.

I turned in early that night but lay in the dark for quite a while before I finally went to sleep. Though I forced myself to wake several times during the night, I was unsuccessful in stopping Jimmy Broda from haunting my dreams.

16

I was nearly done shaving my weekend stubble when Ric Brandon called early Monday morning. He instructed me to change my plans for working on the Avenue and report to the office.

I finished shaving and undid my tie, switching from an Italian print to a wine and olive rep. I changed my side buckle shoes to a relatively more conservative pair of black oxfords that had thin steel plates wrapped around the outside of the toes. I put on a thrift shop Harris Tweed, secured the apartment, and drove to work.

When I reached the receptionist's desk at half past nine, the office was already bustling with Monday morning's full fury. Calls from customers who had been stiffed on their weekend deliveries were automatically being forwarded to the wrong extensions. All terminals were printing, and everyone, though they were moving fairly quickly, carried Styrofoam cups of hot coffee in their hands. The usual line of delivery drivers and warehousemen had formed at the personnel office to complain about Friday's paycheck.

Marsha was screening the call of an angry consumer, but dug deep for a smile as I tapped her desk and set upright the 'Elvis Country' plaque that had been knocked on its side.

Aside from a couple of new plants, the office had not changed in the week of my absence. There were several rows of used metal desks with laminated tops. The desks displayed photographs of children; notes written on small squares of adhesive-backed paper, stuck on the necks of clip-on lamps; rubber figurines from the fast food death-houses, this year's being the California Raisins, running across the tops of computer terminals – all illuminated by the green glow of florescence.

I removed my jacket and had a seat at my desk. Marsha had arranged my mail in stacks, separated by solicitations, trade magazines, and important co-op advertising credits and checks. I tossed the junk mail after a quick glance at the return addresses, then went to the employee lounge for a cup of coffee.

When I returned, Ric Brandon was at my desk, his elbows leaning awkwardly on the soundtreated divider that separated Gary Fisher's cubicle from mine. He was wearing a boxy navy blue suit with a white shirt, and this year's popular tie among the fast-track M.B.A.s, a green print.

'Where's the funeral, Ric?' I said, and sipped my rancid coffee.

'No funeral,' he said a little too cheerfully. He looked down at his black wing tips. 'I'd like to see you in my office at eleven sharp.'

'Sure, Ric. Eleven.'

He put his head over the divider and told Fisher he wanted to speak to him 'right now.' Then Fisher followed Brandon down the hall into his office, where they closed the door behind them.

I checked my watch, pulled the accounts receivable file from my desk, and reconciled my co-op credits. After that I went through my messages. Karen had phoned twice. I took her messages, along with those from the radio and television reps, local newspapers and magazines, and direct mail houses, and threw them all away. I put the remaining stack of customer complains under my phone, to be dealt with after my meeting with Brandon.

Fisher emerged from Brandon's office and shot me a dim glance. He walked in the direction opposite to our desks. As he walked, he stared at his shoes.

In the next fifteen minutes the office became strangely quiet. Though I had seen this many times before, I would not have expected to feel so oddly relieved when it happened to me. Nevertheless, the signs were all around me: the walking in and out of closed doors by management, the avoidance of eye contact, and the whispering into phones as word began to spread by interoffice lines.

I called Patti Dawson and a couple of the vendors with whom I had become close. Then I put on my jacket and walked to the receptionist's desk.

'I'm running out to 7-Eleven,' I said to Marsha. 'You want anything?' Her lips were pursed and there were tears in her eyes. She shook her head, unable to speak. I felt worse for her than I did for myself. 'I'll be back by eleven.'

I passed under the Nutty Nathan's caricature at the foot of the stairs and walked across the parking lot to my car. Then I drove to a hardware store on Sligo Avenue, had a duplicate made of my office key, and returned to headquarters.

At eleven I knocked on the door of Ric Brandon's office. He waved me in. I closed the door and had a seat. He lowered the volume of the news program on the radio, pulled out the bottom drawer of his desk, and rested the soles of his wing tips on the edge of it.

'Nick,' he said, his delicate hands together and pointed at me as if in prayer, 'this is a follow-up to our conversation in this office a week ago. Do you remember the gist of it?'

'Yes.'

'I'd like to reiterate some aspects of it before we continue. In our conversation you basically agreed to play on the management side of the fence in this company, and to work more seriously at your position. This was definitely a fourth down situation, but understand that I allowed *you* to call the play.'

I had spent many nights, lying awake in bed with fists clenched involuntarily, fantasizing about this moment. Usually the fantasy consisted of me firing off a string of cleverly vulgar obscenities, but on weirdly violent nights it ended with me pulling Brandon over his desk by his Brooks Brothers lapels.

Now, looking at his reddening face and hearing his feet slide nervously off the desk drawer that he had only moments before so coolly placed them on, I only wished he'd hurry up and get this done. I must have been grinning, because his plastic smile faded, leaving his fat upper lip stuck momentarily on one of his big front teeth.

'So it was my call, Ric. How did I blow it?'

'Don't think for a moment that I don't wish I was sitting here praising your performance. But when you went to work in our Connecticut Avenue store, you went as a representative of management. And you let us down.'

'How so?'

'A very serious complaint was filed last week. A customer called and claimed that two salesmen, fitting the description of John McGinnes and yourself, were intoxicated during business hours. The customer also reported the smell of marijuana in the store. Can you explain this?'

I looked out of Brandon's tiny window, across the office and through the larger window on the south wall, at the brilliant blue sky. It was one of the last beautifully sunny days of the year.

'Are you letting me go?'

'I'm afraid so, Nick.' His body relaxed in his chair.

'What about McGinnes?'

'I do only what's right for this company. McGinnes is an extremely valuable employee. I'm hoping that a very serious conversation with him will straighten things around. He's the engine that powers that store. Bates and Malone are decent employees, but they're in that store basically because I need some black faces on my D.C. floor. No, I definitely think McGinnes is salvageable.'

'You didn't actually take that complaint yourself, did you Ric?'

'Mr Rosen,' he said unsteadily, 'took the call when I was out. He suggested that there was no alternative but to let you go. Frankly, on this point I agreed. The nature of the complaint constituted a firing offense.'

Through the window of the south wall I watched a flock of blackbirds pass across the blue sky. I rose from my chair. 'Is that all?' I asked. I stared at him until he looked down at his desk, a little gray in the face but basically unmoved.

'I've written up your termination papers, effective immediately,' he said coldly. 'You're eligible for vacation pay, which will come in your final check. I'll pass this on to personnel.'

I walked out of his office and softly closed the door behind me.

It didn't take long to clean out my desk. I was quite certain that I was through with retail. I left behind industry related materials, drawing implements, certificates from management seminars, sales awards, and all other evidence of my tenure in the business. Oddly, the things I put into the plastic bag that a tight-jawed Fisher had wordlessly handed me were the most memorable objects of my career at Nutty Nathan's: a book of matches, on the cover of which was printed 'It Pays to Advertise,' which opened up to a pair of paper legs that spread to expose a thick patch of female 'wool'; a caricature of me that the office girls had commissioned, with what I thought to be a rather lecherous look in my eyes and with a cigarette hanging trashily out the side of my mouth, circa my smoking days; a set of pencils with erasers shaped as dickheads; and a file of vulgarities that is charitably referred to as Xerox 'art.'

All of these things I knew would end up in my apartment's waste-basket. But on that day, like some sentimental pornographer, I couldn't bear to leave them in my desk.

I dropped the duplicate key off with the woman in charge at the personnel office, who was busy cutting out clip art for the company newsletter, a waste of paper so heinous that as 'editor' she should have been convicted of arboricide. Seaton, the controller who peed with his trousers around his ankles, stopped me in the hall to shake my hand and wish me luck. Though he was wrongfully despised by many employees for the cutbacks he was constantly forced to make, he was the only one that day with the guts to say good-bye.

A young woman wearing a Redskins jersey was sitting at the switchboard in Marsha's place. I gave her a questioning look.

'She's in the bathroom,' she said accusingly, 'crying.' She popped her gum and looked me over.

'Tell her I'll talk to her later,' I said.

'Sure, Nick. Take it easy.'

I turned and walked down the stairs, out the door, and across the parking lot, the plastic bag of novelties (the summation of my career) in my hand, a weird grin on my face. It was only eleven-thirty, and therefore a bit early for a cocktail. A cold beer, however, would do just fine.

I was hammering my second can of Bud at the counter of the Good Times Lunch when I noticed a primered Torino parked on the east side of Georgia Avenue. Two men were in the front seat, and one of them was smoking and staring in my direction. Kim was pulling my lunch out of the deep fryer with a pair of tongs.

'I lost my job today, Kim,' I said. He turned his head, looked at the can in my hand, then into my eyes. 'I'm a free man.'

A man seated at the end of the counter wearing an army jacket raised his beer to me in a toast. The radio was playing a half-spoken ballad by a teenage soul singer, barely audible above the jetlike sound of the upright fan.

My lunch was a breaded veal patty with a side of green beans and fries. I ate it quickly, especially rushing through the tastelessness of the veal.

After the lunch crowd had gone, I stayed and had another beer. Once, when Kim walked by, he almost spoke, but passed with only a nod. The primered Torino was still across the street, its occupants still staring into the Good Times Lunch. The last customer walked out as I finished my fourth.

The two men got out of the Torino. I watched them hustle across the street. They were very dark and wiry. They entered the store and moved quickly in my direction.

'What's going on?' I asked in a friendly tone, rising instinctively to face them.

The lead man threw a quick, hard right into my belly that dropped me to one knee. I coughed, fought for breath, and spit up a short blast of beer. I saw his foot coming but was unable to block it. The instep of his boot caught me solidly across the bridge of my nose. I felt the cartilage collapse and a needlelike pain as the force of his kick knocked me back into the base of a booth against the wall.

Kim must have made some sort of move. My attacker looked back and said, 'Fuck you, Chang. This here is *our* business,' then turned to face me. I tasted warm blood pouring down over my lip and into my mouth.

'You can stop all that shit with the boy,' the lead man said. 'Understand?' My nose felt as if it were pointing upward, and the man in front of me got blurry and then it was black for a few dead seconds.

When my vision came back, Kim was vaulting over the lunch counter, a black snub-nosed revolver in his hand. Just as his feet hit the floor, he swung the pistol, striking the second man in the temple with the short barrel and dropping him to the floor. Then he quickly pointed the piece towards the stunned face of the man who had smashed my nose.

The guy seemed to contemplate a break but wisely froze. Kim backed him up to the wall, brought the gun to his face, and tapped the steel of the barrel on the man's front teeth, hard enough so it made a sound.

'You no fuck *me*,' Kim said evenly. 'I fuck *you*.'

The man, hands up, moved slowly away from the wall with as much pride as he could fake. He helped his partner up and they silently backed out of the store. Kim kept the gun on them until they were gone, then locked the door from the inside.

I thought too late to read their plates. By the time I staggered to the door, their car was a fishtailing blur of smoke and burning rubber. I did notice that the plates were out of state, though all I could make out was a design something like a mushroom cloud.

'No cops,' I said as Kim replaced the gun beneath the register. He nodded and pointed to the back room.

I lay on a cot next to a chest freezer, looking up at a shelf stocked with pickle spears and clam juice, holding a compress to my nose. The bleeding had stopped but the pain intensified.

'Help me up, Kim,' I said as he entered the room. He put a hand behind my back and another around my arm, bringing me to a sitting position. The room caved in from both sides, but soon converged into one picture.

'Okay?' he asked.

'I think so. Thanks, Kim.'

'No trouble in my place,' he said with certainty, then smiled rakishly. 'Bad day, Nick.'

'Yeah. Bad day.'

The doctor who worked on me at the Washington Adventist Hospital looked at my paper and asked if I was Italian.

'Greek,' I said.

'Well,' she said cheerfully, 'now you'll have a classic Greek nose to go with your name.'

'Helluva way to legitimize my name. Is it broken?'

'Not badly,' she said, whatever that meant. She wrote out a prescription and handed me the paper. 'These will help.'

I took the script. 'They usually do. They any good?'

She looked at me sternly. 'No alcohol with these, understand?'

'Sure, doc. Thanks a million.'

At my apartment I ate two of the codeines and chased them with a serious shot of Grand-Dad. Then I ran a tub of hot water and lay in it, everything submerged but my head and left hand, which held a cold can of beer.

A couple of hours later I awoke in the tub, now filled with tepid water. The empty can floated near my knee. My cat sat on the radiator and stared at my nose. It was still broken.

I got out of the tub, toweled dry, brushed my teeth, and switched off the light quickly so that I could not catch my image in the bathroom mirror.

The red light on my answering machine was blinking so I pressed down on the bar. The four calls, in succession, were from Karen, Joe Dane, Fisher, and McGinnes. All of the messages, except Karen's, were condolences on the loss of my job. Typically, McGinnes' was the only one with humor and without a trace of awkward sentiment. He ended his pep talk with what I'm sure he considered to be an essential bit of advice: 'Don't let your meat loaf,' he said.

Craving a black sleep, I chewed two more codeines and crawled into the rack.

17

I first met Karen in a bar in Southeast, a new wave club near the Eastern Market run by an Arab named Haddad whom everyone called HaDaddy-O.

This was late in '79 or early in 1980, the watershed years that saw the debut release of the Pretenders, Graham Parker's *Squeezing Out Sparks*, and Elvis Costello's *Get Happy*, three of the finest albums ever produced. That I get nostalgic now when I hear 'You Can't Be Too Strong' or 'New Amsterdam,' or when I smell cigarette smoke in a bar or feel sweat drip down my back in a hot club, may seem incredible today – especially to those who get misty-eyed over Sinatra, or even at the first few chords of 'Satisfaction' – but I'm talking about *my* generation.

Because this club was in a potentially rough section of town, it discouraged the closet Billy Joel lovers and frat boys out to pick up 'punk chicks.' Mostly the patrons consisted of liberal arts majors, waiters who were aspiring actors and writers, and rummies who fell in off the street.

In that particular year the pin-up girl for our crowd was Chrissie Hinde. When I first saw Karen, leaning against the service bar in jeans, short boots, and a black leather motorcycle jacket, it was the only time that the sight of a woman has literally taken my breath away. With her slightly off-center smile, full lips, and heavy black eyeliner, she had that bitch look that I have always chased.

I felt sharp that night – black workboots, 501 jeans, a blue oxford, skinny black tie, and a charcoal patterned sportcoat – but when I approached her and offered to buy her a drink (hardly original, but I was after all, in awe), she declined. I cockily explained that she was blowing a good opportunity.

'Then some day,' she said solemnly, 'I'll look back on this moment with deep regret.' And walked away.

But soon after that I caught her checking me out in the barroom mirror.

A few beers later, keeping an eye on what she was doing and what she was drinking, I watched her walk out the back door, alone, to a patio behind the club. Hurrying up to the bar, I ordered her drink (Bombay with a splash of tonic and two limes) and a beer, and followed her outside.

She smiled and accepted the drink and my company. We sat in wrought-iron garden furniture, drinking and smoking cigarettes and some Lebanese hash I kept in the fold of my wallet for special occasions.

As the band grew trashier (a local female rocker who made up for a serious lack of tone by rubbing her crotch throughout the set) and the joint filled up, that time of night came when men were in the ladies' room pissing in the sink and several minor fights were breaking out. But at this point Karen and I were only concentrating on each other.

Two rounds later we were in the men's room stall, doing coke off the commode (a half Karen scored from the bartender), laughing because we couldn't even see the white on white. We dragged each other out of the place and, climbing into another old Chrysler product I was driving at the time, headed across town.

Then we were on the George Washington Parkway, screaming north at eighty miles per, all four windows down, and listening to Madness' 'Night Boat to Cairo' at maximum volume with the radio dead set on 102.3, the old home of the then-ballsy HFS. We were twisted out of our minds and higher than hippies, and Karen had already unzipped my fly and dug in, and I knew it was going to be amazing, that night and maybe longer.

And it was, but only for about six months. By that time I had graduated from college and we had impulse-married and rented a portion of a house on the east side of the Hill. Soon Karen began wearing her hair differently and lost the eye makeup. She diagnosed me (correctly) as a childish romantic, and pushed me to be more assertive at work and 'go for' management, which I grudgingly did.

We split up less than a year after we were married. Though it seems as if the explanation for our failed marriage should be more complicated, I know it to be just that simple.

When Karen opened the door of her apartment, located in old Arlington, the look of disappointment was plain upon her face. I had cleaned up early Tuesday morning, keeping the bandages on as an alternative to the damage underneath. But the area below both eyes had begun to swell and discolor.

'Don't look so happy,' I said. 'I thought you wanted to see me.'

'I did, but not like this. What the hell happened to you, Nicky?'

'Can't I come in?'

'Sure,' she said, waving me forward with her hand. 'I'm sorry.'

She had on jeans and an oversized pocket T-shirt, which she dowdily wore outside the jeans. As I followed her into the kitchen, I noticed that her hips and bottom were a little fuller, though she carried it well. The wedge cut she was sporting was shaven high and tight on the back of her neck, this year's stylish but not over-the-top hairstyle for the career woman.

There were many labeled cartons lining the hall but no furniture in the apartment. The kitchen was empty except for a live coffeemaker and one cup. There were no chairs so I sat on the linoleum floor, my back against a base cabinet.

Karen washed out the cup in the sink, then handed it to me, filled with fresh coffee. I took a sip and rested the cup on my knee. She had a seat across from me against the bare white wall, and crossed one leg over the other. She still had a look about her.

'Now I know why you've been calling,' I said. 'You're leaving, right?'

'Yes. The company's moving me to Philadelphia this week.'

'Congratulations,' I said, careful to omit any hint of sarcasm. 'I assume it's a good move for you.'

'It's an excellent opportunity. I got a substantial raise, and something like a signing bonus. I'm looking forward to the change.'

'I'm sure you'll do well.'

'I've been trying to call you,' she said. 'I mean, I wouldn't have left without saying good-bye.'

'I'm sorry I didn't get back to you. There's so much been going on.'

'I can see,' she said. 'Are you all right?'

'My nose is broken. In the last week I've been beaten up, twice. Yesterday I lost my job at Nathan's. I'm not exactly on the fast track.'

'Shit, Nicky.' She shook her head slowly. I hadn't meant to go for sympathy, but her news had made me bitter.

We sat for a while without speaking. I listened to the tick of my watch.

'You look good,' I said, cutting the silence. We had often sat like this without awkwardness.

'Thanks. But I've put on a few.'

She leaned forward to stand. I looked down her loose T-shirt guiltlessly. Karen had truly beautiful breasts. I remembered waking before her some mornings and admiring them, slightly flattened as she lay sleeping on her back.

I turned down her offer for more coffee. She washed the cup, and with her back to me said, 'What are you going to do now?'

'I've got a couple of grand in my retirement account. That will get me through the bills for a while. In the meantime, I was hired by this old guy to find his missing grandson.'

'That why you got beaten up?'

'Yeah.'

'A detective now,' she stated flatly, though she might as well have told me just to grow up. I must have looked pathetic, sitting on the floor wearing my little adhesive nose mask. She rubbed her hands dry with a paper towel. Looking down at her feet, she said, 'I'm sorry, Nick. But I've got an awful lot to do today, with moving and all.'

'Sure, Karen,' I said, laboring to my feet. 'I should get going too.'

As she walked me to the door, I felt unsteady, as if another piece of my youth was being torn away. She faced me. The edge in her eyes, the dark side of her that had attracted me, was gone.

'Take care of yourself, Nicky,' she said. 'I'll write from Philly when I get settled.'

'So long,' I said, and kissed her mouth. I felt her warm exhale on my face when she withdrew.

I stepped out and down the walkway. The sound of her door closing behind me was final, like that of a vault.

I crossed the river via Chain Bridge and took Nebraska Avenue through to Connecticut, where I turned right and headed south a few blocks to Pence's building. One look at my battered face convinced him that I was indeed 'on the case'; he stroked me an expense check without flinching.

'Good luck, son!' he shouted, as I bolted out the door.

I spent the remainder of my day doing laundry, listening to music, and taking codeine siestas. By evening I had spoken to my landlord as to the location of the cat food and litter box, and packed my knapsack and overnight bag. When I was done, I phoned McGinnes at his apartment.

'What's going on, Johnny?'

'I'm on vacation till the weekend.'

'Brandon give you a few days off to think about things?'

'Yeah,' he said, 'but the little prick wants me back on the floor by Saturday, so he can make his numbers. How's your early retirement going?'

'Keeping busy. Some guys tried to warn me off the Broda thing yesterday. One of them put a boot to my face to make his point.'

'What now?'

'I'm leaving town for a couple of days to check out a lead. I could use some company.'

He thought it over. 'It beats sucking down draughts in the Zebra Room.'

'Good. I'll pick you up at eight, tomorrow morning.'

'I'll pack the cooler,' he said.

'Fine. And bring a swimsuit.'

'Now you're talkin'. Where we headed?'

'Elizabeth City,' I said. 'North Carolina.'

18

By the time we neared Richmond, traveling south on 95, we had listened to Green on Red's *Gas, Food, Lodging*, and on the other side of the tape, Lou Reed's *Coney Island Baby*. I slid in a fresh cassette, an instrumental mix from the Raybeats, Love Tractor, and the Monochrome Set, and turned off onto 64, heading east towards Norfolk.

'Jesus Christ, man,' McGinnes pleaded, 'pull over! I gotta' pee like a racehorse.'

'I'll pull over when your bladder's ready to burst.'

'It's ready now. Anyway, I didn't know we were being timed on this trip. What is this, the fucking Cannonball Run?'

I found a Stuckey's on one of the turnoffs. He was out of the car before I stopped, running through the pounding rain across the parking lot to the store and rest area. I pumped gas into my Dodge under the sheltering overhang.

'Nice weather,' I said to the attendant, an old guy who stood expressionless in his uniform, shoulders hunched up, hands in his pockets.

'For ducks,' he said.

McGinnes trotted back to the car, a paper bag in his hand, and got in the passenger side. I pulled back onto the highway, turning up the volume on my deck to cover the scraping of my wipers.

'Man, that felt good,' McGinnes said. 'I'm ready now.' He was pulling assorted candies and pecan logs from the bag.

'Careful. You might have bought something healthy. By mistake, I mean.'

'I doubt it,' he said. 'You want a beer?'

'No.'

But an hour later there was a cold can of Bud between my legs and McGinnes was working on his third one.

As we approached the Tidewater area, traffic increased and we crossed several small bridges. McGinnes rolled a joint, which we smoked while driving over and through the Hampton Roads Bridge Tunnel. We had been on the road for just under four hours.

At Route 17 I headed south along the Dismal Swamp Canal. The leaves on the trees had not yet begun to turn here. The rain had stopped and steam rose off the asphalt up ahead. We rolled our windows down. Jonathan Richman was on the stereo, telling his girl to 'drop out of BU.'

I looked over at McGinnes, who was wearing a Hawaiian print shirt with three pens in the breast pocket, a pair of twills, and Chucks. I had never seen him in sneakers.

'I like the shirt,' I said.

'I'm on a holiday,' he said with a Brit accent, holding the shirttail out and pointing it in my direction. 'Do you fancy it?'

'Yeah, I fancy it. But what are the pens for? You plan on writing some business while we're down here?' We crossed the state line into North Carolina, and McGinnes tapped my can with his.

'Just a habit,' he said.

'Hey, maybe you *could* get some work. Nathan Plavin's got a brother in the business down here, has a few retail stores of his own.'

'Yeah, I know. Ned Plavin. Ned's World, it's called. Jerry Rosen worked for him before he worked for Nathan. But his stores are in *South* Carolina, smartass.'

'Nutty Nathan's and Ned's World. Their parents must be proud.'

'Anyway,' he said, '*you're* the one out on his ear. I've still got a job.'

'Thanks.'

'I just hope you know what you're doing,' he said. 'I talked to Andre, told him the whole deal. Let's just say he's more familiar with the types of people you're dealing with now. He says the guys who worked you over aren't going to let that shit lie.'

'What else did Andre say?'

'He said the next time you're in the way, your Korean buddy won't be around to protect you. And then they'll take you down, man.'

'I'm not worried,' I said, and pinched his cheek. 'I've got you.'

We reached the Elizabeth City area before two in the afternoon. McGinnes suggested we drive around to get a feel for the place. In certain residential areas of the city were large Victorians, some with wraparound porches on more than one level. Cypress trees stood handsomely on wide green lawns.

We drove by the waterfront, which seemed to be rundown to the point of decay in several sections. There was little commercial activity on the Pasquotank River that day, though there were a few pleasure boats heading out to the sound.

'This used to be quite a port,' McGinnes said.

'It doesn't look like it was in our lifetime.'

'Not in our lifetime. I'm talking about in the nineteenth century. Some serious Civil War shit went down in these parts. Naval battles. The Union ended up taking this place early in the war.'

'How do you know so much about it?'

'I grew up in this state.'

'Come on, man,' I said. 'You're not talking to one of your customers now.'

'No, I'm serious. My old man was stationed at Lejeune. So we spent some time on the Carolina coast.'

'Then maybe you can steer us to a motel.'

'Is that an order?' he said, and wiggled his eyebrows.

We found a place off the bypass, a row of cottages that looked like toolsheds with stoops. The sign said Gates Motel. McGinnes kept calling it the 'Bates Motel' as we approached it, and insisted we stay there.

The woman in the office had probably seen a few things. But she couldn't help staring when we walked in, announced by the sleigh bells that hung on the inside of the door. McGinnes had on his Hawaiian retailer outfit and a beer in his hand, and I my crisscross adhesive nose mask.

'We'd like a room, please,' McGinnes said.

'Sure,' she wheezed, her slit of a mouth barely moving on her swollen face. 'Eighteen a night, checkout at eleven. How many nights you fellas plan on stayin'?'

'Just tonight for now,' I said. I signed the book and paid her as she suspiciously eyed a smiling McGinnes.

'Anything else?'

'Is there a phone?' I asked. 'I'll be needing to make some local calls.'

She went into a back room and returned with a dial phone and directory, placing them both on the counter in front of me.

'There's a jack in the room. Number nine.'

I took the key and handed her a ten. 'This should cover the phone.'

'That'll do.'

'Any bars around here?' McGinnes asked sheepishly.

'Sure is, son,' she said with a nasty grin. 'But if you was to go into any of 'em, I wouldn't wear that shirt.'

After a shower I sat on one of the twin beds in the room, with the phone in my lap and the white pages spread in front of me. McGinnes was out walking.

There were four Lazarus listings in the directory for the entire region. I began dialing.

My third call was to a T. J. Lazarus. The man who answered sounded old and either drunk or tired.

''Lo,' he said.

'Mr Lazarus?'

'Yes?'

'Kim's father?'

'Yes.'

'My name is Nick Stefanos,' I said quickly. 'I'm a friend of your daughter's.'

'Kim's away,' he said.

'I know. But I was heading south on business and stopped in town for the night. Thought I might meet Kim's folks.'

'Kim's mother passed on last year.'

'I'm sorry.'

'Don't bother yourself,' he said. 'But you just missed Kim. She was in town last week.'

'I'd like to drop by and meet you anyway, sir.'

'I don't know what the hell it is you want,' he said bluntly. 'But if you want to come by, come by. And stop and pick up some beer on your way out, will you?'

'Yessir.' I took his directions, thanked him, and hung up.

I shaved and removed my bandages, deciding I looked more vulnerable and less intimidating that way. McGinnes entered the room.

'There's a train runs behind here,' he said excitedly. 'I walked into the woods out back and down a hill to some tracks.' I didn't answer him. He looked at the keys in my hand. 'Where you headed?'

'I found the Lazarus girl's father,' I said. 'I'm going to talk to him.'

McGinnes drew a beer from the cooler at the foot of the bed. 'Check you later,' he said.

T. J. Lazarus lived on a street of old bungalows set on large pieces of land. His, a gray and white-shuttered affair, badly needed paint.

I crossed the walkway onto a wide wooden porch, where a black Lab rose clumsily to greet me. He sniffed at my jeans, then my hand, and gave me one perfunctory lick. Then he stood next to me and slowly wagged his tail as I knocked on the door.

The man who opened up and stood before me was well into his

seventies. He was tall and thin and rawboned, and wore blue chinos with a faded yellow T-shirt. There was a gardening glove on one of his hands. His eyes were alert and a fluid blue.

'Well, come on in,' he said, taking a good look at me before he shook my hand. 'We'll walk through the house and out back.'

His house was clean and furnished with worn, cushiony armchairs and sofas. A stereo television and VCR were set in the bookshelf, new models that made everything else in the place seem archaic. The dog stayed next to me as I followed Lazarus through the dining room to a back door that led to a screened porch.

'Been in a scuffle?' he said, his back to me.

'Yes,' I said. 'Like my grandfather used to say, I zigged when I should have zagged.'

'Well,' he chuckled, 'no shame in taking a punch now and again.'

We walked back deep into the yard to a garden that ran the width of his property. I pulled two cans of beer off the six I was cradling, holding the remaining four with a finger hooked through the plastic ring. He took them both and opened them, handing one back to me. Sipping the beer, he kept one eye in my direction.

'What was the name again?'

'Nick Stefanos.'

'Okay, Nick. Mine would be T. J.'

'I've been anxious to meet you,' I said.

'You have?' he said almost mockingly. 'Let's step into the garden. We can talk while I do a little work.'

I followed him to a row of tomato plants, where he bent down and untied a stake, tossing it out of the garden.

'Good year?'

He nodded. 'Steady rain last spring, hot and wet all summer. Great for tomatoes. I've cleared out most of the vine vegetables – squash and cucumbers and that sort of thing. Melons were no good this year – went rotten before I got 'em on the tiles.' He waved his hand around the expanse of greenery. 'Still pulling carrots and onions.'

'Kim told me about this garden,' I said, realizing how stupid it sounded as the words were coming from my mouth.

'She did, huh?' That mocking tone again. He squinted up at me. 'Funny. She never took a bit of interest in it all the time she grew up here.'

'Sorry I missed her. Was she alone?'

'No,' he said, tired of the game. 'She wasn't alone.' He rose from his knees and stood to face me. 'Why don't we set up on the porch and knock down these beers?'

120

On the back porch T. J. Lazarus moved two garden chairs together and pulled the remaining beers from my hand, setting them on a low aluminum table between us. He pulled a fresh one off the ring and popped it.

'Who *are* you, son?' he said. 'You sure as hell didn't come here to see my garden, and I don't believe you're a friend of my daughter's. Now I don't appreciate the company of a liar, especially in my own house. But if she's in some kind of trouble, I want to know. You a cop?'

'Private cop,' I said, my own words sounding unreal. I was getting tired of telling lies to honest people. Nevertheless, I handed him my phony ID.

He inspected it. 'I didn't think you were a cop. Cops don't get beat up.'

'So I've been told. I apologize for not being honest with you. But I'm not looking for Kim. I'm after one of the boys she was with. She *was* with two boys, wasn't she?'

'That's right. What's going on?'

'I was hired by the grandfather of one of the boys to find him.'

He studied me. 'Where you from, Nick?'

'Washington, D.C.'

'Murder Capitol, huh?' I didn't answer. 'You just get into town?'

'Yessir.'

'Hungry?'

'I could use something to eat,' I admitted. 'I really could.'

'Like it?'

'I like it fine.'

We were sitting at his kitchen table, eating an early supper of grilled chops, fresh corn, and a tomato and onion salad. The late afternoon sun came in through the west window, brightening the colors on my plate. Lazarus brought a glass out of the cupboard and placed it next to my can.

'Here,' he said. 'Drink it like a white man.'

I poured the beer into the glass. 'What did you think of the boys Kim was with?'

'They only spent the night. The one boy said his name was Eddie, but the younger one called him Red.'

'Redman,' I said.

'That's right. This Redman was the tougher of the two, a brawler from the looks of him. And cocky, like everything was a joke.'

121

'What about Jimmy, the other one?'

'He was trying to be tough, but it wasn't in him. You know what I mean.'

'Where did Kim fit in with the two of them?'

'My daughter was way too old for both of them,' he said bluntly. 'This Redman character clearly thought he had a shot at her. Maybe something was going on between 'em, I don't know. But like everything else, she didn't seem to be too serious about the situation.'

'What do you mean?'

He stared into his beer can. 'Ruth and me had Kimmy late in life. That's not an excuse, but we were a little old to be raising a girl in these times. When she was in her teens, we thought her wildness was just something she'd grow out of, but she went through her twenties the same damn way. After Ruth passed on, I lost touch with her. She sends me expensive gifts on holidays now, but to me it doesn't mean much.'

'Do you have any idea where they've gone?'

'They were headed to the Banks, I think.'

'They tell you that?'

'I heard them talking about it.'

'Where? Nags Head?'

'That would be a start,' he said.

'She have friends there?'

'She worked there years ago, in restaurants. Worked in beaches all along the coast for a while, from Nags Head down to Cape Fear. Yeah, I suppose she's still got some friends on the coast.'

'Where did she work in Nags Head? Specifically.'

He tapped his empty can on the table while he thought. 'It was a Mex place or Spanish. That's all I can remember. It's been a long time.'

'That's plenty of information,' I said, exaggerating. 'Thanks.' There couldn't be too many Mexican joints on the Outer Banks. I was beginning to get a picture of a smalltown girl, attracted to the resort towns by the money and drugs that came with northern tourists, elements that fed her natural wild streak.

'You like what you do, son?' Lazarus asked.

'I don't know yet. It's my first time out. I'm really just bulling my way through it right now. Anyway, it's not like you see on TV or in the movies, I can tell you that.'

'I wouldn't know. I haven't watched either for years. But a man ought to like what he does.'

We polished off the six, and Lazarus walked me to the door. On the way I stopped at a picture of Kim that was, from the looks of her hairstyle, probably ten years old. Lazarus caught my look.

'She got her beauty from my wife,' he explained.

He shook my hand and wished me luck. I thanked him, feeling almost reluctant to leave. I stepped out into his yard. The dog followed me halfway to my car, where he turned and loped back up the porch steps. His tail was still wagging as he watched me drive off.

McGinnes was gone when I returned to our room. I washed up and put on a black sweatshirt over my T-shirt. Then I read the note that he had taped to the phone:

Nick—
   Behind our room are some woods. Walk straight in and down the ridge until you come to a clearing. I'll be by the tracks.
   Johnny

19

The ridge dropped gradually and was dense with pine and the occasional cedar. The ground beneath my feet was soft, in some places almost muddy.

At the bottom of the incline were a clearing and railroad tracks, just as McGinnes had described. A narrow drainage ditch ran along both sides of the track. The clearing looked to be only fifty yards in length. Then it ended and the tracks continued into the forest.

McGinnes was standing at the edge of the clearing, backlit by the sun, which was large and red and dropping quickly below the treeline. He was holding a pint bottle.

'Did you bring any beer?' he asked as I approached him. One of his eyes was covered by a wild strand of hair and the other one told me he was stoned.

I let the knapsack off my shoulder, opened the main flap, and pulled out a cold sixpack. McGinnes reached for one and popped the top. I did the same.

'You've been out here all afternoon?'

'Fuckin' aye,' he said, waving his arm 180 degrees. 'This is great. I haven't had a vacation in years. Here's to Ric Brandon.' He saluted and took a swig from the bottle, then handed it to me. I hit it lightly, tasted peach brandy, and chased it with some beer.

'Where'd you get that?'

'I hitched to the ABC store,' he said. 'Any luck today?'

'A little. I'll tell you later.'

We had a seat on the tracks. I listened as McGinnes described his day. Occasionally he would stand to illustrate a point, center stage as always.

Twilight came and with it bugs and the sounds of bats and small feet scampering through leaves and brush. I felt warm and relaxed.

A small sound like the ocean increased from a faint to audible rumble. McGinnes put his hand on the rail and led me back to the rightmost edge of the clearing.

'You ready?'

'For what?'

'A ride!'

'No way, Johnny.'

'Why not?'

'It's stupid, that's why not.'

'Don't be such a pussy,' he said as the sound of the train grew louder. 'You never did this before?'

'No.'

'All right, listen up. All you do, you pick out a boxcar, an open one if you can, or a flatcar. Then you run alongside it, fast, and grab hold of the ladder or door. Swing up with it, don't try to let it pull you up. Otherwise, you'll go down. This run here is only forty, fifty yards before you hit the trees, so you've gotta be quick.'

'I'm not doing this, man.'

'Okay,' he said. 'Then watch me.'

The train sounded loud enough to be upon us. But a half minute went by before the lead car emerged from the pines and passed. McGinnes dashed out as the lead car vanished into the woods at the other end of the clearing.

He reached it quickly, up the ditch and sprinting alongside the train. He grabbed the ladder of a boxcar and swung up, dragging a foot out first, then putting that foot on the edge of the open car and looking back in my direction. After that he put both feet on the ladder, held an arm out for balance, and let go, running alongside the train and slowing to a walk just as he reached the trees.

He spun like a dancer and bowed. As he swaggered towards me, he bent down once to pick up and toss a rock. I could see that he was stoked.

'Easy, huh?' he said. 'Goddamn, that brings back some memories.'

'You do that often?'

'I did,' he said. When the caboose passed, we walked back on the high side of the ditch and took a seat on the tracks. 'I rode trains all over this state when I was a kid. You had to be careful, though, even then. This was the early sixties. You'd hear stories how these tough-ass railroad men would beat up tramps trying to catch trains out of the yards. Of course, in my old man's day, they'd throw you right in the chain gang if they caught you.'

'You like growing up down here?'

'It was all right,' he said, and passed me the brandy. 'I lived in quite a few places, but I was a teenager in Carolina.' He stared ahead and absently reached back for the bottle, a grin on his face. 'I did some crazy shit, like any kid I guess.'

But I had a feeling that he had been a little more out there than most. He had once shown me a photo of himself as a young man, standing balanced atop a split-rail fence, shirt off and arms crossed and flexed, with one eyebrow devilishly raised below a DI brushcut.

Time passed and the night was uncommonly bright. Black woods surrounded the moonlit clearing. As we killed the last of our beer and brandy, I felt a slight vibration beneath me and heard the low rumble begin.

'Come on,' McGinnes said, and I followed him to the edge of the woods where there was no light.

He pushed down on my shoulder and we crouched in some leaves and soft earth. The rumble increased in volume. A swift wind rushed behind and through us, and I felt my adrenalin pick up.

'Talk to me, man.' I was anxious and a little pickled from the booze.

'All right, Jim,' he said, his hand on my arm. 'When that first car passes and hits the trees, get out of here fast and run to the right side of the clearing, up the ditch and sharp left so you're parallel to the train. I'll be ahead of you. Just watch what I do. Remember, swing up that ladder, don't let it drag you.'

I could barely hear him between the crush of sound that was on us now and the wind that had picked up and was blowing leaves past us into the clearing. My fists were tight as the first car came suddenly out of the trees. I remember feeling that I only wanted to be up and moving away from the blackness around me, up and out and into the light.

'Book!' he shouted, and we were in the clearing and sprinting towards the train, down and up the ditch where I stumbled, then regained my momentum, then alongside it, feeling its power and thinking it was much stronger than I had imagined. McGinnes was in front of me and moving his head back and forth from the train to the trees ahead, then quickly and fluidly grabbing the rung of a boxcar ladder and rising up upon it. He yelled back at me and I saw that the clearing was running out, and I grabbed, white-knuckled the ladder of the car behind him, and ran as he yelled again, and I put one foot on the bottom rung and pushed upward with my shoulders and I was on the machine, tight against the ladder, as the clearing ended and we all roared into the woods together.

I looked behind and the clearing was gone. Around us were only dark forms, and, ahead, the engine cutting a path through the trees. The cars were rocking wildly, and I kept a tight grip on the ladder.

McGinnes was silhouetted against the moonlight and climbing up the side of his car, which was swaying in an irregular pattern to mine. When he reached the top, he let go one arm and one leg, and released a yell and burst of laughter. His hair blew wildly about his head.

'This is great!' he screamed back at me. 'Isn't this fucking great?'

'It is,' I said, and realized I was smiling. My grip loosened and I took a deep breath. The time between the clanging of the rails shortened as we picked up speed.

McGinnes was attempting to open his boxcar with his free hand and foot. I tried the door on my car.

'It's locked,' he shouted.

'So's this one,' I called back. 'What now?'

He looked around the side of the car. 'Swing in between the cars. There's a small platform on either side of the link that you can stand on. And watch your feet.'

I followed his lead and moved gingerly off the ladder and onto a two-foot-wide iron footing, taking my hand off the rung only when I was certain I was secure. McGinnes now faced me across the link that connected our cars. The ground below was a blur that rushed away.

We rode the train for a couple of hours, through smallish towns and low-activity yards and back through woods and clearings. When we crossed a bridge over a wide creek, McGinnes pointed to the moon's reflection on the still water. In one of the railroad yards a dog barked at us briefly. In another, an outline of a man waved slowly.

When we were again in the middle of a long stretch of woods, McGinnes suggested we get off the train. 'It feels like we're slowing down,' he said, and looked out from between the cars and back at me. 'What you want to do is, move back out to the outside ladder. When I tell you, jump off and away from the train. Lean back to counter your momentum, and when you hit, take long strides until you slow down.'

'I'll watch you,' I said.

We moved out to the sides of our cars. The night air had grown cooler. McGinnes waited for a long while until the land gradually leveled out. Then he pushed away from the train, landed on his feet, and slowed to a jog.

I was concentrating on jumping away from the train – it seemed then to be the main objective – and threw myself way out, realizing as I did that my upper body was far ahead of my legs. My feet barely touched the gravel. I rolled until I was stopped by a log and some brush. When McGinnes helped me up, I was a little dazed but relieved.

'You okay?'

'Yeah,' I said, though my back already ached and I could feel a deep scrape below my knee as it rubbed against my jeans.

The caboose passed and with it the noise, leaving only the quiet of the woods. We watched the last of it enter a curve ahead and disappear into the night.

We walked on the tracks in the moonlight, keeping in the direction of the train. He looked at the stars and claimed we were heading northwest. I didn't dispute it as it seemed irrelevant in any case. I was becoming tired and ornery.

'I don't know how you talk me into this shit,' I said.

'Relax, will you?' McGinnes stopped me with his hand on my chest. 'I bet you can't even tell me what you did a week ago today. But when you're drooling in your wheelchair in forty years, you'll remember this night – the way the woods smell right now, the sound of the train. That rush you got when you were running across the clearing. *This* is happening, man, *this* is what's important. Everything else is bullshit.'

We walked on. I related the course of events from the day Pence had called to the present, leaving out nothing. McGinnes was unusually attentive as he listened. At one point he began coughing furiously, then retched and spit up something bilious. I sat on the tracks and waited until he was ready to continue.

Sometime after midnight we reached a railroad yard and found an office with a washroom, where an elderly man let us get some water and clean up. Then we walked into an adjoining town, found its main road, and put our thumbs out.

An hour after that the driver of a jacked-up Malibu slowed and pulled over. McGinnes looked in the passenger window, pointed me to the back seat, and hopped in front.

A young serviceman was behind the wheel. He checked me out in the rearview, looking slightly apprehensive at the sight of my marked face.

'Where you guys headed?' he asked.

'Elizabeth City,' McGinnes said.

'Elizabeth City?' He laughed. 'Hell, you're in Virginia!'

McGinnes looked back at me and then at the kid. 'Where in Virginia?'

'Franklin area,' the kid said. 'What are you, lost?'

'We hopped a train,' McGinnes said proudly.

'No shit!' the kid said.

'Damn straight!' McGinnes said, turning his head slightly so I could see his wink. 'What you got in this thing, a three-oh-seven?'

'Yeah,' he said sheepishly and added, 'but it moves.'

'Good engine. You in the navy?' The kid nodded and McGinnes told him of a base he had once been fictitiously stationed on. We were driving out of town.

'What was it like? Hopping a train, I mean.'

'I'll tell you what,' McGinnes said. 'Let's grab some cold beer, and I'll tell you all about it.'

I hunched down in the seat and folded my arms. I closed my eyes, confident that when I opened them next we would be parked in front of the Gates motel.

I woke early the next morning, hiked back into the woods, and found my knapsack in the clearing. Returning to the room, I woke McGinnes, showered, shaved, and gathered up our gear.

After checking out we stopped for coffee and juice, then got back on the highway and traveled east to 158, then south across a bridge over the intracoastal waterway, our windows down and the radio up.

Less than two hours later we crossed the bridge at Point Harbor and, announcing ourselves with a raucous whoop from McGinnes, rolled onto the Outer Banks.

20

'So, Johnny,' I said. 'Who's Virginia Dare?' We were driving down the beach road that bore her name. To our left were oceanfront cottages and houses on pilings.

'First child born in this country to English parents.'

'I'm impressed.'

'And I'm hungry. Let's get some breakfast,' he said, and then, embarrassed, as if having knowledge of the state history was in some way a feminine trait, added, 'Besides, I gotta' lay some pipe.'

We switched over to the 158 bypass and pulled into the lot of a pancake house. It was warm as summer but there were few patrons. The town was in its off-season.

McGinnes ordered a pot of coffee, french toast topped with a fried egg, sausage, and practically everything else from the kitchen that would clog an artery. I had eggs over easy and scrapple.

When we finished, McGinnes grabbed a section of the *USA Today* he was 'reading' and a book of matches and headed for the bathroom. I borrowed the phone directory and a blank sheet of paper from the cashier and wrote down the names and addresses of several restaurants.

Back in the lot I removed my sweatshirt and tossed it in the backseat. We drove to a variety store on the highway, where McGinnes bought sandwiches, beer, and ice for the cooler. While he did that, I pumped gas into my Dodge, then paid a young attendant who had a back wider than a kitchen table. He sang 'Tennessee Stud' while I gave him the money and kept singing it as he walked back into the garage where he was working.

We returned to the Virginia Dare Trail and drove south out of Kitty Hawk, through Kill Devil Hills, past the Wright Brothers Memorial and into Nags Head. All of these towns were pleasant and indistinguishable from one another. Near the huge dune of Jockeys Ridge we stopped at a motor court named the Arizona and checked in.

We changed into shorts and walked across the road to the beach. We put our gear down in front of a white cottage on stilts that had boarded windows. The tide was receding and the swells were high at four feet and breaking far from the shore.

When I broke a sweat, I jogged to the shoreline and dove in the ocean. The water was pleasantly cold and clean. I swam parallel to the shore for roughly a quarter mile, then breastroked back and rode in a few waves.

McGinnes handed me a cold beer as I toweled off. I drank it sitting upright on the blanket. McGinnes pulled another beer from the cooler and announced that he was going for a walk. I watched him go north, stopping to talk to an old man wearing long pants, a T-shirt, and a baseball cap.

When I finished my beer, I pulled another from the ice and walked up the wooden steps and onto the porch of the white cottage. The window frames were peeling and the rusted storm door was permanently weathered half-open. Wooden Adirondack chairs painted a bright green sat in front of the boarded bay window on the splintering deck. I turned one of them to face the ocean, sat in it, and put my feet up on the railing.

The constant crash of the waves was punctuated by the cries of a flock of gulls that sat on the gravelly beach. A young father was surf fishing a hundred yards down the beach, his tackle box, white bucket, and cooler by his side. His blond little boy looked for shells but stayed close by.

I pushed the hair back off my forehead and finished my beer. The area around my nose and under my eyes no longer ached, confirming my grandfather's claim that saltwater was a cure for every ailment. I crossed my arms and settled into the chair, then drifted to sleep.

McGinnes woke me with a shake. I was sitting half in shade now. I looked at my arms and their deep brown color, quickly regained from my vacation on Assateague three weeks earlier.

'Let's go, man,' McGinnes said. 'You're starting to look like a Puerto Rican.' I poked his red chest with my index finger and brought up a splotch of white.

We returned to the room. I showered and changed into a denim shirt, jeans, and running shoes. McGinnes put on his Hawaiian shirt and went into the bathroom, toothbrush in hand. He began to cough and shut the door.

I sat on the bed and ate one of the sandwiches as I looked over my list. McGinnes came out of the bathroom and wiped his mouth with the back of his hand.

'You all right?' I asked.

He smiled unconvincingly and chin-nodded the list in my hand.

'What's up?'

'Restaurants that Kim Lazarus may have worked in. They should be open by now.'

'Let me check out a couple,' he said quickly.

'Based on what her father told me, I figure there's only three possibilities, unless the place she used to work in is out of business now.' I ripped the bottom of the page off and handed it to him. 'This place has a popular happy hour, judging from the ads, and it's Mexican. Skip the restaurant and check out the bar. I have a feeling they may be trying to off the drugs, and a bar with employees that use would be a perfect spot. If you get a bite, try and find out if they're still in town.'

'No problem,' he said.

'I'll drop you off and check out these other places. Then I'll swing back and pick you up after I've done that. You need bread?'

He put his hand out and I handed him some of my bankroll. He folded it and stashed it in his pocket, then pointed a thumb into his own chest. 'Don't worry about dad,' he said. 'This kinda shit is like cuttin' butter.'

I let McGinnes off in the parking lot of the Casa Grande, which was in a large, old oceanfront hotel in Kitty Hawk.

'I'll see you in the Big House,' he said, and shifted his shoulders in a Cagneyesque manner. I watched him in my rearview as I drove away, feeling an odd sympathy for him as he strolled across the lot in his Hawaiian shirt and polyester slacks.

The first place I hit was in a strip center next to a cluster of movie theaters on the divided highway. It had been advertised as a restaurant but was little more than a carryout serving tacos and burritos.

The kid who was behind the counter when I walked in was busy playing air guitar to the Metallica that was coming from his box. I asked about Kim Lazarus and got a dull-eyed look and a negative response.

My next stop was a free-standing restaurant in Nags Head that was done in a stucco and adobe motif, one of those Tex-Mex chains that American families love specifically for their blandness. It was their dinner rush, and when I saw the waitresses' uniforms – green and gold dresses with some type of elaborate headgear more appropriate on a trotting horse – I had the feeling that Kim Lazarus had never worked here.

The woman behind the register, thin and sharp-featured, seemed to be the only one around not doing anything. I walked up to her and smiled.

'Hi.'

'Hello,' she said. 'The hostess will seat you.' She made a jerky, pigeon-like movement with her head.

'I'm not looking for a table. My cousin works here. I'm on vacation, thought I'd say hi.'

'Everyone's kinda busy, sir. But what's her name? I'll see if I can get her attention.'

'Kimmy,' I said. 'Kim Lazarus.'

'There's no one here by that name,' she said.

'I thought for sure she said this place,' I whined. 'Did she used to work here?'

'Honey, I've been on this station since we opened two years ago. No Kim ever worked here.' She jerked her head again.

'Are there any other places like this?' I asked. 'I guess I got confused.'

'Casa Grande in Kitty Hawk. Or maybe she worked at Carlos Joe's. But they closed down last year. Had some trouble.'

'What happened?' I asked, winking conspiratorially. Then I jerked my head like hers, for punctuation. 'Taxes?'

She leaned in and whispered, 'Owners got in drug trouble.'

'Oh. Anybody work here who used to work at Carlos Joe's? Maybe they know my cousin.'

She pulled back and buttoned up. 'Not that I know.'

'Thanks.'

I walked to my car with my head down. Carlos Joe's was the type of place Kim Lazarus would have been attracted to. But it was closed now, and I had driven into a stone dead end.

The bar at Casa Grande was above the dining room and accessible by a staircase to the left of the hotel entrance. I picked a magazine up off the table in the lobby and went up the stairs.

McGinnes was seated at the bar when I entered. He was leaning across the rather appalled-looking woman to his left, showing her companion a trick involving a swizzle stick. He saw me but averted his eyes. I took a seat at a deuce near the window and the hors d'oeuvre station.

The young cocktail waitress who arrived at my table had that look of false health common to beach employees who party every night, then spend a couple of hours in the sun each day for recovery purposes. She had the scrubbed, Baptist good looks preferred by ACC frat boys, but her best days were already behind her. Her summer tan was fading like an Earl Schieb paint job.

'What can I get you?' she asked with a pained smile, and set a basket of chips and salsa on the table.

'A Dos Equis, please. And some *queso*.'

The place was filled with older, successful men, stag or with younger women, gray-templed gents who tie the arms of their summerweight sweaters around their necks and drink single malt scotch or beer from green bottles.

McGinnes was doing an awful job of buddying up to the bartender, one of those doughy ex-jocks who 'parlay' a summer bartending job into a full-time career that leaves them forty-five at thirty.

The *queso* was spicy and hot. I ordered beef and chicken enchiladas with a side of sour cream and another Dos. I pretended to read the real estate magazine that I had brought up from the lobby.

The food arrived and was of the same quality as the *queso*. Someone in the kitchen obviously liked their job. I watched the bartender whisper something to his barback, then leave his station and walk into the men's room. Half a minute later McGinnes followed him in.

I finished my meal and the waitress removed the plates. The bartender returned to the bar, where he immediately lit a cigarette and drew on it hungrily.

McGinnes emerged from the head and took his seat at the bar, turning to his neighbors and quickly starting a conversation. Then he pulled the rope on a bell that hung from the ceiling. There was applause in the bar, as McGinnes had just bought the house a round.

I raised my bottle in a toast to McGinnes, via the bar mirror. He winked at me, a little too broadly, though he deserved to be somewhat reckless. Clearly he was on to something.

As I finished my beer, McGinnes was in close conversation with the bartender. He looked at me again, then stepped away from the bar, and said loudly, 'What do I owe you, professor?' I left twenty on sixteen, walked down the stairs, and out to my car.

I turned the ignition key and knocked the ocean mist off my windshield with a stroke of the wipers. McGinnes bounded out of the hotel and goose-stepped to my car, settling in on the passenger side. He grinned the same cocky smirk when he closed a major deal.

'What's my name?' he asked childishly.

'Johnny Mac.'

I pulled out onto Virginia Dare, heading south. McGinnes brought the snow seal out of his breast pocket, unfolded it carefully, dipped in with his pinky nail, and did a hit. Then he fed the other nostril the same way.

'What did all that cost me?' I asked.

'Call it a hundred. Thirty for the house round, seventy for the half.'

'Seventy, for a half? You're pretty generous with my money.'

'You got to ante to play the game, Jim. It was worth it, for what I got.' He pointed ahead. 'Pull in there. I'm thirsty.'

'I'll bet you are.'

He was out of the store quickly with a tall brown bag in his arms. He handed me a cold bottle of beer and took one for himself. We drove on.

'Spill it, man.'

'All right,' he said. 'Soon as I walk in the bar, I can see everyone working the place is wired. I strike up a conversation with the barkeep and ask if he remembers Kim Lazarus, used to work there. I'm a good friend of hers from D.C. Not only does he remember her, she was in town last week. I steer the conversation to coke, and how Kim told me I could look him up if I wanted to cop. He gets suspicious now and I ease off. But I get him back on the track when I tell him I'm used to spending one-forty, one-fifty for a gram.' He looked at me and smiled.

'Keep going,' I said.

'This guy can't resist the high dollar. He offers to sell me a half for seventy. I gotta try it first, I say. We go into the john, he turns me on. Let me tell you, this shit is good. I know you've found Jesus and all that, but if this was the old days, you would *concur* on this, Jim.'

'Get to the meat, Johnny.'

'We go back out to the bar. I tell him this freeze is so serious, I've *got* to cop more. How can I get my hands on some quantity?'

'Kim and the boys, right?'

He nodded. 'Let me tell it, man. The bartender, he's juiced now, he's my buddy. He tells me that it was my friend Kim that sold him the shit.'

'Where are they?'

'This bartender was too small-time to take on quantities. There was another guy, though, a surf rat by the name of Charlie Fiora who used to work with Kim at Casa Grande. He's got his own gig now down the coast, a little bar called the Wall. He's the one that Kim and Eddie and your boy Broda went to see to sell their supply to.'

'Where?' I said.

'Wrightsville Beach.' He took a swig and looked at me out of the corner of his eye.

I slapped the steering wheel as we pulled into the lot of the Arizona. 'Good job, man.'

'I know,' he said.

In our room I laid out maps and ferry schedules. McGinnes tapped out some lines on the mirror he had removed from the wall.

'You want a blast?'

'No,' I said. But like any former cokehead, I really did.

He did a couple that had the width of fingers. 'Let's go out and have a few.'

'Not tonight. We've got a shitload of miles to travel in the morning.'

'Wrightsville's *down* there.'

'You want to go, go ahead. My keys are on the dresser.'

'I think I will,' he said. 'For a short one.'

'Thanks for tonight, Johnny.'

'No sweat,' he said casually. 'See you in the A.M.' He took my keys off the dresser and twirled them on his finger. He was coughing as he bolted out the door.

21

Crossing Whalebone junction, we passed the sign for Cape Hatteras National Seashore and blew down Route 12 very early the next morning. The sun sprayed over the dunes to our left, highlighting sea oats and myrtle.

We rolled our windows down as the dawn chill faded, and sipped our coffee from Styrofoam cups. I had a neo-country tape playing in the deck – Golden Palominos, Dwight Yokum, T-Bone Burnette, and Costello, with some Merle Haggard and Johnny Cash thrown in for tradition.

McGinnes was singing along to what he knew, and laughed at my voice as I joined him on the occasional odd chorus. The lines around his eyes crinkled out from behind his aviators.

'This is beautiful!' he said emotionally, his arm straight out the window, his palm catching the wind.

'Everything is Beautiful,' I said.

'Ray Stevens, right? Worst Top Ten song ever recorded.'

'Right about Ray Stevens. Wrong about the honors. They go to "Daddy, Don't You Walk So Fast" by Wayne Newton. *That's* the worst song to crack the Top Ten.'

'You mean, "Daddy, Don't You *Hump* So Fast," don't you?'

'Whatever you say, Johnny.'

Soon we were on the Herbert C. Bonner Bridge over the Oregon Inlet. Scores of trawlers and charter boats were heading out into the ocean. On the other side of the bridge lay the Pea Island Refuge, where flocks of snow geese and shorebirds flew by at regular intervals. Egrets laced the wetlands to our right.

We drove through the nearly empty beachtowns of Rodanthe, Waves, and Salvo, then cruised a long stretch along the coast to Avon and beyond. Near Buxton, McGinnes had me stop at a windsurfing mecca on the soundside called Canadian Hole. He peed on the grass next to my car while I watched the brightly colored sails and their boards ripping across the chop. Then we pulled back onto the highway.

We stopped once more to fill the cooler in the town of Hatteras, then raced to the end of the highway to make the ferry. I pulled into spot number nineteen just as the khaki-uniformed park employees began to board the cars.

We were directed to an area behind a North Carolina Christian Academy school bus, where a tan woman wedged wooden blocks beneath my front tires. A fully restored black and white Chevy with red interior parked to our right. The New Jersey vanity plates read '57 Love.' The driver was bearded and fat and wore an Alf T-shirt.

'Let's get out and enjoy it,' McGinnes said, as the ferry finished loading and pulled away from the dock.

The crowd was an October mixture of elderly couples, young parents with preschool children, and a few tradesmen heading over to the island for work. The tourists began to congregate at the bow, where a woman was throwing bread to a few gulls. Those few gulls turned to dozens very quickly and stayed with the ferry for the entire trip.

McGinnes brought out two beers and handed one to me. I had intended to remain dry that day, but the weather was gorgeous, the final brilliant display of the long Carolina season. I took off my shirt, sat on the hood of my car, put my feet up on the iron rail, and popped the can.

McGinnes drifted away and struck up a conversation with a group of young men standing around a Bronco that had surf rods stuck in tubes mounted around the front fender. I folded my arms and enjoyed my beer and the view.

Forty minutes later we approached the island. The ferry ran parallel to the shore, which was crowded with all-terrain vehicles and fishermen, some of whom were throwing out nets. The family next to me waved at an old man motoring by in a Chris Craft, who waved back, mimicking them playfully. Finally we docked with a thud against the rubber-wrapped pilings.

We drove off the ferry and onto Ocracoke Island. The terrain was flat and covered with shrubs of myrtle, the two-lane road shoulderless and sandy. Many of the cars ahead turned off at beach access trails or state-run campgrounds.

The drive to the other end of the island took only ten minutes. But when we arrived, the Cedar Island ferry was full, and the next available was two hours away. I bought tickets and walked back to the car.

'Don't worry about it,' McGinnes said. 'We made good time getting down here. Let's relax, drive back to the village. I saw a place there.'

We turned the car around and headed back up the road, where McGinnes directed me into the lot of what looked like an old house on pilings. The small gray sign, camouflaged against the gray house it hung on, read 'Jacko's Grille.'

'You coming?' he asked, out of the car before it stopped.

I shook my head. 'I think I'll grab a swim. I'll swing back and pick you up.' He waved me off and ran up the wooden stairs.

I drove to a small turnoff that I had noticed earlier, a place with no facilities and no tourists. I changed into shorts and walked on a path through the shrubs, over a barrier dune, and out onto a wide, white beach.

On my trek to the shoreline there were sandcrabs and shells and no footprints. The swells were small, like those in a bay. I walked out in two feet of water for what seemed like quite a distance. Small fish moved around my feet. I reached deeper water and swam, then walked along the beach until I neared a group of fishermen. I turned and walked back, stopping occasionally to put the more interesting stones and shells in my swimtrunk pockets. Some high clouds drifted in the sky but they never neared the sun.

I changed back into jeans and drove back to the bar. Inside were picnic tables and a jukebox and a small selection of domestic beer. McGinnes was talking to and drinking with a couple of old-timers. I ordered a burger and a beer and took them both out back to the screened-in deck that overlooked the wetlands and the Pamlico Sound.

The Cedar Island ferry was a two-hour trip. I grabbed the opportunity to nap on the hood of my car in the warm sun.

McGinnes shook me awake when we docked. As we prepared to disembark, I noticed the license plates on a car ahead. The 'mushroom cloud' on the plates of the men who attacked me was the state tree of South Carolina. I told McGinnes.

'What difference does it make now?' he said. 'You didn't get the number, so you still don't know dick.'

As we drove off the ferry onto Cedar Island, I saw that the vegetation was more tropical. But the palmettos diminished, then disappeared as Route 12 became 70. We went through the lovely seaside town of Beaufort, then passed the more conventional Morehead City and turned off on 24 south. At two o'clock we entered Camp Lejeune, where McGinnes saluted the MP at the gate and told childhood stories all the way through the grounds and beyond. Then we were on 17 south along the coast, passing billboards advertising surf shops and hamburger stands.

At nearly four in the afternoon we reached Wilmington, a large city in the midst of revitalization, which was still filled with examples of old Southern architecture. McGinnes informed me in the same breath that Wilmington was once the premier city of the state, and that it was the birthplace of Sonny Jurgenson.

Wrightsville Beach was just across the bridge over Bank's Channel. Driving onto its main strip, I saw the large hotels and general congestion of concrete that I associated with the Delmarva Peninsula and the Jersey Shore. We checked into a clean and expensive motel near the fishing pier.

McGinnes was sleeping when I came out of the shower. I dressed quietly, slipped out the door, and walked up to the pier. At its entrance was a snackbar that overlooked the beach. I sat on a red stool and ordered a tuna sandwich with fries and a coke.

The teenage girl behind the counter had black hair and thick eyebrows and wore a Byzantine cross. I asked if she was Greek and she said yes. Her parents owned the concession stand and the adjoining restaurant. I asked her if she knew a place called the Wall.

'It's a surf-rat place,' she said. 'In the summer they rage, but now in the off-season only the hardcores hang out there. If you're not a local and you're not in that crowd, it's not too cool.' She told me where to find it, up near the Strand. I thanked her and left eight on four.

Traffic was light. I found the Wall on the soundside corner of the intersection the girl had mentioned.

The place appeared to be a converted service station. It stood alone on a shell and gravel lot. I was the only one parked in the lot. I sat in my car for half an hour and listened to top forty radio and beach commercials. Then a modified, black VW with two short-boards racked on the top pulled in. The doors opened and two guys got out.

They walked across the lot. The taller one of the two was in oversized baggy shorts and a tie-dyed T-shirt and wore a red duckbilled cap, out of which came white blond hair. He was tall and in swimmer's shape. The smaller one was dressed similarly but had a weak frame and the overly cocky strut of the insecure.

I got out of my car quickly and ran to the door of the bar, just as the tall one was turning the key. I startled him as he turned and for a moment he looked vulnerable, but only for a moment. He had thin eyes and a cruel, thin mouth.

'Hey,' I said, 'how's it going?' He didn't answer but gave me the once-over. 'Is Charlie Fiora around?'

'That's me,' he said in a monotone. 'What do you want?'

'I'm a friend of Kim Lazarus,' I said. His eyes flashed for a second, an emotion that he quickly shut down. 'I heard she was in town. Heard you might know where she's staying.'

'You heard wrong, ace. I don't know any Kim Hazardous,' he said, and his little friend giggled. 'Now I gotta get my place opened up. So later.'

The two of them walked in and shut the door behind them. I heard the lock turn. I stood staring at the door and the painted cinderblocks around it. Then I turned and walked back to my car. I sat there for a while. Nothing happened and I did nothing to make it happen. Finally I turned the ignition key and drove back to the motel.

McGinnes was cleaned up and waiting when I returned to the room. We walked to the restaurant above the arcade and concession stand and had a seat at the bar, which afforded us a view of the pier below. The ocean shimmered orange and gray at dusk. I told McGinnes of my experience at the Wall. Afterwards, he put down his Pilsner glass and looked at me dourly.

'I didn't want to bring this up,' he said, 'but I've got to be at work tomorrow morning. If I don't post, I lose my job.'

'I know.'

I settled the bill after finishing only half my meal. We walked down the stairs and out onto the pier. I turned my collar up against the wind as we neared the end, where some kids were spinning a cast-iron telescope on its base.

'What are you going to do?' McGinnes asked. His hair was blowing back to expose his scalp.

'They're here in Wrightsville,' I said with certainty. 'I didn't go through everything and come all the way down here to drive back to D.C. now with my fucking tail between my legs.'

'You want company?'

'No, not this time. But get everything together at the room. I'll be back in an hour to pick you up.'

He nodded sadly and looked away. I left him there at the end of the pier and walked back, passing a small group gathered around a sand shark that was floundering and dying on the wooden planks.

I found my car in the motel lot, pulled out onto the highway, and headed for the Wall.

22

When I pushed open the heavy door to the Wall, they were blasting *Led Zeppelin IV* through the speaker system.

The place was one big unfinished room, with a couple of pool tables, pinball and video machines, scattered chairs, and a bar. Some of the people that night looked to be underage. It was difficult to pick out the patrons from the employees.

Charlie Fiora was standing outside the service bar area and recognized me as I entered. He said something to his sidekick, who then looked at me and grinned. I walked across the concrete floor to the bar, where I took a seat with my back to the wall on a stool in the corner.

When the bartender was finished ignoring me, he dragged himself down to my end. He was tall with long brown hair and wire-rimmed glasses, which gave the probably false impression of intelligence. I ordered a bottle of Bud and gave him three on two. He didn't thank me but accepted the tip.

I drank the beer and looked around. There were no windows. The area that had once housed the service station's bay doors had been bricked up. The decorations were sparse but effective. Tiny white Christmas lights laced the walls and bar mirrors. Posters, replicating album covers of groups like Siouxsie & the Banshees and the Meat Puppets, hung on the cinderblocks. Styrofoam Flintstone Building Blocks were spraypainted and glued to the ceiling to better the acoustics and insulate the noise. Tie-dyed bedsheets hung like inverted parachutes, and held in their pockets still more Christmas lights. Fiora was nothing if not resourceful.

The crowd here was the dark side of the myth of healthy, bronzed surfers out for clean fun and the perfect wave. The young people who lived in beachtowns like this, long after their peers had returned to school for the fall semester, were strangely joyless hedonists, bitter poseurs who were capable of unrepentant violence.

Fiora was staring at me and I could feel it. I got up and walked across the room, past the pool tables and pinball machines, and into the men's room.

There was one sink, two urinals, and a stall. I stood at one of the urinals and peed. Above me on the wall were two lines of graffiti: 'Michael Stipe sucks my pipe' and 'Any friend of Ted Bundy's is a friend of mine.'

I washed up and returned to my barstool. There was a pretty young blonde in a powder blue sundress standing next to Fiora now. Fiora whispered something in her ear. She looked at me and smiled, then kept her eyes on me as she kissed him on the cheek. They both laughed.

I ordered another beer. They were now well into the second side of the Zeppelin tape. A loaded kid sitting next to me said to his friend on the right, 'I'm tellin' you, dude, the way to get a babe to like you is to make her drink.'

I began to read the cassette titles that were racked behind the bar. There were hundreds of them, arranged alphabetically. When I was finished doing that, I looked at my watch.

Bonham's drum intro to 'When the Levee Breaks' kicked in, followed by harmonica. I finished my beer, got up from my stool, and walked back into the men's room.

I rewashed my hands. I was drying them with a towel and looking in the mirror when Charlie Fiora and his buddy walked in behind me. I threw the paper in the trash and turned to face them.

Fiora had removed his cap, making him appear less boyish. In the blinking Christmas lights his tan skin was drawn tight. Veins popped on his biceps below the rolled-up sleeves of his T-shirt. His right fist was balled.

'All right, ace,' he said. 'What do you want?'

I glanced quickly as his skinny little partner, who was struggling to look tough, then back at Fiora, whom I addressed.

'Tell your girlfriend to beat it,' I said. 'Then we talk.'

The kid took half a step towards me out of pride but stopped short. I thought I saw the beginnings of a grin at the edges of Fiora's mouth.

'Go on, Robo,' Fiora said.

Robo left after giving me one more hard stare. Fiora and I studied each other for a minute or so. The music was thin and distorted, coming through a cheap speaker hung above the mirror.

'I told you earlier what I wanted. Kim Lazarus is in town with two guys and I want to talk to one of them.'

'You some kind of cop?'

'Private,' I said. Fiora relaxed.

'Then why don't you just get the fuck out of here?' he said.

'I could make trouble for you, Charlie. I know Kim sold you some shake, and I know you're dealing it out of this bar.' I shifted my weight to my back foot.

'You want some more?' he said, and pointed his hand very close to my bruised face. I was tired of him and all of it. Most of all, I wouldn't be touched like that again.

I grabbed his outstretched wrist and twisted down, and at the same time yanked him towards me. Then I kicked him with my back foot, pivoting the heel of my front foot in his direction and aiming two feet behind him, as I connected at the bottom of his rib cage.

The sound of it was like that of a hammer through a carton. He veed forward, coughed once, and opened his eyes in pain and surprise. I stepped behind him, one hand still around his wrist, and with the other pushed down violently on his elbow.

His face hit the floor before the rest of him. A sickening sound, like stone against stone, echoed in the bathroom. When a puddle of blood spread between his face and the floor, I knew he had broken his teeth on the concrete.

'Where are they?' I growled. I had pressure on his arm and held it pointed at the ceiling.

'Beachmark Hotel,' he said, and coughed convulsively, adding more blood and phlegm to the floor.

'Where in the hotel?'

'I don't know the number,' he said, and I believed him. But I pressed harder on his arm. 'Last room on the right. Oceanfront.'

'Floor?'

'Second floor.' He made a gurgling sound.

'Repeat it,' I said, and his answer was the same. I let go of him and stepped away without looking back. I pushed the door open and walked quickly across the main room.

Fiora's friend was shocked to see me emerge first. He moved back from my path and stopped against the wall. I felt numb, and a foot taller at the same time. Robert Plant was shouting the blues.

I walked over to the blonde in the blue sundress, took the bottle of beer out of her hand, and drank deeply. I put my other hand behind her neck and pulled her mouth into mine. When she began to kiss me back, I pushed away.

Then I was out of the bar, out in the cool and wet air. I got into my car and watched my hands shake before I tightened them around the wheel, then laughed for no reason. I pulled out of the lot and screamed down the strip, to pick up McGinnes, and, from there, to get Jimmy Broda.

'What's going on, man?' McGinnes said, and looked at me strangely as I entered our room.

'You turn in the room key yet?'

'Yeah.'

'Let's get going, then.'

We were out on the street quickly. I unintentionally caught rubber pulling out of the lot. I felt McGinnes' stare.

'I guess you got your information,' he said.

'That's right.'

'There's blood on your shirt,' he said.

'I know,' I said, pressing down on the accelerator. 'It isn't mine.'

23

The Beachmark was a tan, three-story hotel on the ocean near the Wrightsville Holiday Inn. It was highlighted with green awnings and a diagonal green sign with white lettering announcing its name. I parked and looked over at McGinnes.

'You coming?' I said.

'You want me to?'

'Yeah.'

'What's the plan?'

'There isn't one. Let's just go in and get him.'

There were few cars in the parking lot, and the area around the hotel was still and quiet. The pool's green light tinted our clothing as we walked around it and on past a Coke machine and ice dispenser.

We ascended a metal stairwell, then went through a concrete hall and onto a walkway around the second floor. We walked along the northside wall and turned right at the oceanfront, where the temperature immediately dropped, the air became damper, and the sound of the surf more pronounced.

I found the last door on the right and tried the knob. It was locked. To the left of the door was a small rectangular window and, through it, darkness. My first thought was that I had been had by Fiora. But McGinnes whistled and directed me to the next door in the row.

The door of that room was ajar. Out of it fell a bar of light and the sound of a radio playing AOR at a very low volume.

I knocked on the door and shouted 'Hello.' No response. My knock opened the door halfway. I finished it with a push and stepped onto the green carpet of the living room. McGinnes followed me in.

We walked slowly past the standard bamboo and plastic beach furnishings and the seaside prints that hung on the wall. There appeared to be two bedrooms. I pointed to one, and McGinnes walked in. I walked into the other.

At first I did not recognize the figure lying on the bed. He did not look much like the defiant kid in the photograph his mother had shown me. In the photograph, Eddie Shultz had been alive.

They had gagged him and tied his hands and feet together behind his back, laying him on his side on a dropcloth. Then they had cut his throat down to the windpipe, from left to right. His shirt and jeans were soaked halfway up in blood. Rope burns marked his wrists and his eyes were open. He looked something like a frog.

I fell back against the door, tasted the bile of my dinner, and swallowed my own puke. I felt the blood drain from my face and I thought I heard Maureen Shultz's voice on my answering machine. I stumbled into the other bedroom.

McGinnes was on the bed, cradling a woman in his arms. Her eyes were barely open and her lips were moving but there was no sound. He pushed some hair out of her face.

'She was unconscious when I walked in,' he said. 'I've almost got her around.' He turned his head to look at me and dropped open his mouth. 'What the fuck . . . ?'

'Eddie Shultz is dead, man. Murdered in the other room.'

'Hold her,' he said, and I absently put my arms around the woman as he rushed out. I heard him say, 'Jesus Christ,' then walk around the apartment until he came back, pasty-faced, into the bedroom.

'Is Jimmy Broda . . . ?'

'Nobody else in the apartment,' he said.

'We've got to . . .'

'We don't have to do shit,' he said, his voice shaking. He reached out and grabbed a handful of the front of my shirt. 'Now listen. Did you touch anything besides the front door?'

'I don't know. I mean I don't remember. Probably.'

'You walk downstairs, now, and bring the car around to the stairwell we came up. I'm going to wipe this place down and get her walking. I'll be down in a few minutes. Understand?'

'Yes,' I nodded.

'Do it,' he said, and released my shirt.

I let the woman down gently on the bed, forcing her hand off my back. I walked out of the apartment, around to the north side of the hotel and down the stairwell.

I moved the car past the pool and into the spot nearest the stairwell. I kept the windows rolled up, listened to the tick of my watch, and wiped sweat off my forehead.

McGinnes came down the stairs ten minutes later with the woman.

She was walking, supported by his arm. In his other hand was a suitcase. He put her in the back seat, where she immediately lay down. He stowed the suitcase in the trunk and got into the passenger side.

'I think I got everything,' he said to himself, then looked at me. 'Come on, let's get out of here.'

I found the bridge over Bank's Channel, left Wrightsville Beach, and drove into Wilmington. At a convenience store I parked far away from the entrance.

I bought three large coffees and a pack of Camel filters. I returned to the car, handed McGinnes two of the coffees, and tore a hole in the lid of mine. Then I opened the deck of Camels, shoved one in my mouth, and lit it. I had not smoked in more than three years. The raunch hit my lungs and burned. I kept it there, finally exhaling a stream out the window.

'She know where Broda is?' I said, jerking my head in the direction of the backseat, where she slept.

'No,' McGinnes said. 'Drive.'

He directed me to 421 heading northwest. It was past midnight and there were few cars on the highway. I kicked on my hi-beams with a tap on the floorboard.

'We blew it,' I said, after a long period of silence.

'Bullshit,' he said angrily. 'Everything that's happened has had nothing to do with you. And everything that's going to happen, whether they catch up with the kid or not, you can't change that either. The boy got his hands on some shake that wasn't his, and the guys he took it from, man, they are not to be fucked with. You're way out of your league, Nicky. Forget about it.'

'What about the woman?'

'She'll be all right. I don't think she was hurt bad. I've got to figure that half of her condition right now is from all the drugs they were doing. Take her back to D.C., drop her off, and wash your hands. Then pray we don't get implicated in all this.'

We drove for a couple of hours on 421. When we neared the signs for 95, McGinnes had me pull over.

'I'm going to switch with her and try to get some sleep,' he said. 'It'll do her good to open her eyes for a while.'

We urinated on the shoulder of the road. McGinnes rousted the woman and walked with her down the highway for a block, then back to the car. She slid in next to me on the passenger side. McGinnes lay down on the backseat.

At Dunn, past Fayetteville, I turned off onto 95 and headed north. I offered her a cigarette. She took two from the pack and lit them both with the lighter from the dash, then handed one back to me.

She smoked while staring out the window. Her shoulders began to shake, and I could see that she was sobbing. I turned the radio on to a country station and left the volume very low. When she had stopped crying, she turned her head in my direction.

'Who *are* you guys?' she said. There was that slight Southern accent.

'We're taking you back to Washington. I'm Nick Stefanos. The guy in the back is John McGinnes. Who are you?'

'My name is Kim Lazarus.' She took another cigarette from the pack and lit it off the first. She still had the long brown hair from her father's photograph, and large, round, blue eyes.

'You feel well enough to talk?'

'I think so,' she said, but again began to cry. She shook her head. 'Fucking Eddie. Why?'

I let it go again for twenty minutes. She drank the cold coffee we had saved for her and smoked another cigarette. I kept my eyes on the road.

'I'm not interested in anything other than Jimmy Broda,' I said finally. 'I want you to know that . . . so you can speak freely. I was hired by his grandfather to find him, and that's what I was trying to do when I caught up with you. I know he had coke that wasn't his, and I know you were selling it off as you traveled. But I don't care about any of that.'

'What can I tell you? We were partying for two weeks straight. We had sold most of it, and we were doing the rest of it like a last blowout.' She dragged on her cigarette.

'Keep going,' I said.

'Jimmy went out for some beer late in the afternoon. Pretty soon after that two guys came into our room. I don't remember much after that. Either I hit my head backing up or they knocked me out. Anyway, the next thing was, your friend in the backseat was waking me up.'

I thought about that for a while. 'You recognize the guys?'

'Black dudes,' she said meaninglessly. I didn't ask her any more questions, and after a short time she fell back asleep.

I drove on through the night, into Virginia and around Richmond, stopping once more for gas. Kim slept through, though her body jerked occasionally from speed rushes.

McGinnes awoke outside of Springfield and sat up. He stared out the window for the remainder of the trip. We rolled into D.C. just after dawn on Saturday morning. McGinnes grabbed his gear from the trunk and walked back to the driver's side, leaning his forearm on the door and putting a hand on my shoulder.

'I'll be talking to you,' is all he said. Then he turned and walked into his apartment building, stoop-shouldered and slow, and suddenly old.

I woke Kim Lazarus and got her into my place. While she showered, I put fresh sheets on my bed. She came out looking clean but still drawn. She had only enough energy to thank me and get into bed. I closed the bedroom door and walked out into the living room.

The light on my answering machine was blinking. I let it blink. I lay on the couch and pulled the blanket over me. My cat jumped up and kneaded the blanket. I went to sleep.

I did not dream. But I woke two hours later, thinking of a redheaded boy who looked so horrible in death that I was grateful for never having known him alive. And there was still Jimmy Broda. Either he was caught now, or he was running. I knew with certainty that he was frightened and he was very much alone. The thought of it made the comfort of my apartment seem obscene.

Unable to return to sleep, I rose, and with great impotence, paced the rooms of my apartment.

24

On the television news there was no mention of the out-of-state murder of an area youth.

I erased the tape on my answering machine without listening to the messages. The phone rang twice during the day but I did not pick it up. In the afternoon I gathered all the liquor, beer, and wine from my apartment and made a gift of it to my landlord.

Kim Lazarus woke up at around six in the evening. I cooked her an omelette, fried potatoes, cut a salad, and served it with juice and tea. She ate it and returned to bed, where she slept soundly through the night.

On Sunday morning I prepared a huge breakfast. She came to the table, a bit swollen around the eyes, but with color back in her face. She was wearing Levi's and a blue sweatshirt.

'Thanks,' she said as I poured her some coffee. One side of her mouth rose as she smiled, her thick upper lip arching lazily above her slightly crooked teeth.

'You've been thanking me an awful lot. It's no bother having you here. I figure we both need to chill out for a few days.'

'What day *is* it?' she asked.

'Sunday.'

She ate her breakfast and cleaned her plate with pieces of toast. I refilled her plate and she kept going. She was a big-boned woman with little boy fat but plenty of curves.

When she was finished, the cat, who had already taken to her, jumped up on Kim's lap.

'Do you mind?'

'No,' she said, rubbing behind the cat's ears. 'I like it. How'd she lose her eye?'

'Catfight, I guess. That's how I found her. She was hiding outside behind some latticework, and her eye was just hanging out, hanging by a nerve. I got her to a vet, and he took it out, then sewed the lid shut. After that she stuck around.'

'Kind of like how you adopted me.'

'Until we figure this whole thing out, yeah.'

'Don't you work?' she asked.

'I lost my job last week.'

'Where?'

'I did ads for a retail outfit.'

'Really. Which one?'

'Nutty Nathan's,' I mumbled.

'I know that place,' she said. ' "The Miser Who Works for you." '

'That's the one.'

'Your friend John work there too?'

'Yeah, how'd you guess?'

'He looks like a salesman. You don't.'

'Well, I was – for years. Johnny and I worked the floor together for a long time.'

'Hard to stay friends and not fight over ups and things like that.'

'Oh, we fought over ups, believe me.'

'How did that happen?' she asked, reaching across the table and touching the faded purple area around my nose.

'Looking for Jimmy Broda.'

I refilled our coffee cups and put a fresh pack of smokes on the table between us. She shook one out and lit it, then blew smoke at the window. Her mouth turned down at the edges and her eyes watered up.

'Have you heard anything yet?' she asked.

'Not yesterday. Not on the news today or in the Sunday paper. Frankly, I'm beginning to think that the ones who killed Eddie went back and cleaned up.' I thought of the dropcloth they had placed beneath him. 'I don't think anybody's going to find Eddie, not for a while anyway.'

'And you're not going to report it?'

'Not yet,' I said. 'Can I ask you something?'

'Go ahead.'

'How did you get involved with those guys?'

'Cocaine,' she said. 'The same way I get involved with every guy I know.' She butted her cigarette and lit another, then looked back at me. 'When I moved up to D.C., I didn't have a job, but I had money. I was dealing for a guy. Then we had a falling out, and my supply and income got cut off. I started hanging out in the clubs. One night at the Snake Pit I met Eddie and Jimmy.'

'And Jimmy was holding.'

'Bigtime. And he was generous with it. I think it made him feel like a bigshot, but at the same time he was real nervous about it.'

'Did you know it was stolen?'

'I suspected it at first,' she admitted, 'and then after a while I was certain. But I'm an addict, Nick. I didn't care *where* it came from, only that he had it, and that he didn't mind handing it out.'

'Where did Eddie fit in?'

'He wanted me,' she said.

'Why did the three of you leave town?'

'Like I said, Jimmy was paranoid. I told him how we could off it and take a vacation at the same time. So we drove south.'

'Did he ever say where he got the drugs?'

'No.'

'Come on, Kim, think. Something must have been said. With all the shit you were putting up your noses, there must have been quite a bit of talking going on.'

'I'm certain,' she said bitterly.

I stood up and washed our cups in the sink. I could hear her crying behind me. When I turned, her arms were outstretched.

'I'm sorry,' I said, and put my arms around her.

'I'm so fucked up,' she said. Her tears felt hot on my neck. I was aware of her breasts crushed against my chest, and of my erection. I eased her away.

'You can stay here for as long as you like.'

'I could use a glass of wine or something.'

'There isn't any booze here,' I said. 'I was thinking maybe it would be a good time to start drying out. I could stand it myself.'

She nodded. 'If you're willing to put up with me. But I'll need a few things from my place.'

'Where do you live?'

'I have an apartment in Southwest.'

'I'll take you there.'

'Thanks, Nick.'

Her place was in a low rent hi-rise near the Arena Stage, two blocks back from the river. We rode the elevator up to the eighth floor.

Her apartment seemed to be a part-time residence. There were chairs and stereo equipment and a television, but no tables. The walls were bare. Magazines and newspapers were scattered on the floor, along with several full ashtrays.

As she walked towards the bedroom, she said, 'I'll be out in a minute.'

I had a look in before she closed the door. A sheeted mattress lay on the floor. Next to it was a small reading lamp and a telephone, and another ashtray.

I walked out onto her narrow balcony and lit a smoke. Her view faced north and looked out over other bunker-style buildings. I crushed the butt on the railing and reentered the apartment.

I could hear her muffled voice through the bedroom door as she talked on the telephone. I browsed through her small record collection, a typically seventies example of dead-end rock: Boston's debut, REO Speedwagon, Kansas, etc. Her stereo equipment was high-end; her television, state-of-the-art.

'You ready?' she asked cheerfully, coming out of the room with the suitcase she had emptied, then refilled.

We got on the freeway at Maine Avenue and headed east for a couple of miles, turning off past the Capitol and driving down Pennsylvania. I parked near the Market.

We walked to a restaurant near the strip, one of those places that does a huge Sunday brunch business on the Hill. The television set over the bar was already fired up and set on 'The NFL Today.' They were moving plenty of mimosas and Bloody Marys, though there was also a fair amount of draught beer being sold to those who were past kidding themselves.

We lucked into a window deuce and ordered burgers and coffee. When the coffee came, Kim lit a cigarette.

'Is this going to be your first winter in D.C.?' I asked.

'Yes.' The sun was coming through the window, finding the three or four strands of silver in her long brown hair. 'When does it start getting cold around here?'

'Sometimes this month. Sometimes not till January.'

'How long have you lived here?'

'Practically all my life.'

'Your folks alive?'

'My parents live in Greece.'

'Were you born there?'

'Yes. But I don't remember it.' I sipped my coffee. 'I met your father, you know?'

'When you were following us?' Her eyes narrowed, then softened. 'He's a good man.'

'He is. That home in Elizabeth City might be the right place for you to start again.'

'My childhood's over, Nick.'

'It was only a thought.'

'How about you?' she asked. 'Any plans for a new start?'

'No,' I said. 'I think I'll just hang around.'

'And what?' she asked.

'See what happens.'

After lunch I drove across town and picked up Rock Creek Park just above the Kennedy Center. The leaves on the trees had turned completely. With everything, I had not noticed the change of season.

A car that had been behind us since we entered the park stayed with us as I veered right on Arkansas Avenue. When I made a left onto Thirteenth Street, the car turned right.

The rest of the day I watched football and paced around the apartment while Kim napped. At one point I pulled a chair up to my bed and watched her sleep, then spent the next fifteen minutes wondering why I had done that.

I drove to a Vietnamese fish market on New Hampshire and Eastern Avenue, bought two pieces of flounder, and returned to the apartment. I brushed them with butter and lemon and wrapped them in foil. Kim put them on a small hibachi she had set up outside near the stoop. I sat on the steps with my cat and we watched her grill the fish.

After dinner she washed the dishes while I watched the news. Still no word on Eddie Shultz. Kim entered the living room. She looked healthy and almost beautiful.

'You're nearly there,' I said.

'Goodnight, Nick.' She kissed me on the back of my cheek, where the neck meets the ear. Then she turned and walked into the bedroom. I watched her walk.

That night I slept on the couch. The cat slept on my bed, with Kim Lazarus.

The next morning I used my room to change clothes while Kim showered. She had reorganized my dresser into a makeup stand. Moisturising creams, eye shadows, and lip glosses were mixed in with barrettes and odd pieces of jewelry. A wallet-sized, aged black and white photograph of a German shepherd was wedged in the frame of the mirror that hung over my dresser.

'I guess I kind of took over,' Kim said as she walked into the bedroom wearing my bathrobe. Water dripped from her hair onto her shoulders and over the top curves of her full breasts. 'I'm sorry.'

'Don't be,' I said. 'I like a woman here. The difference of it, I mean. When I was married, my wife was always putting fresh flowers and plant pieces around our place. It's something I would never think to do myself. Now it's one of the few things I remember about our marriage.' I pointed to the picture of the dog on the mirror. 'Who's this?'

'Rio,' she said. 'A shepherd I had when I was a kid.'

'How do you feel?'

'Really good,' she said. 'The mornings are great. I feel so proud waking up, knowing I made it through another day without doing drugs. But the nights are really rough, Nick. I just associate the night-time with getting fucked up.'

'You feel like going for a ride today, look at the leaves?'

'Yeah,' she said, smiling. 'I'd like that.'

We drove out 270 and turned off at the Comus exit, parking in the lot on Sugarloaf Mountain. We hiked the mile to the top.

It was Monday but crowded due to the peak foliage. We found a rock on the edge that was unoccupied, and had a seat. The air was cool and there was a strong breeze. As the clouds moved across the sun, we watched their shadows spread over the trees below.

The temperature began to drop. We didn't speak for quite a while. Kim found my hand with hers and held it. I was thinking of Jimmy Broda and I know she felt it. But she let the afternoon drift by and didn't say a word.

That night I fell asleep on the couch shortly after Kim had gone to bed.

She woke me sometime after midnight with a long kiss on my lips. She was wearing only a T-shirt. She was kneeling beside me, and the T-shirt crept above her pale, round ass as she leaned in.

'Aren't you tired of this arrangement?' she said.

'Yes.'

'Me too.'

She pulled down my blanket and straddled me, easing me into the folds of her dampness. I pushed her breasts together and kissed them, then her neck. Her hips moved with an even liquidity. I let her take me to it, and when I was there, it was as if she were tearing a piece from me to keep in her lambent belly.

Afterwards I remained inside her. She laid her chest on mine and I listened to her breath.

We slept in my bed that night, with the cat between our feet. I woke early, showered, and dressed. I shook her awake and told her I was leaving to run some errands, then kissed her. Her eyes had closed again by the time I reached the door.

When I returned two hours later, she was gone. Her suitcase had been taken, as had all of the makeup and jewelry on the dresser. The rest of the apartment was orderly. There were no signs of struggle.

The photograph of the German shepherd still hung crookedly on the mirror, the only item Kim Lazarus had left behind, like the last discarded fragment of a childhood long since past.

25

The weather that morning suddenly turned, to the kind of gray, windy October day that is a harbinger of winter. I put on my charcoal wool sportjacket over a blue denim shirt, filled the cat's dish, secured the apartment, and headed downtown.

I had the desk clerk ring up Kim's apartment from the lobby of her building. There was no answer and she had not been in to pick up her mail.

Out in the street, I turned my collar up and walked into the wind down the two blocks that ended at the river. I entered a seafood restaurant on the waterfront that was just opening for lunch, and had a seat at the empty bar.

The bartender was a thin man with a thin mustache wearing black slacks and a stained white shirt. He stopped cutting limes, idled over, and dropped a bev-nap on the bar in front of me. Then he ran a waxy fingernail along the edge of his mustache.

'What can I get you?'

'A bottle of Bud. And an Old Grand-Dad. Neat.'

He served me and returned to his cutting board. I downed the shot and lit a smoke, then drank deeply of the beer. When the bottle was empty, I ordered another and a shot to keep it company.

I watched a yacht leave the marina while I killed my second round. I settled up and walked back out, up the street and to my car. Heading northwest, I stopped at a liquor store and bought a sixpack and a pint of Old Crow.

Before my next stop I slammed two cans of beer and had a fierce pull off the bottle. I wasn't really sure where I was going, but it didn't much matter. I knew at that point that I was spiraling down into a black binge.

I parked in front of May's, a glorified pizza parlor on Wisconsin between Georgetown and Tenley Circle. To the left of the dining room was a bar run by a fat Greek named Steve Maroulis. Maroulis also made book from behind the bar.

'*Ella, Niko!*' he shouted when I walked in.

'Steve,' I said, and took a stool at the bar next to a red-faced geezer in an Orioles hat.

'What'll it be?' Maroulis asked cheerfully, with a smile on his melon-like face.

'A Bud and a shot.'

'You still drinkin' Grand-Dad?'

'Yeah.'

He put both in front of me and I drained the shot glass. I lit a smoke and put the matches on top of the pack, then slid them neatly next to my bottle of beer. All settled in.

'Sorry to hear about Big Nick,' Maroulis said.

'He had a life.'

'Tough sonofabitches, those old Greeks.'

'That they were.'

'Not like us.'

'No,' I said. 'Not like us.'

I drank my beer and watched a soap opera on the bar television. A pretty-boy actor was doing his impersonation of a man, while the young actress opposite him was trying to convince the audience that she could love a guy who wore eye makeup.

I ordered another round and finished watching the show. When the next one came on, the same garbage with different theme music, I asked Maroulis to switch the channel.

'Anything,' I said. 'Christ, even "The Love Boat" would be better than this shit. How about a movie?' I was looking at the stacks of tapes Maroulis had lined up next to the VCR.

'No movies!' the geezer next to me declared, and pounded his fist on the bar to make his point. 'Haven't seen a movie since *Ben Hur*. Don't plan to either. They're all shit.'

'All right, old-timer,' I said. 'No movies.'

And, I might have added, 'Welcome to the '90s.' I thought of T. J. Lazarus, another senior who claimed he hadn't seen a movie in years. But there had been a brand-new television and VCR in his house. Probably one of the gifts from Kim that he had mentioned. I thought of Kim's state-of-the-art equipment in her barren apartment. But from the looks of her collection, she hadn't purchased a record since Don Kirschner's heyday. And I thought of Pence, with his unconnected recorder, a pathetic reminder of the gift from his missing grandson. Gifts.

159

The geezer next to me was still talking. I don't know if he was talking to me. I smoked another cigarette and moved the ashes around in the ashtray with the lit end. In my other hand I held the empty shot glass and made circles with it on the bar. I finished my beer.

'Steve,' I said, calling him over. 'You still got that phone in the office upstairs?'

'Yeah?'

'I need to use it.'

'Go ahead.'

He handed me an unsolicited beer as I stepped away from the bar. I put the Camels in my breast pocket and passed the kitchen, tripping once as I went up a narrow staircase. I found the small office and had a seat at a government-issue desk that faced a dirty window overlooking the alley. The phone directory was under the desk.

I looked up the number for the local authorized Kotekna service center and dialed it. After two rings a friendly voice picked up.

'Service,' he said.

'Hi,' I said. 'I've got a problem with my VCR.'

'Is it in warranty, sir?'

'Yes, but it's been serviced twice already. I'm not interested in having another serviceman look at it. What I need from you, is there some sort of eight-hundred number, a customer service line or anything like that?'

'Hold on,' he said, a little less friendly. He got back on the line and gave me the number. I thanked him, hung up, and dialed the number he had given me. A recorded voice instructed me to wait for the next available operator. Before the message ended a live voice broke in on the line.

'Kotekna Video. Customer service.'

'Customer service?' I said lamely. 'I'm sorry. I'm a retailer, not a customer. I was trying to get the sales manager for the mid-Atlantic region. What's his name again?'

'Bruce Baum,' she said.

'Yes, of course. Could you connect me please?' There was a click, then a couple of rings.

'Mr Baum's office,' a sweet voice said.

'This is Gary Fisher,' I said, 'with Nutty Nathan's in Washington. Can I speak to Bruce, please?'

'Let me see if he's in. Hold, please.' A click, more waiting, then, 'I'll connect you.'

'Bruce Baum,' a smooth voice said.

'Bruce,' I said, 'Gary Fisher, the merch manager with Nutty Nathan's.'

'Gary,' he said with false warmth. 'What can I do for you?'

'I'm really calling for some advice on one of your products.'

'Go ahead, Gary.'

'My company purchased a hundred sticks from your people at the CES show in Vegas, a closeout I think.'

'That's right. The KV100, wasn't it? Your GM, Jerry Rosen, cut the deal himself.'

'Yes. Anyway, to be honest with you, I'm having some trouble moving them. I don't know if it's a problem with price point, or if I'm not promoting them correctly, or what?' I heard the slur of my words and let him talk.

'Well,' he said, 'I hope you're not trying to make the full mark on them. After all, even considering they were defects, I practically gave them away.'

'Defects?'

'Yes. Didn't you know?'

'No.'

'Well, then,' he said with a chuckle, 'there's your problem right there. Miscommunication in your office. I had this load of KV100's with defective boards. Jerry Rosen came out to the show and decided to take them off my hands for practically nothing. He said he was going to have your service department order the new parts, fix the units themselves, then blow them out at a strong retail to make an impression in your market. He probably hasn't gotten the parts yet. *That's* why they're still sitting in your barn.'

'The units are shells right now, is that what you're saying?'

'That's right.'

'Thanks, Bruce.'

'*Thank you.* Let me know how you do with them. We've been trying to get our foot in your door for years. Frankly, I cut this deal with Rosen as an entrée.'

'I'll let you know, Bruce. Thanks again.' I hung up.

I put fire to a Camel and leaned back in my chair. A bird flew onto the window ledge, saw me, and flew off. I exhaled a line of smoke and watched it shatter as it hit the glass. I heard cynical laughter and realized it was mine.

There was one more call to make, a detail done so that I could put it all away and return to my cleansing binge. I got South Carolina information on the line.

I contacted the personnel director for Ned's World. I identified myself as the personnel manager of a large retail chain in the Baltimore–Washington corridor. After a couple of questions my suspicions were confirmed.

Then I was downstairs and spilling money on the bar. Steve Maroulis yelled something to my back as I walked out. The temperature had dropped and the sun was buried in a thick cover of clouds. Still, the light burned my eyes. I put on shades and got behind the wheel of my car.

I cut down Thirty-Eighth to Nebraska, across Connecticut and right on Military to Missouri, then left on Georgia. I pulled over and parked across the street from the Good Times Lunch.

Kim shot me a look when I walked in. Some heads turned in the gray-haired group seated near the upright fan and the malt liquor poster featuring Fred 'The Hammer' Williamson. I sat on the stool nearest the front door. Kim walked over with a pad in his hand.

'No food today, Kim. Just give me a can of beer.'

He brought one, set it down, and walked away. I drank half of it in one swallow and lit a cigarette. The fan blew my smoke in the direction of the front door. I killed my beer and shouted for Kim to bring me another.

I dozed off or blacked out for a minute or so. When I opened my eyes, Kim was setting a fresh beer in front of me. I popped the top and drank deeply. Some of the beer ran down my chin.

'Last one,' Kim said.

'Sure, Kim.'

'Go home, Nick.' There was something approaching sadness on his face.

I left the remainder of the beer and a pile of ones on the counter. I stumbled out and stepped off the kerb. A group of kids yelled something from a car that nearly grazed me. The kid riding shotgun flipped me off.

My Dodge came to life. I swung a 'U' on Georgia and headed back downtown. I undid the top of the pint with one hand and took a burning slug. I cracked another beer and wedged it between my thighs.

The car next to me honked and someone yelled. I turned the radio louder. I passed what was once a movie theater and was now a Peoples Drug Store. My thoughts moved back twenty years.

I am ten years old in this summer of 1968. I'm on the bus, the J-2, on my daily trip down Georgia Avenue to F Street, where I'll transfer to another bus that will take me crosstown to papou's carryout. I bag lunches there behind the counter.

The D.C. Transit bus, with its turquoise vinyl seats and orange striping, is not air-conditioned. The ones they commission to this part of town never are. By ten in the morning, when I ride, the bus already reeks with the sweat of working Washington.

This summer things feel different. Georgia Avenue is not the worst of spots, but the fires of April have lapped at this street. Every week I notice more businesses have closed. There seems to be a tension on the bus between blacks and whites, though I'm not afraid. Something is happening and I'm there to see it. Women wear large, plastic florescent earrings that read, 'Black Is Beautiful' over the silhouettes of Afro'ed couples. Lawyers have long hair and wear wide, flowery ties. The ultra-square DJ, Fred Fiske on 1260 AM, is playing the Youngblood's 'Get Together' in heavy rotation.

I read the changing marquees of the neighborhood movie theaters that line Georgia Avenue: Eleanor Parker and Michael Sarrazin in Eye of the Cat; *George Peppard and Orson Welles in* House of Cards; *Alex Cord in Harold Robbins'* Stiletto. *Downtown, at the Trans-Lux,* The Great Bank Robbery, *with Clint Walker and Kim Novak, has just opened.*

At three in the afternoon, after the lunch rush is over at papou's store, a man drops a stack of Daily News *on top of the cigarette machine. I take one to a booth and read the reviews of the films whose titles I have seen splashed across the marquees earlier in the day.*

I look behind the counter at my grandfather. He is slicing a tomato that he holds in his hand. The juice of the tomato stains the yellowish apron he wears around his ample middle. There is a Band-Aid on his thumb from his accident on the meat slicer earlier in the day. He sees the tabloid open in front of me and knows my daily ritual.

'Anything good today at the movies, Nicko?' he shouts across the store.

'Nothing much, Papou.'

'Okay, boy,' he says, and continues to slice the tomato. There is a smile on his wide, pink face.

I threw my head back and killed another beer. More horns sounded. I pulled back within the lines of my lane and turned left on Florida Avenue, heading east.

I ran the red at North Capitol and bore left onto Lincoln Road. I passed houses with rotting back porches, alleys littered with garbage, and packs of young men grouped like predators on street corners.

Then I was veering left, passing under the black, arched iron gate of the Glenwood Cemetery. I pulled the top on another beer and stayed to the right, driving slowly around long curves and lazy inclines, by rows of headstones and monuments crammed together, their symmetry broken only by the occasional dogwood or pine.

As the names on the headstones changed from Protestant to ethnic, I slowed down. When I reached a section that only contained the graves of Greeks, I stopped the car.

I remained seated and drank my last beer. When I finished it, I crushed the can, tossed it into the backseat, and slipped the pint bottle inside my jacket. I got out of the car and staggered onto the grass.

Spartan immigrants had chosen to lie here. They were buried on a long hill overlooking the road and a junior-high playground. A few of the headstones mentioned their native villages and the year in which they came to America.

I recognized many of the family names. Some had been friends with, or had known my grandfather: Kerasiotas, Kalavratinos, Stathopoulos, Psarakis. On the headstone of a guy named Vlatos, the inscription read, 'I Wish I Was in Vegas.'

I had a seat under an oak tree across from my grandfather's headstone. I reached into my jacket and pulled out the pint, tilted it back to my mouth, and watched bubbles rise to its upturned base. I swallowed, toasted my grandfather with the bottle, and replaced the cap.

Though it was probably very cool, I felt comfortable. I listened to the faint laughter and yells of the boys playing ball on the playground at the foot of the hill. The wind blew small yellow leaves around my feet. And I stared at the headstone that bore my name: Nicholas J. Stefanos.

I stayed in that position for the remainder of the afternoon. I was unable to focus my thoughts on any one thing; all of my emotions seemed to flow through me at once. In the end there were only a few pathetic certainties: I was thirty years old, unemployed, and sitting dead drunk in a graveyard, an empty pint of rotgut bourbon in my hand.

Sometime after the skies had darkened and the sounds of the playground had died away, a man in a caretaker's uniform walked towards me. He kicked the soles of my shoes lightly. The name stitched across his chest, on a white patch, was Raymond.

'You better get on up,' he said. 'They'll be lockin' the gates, and just before that the police cruise through.'

'Thanks,' I said, using his arm to help me up.

'You all right, man?'

'Yeah, Raymond. Thanks a million.'

I don't remember the ride home, except that there was shouting and more hornblowing. There was also a nasty bit of business at the National Shrine, when I attracted a small crowd when I pulled over to vomit.

I woke up early the next morning, halfway on my bed and fully clothed. There was some puke splashed across my denim shirt, and a dried clump of it on my chin.

I had a cold shower. After that, I put on side two of the Replacements' *Tim*, the most violently melodic rock and roll I owned. I cleared the room and forced myself to jump rope.

By the time Bob Stinson's blustering guitar solo kicked in, on 'Little Mascara,' my eyes were closed and I was working the rope, my body soaked with sweat and alcohol.

I took another shower, as hot as I could stand it, and shaved. I cooked breakfast, made a pot of coffee, and finished them both. I put on clean clothes and ran fresh water into the cat's dish.

Then I climbed into my Dodge and pointed it in the direction of James Pence.

26

The buzzer unlocked the glass doors automatically. I stepped into the building, past the security guard and the woman at the switchboard, and into the elevator. I rode it to the tenth floor and walked the narrow carpeted hallway to Pence's apartment. The door was open as I arrived.

The final drag of Pence's cigarette burned between his fingers. The familiar smell of Old Spice and whiskey drifted towards me.

'You look like hell,' he said.

'May I come in?'

'Certainly.' He stepped aside as I passed.

I walked into the living room, hearing his padded footsteps behind me. I turned to look at him. The grief of the last weeks had taken years from him, years he didn't have.

'Coffee?' he asked.

'No coffee. Why don't you just get me a screwdriver. A Phillips head, can you do that?'

'Yes,' he said. 'I own one.'

'Then do it.'

I heard him rummage through a drawer in the kitchen. I picked up the VCR from the lower shelf of the television stand and moved it over to the dining room table. It felt very light.

Pence brought me the screwdriver. I took it and worked on the back of the recorder. He lit another cigarette and sat watching me from the end of the table. His face was reddening from embarrassment, but there was also a look on him something like relief.

When the screws were off, I lifted the back panel and put it aside. I reached in and felt around, then looked it over with a perfunctory glance. I sat back in my chair and stared at Pence. He looked away.

'It's empty,' I said. 'But you knew that.'

'Yes.' He looked at his lap boyishly and blew some smoke at his knees.

I walked over to the window and raised the blinds. Then I cranked open the casement window and breathed cool air.

'Is my grandson alive?' Pence said in a small voice.

'I don't know.'

'What *do* you know, Mr Stefanos?'

I turned and looked at him angrily. 'I know now what you've suspected for weeks. The people I used to work for are involved in some sort of drug trafficking. They're moving the drugs through the warehouse in these VCRs. I think that Jimmy stole one and brought it home. Do we agree so far?'

'Yes.'

'When he got it home and saw it was dead, he opened up the back and found its contents. He was never fired from Nathan's, he just never went back. But he knew they'd figure out eventually who took the VCR. So he got scared and left town with the drugs and a couple of friends he made along the way. You figured all this out and came to me for help. Then you put the VCR out where I could see it, knowing I'd notice it, right?'

'That's right,' he said. 'Believe me, I'm not proud of how I got you into this. Playing on your sympathies, and so forth.'

'So forth. You mean *lying*, don't you?'

'Yes. I'd do more than that, to protect my grandson. When you have children, you'll understand.'

'I'm not interested in understanding your motives.' I shook a cigarette out of his pack and lit it, then dropped his Zippo on the table. 'Why did you come to me?'

'After I found the empty recorder in Jimmy's room and linked it with his rather erratic behavior and the company he was keeping, I didn't know what to do. Going to the police seemed out of the question. After all, Jimmy was involved, in a criminal sense. I went to Mr McGinnes for help – he was the only one in the organization I knew – and he suggested you. When he said your name, I recognized it. Jimmy *had* mentioned you to me, several times. It wasn't all a lie, Mr Stefanos.'

'But why didn't you come clean with me from the beginning?'

'Obviously there's more than one person at Nutty Nathan's who's dirty,' he said. 'I wasn't sure if I could trust you.'

I raised my open hand without thought, then lowered it. My voice shook.

'You stupid old bastard,' I said slowly. 'You just don't understand, do

167

you?' He stared at me blankly. I butted the cigarette, walked to the door, and turned the knob.

'I'd like to help,' he said weakly.

'No.'

'What are you going to do?'

'Finish it.'

McGinnes watched me enter Nathan's on the Avenue, and kept watching, his arms folded as he leaned against a microwave oven display.

Lee was behind the counter to my right. She was wearing a jade green shirt, buttoned to the top, and a jean skirt, out of which came her stout little wheels. First she smiled, then her brow wrinkled.

'You look terrible,' she said.

'So I've been told.'

'Sorry about your job.'

'Don't worry about it, Lee. Listen, I've been awful busy.'

'You don't have to explain,' she said.

I glanced back at McGinnes. 'Lee, I don't mean to cut you short, but I've got to talk to Johnny.'

'Go ahead,' she said. 'We'll talk later.'

I head-motioned McGinnes. We walked the length of the store through the back to the radio room.

'You want a beer?' he asked.

'No.'

'Suit yourself,' he said, and pulled a malt liquor from his usual spot. He popped the tab and drank.

'Where's Andre and Louie?'

'Andre's off. Louie's out making a deposit. What's up?'

'Can we talk for a few minutes?'

'Yeah, the floor is dead. If this is about the Broda thing, I can tell you that I've been keeping an eye on the news, and that Shultz boy was never found.'

'I know. But there's more.'

I told him everything that I was certain of, and some of my guesses. He whistled softly when I was finished and then stared at his feet. Some color had gone out of his face.

'What do we do now?' he said.

'I only wanted you to be aware of the situation, in case they think you're involved. They haven't made any kind of play on me yet. Maybe they think the Shultz murder scared us off.'

'What happened to the girl?'

'She's gone,' I said. 'Listen, Johnny, I need one more favor of you, man, then it's over for you.'

'What is it?'

'I know you keep a few pieces that you collect, the unregistered kind. I'll be needing to borrow one.'

He looked at me as he finished his beer. He moved the can around in his hand and then crushed it.

'You come in here,' he said, 'and tell me all this shit, and I haven't even got it all digested yet, and now you want a gun? You're fuckin' nuts, man. Why don't you just ask me to put one to your head and pull the trigger?'

'Listen,' I said. 'I'm going on with this thing. I don't *have* any options, Johnny. And I need something behind me if I'm going to get this kid.'

'I don't think so, Nick,' he said, and shook his head as he walked away. 'I gotta get back out on the floor.'

'Think about it,' I yelled to his back. But he was already out the door.

Late in the afternoon I stopped in the Good Times Lunch and had a seat at the counter. Kim came over with a pad in his hand.

'The special, Kim,' I said sheepishly, 'and a coffee, black.'

He nodded and returned shortly with a fried-fish platter. I shoveled it in and had a cigarette with my coffee. After that I paid the check that Kim laid in front of me.

'Kim,' I said, and he turned back around. 'I'm sorry about yesterday. I was out of control. It won't happen again.'

'No problem, Nick,' he said. 'But you should get rest. You don't look so good.'

The red light on my answering machine was blinking when I entered my apartment. I pushed down on the bar.

The first message, from McGinnes, told me to meet him at the store tomorrow. He would have what I wanted. The second message was from Joe Dane. I called him at home, and he picked up on the third ring.

'Hello?'

'Joe, it's Nick, calling you back.'

'Nick, we need to talk.'

'I think it's time. How about right now?'

'No, not now. I'm busy tonight. Tomorrow morning in the park.'

'Tomorrow's fine, but not in the park. Someplace more public.'

He hesitated. 'So it's like that.'

'That's right,' I said. 'Tomorrow morning at ten, in the bell tower at the Old Post Office downtown.'

'Okay, Nick,' he said. 'Ten o'clock.'

27

To get into the tower of the Old Post Office at Twelfth and Penn, one has to take the tour. I stood amid a group of eight tourists on the ground level, around a brightly lit, U-shaped counter.

A gangly Park Service employee was giving us a brief history of the Post Office. He mumbled into a microphone in a barely intelligible, nasal voice. The man next to me was taping him with a video camera.

After his speech we were ushered into a glass elevator and began our ascent to the tower base. The checkerboard floor of the Pavilion fell away rapidly as we rose higher. A little girl near me said to her father, 'Daddy, if we fell now, we'd be dead, right?' An older woman who already looked a little frightened touched her collar and laughed nervously.

The doors opened and we walked out to a circle of white and red ropes that rang the Congress Bells. A rotund guide informed us that the bells, a gift from Great Britain, were rung on the opening and closing days of Congress, and on all national holidays. The only other instances when they were rung, she said, were in honor of the Challenger's crew, and 'when the Redskins won the Super Bowl.'

Then the guide herded us into another elevator. She reached in and pushed the floor button from the outside. 'You picked a great day for the tower,' she said, as the doors closed and her fat, bespectacled face disappeared.

When the doors opened again, the group walked out into the open-air tower and scattered. The clock mechanism was housed in a raised platform in the center. A Park Ranger sat on the platform and looked through binoculars.

A circular walkway afforded a view of the city in all directions. Three of the sides were strung with narrowly spaced wire to discourage jumpers. The south side had a Plexiglas shield. Joe Dane was standing on the east side, looking out. I tapped his shoulder.

He turned without surprise. Though his clothes were clean, he looked as disheveled as always. There was a dead look to his watery brown eyes.

'I don't really like this view,' he said, turning his head towards the expanse of Pennsylvania, Constitution, and the Capitol.

'We can move,' I said.

We walked past the southern view of the Potomac and the Jefferson Memorial, and over to the west wall. Dane stared through the wires. The curving lines of the Federal Building below were like a horseshoe framing the Mall and the Lincoln Memorial.

'All those tourists,' he said. 'They waste their time standing in line to get up the Washington Monument, when the best view of D.C. is right here.' He smiled. 'Remember when you and me and Sarah and Karen used to come down here on Sundays? Smoke a joint out in the car, then come up and take pictures with our heads through the wires and shit like that? After that spend a couple of hours munching our way through the eatery downstairs.'

'Joe,' I said. 'Let's just get down to it, all right?'

'All right, Nick,' he said softly. His smile faded, and he buried his hands in his pockets.

'Give it to me straight up. Did they get Jimmy Broda?'

'Yes.'

'Is he alive?'

'Yes.'

I smiled and slapped the wall. The ranger and a couple of tourists looked my way. I wanted to hug Dane but didn't show it. I wasn't finished with him.

'Why are you here, Joe?'

'Last shot at redemption, I guess.' He shook his head. 'I don't know.'

'Are you still with them?'

'No. But they don't know that.'

'Tell me about it.'

He shrugged. 'It's not all that complicated. It's a small operation, smaller than you think. Only a few people involved. And this was their first time at this sort of thing. At least it was for Rosen.'

'Jerry Rosen in charge of it all?'

'On the D.C. end.'

'What about Nathan Plavin?'

'No. It was easy to keep him out of it. Rosen had him insulated from the day-to-day aspects of the business, anyway.'

'Who else at Nathan's? Brandon?'

'No.'

'How did you get in, Joe?'

'Rosen knew I was hard up for money,' he said. 'He came to me with a proposal. Supervise the shipment, in and out, and keep an eye on it while it was in the barn. The payoff was pretty sweet. And I rationalized it with that old mentality you and I grew up with – drugs are innocent, done by innocent people.'

'That was a long time ago.'

He looked down at his shoes. 'When one of the warehouse guys tipped me that the Broda kid had stolen the VCR, I knew things were going to fall apart. Then you started to poke around. I wanted to tell you and get out then, but I had to make a choice . . . I had to make a choice between warning you and looking out for Sarah.' He spread his hands out.

'Keep talking,' I said.

'I went to Rosen,' he said, still looking at his shoes. 'He had Brandon fire you, then had his boys beat you up to warn you off. They followed the kids south. The Shultz boy was killed. Then they caught Broda and brought him back.'

'Why didn't they kill Broda too?'

Some tourists walked by. Dane stopped talking until they passed. 'They don't know *what* to do with him,' he said. 'Listen, Nick, I know you feel like a sucker. But the reason that kid is still alive is you. They know you've stuck with this thing, and that you're not going to leave it alone. They *can't* get rid of the kid while you're still looking, and they can't let him go. It's a stalemate now.'

'Don't bullshit me, Joe.' I eyed him suspiciously. 'Let me get this straight. Jerry Rosen was a fair-haired boy when he worked for Ned's World in South Carolina. When he moved to D.C. to work for Nathan, he saw the drug market up here and decided to get a piece of it. Those two guys who roughed me up – did he recruit them from the South Carolina warehouse?'

'Yes.'

'Who else?'

'There's the Jamaicans who work with me.'

'I met them,' I said. 'A tall albino and his shadow. So there's them, Rosen, and two from Carolina, you – and the man who bankrolled the whole deal. Ned Plavin, right?'

'That's right.'

I thought for a minute. 'Are the drugs out of the warehouse yet?'

'Not entirely,' he said. 'It was a hundred sticks to start out with. They moved fifty in two consecutive nights last week, and another twenty-five on Tuesday. Tomorrow night they move the last twenty-four.'

'How?'

'What do you mean?'

'The setup. Where, who comes for it, how it's done, the money, all of it.'

'Shit, Nicky.' He studied my face. 'The way it was done the other times, two buyers come. They bring a hundred-fifty grand in a suitcase. We meet in the back of the warehouse, where the VCRs are stacked. Our guys load them up, they leave the suitcase.'

'Guns?'

'Yeah, everyone.'

'What time does it go down?'

'Ten o'clock.'

'Are you going to be there?'

'I'm gone, Nick. Sarah and I packed last night. I called in sick today. We're leaving this afternoon, all of us.'

'Just walk, then everything's all right.'

'No,' he said, 'it's never going to be all right. I was part of something that got a kid killed. Maybe someday I'll put a gun in my mouth to help me forget. Probably not. But for the time being my job is to protect my family.'

'You'd better get going then, Joe.'

'One more thing,' he said, and grabbed my arm before I could pull it away. 'These guys are just a bunch of dumbshit cowboys. You go up against them, man, you're gonna die.'

'You know where they've got the kid?'

'No.' He took his hand off my arm. 'I'm sorry, Nick. I really am.'

'So long, Joe.'

He turned and headed for the stairwell. When the door closed behind him, I wished him luck.

Louie was behind the front counter when I walked into the store. He gave me a nod with his chin, then stared at me over the tops of his reading glasses.

'How's it going, Louie?'

'Oh, I'm makin' it, Youngblood. How about you? Anything goin' on?'

'I'm weighing the possibilities.'

'Well, you got all the time in the world now. To find out what's *important*.'

'Is Johnny in?'

'In the back, takin' his medicine.'

I negotiated the maze of floor display and passed under the BB-riddled caricature of Nathan. I took the stairs down to the stockroom.

McGinnes was sitting on a carton in the back. Malone was standing next to him, a live Newport between his long fingers. I walked through a stagnant cloud of tobacco and pot smoke to get to them. I shook Malone's hand and shot a look at McGinnes.

'Andre knows everything,' McGinnes said unapologetically.

'He ran it all down to me,' Malone said quickly, 'in the hopes that the two of us could talk you out of whatever it is you plannin' to do.' He gave me the once-over, dragged on his cigarette, exhaled, and threw me a hundred dollar smile. 'You really stepped in some shit this time, didn't you, Country?'

'It's deeper than you think.'

I told them just how deep it was. Malone's brow was wrinkled the entire time I spoke. When I was finished, he ran a thumbnail between his front teeth, keeping his eyes on mine.

'So,' McGinnes said. 'They've got the boy.'

'If you don't mind, Johnny,' I said, 'I'll take what I came here for.'

McGinnes went to the corner of the stockroom, moved some boxes, and returned with something in his arms. He unwrapped the oilcloth it was in and brought it out.

'I wasn't sure what you wanted,' he said. 'So I brought a solid automatic. Nine-millimeter Browning Hi-Power. Push button magazine release.' With a quick jerk of his wrist the clip slid out into his palm. 'Holds thirteen with one in the chamber. Right here is the safety – you can operate it with your thumb while your hand's still on the grip. If you're not sure the safety's on, try cocking the hammer.'

'Thanks.' I held out my hand.

'I brought an extra clip.' He pulled that out, placed it with the pistol, and put them both in my hand. 'It's your up, man.'

I rewrapped everything in the oilcloth and put it in my knapsack, then hung it over my shoulder.

'You guys coming upstairs?'

'I am,' Andre said.

'I think I'll hang,' McGinnes said. 'Catch a buzz.'

Malone and I climbed the stairs. As we neared the landing, we heard McGinnes coughing below. Malone stayed with me all the way to the front door, where he stopped me with a grip on my arm.

'Hey, Brother Lou,' he shouted at Louie, who was still behind the counter. 'I'll be takin' a break.'

'You already had a break,' Louie said tiredly.

'Then I'll be takin' another.'

'What's up, Andre?' I asked.

'Let's go for a ride,' Malone said. 'I got a proposition for you, Country.'

28

Malone said, 'Pull on over, man.'

We were in the southbound lane of North Capitol, near the Florida Avenue intersection. I pulled over and cut the engine. Malone rolled the window down, leaned his arm on its edge, and put fire to a Newport.

On the east side of the street was a casket company, a beauty parlor, and a sign that read, 'FISH, UBS.' Hand-painted on the door, in dripping, wide red brushstrokes, was 'Closed for Good.' To our right stood a Plexiglas bus shelter on a triangle of dirt that the city called a park. A man in a brown plaid overcoat slept in front of the shelter's bench, where another graybeard sat and drank from a bagged bottle. Further down the street, near P, a Moorish carryout and a 'Hi-Tech' shoeshine parlor graced the block.

The sidewalks were teeming with activity. Those not seated on stoops paced within the confines of their block. A woman in a two-piece, turquoise jogging suit stood with her hands on her hips and yelled gibberish at the unconcerned people walking past. Her flat buttocks sagged much like her sloping shoulders. Straight ahead, less than two miles down the strip, rose the Capitol dome.

'Look at it,' Malone said. 'This is our city, man. Just *look* at it. Right in the shadow of the motherfuckin' Capitol. And they be throwin' eighty million dollar inauguration parties.'

'You came from a neighborhood just like this,' I said, 'and you made it out. It's no different than it was twenty years ago.'

He chuckled cynically and blew out some smoke. 'Don't tell me it's no different, man. On these streets they kill you now for a ten dollar rock. And the media, all they be talkin' about: "The Mayor Snorts Coke." But nobody really cares about these people, because it ain't goin' down in Ward Three. It's just niggers killin' niggers. Meanwhile, you read the *Washington Post* – they supposed to be "the liberal watchdog of the community," right? – well, check it out. Some white woman gets raped in the suburbs, it makes page one. Now go to the back of the Metro section, where they got a special spot reserved for the niggers. They call it "Around the Area," some shit like that. And it's always the same little boldfaced type: "Southeast Man Slain, Northeast Man Fatally Shot."' He tossed his butt out the window. 'One little paragraph, buried in the back of the paper, for the niggers.'

'You and me have talked about this a hundred times, Andre. What's it got to do with today?'

He looked out the window and squinted, then ran a finger along the top of his thick mustache. 'I remember my first day of work at Nathan's. I got dressed that morning, real sharp. When I walked out of my place that day, I *knew* I was serious, I was so hooked up, I was *proud*.'

'I remember,' I said, and smiled at the thought of it. But I wondered where he was going with it.

'Anyway, I was all fired up, like anyone on their first day of the job. After a year, I had me enough to rent my place on Harvard, out of the old neighborhood. But then I started to notice some shit. The company was always sending other guys to seminars, putting other guys in management training. When the big dogs came into the store, I got no recognition, man, nary a nod. I doubt they even knew my name. And then they started cutting our commissions, changing payplans every six months. I woke up one day, I saw I was sliding back to where I came from.'

'What are you telling me?'

He waved his hand the width of the block. 'I don't want to come back to these streets man. I *won't* come back to these streets, understand?' He lit another smoke and pitched the match out the window. 'When I was listening to you earlier, I started to think. We both got a problem we need to work out. How could we take that situation they got down in that warehouse and turn it around to our advantage?'

'And?'

'I ain't got it all nailed down yet, see what I'm sayin'? But it would involve other people.'

'Not McGinnes,' I said quickly. 'There's something wrong with him. I mean he's not well.'

'Yeah, I think he's getting ready to bottom on out. Besides, all the man wants is to sell televisions.'

'And what do you want?'

'I'm still thinkin' on it,' he said. 'Hold up a minute while I make a call.'

He left the car and walked to a payphone at the gas station on the intersection. I had a Camel while he talked on the phone. By the time I finished it, he was back on the seat at my side.

'We got an appointment to see some fellas,' he said.

'Who?'

'Just younguns, that's all. They all right.'

'This is getting too complicated,' I said.

'Not complicated. Simple. Look here.' He slid closer to me on the seat. 'You want the boy, that's as plain as the light. But you got nothin' to deal with. When that last shipment of goods leaves the warehouse tomorrow night, and they tighten up the loose ends, they gonna do that boy just like they done the one down in Carolina.'

'I could go to the cops,' I said, 'like I should have done from the beginning.'

'Too late for that. You might get the boy killed, and take a fall yourself. No, man, there's a better way.'

'Talk about it.'

'Twenty-five percent of the man's goods,' he said. 'That's a big bargaining chip to sit down with at the table.'

I thought about that. 'You mean, steal the rest of the cocaine.'

'That's right, Country. Then trade it back to Rosen for the boy.'

I lit another cigarette and tossed the match, taking a deep lungful of the deathly smog. Then I watched my exhale stream out the window and disappear as it met the wind.

'What's your angle?' I said.

'My angle? A way out. All the way out. The way you tell, there's gonna be some money changin' hands tomorrow night. The money will be mine. A hundred-thirty for me, twenty for the boys I just called.'

'So you think we can just walk in and grab it – all of it, the money and the shake – from these guys? You said yourself, these people don't play.'

'Then neither will we.'

'You'd have to leave town. You'd never work or live in D.C. again. Have you thought about that?'

'This shit goes down in the street every day. As for work, well, a hundred and thirty grand is quite a start. For me, some things I've wanted for my mom. Yeah, I've thought about it.'

'It's too fucking crazy, Andre.' I dismissed the idea with a motion of my hand. But even as I did so, I was picturing in my mind the layout of the warehouse.

Andre pointed to the key in the ignition. 'Kick this bitch over,' he said. 'I want you to meet my boys.'

We veered off of Florida and climbed sharply up Thirteenth Street. On our right was Cardoza High School; to our left were the Clifton Terrace apartments. At the crest of the hill, just past Thirteenth and Clifton, I made a 'U' in the middle of the street and pulled the car over to the kerb at Andre's command.

Children kicked a ball around the glass-covered courtyard of the apartments. Boys walked from the high school, hunched and slower than old men. The downtown skyline rose below us majestically.

'Top of the motherfuckin' town,' Malone said without emotion. He pointed left to the Highview Apartments. 'They'll be coming out of there.'

'You grew up right around here, didn't you?'

'Yeah.'

We sat there for about ten minutes without speaking. Then Malone tapped me on the shoulder and I looked left. Two young men were crossing the street.

They were still in their teens. The taller of the two was lanky and wore a red sweatsuit with high-tops, and walked with an exaggerated down-step. There was a fixed scowl on his face. The other one was short and slender at the waist, with a boxer's upper body. He wore Lee jeans and a T-shirt. Both of their heads were shaved close to the scalp, with off-center parts like scars. They climbed into the backseat of my car.

'All right, Home,' the short one said to Malone, and they touched knuckles.

'Tony,' Malone said to the short one. 'Who's your friend?'

'His name's Wayne,' Tony said. 'He in my crew.'

'This is Nick,' Malone said. Tony nodded slightly. Wayne did nothing. We stared at each other in my rearview. 'Where's your big brother at, Tony?'

'You mean Charles?' Tony said and tilted his head.

'Yeah.'

'Chillin' in Lorton.'

'What happened?' Malone asked.

Tony said, 'Charles always be tellin' me, "Don't be shakin', messin' with guns and shit." One day this nigger dissed his ass in the street. Charles steals the motherfucker in the jaw. The nigger gets up for more. Charles double-steals the motherfucker. Nigger hits his head on the street. Dead. Charles doin' six to twelve, second degree.'

Wayne said to Malone, 'What'd you call us for, Home?'

'A job,' Malone said slowly. 'Tomorrow night.'

'What kind of job?' Tony asked.

'Robbin' a cocaine deal.'

'Where?'

'A warehouse, just over the line.'

'Talk about the pay,' Wayne said.

'If it goes down right, twenty thousand for the two of you,' Malone said. In the rearview I saw Wayne grin and tap Tony's hand with his own.

'How many guns?' Tony asked.

Malone said, 'We lookin' at maybe six.' If this impressed them, they didn't show it.

'What about the 'caine,' Wayne asked.

'The cocaine goes to Nick.'

'Who?' Wayne said and smiled.

Malone glared at him. 'You heard me. And he's in charge.' Wayne and Tony stared back but didn't speak. Malone continued. 'We're going to need guns, and a van.'

'We got guns,' Tony said. 'We can get a van.'

I cleared my throat and spoke for the first time. 'The guns are for show, understand? They're not to be used.' My voice sounded awkward and lily-white.

Tony said to Malone, 'You better tell your boy what time it is. If a man holdin' a gun on you, and he willin' to use it, you *got* to fire down on his ass.'

'He knows that,' Malone said unconvincingly.

'That's all for now,' I said abruptly, and turned over the ignition. I could feel their stares. 'We'll let you know tomorrow if it's going to happen. We'll let you know.'

Tony and Wayne slid out of the car. Tony leaned in the passenger window.

Malone said, 'How the pay sound?'

Tony said, 'Pay sound good, Home.'

'I'll call you tomorrow,' Malone said, 'first thing.'

I yanked the column shift down into drive and pulled away from the kerb. Fifteen minutes later I dropped Malone at the door of the Avenue.

That evening I drew a diagram of the warehouse and studied it. After that I phoned Malone.

'Andre, it's Nick.'

'Nick. What's up?'

'It's on for tomorrow night.'

'Good.'

'Call Wayne and Tony. Tell them to meet us, with the van, on top of the Silver Spring parking garage, the one next to and on the same side of the street as the Metro station. All the way up, at seven-thirty sharp. You got that?'

'That it?'

'You want out, I mean up to the last minute?'

'I'm in, Nick.'

I hung up and smoked a couple of cigarettes at the kitchen table. The cat sat on the radiator and watched me smoke. When I was finished, I washed up, locked the front door, and went to bed. I fell asleep quickly and did not dream.

I rose early the next morning and got permission from a high school friend to visit his property out around Thurmont, north of Frederick. An hour and a half later I was parked in front of a padlocked barn. I walked across a plowed field and into the woods.

I found the clearing where my friend kept his personal garden of vegetables and marijuana. Both had been harvested by now. I pulled a few rusty beer cans from a steel drum on the edge of the clearing and set most of them upright on stumps. I hung the remainder on the low branches of trees.

I walked to the middle of the garden, removed the Browning from my knapsack, loaded it, and undid the safety. I took my time firing at the beer cans. Eventually I emptied a full clip. When I was done, I had a reasonable approximation of the sight, and a good feel for the kick.

I replaced the gun in my knapsack and walked back into the woods. I came across a deer blind and climbed up into it, using the wooden blocks that had been hammered to the tree trunk.

For the next hour I sat in the blind smoking cigarettes and listening to the silence. There were not many birds this time of day. A rabbit bolted across some dry leaves, then down the bluff of a nearby creek.

I climbed off the tree and walked through the woods and across the field to my car, then drove back to D.C.

In my apartment I cleared out the center of my bedroom, turned my stereo up, and began to jump rope. Twenty minutes later I removed wet clothing and had a hot shower.

I shaved and dressed in jeans, a black sweatshirt, and running shoes. I had a sandwich, a cup of coffee, and, with that, a smoke. I put some dry food in the cat's dish. I loaded the Browning and placed it in my knapsack. Then I left the apartment to pick up Malone.

We drove onto the roof of the parking garage at about seven-twenty. A thin, purple line of sunset ran between a thick mass of clouds on the western horizon.

'That would be them,' Malone said, pointing to a green, windowless Ford van parked in the far corner.

'Is it stolen?' I asked, and drove towards it.

'That's a bet,' he said. I pulled up next to them.

We got out of my car and locked it. Malone walked around to the driver's side. They were up front in the buckets, both wearing jeans and blue, zip-up windbreakers.

'Give me the keys and move in the back,' Malone said. They did it, but slowly. Malone got behind the wheel, and I took the passenger seat. There were no seats in the back. Tony and Wayne sat with their backs against the interior walls, a blanket-covered mound between them at their feet.

'All right,' I said, pulling the diagram from my knapsack and crawling back with them. 'Andre and I have already gone over this, so listen up.' They moved in close and looked at the drawing. 'I have a key to the office, and I know the alarm code. But the code to the warehouse is different. We'll have to wait until they come to make the transaction before we can enter the warehouse.'

'Where they gonna be?' Tony asked.

I pointed to the diagram. 'The goods are in the rear left corner. Here. Wayne, you're going to go down the center aisle and cut left at the break in the row. You just move in and cover them from the side. Andre and me are going to walk right in on them, straight up the aisle they're in. That way they'll be covered on two sides. The other two sides are walls.' Wayne nodded and concentrated on the diagram.

'Where am I?' Tony asked.

'You enter the warehouse from the loft. Here. Then you climb over the railing and drop down to the top of the stock in the center aisle. Crawl along the top of it until you get to where the deal is happening, in the back. You cover us all from above.'

'What you gonna do,' Wayne said, 'ask 'em, "Please, can I have the 'caine?"' I didn't answer.

Malone said, 'What about the guns?'

'Right here, Home.' Tony pulled back the blanket and tossed it to the side. He reached in the pile and handed Malone a blue steel pistol. 'Three-eighty Beretta, holds eight rounds. Bad little gun, too.'

Malone felt the weight of the piece and checked the action. I watched

Wayne slide a nine-millimeter Colt into his jacket. Tony held up some sort of semiautomatic assault pistol.

Malone said, 'What you plan on doin' with that, Tony?'

'Spray the motherfucker,' Tony said, 'if I have to. MAC ten. Thirty-two rounds in the clip. Can't *nobody* fuck with it.' The short barrel passed in front of me as he moved the gun to his other hand. I grabbed the barrel and glared at Tony.

'Remember what I told you,' I said.

'Sure, chief,' Tony said, and Wayne chuckled joylessly.

Malone turned the key in the ignition, and the van came alive.

We parked in the body shop lot across the street from the Nutty Nathan's headquarters. The trucks near the warehouse were closed and locked. The showroom doors stood open. A couple of employee cars sat parked near the entrance. The office windows above the showroom remained dark.

'How long?' Tony said.

'They'll be leaving any time now,' I said. 'Then we go.'

Night came quickly. The air was heavy with the smell of rain. A salesman left the showroom and drove away. Moments later the lights went out and the store manager emerged. He locked the glass doors, walked to his car, and was gone.

'Okay,' I said, exhaling a nervous breath. 'I'll go in through the employee entrance. When I signal, the three of you follow. Move quick and low, and keep the guns in your jackets.'

Malone tried to smile, then shook my hand.

Wayne said to Tony, 'You ready, man?'

'Yeah,' Tony said, and they tapped fists. 'Let's get paid.'

29

I walked to the kerb with my knapsack slung across my back. A car approached, and I turned my face in the direction it was heading, letting it pass. When the car disappeared around a curve, I ran quickly across the street, through the Nutty Nathan's parking lot to the double glass doors of the employee entrance.

I felt my hand shaking a bit as I put the key in the lock. The key began to turn but then stopped. I pulled back slightly on the door and put pressure on the key. It caught and turned.

A high-pitched note sounded as I entered. I pressed the numbers one, two, four, and three in sequence on the keypad of the alarm box. The red light above the keys turned to green and the sound stopped.

I pulled a penlight from my pocket, pointed it at the van, and flashed it twice. A car drove by on the road and then another. I stepped back into the darkness of the stairwell.

The three of them were running across the road as the second set of taillights passed. Malone was in front, the others close behind. As they passed through the light of the parking lot, their features became more distinct. Malone's face seemed to be stretched back. Wayne and Tony were expressionless.

I pushed the door open enough for them to slide in. Though it was a short sprint across the lot, Malone was fighting for breath. Wayne coolly unzipped his jacket and drew the Colt. Tony's weapon hung over his shoulder by a strap. I relocked the door and motioned them up the stairs with my thumb. We passed under Nathan's caricature on the way. At the top of the stairs I halted them with my palm.

Though the florescents were off, the office was drawing light from the crime bulbs out in the lot. Some of the terminals had been left on, their amber screens displaying blinking cursors. The office was nearly unrecognizable in its stillness and in the faint yellow glow.

I crouched down and moved along the wall towards my old cubicle.

The others were behind me. When I reached my desk, I sat on the floor near my chair and put my knapsack beside me. Malone sat close by.

'Relax,' I said unconvincingly. 'Five minutes.'

Tony and Wayne were whispering behind the divider that separated Fisher's cubicle from mine. There was also the low, unidentifiable hum that exists in all commercial buildings late at night. I stared up at the drop ceiling.

The alarm company phoned ten minutes later. I gave the woman my employee ID number and explained that I would be working for a couple more hours. She thanked me and hung up. Though I had been gone more than a week, our personnel director had not called the alarm company to have my name stricken from the list. I had counted on her inefficiency.

'All right,' I said, 'let's go.'

We were back against the wall and retracing our steps. At Marsha's desk I made a right, the others following. I turned the knob on the third door to the left, opened it, and stepped in.

Except for a block of light that fell in from a large rectangular window on the eastern wall, the room was black. The window looked out into the warehouse. Next to the window was a door, which led to the stair-well landing, which led to the door of the loft. At the bottom of the stairs another door opened to the warehouse itself.

I tugged on Tony's windbreaker and pulled him closer. I pointed out to the loft and then to the second row of stock that rose up to meet it from the warehouse below.

'Tony, when I let you into the loft, get over to the railing and drop down onto the boxes in that row. You've got a long way to crawl to get to the back of the warehouse, but you've got time, understand?'

'Yeah,' he said, staring out the window with his mouth open. 'When?'

'They should be here soon.'

'What then?' Wayne said.

'There's an office downstairs with glass walls. We'll go down the stairwell, out the door to the warehouse, then get into that office – as far back into it as we can. When they're all together in the back, we make our move.' I pointed to the break in the middle row. 'That's where you cut in, Wayne.'

'Ain't no thing,' he said, and looked at Tony.

After fifteen minutes a sound came up from below, far away but heavy. We stepped back from the light of the window. One drop of cool sweat rolled down my back.

A figure emerged from below the loft and walked slowly towards the left aisle. The loose-limbed Jamaican was wearing his knit cap and vest. The grip of a pistol stuck up above his rearmost beltloop. He was followed by the tall albino with the single braid. The albino was cradling a shotgun that had a pistollike grip.

'Check that shit out,' Wayne mumbled.

'Mossberg,' Tony said. 'Twelve gauge.' For the first time there was a hint of apprehension on his young face.

'When it goes down,' Malone said, his eyes straight ahead, 'I'll be coverin' that yellow motherfucker. Everybody got that?' The others nodded.

'I go now?' Tony asked.

'No,' I said. 'There's two more, be along soon.'

As I said that, two others followed from beneath the loft. The first man was the one who smashed my face. Both wore heavy jackets that stopped at the waist. I could not see if they were armed.

'Wayne,' I said, before they left our sight. 'The man in front has killed before. When you step out, you cover him.'

'They all look like they done some killin', chief,' Wayne said.

'Maybe so,' I said. 'But I'm sure about him. Let's go, while they're in the back.'

They followed me to the door in the left corner of the room. We moved out to the stairwell landing. The steel below our feet gave off a soft echo. My key unlocked the next door. I opened it a few inches and looked out at the loft and the warehouse. I jerked my head to Tony in the direction of the railing.

Tony tightened his gunstrap. The MAC hung snugly against his back. He looked back at Wayne, tucked in his head, and was out the door.

He moved quickly across the loft. He climbed over the railing above the second row of stock. He stepped off about two feet to a console carton below. The carton moved under his weight. Then it stopped moving and he was on his stomach, crawling towards the back of the warehouse.

I eased the door closed and pointed down the stairs. The rain had begun, and muffled the vibration of the steps as we descended. I reached for the knob, and turned it slowly until there was a small click. I cracked open the door and looked out.

I heard faraway voices and the rain. I slid out the door and moved along the wall to Dane's office door. The knob turned in my hand. I left the door ajar as I moved into the darkness.

Malone and Wayne followed me in. Wayne closed the door behind him. They found me in the rear of the office, sitting on the floor with my back to the wall. They sat near me. I felt clammy and wet. I pulled the gun from my knapsack and tossed the knapsack aside.

A motor kicked in. The sound of it grew louder. A spinning shaft of yellow light approached with the sound. I held the Browning tightly between my legs. Then the sound diminished and the light faded.

'Forklift,' I said quietly and saw Malone nod.

There were more voices. I crouched up on the balls of my feet. Two tallish, thin men I didn't recognize were standing with the albino thirty yards from the office. They would be the buyers. One of them wore his dreadlocks long and out, and carried a briefcase in his right hand. He kept his other hand in his jacket pocket. So did his partner. The albino and one of the buyers traded unsmiling nods, then were gone behind the last row of stock.

'All here now,' I said.

We listened to the rain and each other's breathing. Some time went by like that, then Malone spoke.

'We best go, Country,' he said quietly.

'Okay,' I said.

I stood up and moved to the door. I undid the safety on my gun. I looked out, saw no one, and opened the door.

Wayne was out without a word, bolting across the floor to the center aisle. He held his gun up next to his head and pressed his back against the cartons. He began to edge his way to the back of the warehouse. I could see sweat reflecting off his forehead.

I walked out and moved quickly to the end cap of the second row. I felt Malone move with me. We glanced at one another. He moved his pistol from his left to his right hand. I wiped my palm across my jeans, got that hand around the grip of the Browning, and jacked a round into the chamber.

The rain had intensified. It beat against the metal roof with a steady rumble. Below that sound was the bass of their voices. We stepped away from the boxes, moved into the aisle, and walked towards them.

They were standing in a group at the end of the aisle. The buyers had their backs to us and the briefcase was at their feet. The other four were facing them. Everyone was armed.

We came within twenty yards of them. Then the loose-limbed Jamaican, the one who had blown me a kiss, locked his eyes into mine and stiffened. I stopped and raised my gun, pointing it in his direction. The buyers turned to face us.

'Don't nobody move,' Malone said evenly.

Wayne appeared suddenly from the right, stepped in quickly, and put the barrel of the Colt to the head of the South Carolinian who had broken my nose. He pulled back the automatic's hammer. It locked with a click that rode over the sound of the rain. The man dropped his gun from his left hand and let it fall to the concrete floor.

The Jamaican seemed to study me and then grinned. I squinted and looked down the sight of my gun to his chest, but it wasn't enough. A cowboy, just like Dane said.

He began to raise his gun from his side. He must have crouched down into a shooting position just as I squeezed the trigger.

The slug tore into him above his shirt collar, on the Adam's apple. A small puff of white smoke and some fluid shot away from his neck as he was blown back to the floor.

Wayne squeezed a round off into the head of the South Carolinian. His scalp lifted and his forehead came apart like an August peach. Then Wayne moved his gun to the face of the man's startled partner and shot him twice at close range. As he fell back, I saw a nickel-sized spot steaming above the bridge of his nose. His mouth was moving as he went down, but he was dead before he hit the ground.

Malone had shot the albino twice in the chest. The tall man stumbled, and still standing, pumped off two loads in succession from his shotgun. Malone screamed. In my side vision I saw him falling backwards in a 'V', still firing. The albino was tripping forward. I emptied two more rounds into his long torso.

The dreadlocked buyer was spinning slowly from the rapid fire of Wayne's automatic. The second buyer raised his gun in my direction. I screamed Tony's name.

I saw fire spitting down from above. I covered my face with my arms. There was the sound of ripping cardboard, splintering wood, and concrete ricochet. Glass exploded around me, and I went to my knees.

Then there was only the sound of the rain hitting the roof. I stood up. Tony dropped the empty clip from above. It hit the floor and bounced once. He slapped in another clip.

Wayne walked towards me through the smoke, his feet crushing glass. He stopped at the second buyer. The man was kneeling with his head tucked between his knees. Wayne pointed his gun at the back of the man's neck and looked at me. I shook my head.

The powder smell was heavy. I waved smoke from my face and turned. Behind me someone screamed out for Jesus and moaned, then stopped moaning. I knelt down over Malone's body.

He had taken a blast low in the abdomen and one in the chest. The gunshot had opened him. His upper lip had curled up and stuck on one of his teeth, so that it looked as if he were sneering. I pulled the lip away and down. Then I closed his eyes.

'Let's move, chief,' Wayne said.

I reached into Malone's wet trouser pocket and pulled out keys. His blood stained my fingers. I tossed the keys back to Wayne.

'Get the van,' I said. 'Pull it up to the warehouse door.'

Wayne walked away. I held my gun on the buyer until Tony made it down to the floor. He nodded, saw Malone, and looked back at me. I picked up the suitcase and turned to the man still kneeling on the floor.

'Get the forklift going,' I said, 'and load the van with the goods. Do it and you'll live.'

He got started. I sat against a carton and smoked a cigarette while he moved the bodies to the side. Tony rode the forklift with the man for several trips until the VCRs were all loaded. Tony walked back and stood over me.

'It's done,' he said. 'What now?'

'Put him in the van,' I said, motioning towards Malone. 'Tie the other one up and wait for me. I'll be out in five minutes.'

I switched on the light in Dane's office, found my knapsack, and pulled a phone number from its front compartment. I put the Browning in my knapsack and carried it and the briefcase to Dane's desk. I lit another cigarette and dialed the phone number.

'Hello.'

'Jerry Rosen, please.'

'This is he.' The voice was deep and rich.

'This is Nick Stefanos.'

'I'm sorry, Nick, but it's very late. If this is about your termination—'

'Shut up,' I said. 'Don't say a word, understand? Just shut up and listen.' I heard him swallow. 'I busted up your deal tonight. All four of your employees and one of your customers are lying dead in the warehouse.' He cleared his throat. 'I own the remainder of your supply now. If you want it back, bring Jimmy Broda with you to the roof of the Silver Spring parking garage tomorrow morning at nine o'clock sharp. We'll make the trade there.'

'I don't—'

'I told you, no talking. Now you'd better get down here. Someone will be waiting for you to confirm everything I've told you.' I hung up and stubbed out my cigarette. I grabbed my knapsack and the briefcase, and left the warehouse.

The wipers struggled to clear the rain from the van's windshield. I was driving south on Eleventh Street, into the darkest center of the city. The liquor and convenience stores were closed now and few of the street-lights were lit. People walked through the rain, drenched and unprotected, in slow, druggy steps.

The briefcase was next to me on the seat. Tony and Wayne sat in back, on opposite sides of the cartons. Malone lay between them, covered by the blanket.

Tony pointed me into an alley near a Bible Way church. I stopped at the head of it and cut the lights. A stream carried small bits of trash down the center of the alley.

Tony said, 'Wait for me in there, Wayne.'

Wayne exited the van through the back door. He walked into an open garage and was consumed by its blackness. I continued down the alley with the headlights off until Tony told me to stop.

'What you gonna do with all this 'caine?' he asked.

'I've got plans for it.'

'You make more at the cookin' house,' he said, and looked me over slowly. 'You got plans for Homeboy's money, too?'

'Yeah,' I said, and stared him down with all the energy I had left.

'I'll take mine,' he said.

I counted twenty thousand in worn bills from the briefcase. He shoved the stack into his jacket. I looked at the lumpen figure in the back and then at Tony.

He nodded and pulled the blanket off Malone. I grabbed him under the arms and lifted. Tony held his feet. We stepped out of the back of the van and carried him into the rain.

'Set him down,' Tony said, and we placed him in the middle of the alley.

For some reason I straightened Malone's shirt. I looked up from where I knelt. Tony was standing over me, dripping wet and staring into my eyes.

'Just another dead nigger,' he said. 'Right?'

He turned and walked away. I watched him meet Wayne at the door of the garage. They passed under the glow of the alley light, then disappeared into the night.

I let go of Malone's hand and returned to the van. I drove slowly to the end of the alley and began to turn out. In my side mirror I saw Malone's body shift and move, carried by the stream. Then it stopped moving. I accelerated out of the alley.

I drove to upper Northwest and parked on a side street in a residential neighborhood. I moved to the back of the van.

I didn't sleep. For the rest of the night I stared at the cartons and listened to the rain. And with one wringing hand I clutched the blanket that was smeared with Malone's blood.

30

The rain had tapered off by dawn. I started the van and drove north. Just over the district line I stopped at a convenience store that had a public rest room.

I cleaned up in the rest room, then bought two coffees, an orange juice, a bag of nuts, some beef jerky, and a deck of Camels. I returned to the van, drank the orange juice and one of the coffees, and ate the nuts and jerky.

After that, I drove the half mile to the parking garage and took the van up to the roof. I parked next to my Dodge and locked the briefcase in my trunk. I shoved the barrel of the Browning in my jeans and covered the grip with my sweatshirt. Then I drove the van to a sub-roof four floors down and locked it up. I walked back up the open-air stairwell to the roof.

I leaned against my car and drank the second coffee. I had a cigarette with the coffee, then another. The sky was already clearing though the wind carried quite a chill.

A long, late-model Cadillac rolled up the ramp and onto the roof, passing me slowly. Rosen was driving. The buyer we had left in the warehouse was in the backseat. Next to him sat Jimmy Broda. He glanced at me blankly as they passed.

They parked in the far corner of the roof. I remained against my car. A few minutes passed, then Rosen got out of the car and walked towards me. I blew out the rest of my smoke and crushed the butt under my shoe.

Rosen was a heavy man of medium height with a tendency to put on pounds. His scalp showed through his thin permanent, and he wore a beard that only partially masked the fatty rolls of his neck. There were dark semicircles beneath his eyes.

Rosen extended his hand as he reached me. He had on one of those diamond horseshoe rings that are impressive only to the pompous shitheels who wear them. I refused his handshake. He placed his hand back in his cashmere overcoat.

'Nick,' he said solemnly. 'Let's make this civil, shall we?'

'Is everything in order?'

'The warehouse, you mean? Yes. Though you left me quite a mess. Fortunately, the man you left behind decided to join me rather than return to his people empty-handed. He handled most of the mop-up work. No one will miss them. As for the inventory that was destroyed, I'll have my accountants write that off as pilferage.' He stroked the tip of his beard. 'What are you going to do with all the money, Nick?'

'It's already gone,' I lied.

'That's right,' he said. 'You had to pay off your little army. But you lost one, didn't you? From my man's description, that would be your friend Malone, from our Connecticut Avenue store, correct?' I didn't answer. 'My sympathies. Of course, no one had to die. They should have let you take it. We would have settled it later. But they had to make a play. Fucking *Schwartzes*.'

'You talk too much,' I said.

'I'm sorry. It's because I'm nervous. This is all new to me.'

'Why'd you get into it in the first place, then?'

'I *wanted* it,' he said. 'When I saw Ned Plavin's ambitions were in line with mine, I convinced him to bankroll the operation up here. I chose D.C. for the same reason all the gangs come down from New York. Law enforcement here – face it, Stefanos, it's a joke. The cops are passing out jaywalking tickets downtown. And the mayor? Well, maybe he could take care of things. If only he could pull his head up off the mirror.'

'Get back to our business,' I said.

'You're going to think I'm blowing smoke up your ass, but frankly, Nick, you did me a favor last night. I've been wanting this whole thing to end. I know where I made my mistakes. It was stupid to try and move the goods through the warehouse. Plus, those guys who worked for me' – he waved his hand in front of his face – '*they* killed that Shultz boy, on their own. I never ordered that. And I didn't know what to do with the Broda kid.' He spread the fingers in both of his hands out to suggest helplessness.

'What else?'

'Like I said, in a roundabout way you did me a favor. I'm going to get my goods back, but nobody has to know that, understand what I'm saying? Now I can turn this last batch over on pure profit. That makes me an independent. Which is what I wanted all along.'

'Let's go to the car.' We walked in the direction of the Cadillac. 'Is the boy all right?'

Rosen shrugged. 'He's an addict, I'm sure of that. Some associates of the ones you took down last night were keeping him busy in the crackhouse. He'll need treatment.'

'That kind of treatment is expensive,' I said. 'And often it doesn't take.'

'He's lucky to be alive.' Rosen stopped walking and narrowed his eyes. 'So are you.'

'We should get something straight before this is over. Because when I take that boy out of here, it *is* over. I've written several identical letters to my contacts at the *Post*, explaining in detail the history and players of your operation. These letters won't be read, unless something happens to me, or the boy, or his grandfather, or anybody I know for that matter. That includes John McGinnes, and Joe Dane, *and* Dane's family.'

'McGinnes,' he said, 'will have to be terminated. He can't continue to be employed at Nathan's. You can understand that.'

'McGinnes can make a living anywhere. He's a salesman. But he's not to be touched.'

'Anything else?' he asked, irritated.

'One thing,' I said. 'Where's the girl?'

He chuckled. 'You're so predictable.' He shook his head, but gave me the address.

We reached the car. Rosen signaled his new ally, who got out, threw me a requisite, half-hearted, hard-guy look, and walked around to the other side of the Caddy. He opened the door and helped the boy out.

Jimmy Broda's color was just short of gray. His trousers were crimped at the waist by a severely tightened leather belt. His jean jacket fit his shoulders as if it were hung on a wire hanger.

The buyer walked him towards me. Broda's eyes widened almost imperceptively as recognition seeped in. He quickened his step and reached out in my direction. I pulled him in with one hand and put my arm around his shoulder, holding him up. He had the weight of a paper bag.

'You've got him now,' Rosen said impatiently. 'Where are my goods?'

'Follow me,' I said. 'The van is parked a few floors down. Your boy here knows which one it is.' I tossed the keys to the buyer.

Rosen said, 'Don't even consider fucking me.'

I let him have the last word and, with Broda under my arm, walked slowly across the roof. I was aware that they were still standing by the

Cadillac, watching us. I instructed the boy to continue moving in the direction of my car.

I let him into the passenger side and got behind the wheel. His hands were folded in his lap, and he was staring straight ahead. I reversed out of my spot and rolled down the ramp.

They were tailing me slowly. Jimmy turned his head back, saw them, became startled, and looked at me.

'Just look ahead,' I said. 'We're almost out of here.'

We wound around the garage. Four floors down I stopped my car, rolled down the window, and pointed my arm out to the sub-roof. Then I continued down the ramp. I saw them in my rearview, veering off to the right.

I accelerated when I reached the ground floor and blew off the stop sign at the exit. I lit a cigarette and turned down North Portal at the Sixteenth Street circle. WHFS was playing Graham Parker's 'Howling Wind,' and I kicked up the volume. An Afghan hound was running alongside our car, and Broda watched him until he broke stride. Orange leaves blew out of our path as we entered the park.

Between the double glass doors of the apartment house on Connecticut Avenue, I dialed up Pence's number.

'Yes?' he said.

'Nick Stefanos. Buzz me in, will you?'

'Certainly. Would you like me to meet you?'

'No,' I said. 'I'll be right up.'

We exited the elevator at the tenth floor and followed the carpeted hallway. Pence opened the door on the second knock. His eyes widened and both hands reached out. He pulled Jimmy Broda through the door and into his arms.

The old man shut his eyes and mumbled something as they held each other. Their faces crushed together. I stood in the hallway, my hands shoved into my pockets, and looked down at my shoes.

'Please, come in, Nick,' Pence said finally over the boy's shoulder.

'I can't right now,' I said. 'But call me later at my apartment. There are some things you need to know.'

'Your compensation. Of course.'

'That, and other things. Good-bye.'

Before he could object, I pulled the door shut from the outside. I stood there for quite a while and listened to the muffled cadence of their voices on the other side of the door. Then I stepped away and walked slowly down the dimly lit corridor.

Early Monday morning I dialed the number for Ned's World in South Carolina.

'Ned's World, how may I help you?'

'This is Roy Lutz,' I said, 'regional director for Panasonic, confirming my lunch appointment with Ned Plavin. Is he in, please?'

'I'll see if he's at his desk. Hold please.' A click, some whale music, then another click. 'I'll transfer you now.'

A gravelly voice answered after two rings. 'Roy!' Plavin said with forced excitement. 'I didn't know we were on for today.'

'This isn't Roy,' I said.

'Well, then, our lines must have gotten crossed—'

'Our lines didn't get crossed. This concerns the Kotekna VCR deal that got soured up in Washington, D.C., over the weekend.'

'I'm not familiar with any "deal" in Washington,' he said thickly. 'Who is this?'

'If you're not interested in what I have to say, hang up now. If you are, I'll continue.' There was a silence while he thought it over. 'Can we talk on this line?'

'Go ahead,' he said.

'I'm not sure what you've been told about the events of this past weekend. I suspect you know only part of the truth. I'll condense it for you. I was one of the group that stopped the deal in the warehouse. We took the merchandise and the money. I kept the money. I traded the merchandise back to your people in exchange for a boy they were holding.'

Ned Plavin cleared his throat. 'My people?' he said. 'Who did you give my goods to?'

'Jerry Rosen.' I said. I watched my cat chase a large bug that was crawling across the rug to the safety of the baseboards.

'Do you have any proof of this?' Plavin asked.

'No.'

'What do you want?'

'I don't trust Rosen,' I said. 'I want this all to be over with, now. I want Rosen out of Washington. And I don't think *you* want a business partner who plans on going solo with goods that you bankrolled. He's the proverbial loose cannon, Ned. Do something about it.'

This time the silence was longer. My cat trapped the bug under its paw, examined it, then walked away. The bug continued on its path to the wall.

'I'll look into it,' Plavin said. 'If what you say is true, I'll act on it.'

'Do it quickly, Ned. Good-bye.'

I hung up the phone and lit a cigarette. I dialed the number for the Connecticut Avenue store and got McGinnes on the line.

'What's happening, Nick?'

'Too early to meet me for a cocktail?'

'Hell, no,' he said. 'But things are a little hectic right now. Andre didn't post on Saturday, or today. Louie's ready to can his ass. I don't think I can get out till eleven.'

'Eleven's fine,' I said.

'Where?'

'La Fortresse, in the back.'

'La FurPiece?'

'Yeah, Johnny. La FurPiece.'

31

The bartender was fanning out cocktail napkins with a tumbler when I entered La Fortresse sometime after eleven. I passed him with a nod and walked towards the back room.

McGinnes sat at a deuce, halfway into a cold bottle of beer. He saluted mockingly and shook my hand as I sat down. I put the briefcase on the floor, between our feet.

'What'ya got in there,' he asked, 'a bomb or something?'

'Something like a bomb,' I said cryptically.

He waved a hand in front of his face and finished the beer left in his bottle. Our fine-skinned waitress came over to the table. Her white shirt had a start-of-shift crispness. She smiled.

'What can I get you, Nick?'

'A Coke,' I said. 'Bottled, please, not from the gun. Thanks.'

'One more for me, darling,' McGinnes said, pointing at his bottle. He frowned at me. 'You on the wagon, man?'

'No.'

The waitress brought our order. I poured from the bottle to a glass full of ice and waited for the foam to retreat. By the time I took the first sip McGinnes had killed much of his second beer. Some of his straight black hair fell across his forehead as he set his bottle down.

'You seen Andre?' McGinnes asked.

'Yeah.'

'He'd better drag his black ass back to work. The man is in some shit. And you know what it's like to work with Void, full time? That shit-for-brains can't close one deal – hell, he can't even close his fly.'

'Andre's not coming back, Johnny,' I said. 'He's dead.'

McGinnes' mouth opened, then the corners of it turned down. One tear immediately fell from his left eye and rolled down and off his cheek. He swept the bottle off the table with the back of his hand, sending it to

199

the floor. Foam poured from its neck. McGinnes made a fist and dug knuckles into his forehead.

Our waitress came back into the room. She saw the bottle and McGinnes, then looked at me.

'Bring him another,' I said. She nodded and left quickly. She returned just as quickly, set a fresh beer in front of McGinnes, picked the old up off the floor, and left the room. McGinnes stared straight ahead with watery eyes and slowly shook his head.

'You stupid bastards,' he muttered. 'You stupid, stupid bastards.'

I waited until he looked at me again. 'Andre and me,' I said carefully, 'and a couple of guys from his old neighborhood interrupted the tail end of Rosen's drug deal on Friday night. The idea was to heist the money and the drugs and trade the drugs back to them for the boy. Andre was to keep the money. But Rosen's people turned out to be gunslingers. When it was over, most of them were dead. Andre died quickly.' I drank some soda. 'On Saturday morning I got the boy back. He's safe, Johnny. He's with his grandfather.'

'That's it, huh?' he said emotionally. 'The boy's safe, Andre's dead, you and me just walk away into the sunset.'

'Nobody will touch us,' I said vaguely. 'I fixed it.'

'You fixed it,' McGinnes said, and snorted. I slid the briefcase along the floor with my foot, until it touched his own. He looked down, then back at me.

'There's a hundred and twenty grand in that case,' I said. 'It goes to Andre's mother. I think that's what he was planning to do with it, regardless of the outcome. Do me a favor and see that she gets it.'

'How much did you skim?'

'I took ten, to keep me on my feet. Until I figure out what's next.'

McGinnes chugged the rest of his beer and slammed the bottle on the table, loud enough to cause the waitress to poke her head back into the room. He signaled her for another. She served it without looking at either of us.

'So, Nicky. Was it worth it?' McGinnes squinted at me. His voice shook as he spoke.

'I don't know.'

'How did it feel to deliver the kid?'

I thought about it and said, 'It felt good.'

'You know what I mean,' he said impatiently. 'Did you find *your* parents, too? Did you say good-bye to your grandfather?'

I stood up and reached into my pocket. I found a five and dropped it on the table.

'Make sure Andre's mother gets the money,' I said.

'To Andre,' McGinnes said, and raised his bottle in a toast. 'The only hero in this whole damn thing.'

I grabbed a handful of McGinnes' shirt and pulled him up out of his seat. When I looked into his frightened eyes, I let him down gently but still held on. His breath was sour and sickly, like an old man's.

'Andre's no hero,' I said softly. 'He was, when he was alive. But he died, and then he was nothing. I dumped him in a fucking alley, like a sack of shit. So don't romanticize it, understand?' I released my grip on his shirt.

'Sure, Nick, I understand.' He tilted the bottle back to his lips.

I wiped tears off my face with a shaky hand. 'Try not to sit here all day,' I said.

'The stuff tastes awful good today, Nicky.' I walked to the doorway. 'So long, man,' he said behind me.

I looked back to the table. 'So long, Johnny.'

I left him there, staring into his bottle. I crossed the dark barroom, passed through the door, and stepped out into the light.

The corridor I had entered marked the beginning of the hospital's original wing. I followed its worn carpeting as it snaked towards the ward. Small hexagonal windows had black bars radiating spiderlike from their centers, and were spaced at intervals on the yellowing walls to my left.

At the end of the corridor I pushed open one of two swinging metal doors and stepped into the ward's reception area. I signed my name and recorded the time in a notebook on the desk. Behind the desk sat a young man wearing a flannel shirt and a brush mustache. I asked him for her room number.

'She stays in eight-oh-two,' he said. 'But this time of day you might try the rec room.'

'Thanks,' I said, and headed down the hallway.

I had visited friends on several occasions in places such as this. The alky wards were usually populated by middle-aged individuals who drifted slowly and deliberately, like ghosts, in and out of doorways. In this place they separated the boozers from the druggies. The k-heads and cocaine kids moved about these rooms like hopped-up insects.

I passed a large room that had a shield of gray smoke at its entrance. There were Ping-Pong tables and board games, but everyone was seated in vinyl furniture watching a television mounted high on the wall. A couple of them were laughing.

I stopped at eight-oh-two and knocked on a partially closed door. She told me to come in. I pushed the door open.

There were two cots in the room, with a night table and reading lamp in between. On the night table was some propaganda, and under that a notebook. Next to the notebook was a flat aluminum ashtray filled with crushed filters. She sat on the edge of the bed nearest the window, a live cigarette between her fingers.

'Nicky,' she said, without emotion.

'Kim. May I come in?'

She nodded and I entered. She was wearing jeans and a T-shirt, with a sweater vest over that. Her hair had been cut short and spiky, which made her big eyes even more pronounced above her hollow cheeks. She had the pallid color of the very ill.

'Cigarette?' she asked, rustling the pack in my direction.

'No thanks. I won't be staying long.'

She took a drag and blew some my way. 'I knew you'd be by, eventually. You're not particularly bright. But you are persistent.'

I let that go and asked, 'How's it going?'

'I've been through all this before,' she said with a small sweeping gesture of her hand. 'Several times. They tell you to surrender your will to a higher being. Trouble is, I don't know if there *is* one.'

'Let's assume there is,' I said. 'But then you still would have a problem. There's certain people, even He has no interest in saving.'

She calmly shook a cigarette out of her pack and lit it off the one still burning. She butted the shorter one of the two and exhaled a wide cloud that spread around me.

'How did you get on to me?' she asked.

'Nothing set right with you from the beginning,' I said. 'Like what you were doing with those kids in the first place. And the fact that you were barely hurt, much less alive, when we found you. I buried those suspicions, though, as I became more attracted to you. At that point I was letting my dick do all the thinking.' I waited for a reaction to the twisting knife. There wasn't one. I folded my arms and leaned against the wall. 'After you left me, I met a geezer in a bar who reminded me of your old man. I started to think about his unused video equipment, and the new stereo in your apartment. And how Maureen Shultz told me that you had worked in some stores in the South before coming up here. Then there was the time you asked about me and Johnny taking "ups." Only a retail salesperson would know that expression. I made the connection to Rosen and called Ned's World in South Carolina. You had been on the payroll at one time.'

She nodded. 'I was a cashier in one of the stores down there when Jerry Rosen was sales manager. It wasn't long before he was fucking me, and supplying me with all the coke I needed. We moved up to D.C., I got heavier into drugs, and he lost interest in me. In the end, he only kept me around to help out with his business.'

'He had you hook into Jimmy Broda,' I said, 'when he discovered the missing VCR. You were to keep an eye on him and the drugs, maybe take him out of town, someplace where Rosen's boys could take care of things without much scrutiny, right?'

'Yes,' she said, and looked away. 'I didn't know anybody would be hurt. It was just another free party for me. And for a change, I didn't have to sleep with anybody to do it.'

Tired laughter ebbed briefly from the television room down the hall. 'Back to Wrightsville Beach,' I said. 'Jimmy never went out for beer like you said. He was there when Rosen's boys came in. You must have signaled them somehow. But why didn't they kill Broda too?'

She blew some smoke at her feet and spoke softly. 'After you fought, Charlie Fiora called me at the motel to tip me off that you were on the way. They had just killed Eddie. There wasn't time to do anything but take Jimmy and leave me behind, to slow you up.' She looked up at me with pleading eyes and began to cry, but I stopped it.

'You can save the crocodile tears,' I said coldly. 'I don't think I'll ever forget the way Eddie looked, tied up on that bed. His throat had been cut, left to right. You could tell by the entry wound on the left, and by the direction of the skin as it folded out from the slice. Assuming he was killed from behind, that would have to be done by a right-handed person.' I stepped away from the wall and unfolded my arms. 'The other night, I faced the man I thought had killed Eddie Shultz. He proved to me that he didn't have the stomach for that sort of thing. In fact, before his brains were blown out, he dropped his weapon. And he dropped it from his left hand.' I paused and stared at the cigarette in her right hand, then into her eyes. 'You cooled Eddie Shultz.'

The silence between us was heavy and long. Finally she spoke just above a whisper and with her eyes down. 'They couldn't do it,' she said. 'They were tough, but even they couldn't do that, not to a kid. They didn't know Redman like I knew him. Him and his Nazi friends. They would have queered the whole deal, believe me. He *had* to die.'

'Everybody has to,' I said. 'But nobody has to like that. What were you going to do about me?'

'Nothing,' she said, her voice rising. 'Jerry just wanted me to keep you occupied until he could figure out what to do.'

'Relax. I'm not going to turn you in. They'd only treat you and set you free. I'd only be doing you a favor.'

'I know what I did was horribly wrong,' she said. 'But this program here . . . I'm going to clean up.'

'There isn't going to be any program. Not much longer. Your benefactor is going to be leaving town any day now. When the well dries up, you're out. You're a junkie, Kim. That's your future.'

'I'll make it,' she said.

'I don't think so.'

My landlord had wedged my mail in the screen door of my apartment. The cat nudged my calf as I carried in the letters and sorted them out.

There was a phone bill, which I kept, and a credit card offer, which I tossed. The last item in the stack from the D.C. government. My application for a private investigator's licence had been accepted. The notice instructed me where and when to pick it up.

I fed the cat, brewed some coffee, and took a mug of it and a pack of smokes out to the living room. I settled on the couch to read the Monday *Post*.

Andre Malone's two little paragraphs were buried in the back of Metro, under a group head called 'Around the Region.' He was 'an unidentified N.W. man.' He died of 'gunshot wounds to the chest and lower abdomen.' Police believed the killing, the article said, to be 'drug related.'

One week later, McGinnes phoned.

'Nick?'

'Yeah?'

'Johnny.'

'Hey, Johnny. Where you at, man?'

'The Sleep Senter,' he said.

'That the place that spells *Center* with an *S*?'

'The same.'

'Uh-huh,' I said.

'The way they explained it to me, it has a double meaning. The sleep *sent-her*, get it? Like this place really sends her, it's some kind of out-of-body experience.'

'Clever.'

'Yeah,' he said. 'This place is okay. They got a bunch of *schmoes* on the floor, but they're an all right bunch of guys. And dig this – they put a fifty dollar pop on the reconditioned mattresses. Fifty big ones, man, for something that's recession proof. Everybody's gotta sleep, right, Jim? Anyway, mattresses, electronics, what the hell's the difference? I could sell my mother if they'd tack a dollar bill on her.'

'When did you make the move?'

'Today's my first day. The last day I saw you, I kinda fell into a black hole. When I crawled out the next day, I quit my job at Nathan's. Good thing I did. I talked to Fisher – they had some serious shake-ups after I left.'

'Such as?'

'Rosen resigned on Wednesday, effective that day.'

'Who's running the show?'

'They booted Ric Brandon up to general manager. You believe that shit?'

'The cream always rises to the top,' I said.

'Yeah.' He laughed briefly, then coughed into the phone. 'Listen, Nick, I gotta go take an up. I don't want these *putzes* to think I'm weak. Talk to you later, hear?'

'All right, Johnny. Talk to you later.'

The next morning I was folding my clothes from the laundromat when some shells and stones fell from the pockets of my swimtrunks. An hour later I was driving south on 95, headed for the Outer Banks and Ocracoke Island.

The ferry was nearly empty that early November day, as was the island campground. I pitched my tent on a spot near the showers and, wearing a sweatshirt beneath my jean jacket, unfolded a chair on the beach.

I spent the first day reading the rather seedy biography of a relentlessly hedonistic musician, a story I lost interest in long before the inevitable overdose. Later I wrote a long letter to Karen that took two hours to compose and only a few seconds to shred. In between those activities I walked on the beach and stopped occasionally to talk with fishermen who were wading in the surf. In the evening I cooked hot dogs and ate a can of beans, and then crawled into my sleeping bag as soon as it was dark, as there was little else to do.

By the middle of the second day, I realized once again that being away from home clarifies nothing. Despite romantic notions, that's been the case in every instance that I've left town to 'think about things.'

An approaching northeaster shook me out of my stupor late in the afternoon. I broke camp as the slate sky blew in, and was packed and in my car when the rain came down, suddenly and quite violently, from the clouds.

I started my Dodge and drove through the storm to the gray house on pilings with the small gray sign. Running through the rain and up the wooden stairs, I entered Jacko's Grille.

The door slammed behind me when I entered and most of the heads in the place turned my way. There was a group of older locals in plaid flannel shirts and dirty baseball caps, all sitting at a couple of picnic tables that they had pushed together. Empty cans of beer dotted the tables. Full ones were in the men's hands. Water dripped down through holes in the roof into more than a few spots in the room, though no one was taking much notice. The sound of the rain competed with the country music coming from the jukebox.

I nodded to the men and pushed wet hair back off my forehead. A couple of them nodded back. One of them smiled and said, in a startling island accent more northern European than American South, 'Wet enough for ya?' I said it was and stepped up to the bar, where I ordered a burger and a beer.

I took the beer out to the screened-in deck and drank it while I watched the hard rain dimple the wetlands as it blew across the sound. The beer was cold but warmed me going down, and I ordered another when I picked up my burger.

I ate the burger and drank the beer out on the deck. When I was finished, the first, beautiful verse of 'Me and Bobby McGee' came from the juke, and the men inside began to sing. I listened as their drunken voices welled up on the achingly true chorus. When I went to the counter for another beer, one of them waved me over and I joined them.

I bought what was the first of many rounds. The water was coming in now all around the bar, and someone had turned up the jukebox to its maximum volume. One of the men produced a fifth of whiskey and some glasses, and we started in on that.

The corners of the room bled into the walls. There was laughter and it was warm and I was away from my world, and everything was cleaner and more clear.

With time came darkness, and the rain continued to fall outside and into the barroom. My friends told jokes and sang, then joined me in a toast, to a Greek immigrant everyone had called Big Nick. For a moment I wondered what he would think, seeing me now, so twisted and so far from home; that moment burned away with my next taste of whiskey, stronger than reason, stronger than love.

Nick's Trip

To my son Nicholas,
and to Lou Reed

1

The night Billy Goodrich walked in I was tending bar at a place called the Spot, a bunker of painted cinder block and forty-watt bulbs at the northwest corner of Eighth and G in Southeast. The common wisdom holds that there are no neighborhood joints left in D.C., places where a man can get lost and smoke cigarettes down to the filter and drink beer backed with whiskey. The truth is you have to know where to find them. Where you can find them is down by the river, near the barracks and east of the Hill.

An Arctic wind had dropped into town that evening with the suddenness of a distaff emotion, transforming a chilly December rain into soft, wet snow. At first flake's notice most of my patrons had bolted out of the warped and rotting door of the Spot, and now, as the snow began to freeze and cover the cold black streets, only a few hard drinkers remained.

One of them, a gin-drenched gentleman by the name of Melvin, sat directly in front of me at the bar. Melvin squinted and attempted to read the titles of the cassettes behind my back. I wiped my hands lethargically on a blue rag that hung from the side of my trousers, and waited with great patience for Melvin to choose the evening's next musical selection.

Melvin said, 'Put on some Barry.'

I nodded and began to fumble through the stack of loose cassettes that were randomly scattered near the lowest row of call. The one I was looking for was close to the bottom, and its plastic casing was stained green with Rose's lime. It was Barry White's first recording, 'I've Got So Much to Give,' from 1973. The cover art showed the Corpulent One holding three miniaturized women in his cupped hands.

'This the one, Mel?' I palmed it in front of his face. Mel nodded as I slipped the tape in and touched the PLAY button.

Mel said, 'Let me tell you somethin' 'bout my boy Barry. You done been on a bad trip with your girlfriend – you put on Barry. Barry be talkin' real pretty and shit, all of a sudden you sayin', "I learned, baby. I sweeeear I learned."' The bass of the Barrance came through the grilleless Realistic speakers, and Mel sensually joined in: 'Don't do that. Baby, pleeease don't do that.'

Melvin Jeffers had just sunk his fifth rail martini. He had begun to sing and in all probability would continue to sing for the remainder of the night. I eyed my options down the bar.

Buddy and Bubba were in place at the far right corner, seated next to the Redskins schedule that was taped to the wall, the one with the placekicker booting the pigskin through goal-posts shaped suspiciously like long-necked bottles of Bud. Buddy was short and cubically muscular with an angular face and white blond hair. Like many men who took up body building for the wrong reason, he had found to his dismay that having a pumped-up physique did nothing to diminish the huge chip that was on his shoulder. His friend Bubba also considered himself to be an athlete but was simply broad-shouldered and fat. Bubba had the pink, rubbery face that some unlucky alcoholics get and then keep after their thirtieth birthday.

I moved down the bar, picked up Buddy's mug, and with my raised brow asked him if he wanted another. Buddy shook his head and made sure I saw him look me over. I turned my attention to Bubba.

'How 'bout you, Bubber?' I asked in my best whiny, mid-sixties Brando. 'You want one?'

Bubba said, 'Uh-uh,' then looked at his friend inquisitively, something he did every time I addressed him in this manner. In *The Chase*, a film that barely contained one of Marlon Brando's most eccentric performances, the legendary actor continually mispronounced the name of Bubba, Robert Redford's character, as 'Bubber.' It was a film that the Spot's Bubba had obviously missed.

I left them and, as I passed, avoided eye contact with the only remaining customer, a cop named Boyle. Buddy and Bubba were one thing, rednecks wearing ties, but I was in no mood to open that particularly poisonous, psychotic can of worms named Dan Boyle.

Instead I turned my back on all of them and began to wipe down the bottles on the call rack. I caught a sliver of my reflection in the bar mirror between liters of Captain Morgan's and Bacardi Dark, then looked away.

Almost a year had passed since I had taken my first case, a disaster that had ended with a close friend being numbered among the dead. I emerged relatively unscathed but had caught a glimpse of my mortality and, more startling than that, a fairly obvious map for the remainder of the trip. I had three grand in the bank and a District of Columbia private investigator's license in my wallet. In my license photograph I sported a blue-black shiner below my left eye, a trophy I had earned in a Eurotrash disco while on a particularly ugly binge. Clearly I was on my way.

Though my tenure in retail electronics was over (I had made the poor career move of staging a gunfight in my former employer's warehouse), I began the year with energy. I made the yellow pages deadline, listing myself as 'Nicholas J. Stefanos, Investigator,' even stepping up for the boldfaced type. I bought a used pair of binoculars and a long-lensed Pentax, printed report forms and business cards, and hooked myself up with an answering service. Then I sat back and waited for the cases to roll in.

When they didn't, I began to take long, daily walks through D.C. I visited galleries and museums, spending more than one afternoon studying the large paintings of Jack Dempsey and Joe Louis in the National Portrait Gallery at Eighth and F. Several times on these visits I was followed through the cavernous halls by suspicious security guards, something I attributed to their boredom and to my progressively hangdog appearance. When I had exhausted the museums, I went to the Martin Luther King Jr. Memorial Library and renewed my card, then spent the next week in the Washingtoniana Room on the third floor, mainly in the company of street people who slept silently at the various tables with newspapers wedged in their hands. In that week I read most of the *Washington Star*'s morgue material printed between 1958 and 1961, in an effort to get a feel for those years of my life of which I had no recollection. I then discovered the European reading room at the Library of Congress and read modern history for two weeks in a row, sitting across from an ultrawhite eunuch who wore a bow tie every day and never once looked in my direction. One day I walked the pale yellow tunnel from the Jefferson Building to the Madison Building and stumbled upon the Motion Picture and Television Reading Room on the third floor. I spent the month of March in that room, reading everything from scholarly works on the spaghetti western to André Bazin to something called *A Cinema of Loneliness* by a guy named Kolker. Though the room was reserved for professionals, no one questioned my presence or bothered me in any way. In fact, no one spoke to me at all. Spring came and I began to haunt the parks and gardens of the city, returning with frequency to the Bishop's Garden at the National Cathedral. Some days I would walk through cemeteries finding them a curious combination of the enigmatic and the starkly real. The Rock Creek Cemetery, with its Adams Monuments, was a particular favorite.

Sometime in May I was suddenly overcome with the natural feeling that it was time to 'do' something. The next morning I tied my first Windsor knot in five months and rode the Metro to Gallery Place, where I walked to the offices of Bartell Investigative Services on Eighth at H., located smack in the middle of Chinatown.

I had picked them out of the phone book at random, preferring to work in that section of town, and was surprised upon entering and filling out an application that they would interview me on the spot. But as I stood in a reception area at the front of the office, I studied the other operatives at their desks, beefy guys in tight gray suits with prison haircuts who had the appearance of aging high school linemen, and decided it wasn't for me. I stuffed the application in my breast pocket, thanked the nicotine-throated grandmother type at the desk, and walked out into the street.

I had been all right up to that point, but the experience made me aware of just how irrevocably far from the mainstream I had strayed. I entered the Ruby Restaurant around the corner and had a bowl of hot and sour soup and some sautéed squid. Then I walked to Metro Center and boarded the Orange Line for a short trip to the Eastern Market station. I crossed Pennsylvania and headed down Eighth Street.

On the corner was the bar in which I first met my ex-wife Karen. They had changed both the ownership and the decor, from early eighties new wave to rustic wild West saloon. I looked in the plate-glass window and saw cigarette-smoking Cambodians shooting pool and arguing. One of them had a wad of ones grasped tightly in his fist, his features taut as he shook the bills in his opponent's face. I kept walking.

I passed carryouts and convenience stores and cheap ethnic restaurants. I passed the neighborhood movie theater so hopelessly run down that it was no longer advertised in the *Post*, and a record-and-drug store. I passed two bars that catered to lesbians. I passed a bus stop shielding loud groups of young men wearing L.A. Raiders caps and red jackets, and quiet older folks who could no longer laugh, even in cynicism, at their surroundings. Karen and I had lived in this neighborhood during the early days of our marriage.

Toward the end of the street an MP in full dress was directing traffic near the barracks. I crossed over and headed to a bar whose simple sign had caught my eye: THE SPOT. Other than the rectangular glass in the transom, there were no windows. I pushed on the heavy oak door and stepped in.

There was a room to my right painted dark green, housing a few empty deuces and four-tops. Beer posters were tacked to three of the walls and on the fourth was a dart board.

I stepped down into the main bar, which was to the left and ran the length of the room. There were two hanging conical lamps, which dimly illuminated columnar blocks of smoke. A blue neon Schlitz sign burned over the center of the bar. Billie Holiday was singing in mono through the speakers hung on either side of the room. There were a couple of regulars who didn't glance my way and a redheaded woman behind the bar who did. I had a seat at the stool in front of the area she was wiping down.

'What can I get you?' she asked, seeming mildly interested to see a new face. She was in her twenties but had crossed the line from youthful optimism to drugged resignation.

'I'll have a Bud,' I said, breaking my daytime drinking resolution.

She pulled a long-neck from the cooler and popped it with a steel opener that looked heavy as a weapon. I waved off a glass as she set down the bottle on a moldy coaster touting Cuervo Gold. After she did that she didn't walk away.

'What's your name?' I asked.

'Sherry,' she said.

There was more silence as she stood there, so I pulled a Camel filter from my jacket and lit it. I blew the smoke down, but some of it bounced off the pocked mahogany bar and drifted in her direction. She still didn't move. I thought of something to say, came up blank, then looked up at the cursive neon tubes above my head.

'So,' I said lamely, 'you sell much Schlitz here, Sherry?'

'We don't sell it at all,' she said.

'I thought, you know, with the sign and all . . .'

'We put up whatever the liquor distributors give us,' she said, then shrugged and gave me a weak smile. 'Fuck it. You know?'

Yeah, I knew. It was my kind of place and I was due. I returned there every day for the next two weeks and drank with clear intent.

In those two weeks I got to know some of the regulars and became a familiar face to the small staff. Sherry was, predictably, looking for other work, as was the other shift bartender, a stout-faced, square-jawed German woman named Mai who had married and then left a young marine as soon as her green card had come through. There was an all-purpose busboy/cleanup man named Ramon, a little Salvadoran with a cocky, gold-toothed smile who didn't understand English except when it had something to do with quiff or his paycheck. The cook, Darnell, worked in a small kitchen to the side of the bar. Mostly I saw his long, skinny arms as he placed food on the platform of the reach-through.

Phil Saylor was the proprietor of the Spot. He came in for a couple of hours in the afternoon and I presumed at closing time to do the book work. Saylor was an unlikely looking – short, soft in the middle, wire-rim spectacles – ex-D.C. cop, originally from South Texas, who had quit the force a couple of years earlier and opened this place. He seemed to make a living at it and to enjoy it. Certainly he enjoyed his abominable bourbon and Diet Cokes, which as owner he inexplicably opted to drink with Mattingly and Moore, the house rotgut.

Saylor's past explained the unusually large percentage of detectives on the D.C. squad who were regulars. Though the Fraternal Order of Police bar in lower Northwest was still popular with D.C.'s finest, this was a place where cops could drink without restraint and in private. And unlike at the FOP, where they were expected to unwind with 'a few' after work, they could do their unscrutinized drinking at the Spot while still on duty. In fact, in my two weeks spent with bent elbows at the bar of the Spot, it became obvious that this was a place where serious drinkers from all across the city came to get tanked in peace, without the presence of coworkers, hanging plants, brass rails, or waitresses who overfamiliarly (and falsely) addressed them as 'gentlemen.'

One Monday late in May I watched the bar as Sherry and Saylor retired to the kitchen for a short discussion. I was alone in the place and had gained Saylor's trust to the point where I was allowed to help myself. I reached into the cooler and popped a Bud and nursed it for the next fifteen minutes while I listened to Ma Rainey on the deck.

Sherry emerged from the kitchen and began to gather up what looked to be her things, stuffing a romance paperback into her purse and then picking up a dusty umbrella from the side of the cooler. Her eyes were a little watery as she leaned in and kissed me lightly on the cheek before walking from behind the bar and then out the front door.

Saylor came out of the kitchen a little later and poured himself a straight shot of Mattingly and Moore. He adjusted the wire rims on his nose as if he were going to do something smart, but instead did something stupid and fired back the shot.

When he caught his breath he looked through me and said, 'God, I hate that.' His face was screwed tight, but I guessed he wasn't talking about the speed-rail bourbon. 'I knew she was giving away drinks to jack up her tips – all of 'em do it, even the honest ones – but there was money missing, five, ten a day, all this past month. I had to let her go, man; I didn't have any choice.'

'Don't worry about it, Phil.' I had pegged Sherry for a gonif the first day I met her but felt I had no duty to inform Saylor. I didn't owe him anything, not yet. 'You still got Mai,' I said.

He nodded weakly. 'Yeah, and she wants more shifts. But she's got a temper, man, with me *and* the customers. I don't think I can handle that German wench in here all the time.' His hands spread out. 'I guess I gotta go through the process of looking for a new girl.'

I looked at my beer bottle and saw a thousand more like it on a hundred more dark afternoons. Then I looked into the bar mirror and saw my lips moving. They said, 'Hell, I'll bartend for ya, Phil.'

He pushed his glasses up again and said, 'You kidding?'

'Why not? The cases aren't exactly building up,' I said with understatement, then told the biggest lie of the day. 'Besides, I've done some bartending in my time.'

Saylor thought it over. 'I never had a man behind the bar here. Can't say any of these guys would notice the difference.' I lit a Camel while he talked himself into it. 'I guess I could give you a few shifts, try it out. You start tomorrow?'

'Yeah,' I said with the misguided, giddy enthusiasm common in long-term unemployment cases. 'Tomorrow.'

On the way home I stopped at the MLK Library and borrowed a book on mixology called *Karla's Kocktail Kourse*, then took it back to my apartment in the Shepherd Park area of Northwest. The book was fine (except for those ridiculous *K*'s in the title) and entertaining with its modern fifties, triangularly matted illustrations, complete with hostesses serving drinks in June Cleaver dresses and the author's insistence on displaying cocktails set next to burning cigarettes. I studied into the night; my cat, confused by my diligence, alternately circled and slept on my feet the entire time. When morning came I was ready.

But I was never really put to the test. I found, with some disappointment, that the patrons of the Spot were hardly the type to call for Rob Roys or sidecars, or any of the book's other extravagant concoctions whose ingredients I had memorized. Neither were they, as Saylor had predicted, unhappy (or happy, for that matter) to see me behind the bar. Generally, their nostalgia for the Sherry dynasty faded with my first shift and their first pop of the day.

As the weeks went by I got quicker with the bottles and memorized most of the regulars' drinks. I snuck my own music onto the deck and received only a couple of belches, and kept the promise to myself never to drink on shift, which made that first one at the end of the day go down even better. I made few mistakes, though the ones I did make were memorable.

There was a guy I called Happy, partly because of what I am convinced was his inability to smile. Happy had hair like gray seaweed, a flat, veined nose, and heavily bagged eyes. He was taken to wearing baby-shit brown sport jackets with white stitching at the seams. The jackets appeared to have the texture of Styrofoam. Often he'd fall asleep at the bar with his hand limply wrapped around his drink glass. One afternoon he spit a mouthful of manhattan over the bar shortly after I served it to him. I looked his way.

'I asked for a manhattan,' he mumbled loudly.

I thought of the only explanation. 'Sorry. I must have used the dry vermouth instead of the sweet vermouth.'

'Listen,' he said with a fierce stare and a voice informed by sixty Chesterfields a day. 'When I order a manhattan, I don't want *any* kind of vermouth, you hear? Pour an ounce of bourbon into a martini glass and drop a fuckin' cherry in it. Understand?'

I nodded that I did.

For the summer I had four shifts a week and accumulated quite a bit of cash in the bottom drawer of my dresser. Ironically, I picked up some investigative work soon after I started at the Spot.

The first was a shadow job on the wife of a greeting-card salesman who suspected her of adultery. The salesman had out-of-town accounts and subsequently was away from home three days a week. I spent a good amount of time sitting in my Dodge at the parking lot of her office building in Rockville, smoking too many cigarettes and listening to what was becoming a decidedly boring, unprogressive WHFS. At noon I'd follow her and a couple of her friends to their lunch destination, then follow her back to the office. It wasn't until her husband left town, however, that she cut loose. On the day of his departure she left work early and drove to some garden apartments off the Pike. Two hours later she was gone and I was reading the name off her lover's mailbox. The next day they met at Romeo's apartment for a lunch boff, and I snapped his picture as he walked out the door to return to work. I gave the photos to the husband and watched his lips twitch as he wrote me a check for seven hundred and fifty dollars. It took the better half of a fifth of Grand-Dad that night to wash his broken face from my mind.

Shortly thereafter, the parents of a high school sophomore in Potomac signed me on to get to the bottom of what they hysterically perceived to be their daughter's growing interest in satanism. I hooked up with her fairly easily through her mall-rat friends and we had lunch. She seemed bright, though unimaginative, and her devil worship turned out to be no more than hero worship. She was into Jim Morrison and her ambition, man, was to visit his grave in Paris. In the conference with her parents I told them that in my youth I had survived a fling with Black Sabbath and early Blue Öyster Cult without killing a single cat. They didn't smile, so I told them to relax; in six years their daughter would be driving to law school in her VW Cabriolet and listening to Kenny G like all her other friends from Churchill High. They liked that better and stroked me a check for two hundred and a half. After that I resolved to be more selective in my cases (my bar shifts were keeping me solvent), but I'll never know if I would have held to it since in any case the phone, for the remainder of the year, neglected to ring.

Summer passed and then the fall. When I wasn't at the bar I spent my time reading, jumping rope, riding my ten-speed and, once a week, sparring with my physician, Rodney White, who in addition to being a reliable general practitioner was a second-degree black belt. Occasionally I kept company and slept with my friend Lee, a senior at American University.

The mayor's arrest on charges of possession was big news, though that event was more significant for the local media's shameful self-congratulatory arrogance and their inability to see the real story: the murder rate was at another record high and the gap was widening between the races, socially and economically, every day. But of course there was no story there, no angle. The colonizer and the colonized, just like the textbooks say.

This was also the year that I was to both lose and make two special friends. The friend I made was Jackie Kahn, a bartender at a woman's club called Athena's, located two doors down from the Spot. As I was walking past the windowless establishment one evening in late September, I noticed a flier tacked on the door concerning an upcoming 'womyn's' march. I stepped inside and, ignoring a few mildly unfriendly stares, went directly to the bar and had a seat. The bartender gave me the once-over before she asked me what I'd have. She had short black hair and high cheekbones, and deep brown, intelligent eyes. I asked her name first and she said it was Jackie. I ordered a Bud.

After she served it she said tiredly, 'Why do you want to come in here, make trouble or something? I mean, we don't mind getting a few guys now and then. But they're usually the New York Mary types, you know what I'm saying?'

'I'm a high school English teacher,' I said, feeling a sudden rush from the two bourbons I had rocketed before closing the Spot. 'I noticed a misspelling on your flier outside. You have *women* with a *y*. Just thought I'd point it out.'

'That's the way *we* spell it,' said a humorless type with slicked-back hair sitting to my left. I had the feeling this one didn't like me much. She confirmed it with her next suggestion: 'Why don't you just move it the fuck on out of here, chief?'

'He's all right,' Jackie said, surprising me. She was looking at me with a smile threatening to break across her face. 'What do you *really* want?'

'A beer,' I said, and extended my hand. She shook it. 'My name's Nick. I bartend over at the Spot. Didn't feel like having that last one alone tonight.' I chin-nodded to the table in the corner. 'Thought I'd shoot a game of pool while I was in here. That all right, Jackie?'

'Sure.' She nodded, then leaned in close and, with an amazingly quick read of my personality, said, 'But do me a favor, Nick – don't be an asshole. Okay?'

I began to frequent Athena's fairly regularly after work for a beer and a game of pool. An ex-Brooklyner named Mattie would wait for me to come in and we'd shoot one game of eight ball for a five spot. Athena's was typical of most of the women's bars in Washington. It was owned by men who saw it only as an exploitable market niche and therefore tended to neglect it in terms of cleanliness and decor. But it was a place to go. To sensationalize the scene would be to give it too much credit; lesbian bars were the same as any other singles bars, with the identical forced gaiety and underlying streams of sadness. People met and fucked or resisted and went home alone.

Jackie and I began to spend time together outside of our jobs, going to the movies or having a beer or two at some of the saner places on the Hill. She was an accountant at a Big Eight firm downtown and moonlighted at Athena's for relaxation and to escape the masquerade that was apparently more necessary for gay women than it was for their male counterparts. Occasionally she'd poke her head in the Spot to say hello, and invariably one of my regulars would boast that he could 'turn one of those "rug munchers" around' if he had the chance. This was especially exasperating coming from guys who hadn't even been mercy-fucked by their own wives for years. As our friendship developed I began to pat myself on the back for finally having a close relationship with a woman that didn't involve sex. It had only taken me three and a half decades to learn. What I didn't know then was that Jackie Kahn would have the largest role in the single most important thing that I have ever done.

The friend I lost was William Henry. Henry was a deceptively quiet young man with an offbeat sense of humor who had migrated from the South to take his first job out of college as a reporter for a local alternative weekly. I met him when he sat in on a meeting where his tabloid's sales manager pitched me on buying space when I was advertising director for Nutty Nathan's. Though I didn't step up for any ads, Henry and I discovered from that meeting that we had very similar tastes in music. I hooked up with him downtown a couple of times – once to see Love Tractor at the Snake Pit and on another night to check out a hot D.C. zydeco band, Little Red and the Renegades, at the Knight's Work – but after my career at Nathan's blew up, I heard from him only through the mail. He was that type of friend who, without an explanation, would send me headlines from the *New York Post* or buy me unsolicited subscriptions to Australian biker mags, publications with names like *Chrome and TaTas*.

In July, William Henry was found murdered in his condo above Sixteenth and U, just around the corner from the Third District police station. He had been stabbed repeatedly with a serrated knife. A witness had seen a thirtyish man with a medium build leave the building at the time of the murder. The man was light-skinned and wore a blue T-shirt that appeared to have been stained with blood. The Metropolitan Police spokesman said in the *Washington Post* that an arrest was 'eminent.'

For a few days after that the *Post* ran a daily article on the slaying, returning to their favorite theme of Small-Town Boy Comes to Murder City and Meets His Fate. But when it was clear that the story would not have a pat ending, the articles stopped, and William Henry's killer was never found.

I was thinking of Henry when I stepped up to Boyle that night and gave last call. Buddy and Bubber were gone, as was Melvin. He had left when I put George Jones on the deck. The tape always sent him out the door. Darnell was in the kitchen, cleaning up. I could see his willowy torso in the reach-through and hear the clatter of china, muted by the sound of his cheap radio, as he emptied the dishwasher.

Dan Boyle placed his palm over the top of his shot glass to signal he was done, then drank the rest of the beer from the bottle sitting next to it. I asked if he wanted to put the night on his tab and he nodded, seeming to look both to my right and to my left simultaneously.

Boyle was square-jawed and built like a heavyweight prize-fighter, with stubbornly short, dirty blond, Steve McQueen-style hair, circa *Bullitt*. The age in his bleached blue eyes exceeded his thirty years. He drank methodically, and when he spoke it was through the tight teeth of an angry dog.

Many of the on-duty detectives who frequented the Spot wore their guns in the bar (it was, in fact, a police regulation that they do so), and most of them got tanked up and weaved out into the night without incident. But it wasn't Boyle's weapon (the grip of his Python always showed from beneath his wool jacket where it was holstered) that was disturbing, or the fact that he even carried one. He was clearly on the edge, and he was the last guy in the bar who I ever would have fucked with.

'Hear anything more on the William Henry case?' I asked him carefully. I bent into one of the three sinks and rinsed out the green bar netting.

'You knew him, didn't you?'

'Yeah.'

'Haven't heard anything,' he said. 'But I'll lay you ten to one your friend got burned for drug money. In this town, it all boils down to drugs. Let me tell you what it is. It's' – he glanced around the room – 'it's fuckin' boofers. You know what they ought to do about the drug problem in this city?' I didn't answer, having heard his solution a dozen times. 'Take 'em out in the middle of the street and shoot 'em in the head. Public fuckin' executions.'

I said, 'Check on the Henry case for me, will you, Boyle?' He rose clumsily, nodded, and with a tilted, heavy gait made his way across the room and out the front door. A trace of snow blew through before the door closed.

The lights dimmed in Darnell's kitchen. He walked out, wearing a leather kufi on his head and a brown overcoat. Darnell was tall and bone-skinny and pushing forty. He had done time and from that had gotten a thick white scar from the back of his ear to the underside of his chin. The scar made him look tough but, whatever he had been, that part of his life was clearly over. He was soft-spoken and introspective now, and though it was obvious that he would never rise above his position in the kitchen, that futility did not prevent him from reporting to work every single day. He was, as one of my regulars had described him with special emphasis on the word, a man.

Darnell and I looked through the transom window and watched the steady diagonal fall of thick flakes, a picture that seemed unreal from our warm vantage point. Darnell, hoping for some company, said, 'You headin' up my way?'

'I've got some work to do,' I said. 'Think I'll stick around, check my antifreeze.'

Darnell looked at the pyramid of liquor on the wall and then back at me. 'What you want to drink that nasty shit for? Shit kills your spirit, man.' He shook his head and walked to the door, then turned. 'You want me to lock up?'

'No, I'll get it. Thanks, Darnell.'

'Check you tomorrow, hear?' He waved and then he was gone.

Dimming the lights even further, I finished wiping down the bar, placing all the ashtrays but one in the soak sink. Then I slipped Robyn Hitchcock's *Queen Elvis* into the deck and listened to the quiet intro to 'Wax Doll' as I poured myself two fingers of Grand-Dad. I brought the shot glass to my lips and with closed eyes tasted sweet velvet.

I opened my eyes to a shock of cold air and a memory fifteen years old. Billy Goodrich glided across the dark room and had a seat at the bar.

'Hey, Greek,' he said. 'Aren't you gonna' offer me a drink?'

2

The first time I met Billy Goodrich he was sitting on a wooden bench in Sligo Creek Park, rolling a huge spliff with the care and precision of an artisan. This was in the fall of my junior year, and my first semester at Blair High in Silver Spring. My grandfather had used a Maryland relative's address to get me in, alarmed as he was at my subpar sophomore performance in the D.C. public school system.

Billy yelled, 'Hey, Greek,' and I did a double take, surprised that one of the more popular students even knew who I was. 'Come on over here and help me out with this number,' he said.

We split the joint (the handshake of my generation) and then laughed awhile over nothing. After that we played one-on-one at the park courts for the rest of the afternoon and our friendship, with the uncluttered reasoning that accompanies those years, was sealed.

Billy Goodrich was one of the better-liked kids in school, though not for the usual reasons. He wasn't the best-looking or most athletic guy; neither was he the friendly intellectual who even the most brutal students grudgingly learn to respect. What he had was that rare ability to fit in at the fringe of every group – hippies, grits, geeks, jocks – without conforming to their constrictively rigid codes of behavior and dress. He did it with an infectious smile and a load of self-confidence that bordered on, but never slipped into, conceit. As I had always hung with Jews and Italians and other Greeks, he was also the first truly white-bread friend I had ever had.

The details of those years are unimportant and certainly not unusual. Billy had a '69 Camaro (the last year that car made any difference) with a 327 under the hood and Hi-Jackers in the rear. There was a Pioneer eight-track mounted under the AM radio and two Superthruster speakers on the rear panel. On weekend nights we drank Schlitz from cans and raced that car up and down University Boulevard and Colesville Road, trolling for girls and parties. On the nights when we got too drunk the cops would pull us over and, in those days, simply tell us to get on home. Our friends enacted roughly the same ritual, and amazingly none of us died.

I had part-time work as a stock boy, but on the days I had off, Billy and I shot hoops. Every Saturday afternoon we'd blow a monster joint, then head down to Candy Cane City in Rock Creek Park and engage in pickup games for hours on end. The teams always ended up being 'salt and pepper,' and the losers did push-ups. Billy had a cheap portable eight-track player, and on those rare occasions when we'd win, he would blast J Geils's 'Serve You Right to Suffer' over the bobbing heads of the losing team. Eventually our overconfidence (and the desire to unearth the wet treasures that simmered beneath the red panties of our Blazer cheerleading squad) pushed us to try out for the varsity team, but Billy didn't have the heart and I, in truth, lacked the ability. The day we were cut we walked the path in the park and, with laughter and some degree of relief, split a bumper of beer and huffed half a pack of Marlboros.

After graduation Billy, who had already been accepted to an out-of-state school, took a construction job, and I continued to work as a stock boy at Nutty Nathan's on Connecticut Avenue. The prospect of another humid season carrying air conditioners up and down stairs was upon me, so when a customer I had befriended offered me the opportunity to tow his ski boat down to the Keys for two hundred bucks, I accepted. Billy's construction job was kicking his ass so he asked to come along. I secured a leave of absence from Nathan's with the help of my friend and mentor Johnny McGinnes; Billy simply quit. We made plans to stay in D.C. through the Fourth of July and leave the following day.

The summer of '76 was not just the tail end of my childhood, a fact of which even then I was vaguely aware, but also the end of an optimistic era for an entire generation. The innocence of marijuana had not yet, to use the most emblematic example, become the horror of cocaine, and the economic and political emergence of minorities hadn't yet been crushed by the moral bankruptcy of the Reagan years. But our Bicentennial celebration reflected none of this, and what I witnessed on Independence Night was simply the most spectacular party ever thrown in downtown D.C.

The next day Billy and I prepared to leave. We attached a hitch to his car (mine, a '64 Valiant with push-button transmission on the dash, never would have made it), changed his oil, and filled up the tape box. The tapes we were to return to most were Lou Reed's *Sally Can't Dance* (I can't hear 'Kill Your Sons' now without the druggy heat of that summer burning through my memory), Robin Trower's *Twice Removed from Yesterday*, Bowie's *Station to Station*, Hendrix's mind-blowing *Axis: Bold as Love*, and the debut from Bad Company. We cut the black BAD CO. logo off that tape's carton and glued it, facing out, on the Camaro's windshield, to let any doubters know just who we were. There was also the odd business of a plastic grenade hung from the rearview, and new bumper sticker that read MOTT THE HOOPLE: TELL CHUCK BERRY THE NEWS. For recreation we had copped, from Johnny McGinnes, an ounce of Mexican, a vial filled to the lid with black beauties, and half a dozen tabs of purple haze; there were also several packs of Marlboros scattered on the dash. We were eighteen years old and certain that the world's balls were in our young hands.

And so we took off. We put together four hundred dollars between us, and our plan was to travel around the South until the money ran out. Billy picked me up, and my grandfather stood and watched us from the front of our apartment house, tight-lipped and with his hands dug deep into his pockets, until we were out of sight. His shoulders were hunched up, and he grew smaller in the rearview as we headed down the block.

A half hour later we had secured the Larson on the hitch of the Camaro and said good-bye to the surprisingly trusting owner of the boat. We stopped once more for a cold six-pack, got on the Capital Beltway, and headed for 95 South.

That night we pulled into Virginia Beach and crashed at the place of a friend who was working in a pizza parlor for the season. In the grand tradition of resort employee living quarters, there were several burnouts staying in his two-room flat, where pot was always lit and the TV and stereo were always competing in loud unison. Since there were no cooking facilities, I can only guess that these guys ate pizza the entire summer. The decor consisted of a fisherman's net tacked to the wall (during our stay someone had hung a dead sea bass in its webbing) and a bright green carpet, which was stained alternately with puke and bong water. The next day we swam and then in the early evening Billy and I each ate a tab of purple haze and bought tickets to the B. B. King show at the local civic auditorium. We arrived and found we were the youngest and most sloppily dressed in the mostly black crowd of oldish fans, some of whom were sweating through their three-piece suits and evening dresses in the liquid heat. I began to get off on the acid during a tune where Mr King sang, with his hands off Lucille and one fist clenched, 'I asked my baby for a nickel / She gave me a fifty-dollar bill / I asked my baby for a sip of whiskey / She gave me the whole gotdamn still.' Billy and I smoked joints for the rest of the show to notch us down, and the folks around us were all quite happy to join in. I kept a log on that trip, in which I critiqued B. B. King's performance in the following manner: he had 'turned that shit out.' Afterward a bespectacled guy wearing khaki shorts and a pith helmet accompanied us as we wandered from one late-night establishment to the next, fluorescently lit cafés that were indistinguishable in that they glowed and buzzed with identical intensity. We lost our friend sometime before dawn and ended up on the beach for what I thought was the most blazingly orange sunrise I had ever seen. Billy was sleeping by then, with his face in the sand, and I watched his body twitch as a deerfly continually had its way with his leg. I never once thought to brush it away.

We slept that morning and, after stopping to say goodbye to our host (he was scarfing down a slice of pizza as he waved us off), headed south. The drive lasted into the evening and ended when we pulled into a motel called the Pennsylvania on Twenty-first Street in Myrtle Beach, South Carolina. We hung out on the beach and swam the next two days in the piss-warm wavelets of the Atlantic. On the second night we felt rejuvenated enough to party and returned to it with a vengeance. By the time we got to the Spanish Galleon, the resort's most popular nightclub, which was packed with raucous innocents (in a way that only Southern bars can be), Billy and I were raped on beer and tequila and determined to score. We had by now developed a contest involving the number of women we could rack up on the trip (Billy dubbed it our 'cock test'), and I immediately crossed a busy concrete dance floor where college kids were doing the shag to Chairman of the Board's 'Give Me Just a Little More Time,' and proceeded to slip my tongue into the mouth of a hideous but willing biker queen who had been standing by herself. From out of the corner of my eye I could see Billy laughing as I rolled my tongue in her cankerous orifice, and now, with spiteful determination, I led her out to the beach for the long walk down to the surf where I 'made love' to her near the breakers. After I came in her doughy box her face changed from the merely ugly to the truly frightening, and when she demanded that I 'fuck' her again, I obeyed, her oily black hair buried in the sand by my dutiful thrusts. Somehow I lost her in the Galleon and hitched to the motel, where an unrelenting Billy was waiting for me with an evil grin. For the next three days he teased me about the clap (and every time I urinated I could hear his laughter outside the bathroom door), but miraculously it didn't surface, and the next morning, my head pounding and down in disgust, we left Myrtle and continued south.

Our next stop was Charleston, the Jewel of the South, which at first glance promised to be a genteel blend of white-gloved belles and dripping cypress. We planned to visit Billy's friend Dan Ballenger, who for reasons I can't recall was nicknamed and preferred to be called Pooter. Pooter was an amiable squid who lived off base in a decaying suburb of the city. Pooter's cottage was small and not even air-conditioned with window shakers, so there was little else to do in that oppressive heat but lie around on his sticky green vinyl furniture and do bong hits while watching the Summer Olympics. This was the year the young man from Palmer Park took the gold medal in boxing, and I cannot remember anytime being quite so proud to carry the label of Washingtonian. On the second night of our stay Pooter took us to a shotgun shack of a bar on the edge of town where aggressively plain girls were employed to wear negligees and con the customers into buying them seven-dollar wine coolers. One of them, an emaciated, pimply little teenager, sat on my lap and then got pissed when I refused to step up for the drink. By now Pooter was nervous, as there were several sinewy, long-haired types scattered around the place who looked more than happy to dispatch wise-asses such as us. Billy made a point of finding the owner and telling him what a 'classy place' he had, and that was when we all decided it was time to go. In the car Billy and I ate two more tabs of haze and drove to a Piggly Wiggly, where we stole a watermelon from the outdoor rack and, as a startlingly quick clerk chased us on foot, peeled out of the parking lot and into the thick night. The watermelon was as warm as the air and we dumped it after a disappointing taste. Then we found a movie theater and bought tickets to *The Outlaw Josie Wales*. After Joseph Bottoms's wonderfully acted death scene – 'I was prouder than a game rooster to have ridden with ye, Josie' – I remember very little, since the acid kicked in and I focused, for the remainder of the film, on the colorful, dust-filled tubes of light that traveled from the projector to the screen. When the film ended we drove to the Battery, which seemed to be the only spot in Charleston that carried a breeze, and got high, and talked with a young man named Spit who claimed he didn't care for 'ofay motherfuckers' but had no problem with smoking their weed. The whole time we were doing this, Pooter slept (I still don't know how) in the backseat of the Camaro, his head back between the Superthruster speakers that were now blowing thirty distorted watts of Hendrix out across the intracoastal waterway. We slept that whole next day and, at six in the evening, said good-bye to a rather relieved-looking Pooter.

Soon after we hit the highway we agreed that we needed to clear our heads. Each of us swallowed a black beauty and then, as that cranial tingle began, we pulled over in Columbia and bought two large bottles of burgundy. After Columbia the speed tore in, and from then on it was all cigarettes, wine, open windows, and maximum volume (we blew one of the speakers that night, during Earl Slick's screaming guitar solo on Bowie's 'Stay'). In Augusta we stopped for more wine, were thrown out of a rock-and-roll club for something Billy said to the doorman, then wandered into an all-black disco and danced with an amphetaminic frenzy until 3:00 A.M. (I was fairly proficient then in a jerky, popular dance called the Robot.) I drove the rest of the night, nervously picking at my thumb the entire way, which resulted in a good bit of blood on my hand by the time we reached our destination. We pulled into Atlanta at 6:30 in the morning.

The first hotel we saw was on Houston Street, and it was there, a ten-dollar-a-night wino flophouse, that we took a room. We only stayed in Atlanta a couple of days, finding it in general to be neither friendly nor safe, though I did get a date on the first night with a young, green-eyed strawberry blonde, a hawker for one of the clubs in the Underground. She had no intention of sleeping with me – she was too smart for that – but we enjoyed a quiet, air-conditioned evening together in her apartment, where she lent me the use of her blessedly clean shower. I think I reminded her of her brother from whatever small midwestern town she had mistakenly fled. The next day a junkie tried to pay Billy and me to pick up his 'pharmaceutical' prescription for Quaaludes, and we came very close to doing it. We decided then to think about leaving, as our part of town was clearly no place for a couple of Yankee white boys, and of course there was the matter of the expensive boat parked in the lot behind the hotel. That night I sat almost naked in the window box of our room (the only spot that wasn't hellish), smoking cigarettes and thinking about home, while Billy stretched out in a bathtub filled with cold water. We left the next morning.

The trip to Key West was sickeningly hot and seemed to take the better part of two days. Once there, we dropped the boat off quickly to some middle-aged hippie and collected our two hundred dollars. We walked around the town but, our spirits drained, found its surreal trapping snot to our mutual taste. There was a fully clothed, sun-blistered young man lying in the middle of Truman Street with pennies stuck in his eyes. That is what I remember of Key West.

An hour north on A1-A we smoked a huge, celebratory joint, which had me peaking just as we rolled onto the old Seven Mile Bridge and gave me the most panicky few minutes I have spent on any stretch of road. Liberated from the boat, Billy's Camaro seemed to be mounted on mattress springs rather than shocks, and it was all I could do to keep the goddamn vehicle from becoming airborne as other similarly drugged and sailing individuals sped toward us, missing collision by what seemed like inches. When we got off the bridge we were both ready for a beer or two, and we stopped in Marathon at what looked to be a peaceful dive called Dave's Dockside. Never having experienced the novelty of a twenty-four-hour bar, Billy and I began a long, boozy evening in which we lost all but fifty dollars of our payoff money shooting pool. The whole thing ended around dawn when a pirate type (yes, wearing a black eye patch) took a swing at me for talking to his girlfriend. He was too drunk to connect, but suddenly our former friends all looked like badassed, raw-knuckled locals, and we walked out to the car and pointed it north.

After another day of hot, conversationless travel, we stopped in Daytona, for no reason other than to satisfy Billy's desire to drive his car on the beach. We checked in to a cheap motel and spent a sleepless night knocking biting, armored cockroaches the size of thumbs off our beds. After breakfast the following morning we were totally broke. We walked around and asked about work but understandably got no takers, as we were beginning to look like every other K-head biker in town. That night Billy, on sheer charm, picked up an Italian girl and got both a life-affirming blow job and a clean, cool place to sleep, while I settled for the spine-wrenching backseat of the Camaro. (For the rest of the trip Billy did not stop describing the determined look on the poor girl's face as she attempted to swallow, as he put it, 'a month's worth of jizz.') The following day we halfheartedly tried to find a job in the one-hundred-and-two-degree heat, but by now we both knew it was over. Sometime after noon we simultaneously fell asleep or passed out on the sidewalk in front of a major hotel and were awakened two hours later by the cops, who threatened to book us for vagrancy unless we left town. We agreed but drove only a few blocks down the road, since at this point we had not even enough money for gas. At dinnertime I created a diversion in a convenience store by breaking a bottle of orange juice, while Billy grabbed candy bars, nuts, and several Slim Jims, and shoved them into his jeans. We ate this bounty seated at some memorial, which (we should have known) turned out to be the favorite cruising spot for Daytona's homosexuals. One of them, a birdlike boy our age who had the unfortunate, swishy mannerisms that Catskill comedians and conservative politicians so love to exploit, had a seat next to us and offered a small bit of money and a place to sleep if we cared to 'indulge.' We both answered with emphatic negatives, but when the kid persisted, Billy winked at me and told me to wait for him at the car. An hour later he returned with a wad of money in his fist and the explanation that he had persuaded the boy to give us a loan. When I asked him, with a smirk on my face, what he had to do to get it, Billy threw me up against the car with an explosion of fury I'd never suspected in him. We drove on and I didn't mention it again, but after that things were not quite the same between me and Billy.

There is not much to say about the next couple of days except that we found Route 10 and headed west. I do remember the surprisingly green and hilly terrain of northwestern Florida; and of the night we spent in Mobile, I have only the strange recollection of a downtown building painted black.

Sometime early in August we made it to New Orleans. I had Billy blast Robin Trower's 'I Can't Wait Much Longer' ('I'll get my coat and catch a train / Make my way to New Orleans') through the speakers as we rolled into town. We chose to stay in a nine-buck-a-night cottage at a place called the Carmen D Motel on Chef Menteur Highway. The plump, elderly proprietors were rosy-cheeked and friendly, and there were chickens running around in the yard of willowy trees that the cottages surrounded. Billy and I found night work quickly on a movie theater cleaning crew. The manager of the theater was to lock us in at around midnight and let us out in the morning, but this was to last only one night. On that first night we smoked a couple of joints as soon as the owner had split and then decided, to the knowing looks and chuckles of our Mexican coworkers, that scraping chewing gum off the underside of seats just wasn't our thing. After that we resolved to stop thinking about work and simply enjoy ourselves until the money ran out. There seemed to be bars everywhere in that city, and in the next two weeks we did little more than sleep through the mornings, then spend the humid afternoons shooting pool and drinking Dixie. In one of those bars we met two sisters, older women named Viv and Julliette, who took a liking to us and then proceeded, for eighteen hours straight, to screw us raw in their respective beds. Billy had chosen Julliette (she was the better-looking of the two) but I was secretly happy to go with the redheaded Viv, who was witty and had a throaty laugh and full, buttery breasts. They had a name for that particular summer's high murder rate down there (I think they called it the Summer of Blood), but I cannot believe there is a place in this country so dedicated as New Orleans to the proposition of having fun. On our last night in town Billy caught one of the chickens in the yard, marked his leg with a twist tie, and fed him a hit of purple haze hidden in a piece of popcorn. Then we each had a tab, the end of our supply. Later, in our room, we began to trip our asses off while watching *The Wild Bunch* on our black-and-white set, howling as we mimicked the classic lines of dialogue, the images becoming progressively amorphic on the small TV screen set against the green wall, the corners of which by now had completely dissolved. On the stoop later, we sat and drank beer, chain-smoking cigarettes while talking about the road ahead. Our lone chicken was out there, traversing the yard in wild circles, wired to the hilt. Billy was distracted by this and remorseful to the point where he suggested we pack up and leave. I don't think he wanted to see that chicken dead, something that was certainly going to happen before morning. So we gassed up the Camaro, swallowed the remainder of our black beauties, and were out of New Orleans before dawn's first light. Twenty-four hours and twelve hundred miles later I was in my bed in the back room of my grandfather's apartment, and that is where I slept for the next two days.

The next week Billy reported to some ACC college in North Carolina, and I began classes at the state university shortly thereafter. We wrote a couple of letters in the fall, and then I saw him over Thanksgiving. The night we went out he was with one of his new fraternity brothers, a guy Billy called Digger Dog, and we went to a local pub where they talked about 'brew' and 'sport-fucking' and 'DG girls' while I faded into my booth seat and got quietly drunk. High school friendships either die or continue in that crucial first semester, and ours simply didn't make it.

But none of that really matters. There is a photograph of Billy and me, taken by a tourist, that to this day is in an envelope at the bottom of my dresser. In the photograph we are sitting high up on a fire escape near Bourbon Street. Billy's hand is on my shoulder, and our hair is long and uncombed and past our shoulders, and we are both smoking cigarettes. There is that look on both of our faces, that look that almost shouts that it has all been grand and that it is never, ever going to end.

In everything that I have done since, and everything that I will ever do, there is nothing that will equal the wondrous, immortal summer that I experienced in 1976. Now Billy Goodrich had walked into my bar, fifteen years later, and brought it all back home.

3

'How you doin', man?'

'Good,' he said, nodding slowly as he smiled. 'I'm doing good.'

I stood there looking at him from behind the bar. He hadn't changed much. The blond hair was there, but it started farther back, and it was short and swept back. His face was still smooth and unlined, though there was a cool hardness now around his mouth and the edges of his azure eyes. He glanced at my shot glass, then up at me.

'Call it,' I said.

'Anything in a green bottle. If you're buying.'

I grabbed him a Heineken from the cooler and a Bud to go with my bourbon. Billy removed his jacket – he was wearing suspenders, a very bad sign – and folded it up on the stool to his left. Then he had a pull off the import.

'Well,' I said, 'you gonna tell me?'

'Tell you what?'

'How the hell you found me.'

He furrowed his brow theatrically. 'Who said I was looking for you? I was in the neighborhood . . .'

'Bullshit,' I said, going over his clothing. 'Guys like you are never in *this* neighborhood.'

'You're right about that.'

'Well?'

'I tripped over your name in the phone book, to tell you the truth.' Billy paused. 'I was in the market for a private investigator.'

'And?'

'I called your answering service, and the girl said . . .'

'She's a grandmother.'

'Okay, the *old lady* said I could get you down here. I was surprised she gave me the information so easily.'

'She's the motherly type. Probably thought she was doing me a favor. Business has been slow, to say the least.'

'Well,' he said, 'the whole thing was a shock to me. I mean, I ran into Teddy Ball a couple of years ago, remember him from high school?' I nodded, though I didn't really. 'Anyway, he told me he heard you were some advertising bigwig for one of those electronics retailers.'

'I was,' I said, and let it go at that. 'Now I do this.'

'Hey, that's great,' Billy said, in the tone of voice one uses when soothing a sensitive child. 'If that's what you want, great.'

'How about you, man? What are you up to?'

He shrugged with studied carelessness and said, 'A little bit of everything. My Ten-Forty says I sell commercial real estate' – and here Billy winked – 'but I have an interest in a couple of cash businesses in the suburbs. Restaurants, carryouts, you know what I'm saying?'

'Yeah, sure.'

'Things are okay,' he said, then looked at the remainder of his beer and finished it off. Billy held the bottle up. 'How about another one of these Green Guys?'

I found him one and killed off the rest of my Grand-Dad, then poured myself another shot. While I did that I watched him nail half the bottle of Heineken. He looked up my way and stared at me for an uncomfortably long time.

'It's good to see you, Nicky,' he said finally.

'It's good to see you too, man.'

After that there was another block of silence. I had a taste of bourbon and chased it with some beer while he looked away. The music had stopped, but he was drumming his fingers on the bar. I moved down to the stereo and switched it over to WDCU, to give him something to drum about. They were playing Charlie Parker's 'Lester Leaps In.' When I walked back Billy was grinning. It was still an ingratiating grin but a little forced now, as if he were attempting to smile against a cold wind.

'So,' he said, 'I never would have figured you to end up as a detective.'

'It just happened. Anyway, I'd hate to think I *ended up* as any one thing.'

'You know what I mean.'

'All too well. You meet somebody, right away, what's the first thing they ask you? "What do you *do?*" I never know how to answer that. I mean, I do a lot of things. I'm a bartender, I read books, I'm a private investigator, I go to movies, I drink, I box, I listen to music, I fuck – which activity are they referring to?'

'I doubt they're referring to the last one.' Billy shook his head and chuckled condescendingly. 'You haven't changed one bit, man.'

'Maybe,' I said. 'But you probably knew that. And you came down here anyway to ask for my help. Right?'

Billy finished his beer and replaced the bottle softly on the bar, then looked at me. 'That's right.'

'You want to talk about it?'

'I'd feel better if we went somewhere else.' Billy had a look around the bar. 'I mean, this place is so depressing. Don't you think it could use a few . . .'

'Plants?'

'Yeah, something.'

'I don't know. I kind of like it the way it is.'

We were gliding north on Fourteenth Street in Billy's sleek white Maxima, the glow of the dash lights rendering our complexions pale green. There was a car phone between the saddle leather buckets. The numbers on the car phone were also illuminated in green. A notepad filled with blank white paper was suctioned to the dash.

Billy had a pull off one of the road beers I had grabbed before locking up the Spot, then wedged the bottle between his thighs. I flipped through his CD selection and tried to find something listenable, but all he owned – Steve Winwood, Clapton, Phil Collins, the Who ('Hope I die before I get old,' indeed – why didn't you, then?) – were forty-minute beer commercials. I closed the box and settled for the soft, intermittent rush of the Maxima's wipers.

Outside, the snow was drifting down in chunked, feathery flakes. Soft, radiant halos capped the streetlights ahead. Children were out, laughing and running on the sidewalks and in the street. One of them, a boy no older than eight who wore only a red windbreaker, threw a powdery snowball that hit our windshield and dissolved. I made a mocking fist and shook it at him as we passed, and he smiled and shook his own fist back. Billy locked the doors with a rather awkward, fumbling push of a button.

Just past Fourteenth and Irving we passed the remains of the Tivoli Theater. My grandfather had taken me there in 1963 to see *Jason and the Argonauts*, a film noted as the pinnacle of Ray Harryhausen's work in stop-motion photography. The scene in which the skeletons come to life to do battle with Jason inspired some of the most frighteningly memorable, sheet-soaked nightmares of my childhood. The night of the film my grandfather and I had walked through a heavy snowstorm from our apartment to the theater. I can still feel the warmth of his huge and callused hand in mine as we made a path through the snow.

'Hey,' Billy said. 'Your papa still around?'

'*Papou*,' I said. 'He died a couple of years back.'

'How about your folks? You ever hear from them?'

'No.'

At my direction Billy pulled over and parked near the intersection of Fourteenth and Colorado. He double-checked all the locks before we headed down the block, turning his head back twice to look at the car as we walked.

'Relax, will you?'

'That's twenty-five thousand dollars' worth of car,' he said. 'I don't want to see it up on cinder blocks when I come out of this place.'

'You worry too much,' I said, but judging from the pale look on Billy's face, that bit of analysis didn't help. I pulled on the thin door and we entered Slim's.

Slim's was a small jazz-and-reggae club owned and run by a couple of East Africans, neither of whom was named Slim. At night there was always a live but unobtrusive band, and the Ethiopian food was top-notch. Slim's had a ten-dollar minimum tab, a quota I never once had trouble making, to keep out any undesirables. I stopped in once in a while on my way home and had a couple of quiet drinks at the bar while I listened to some of the cleanest jazz, mostly of the bebop variety, in town.

We crossed the room to a deuce in the back that was centered under a stylized portrait of Haile Selassie. Our waitress showed momentarily and took our order for two beers. Her name was Cissy. She was wearing a plain white T-shirt and blue jeans, and had beautifully unblemished burnt-sienna skin.

The band that night was the club's regular sextet – trumpet, sax, piano, drums, guitar, upright bass – whose members took turns soloing on practically every number. The turban-headed trumpeter was the coleader, though oddly the least talented of the group, and his partner was the saxman, an aging, bottom-heavy Greek I had seen around town who took his scotch through a straw. The youngest man of the bunch was the guitarist, and also the musician with the most potential, but obviously a heavy user. When he wasn't soloing he sat on a wooden stool with his chin on his chest, a crooked knit cap pushed over his brow, deep in his down world.

Billy and I sat through the rest of the band's set without speaking. Cissy had given us two unsolicited Jim Beam Blacks (a very smooth bourbon that is in fact too smooth for my taste) and served them in juice glasses halfway full to the lip. The band ended its set with a pumped-up version of Miles Davis's 'Milestones.' The young bartender put some low-volume Jamaican dub on the house stereo. Billy, who was starting to look a little pickled, leaned my way.

'Let's talk business,' he said.

'All right.' I pulled the deck of Camels from my overcoat and shook it in his direction. He started to reach for one but then waved it away. I slid one out, lit it, and took in a lungful.

Billy said, 'I guess you've noticed the ring on my finger.'

I nodded and said, 'So?'

'This is about that.'

'I don't tail wives or husbands anymore. I should tell you that straight up. My bartending job keeps me off that sort of thing.'

'It's not what you think,' he said.

'What is it then?'

'My wife has left me, Nick.' Billy took the matches that rested on the top of my cigarettes and pulled one off the pack. He struck it, watched it flare, then blew it out. 'She walked on her own accord. You'd call it desertion, I guess, if it was a man doing the walking.'

'Kids?'

'None. We tried for a couple of years, but it wasn't in the cards.'

I had a sip of bourbon then followed it with a deep drag off my cigarette. When I exhaled I blew the smoke past his head and tried not to look into his eyes. 'Like you said, Bill, this is business. I'm going to ask you some questions that are personal . . .'

'Go ahead.'

'This type of thing – and not to make it seem small – well, it happens every day. Hell, man, in a way it happened to me. So why hire a detective?'

'I'm worried about her,' he said. 'It's that simple. And since there's no evidence of foul play, the cops won't give it the time of day.'

'You've been to them?'

'Yeah, I reported it the first day. They came around, asked me a couple of questions, I never head from them again.'

I had a last pull off my smoke and butted it. 'What do you want me to do?'

'Find her, that's it. You don't even have to talk to her. Just report her location back to me, and I'll do the talking. If she doesn't want to come home, then at least I gave it a shot.' Billy looked at me briefly and then looked away.

'What else?' I said.

'Like?' He nodded me on with his chin.

'Did she leave you for someone else?' Instead of answering, Billy finished the bourbon in his glass, an answer in itself. I signaled Cissy for two more. 'Do you know him?' I asked.

'Yeah, I know him. He was a man I did business with.' The waitress brought our Beams and two more beers. Billy and I lightly touched glasses, and I had a drink while he continued. 'I met this guy as a client. I was showing him around town, some spots for a chain of carryouts he was thinking of opening. Anyway, I did him a couple of serious solids in terms of negotiating leases, that sort of thing. He liked my style, and he put me on the payroll of his corporation in a retainer capacity.'

'You kept your job with the real estate company?'

'Yes.'

'Kind of a conflict of interest there, wasn't it?'

'It depends on how you look at things, I suppose. I've learned some very creative ways of putting deals together, and I guess Mr DiGeordano didn't want me doing that for anyone else but him.'

'Joey DiGeordano?'

'That's right.'

I whistled softly. 'You got yourself pretty connected, didn't you, Bill?'

'You've heard of him, then.'

'I read the paper,' I said, leaving out the fact that my grandfather had known the old man. 'The DiGeordanos have been in it once or twice through the years. They're what passes for a small-time crime family in this town. Nothing serious, by today's standards – a little gambling, some Jewish Lightning in the old days.'

'I'm aware of those things,' he mumbled.

'Keep going,' I said.

'April and I – April, that's my wife's name – we socialized with Joey and his wife a few times early on. Right from the beginning I could see Joey had the eye for April. But that didn't bother me much. I mean, I was used to it. April is a very good-looking woman.'

'Did they have an affair?'

'I can't prove it if they did,' he said. 'Let's say it was a suspicion I had.'

'What was your relationship like when she left?'

'I thought it was good. We had our problems, but in general I was pretty content. And I was willing to work at it, that's the thing. Then I came home one day and she was just gone. Her closet was emptied and there was a note, and that was that.'

'When was that?' I asked.

'A week ago yesterday,' he said. 'Wednesday.'

'Anything unusual about the note?'

Billy considered that. 'It came off a printer. I guess that's unusual, huh? A typed Dear John.'

'Any idea why?'

'She ran the thing off on my computer. That was always a sticking point with her – I'd come home from work and immediately get on my computer and start running spreadsheets and figures. I guess I was pretty obsessed with making it and all that. Anyway, she certainly thought so. And the note was just her way of twisting the knife.'

I thought that over and said, 'What about Joey DiGeordano? Are you still doing business with him?'

Billy said, 'Our business relationship has become strained. I can't exactly talk to him about it, even though I think he might have some idea where she is. That's where you come in.'

I lit another cigarette and exhaled a thin gray veil that settled between us. 'I'll need to know a few things about your wife. Her history, family, that sort of thing. A recent picture.'

'Then you'll help me.'

I nodded and said, 'Yeah.'

'Thanks, Nick.' Billy shook my hand and held it for more than a few seconds. His felt cool. 'I want you to understand that I didn't come to you for any friendship deals.'

'There won't be any,' I said. 'I get two-fifty a day plus expenses, with a day's worth up front.'

'No problem.' A few strands of his moussed hair had fallen across his forehead, and he brushed it back. 'Listen, man, I'm a little drunk right now.'

'Me too,' I admitted.

'Anyway,' he said, 'it's as good a time as any to apologize for all the years that went by. The thing is, Nick, I think of life as being more . . . linear than you do, you know what I mean? High school, college, career, marriage, family, retirement – and I have no trouble leaving the last phase behind me when I start a new one. Anyway, when I went away to school, I could see you just weren't going to come along. I just don't want you to think I forgot about you, man. I never did.'

'Don't worry about it,' I said. 'You're calling it straight. That's exactly the way it is.'

The band was gathering for their next set. Billy reached for his wallet and said, 'Come on, let's get out of here. I've had enough.'

'You go on,' I said. 'I only live a couple of blocks away. I'll walk home.'

'You sure?'

'Yeah.'

Billy shrugged and left a twenty on the table. I let him do it and watched him button his coat. 'I'll courier all that stuff to you tomorrow.'

'Send it here,' I said, and we traded business cards. His said WILLIAM GOODRICH.

'Thanks again, Nick.'

I nodded and he walked away. As I watched him cross the room, I felt an odd sadness, that sense of irrevocable loss one feels upon seeing a friend who has changed so drastically over so many years. I recognized the feeling as little more than a burst of self-pity for my own youth, a youth that had quietly slipped away. But the recognition in itself didn't seem to help.

He was right when he said that I had chosen not to come along, but it was not really something I was sorry for. He had become that characterless, you-can-have-it-all predator that was everything I had come to hate. But somewhere in that cadaver was the long-haired kid who had called out to me one day in the park, and now he was calling out again. William Goodrich had hired me, but it was for Billy that I was taking the case.

I had another bourbon while I watched the last set, then settled up my tab. Out on the sidewalk, I tucked a scarf into my black overcoat and weaved north. The branches of the trees were heavy with powder, and the streets were still. The snow was ending, but its last flakes were still visible in the light of the street lamps. The snow made a sound like paper cutting skin as it fell. Tomorrow there would be a quick melt and a nightmare rush hour, a city of horns and tight neckties. But tonight D.C. was a silent, idyllic small town.

I turned the corner of my block and saw my cat huddled on the stoop of my apartment. I watched her figure slip down and cross the yard, a ball of black moving across a white blanket. Her grainy nose touched the fingertips of my outstretched hand.

4

Friday afternoon's lunch had been typically hectic.

Our regulars had arrived early, shuffling in and nodding hello with pleading doe eyes while I hurriedly sliced fruit and tossed bleach tablets into the rinse sink. The patrons were eager to start their weekend binges. Darnell's Fish Platter, a house favorite, began to get a lot of action, and at one point he was sliding the plates onto the platform of the reach-through faster than I could serve them. Ramon was lurking around somewhere, but, having blown a stick of sensimillion in the basement just before opening time, he was virtually useless.

That, however, had been the easy part of my day. When the rush ended I was left to baby-sit those few drinkers who had decided, as early as their first beer, not to return to work. Today this group of geniuses included Happy, who in his perfect world would someday be buried with one hand rigor mortised into a glass-holding *C*, the other in a horizontal victory sign, the fingers spread just wide enough to ac-commodate a Chesterfield; Buddy and Bubba, today arguing about boxing (confusing it with bullying) and splitting a pitcher with such intense closeness that they appeared to be joined at the hip; an alcoholic Dutch secretary named Petra for whom we exclusively stocked Geneve, a syrupy gin that was rumoured to have the power to induce hallucina-tions; and, least tolerable of all, a fat federal judge by the name of Len.

The fact that Len Dorfman was a federal judge is a point worth mentioning only in relation to his repulsive personality. Len would swagger in after a tough morning on the bench, announce to our deaf ears that he had just 'worked out' at the gym (I would wager any amount that he could not, if a gun were to be placed in his mouth, execute one sit-up), and order a Grand Marnier because, he claimed, he had 'earned' it. After one snifter he would check over the clientele and begin to brag about all the 'savages' he had put away that morning, adding with bluster that he had 'thrown away the key.' Then, like some third-rate Don Rickles ('Hey, if we can't make fun of ourselves, who can we make fun of?'), he would launch into his 'I'm a cheap Jew' routine, a tired shtick that had everyone at the bar staring into their drinks in embarrassment. The fact that Len himself was Jewish made it, contrary to his belief, no less offensive. Finally, after his third round, he would begin to trash gays with a lispy, plump-mouthed imitation so filled with vicious self-hatred that there was no doubt in anyone's mind that Len was a man who had, on several occasions and probably in some bathroom stall in our very hallowed halls of justice, fallen to his soft knees and, with a fervor equal in enthusiasm to his flamboyant bar soliloquies, sucked cock.

He was doing that imitation when Dan Boyle walked into the bar. Boyle hated Dorfman, not for his ignorant slurs (they shared roughly the same prejudices) but for what he perceived to be Len's soft stance on criminals. Dorfman knew it and consequently settled up quietly and exited the Spot. The customers, even Happy, gave Boyle a round of applause.

I did my part and had a mug of draught in front of Boyle before his ass spread over the wood of his barstool. His eyes traveled up and lit on the stack of shot glasses. I separated the top one from the stack and set it next to his mug. Then I poured two inches of Jack Daniels into the glass.

'This one's on the house.'

'You're the greatest,' Boyle said.

'You Irish boys get so sentimental about your bartenders.'

'Leave me alone. It's been a bad fuckin' day.'

'Out on those mean streets, you mean?'

'Go ahead and laugh. After you walk a mile in my shoes.'

'"Walk a Mile in My Shoes"?' I said. 'Joe South, nineteen-sixty-nine.'

'Huh?'

'Forget it.'

I heard a sharp whistle and turned. Petra had done the whistling and now she was, with a perfectly angelic smile and the middle finger of her left hand pointed straight at the ceiling, flipping me off. Though she surely knew the meaning of that most universal symbol, some joker had convinced her one night that, in Washington's bars, this was also an accepted method of ordering a quick drink.

Boyle said, 'I think that Dutch broad needs another hit.'

I poured her a short one and while I was on that end drew a fresh pitcher for Buddy and Bubba. Buddy was a sawed-off little guy, and even while sitting straight, his wide shoulders barely cleared the lip of the bar. Now he was slouched and his blond head seemed to be sprouting directly up out of the mahogany. I placed the pitcher in front of that head. He nodded and then growled.

I changed all the full ashtrays into empties and moved back down to Boyle. He had taken off his overcoat and beneath that was wearing an old tweed with suede patches sewn on the elbows. As he turned to fold his coat on the adjacent barstool, I could see the bulge of his Colt Python protruding from the small of his back. I slid him another mugful of draught and washed out the empty in the soap sink.

'I checked into that thing for you,' Boyle said.

'William Henry?'

'Yeah.'

'What's happening?'

'Nothing, really. No new leads, not since the initial investigation.'

'What do you think?' I said.

Boyle had a long drink from his mug, then wiped his mouth with the sleeve of his sport coat. 'It's not in my jurisdiction,' he said. 'I only looked at the jacket last night.'

'At a glance, then.'

'At a glance? Your friend probably knew his attacker. There weren't any signs of forced entry. He had solid dead bolts on the door and an auxiliary lock; none of the jams were splintered. The ME's report said he was stabbed over twenty times with a serrated knife, like the kind your buddy Darnell uses in his kitchen. Henry was probably dead or in shock before the guy was finished knifing him.'

'What does all that mean?'

'It could mean a lot of things. The intent was clear – he didn't want to wound Henry, he wanted him dead. It could have been a drug deal gone bad. Or it was a crime of passion. You know, a homo burn.'

'A homo burn?' I frowned. 'Come on, Boyle, what the hell is that?'

'We explore every possibility, Nick. That building he lived in, it had a history of homosexual tenants.'

I sighed and drummed my fingers on the bar. 'Keep going.'

Boyle pointed to his empty shot glass. I reached behind me to the second row of call, grabbed the black-labeled bottle of Jack, and poured him some sour mash. He sipped it, chased it with some draught. 'The main point I got out of the report, the angle I'd go for if I was looking into it, was how he got past the security guard in the lobby.' Boyle winked. 'That's, like I say, if I was going to look into it.'

'What was the security guard's name, Boyle? The one that was on duty.'

'I'll deny this if it ever gets out.' I nodded and looked around the bar. Our regulars were drinking peacefully. A couple of them had solemnly closed their eyes and were mouthing the words to Joe Jackson's version of 'What's the Use of Getting Sober? (When You're Gonna Get Drunk Again)' as it came through the speakers. Boyle said, 'James Thomas.'

I wrote down the name and said, 'Any progress on the case?'

Boyle snorted and closed his eyes slowly as he sipped from the shot glass he held in his thick hand. When he was finished he put the glass down. 'A case gets cold after a few days, Nick. And there's always something else. Right now we've got hookers gettin' whacked down in the Midnight Zone. Detectives working double shifts.' Boyle drained half of what was left in the mug. 'The thing you got to remember is, almost one out of two homicides in the District go unsolved. Pretty good odds for the bad guys, huh? You kill someone in this town, you got a fifty percent shot at getting away with it.'

'What are you saying?'

'We're never going to find that boy's killer, Nick. That's a fuckin' bet.'

'Thanks for the information.'

Boyle leaned in and stared hard. He was attempting to focus his jittery pale blue eyes on mine. 'If you need anything else, partner, you let me know.'

'I will. In the meantime, I gotta be getting out of here.' I wiped the area in front of him with my bar rag. 'Believe it or not, I've got a date.'

'I remember those days,' Boyle said. 'Dates. Now all's I got is rotten screaming kids.'

'There's a solution to that.'

'What would that be?' he said.

'Take 'em out in the street,' I said, 'and shoot 'em in the head. Public fuckin' executions.'

On the way home I stopped and picked up my package at the office of my answering service on Georgia Avenue. After that I headed west a few blocks and parked the Dodge in front of my apartment. The afternoon sun had taken care of most of the snow. What was left was gray now and in mounds near the kerb. My cat ran out as I stepped along the walk. She rolled onto her back and let me scratch her stomach. As I did this her left rear paw boxed the air convulsively. When her paw stopped moving I tickled the scar tissue where her right eye had been, then entered my place.

I changed into sweat clothes while the water boiled. Then I made coffee and took the coffee and my package to a small desk I had set up in my bedroom. I opened the package and spread its contents out on the oak top.

Billy Goodrich had organized his wife's file with all the efficiency and warmth of a client's prospectus. There was a cover letter and a photograph that appeared to have been professionally taken. I tacked that one to the bulletin board that hung over my desk. I glanced over the rest of the material – family and medical history, doctors, a résumé – and placed it back in the package.

After that I drove west and met Rodney White at a junior high gymnasium in upper Northwest. I did ten sets of abs and several sets of lat and tricep push-ups, then jumped rope while he taught his class. When he had dismissed his students we put on our sparring equipment and went to it.

'Move to the side, Home,' Rodney said after I had taken a particularly vicious flurry of punches and squared off in front of him. 'Just slide over, man, then make your move.' He demonstrated, suddenly springing to the left, throwing mock jabs to my kidneys. I was facing away from him.

'What about doing that Hemingway thing, standing in there, going toe-to-toe?'

'Only in gladiator movies, Nick.'

We spared for another fifteen minutes, until my hands became too heavy to hold up in front of my face. Rodney White removed his mouthpiece and rubbed it dry on the arm of his gi.

'All right, that ought to do you for tonight.' He pulled a towel from his bag and wiped the sweat from his forehead. 'Say,' he said. 'Been a while since you've been in to see me, for a checkup.'

I pulled out my own mouthpiece. A string of bloody saliva ran from the side of it and clung to my mouth. 'A checkup?' I said, fighting for some air. 'Doctor, I believe I could use one. Right about now.'

A half hour later I was back in my apartment. I threw my wet clothes into the hamper, showered, shaved, dressed in a rented monkey suit, and fed and watered the cat. I got into my black forty-dollar Robert Hall overcoat and slipped a fresh deck of Camels into its breast pocket. Then I locked my apartment, ignitioned my Dodge Dart, and went to pick up Jackie.

Jackie Kahn lived in a two-bedroom condo with her lover, a woman named Sherron, in a three-story building on the edge of Kalorama. The D.C. guidebooks all claim that Kalorama means 'beautiful view,' from the Greek *kalo*. Not to split hairs, but *kalo* is actually the Greek word for 'good.' The word for beautiful is, phonetically, *orayo*, but I would never lobby for the change – Orayorama sounds a little like the gimmick for a fifties horror movie.

Jackie's building was an elaborate Grecian knockoff with egg-and-tongue molding that ran below the roofline, with an urn pediment centered above the stone portico. It was quite regal, and I supposed she was paying for it. I entered an unlocked set of glass doors and pushed her buzzer. After the usual formalities I made it through the second set of doors and took the gated, open lift to her floor.

Sherron opened the door on my first knock. She was wearing winter white pleated slacks and a black sweater with black buttons sewn along the top of the shoulder. On the front of the sweater hung a necklace of spheres that may or may not have been made of gold and that grew progressively larger as they converged at the center. She was taller than me and had wonderfully long legs, and in total she had the build of a Thoroughbred. I had seen reasonably intelligent men commit public stupidities in her presence.

'Can Jackie come out and play?'

'Come on in,' she said in an accent laced with Puerto Rican.

'Thanks.' I kissed her hello and caught the edge of her ripe mouth. She frowned and led me through a marble foyer to an airy living room painted primarily in lavender. There was a fire burning in a marble-manteled fireplace that was centered in the west wall.

'You look different dressed up,' she said, her idea of a compliment. 'Have a seat and I'll fix you a drink. Jackie will be out in a few minutes.'

'Bourbon rocks,' I said. Sherron left the room, and I watched her do it. After a few minutes she came back in and placed a tumbler filled with bourbon whiskey and cubes on a cork coaster edged with a silver ring. I had a long pull, tasted Wild Turkey, and set the glass back down on the tumbler. Sherron had a seat on the divan against the wall across from my chair. She looked me over as if I were a marked-down dress, then crossed one lovely leg over the other.

'So,' she said. 'Been peeping in any windows lately?'

'It's very pane-full.' I drew out the last word so she could get it, but humor wasn't her shtick. In fact I had never seen her smile. I lit a cigarette because I knew she didn't like it and childishly bounced the match off the side of the crystal ashtray that was next to the coaster. Some smoke drifted her way and she made a small wave of her long, thin hand, like she was shaking off a bug. Mercifully, that was when Jackie walked into the room.

She was wearing an above-the-knee black evening dress with multi-colored Mylar buttons down the front and gold piping around the neckline. Above the curve of the neckline was the top of her firm cleavage, the ridge of her sternum, and the tightly muscled traps of her shoulders. She had on patterned black stockings, and on the ends of those stockings were medium-heeled black pumps. There was a black patent leather belt that was tight enough to showcase her thin waist and the curve of her hips. Her black hair was swept up on one side and held in place by a thin diamond barrette. I thought I could see a bit of the flames from the fireplace reflecting off her bright brown eyes.

'How do I look?' she asked.

Sherron said, 'Hot.'

I said, 'I'll say.'

Sherron ignored that, and I finished the rest of my drink while they kissed. Sherron helped Jackie on with her cashmere coat, smoothed the front of it, and walked us to the door. We said our tearful good-byes and then Jackie and I were alone and out in the hall. We walked to the elevator, called for it, and waited.

'You do look good,' I said.

'So do you,' she said. 'You clean up very nicely.'

'I don't think Sherron likes me too much.'

'She's really nice, Nick. But you can lay on that Peck's Bad Boy act a little thick. And she's probably a little jealous. Wouldn't you be?'

'Yep.'

The elevator arrived and we got into it. I closed the accordion gate and through it watched the marble staircase as it appeared to rise while we descended through its center.

'I used to love these things when I was a kid. The old Dupont Building, where Connecticut and Nineteenth meet at the Circle, had a gated elevator and a uniformed operator to go with it.'

'Me too,' she said. 'I think this elevator was what closed the deal for me on this place.'

'So who am I supposed to be tonight?'

'Anyone you want. Let 'em guess. These company Christmas parties get pretty rowdy, and I figured I could use an escort.'

'Rowdy accountants?'

'Yeah. Once a year they're expected to cut loose.'

'Sounds like my meat,' I said.

'Do me a favor, Nick. Don't be an asshole.'

The party was in the penthouse of a new office building on the east edge of Alexandria and on the river, past National and just past Dangerfield Island. We parked Jackie's Subaru in the garage and, with a couple of foxy receptionists who had arrived at the same time, took the elevator up as far as it would go.

A mustachioed young man tediously took our coats when we stepped off the elevator. I retrieved my cigarettes and switched them to my jacket pocket, and we entered the party room. It was situated on the northeast corner of the building, and two of the walls were thick glass. The north view stretched past the lights of National to the Mall and the major monuments. The east view shot over Goose Island in the Potomac to Bolling Air Force Base and then into Anacostia and P.G. County.

The floor was shiny and veined to approximate black marble. There were several freestanding Corinthian columns scattered about the room that looked to be made of papier-mâché, their shafts painted a poinsettia red. Thick green ribbons were tied and bowed around the columns that I assumed had been rented for the affair. A swing combo situated on a narrow balcony was playing jazzy Christmas standards. The violinist had Stephanne Grapelli's style and tone down perfectly.

The room was already crowded and predominantly suited in black. Many of the men sported red bow ties with their tuxes, and most of the women were also in black, though there were a few seasonal reds and, at a glance, one blonde squeezed into gold lamé. I took Jackie's order and made a beeline for the bar.

The bar was set up in the left rear corner. As I approached it I saw the offerings grouped on the white-clothed table. The bottle with the familiar orange label, the gold lettering THE HEAD OF THE BOURBON FAMILY, and the gold oval-framed granite bust in the center that had a fitting resemblance to both LBJ and Buddy Ebsen was right out front, in all its eighty-six proof Kentucky glory. I stood behind the other kids in line and waited my turn.

'Yes, sir?' asked a built brunette as I stepped up to the table. She had on a tuxedo shirt and a turquoise tie that was close to the color of the lenses in her wicked eyes.

'A vodka tonic, please. And an Old Grand-Dad, rocks.'

She marked me with one long motherly look and poured our drinks. There was a pitcher set next to the bottles that was half filled with one dollar bills, probably her own. Good bartenders always place a tip receptacle on the bar and start it off with their own money. Wish fulfilment. I put two of mine in the pitcher, she thanked me with a wink, and I rejoined Jackie.

Jackie was with a tall man, and they were laughing about something as I handed over her drink. He was close to my age and his face was boyish, but his hair was steel gray. Two pieces of it, like the tines of a grilling fork, had fallen over his forehead, giving him the reckless look of, say, a young millionaire who raced cars.

'Nicky, this is John Wattersly. John, my friend Nick Stefanos.'

We sized each other up and shook hands. 'Good to meet you, Nick,' he said in a smooth baritone.

'Same here.'

'John's a senior,' Jackie offered.

'Really,' I said. 'When do you graduate?'

Wattersly laughed and then showed me a warm smile that had probably opened plenty of doors for him during his climb. He seemed intelligent but not arrogant, and I sort of liked him, but he was certainly turning that smile in Jackie's direction an awful lot.

Jackie said, 'I meant he's a senior manager. He's on his way to partner.'

'I knew that, sweetheart,' I said, and kissed her on the cheek as I squeezed her arm. Mine was now around her shoulder.

The next time Wattersly turned his head, Jackie ground the stiletto heel of her pump into the toe area of my shoe. The pain ricocheted off my Achilles tendon, sped up my calf, and watered my eyes. By the time Wattersly faced me again I had released Jackie and was wiping my face with a handkerchief.

'What do you do, Nick?' he said.

'International finance,' I said.

'Interesting work. Who are you with?'

'Fitzgerald and O'Malley,' I said, digging my grave as I pulled two names out of the air and stared at my shoes. 'Gold bars, bullion, currency exchange.' I winked. 'That sort of thing.'

I gulped half my drink as Wattersly winked back.

The evening continued to degenerate along those lines, but happily I was not alone. These accountants and their dates were certainly not averse to having a good time. Someone pulled the plug on the Christmas combo early on, and a boom box was set up, and everything from Motown to Springsteen to Depeche Mode began to turn the place on. There were also several art director types flitting about who, I was later informed, were members of the firm's in-house advertising department. Their leader was a popinjay who had grown his hair in front of his face precisely so that he could shake it out of that smug face with a casual toss of his head; he was running about the room taking clever Polaroids of the accountants whom he obviously thought he was so far above. After my fourth trip to the bar, I decided that it was a wonderful party and these were all very nice people and I was perhaps the wittiest individual in the room.

My responses to that ice-breaking question 'What do you do?' began to range from the unlikely to the absurd. To Jackie's boss I was a university professor who was teaching a course this semester entitled Existentialism and Top 40. I explained that the course placed a special emphasis on the works of Neil Diamond (just 'Neil!' to his legion of fans) and to his perplexed expression contended that 'I Am . . . I Said' was one of the most deceptively simple yet brilliant songs of the last twenty years. To another executive I made the ridiculous claim to being the sole heir to the WHAM-O fortune. And to shut down a guy who would not stop talking to me about his son's high school football program, I proudly proclaimed, with a subtle flutter of my eyes, that I was studying to be a male nurse, explaining that I had chosen the profession 'for the uniforms.'

Late in the evening I followed the stunning blonde in the gold lamé dress to an area near the glass wall. One of my new accountant buddies had explained, with a remorseful shrug, that she was 'with' one of the senior partners, a fact that may have frightened off most of the martinets in attendance but at this point did not affect me. When she was alone I touched her on the arm and she turned.

'Hi,' I said.

'Hello,' she said evenly, with the weary resistance born in beauties like her. Her push-up bra had set her lightly freckled, perfectly rounded breasts to a point where they touched and hung like trophies on the edge of her low-cut gown. She had a mane of wheat hair and a black mole above her arched lip. In the midsixties I had experienced one of my first erections while admiring such a mole on Anne Francis's lip during an episode of 'Honey West,' though at the time I did not even possess the beneficial knowledge of self-relief.

'I'm not an accountant,' I said, and hit my bourbon. By now I had forgone the ice, which was taking up far too much room in the glass.

'Really,' she declared aridly. 'What are you, then?'

'A mole,' I said, still watching her lip. 'I mean, as in spy. I was sent by an industrial espionage firm to infiltrate this party.'

She caught the reptilian gleam of my eye. 'Don't even think about it,' she said, without the barest trace of levity, 'unless you are a mole who happens to be very, very wealthy.' Then she walked to the glass and turned her back to me, sipping her drink as she took in the view.

I was studying the arrogant little ball of her calf and the manner in which her dress was painted onto her luscious championship ass when Jackie walked over and stood by my side. Thankfully she was smiling.

'What's slithering around in that mind of yours right now?' she asked.

'The truth?' I said.

She nodded. 'Yeah.'

'I was thinking how, right now, I'd like to see her place her palms on that glass and lean over just a bit. How I'd lift up that dress, lift it with my forearms as my hands slid up the back of those tanned thighs. How I'd pull down those sweet panties, put one of my hands on the glass for support, and the other on her fine ass. How I'd enter that moist mound, not too gently mind you, hard enough to see her bite down on her lip and shut her eyes, shut her eyes slowly and peacefully like some Disney deer.' I gulped some bourbon, rocked back on my heels, and exhaled. 'So, in answer to your question, I was just thinking what I'd do with that if I had the chance. What were you thinking?'

'Same thing, brother,' Jackie said with a low, sinister chuckle. 'Different method.'

On the way home Jackie and I stopped at Rio Loco's, a neighborhood Tex-Mex bar at Sixteenth and U and found a couple of stools in the back near the juke. Lou Reed's 'Vicious' was just ending. Our blue-jeaned waitress set down a juice glass that contained two inches of Grand-Dad, and a mug of coffee for Jackie. We tapped receptacles and sipped our respective poisons.

'You mad at me?' I asked.

'Uh-uh. You were a hit tonight. A bunch of my friends asked me about you.'

'Sorry about the kiss. The weird thing was, when Smiley was coming on to you, I was jealous.'

'You're loaded,' she said flatly. 'So don't start analysing things, not tonight.'

'Right.' I winked and had another taste. The juke was now playing 'A Whiter Shade of Pale.'

'There must be something missing in your life,' she said, avoiding my eyes. 'I mean there must be a reason why you drink like you do.'

'Christ, Jackie, not now. There's work time and there's drinking time.' I raised my glass. 'Okay?'

'Yeah. Sorry. But I want to talk to you about something, something really important.'

'Sure,' I said, and put a cigarette in my mouth. Jackie lit a match, and

I pulled her hand in until the flame touched the tobacco. I blew the match out with my exhale. 'Let's talk.'

'Not tonight. It's too important, like I said. I want your head to be clear when we discuss it.'

'When, then?'

'You free for dinner Sunday night?'

'I guess so.'

'Good,' she said. 'I'll pick you up at eight.'

I kissed Jackie good night and climbed into my icy Dart. It started after a few attempts and I pointed it northwest. There wasn't much action on the streets except for other drunks and cops too warm in their cars to bother. I parked in front of Lee's apartment building and listened to 'Cemetry Gates' on the radio until it was finished. Then I ran across the hard frozen ground to her stairwell and rang her buzzer.

After what seemed like a very long while her door opened. She was wearing a brown-and-green flannel shirt and, from what I could tell, little else. She began to shiver as soon as the door was open. I had woken her up and she wasn't smiling. Her very green eyes had picked up the green off the shirt.

'Aren't you going to ask me in?' My tongue was thick and I was leaning on the door frame for support.

'It's late, Nick. I've got a final tomorrow.'

'I'm sorry, Lee.' I smiled hopelessly and felt my upper lip stick clumsily to my front teeth. 'I thought . . .'

'I know what you thought,' she said in a low voice that began to build. 'There's lipstick on your cheek, hard liquor on your breath, it's three o'clock in the morning, and you've got a hard-on. You *thought* you'd slide on in here and relieve yourself, that's what you thought. Well, think about this. You mean something to me, Nick, in a strange way, but the next time you disrespect me like this, it's going to be the last time. Understand?'

Before I could tell her that I certainly did, the door was closing with a thudding finality. I stared at it for a minute and then walked back to my car. I drove around the corner to May's on Wisconsin where my bookie friend Steve Maroulis let me in the bar entrance. We had a nightcap together under the cruel lights of last call. I asked him a couple of questions about local gambling and wrote down the answers so I wouldn't have to ask him again. I think I downed another drink while he closed up and did the paperwork. It wasn't until the next morning, when I awoke fully clothed on a made bed, that I realized I had driven myself home.

5

There was a story that used to be told around town concerning my grandfather and Lou DiGeordano that almost attained the status of local folklore, until the men telling it began to die off and it began to die off with them.

My grandfather, Nicholas ('Big Nick) Stefanos, came to this country from a village in Sparta just after World War I, leaving behind his wife and young son. Like almost three quarters of Sparta's male population in those years, he came to America to make a quick fortune and to escape the horrible rural poverty that resulted from the new government's disorder and indifference after the Greek War of Independence. He had every good intention of returning to Sparta, but as it happened his wife died from tuberculosis and his son was raised by relatives in the village. His son eventually married another young woman in the village and out of that union I was born. My parents sent me to the States at a very early age with the intention of joining me in a year or two, but again, as things happen, they never made it. Consequently I was raised by my grandfather in D.C. Having never known my parents, I can almost truly say that I've never missed them, though I'm sure some eager psychiatrist could bleed me dry with a lifetime of sessions and related explanations as to why I've become this person that I have.

Big Nick spent Prohibition living with relatives and driving a bootlegger's truck in upstate New York. I imagine he was also some sort of a strong-arm man, as he had the bulk, and I've heard several old-timers claim that he was quick with his clubbish hands. He himself told me, without remorse and in fact with a bit of light in his eyes, that he had done some 'bad things' in those years to get by. I know he packed a pistol; an Italian .22 had blown up in his face around that time and given him a lifelong scar on his cheek, which explained his fondness for American firearms, witnessed by the fact that he carried a pearl-handled

.38 Smith & Wesson in his jacket pocket until he died. There is a photograph of him in my possession that says more about those years than he could ever. He is in a dark, wide-lapelled pin-striped suit, and he's wearing a wide-brimmed hat. The hat is pulled down over one eye. There is a young blonde wearing a floral-print dress in the edge of the photograph, obviously an American woman, and she is looking up at him and laughing. It's easy to guess from his cocksure grin why that young man never returned to the village.

But something, some trouble maybe, made Big Nick decide to drift south and end up, with relatives again, in Southeast Washington in the thirties. He had brought some cash with him, and the cash staked him in a vegetable stand in the old Southeast Market. His life here was more austere, though reportedly he was a heavy drinker and enjoyed fairly high-stakes poker and occasionally games involving dice. One night, according to the story, he had a dream of his mother, alarming in itself, since Greeks in general did not believe it was likely to dream about the dead. In the dream she was behind the door of an apartment, and what he talked about with her is relatively unimportant. What he remembered when he woke up is that the number on the apartment door was 807.

The next day Big Nick put twenty bucks on 807 with a young numbers runner by the name of Louis DiGeordano. Little is known of DiGeordano's history before that day except that he was a Sicilian immigrant of my grandfather's generation who up to that point had not experienced the luck of Big Nick. He pushed a fruit-and-candy cart in the streets and lived near Chinatown in a two-room apartment with ten other relatives.

When the number hit, DiGeordano delivered the payoff to my grandfather. The hit was in the neighborhood of forty thousand dollars, a fortune in those days. The legend has it that when DiGeordano gave Big Nick the bankroll, my grandfather peeled off two thousand dollars and handed it to Lou. DiGeordano supposedly dropped to his knees (an embellishment, I think, that has been tacked on to the story over time), but my grandfather pulled him back up. It was a curious act of generosity that my grandfather never explained or claimed to regret.

Life after that took unexpected turns for both of them. My grandfather invested in a couple of downtown buildings and owned and operated a series of modest coffee shops until his death. He never flashed his money around, decreased his card playing over the years, and even quit drinking when I entered the picture. Lou DiGeordano opened his own carryout with the two thousand and began a loan-sharking business and an organized gambling operation that grew into a small, bloodless crime empire in D.C. that lasted well into the sixties. Lou was still alive, but his business had deteriorated and had been run into the ground, as businesses usually are, by his son, a man named Joey.

Now, on this bright, biting Saturday in December, I was driving my Dodge Dart south on Georgia Avenue with the window down, letting in as much cold air as I could stand in a vain attempt to slap away my hangover, and I was on my way to see the DiGeordanos. The cigarette I was smoking tasted like the poison it was, and I pitched it out the window. I tried a breath mint, but that was worse, and it followed the path of the cigarette.

I pulled over and parked on Georgia just past Missouri, in front of an R & B nightclub and across the street from a Chevy dealership and a Chinese restaurant facaded as a pagoda. Next to the nightclub was a pawnshop and next to that was Geordano's Market and Deli. The sign on the window was small, but there was a larger fluorescent sign below it advertising cold beer and wine to go. I walked around a man with mad black eyes who looked seventy but could have been forty. He was wearing a brown wool overcoat that was ripped open beneath both arms. The coat smelled, even with the wind behind us, of body odor and urine. The man said something unintelligible as I passed and entered Geordano's.

A small bell sounded as the door closed behind me. The air was heavy with the tang of garlic and spice. I went by tall shelves stacked with small red-and-blue cans and large gold cans of olive oil. Past the shelves were two coolers stocked with beer, fortified wine and sweet sodas, and past that a row of barrels with clear hinged lids containing various types of olives and spiced peppers. The barrels were lined across a Formica counter on which sat an old register. Beyond the counter was a work area and the entrance to a back room of sorts. In front of the entrance was a chair and next to that a steel prep table on wheels. Dried beans were scattered on the top of the table, and next to the table sat a burlap sack half filled with the beans. An old man was sitting in the chair, and he was looking closely at the beans on the prep table before he pushed small groups of them into his hand and dumped them into another burlap sack. He looked up at me as I approached the counter. Thin pink lips smiled beneath a broad gray mustache.

'Nicky,' he said.

'Mr DiGeordano.'

I walked around the counter before he could stand and shook his hand. His grip was still strong, but the flesh was cool, and the bones below it felt hollow. His aging was not a shock – he was in his mideighties, after all, and I had seen him at my grandfather's funeral – but the frailty that went with it always was. He was wearing a brown flannel shirt buttoned to the neck and over that a full white apron. The apron had yellowed in spots, and there were reddish brown smudges of blood near the hemline where he had wiped his hands. He wore black twill slacks and black oilskin work shoes with white socks, an arrangement fashionable with kids sixty-five years his junior in some of the clubs downtown.

'I wasn't sure if this was your place,' I said. 'The name I mean. When did you drop the *Di*?'

'A couple of years ago,' he said in the high rasp common in Mediterranean males his age. 'Only on the sign out front. No use making it tougher on our customers to remember our name than it already is. We still get some of the old-timers, but mainly what we get is neighborhood people. Beer and cheap wine is our main seller. You can imagine.'

I nodded and then we stared at each other without speaking. His eyes were brown and wet like riverbed stones. His hair was whiter than his mustache, full and combed high and then swept back. Deep ridges ran from the corners of his eyes to the corners of his mouth. The mouth was moving a bit, though he still wasn't talking.

'What are you doing?' I said, glancing at the table.

'Checking the beans for rocks,' he said. 'There's always a rock or two in the bag. You have to go through them by hand. A customer breaks his tooth on a rock, you got a lawsuit, you lose your business.' He shrugged.

'Is Joey in? I'd like to talk to him if he has a minute.'

'Anything I can help you with?'

'Nothing that serious,' I said.

'In the office,' he said, and made a small backward wave with the point of his index finger. Then he yelled for his son.

Joey DiGeordano stepped out momentarily. He was rubbing his hands with a towel, and he looked at me briefly before he looked over to his father. Joey wore a dark suit and a blue textured dress shirt more poly than cotton, with a plain lavender tie that was tacked to the shirt by a pearl button. He was street slender, and his hairline was identical to his father's, and it was pompadoured identically but was black and slicked with some sort of oil-based gel. The smell of a barbershop entered the room with him.

'Yeah, Pop.'

'This is Nick Stefanos.' Joey glanced my way again, this time with more interest. 'Big Nick's grandson.'

'How ya' doin',' Joey said in a tone that was inching its way up the scale toward his old man's.

'Good,' I said. 'You got a couple of minutes?'

'Sure,' he said, and jerked his head just a little. 'Come on back.' I could feel the old man's appraisal as we walked by.

I followed Joey through a long storage room Metro-shelved with dry goods into a wider room that housed a metal desk and a couple of chairs. On the desk was a phone and an empty plastic in-basket and not much else. A calendar that featured a topless blonde holding a crescent wrench hung over the desk. Beyond the desk was a narrow hall containing a small bathroom and beyond that a padlocked door that opened to the alley.

A broad-shouldered lummox stained the bare wall across from the desk. He was also wearing a suit, but the suit did not hit the intended mark. His arms barely reached past his hips, his mouth was open, and his spiky haircut was some suburban hairstylist's idea of new wave. His eyes shifted beneath heavy lids as I entered the room.

Joey motioned me into a chair upholstered in green corduroy. I folded my overcoat on the back of it before I sat. He took his seat at the desk. He removed a pencil from a mug full of them and tapped its eraser on the edge of the metal desk. His olive skin was lightly pocked and his sideburns reached almost to the lobes of his ears. I had seen him in May's quite often, though we had never spoken. Usually he sat with a group of aging, scotch-drinking hipsters whose conversations ran from Vegas to 'broads' to Sinatra and back again, guys who were weirdly nostalgic for a time and a place that they had never known. I placed his age at about forty-eight.

'Who's he?' I said to Joey, jerking my head slightly in the direction of the lummox.

'Bobby Caruso. You want some java?'

'Black,' I said. 'Thanks.'

Joey signaled Caruso, the first time since we entered the room that he had acknowledged his presence. Caruso left but brushed my back with his heavy arm before he did it. I pulled a business card from my inside breast pocket and slid it across the desk until it touched Joey's fingers.

He read it without lifting it off the table and then tapped the eraser on the desk as he looked back my way.

'What can I do for you, Nick?'

'I've been hired by Bill Goodrich,' I said, 'to find his wife.' I let that hang in the air and studied his cool reaction. 'He thought you might be able to point me in the right direction.'

Joey chuckled and shook his head. He made a tent with his hands and didn't say a word, and then Caruso lumbered back into the room and set a small cup of espresso on the edge of the desk nearest my elbow. I nodded by way of thanks, and in response he tried to sneer, showing me some large front teeth that would have been attractive had they belonged to an aquatic rodent. I had a sip of the bitter coffee.

Joey said evenly, 'I don't think I can help you.'

'Bill Goodrich thinks you can.' There was more silence as Joey and I stared at each other meaninglessly and without malice. Finally I said, 'Let's talk about this, Joey. Alone.'

Joey looked over my shoulder and moved only his eyes in the direction of the doorway. I felt the heavy arm bump my back, harder this time, and then heard plodding footsteps fade. Joey used a thin gold lighter to fire up a white-filtered cigarette, then slipped the lighter into his suit pocket.

'Who's the sweetheart?' I said.

'Bobby's a young cousin of mine. I apologize for him. He's very protective of me and my father. Hangs around 'cause he's got visions of getting into "the business." Of course there is no business anymore. But I haven't been able to convince him of that.'

'Keep him away from me,' I said.

'You said you wanted to talk,' said Joey, his dark eyes narrowing.

'Okay.' I sat back. 'Goodrich thinks you were having an affair with his wife. He doesn't seem too stoked about that, to tell you the truth. He just wants to make sure she's all right.'

'What's your angle?'

'No angle. It's a job. Goodrich is paying me to locate her and that's it. It should be very simple if we all cooperate.'

'How did you two hook up?'

'Old friends,' I said.

Joey's eyes lingered on my wrinkled blue oxford and loosened knit tie. 'I don't make you guys as peas in a pod.'

'We were once,' I said, and killed it at that. 'How about you? How did you hook up with him?'

'Your friend's a very ambitious young man,' Joey said. 'He was persistent early on, calling me every day, trying to interest me in locations for carryout shops I was thinking of opening at the time. Finally I let him drive me around to look at some spots. I could see right away he was more interested in my business than in brokering locations. I guess Goodrich bought into all that fiction they print in the newspaper.'

'It's not all fiction.'

'No, but it *is* ancient history. The loan-sharking, the necessary arsons – they might as well have gone down a thousand years ago. We're involved in a little bookmaking here and there, and that's all – college basketball, and so on.'

'So Goodrich was ambitious,' I said, filling in the common blanks. 'You met his wife over dinner, and he says you gave her the eye.'

'Listen,' Joey said. 'I'll speed this up for you.' He flicked an inch of ash to the linoleum floor and leaned forward. 'I not only gave her the eye, my friend, I gave her this.' Joey grabbed his crotch for emphasis and shook its contents. 'All right? I gave it to her all over her beautiful body and anywhere else I damn well pleased. And all the while I had the distinct impression that your young friend was pimping his wife to me for just that purpose.'

I shook a Camel from the deck. Joey leaned over with his gold lighter and set it on fire. I blew some smoke across the room that mingled with his. He slid the lighter back into his pocket.

'How so?' I said.

'Goodrich didn't care about that broad any more than I did, that's how so. I could see she had no class the first night I met her, and class is something I know a thing or two about.'

I looked at the blonde mechanic on the calendar and then back at him. 'A thing or two at the most, maybe.' The shot glanced off him, so I plowed on. 'What was your deal with Goodrich?'

'I put him on the payroll as a real estate adviser. He was paid in cash, always in cash. It's something he asked for, and it's something guys like him can really appreciate. After a while their high salaries just become a blur of numbers. But cash – it's real, you can feel it in your hand, and it's dangerous, you know what I'm saying? Let's face it, there's no reason to be in business for yourself unless you can steal from the IRS. He wanted a piece of it. I gave him what he wanted, and I took what I wanted from his wife.'

The comment lingered in the air like a bad odor. 'Joey,' I said, 'do you know where April Goodrich is?'

Joey DiGeordano barked a short laugh that turned into a cough. When he was finished coughing he wiped his eyes with a handkerchief that he drew from the breast pocket of his suit jacket. Then he studied my eyes and grinned. 'Big private eye,' he said, and shook his head. 'You really don't know a damn thing, do you?'

'Educate me,' I said.

'I don't know where April Goodrich is,' he said. 'But I'll give you ten grand if you find her and bring her to me.'

I considered that after a drag off my cigarette. 'I thought you didn't care about her.'

'I don't. But she's got something of mine.'

'What would that be?' I said.

Joey said, 'Two hundred grand.'

I finished my espresso and had a last pull off my cigarette before crushing it on the floor. I heard Caruso's heavy breathing in the hallway and below that the faint tick of my wristwatch.

'You going to tell me about it?'

'Why not?' he said. 'Everybody in town knows I got took for a ride. I have an apartment I keep downtown. I take my friends, girlfriends there, for parties, whatever. I also keep my bankroll there. Being in the cash business has its disadvantages. One of them is you can't use the banks.'

'April knew about it?'

'Yeah. She was at the apartment on a regular basis for quite a while, and occasionally she needed cash. I didn't have a safe or anything, and I knew how much was there, so I figured it couldn't do any harm to let her in on it.'

'You trusted her?'

'It wasn't so much as trust. She was a hillbilly piece of ass – from southern Maryland, for Christ's sake. I just didn't think she'd pull anything like that.'

'Go on,' I said.

'She had a key to my place. One night—'

'What night was that?'

'Monday, last week. She was supposed to meet me at the apartment. She *was* there – I called her at about six o'clock. But when I got there she was gone. So was the bread.'

'How do you know she took it?'

'I *don't* know,' he said. 'Anything can go down, right? But my money's missing, and she's missing, and that's what I've got.'

I thought things over. Bill Goodrich had said that April had disappeared a week ago Wednesday. The money was stolen on the Monday of that week. That left a day in between.

'Will you help me?' Joey said.

'I work for Goodrich,' I said, rising from my chair as I put on my overcoat. 'But if I find the girl, and she has the money, you'll get it back.'

'Fair enough,' Joey said. 'But understand this. I've got people out looking for her. If they find her before you do, I can't guarantee they're going to be too gentle.'

'People like Caruso?' I said, pointing my chin to the hallway. 'He couldn't find his dick in the shower.'

'Others too. There's a lot of people in this town, Nick, they owe me favors.'

'So long, Joey.'

'Be in touch.'

'So long.'

I turned and headed through the doorway. Caruso was off to the side, his back against the shelving. I don't know why he decided to make a play. Maybe he didn't like the way I talked to his boss, or maybe he just didn't like my looks. It didn't really matter. Guys like him always do the wrong thing, and they always keep doing it; he telegraphed his move by trying to look too casual. But casual hung on Caruso like his tight shiny suit. When I was one step away he jerked his arm up in my direction.

I grabbed the arm with my left hand and twisted it back. Then I boxed his ear with my open right hand and swung the elbow of that arm across his mouth. It sent him into the steel shelving with a force that rocked it back and knocked cans to the floor. I bunched his shirt and got up in his fat, sweaty face. A small amount of blood seeped off his gums and pinkened his beaverlike teeth.

'Now, listen, you fucking Guinea. You touch that arm to me again,' I said, 'and I'll cripple you. Understand?'

'Let him go,' Joey said tiredly from the office to my right.

I looked to my left. The old man was in the doorway that led to the store, slicing me open with his watery brown eyes. I released Caruso's shirt and straightened my overcoat, shifting my shoulders underneath. Caruso exhaled and attempted a vicious stare but didn't say a word. I walked out into the store, sidestepping the old man. The old man followed. Finally I reached the front door.

'I'm sorry, Mr DiGeordano,' I said. 'He had that coming.'

'Not in my place, he didn't.'

'I apologize.'

'You have your grandfather's quick hands,' he said. 'But you don't have his class.' Lou DiGeordano looked me up and down and made sure I saw it.

I pushed on the door and walked to my car, where I slid behind the wheel. I watched my hand shake as I touched the key to the ignition. The car came alive. I swung it out onto Georgia Avenue and ignored an angry salutation of blaring horns.

6

'Say that again?'

Jackie Kahn said, 'You heard me.'

We were seated at a four-top near the kitchen in a restaurant called Giorgaki's on Pennsylvania Avenue in Southeast, a place that was decorated to approximate one of those sparse, white-stuccoed *cafenions* that are all over Greece. On the wall next to our table was a large framed photograph of the windmills of Mykonos. Waiters were hurrying through the outward swinging metal doors, and when they came out from the kitchen the excited shouts of argumentative Greeks came out with them. Jackie dipped her bread in the *tarama* that was dolloped next to the *tzaziki* on the appetizer tray and kept her eyes on mine as she tore a bit off with her teeth.

'I heard you,' I admitted. 'But why me?'

'You've got good genes. And you're . . . reasonably attractive.'

Our African waiter arrived and set down a plate of marinated octopus just as Jackie spoke. He asked, in Greek more fluent and correctly accented than mine, if there would be anything else. I ordered an American beer and a retsina for Jackie. The waiter winked at me before he left. I squeezed some lemon over the octopus and had a taste.

'Knock if off, Jackie,' I said as I swallowed a rubbery cube of octopus.

'There's nothing to knock off, Nick.' Jackie rearranged the silverware around her plate and folded her hands. 'Listen. I'm a person who's generally content. In that respect I'm very lucky. And I'm very comfortable with my sexual proclivity. I have a wonderful career, and I've found an extremely compatible person to share it with. There's only one thing now that I'm missing, and I see no reason why I can't have it.'

'A child.'

'Right.'

'So adopt one,' I said. 'There's laws now that prevent discrimination against gay couples who want to adopt.'

'I'm not interested in getting into some long, protracted process involving miles of red tape, or the expense that goes along with it. And like most people, I prefer to bear a child from my own blood, especially if I'm able.'

The waiter brought our drinks and took our dinner order. Jackie asked for a country salad, and I ordered *souzoukakia,* a meatball dish in a spicy tomato sauce served over rice. He left and I had a pull off my beer, then studied Jackie's face.

'You're serious, aren't you?'

'Never been more serious, Nicky.'

'How do I fit in?' I said. 'So to speak.'

Jackie smirked. 'I thought that part would interest you.'

'Only in the scientific sense.'

'Uh-huh.' She sipped her retsina and set down the glass. 'Actually, the ball is rolling right now. A week from now I'm scheduled for a sonogram. If everything goes according to schedule – that is, if I'm ovulating – we could have intercourse next Sunday night.'

'Intercourse? You make it sound so romantic.'

'I just want to be efficient. It's not that the thought of being with you is so awfully repulsive.'

'Now, stop. You'll make me blush.'

'What do you think?' she asked.

I lit a cigarette and aimed the exhale away from her face. 'Normally, I'd say something wise. But I can see you're not bullshitting me. I can tell you right off the bat that a guy like me has no business being a father.'

'You wouldn't be, not in that way. I've had my lawyer draw up a waiver that would limit any parental rights you might have, even if you were to have a change of heart up the road. Of course I'd never stop you from seeing the child, if that's what you wanted.'

'You've thought of everything.'

'That's right,' she said, and her eyes softened. 'What else?'

'I'll tell you the first thing that came to my mind. Bringing a kid into this world – it's a huge decision, and sometimes it's one based entirely on selfishness. And I've got to admit, you know, as much as I wear my heart on my sleeve, who's to say that the fact that you're gay is not rattling around somewhere in the back of my mind?'

'What bothers you about it?'

'Are a gay couple going to make proper parents? I don't know. I don't know if it does bother me. I'm just being honest with you. I've gotta think about it. All of it.'

'I didn't expect you to decide right here,' she said. 'But don't drag your feet. I've scheduled you for an appointment at the clinic on Wednesday morning. I want you to have a blood test, and I want them to check your sperm count while you're there.'

'Don't trust me, huh?'

'If your sperm count's low, there's no reason to go through with it. As for the blood test, the fact is that I'm monogamous. And you're an active heterosexual. I'm not taking any chances.'

'No chances, huh? Kind of takes the fun out of it.'

'Fun?' Jackie said. 'You'll find a way.'

I dropped Jackie off and drove north on Wisconsin through an alternation of flurries and freezing drizzle. The radio was on, a sports-talk program on WHUR. The caller was saying something derogatory about Larry Bird. He called and said roughly the same thing at about the same time every week. What he really objected to was the fact that Bird was white. But tonight I wasn't listening. I was thinking about Billy Goodrich.

I called him at his house in Scaggsville after my meeting with DiGeordano. There had been a pause on his end when I told him about the money. The pause in itself could have meant a lot of things – shock, fear for his wife, a moment to strategize – and as I was waiting for his response, I realized my mistake. I should have brought the matter up in his presence; there are, after all, more clues in one face than in a hundred telephone conversations. In any case, when I hung up with Billy, he knew more than I did, and I knew nothing.

I found a spot near Lee's apartment in Tenleytown and killed the engine. On the way to her stairwell I hawked the remainder of a mint onto the brown lawn of the property. At Lee's door I straightened my overcoat and knocked twice. I watched my breath hit the metal door until the door swung open.

Lee had on a jade green shirt, buttoned to the top, the one that made her green eyes seem violently alive. The large brown speck in one of those eyes appeared hazel in the yellowish light of the stairwell. Her dark hair was drawn back, but a twist of it had come unbound and had fallen across her forehead and then down the side of her angular face. Her smile caused small lines to flower at the corners of her eyes.

'Hello,' she said.

'Hi.'

'How are you?'

'Sober. Get my flowers?'

'Uh-huh. Not very original. But the note was.'

'You liked it?'

'Yeah,' she said.' I got the part about you being a perfect slob. And the apology. But what are you now, an Indian? I mean you signed the note "Tongue of Snake." What's that got to do with the price of beans?'

'If you'd like' I said, 'I'll just come on in and show you.'

A moment later we were against the wall near the hall closet where, in a mindless rush, I penetrated her with my trousers heaped down around my shoes. Then, carrying her, still inside her, with a Chaplinesque waddle (my pants still binding my ankles) to the living room rocker, I set her down, pulled out, and with my chin scraping the perforated cane seat, her legs veed out over the Brentwood's lacquered arms, I chased the sliding chair across the hardwood floor, as I sunk my face into that slippery thicket of sweet brine, and showed her, with workmanlike pride, just what my tongue had to do with 'the price of beans.' During the first orgasm, her muscular thighs clamped down so tightly on my head that I thought for a moment she had dislodged some vertebrae. Her second spasm, marked by her cool dry lips and a visible shudder of her damp shoulders, was less dramatic. Then we were down on the floor and I was inside her once again, in an undulating crab walk that ended with her head tilted against the base of the sofa and me baying unashamedly, like the dog I was, at the low white ceiling.

Afterward we sat naked on the couch and drank a bottle of Chilean cabernet and listened to the 'Reggae Splashdown' on HFS. We were both fairly quiet that night and both of us wanted it that way. The sex and the wine and our nakedness had thrown a calming blanket over us and the entire room. Somewhere in the evening I told her about Jackie Kahn's proposition.

'What are you going to do?' she asked. I searched for a trace of jealousy in Lee's voice, but there wasn't one. Instead there was interest and the genuine concern that I was not setting myself up for a brass-knuckled punch in the heart.

'She's going through with it,' I said, 'whether I agree to be the one or not. We're friends. I can't turn her down.'

'How does it make you feel, to think you might become a father? Even though, you know, you're not really going to have the responsibility.'

The chugging rhythms of Peter Tosh's 'Legalize It' filled the room. I finished off the goblet of wine and placed it on the glass table in front of the couch. Lee leaned into my shoulder and I put my arm around hers. 'There was a long while, after my marriage flamed out, I resigned myself to the fact that I was never going to have any kids. It's not an easy thing to come to terms with, believe me. Having kids always seemed to me to be the most elemental thing to do. But there's certain people maybe shouldn't have kids, even if they want to. I'm probably one of them.'

'Cut it out,' she said.

'It's not self-pity,' I said. 'What's the old expression? "Kids shouldn't have kids" – Lee, that's all I'm saying. But when Jackie explained the deal, I've got to admit, I got excited. I can be a father, Lee. I *can* be. And I don't have to screw anybody up by doing it.'

'You're just too hard,' Lee said, and kissed me on the mouth. But she knew I was right, and she couldn't look me in the eye.

'I know who I am,' I said. 'That's all.'

The clock on the nightstand read 4:39 when I awoke in Lee's bed. Lee's hip was warm against mine, and her breathing was like a faint wind slipping through the crack of a pane. I watched a tree's shadow shimmer across the bare white wall of her room. The shadow became more detailed as my eyes adjusted to the light. I thought about the weekend and felt my blood jump and knew then that it would be a while before I would return to sleep. I reached for the pack of Camels on the nightstand, found a matchbook, and struck a flame to the tobaccoed end.

The first lungful was toxic with sulfur, but I held it in and tried to watch the smoke of my exhale drift up toward the ceiling. What I saw was a subtle change of the spare light, like the slow movement of deep water on a moonlit night. I studied the lit end of the smoke and made a trail of it with a small circular motion of my hand. Lee woke and got up on one elbow. She put one small hand on my chest and with the other brushed the hair back away from her face.

'What's up, Nicky?' she said.

'Just thinking,' I said. 'The thinking woke me up, and now it's keeping me up.'

'Thinking about what?'

I took a deep drag off the cigarette. 'I had a run-in with this guy yesterday. This guy just happened to be Italian. Anyway, I belted him across the mouth. And after I did that I called him a name.'

'What kind of name?'

'A Guinea. A dago. I don't remember.'

'Go to sleep, Nicky. You didn't mean anything.'

'Something like that always means something.'

'Go to sleep.'

'I got a feeling here,' I said. 'That this whole thing with Billy Goodrich – his wife, the DiGeordanos, all of it – there's something not right about it. Nothing ever good comes from situations like that, Lee. It's going to turn out bad.'

7

Washington, D.C., is laid out in quadrants with the Capitol serving as the point at which they all meet. Numbered streets progress, well, numerically, and run north to south. Lettered streets are arranged alphabetically and run east to west. At the border of each quadrant this numerical progression begins again. Thus it is nearly impossible to get lost in our nation's capital. Unless, of course, one hails from some hotbed of logic like, say, Baltimore.

I had parked my Dodge early Monday morning on Florida Avenue, facing west. Florida Avenue bisects the city at the fall line of the Piedmont Plateau. It is no accident that well-to-do whites live on the more stable high ground of upper Northwest, while moderate to poor blacks reside in North and Southeast; rather it is a geographic divination that seems to evolve in all the major cities of the Northeast. It is also no accident, then, though it can be said to have been mildly prophetic, that Florida Avenue once went by the name of Boundary Street.

I turned the collar of my overcoat up to warm my neck against the stinging wind and walked beside a retaining wall toward Sixteenth. On the wall was spray-painted, in red, STOP THE PHONY U.S. DRUG WAR IN PANAMA. At the corner of Sixteenth and Florida, on the opposite side of the street, was the apartment building gone condo where William Henry had lived and died. I gave it an uncritical eye as I waited for the light to change. The light changed, and I crossed Sixteenth and passed beneath a concrete archway, on which was painted the slogan CHE LIVES!. When I was through the archway, I was in Meridian Hill Park.

Meridian Hill Park could have been the most beautiful park in the city, a cross between a European palazzo and a garden. Neighborhood people in the pre-air-conditioned forties used to sleep here on summer nights and enjoy starlit concerts ranging from classical to swing. The park also had a grand view of downtown, until a high rise erected at Florida and New Hampshire avenues put an end to that. Sometime in the seventies the D.C. government renamed it Malcolm X Park, though since they had no legal right to do so (the Feds owned it), the place is still known officially as Meridian Hill. Most people who follow the teachings of Malcolm X agree that this is for the better, since Meridian Hill Park is now little more than a drug market.

I walked across a balustraded promenade that spanned an empty pool situated at the foot of a graduated series of empty fountains. I passed the large statue of James Buchanan on the east side of the park and climbed a set of concrete steps that led to the mall. On the wall that bordered the steps was painted the names of the members of a local gang called the Crew – Easy E, Duck Derrick, and Million $ Eric.

All of the activity that day was on the terrace at the crest of the park. Some kids were playing an informal soccer game on the grassy mall, where several posted signs forbid such activities. Though the air was quite cold, the game's participants wore light jackets, and a couple of them were in shirtsleeves. The curly-haired forward who was controlling the ball had his shirttail in his mouth as he dribbled upfield.

Everyone else in that part of the park was in the process of either buying or selling drugs. They were walking the perimeter of the mall – nobody was standing still – and there was the occasional brief hand contact as the deals went down. Some of the walkers were obviously cops, with their fatigue jackets and knit caps. Nobody, however, was being busted.

A Latino in a matching jean outfit with black shoes and white socks quickly glanced up as he approached in my path. He mumbled, 'Sense! Sense!' as I shook my head and passed him on my way to the center of the terrace. At the front of the Joan of Arc statue, I stopped and leaned on the concrete wall that overlooked the fountains and the pool.

Some skateboarders with shaved heads were traversing the bowl of the last fountain in the grotto below. A boom box was set next to the bowl, out of which came a cut from local heroes Fugazi. A young man in a sweatsuit stood at the wall to my right, looked at me, and then yelled at the skateboarders, 'I hope you break your muthafuckin' heads.' Then he walked away.

I watched a thin figure emerge at the spot where I had entered the park minutes earlier. The man pointed a one-finger wave in my direction as he crossed the promenade. His hair had grown gray since I had seen him last, but there was still the quickness in his step. Winchester Luzon had kept our appointment.

I first met Winnie Luzon on my premier day as a stock boy at Nutty Nathan's on Connecticut Avenue, in early summer of 1973. I had wandered into the employee lounge at the back of the store, with a dust rag in my hand and a look of stoned innocence across my face. I had just been given my first words of direction from Phil Omajian, a sweet-natured down freak who was the store manager at the time: 'Never walk *into* the stockroom without something in your hands, and never walk *out* of the stockroom without something in your hands.' So I had picked up a rag and, coming down from the joint I had blown on my way to work (I hitched down Connecticut in those days, and invariably my patron driver would produce some weed – even strangers got strangers high in the early seventies), I entered the lounge with every intention of doing nearly nothing until my shift was done.

Luzon was sitting at Omajian's desk when I walked in, licking the seal of a manila envelope. His pink tongue continued to slide along the edge of it as his eyes shifted in my direction. I was wearing a Nutty Nathan's T-shirt that day, the one with the old logo that made Nathan look like, in the words of one outraged customer, 'a goddamned mongoloid.' (I could not have known then that years later, as advertising director for the company, I would design a new caricature of Nathan that was less offensive but equally ridiculous.)

Luzon squinted through the smoke of his filterless cigarette and said, with the accent and brown hairless skin of a Filipino Charles Boyer, 'You work here, kid?'

'Yes,' I said, phrasing it as a question.

Luzon tossed me the envelope, rose from the chair, and produced a five from the pocket of his brocaded slacks, placing the bill in my hand. 'Run the envelope down to the mechanic at the Amoco, a big cat named Spade. Black dude,' he added redundantly. 'On the way back pick me up a Mighty Moe from the Hot Shoppes. Tell Mary at the counter it's for Winnie – she'll toothpick an extra pickle to the top. Use the five and keep the rest for yourself. Hear?'

I nodded and did it. In fact, I delivered that package and picked up his food every day for the remainder of the summer. Though I knew there was something 'wrong' in those envelopes, I was hardly concerned with questions of morality. If it was gambling chits (which I now know it to have been), well, gambling was something that was part of my life with Papou. And if it was drugs, then my opinion was equally neutral. Doing and moving pot was, after all, almost a duty for kids my age in those years. That was, of course, before cocaine crept into town and made the whole party a bloody nightmare.

Winchester Luzon was not the biggest character I met that summer (those honors go to the amazing Johnny McGinnes), and we never became too close. There was the wet-eyed Omajian, who drove me home on those sticky summer nights and waxed with a barbiturate deliberateness about the brevity of life: 'Nicky, does it seem as if it's all moving so quickly?' (For him, it was – he died in 1975 of a massive coronary. The makeup men at Gawler's had, for once, done a fitting job when they froze a boyish smile across his ashen face.) Gary Fisher was the store's audio man, a good salesman who was fond of gadgetry and Columbian and who played Steely Dan's *Pretzel Logic* and a group called If in the sound room all day long. There was my friend Andre Malone, audio enthusiast and stone-free lover, fresh then with the bottomless energy and optimism of youth. There was part-time salesman Lloyd Danker ('Void Wanker,' we called him, to his face), a zombified Jesus freak who was my tormentor. And of course there were the cashiers, Lisa and Lois, two young women whom I was to alternately feel and fuck in various locations of the store over the course of the summer. With all the giggly, pot-induced laughter, the music, the camaraderie of my sagelike new friends, and of course with all that sweet, sweet teenage lust, those dry humps against chipped wallboards in musty stock-rooms, those rushed blue-balled moments at closing time, those achingly pungent smells of cheap musk and thick vaginal heat, it was natural that I couldn't wait to wake up on those hot mornings and head downtown for my next day of work.

Nevertheless, Winnie Luzon was a character. Everything about him, from his tight black poodle curls to his pointed, tin-man nose, to the crease on his slacks, to the toes of his Italian shoes, was sharp. He reminded me at times, especially in profile, as we watched the Watergate hearings that summer on the fifty television sets that lined the wall, smoke dribbling from his thin mouth as he slowly shook his head, of a cardboard devil.

Luzon had been fired late in August that summer, as I prepared for my junior year at a new high school. Omajian had found some clock radios in the Dumpster out behind the store, on a day when Luzon had uncharacteristically offered to empty the trash. Omajian reluctantly let him go, then ate a soper and drank some beers at his desk and brooded about it for the rest of the evening. I had not seen Luzon since, though Johnny McGinnes continued to cop from him on a monthly basis. It was from McGinnes that I had gotten Winnie Luzon's number.

Now Luzon was upon me, with the slight, gassy smile that twisted up on one side of his face. His hair was slick and still high and tight, though any hint of blackness was gone. I figured him at about fifty, but the seventeen years that had passed had turned him into an old man. His face was lined and swollen.

'What's going on, Nick?' he said as I shook his callused hand.

'Nothing much, Winnie. Thanks for coming.'

'Hey, bro', you said nine o'clock at Joanie on the Pony, I'm here.' Luzon pointed at the statue, with its broken lance. Joan of Arc's eyes had been painted red. 'Shame what they did to her, huh? They fucked up this whole park, man.'

'The dealers?'

'No, man, not the dealers. We do business here, we keep it clean. I'm talkin' about the fuckin' trashheads, bro'.'

'You work out of here, Winnie?'

'Yeah,' he said, then reached into his overcoat and drew a trademark white cigarette. Luzon lit it, coughed, then took a second drag. 'I sell herb only, man, dime bags. The *Post* calls this a drug market, but nobody's selling crack, love boat, none of that shit. It's safe here, man, you want herb, you come up into the park, it's like the fuckin' Safeway, Holmes.'

'You sell information too? McGinnes said you knew most of what was going on around town.'

'Maybe for you, Nicky, I give it away. You were a good kid, man, you did me some solids.' Luzon looked me over. 'You put on some weight too. Some meat on those bones.' His forehead wrinkled. 'You wouldn't be no undercover man, would you?'

'I'm in business for myself,' I said. 'And anyway, I wouldn't blindside you, Winnie.'

'Course not. Like I said, you were a good kid.'

'I was sixteen.'

'Sixteen. Shit.' Luzon looked down at the wrinkled hand that held the smoke, then brought it to his mouth, as he stared over the wall at the skateboarders in the fountain below. 'What do you want to know, Nicky?'

'The DiGeordano family.'

'Yeah?'

'What do you know about them? Lately.'

Luzon shrugged. 'There's not much to know, man, not anymore.'

'They a factor?'

'What?'

'Are they important? Are they still players?'

'Small players,' Luzon said. 'Very small. The old man's always had a numbers runner's mentality, never any big-time stakes. When the legal game happened, the business dried up for everybody but the big guys. Yours truly included.'

'I know all about the old man,' I said. 'What about Joey?'

Luzon pursed his thin lips and slowly shook his head. 'He's nothing. Hangs out at May's with all those other ring-a-ding-ding boys and dreams about the fifties. Places a few bets every so often, and sometimes he hits. Mostly track action. Long shots.'

'I heard he got burned pretty bad recently,' I said.

'On the odds?'

'Uh-uh. A woman.'

'Oh, that,' Luzon said, making a small wave with his hand. 'I heard something too.'

'You don't seem too surprised.'

'It's not the first time a woman took DiGeordano to the cleaners. Joey D's been chasin' pussy all his life. Sometimes the pussy bites back.'

'They say it bit back to the tune of two hundred grand.'

Luzon chuckled. 'Then that's some serious shit, Holmes.'

'I'm looking for the woman who did it,' I said.

'I guess Joey is too.'

'That's right.'

'You working for Joey?'

I shook my head. 'The woman's husband.'

'What's her name?'

'April Goodrich.'

Luzon said, 'I'll ask around.'

'One more thing,' I said.

'Talk about it.'

'You remember hearing about that boy got killed across the street, earlier this year? At the Piedmont, in his apartment.'

'White boy?' Luzon said.

'Yeah.'

'Knife job, right?'

'Uh-huh.'

'Heard some talk about it that day. Then the next dude got offed somewhere else, and that took its place in the conversation sweepstakes. You know how it goes around here.'

'What was the word on the boy?'

'You saw the papers, just like me. Nobody knows anything, and if they did, who would they tell? I mean, what for? Just another punk-ass bitch, dead. We got our own problems, real ones, man.' Luzon blew me a kiss and said, 'He a friend of yours, man?'

'That's right,' I said as Luzon's smile turned down. 'And I'd like to know what happened.'

'They say a light-skinned dude—'

'I read that already.'

'Listen, Nicky. The only thing I know, they got the Piedmont locked down tighter than a schoolgirl, man.'

'You've tried to get in, then.'

Luzon looked up, sheepishly. 'I've made some attempts, yes.'

'What's your point?'

'That "light-skinned dude in a blue shirt" routine – it's just smoke, man. That way the public thinks it's just a junkie kill, from the neighborhood. But no junkie got into that building unless he greased somebody's palm or unless that boy let him up. You see what I'm sayin'?'

'Yeah. Thanks, Winnie. See what you can dig up on that too, hear?'

'Sure, Nicky.' Luzon shifted his feet and looked down at his shoes. 'You positive you don't want no smoke?'

I drew a folded twenty from my pocket and my business card and placed them both in his palm. 'Keep the weed,' I said, 'and call me.'

Luzon eyeballed the card, smiled, and shook his head. 'Good to see you again, Nicky. Or is it Nicholas?'

'Nicky,' I said.

Luzon smiled again before he turned and walked smoothly back along the walkway that encircled the grassy mall. I eyed him until he became too small to watch, shoulders up with a white curl of smoke that seemed to circle around his head. If there is one thing I cannot reconcile, one inevitable, it is the slow, sad progression of decay.

William Henry's building stood at the intersection of Sixteenth and Florida and was on the way to my car. I stepped behind the building and had a cigarette while I watched a delivery being made to the truck bay in the alley. An unsmiling man in a blue maintenance uniform checked the delivery in and then pulled the doors closed from the inside when the process was done. There were no outside handles on those steel doors and only one similarly fashioned door on the left side of the building. I crushed the butt under my shoe and walked around to the front.

The Piedmont was gray stone and six stories tall, with swirled detail work above each window. Black wrought-iron balconies had been added to the apartments at the time of their condo conversion, adding to the price tag but adding little in the way of practical use, since the balconies appeared to be only three feet deep. A couple of bicycles were chained to the railings, a few of which were strung with Christmas lights. I moved along the front walk to an open heavy glass door. Inside I encountered a locked set of similar doors and a black telephone on the gray wall. Next to the telephone was a slot for a magnetic card that I presumed would allow tenants to gain entrance. The telephone had no dial or numbers. I picked it up and heard a ring on the other end.

'Yes,' said a large voice.

'Detective Stefanos,' I said. 'I'd like to ask you a couple of questions.'

'Metropolitan Police?'

'That's right,' I lied.

The phone clicked dead, and then a man as large as his voice walked across the marble lobby to the glass doors. This one was a hard two-fifty if he was a pound. He stopped on the other side of the door, folded his thick arms, and looked down into my eyes. The aluminum tag clipped to his shirt pocket read RUDOLPH. On the arm of his shirt, above the bicep, was sewn a red patch with the coat-of-arms logo of the Four-S Security Systems company.

Rudolph raised his eyebrows as I put my business card against the glass and quickly pulled it back. He pointed to the badge on his chest and then made a come-on gesture with his fingers. I put the card back up on the glass along with a ten spot that I produced from my slacks. Rudolph stared at me until I squeezed out another ten and put it behind the first one. He kept staring while he pointed once again to his badge and then at me. When I didn't produce one he walked away. He was still walking as I tapped my fingers on the glass.

Out on the street I buttoned up my black overcoat and found a pay phone on the corner nearest my car. I dropped a quarter getting the number of Four-S, then another dialing that number. After a few minutes I was directed into the office of personnel.

'How may I help you?' said an aging female voice.

'Jim Piedmont,' I said, as I looked at William Henry's building across the way. 'Bartell Investigative.'

'Yes, Jim, what can I do for you?'

'I'm doing an employment check on a James Thomas, just on the essentials. Do you mind?'

'I'll help where I can,' she said coolly.

'I just need to verify his current address. I have him at Fourteen-twelve P Street, in Northwest. Is that correct?'

'Hold on and I'll check,' she said. I listened to the tapping of a computer keyboard while I wondered if there was any such address at Fourteenth and P. The woman got back on the line.

'I have him at Thirteen-forty-three Hamlin Street in North-east.'

'Over in Brookland area, right?'

'That I don't know.'

'Can you tell me, Miss—?'

'Sheridan.'

'Miss Sheridan, can you tell me the circumstances of Mr Thomas's severance with the company?'

'No,' Miss Sheridan said, 'I can't.'

'I understand,' I said. 'One more thing. I recently met one of your employees, a big fellow by the name of Rudolph.'

'Yes?'

'I just wanted to tell you – he's doing one hell of a job.'

'Thank you,' she said.

'Thank *you*,' I said, and hung up the phone.

I ripped a ticket off the Dart's windshield and threw it in the glovebox with all the others. Then I swung a U on Florida and headed across town to the Brookland section of Northeast.

8

James Thomas lived in a pale green two-story house with pine green shutters, on a gently graded piece of Hamlin Street between Thirteenth and Fourteenth in Northeast. The lots were large in this part of town, with wide yards whose once-grand homes were set far back from the kerb.

My grandfather had still owned some Brookland property in the midsixties, when we would drive across town in his black Buick Wildcat once a month on Sunday to collect the rent. Papou's property was a brick warehouse on Ninth Street that faced railroad tracks that later were to parallel those of the Metro. The dark-skinned man we met each month was elderly and bald, except for two neatly trimmed patches of gray above each ear, and he paid my grandfather with a roll of twenties that he had ready as we pulled up to the lot. His name was Jonas Brown, and he ran a clean little auto body shop out of the space, and he called my grandfather 'Mister Nick' and me 'Young Nick.'

After the riots, Papou sold the warehouse to Jonas Brown, and I had since rarely returned to Brookland. I remembered it as being as peaceful as any section of D.C., with its stately Victorians surrounded by huge clusters of azaleas in the spring. In my gauzy childhood visions, middle-class black families walked slowly down city streets, the men wearing striped suits and brown felt hats, the women in brightly colored dresses cinched with white ribbons, and Brookland was always Sunday morning.

So the drive that day down Twelfth Street, the neighborhood's main avenue, saddened me. A painfully thin, coatless woman stood at the corner of Twelfth and Monroe in what looked to be a chiffon Easter dress, her head bowed as she fought to remain upright against the strong, cold wind. At Michigan Liquors a young man in a thick red down coat stood talking into a pay phone, gesturing broadly with his free hand, his beeper clipped to the waistband of his sweatpants, the door open to his window-tinted Chevy Blazer that sat idling near his side. I noticed several other drug cars, Jags and Mercedes with gold wheels and spoilers and gold-framed licence plates, parked in the lot of the Pentecostal Church of Christ. The movie theater was gone, replaced by a chain drugstore. There were hair salons and dry cleaners and delis; outside their doors teenage boys heavily paced the sidewalks. At Lucky's Cocktail Lounge a warping sign depicted a logo of a forked-tongue Satan. Under the Satan a slogan was printed with red bravado: WHERE THE DEVILS PLAY, AND THE LADIES MAY.

I had parked my Dart two doors up from the Thomas residence, in front of a leaning Victorian that was fronted with stone steps leading up to a rotting porch. Two young men sat on those steps and watched me as I walked by. Ice T's 'Drama' was coming out of their box. One of the boys smiled malignantly in my direction as the words 'Fuck the damn police' rapped out of the speakers. All of the house windows were barred on this street, and the deep barks of large-breed dogs were alternately close and distant in the air. I walked on.

On the porch of the Thomas residence I knocked on a heavy oak door. After my second knock there were muted footsteps and the darkening of the peephole centered in the door. Then the release of deadbolts and the metallic slide of a chain. The door opened, and a tiny dark woman in a print housedress stood before me, looking up with quizzical, kindly brown eyes. Her hair was thin and white; her deeply lined features nearly aboriginal.

'Yes?' she said in a manner that wedded curiosity to trepidation.

'Is James Thomas in, ma'am?' I gave her my card along with my least threatening smile. She handed back the card after a brief inspection.

'That would depend on your business with him, Mr . . . ?'

'Stefanos.'

'What is your business with him, Mr Stefanos?' she repeated, with the greatest degree of forced unpleasantness that a woman of her frailty could muster.

'It concerns a case I'm working on,' I said, adding, 'I'm not with the police, ma'am.'

She considered that as the December chill continued to intrude upon her house through the open doorway, along with the rap from the boom box on the porch of the house to her right. Her shoulders finally slumped in visible submission as she motioned me in. I thanked her and followed as she led me into a den furnished with throw rugs and faded overstuffed furniture.

Mrs Thomas had a seat on the couch; I took mine in a cushiony chair.

She folded a slim pair of hands in her lap after pulling the hem of her housedress down to her knees, then looked into my eyes. I don't know what she was looking for, or if the look was meant to intimidate me. It did. There were seventy years of hard life in those eyes, seventy years of churchgoing faith and hope in answer to deterioration and dis- appointment and death. The wooden clock on the fireplace mantelpiece ticked loudly in the otherwise silent room.

'I'd like to see your son,' I said. 'If he has a few minutes.'

'Does this concern the young man's death at the Piedmont?'

'Yes, it does.'

Mrs Thomas sighed slightly but retained her posture. 'The District police have gone over the case with us very thoroughly, Mr Stefanos. I believe they were satisfied that my son had nothing to do with that boy's death.'

'I'm not working with the police,' I said. 'So I'm not privy to what was said between them and your son. But I do have an interest in seeing that the murderer is found. William Henry was my friend, Mrs Thomas.'

Her hands moved together in a washing motion in her lap, as if it were her hands that were doing the deliberating. She looked away briefly and up the stairs, where I assumed James Thomas was residing. Then she looked back at me, her features softened but unresigned.

'When one person dies, his suffering is over, Mr Stefanos. Those left behind often bear the weight of the hardship. I didn't know that Henry boy. The papers and the police said he was an innocent young man. Anyway, he's in the hands of the Lord now – neither you nor I can help him. But my son has been hurt enough. He's lost his job and he's lost all his self-respect. He sits in that room upstairs all day, and he doesn't come out, except for dinner and to walk down to the liquor store.' Mrs Thomas looked down at her lap. 'I couldn't help that young man. It wasn't my job to help that young man. But it *is* my job to protect my son. And I don't want him hurting anymore.'

'I didn't come here to hurt your son. I came here for a few simple answers. You believe in justice in heaven. I respect that belief, if a person can be satisfied with it. I can't. So I have to believe in justice on earth.' I rose slowly, walked in her direction, and stood over her. 'Let me have a couple of minutes with your son, and I'll be on my way.'

'I'll ask if he'd like to see you,' she said.

I stepped aside to let her pass and watched her ascend the stairs. She held the wooden banister as she did it. Soon after that was the opening of a door and her voice, then a voice intermingled with hers that was low but gentle. In a few minutes she moved back down the stairs and stood before me.

'James will see you,' she said. 'Please don't stay too long.' It was less a command than it was a solicitous request. I nodded and moved away.

At the top of the stairs was a half-shut beveled door stained dark cherry. Above the door a transom window was cracked open just a bit; a barely visible fall of smoke flowed out from the crack. I knocked on the door and pushed as I did it. Then I stepped into the room.

It was a bedroom, probably the same bedroom James Thomas had been raised in. The oak furniture was scratched; its copper hardware pulls had long ago tarnished. An ashtray spilling over with butts was on the dresser and another ashtray just like it was on the nightstand next to the unmade bed. By the nightstand was a wastebasket lined with a brown paper bag. The neck of a fifth leaned out from the top of the bag. James Thomas sat in a small wooden chair facing the window, a smoking Kool Long in his hand. There was a third ashtray balanced on one very thick thigh.

He stared out the window, took a long drag off his smoke, and said, 'Come on in.'

'Thanks.' I removed my overcoat and folded it over my forearm.

'You don't need to be doin' that,' Thomas said. 'You won't be stayin' long. I said I'd see you because my mom asked me to. But now that I have, I want it short.'

'That's the way I want it too, James.' I had a seat on the edge of his bed. Closer to him now, I caught the stale stench of yesterday's cheap liquor seeping through his pores.

James Thomas turned his head in my direction. He was wearing a brown-and-orange-plaid flannel shirt that gapped at the buttons, stretched as it was from his barrel chest. His head was round, dark, and cubbish. He had not shaved in days, though his facial hair was faint and spotty. His eyes were watery and rimmed red, the full-blown badge of a burned-down drunk.

'Let's get to it,' he said.

'All right.' I handed him my card. He stubbed the butt in the aluminum ashtray that rested on his thigh, then blew smoke at the card while he looked it over. Thomas folded the card and slipped it into his breast pocket.

'So?' he said.

'I'm working on the William Henry case,' I said.

'Workin' for who?'

'William Henry.'

'Guess you don't plan on bein' paid,' he said.

'*Somebody* got paid,' I said.

Thomas shook a Kool from the deck on the windowsill and put the filtered end to his mouth. I produced a matchbook from my trouser pocket and tore one off the pack. He watched my eyes as I fired him up.

'Say what you got to say,' he said.

'Okay,' I said. 'I'll keep it simple. I've looked over the file on the William Henry case. I've talked to some people in the neighborhood, and I've been to the Piedmont. Nobody gets into that building unless they live there or unless they've been invited. I even tried to buy my way in. It didn't happen. Not with the guy they've got on duty now.'

Thomas's jaw tightened. 'I told you to say what the fuck you got to say. Now, do it.'

I stood and walked to the window. Out on the street was an old Bonneville, a white BMW with dark tinted glass, and a new maroon Buick Regal. I pointed to the Regal, looked at Thomas, and said, 'That you?'

'Yeah.'

'Not a tough call. I don't make you for a dealer – that eliminates the drug car. And that shit-wagon Pontiac isn't your style. No, a guy from your generation – what are you, early forties? – a guy your age who just came into some money would probably head right down to the car dealership, first thing, and pick out a brand new Buick. Cash on the line. Am I right?'

'Got me all figured out,' Thomas said. 'Nigger with some cash money, burnin' a hole in his motherfuckin' pocket. "Nigger rich." That what you and your boys say when you're sittin' around drinkin' brew, tryin' to feel all superior about yourselves?'

'That *is* your car, isn't it, James?'

'It's mine.' Thomas hung his head and glanced down at the floor. His anger was there, but it was weak, with only the residual strength of a cut nerve. He sighed. 'Company gave me what they call a "golden handshake." They let me go after the Henry case made the TV news. Gave me a bunch of money to go real quiet. So that's what I did. And now I got a new ride, all paid up.' He looked at it through the window and lowered his eyes once again.

'How much did they give you, James? Twelve thousand? Fifteen? Because that's about what that car costs.'

'Ain't none of your damn business what they gave me.'

'It's easy enough to find out.'

'Then go on and do it,' he said angrily. I put on my overcoat and shifted my shoulders beneath it to let it fall. When I walked to the door I turned to face him.

'I am going to do it, James. But it won't change what we both know, right now. You didn't kill that boy. You didn't even have an idea that he was going to be hurt, or what it was all about. But you let somebody in the Piedmont that night for money, and because of it my friend got greased.' I fastened the buttons of my overcoat. 'You see the body, James? He was stabbed with a serrated knife. Stabbed in the chest and in the stomach and in the legs. Through the hand when he was holding it up, to protect his face. And in the mouth, James. Twenty times.' I shoved a hand in my pocket. 'You know the details – you've been swimming in a bottle of Early Times ever since. When you're ready to crawl out, you reach for my card and you call me, hear?'

Thomas cocked his head and squinted. 'What do you want?' he said slowly.

'Same thing as you,' I said. 'To sleep at night. And no bad dreams.'

We looked each other over for a while. Then I closed the door behind me and descended the stairs. Mrs Thomas was standing at the bottom, her hand resting on the scrolled end of the banister.

'I'll see myself out,' I said with a nod. 'I'm sorry for disturbing your day.'

'Did you get the information you wanted?'

'Yes.'

'My son didn't kill that boy,' she offered with commitment. 'I don't think he had one thing to do with it.'

'I don't think so either. But he can point me in the direction of the ones who did.' She walked me to the door, and once more we stood together. I asked her before leaving, Do you know a Jonas Brown? He had an auto body shop down by the tracks.'

Mrs Thomas's facial features converged into an amalgamation of smile lines and rounded cheeks. 'Yes, I knew Mr Brown quite well. He was in the congregation. He's been gone ten years. Now he's resting with the Lord.'

'Good-bye, Mrs Thomas.'

'Good-bye.'

Out on Hamlin, I put the key to the lock of my sedan. The boys on the steps next door were gone, though somewhere close a drum machine ticked out from a boom box. I looked up and caught a glimpse of James Thomas.

It was the last I saw of him. He was framed behind the window of his bedroom in the second story of the house, expressionless as he watched me climb into the driver's side of my Dart. I lit a cigarette and stared at the growing end of ash, thinking of how things burn and fade, before I drove away.

9

The Health Pro Center was a bunkerlike structure that end-capped a ubiquitous strip shopping center in the South Gaithersburg area of Montgomery County. I had driven out Rockville Pike early Wednesday morning with a quarter-inch of frost on my windshield, an ice sheet that had only begun to dissipate as my car neared the outer loop of the Beltway.

Rockville Pike is a track of fluorescence and concrete and traffic signals, five miles of heaven for the nouveaux riches who live to shop. To be fair to Maryland, all metropolitan areas seem to breed such cultureless outlying strips. The state of Virginia, in fact, has its own Rockville Pike. On that side of the river they call it Tysons Corner.

The sky was lightening as the hour neared seven. My Dart chugged north against the traffic that was already beginning to build. Sometime after the Pike changed over to its interstate moniker, 355, I hung a left onto Shady Grove Road and followed that for another mile until I reached my destination. I pulled in, killed the engine, and walked across the lot to the doors of the bunker.

The glass doors were locked. I pushed a yellow button to the right of the doors and watched the barely lit lobby for some signs of life. After a few minutes of shuffling about in the cold air that by now had triggered an ache in my temples, a large man in a white smock waved from inside and strode toward me.

He unlocked the doors, and I stepped inside. The man was wearing jeans beneath his smock, the sleeves of which were rolled up to the elbow to reveal thick, hairy forearms. With his lumberjack–meets–Gomer Pyle appearance (his smile matched that rube character's jaw-jutting grin), it was difficult to tell if he was on the medical or the custodial staff. I asked him for a cup of coffee.

'No coffee,' he said, shaking his head slowly as he maintained that silly smirk. 'It hinders the sample.'

'Oh.'

'Walk this way, please.'

I immediately thought of the old gag, of course, but walking behind him in an elephantine manner would have been pointless, since there was no one around to serve as an audience, and at any rate it was way too early for that type of nonsense. I followed him down a corridor and asked, to his back, 'Why did the appointment have to be at seven in the morning?'

'Policy,' he said, stopping at an unmarked door, the smile fading for the first time. 'We determined that most men find the procedure socially embarrassing. So we do it early in the morning, before anyone's around. As a matter of course.'

He opened the door to a nondescript room that had a desk and a chair and a small Formica counter and cabinet arrangement. Beneath one of the cabinets hung a roll of paper towels. There were no prints on the white walls, and both the blinds and curtains were drawn, giving the whole deal the foreboding look of one of those emergency room side offices where doctors tell you, with studied evenness and with theatrically lowered eyes, that your loved one 'didn't make it.'

I followed the man into the room as he walked me over to the counter, where he pointed to (but did not touch) a capped plastic bottle sitting atop a magazine. A piece of tape with N. STEFANOS written across it was affixed to the jar.

'Just leave the bottle on the counter when you're done, and you can leave. There's paper towels if you need to clean up.' His hick smile was beginning to appear once again.

'Are there any directions?' I said. 'I mean, you're just assuming that I've done this before.'

His smile was gone now. 'Ninety-nine percent of adult men masturbate, Mr Stefanos. And the other one percent,' he said solemnly, 'are liars.' He walked to the door and kept his eyes on me as he closed it behind him. I'm not certain, but before he closed it, I believe he winked.

The first thing I did was check the lock. Then I walked over to the counter, dropped my trousers, and flung my tie back behind my shoulders. I unscrewed the lid on the jar, moved it to the side, and picked up the magazine. The title of it was *Girls Who Crave Huge Ones*, leading me to believe that if this was not one of the classier clinics in the area, it certainly had some very bizarre smart alecks working in the acquisitions department.

Between the ethnic young ladies in the front of the mag and the little scenario I was now developing in my mind (in which a checkout girl from my local market named Theresa lured me into the stockroom so that we could 'log in' a shipment of olive oil), it wasn't long before my compass had begun to point north. But, flipping through the pages of *Girls Who Crave Huge Ones*, trying (rather feverishly now) to find that one perfect photograph that would send me flailing away into bug-eyed nirvana, I came upon (I mean, stumbled upon) a rather odd pictorial.

It was a series of Polaroid photographs of a certain aging rock-and-roll singer, a man who had cut a classic single in the fifties about the relationship between a backwoods young man and his guitar. Strangely enough, that single was never a number one record – it took a novelty hit, years later, called 'My Wing-Dang-Doodle,' to propel that singer to the top of the charts. And now, under the border-to-border headline of HIS WING-DANG-DOODLE, were several photographs of the totally naked singer, his arm around various young, equally naked women (their eyes masked in black to 'protect their identities'), a lizardly lascivious smile on his aging face.

And what of his 'Wang-Dang-Doodle'? Well, for one thing, it appeared to be longer and thicker than my own forearm. And the result was that this strange pictorial spread that had both grabbed my rapt attention and taken the bark out of my angry dog only delayed my mission at the clinic, so that it wasn't until fifteen minutes and several stop-and-go fantasies later (not to mention two more waddles across the room to check on that lock), that I tossed the paper towel in the wastebasket, cavalierly zipped up my fly, and walked with as much dignity as I could muster out to the lobby, where I signed out in a lined logbook.

'Everything go all right?' asked Gomer, who was now behind the desk.'

'Like the Fourth of July,' I said. 'Do you mind if I smoke?'

The white-smocked man lowered his reddening face and pretended to go over some paperwork. He was slowly shaking his head as I walked out the door.

My next stop was at the private office of another doctor, just a few miles away from the Health Pro Clinic, in a low-rise medical building south on the Pike. After filling out a new-patient form on a clipboard, on which I left both the insurance section and the emergency contact sections blank, I settled in among the mostly geriatric crowd in the white lobby and picked up a magazine.

I don't quite know how long I sat waiting, but I managed to finish a fairly long magazine article in *Washingtonian*, written by a friend of mine from college named Marcel DuChamp. DuChamp had been a copywriter around town for years until he decided to be a man and put his name (well, not exactly *his* name – he was called Mark Glick when I knew him) and reputation on the byline. Copywriters, of course, have as much in common with writers as bowlers do to athletes, but at least M. DuChamp was making a go of it. The last time I saw him he claimed, with just a trace of bitterness, that at a party one could always tell the writers from the copywriters. The writers drink straight liquor and situate their frumpy selves in front of their host's bookshelves, while the copywriters stand together in a well-dressed circle with their well-dressed wives and tell 'off-color' jokes. The wives of the writers, Marcel said, stand alone and stare with envy at the wives of the copywriters.

By the time I had finished Marcel's article, a somewhat severe middle-aged woman had emerged from a mysterious door and called my name. I followed her back into a hall, past a large scale and a wall-mounted Dictaphone, and into an office.

The office contained a table padded in maroon Leatherette that was half-covered with a strip of industrial paper. There was a folding chair next to the table, and several cabinets with thin drawers that I immediately knew contained all varieties of needles and clamps and other instruments that inflicted pain in the name of health care.

'Take your shirt off and have a seat on the end of the table, Mr Stefanos,' the nurse said. 'Dr Burn will be in shortly.' She exited the room.

I undid the buttons on my shirt and made myself comfortable on the edge of the Leatherette table. The paper crinkled beneath me as I sat. As I waited, I mulled over how many children had been scared witless in anticipation of a visit with a man named Dr Burn, and wondered why he, like my imaginative copywriter friend, didn't change his name to something less ominous.

But it wasn't long until the good doctor arrived, closing the door softly behind him. He was tall and lean, with the genetically regal gray temples of the profession and the glow of a man whose bronze hands were wrapped around a nine iron more often than they were around a stethoscope.

'Good morning,' he said, looking over my blank chart.

'Dr Burn,' I said.

'What brings you in today?' he said.

'Just a blood test,' he said.

'Getting married, are you?'

'Nope.'

'Roll up your sleeve and make a fist,' he said. I made a tight fist for the second time that day.

Dr Burn hadn't looked me in the eye yet, and he didn't now, as he crossed in front of me and opened one of the thin metal drawers. He pulled a syringe out of its wrapping and wet some cotton in alcohol, then stood in front of me and dabbed the alcohol at the vein that was visible at the base of my bicep.

I looked away and felt a sharp sting, then I felt nothing. I said, 'You get it, Doc?'

'No, I didn't, as a matter of fact,' he said tiredly. 'Your vein's a little tough. Do you drink very often, Mr Stefanos?'

'Only on special occasions,' I said.

'Right,' he said; then I felt the sting again and turned to watch the burgundy black liquid fill the tube. Dr Burn capped it off and handed me the plastic cylinder. I felt the sickening but reaffirming warmth of my blood thorugh the plastic. 'Hold this while I wash up.' He returned after washing and took the sample from my hand. 'What's the sample for?'

'I'm going to be a father,' I offered, in response to his coercive gaze. 'The mother wanted me checked out before we went through with the process.'

'The process?'

'I'm a surrogate,' I said, the words clipped with clinical sterility.

'That's very intelligent of her,' he said, and added, before I could take it the wrong way, 'and noble of you.' He tapped his pencil on the clipboard. 'But I'm curious. Why come to me for a simple blood test? Any of the in-and-out clinics would have done.'

'That's true. In fact, I just came from a clinic where I could have had it done. But I wanted to speak to you. I was referred by William Goodrich.'

'I saw that on your chart,' he said. 'Which is stranger still. William Goodrich isn't a patient of mine. His wife April is.'

'I said I was referred by Billy Goodrich, Dr Burn. I didn't say it was a medical matter.' I buttoned my shirt and looked up at the doctor. 'April Goodrich is missing. Her husband hired me to find her.'

I handed the doctor one of my cards. He cleared his throat as he looked it over, then handed the card back to me.

'I'm afraid I can't discuss my patients with anyone without their consent. That is something that I think you can understand.'

'Of course. But I'm not here to ask you if you know her whereabouts. I wouldn't ask you,' I lied, 'to compromise your professional relationship with your patient.'

Dr Burn had a seat on the folding chair and crossed one long leg over the other. He removed his reading glasses and placed them on the counter to his left. 'Then what is this about? Is April in any danger?'

'I don't know. She may have just walked away and made a clean break from her marriage. Even if that's the case, I still intend to find her. It's what I was hired for. But if something's happened to her, it would help to know of any medical difficulties she may have. It could increase her chances.'

'You mean, if she's been kidnapped.'

'That's right.'

'I would need to check this out with the police first, before I spoke to you. I assume they know.'

'They have a record of her disappearance,' I said.

Dr Burn said, 'I'll call you.'

The phone rang shortly after I arrived at my apartment.

'I spoke to the police,' Dr Burn said.

'Well?'

'Your story checks out.'

'So? Is there anything I need to know on the medical end about April?'

'She's a healthy young woman,' he said carefully, 'as long as she watches herself.'

'What's wrong with her, Doc?'

Dr Burn chuckled without joy. 'She's got a very minor problem, one that you would benefit from greatly,' he said. 'She's allergic to booze.'

'No shit.'

'Precisely.'

'So April Goodrich can't take a drink.'

'Not exactly,' he said. 'April is both corn- and grape-sensitive. Most liquor is out, of course, and it goes without saying that wine is too. The majority of rum sold in this country is shipped in hogshead barrels, blended with grape brandy before bottling. So that's out too. But rum bottled in Jamaica is a different story.'

'You lost me.'

'April can drink liquor that's free of corn or grape, and drink it she does, Mr Stefanos – to excess. She's damn near what we used to call a Jamaican rummy.'

'And if she drinks something else?'

'She knows not to. She'd get violently ill.'

'Anything else?'

'Nothing on the medical end, as you say. Nothing else particularly unusual.'

'What about on the personal end?'

'It's none of my business, of course' he said. 'But I'll tell you this: on more than one examination, I noticed various . . . markings about her wrists. Sometimes similar markings were around her ankles.'

'What kind of markings?'

'Burns of a sort. Hemp or wire.'

'You think she was tied up?'

'The markings would seem to indicate some sort of bondage, yes.'

'April ever mention it? Complain about it?'

'No.'

'Consenting adults, Doc. It's not my thing, but it's not illegal.'

'Maybe not. But I met her husband once on a consultation, when they were considering having a child. Let's just say that I don't think April left home involuntarily. He seems to have had a proclivity for sudden anger, an anger perhaps that could have manifested itself in violence. Does that paint any type of picture for you?'

'It's vivid enough.'

'Good luck, then,' he said abruptly. 'And good luck with fatherhood too. Your blood specimen was fine, by the way. Though you ought to take it easy on the sauce, as a general matter of health.'

'It's under control,' I said.

'I don't think so,' he said.

'Thanks for the advice, Doc, and thanks for the information. You've been a big help.'

10

Thursday's *Post* was light on news but heavy with inserts. I read it that morning as I sat on my convertible couch, a mug of coffee resting on the couch's arm. My cat sat next to me, her thin body barely touching mine, licking her paws with deliberate, efficient zeal. Occasionally I reached over and scratched around the scarred socket that had once housed her right eye.

The headline of the Metro section screamed that the homicide numbers had exceeded the previous year's, with three weeks to spare before New Years Day. Arsons and gay bashings were on the increase as well. Several related articles described the 'faces behind the victims' of the street crimes that were now spreading 'west of Rock Creek Park,' a D.C. code phrase for whites. This from a newspaper that routinely buried the violent deaths of its black readership in the back of the section.

After my second cup of coffee I laid Dream Syndicate's *Medicine Show* on the turntable, cranked up the volume, and cleared the rocker out from the center of my bedroom. I jumped rope for the duration of the album's first side; for the B-side I did abs and several sets of push-ups. Then I showered, shaved, dressed, and had another cup of java and a cigarette. The cat slid out the door with me as I left the apartment. I tapped her head slightly before she scampered away into the depths of the backyard.

The platform of the Takoma Metro was empty at midmorning. I caught a Red Line car and grabbed an early copy of *City Paper* that had been left beneath my seat. By the time I had finished the weekly's arts reviews, I was ready to transfer to the Orange Line at Metro Center. Six stops east I exited at Eastern Market and headed down Eighth to the Spot.

Darnell was standing by the door, waiting as I arrived, his hands deep in the pockets of his brown car coat. Next to Darnell was the tiny man-child Ramon, smiling his gold-toothed smile. Ramon had on a pair of Acme boots and wore a cheap cowboy hat with a red feather in the brim. Though there weren't many Western types left in D.C. (the garb was still mildly popular with Latins), there had been a short craze of it in the gay community centered around the 1980 release of *Urban Cowboy*. At that time it was nearly impossible to walk around the P Street area without witnessing a sea of cowboy hats. My friend Johnny McGinnes, never accused of being too sensitive, had dubbed the headwear 'homo helmets.'

'Gentlemen,' I said as I pulled the keys from my pockets and put the correct one to the lock.

'Same shit,' Darnell said. 'Different day.'

The lunch hour was over, and pensive drinking had begun. A fiddle screeched, and Dwight Yoakam sang, 'It won't hurt when I fall from this barstool . . .' Happy stared straight ahead, his hand gripping a rocks glass filled with Mattingly and Moore. At the sports corner of the bar, Buddy and Bubba were splitting a pitcher, while a pompadoured guy from Bladensburg named Richard blew smoke in Buddy's tight-jawed face and loudly insisted, 'I'll bet you a goddamned C-note, goddamn it, that Tampa Bay did too make it to the fuckin' play-offs!' Melvin Jeffers's eyes were closed as he sat alone at the other end of the bar, mouthing the words along with Dwight Yoakam. I sipped a ginger ale and chewed ice from the glass.

Dan Boyle entered the Spot at three o'clock, had a seat at the bar, and exhaled slowly. His eyes, like a bashful old hound dog's, slid up the call rack to the Jackie D. I put a mug of draught in front of him and poured two fingers of the mash into a shot glass, placing the glass on a damp Bushmill's coaster. Boyle shut his eyes and drained the shot, then chased it with some beer.

'How's it goin' Boyle?'

'*Bad Day at Black Rock.*'

'Ernest Borgnine,' I said. 'And Lee Marvin.'

'I'm not kidding, man. Been over at Edgewood Terrace all day, in Northeast. Twelve-year-old kid got blown away over a pair of Nikes. Shotgun load to the chest. You could drive a truck through the fuckin' hole. And the look on the kid's face by the time we got to him – twelve years old. I seen a lot of death, man. I seen too much death.' Boyle rubbed his face with one large hand while I free-poured another shot. This one he sipped.

'You got a kid about twelve, don't you, Boyle?'

'A girl,' he said. 'It never gets any better, to see a kid get it, no matter who it is.'

'Even when it's just a spade, right?'

Boyle had some more whiskey and some beer behind that, then focused his pale eyes on mine. 'Don't be so fuckin' self-righteous, hombre.' He was right, and I let him give it to me. I looked down at the bar until his voice softened. 'Anything happening on the Henry deal?'

'Something will shake out.'

'You let me know when it does,' he said.

'Bet on it, Boyle. I will.'

An hour later only Happy remained at the bar. A Chesterfield burned down in his right hand as he slept. For a while I watched it burn, then lost interest. Shirley Horn was smoothly pouring from the house speakers. Drinking music. I began to eyeball the Grand-Dad on the call rack and was contemplating a short one when the phone rang. I stubbed out my own smoke and picked up the receiver.

'The Spot.'

'Nicky, that you?'

'Billy?'

'Yeah.'

'It's hard to make you out, man.'

'I'm on the car phone, on Two-ninety-five.'

'What's up?'

'What's up with you? Anything on April?'

'Nothing,' I admitted, then waited for his reaction. Hearing only static, I continued. 'I was thinking of heading down to southern Maryland on Saturday. Talk to her family, see if she's been through.'

'Want some company?'

'I'm a big boy.'

'Sure you are,' he said. 'A big city boy – you'll be a fish on dry dock in that part of the country.' Billy paused. 'Me and April spent a lot of time together down there, Nick. And I've got a key to the trailer on her property. We can stay there tonight.'

I thought about that. 'I've got to make arrangements to have Mai take my shifts tomorrow. And I've got to go home, to feed the cat.'

'Fuck the cat,' Billy said with annoyance. 'Listen, I'll pick you up in an hour, hear? I've got another sales call, then I'll swing by. We can go by my house first – there's something I want you to hear.'

'I need warm clothes.'

'You can wear some of mine.'

'The ones with guys playing polo on them?'

'Turn 'em inside out, wise guy.'

'All right, Billy. See you then,' I said just before the click.

I glanced over at Happy to make sure there was still some paper left on his smoke. I dialed the number of my landlord and let it ring several times. No answer. Then I dialed Jackie's work number and made it through an army of secretaries before I got her on the line.

'What's going on, Nick?'

'Just checking in,' I said. 'Trying to picture you right now. Got your wing tips up on the desk, leaning back in your chair?'

'Yeah, it's just a white-collar picnic around here. Come on, Nicky, I'm really busy. What's up?'

'I got a clean bill of health, Jackie. So I just wanted you to know that I haven't forgotten our date Sunday night.'

'Somehow I didn't think you would,' she said.

'What time?'

'Make it seven,' she said.

'Okay. And Jackie – wear something provocative.' I heard her groan. 'Anything you want me to wear?' I added cheerfully.

'Not particularly,' she said. 'But there is something I don't want you to wear.'

'What would that be?'

'That silly little grin,' she said, 'that you're wearing on your face right now.'

'Right,' I said. 'Seven it is.'

I hung up the receiver, walked over to Happy, dislodged the butt from his callused hand, and crushed it in the ashtray. It woke him up, or at least a half of him. One of his eyes opened and he looked into mine and mumbled something brusquely, something I couldn't make out.

'What?' I said.

'Gimme a fuckin' manhattan,' he said. 'That's what.'

Billy Goodrich was the picture of Young Turk affluence, D.C. style. In the driver's seat of his white Maxima, with his somber, subtly plaided Britches suit, suspenders, thinly striped shirt with spread collar, maroon-and-gold retro tie, and forty-dollar haircut, he oozed mindless ambition. Billy threw a glance in the direction of the passenger seat, where I was tapping the side of my index finger against the window.

'April called,' he said, 'and left a message on my machine.'

'When?'

'Today. I called home for my messages and there it was.'

I spread my hands. 'Well?'

Billy said, 'You'll hear it. We're almost there.'

We had turned off 29 onto 214, a winding, gently rising road between the towns of Scaggsville and Highland. Only twenty minutes north of the District line over the Patuxent and into Howard County, the area was a mix of farmland broken by the creeping beginnings of development. Livestock dotted the landscape patched with last week's snowstorm as the sun burned down in the west. I lowered the passenger visor and sat back.

About a mile past a small shopping center that housed a pizza parlor and video rental store, Billy hung a right onto a gravely two-lane road. He eased into a circular driveway and cut the engine. The sun had dropped now, leaving his house, a long rambler of brick and stone, in shadow.

'Nice,' I said.

'I stole it,' Billy said. 'Come on.'

We walked to his door, behind which we heard three deep barks and then some impatient crying from what sounded to be a large breed of dog. Billy turned the locks and a brown-eyed shepherd-Lab mix with a yellow coat appeared, her tail wagging slowly. She licked Billy's glove and smelled mine, and we entered the house.

I followed Billy through a marbled foyer and past a living room elegantly but rather self-consciously appointed in Louis Quatorze furniture. The dog walked clumsily beside me, bumping my leg and looking up at me as she did it. We reached a kitchen done in white custom cabinetry with white appliances and a white Corian countertop ending in the shape of a modified mushroom cap.

'Take your coat off and have a seat,' Billy said. 'Want a beer?'

'Sure.'

Billy pulled on the weighted door of the build-in refrigerator and withdrew a bottle of Sam Adams. He removed the cap with an opener and handed me the bottle. I had a pull of the cool, sweet lager and then another.

Billy said, 'Listen.' He went to a small oak table with scrolled feet, on which rested an answering machine, telephone, large notepad, and a Ball jar of pencils and pens. He pushed the bar on the answering machine.

A female voice began to speak on the tape. It was a calm voice, the words spoken plainly and without anxiety, with the upward inflection at the end of each sentence that is the vocal trademark of the mid-Atlantic South.

'Hello, Bill . . . It's me, baby. You got my note I guess . . . I guess the note kinda said it all. But I wanted to tell you, 'cause I figure you'd want to know . . . I figured you'd want to know that I'm all right, Bill. I went to see Tommy one last time and then I left, and now I'm . . . away. But I wanted you to know that I'm okay. Take care of Maybelle, baby, that's all I'm going to ask . . . I'm not scared, Bill . . . Take care.'

Billy stopped the tape and hit the rewind. I stared at him as I listened to the whir of the machine.

'That her?' I said.

'Yeah.'

'She sound all right?'

'She sounded real calm, buddy. Real calm.'

'Who's Maybelle?'

Billy chin-nodded the Lab and said, 'Her dog.'

'And Tommy?'

'An old friend. An old boyfriend, I should say. In southern Maryland.'

'Then we're headed in the right direction.'

'I'd say so,' he said unemotionally.

'You gonna play this for the cops?'

'Should I?'

'Don't erase it,' I said. 'But I don't think you need to bring them in again, not yet.'

Billy nodded. 'Relax while I get some things together. I'll be out in a few minutes.'

When he was gone I walked to the kitchen's bay window and looked out into the dusk that was rapidly turning to darkness. Maybelle stayed with me and smelled the leg of my jeans. 'That's my cat you're smelling, girl.' I scratched behind her ears and rubbed the bridge of her snout. She licked my hand furiously, cementing our friendship.

Walking to the phone, I dialed my landlord. Still no answer. I finished my beer and tossed the bottle into a wastebasket that I found under the white porcelain sink. I drew another Sam Adams from the Sub-Zero and moved a chair to the bay window, where I drank it facing out into the night. Maybelle lay at my feet, breathing slowly.

Fifteen minutes later Billy emerged from the shadows of the hall and dropped a duffel bag at my feet. 'Road trip,' he said, smiling. 'Like the old days, Greek.'

'Right.' I found a black cotton turtleneck and navy shaker-knit sweater in the bag and put them on. Billy handed me a blue Hollofil jacket. I zipped that up over the sweater and transferred my smokes from my overcoat to the jacket pocket. I patted the pocket. 'What about Maybelle?'

'My neighbors can walk her tomorrow.'

'Let's bring her.'

'She'll be a pain in the ass.'

'She's April's. Let's bring her.'

The mutt's tail was already wagging. Billy shrugged and the dog woofed and trotted to the front door of the house. We followed and Billy locked the door behind him. Out in the driveway we walked to the car, where Maybelle waited patiently for Billy to release the front seat of the Maxima. Maybelle leaped into the backseat as I entered the passenger side.

'Thirsty?' Billy asked as he ignitioned the car.

'I could stand it.'

'We'll stop in the old neighborhood on the way out,' he said, a trace of boyish mischief peeking through his smile. 'For a short one.'

Billy tapped on the brights as we pulled out onto the gravely road. In the vanity mirror of the visor I saw Maybelle staring out into the blackness. Her breath formed crystal gray spiders on the tinted glass.

11

At 29 we stopped at a deli for a six of Bud cans and drank two of those on our way into Silver Spring. Billy talked about the soft real estate market the whole way in, shaking his head solemnly between swigs of beer. He was wearing jeans and oilskin Timberland boots and a logoed, royal blue jacket over a heavy wool shirt. We kept the radio off, the low, steady hum of the engine the only sound around our silences.

Billy parked in Wheaton and cut the engine in front of Captain Wright's, near the intersection of Georgia and University. Captain Wright's had stood stubbornly at that corner through twenty years of modernization, and though it was in the geographical domain of the now-closed Northwood High, it had always been the hangout for students and 'alumni' of Blair. Blair boys liked to think that their Territorial Wrights (as they called them) had evolved from the fact that the place was just too tough for Northwood boys, but in truth many of the bars in that part of the county, from Silver Spring to Aspen Hill, were roughly alike. It was a headbanger's bar, with the stale, vinegary smell of cheap liquor oiled into every wooden crack. A suburban boy on his way to a rotten liver could maybe get laid there, and if not, he could always skin his knuckles. The sign outside read CAPTAIN WRIGHT'S, but every teenager who gunned his glass-pack Firebird or muscle car Malibu up Georgia and University in the seventies had called this place, with some misplaced degree of affection, 'Captain Fights.'

I patted Maybelle on the head and cracked a window for her before we headed into Wright's. Over the door a plastic marquee announced that the Jailbaiter Boyz (from Frederick, no doubt, in that all the boogie/glam-metal outfits from that part of the state substituted their *s*'s with *z*'s) were the headliners that evening. We pushed on a thick door and left fresh air behind for stale as we entered.

The Jailbaiter Boyz, pale and strangers to exercise, were in midset, pounding out their deafening rendition of 'Sweet Home Alabama.' A confederate flag hung over the empty dance floor, surrounded by unaligned four-tops filled with flanneled and T-shirted young men drinking long-necked Buds and Lights. Few heads were moving to the music. We caught the perfunctory hard stares from the most insecure members of each group as we passed and made our way through the maze of tables to the dart room.

In the dart room several groups were in play. Some of the male players had their sleeves rolled up past their biceps and all had Marlboro hardpacks in their breast pockets. I recognized one woman as a high school acquaintance, her features heavy now and swollen from drink. She had been part of a group of wild ones who rode around in a lavender Gremlin on weekends, a car that Blair's males had collectively dubbed the Meatwagon. I had made out with her one night in someone's dark basement while Billy had had his way with one of her friends in the side room. I nodded to her, but she didn't know me, and I walked on.

In the back room Billy and I stepped up and leaned on the bar. A wiry ex-wrestler from Blair named Jimmy Flynn was tending, where he had been since graduation. Flynn had always managed to make weight and go to the mat in the one-twenty-nine class; there wasn't much more of him now. He nodded and said, 'I see you two jokers are still hanging out together.'

Billy said, 'And you're still pushing beer.'

'Yeah.'

'Give us two Buds, then.'

'I'll have a bourbon with mine, Jimmy,' I said.

'What'll it be?'

'Grand-Dad, if you've got it.'

Flynn pointed to the unlit call rack. 'Jack and Beam is what it is.'

'The Jim Beam will do it,' I said.

Billy put money on the bar and walked back toward the dart room, where I saw him move toward a woman in a half-length black leather coat. Her hair was as black as the coat, and she wore blue jeans and a loose purple sweater that didn't work at hiding her lush shape, if that was what she was after. She smiled at something Billy said, and he leaned into her slightly and returned one of his patented pretty-boy grins. I looked around the bar.

I knew one guy standing up, an alcoholic named Denneman who was memorable for having thrown up whiskey one morning in junior high first period industrial arts, thrown it up with stunning ferocity on the varnished oak of the center drafting table. His young porcine features had mutated into an obese mask of pink splotches and scars. Someone bumped my back – on purpose, I supposed – and I didn't bother to find out why. Instead I searched for a friendly face.

There was one – a guy I knew who had worked for years at the local Shell, sitting at a deuce away from the crowd with his girl, a plump young woman in a waitress uniform of white oxford shirt and black skirt. I grabbed my beer and whiskey off the bar and moved across the room to join them.

Thankfully, the guy's name was stitched across his shirt. 'Hey, John,' I said, shaking his hand.

'Nick, right?' He smiled crookedly but with warmth as I nodded. 'Have a seat, man. This is my girlfriend, Toni.'

Toni looked a little looped but still conscious and I shook her clammy hand as I sat. I was relieved to find that John was as genuinely nice as I remembered him, and the conversation stayed dead set on what type of Chrysler product I was driving now. But John had to go and screw things up by excusing himself to play a game of darts, leaving me to sit with Toni, who was becoming alarmingly more drunk with each rum and pineapple she was firing down.

Toni excused herself and stepped up to the bar. I waved my arm to get Billy's attention, but he was deep in conversation with the woman in black leather. And John, a lit cigarette drooping out the corner of his mouth, was playing his darts.

Toni returned with a bar tray, on which were set two rum drinks and another round for me. She served the drinks, left the tray on the sticky wood table, and slid the bourbon and beer in front of my forearms.

'Drink up,' she said. 'I can tell you like it.'

I shrugged and had a pull off the fresh beer. The Jailbaiter Boyz were playing at Guns N' Roses cover amid some competing activity in the main room, most likely a spiritless fight.

'So, Toni. Where do you work?'

Toni made me pay for that innocent question by launching into a tirade against the management of the Brave Bull, a steak house around the corner on the mistakenly named Grandview Avenue. Then she got right up in my face (hers was now ghoulishly contorted) with graphically venomous descriptions of her unfortunate coworkers, and it became apparent that she hated all of them, save the Greek chef she called Uncle Baba, who was the 'undisputed master' at carving 'fuckin' sides o' beef' and 'fuckin' cuts o' veal,' a point that she argued with the vehemence of a litigator at the Nuremburg Trials.

'If you hate the place so much,' I said tiredly behind a slug of Beam, 'why don't you leave?'

''Cause I can't get a good job,' she said indignantly, looking around carefully (as if there would be an African-American face within miles of Captain Wright's), ''cause the colored women get all the good jobs.'

'Where'd you get that idea?' I said, realizing as I did that I had made a huge mistake.

'Where? Where? I'll tell you where. I know it's true 'cause my ex-old man used to work for Montgomery County Social Services. That's how I fuckin' know.'

For some reason I said, 'Your ex-old man? Bullshit.' And then I watched her fat little face turn red.

Seeing the hopelessness of the hole I had admittedly dug and then leaped into, I began to look around the bar for help. Toni wouldn't let it die, though, and she reached her flabby right arm across the table (her tricep was shimmying flatulently like one of Uncle Baba's cuts o' meat) and began to sock me on the shoulder with progressively harder punches, yelling, between each slug, 'Huh? Huh?'

I realized then that she actually wanted to fight, and for a brief moment I indeed considered what a kick it would be to see her rubbery face cave in as I smacked her across the barroom, but John was a truly good guy, and then there was the tiny obstacle of the six-and-a-half-foot bouncer of indeterminate lineage in the black Harley T-shirt who was now eyeing me out the corner of his narrowed eyes. I finished my shot, then my beer, and set the bottle on the table.

'Have a nice night,' I said, and went to recover Billy.

I pulled him away from his friend and gave him a nudge for the front door. Somebody at one of the tables near the dance floor yelled something at Billy, but when we glanced in that direction no one was looking our way. The Jailbaiter Boyz were destroying Free's 'Fire and Water' as we headed out the door and into the cool, fresh air.

Billy was laughing as we climbed into the Maxima. Maybelle's tail thumped the backseat. 'You saved me, man.'

'I saved myself,' I said. 'Who was the lady?'

'No lady.' Billy shook his head as he started the engine and pushed a button for the heat. 'I met her in here one night, about a year before I met April. Took her over to my car in front of Wheaton Guns, that night, and fucked her right in the parking lot. She made me pull out before I came – she didn't want to get pregnant "again,", she said. Man, I shot off all over her leather jacket, the same motherfucker she was wearing tonight. She got some hankies out of the glove box, real calm, and wiped all that jism off, like it was nothing. And we just walked back into Cap'n Fights and had a couple more beers.'

'You're a hopeless romantic, you know it?'

Billy chuckled. 'She called me a couple of times after that. Described on the phone how she wanted to do all this funky shit to me – leather and shit – shit I'm just not into, man. So I didn't hook up. I never saw her again, until tonight. But I gotta love that jacket.'

'A sensitive guy, Billy. To the end.'

'That's me, Greek.' He smiled. 'How about another beer?'

'Okay.'

'We're on a roll tonight, aren't we?' Billy handed me a beer and opened one for himself.

'Yeah, Billy. I believe we are.'

I found WMUC on Billy's radio. They were just crashing into the intro to the Replacements' 'Seen Your Video.' I clock-wised the volume as we pulled out of the lot and headed south on University, toward the entry ramp to 495.

12

The Maxima cut a swift southeast arc on the inner loop of the Beltway. We followed and then passed taillights of various geometric mutations, using the leftmost lane for the pass and then returning to the center. Billy seemed to be holding his booze fairly well, though the fact that he was driving did not seem to influence his rate of drinking. He was on a tear, and I was right there with him.

We exited at Route 5 and headed south, stopping at the first bar we saw, a strip joint named the Fourway at a traffic crossroads in Clinton, to cop a six of long-necks. I waited in the car and kept an eye on the movement behind the fogged car windows in the lot. Billy emerged from the bar, the thump of bass briefly chasing him until the door behind him swung closed, and hustled to the car. We popped the caps on two of the beers, swung back out onto the highway, and once again drove south.

The road went to four lanes with a wide, bare median, the terrain hilly at first and then flattened out. In the southeastern sky the bright yellow moon was full and large. We passed pickup cap depots and parts yards and outdoor ornamental pottery shops, broken by the odd stretches of undeveloped land. Ten miles of that, and the low lights of Waldorf appeared ahead.

Charles County's Waldorf stood where Route 5 met 301. It had once been a gambling mecca for Washingtonians who had a taste for the slots, but that had ended by law sometime early in the sixties. Scattered remnants of Little Vegas remained – the Wigwam 'casino' had been converted for a while into a bakery, and now the peaked structure was nothing but an empty glass tepee – but Waldorf had been reborn initially as a five-mile stretch of car dealerships, Taco Bells, and strip shopping centers whose tenants consisted primarily of liquor stores, electronics franchises, low-end clothiers, knockoff booteries, and convenience markets. Now the area had entered another phase, as its predestined growth pushed it into the league of Washington Suburb. A mall at the south end of town, anchored by two mildly upscale retailers, had opened to much fanfare, bringing with it the legitimisation of a ten-plex cinema and a new Holiday Inn.

But all the swirling logos and white-handled shopping bags could not mask the fact that Waldorf was still Waldorf – the memory of the abandoned 301 Drive-In still loomed like a decaying gray ghost over the highway, and it still took fifteen minutes to get an ice-cream cone from the geriatric hair-netted help at Bob-Lu's Diner. Then there was Reb's Fireplace (the sign had two silhouetted swingers dancing the night away over the tag line LET'S PARTY TONIGHT!), aptly named since it had become a raging inferno one night three years earlier and had remained undemolished, a charred shell and unforgivable eyesore to the occupants of the Volvos who cruised by nightly on their commute home to the planned 'city' of Saint Charles.

Billy pulled the car into the next lot down from Reb's, where a nightclub called the Blue Diamond stood windowless and alone. The lot was filled with Ford and Chevy pickups, late-model American sedans, and Mustangs and Firebirds. We parked next to a black El Camino that had a blue tarp in the bed covering varying lengths of PVC pipe.

'What's going on?'

'One of April's haunts,' Billy said. 'She used to stop here on the trip home, and usually on the way back. Maybe someone's seen her.'

I patted the dog, who had instinctively lain down when Billy cut the engine. We locked up and walked across the lot. A couple of young men exited the club as we approached. They didn't look at us, and they didn't hold the door. The Top 40 rock coming from inside faded and then blared out as I pulled the door open once again.

The Blue Diamond had two circular bars on either side of the room and a large dance floor in the middle, with a live band playing on a barely elevated stage in front of it. The band was finishing up their set with 'Glory Days,' the vocals buried somewhere in the heavily synthes-ized mix. A sea of acid-washed jeans, high-tops, and ruffled shirts moved on the dance floor. A glitzy banner behind the band announced that they were FRIDAY'S CHILD.

Two mustachioed bouncers, both twig-legged but heavy in the chest, checked our IDs. We moved to the bar and ordered a couple of domestics. I paid the tab and added a healthy tip, and the neckless bartender took both without a nod. Billy and I turned and leaned our backs against the bar.

No one spoke to us while we drank or even gave us a hard stare. Finally I turned to Billy. 'Come here often?'

'I like it like cancer.'

'We're way too old for this shit. Nobody even wants to kick our asses.'

'I know,' he said. 'Let me ask around, then we'll split.'

'That's my job.'

'And you can do it. But I'll do it here. I know some of these guys.'

'Go ahead.'

I grabbed my beer off the bar and walked into the men's room. After I drained I washed up in a dirty sink and ran a wet paper towel across my face. When I walked out Billy was on the other side of the room talking to the barkeep. He was putting something back into his wallet while he talked. He nodded and headed back in my direction. I finished my beer and placed it on the Formica-topped bar as he arrived.

'Let's go,' he said.

'Any luck?'

Billy shook his head quickly. 'These brain-deads don't know a fuckin' thing.'

We moved across the empty dance floor to the entranceway. I noticed the blue vein of determination on Billy's temple, and I knew he was going to crack on the doorman, knew it like I knew the sun was going to rise, knew it from all the teenage years we had spent together in bars more dangerous than this. When we reached the door, Billy turned to the larger of the two bouncers and smiled.

'Thanks,' he said. 'We had a great time. And oh yeah' – Billy whacked his own forehead thoughtfully – 'I meant to tell you when we walked in. I really like those jeans you're wearing tonight.'

'Yeah?' the doorman said with hesitance.

'Yeah,' Billy said, the smile turning down on his face. 'My sister's got a pair just like 'em.'

The doorman sighed and said, 'You guys have a nice evening,' holding the door open for us as we walked out. I zipped up my jacket as we moved across the lot.

'What the hell you do that for?' I said.

'It's his job to take shit.'

'You always had to do that, Billy. You always were a mean drunk.'

'Drunk?' Billy said, showing me his young-boy grin. 'Man, I'm not even halfway there.'

We climbed into the car, and Billy started it up while I fixed him a beer. Maybelle's nose touched the back of my neck. Billy caught rubber and tilted back his bottle as he pulled back out onto 301.

Waldorf ended abruptly, and then the highway was the same as it had been before – flat road and forest with the occasional strip shops, failed antique stores, and billboards. Billy kept the needle at seventy, and ten minutes later we hit La Plata, much like Waldorf only less. Past La Plata were last-chance liquor stores and low-rise motels with Plymouth Dusters and Dodge Chargers and Chevy half-tons parked in their gravel lots. Billy aimed the Maxima for a red-and-blue neon sign touting on/off sale as we both drained the last of our beers.

'You go in,' Billy said, cutting the engine. 'I'll pitch the empties in that can.' He nodded to a rusted oil barrel open on one end that stood near the bar entrance.

We were parked in front of a wide, noncurtained plate-glass window. The bar – it had no name – was cinder block painted white. Through the window I could see a small group of men in their thirties and forties shooting pool. 'I'll be right back.'

I left the car, walked to a glass door, pulled it open, and entered. It was only ten o'clock, but the place was lit up like last call. I guessed they didn't go much for atmosphere – a look around the place con-firmed it. There were three scarred pool tables standing on the industrial-tiled floor, with some metal folding chairs scattered around the tables. A jukebox was against the left wall, though it wasn't lit and there was no music playing. A narrow wooden bar stood against the back wall, also unlit, with a small selection of low-call liquor racked behind it.

There were two games being shot, and the entire patronage of the bar was grouped around the games. The men wore designer jeans circa 1978 and sweatshirts with the sleeves pushed back to reveal uniformly pale and hairy forearms. The few women in the joint, teased hair and also in jeans, sat in the folding chairs drinking beer and smoking cigarettes, the ashes of which they flicked to the floor. The men's cigarettes were balanced on the edges of the pool tables, lit end out.

I moved to the bar and on the way got a chin nod from one of the players, a nod that I returned. The woman behind the bar was blonde and maybe fifty, with a raspberry birthmark on her right cheek.

'What can I get you?' she said in a businesslike but upbeat way.

'Two sixes of Bud bottles to go,' I said, 'and a pint of Old Grand-Dad. Thanks.'

'Don't have the Grand-Dad. Something else?'

'A pint of Beam, then.'

'The Black or White?'

'Make it the White.'

She wrapped the bourbon and handed me the bag. 'Let me go in the back and get you the beer.' She winked. 'Rather not pull it from here, have to restock the cooler later.'

She left the bar and entered a walk-in to the left of it. I turned, rested my back on the bar, and looked out the plate-glass window onto 301. Billy was standing in the gravel next to the Maxima, looking down at the rush of his own steaming urine as he peed toward the window. His hair was unmoussed now, full and ruffled as I remembered it from his youth, and his mouth was slightly open, with that dumb look of stoned concentration he had perpetually worn as a teenager. I felt a sudden sting of guilt and looked away. I drew a cigarette from my jacket and lit it, keeping the hot smoke in and giving it a long exhale. Someone tapped my shoulder.

One of the pool players stood next to me. He had long black hair thinning on the top, and he was skinny and nearing forty. His small potbelly barely hung over the waistband of his Sergio Valente jeans.

'That your friend out there?' he said in a direct but not unfriendly way, pointing out the front window.

'Yeah,' I admitted.

'I'd appreciate it,' he said, giving a quick nod to a woman in one of the folding chairs, 'if next time he wouldn't be so quick to show off in front of my wife.'

'I'll tell him,' I said.

He nodded and smiled. 'You take care, buddy.'

'You too.'

I paid and thanked the woman behind the bar, put the bourbon in the larger sack, and moved toward the door. On the way out I smiled apologetically at the man's wife and got a smile back. Out in the lot I took a last drag, tossed the butt, put the beers in the backseat, transferred the pint to my jacket pocket, and patted the dog on the head. Two of the beers came out of the bag before I settled in.

Billy grabbed one, popped it, and tapped my bottle with his. He drank deeply and turned the bottle to admire the label. 'That's what I'm talkin' about.'

'You ready? Or you going to do a beer commercial.'

'No, I'm ready. But I really had to let one fly.'

'I noticed. So did all those folks inside.'

'You talkin' about those rednecks?' Billy said, pointing in the window. '*Fuck* them.'

We continued south. The road ahead was free of commercial activity and hilly once again as we neared the Potomac. I lodged my beer between my thighs and withdrew the pint of Beam from my jacket. I twisted the cap, broke the seal, and handed the bottle to Billy. He had his and then passed me the bottle as he chased it with some beer.

'That's good,' he said, wiping his mouth with his shirt-sleeve. 'Been a long time since I took whiskey from a bottle.'

'Listen, Billy . . .'

'What?'

'I was looking at you, back there, pissin' on the highway. I saw you for a second, like it was you, man, fifteen years ago.'

'Yeah?' Billy looked at me briefly with a blank smile and returned his gaze to the road.

'I'm trying to apologize,' I said. 'That's what I'm trying to do. I've been kind of ice cold, man, since you walked into the Spot. I expected things to be like they were with us, when we were kids – like *you* were. You understand?'

'You're drunk, Greek,' Billy said, turning his face in my direction again. Half of his was lit green from the dashboard lights. 'You *are* drunk, aren't you?' He smiled. 'Or are you trippin'?'

'I guess I'm just drunk.' I had a slow pull of bourbon, then beer. 'Not trippin', though. Last time I did that I was with you. Right before you went away to school. Remember?'

Billy reached for the bottle. I put it in his hand. 'That time in the park, right?'

I nodded, thinking back. The blurred dark limbs of trees rushed by against the night as I stared through the passenger window and recounted that night for Billy.

On a late August afternoon, at the tail end of the summer of 1976, Billy and I had eaten a couple of hits of blotter that I had copped through the back door of Nutty Nathan's from Johnny McGinnes. We smoked a joint on the way down to Candy Cane City and once there began a round of pickup ball with a group of Northwest boys we had come to know. For the first hour we were on our game, but that ended when the acid began to seep in, and after a while our laughter caused us to drop out. I went home and took a shower, sneaking around my grandfather, unable to look him in the eye. Then Billy came by and picked me up in his Camaro.

That night had started like any other – we had no clue at first as to where we were headed, only that we were headed out. Neither of us talked about the buzz – that would have been uncool – but when Billy asked me to drive I knew he was tripping as hard as I was; he had never let me drive his car, even on his most twisted nights.

307

Billy was wearing straight-leg Levi's that night, rolled up once at the cuff, and one of those glitter-boy rayon shirts, from a store named Solar Plexus, in Silver Spring. The red lid of a Marlboro box peeked out over the top of the shirt pocket. On his feet were the denim stacks that he had bought at Daily Planet, a pair of shoes that he knew I had always wanted to own.

For some reason we ended up on Beach Drive in Rock Creek Park. I had begun to hallucinate mildly, but it was under control, and my driving up to that point had been okay. But then Billy popped *Eat a Peach* into the eight-track, and he turned up the volume, and when 'Blue Sky' came on, and Dickey Betts moved into his monster guitar solo, I lost my shit. It was at that point that I was convinced that the car was going to lift up and fly right off the parkway.

I pulled over at a picnic area, Billy laughing over the sound of the tape, and he walked me down to a patch of dark, gravelly beach at the creek. I lay down by the creek and stared at the top branches of the oaks that lined the east side and listened to the rush of the brown water over the rocks and the loopy liquid guitar that was still flowing through my head. Then Billy took my shoes off and put his – the denim stacks I had coveted throughout our friendship – on my feet. And he talked to me for at least two hours. By then the branches had melted into the flannel gray of the sky, and there was a small throb in my stomach, and I had begun to come down.

'That was a night,' Billy said when I was finished. 'After that we went down to some hippie bar, right next to the Brickskeller at Twenty-second and P, second floor, got sober on alcohol. Some band was playing, some cat blazing on lap steel, right?'

I nodded. 'Danny Gatton.'

'How do you remember all that shit?'

'The funny thing is, I almost forgot. And the thing is, the thing you did for me that night, *those* kind of things are the only things worth remembering. Am I making any sense?'

'Yeah, pardner, you're making sense. Hang on.' Billy eased off the gas and swung the Maxima into the turn lane. He pulled left across the highway onto Route 257. We passed a gas station and liquor store, then drove southeast, into a shroud of darkness.

13

We followed 257 for a quarter-mile, blowing by a hardware-and-bait shop lit only by a John Deere sign in the window. Then Billy abruptly veered left off the interstate, onto a roughly paved, unlit road that swept up into a grove of high shrub and pine, then opened to acres of flat field.

'Where we goin'? I thought April's property was off Two-fifty-seven.'

'It is. Mount Victoria road parallels Two-fifty-seven. We'll come back out onto it at Tompkinsville.' Billy winked. 'Watch this, Greek,' he said. Then he cut the headlights of the Maxima.

For a couple of seconds Billy and I were green, and everything outside the car was black. I grabbed the handle of the door and gripped it until the road ahead began to appear, slowly, in a bluish light. The moon was bright and almost directly overhead.

'You sure you want to do this, man?'

'Like we used to do, on that stretch of Oregon Avenue, down in the park.'

'We knew that road.'

'I know this one,' Billy said. 'Roll your window down, man, it's not too cold. Enjoy it.'

I did, as Billy maxxed out the heater fan, then rolled his own window down. Maybelle came forward and laid her head partly on my arm, partly on the door, leaving her face out, letting the wind blow back her ears. She closed her eyes.

The sound of the heater meshed with the wind. I had a slug of bourbon and passed it to Billy. Through the glass of Billy's roof the moon shimmered above as if it were submerged in water. We passed a small gas station with an old Sunoco sign lit and suspended from two chains at the corner of a two-lane intersection, then moved on. No headlights approached from ahead or from behind.

Low trees began to appear on either side of the road, and the road grew darker. Billy saw something just ahead of his path, or maybe he didn't, and he laughed piercingly and swerved, and we drove onto a shoulder of loose gravel. There was a sharp, screaming metallic scrape. Maybelle yelped, and there were sparks, and I drew back my face just as something shaved it like a quick, cold razor. I turned and looked through the rear window, and saw a roadside mailbox uprooted and tumbling back onto the shoulder in the fading rouge glow of our brake lights. I checked Maybelle and she was all right, though now she was lying belly-flat on the backseat, her head resting firmly between her two front paws.

Billy's laughter was softly manic. I cackled with him and rubbed my right cheek, feeling raw skin but no blood. Then we were in a forest of pine, and there was almost total blackness, except for the light through the space between the tree line above, a light that snaked parallel with the road. Billy's laughter ebbed and he shifted his sight from the road to the tree line and back again, navigating the course while negotiating the serpentine curves. At the bottom of a steep incline the road seemed to end in a finality of shadow, but Billy turned the wheel sharp right just as we seemed on the edge of the chasm, and then we were suddenly out of the trees and on the flat blue road again, the vast, open, moonlit fields on either side.

After another mile Billy tapped on the headlights, and we merged back onto 257, turning left. I cracked two more beers, handed one to Billy, and lit a cigarette for myself. We passed a Methodist church and several bungalows with screened porches set back from the highway, Pontiacs and Buicks parked in the yards. A couple of markets that sold gas and liquor and lottery tickets slid by. Both the markets and the houses were closed and unlit.

Two miles later Billy turned right at 254 and accelerated down a straight stretch of highway toward the lights of Cobb Island. He slowed as we neared the water and drove by two crab houses and bars on opposite sides of the road. The bar on the right had lit Christmas lights strung around its low-rise white facade, with lights that ran along the dock as well, out into the channel beyond a gas pump and boat ramp. The road rose as we crossed a bridge with cement rails that arced over the channel and connected the mainland to the island. When we rolled onto the island, Billy pulled the car into a lot past an IGF grocery store and killed the engine in front of a small bar called the Pony Point.

'A nightcap?' Billy said.

'How's my face?'

Billy grabbed my chin and turned my head into the light. 'You'll make it.'

'Let's go.'

We chugged the rest of our beers and put the empties in the backseat, where Maybelle now slept. Out in the lot I tripped stepping up over a concrete divider and felt Billy grab my jacket and yank me back into balance.

'Keep your shit,' he said. 'Let's have some fun.'

We stepped into the Pony Point. The place consisted of one small room paneled in knotty pine with a U-shaped bar extending out from the wall that divided the front of the house from the back kitchen. The bar was nearly filled. 'Tight Fittin' Jeans' by Conway Twitty was shrieking out of the tinny jukebox. I felt heavy and slow as I moved toward the bar, but by now I had acquired that singular glow of imagined invincibility that is bestowed upon certain drunks during particularly blessed binges.

Billy and I found two empty red vinyl stools on the west end of the U and bellied up. A large jar of pickled pig's feet rested on the bar between us. I signaled the barmaid, a woman in her sixties with steel gray hair flipped on one side. She moved slowly to our curve in the U as she wiped an aquamarine bar rag across her hands. When she reached us she kicked her chin up just a bit to signal for our order. One of her spotted hands, with short, hard nails painted apple red to match the color drawn across her lips, rested on her hip. That hip, which still had a shape distinct from the rest of her, was slightly cocked. Grandma, with a fistful of rolled nickels.

'What can I get you fellas?'

'Two beers and two whiskeys,' I said. 'Make the beers Budweisers and the whiskeys Grand-Dad.'

'I suppose you take your bourbon straight up,' she said, and tilted her chin up once again to let her eyes look us over.

'Yes, ma'am.'

She served the beers at once and rooted around the rack for a couple of shot glasses. While she did that, Billy and I tapped bottles and drank deeply. Then I had a look around the Pony Point.

On the east curve of the U sat three drunken men, their shoulders touching as if joined. The man in the middle was young, with a flattop and pale skin and an over-the-lip wisp of light brown hair masquerading as a mustache. He was bookended by two older men, one of whom was a well-worn version of flattop. Several beers sat in front of the three of them. The two older men looked quickly over to flattop and sang, in ravaged unison, 'I'm gonna stick . . . like glue.'

Flattop looked into my eyes from across the bar and yelled, with a crooked smile, 'Tomorrow ah'm a fuckin' marine!' The Pony Point was filled with noise, but I could have heard the kid from out in the parking lot.

Our bourbons were served, and I raised my glass to Flattop before tapping Billy's and tipping the shot to my lips. The warm liquor slid down with slow-jazz ease. I savored the afterburn, then asked the barmaid her name.

'Wanda,' she said.

'Wanda, buy those two older ones their next round. And give the soldier in the middle whatever he wants.'

'Sure thing.'

Billy said, 'And we'll take a couple of those pig's feet, honey.'

Wanda said, 'You got it.'

A hand wrapped around my arm. It was attached to a little man in a Cubs cap who was sliding onto the stool to my right. The man was not very old, but he had lost his teeth and on this night at least was not wearing the replacements. He used my arm for support as he adjusted his butt to the center of the stool.

'Thanks,' he said, and removed the cap to wipe a fuzzy, rather bullet-shaped head.

'No problem.'

'I see you're buyin',' he said matter-of-factly. He was trying to look up at me, but his gray eyes were missing the mark, shooting up toward the beamed ceiling.

'Why not? What are you drinking?'

'I'd love some whiskey. You like Conway Twitty?'

'No. But I dig Merle Haggard.'

'My name's Ken.'

I shook his hand and said, 'Nick.'

Wanda served our pig's feet on paper plates set next to plastic forks and then poured Ken a shot of rail whiskey. Ken knocked back half of it posthaste and cupped his hand protectively around the glass as he set it down on the bar. Billy ignored the fork, picked up the pig's foot, and began to chew meat off the bone. I tasted a sliver of mine, rejected the texture, and pushed the plate in front of Billy. The juke was playing Dolly Parton's 'Jolene.' I lit a cigarette and ran my hand back through my hair.

Two men stood by the kitchen door at the far side of the room. One was heavy and dark-skinned and wore an eggshell apron stained brown around his waist. The other was tall and lean and wore Wrangler jeans and a brown flannel shirt unbuttoned once to expose a triangle of white

T-shirt at the base of the neck. Both of them stared at me until I looked away. When I looked back their attention remained fixed. I turned to Ken.

Ken said, 'You like Randy Travis?'

'Uh-uh.' I said. 'You ever listen to Gram Parsons?' Ken's eyes traveled back up to the ceiling as he thought it over and shook his head. 'How about Rodney Crowell?'

'That's that boy married to Johnny Cash's girl, right?'

I nodded. 'Had a great single on the country charts, seven or eight years back – "Ashes by Now."'

'Yeah,' Ken said. 'I remember it. He's pretty damn good.'

I turned my head to the left. Billy dropped what was left of the pink-and-yellow pig's foot to the plate and wiped a paper napkin across his mouth. He chin-nodded the two by the kitchen door. The tall one nodded back without emotion.

I said, 'I don't think those two like us.'

'They're all right.'

'You know 'em?'

Billy had a long, even taste of the bourbon and winced. He set the glass back down on the bar. 'Black dude with the apron's named Russel. Local boy, knew April when they were young. The tall hard guy's Hendricks – a state cop. Grew up in Nanjemoy on the other side of Three-oh-one. Rides out of La Plata but spends a lot of time around the island. Don't take it personal. It's me they don't like.'

'Maybe I should talk to 'em.'

'Suit yourself. Want an introduction?'

'No.'

I killed my bourbon, stubbed my smoke, and picked up my beer. Ken suggested another round, but I ignored him as I pushed away from the bar and followed the curve of the U. I swerved by two old guys with winter sunburns and dirty hands and was clapped on the shoulder by one of Flattop's crew as I passed his back. His crossed eyes zeroed in on my chest as he sang, 'I'm gonna stick . . . like glue.'

The one with the apron, Russel, turned on his heels as I approached. By the time I reached the end of the bar, he had retreated into the fluorescence of the kitchen. That left me and Hendricks.

Hendricks looked in my eyes evenly and for a long time. I studied his as he did it. He had the clean, open face of a man who works hard every day and likes it. His eyes were dark blue, framed by short bursts of lines and set wide; his broad mouth stretched out across a stone jaw. I put him at about my age, though weathered by the elements.

313

'How's it goin'?' he said.

'It's goin' good.'

'You about done nursin' that beer?'

'Yeah.'

'Let's have another.'

'Sounds good.' I finished off the bottle. 'But I'm buying, okay? Makes sense to buy the local cop a beer when you're in his county.'

Hendricks grinned just enough to lift one cheek. 'I won't stop you,' he said.

'My name's Nick Stefanos.'

'Hendricks.'

I signaled Wanda with a sweeping victory sign and had her serve another shot to Ken. Billy was off and talking to a huge bearded man in a Red Man cap who stood blocking the front door like a bear in overalls. The bearman's narrow eyes were obtusely pointed to the floor as Billy talked. When the beers came I raised mine to Hendricks and had a swig. The floor tilted somewhat beneath my feet. I wrapped a hand around the curved lip of the bar.

Hendricks said, 'Which one of you lovers is drivin'?'

I pointed the neck of the Bud at Billy. 'We're not going far. Sleeping at April Goodrich's farm tonight.' I closed one eye a bit to focus on Hendricks. 'You know her?'

'Knew her before she was named Goodrich,' he said.

'Seen her lately?'

'That what you came down here for? Lookin' for April?'

'That's right.'

'What's it about. Personal?'

'It is for him.' I glanced quickly toward Billy and back to Hendricks. 'For me it's a job.'

Hendricks said, 'You're no cop.'

I shook my head. 'Private.'

Hendricks thought about that over a long, slow pull of beer. He placed the bottle softly on the bar, looked my way, and relaxed his shoulders. 'So what happened to your face?'

I rubbed it and felt the swell. 'To tell you the truth, I don't remember. We made a night of it, I guess.'

'It's not a bad face,' Hendricks said frankly. 'But you can't tell a thing about a man when you meet him on a drunk. And right now I don't know nuthin' about you but your name. You want to talk to me, I'll be around the island tomorrow.'

'Fair enough.' I shook his hand.

'You take care, now.'

Just then Hank Williams Jr., roared out of the juke and Ken began to yell, from across the bar, 'Bocephus! Boceeeephus!' He was pointing at me and smiling and with one hand keeping the cap on his head as he bucked like a rodeo clown on the red vinyl stool. I weaved recklessly across the smoky bar, past Flattop and his send-off crew (his uncle or father appeared to be holding the young man upright now at the bar), and made it over to Billy. Ken was off his stool and at my side by the time I reached Billy and the bearman.

'Let's get out of here,' I said.

Billy tried to focus one eye. A block of his blond hair had fallen over the other. 'Had enough?'

'Yeah.'

'One more stop, though.'

'Where?'

'Place called Rock Point.'

Ken let out a small whoop and I thought I saw the bearman break a tobacco-stained smile. I handed Billy some bills and he put those together with some of his own and left them all in a leafy heap on the bar. Wanda flicked her chin at him and then at me by way of thanks. Hank Williams, Jr., was still pumping out the bar-band jam as the four of us proceeded to fall out the front door. When I turned around for one final glance at the joint, Russel and Hendricks were standing in the entranceway to the kitchen. They were talking to each other, but they were looking dead straight at me.

The four of us crashed like a wave into Billy's Maxima and headed north on 254. I handed a tape I had lifted from the Spot over the seat to the bearman and had him slip it into the deck. Steve Earle's 'I'm the Other Kind' immediately boomed out of the rear-mounted speakers like some Wagnerian, biker-bar anthem. The bearman turned up the volume and clumsily moved his head to the beat. I watched it bob from behind like a hairy, floating melon. Ken sang the romantic wind-road-and-bike chorus (in between screaming praise about Earle's band, the Dukes – he called them the 'Dee-yukes') and passed beers all around.

At 257 Billy turned sharply right, spit gravel, then recovered his course onto a crudely paved road that soon narrowed to one lane. We passed a shack of a general store – an old man in a down coat sat in a lighted telephone booth and waved as we drove by – and some screened bungalows set far back on properties bulkheading the Wicomico. The road ahead, veined now with deep fissures and cracks, seemed to narrow even further. And then, without warning of any kind, the road simply ended.

We parked the car in front of a steel guardrail serving as a barrier. To the right, on a raised plot of dirt and naked turf, stood a post office the size of a tollbooth. Billy and the bearman got out of the Maxima, and Maybelle scrambled over my legs to follow. Ken was next out, and then me. I felt the temperature drop sharply as my face met the winter wind that was coming out of the southeast and off the river.

Billy cut the engine and the lights; the music still played. I trailed the group – Maybelle had trotted off into a wooden area to the right – and climbed over the barrier, on which was posted a NO TRESPASSING notice peppered with buckshot. What was left of the concrete road continued, buckled and in pieces, on a downward slope to the river. The swells of the Wicomico shimmered from the light of the moon and moved diagonally toward the shore in rough cadence with the wind. South beyond the point the Potomac merged with the Wicomico in cold, deep current. I zipped my jacket to the collar.

Ken and the bearman stopped at the waterline; one of Ken's fists dug into his jean pocket, the other gripping the neck of the Bud. The bearman appeared to be rolling a joint – he was carefully twisting it now, his muttonchop hands working the papers very closely to his small eyes – and Billy, with the cheesecloth bladder that had plagued him since childhood, was pissing like a filly near a grove of sycamores on the edge of the gravelly beach. I drew the pint from my jacket and knocked back an inch of bourbon.

Down on the beach I joined Billy and passed him the bottle. He had his taste and then we both followed it with beer. The wind was lifting Billy's hair off his scalp and blowing it about his face. Music came from the road and through the trees – Steve Earle had yielded now to Neil Young on the tape. The feedback and grunge of twin Les Pauls and Young's wailing vocals pierced the rush of the wind.

'The road ends at Rock Point,' Billy said out of nowhere, stating the obvious and pointing his beer bottle toward the river with uncharacter-istic dramatic punctuation. 'I used to come here all the time, that first summer when me and April got together. She didn't understand the attraction – to her it was the place where she and her friends came to smoke pot and drink and screw when they were growing up – but there was something to it for me. Something about the road running right into the fucking sea.'

'What about now?'

'It went to seed,' he said, adding, with a bitter edge, 'like everything else in this life.' Billy drank his beer and wiped the backwash on his jacket sleeve. 'Rubbers and beer cans, and gooks fishing for spot. That's all this place is now.'

I nodded in the direction of our new friends. 'You know those guys?' The bearman head lit the joint and was stooping low as he shotgunned Ken, the Cubs hat now set far back on the little man's head. Ken had cupped his hands around the bearman's face to get it all, and the cloud of smoke emanating from their union was great and wide. Ken's head appeared to be on fire.

'I've seen 'em around the island before. Barflies.' Billy looked at them and chuckled. 'That's just what April'd be doing right now, if she hadn't met me. Gettin' high and hangin' out.'

'There's more to this place than that. After all, she keeps coming back.'

'Most people don't have enough sense to stay away from home, even after they outgrow it.' Billy finished his beer. 'Come on, man, let's get out of here.'

'What about those guys?'

'They'll want to stay down here,' he said. 'Come on.'

Billy and I walked back up the buckled fun house road and climbed over the barrier. Neil Young was shouting 'Come On Baby Let's Go Downtown,' backed by the primal electric rage of Crazy Horse; the wind kicked at our backs. I looked back to see if the bearman and Ken were following, but Billy was right – they had drifted. The bearman was doing a slow shuffle on the beach, and Ken had leaped out into the river to a slab of concrete that the tide had not yet covered. He was dancing some sort of whacked jig, and he appeared to be singing toward the sky.

We climbed into the Maxima, Maybelle appearing suddenly from the trees and taking her place in the backseat. Billy lowered the music and cranked up the heat, rolling the windows up as he did it. I looked back through the rear window. The music no longer reached his ears, but Ken continued to dance out on the concrete slab in the river. The bearman stood with his hands buried in his pockets, a stoned stare focused up at the full December moon.

The gravel road to April Goodrich's property was at an unmarked turnoff two miles back up 257. We followed it straight into a wooded area, and then it turned to hard dirt as it continued out into several acres of plowed field. The road ran through a field bordered by woods on three sides and on the fourth by a wide, still creek. In the center of the field stood a hickory tree, under which a small trailer was mounted on concrete. It had a poured concrete patio in front and a corrugated Plexiglas eave hanging over it. The road from there went back through the field and down to a dock that ran out and into the creek. We passed the trailer and drove down to where the road ended at an open boathouse that stood near the first planks of the dock.

Billy cut the engine and the lights. I could hear Maybelle's tail excitedly thumping the backseat, but beyond that there was just the deep silence that exists at night and only in the country.

'What now?'

Billy said, 'Let's get out and feel the water. Finish the whiskey.'

We exited the Maxima. Maybelle bounded out before us and ran out onto the dock. I waited for Billy to lead the way and then stepped out onto the vertical planks that bridged the severely eroded bank to the dock. Beneath my feet the wood was white with the excrement of gulls. The wind had abated here, though the air was damp and bitter.

The dock ended in the head of a T. I sat on a piling and buried my hands in my jacket pockets. Maybelle lay on her stomach to my right. Billy climbed down an aluminum stepladder that had been halved and lashed with thick rope to the pilings on the eastern corner. He was out of sight now, but I heard his hand splashing in the freezing water.

'Ice cold,' his voice said. 'Not frozen yet, though.'

I'm not comin' in for your ass if you fall in.'

Billy climbed back up the ladder and said, 'Sure, you would. If there's one thing I know, that's it.' Billy rubbed his hand dry on his jeans and had a seat next to me. He leaned back on one elbow and pointed at my jacket. 'Let's have a drink and a couple of those smokes.'

'Sure.'

I brought the pint and the Camels out from my jacket and rustled the pack in his direction. Billy drew one from the deck and put it to his lips. I fired his up, put one in my mouth, and lit it off the same match. The tobacco hit my lungs and I kept it there. I watched the silver exhale drift slowly in the motionless air like a ghost and spread out over the creek.

Billy took the Beam off the dock, uncapped it, and had a drink. He sighed comfortably and stretched like a waking animal. 'Good night,' he said.

Across the creek one prefab rambler stood in a clearing in the woods. Mounted atop a pole in front of the rambler was a spotlight that illuminated the property. A horse stood beneath the spotlight inside a small grassy area framed by a split-rail fence. The horse's breath, backlit and haloed, poured from its nostrils and widened into two even streams.

Some time passed. Billy pitched his cigarette out over the dock and into the creek. I followed the orange trail and listened to the quick, dull finality of the fire hitting water. Then I had a last drag of my cigarette and threw what was left of it in the direction of his.

'Your head's rolling,' Billy said. 'Let's go on up to the trailer.'

I looked around at the dock. 'Where's the dog?'

'You've been noddin'. I was waiting for that smoke to burn down into your fingers – would have let it too. But you woke up.' Billy stood and reached for my hand. 'Maybelle ran off. She'll be all right.'

I stood with Billy's help. 'We ought to find her. She'll freeze.'

'Not cold enough. Come on, let's turn in.'

We walked off the dock and onto the dirt road that cut through the field. Some clouds had drifted across the sky; the darkness seemed denser now. At the trailer Billy jiggled a key in the lock and opened the door. I followed him into the narrow space and closed the door behind me. Billy found a candle in a drawer and forced it into the neck of an empty bottle of Rolling Rock. He struck a match and lit the candle.

The trailer appeared smaller lighted. An old double-barreled shotgun rested in the hooks of a rack mounted above a narrow kitchenette. I thought I heard something move beneath one of two bunks that end-capped the trailer's interior, and raised an eyebrow in Billy's direction.

Billy smiled and shook his head. 'If there's snakes in here, they're sleeping. Field mice, if anything.'

'Oh.'

'Here.' Billy tossed me a rolled sleeping bag and pointed to the bunk where I had heard the noise. I ignored his direction and spread the bag out on the other bunk. Then I stripped naked and zipped myself in. I balled up shivering, waiting for the ache of cold to subside. The objects on the kitchenette and then the kitchenette itself began to move and float. I fell into an open-mouthed sleep.

I awoke some time later. A dull throb had entered my temple, and my mouth was glutinous and dry. There was a bit of natural light in the cabin now; dawn had begun encroaching on the night. I looked over at Billy.

He was up on one elbow, half out of his sleeping bag, smoking one of my cigarettes and staring into my eyes. His eyes reflected the flame of the candle that still burned in the green bottle. The lower right portion of his face was in shadow. We kept each other's gaze for a while – then I drifted back to sleep. When I opened my eyes, Billy was still staring. Now there was a cool smile across his smooth face. He dragged off the cigarette and thumb-flicked some ash onto a piece of foil set on the Formica counter that held the candle.

I said, 'Something's not right, Billy. Let's talk about it.'

'You're coming down off a drunk, that's all. You gonna be sick?'

'I don't mean that.'

'What, then?'

'This whole thing.' I sat up in my bunk and wiped the back of my hand across my mouth. 'Who's Tommy?'

'Tommy?'

'The guy April talked about on the answering machine.'

'Tommy Crane.' Billy sighed. 'Fuckin' pig farmer. Lives up Two-fifty-seven a few miles. April used to do him and maybe she still does. She said on the tape she was coming down here to kiss him good-bye. That's what we're doing down here, remember?'

'An old boyfriend, right? Like Joey DiGeordano. And that guy at the Pony Point, Russel – another old boyfriend. Maybe Hendricks too. All these old boyfriends – and you don't seem too shook about it, Billy. That's what the fuck is bothering me, man. It's been gnawin' at my ass since you hired me.'

Billy squinted against his own smoke. 'What's your point?'

'Do you love her?'

He looked down at the table as he butted the cigarette in the foil. His face had fallen into shadow, but when he looked back up again it was lit by the fork of the flame. 'No, Nick, I don't love her. I'm not sure if I've ever been in love, to tell you the truth. But I'm sure I never was in love with her.'

I struggled against a curtain of alcohol that now pushed down upon my consciousness. 'I don't mind being a sucker, Billy – it's happened to me before – but I don't want to be *your* sucker, understand? We've got too much behind us, man, too many years.'

'Sure,' he said. 'Let's clear it.'

'You put April onto the DiGeordano heist, didn't you?' Billy nodded with hesitation. 'Joey called it the first time I sat with him. He said you were pimping your own wife. I didn't want to believe him. Now I do.'

Billy nodded again and lowered his eyes. 'I'm sorry, man.'

'You two were going to split the two hundred grand down the middle, then April was supposed to disappear. But April got wise. She booked with the full take and left you out in the cold. Now you want to find her and take back your share. That's what you really hired me for – right, Billy?'

'That's right, Greek,' he said. 'That bitch took what was mine, understand? And now I want it back.' The shadow of the candle's flame danced across Billy's smile.

My eyes closed, watching him. The trailer darkened, and then it was black. I dreamed of high school, Billy, me, our teachers, our friends. Dead now, all of us.

14

There was a tightness in my chest, and in my sinuses the suffocating stench of stale smoke. I unzipped my bag and sat up naked on the edge of the bunk. My feet dangled, and I let my toes touch the cold linoleum of the trailer floor. I pushed the hair away from my eyes and rubbed my face for a long while. Then I dressed slowly, turned the knob of the trailer door, and stepped down onto the concrete patio, out into the light.

It was a clear and cold sunny day. Billy stood down by the bank, scrubbing Maybelle with a thick-bristled brush that he dipped in the brackish water of the creek. I zipped my jacket to the neck and walked across a field ridged with hard brown mud and a ground cover of freshly sprouted winter wheat. By the time I reached Billy, he was drying Maybelle with a yellowed towel. Maybelle shook off, snorted, and ran up the bank to greet me, her tail moving excitedly. I rubbed the top of her head as she pushed the side of her snout against my leg.

Billy's car was parked by the boat shed. A deep scrape was etched in the white paint and ran from the rear quarter panel to the mirror on the passenger side. I looked at it and then at Billy.

'I don't want to talk about it,' he said. 'I'm feeling bad enough, so let's not talk about it, okay?' I nodded. 'How you doing?'

'A little rough,' I said.

Billy put his fists in his pockets and tried to widen his eyes. 'Want some breakfast?'

'Sure.'

The Pony Point was open for business. We parked in front and left Maybelle behind. By now she had used her paws to form a bed from the yellowed towel.

A small bell sounded as we opened the front door and stepped inside. Wanda was behind the bar. She flicked her chin in our direction and threw us a tight smirk as she looked us over. I kept my eyes on my shoes and followed Billy to a booth.

A square-headed guy wearing a camouflage hat sat alone drinking coffee in the booth behind Billy's back. At the bar sat Flattop and his two older companions, beers in front of them all. They were still alive but barely conscious – one of Flattop's eyes had rolled up into his head while the other stared straight ahead. The uncle leaned his weight into Flattop, in an effort to keep them both upright. The other man was sleeping, his posture still erect, his hand wrapped around the body of the Bud.

I looked over at the hunter and then at Billy. 'What's in season?'

'Rabbit,' Billy said.

Wanda stood before us, her shapely septuagenarian hip slightly cocked. She tapped the pencil on the order pad and dished Billy with her smirk. 'Bloody Marys?'

Billy said, 'I'll have one in a mug.'

I said, 'Just coffee for me. And breakfast. Eggs over easy, with toast and scrapple.'

Billy nodded. 'I'll have the same.'

Wanda wrote it down and then spun on her heels. She walked back behind the bar and tore the check off the pad, sliding it through the reach-through. I saw an eggshell apron fill the space and a brown hand grab the order. Flattop's uncle snapped his fingers with an on-the-one beat and sang, 'I'm gonna stick . . . like glue.'

'I'll be back in a minute, Billy.'

I rose with difficulty and shook the dizziness from my head. At the bar I took a thick white diner mug from a stack and poured some coffee from the fullest pot heating on the Bunn-Omatic. I had a sip standing there, then walked around the U of the bar to the kitchen's entrance.

Inside, Russel was standing over a large grill. On one side of the grill a dozen hand-packed burgers precooked slowly on the breakfast-level heat. Russel poured some grease from a coffee pot onto the other side. It spread into a pool the size of a dinner plate and began to sizzle.

'How's it going?' I said.

'It's goin',' he said without looking up. Russel took a thick black-handled knife from the rack and cut two slices from a wax-papered block of scrapple. He laid the scrapple carefully into the grease, then turned to face me.

Russel's hair was cut in a modified fade. His eyes were baby-round and olive green. Two black moles dotted the brown skin of his left cheek.

'I'm Nick Stefanos.' I walked across the brick-colored tiles and shook his hand. His grip was tentative.

'I know your name,' he said, and grinned slightly. 'But I would have recognized you anyway. You're wearin' the same tired shit you had on last night.'

'Didn't bring a change of clothes.'

'Uh-huh.'

He faced the grill again and turned the scrapple. I walked over to the opposite wall and leaned my back against a stainless-steel refrigerator. The kitchen was warm, and Russel had opened the back door. Some sun fell in through the wood-framed screen. Through the screen I watched a large black cat lick her kittens clean on a concrete porch. Beyond that, on a worn patch of brown grass, a three-legged German shepherd slept. I had a deep swig of coffee and lit a cigarette. The smoke of my exhale hovered and shimmered in the oblong wedge of sun.

'I'm looking for April Goodrich,' I said.

'Hendricks told me.'

'Can you help me?'

Russel used a spatula to retrieve the scrapple from the grill. He slid the scrapple onto a plate that he had lined with paper towels to absorb the grease. Then he broke two eggs using one hand, and another two after that. Russel carefully pushed the spatula around the white edges of the eggs.

'Depends on what you want to know,' he said.

'Was she here?'

He nodded. 'She was down here.'

'When?'

'About a week ago, I guess.'

'When exactly?'

Russel thought it over, the spatula pointed upward like a barometer. 'Middle of the week, about then.'

'In this place?' I dragged on my cigarette and let the smoke drift.

'She doesn't come here,' he said. 'On the other side of the bridge, at Polanski's.'

'Doin' what?'

'Drinkin' Jamaican rum,' Russel said, chuckling. 'Like she always do.'

'Who with?'

His smile faded. 'Tommy Crane.'

'How'd they look?'

'Drunk. Crane had two beers in front of him and April was all over him.'

'Why doesn't she do her drinking in the Pony Point? Avoiding you, Russel?'

'I don't think so,' he said. 'That was a long time ago. She's forgotten all about me, man.'

'What about you?'

'Like I say, that was a long time ago.'

'You still in love with her?'

Russel turned the eggs without breaking the yolk, then leaned his wide ass against the cutting board that fronted the grill. He crossed his arms and looked me over. 'You ask a lot of questions, man.'

'It's my job to ask questions.'

He sighed and looked toward the wall. 'I can't say if I was in love with her. I don't know. It's easy to confuse being in love with just lovin' the memory of a certain time. A certain time in your life, I mean. When anything's possible, all the shit's out in front of you. Before the world gets real, beats you down.'

'Pretty philosophical.'

'That's me. Two years at Howard, and that's what I got. Goethe, Sartre. Existentialism and the Absurd – the last class I took before I booked. Absurd is right. None of that shit had a goddamn thing to do with what's reality.'

I looked at Russel's apron and then into his intelligent eyes. 'What are you doing down here?'

He chuckled. 'How's D.C.?'

'You know how it is.'

'Where you live?'

'Shepherd Park.'

'Uptown.'

'Uptown, and east of the park.'

'Yeah, I know how it is, all right. Rough two years I spent up there – for a country boy. In D.C. I wasn't nothin' but a 'bama.' Russel relaxed his shoulders. 'So that's what I'm doing here. I like this place. I like to walk at night, and I like to fish and I like to hunt. And I like my animals, man.' He glanced out the screen door. 'My cats and my dogs.'

'You seen April since that night at Polanski's?'

'Uh-uh,' he said, shaking his head.

'Why's she hooked up with Tommy Crane?'

'April likes the wheel, and Crane's holdin' serious weight. That boy's damn near a legend.'

'I don't follow.'

Russel said, 'If Crane had any more dick, he'd be wearin' three shoes. You follow now?'

I had a last drag and pitched the rest of my cigarette out through the gap in the screen door and into a mound of dirt. Russel lifted the eggs off the grill and dropped them onto two plates. He added the scrapple and some buttered toast from a stack, then placed both plates on the platform of the reach-through.

'Your breakfast is up, man.'

'Thanks for the information.'

'You got honest eyes. I didn't talk for you, though. And I sure didn't talk for that gray husband of hers. If April's runnin' from him, then I wish her luck. But her hangin' with Tommy Crane can only come to bad.'

'I'm going out to his place now, to talk to him.'

'Then you take care,' Russel said. ' 'Cause that's one crazy mother-fucker.'

Breakfast worked. I had two more cups of coffee, then voided my rotten bowels in the men's room and washed up. When I walked out, Billy, who still looked somewhat ashen, took my place in the sole stall. I made a go-cup of coffee at the bar, thanked Wanda, and stepped out into the parking lot for some clean air.

Hendricks was sitting in his unmarked Ford, the powerful engine idling. He stepped out of the white car without cutting the ignition and strode slowly in my direction. He was in his brown uniform now, though his general appearance hadn't changed. He had looked exactly the same the night before – like a cop.

'So,' he said, hooking his thumbs through the belt loops of his slacks. 'How you feelin' today?'

'Better now. Thanks.'

'Nothin' a good breakfast can't cure, right?'

'Russel's a good cook.'

'Best in this part of the country.'

I glanced at the .357 Smith & Wesson that was holstered on his hip. The lacquered walnut stock gleamed in the sun. 'I see you favor the four-inch barrel.'

Hendricks frowned with interest. 'Now, how you know that, Stefanos?'

'My grandfather was an S & W man. So I heard enough trivia over the years for some to stick. Your gun's squared on the butt – and they only square it on the four-inch. Smith and Wesson rounds the butt on the three-inch barrel.'

'That's right.' Hendricks patted the holster. 'It's not that the barrel size makes a damn bit of difference to me. But it makes a hell of a better . . . impression if you have to draw it.'

'You have to much, down here?'

'It happens,' he said. 'But I can't say I favor this one at all. Fact is, the son of a bitch sights low. Much as I try to correct, I hit a full foot higher than I aim.'

'Aim low, then.'

'Thanks for the big-city tip.' Hendricks winked, looked over my shoulder, and smiled with satisfaction as he followed Billy's labored trek from the door to the Maxima. I heard the engine start behind my back.

'I better get going,' I said.

'Where to?'

'See if Tommy Crane's around. He was drinking with April at Polanski's a week ago. Maybe he can tell me where she went.'

Hendricks said, 'You don't want to be messing with that guy, if you can help it.'

'Russel said the same.'

'Well, he knows. Crane nearly beat the life outta Russel one night at Rock Point, for nothing at all. I was doing a routine drive-by and ran right up on it. By that time Russel was on the ground spittin' blood and froth, and Crane was still kickin' in his ribs.'

'I'll watch myself.'

'I'm not kidding,' Hendricks said.

'I'm not either,' I said. 'This is just a job to me. And I don't want to die.'

Billy and I crossed the bridge over the channel and turned left onto 257, then followed the highway for two or three miles. At a steepled church Billy turned right and drove back southeast toward the Wicomico. The road was narrow, though smoothly paved. Billy slowed at a gravel road on the left that broke into a thick forest of oak. He was turning in when I told him to cut the engine. Billy parked on the gravel road.

'What is it?' he said.

'Crane live back in there?'

'That's right.'

'How do you know? You been here before?'

'Long time ago, when me and April were first coming down here. She

327

introduced me; I didn't know there was anything between them.' Billy looked me over. 'What's wrong with you, man?'

'I don't want any surprises, that's all. I want everything up front before I talk to this guy.' I cracked my window and stared straight ahead. 'Joey DiGeordano told me that April took the money on Monday last. You say she took off on Wednesday. What happened in between?'

Billy glanced at his lap and brushed air off his leg. 'We celebrated.'

'Where?'

'I don't know. What difference does it make?'

'Tell me everything you did between the time she glommed the cash and the time she left you.'

Billy sighed with annoyance. 'All right. The night she came home with it, we stayed in. We paced a lot, didn't sleep much. The next day I worked and April stayed home. That night – Tuesday night – we went out. We were getting a little nervous then – about having all that cash, about when DiGeordano's boys were going to get around to come looking for it. And we planned to leave town the next day, cool our heels, whatever. Fact is, we didn't have a plan.' Billy paused as he cracked his own window. Some sweat had appeared on his forehead. 'Anyway, like I say, we went out. To a movie.'

'What'd you see?'

'I don't know, some bogus action flick at the Laurel Ten. You know, the new one, with the guy's got a ponytail.'

'What about after that?'

'We went out for a few.'

'Where?'

Billy thought it over and waved a hand in my direction. 'I can't remember the name, a chain joint. One of those phony Irish names, they have drinks comin' out of machines. Right in front of Laurel Mall. O'Tooligan's, MacManley's, some shit like that.'

'April get drunk?'

'She always gets drunk.'

'She get drunk enough to give you any idea she was going to split?'

'She was drunk enough. But no, she didn't say a word.'

'And she left the next day.'

'That's right. I went to work, and when I came home she was gone.'

'No note, right? I mean, that computerized Dear John you told me about, that was all bullshit, right, Billy?'

Billy narrowed his eyes. 'I apologized already, last night. You've busted my balls enough, don't you think? I've got nothing else to tell you.'

'All right,' I said, pointing down the road. 'Let's go see Crane.'

15

Tommy Crane's cottage was in a half-acre clearing about a quarter-mile through the woods. Fifty yards from the house was a cinder-block structure larger than the cottage. We parked the Maxima beside a red F-150 truck on a plot of hard sand under a single oak that stood next to the cottage.

I pointed to the cinder-block structure. 'What's that?'

'Pig compound. He houses and feeds them in there. Slaughters 'em in there as well, from what I can remember.'

I thought things over. 'Crane probably won't let me in his house, if he's got something to hide. At the very least, maybe I can get in to use his bathroom. If he does let me in, I'm going to need as much time as I can in there alone, to look around. Do your best and keep him occupied, even if it's only for a few minutes. You'll know when to do it. But for now, just stay in the car, okay? I don't need any distractions up front.'

'It's all you now, man. Go on.'

I climbed out of the car and pushed Maybelle's head back in – she was trying to slide out with me – before closing the door. A fat sound, the movement of animals, came from the direction of the compound. The air felt colder as I passed beneath the naked branches of the oak. The branches cast shadows like black arthritic arms on the hard earth.

I stepped up onto a wooden porch whose planks were painted gray. There was a screen door and after that a solid one. I pulled open the screen door and knocked on the other.

The door unlocked quickly, and Tommy Crane stood before me. He was wearing a blue chamois shirt over a thermal undershirt, and loose-fitting jeans. Over the shirt was a black down vest that bulged on the left side of his chest. On the side of his hip a knife was secured in a thin brown-leather sheath. The knife's handle was wrapped tightly with black electrician's tape. The long blade of the knife took up the balance of the sheath. The sheath ran halfway down Crane's thigh.

'Yes?' Crane said. The voice was controlled and uncomfortably gentle – for a man his height and weight, it didn't fit. His tan hands were long and densely veined, and his rawboned wrists filled and stretched the cuffs of the chamois shirt. The wrists had the thickness and mass of redwood.

'My name's Nick Stefanos.'

'That supposed to mean something to me?' Crane squinted and scratched his black beard. A wire-thin scar veed deeply into the right side of the beard.

'I work for Billy Goodrich,' I said, turning my head briefly in the direction of the Maxima. Crane looked toward the car and saw Billy in the driver's seat, then looked back at me. There was lack of interest and mild annoyance in his thin black eyes. I shifted my feet to simulate discomfort as I handed him my card. 'Mind if I come in?'

He gave the card a contemptuous glance. 'For what?'

'I'm looking for April Goodrich. I understand she was down here and she was with you.'

'She was down here,' he said, and as he said it he stepped out onto the porch and closed the door behind him. Crane ran one hand through his thick black hair and pulled the bulk of it back behind his ears. Then he hitched up his jeans and puffed out his broad chest. 'You want to talk to me, come on, but make it quick. I got work to do, and plenty of it.'

Crane skipped the steps, jumped down off the porch, and landed walking, taking long strides toward the pig compound. I looked quickly at Billy. Billy shrugged, and I followed Crane.

I trailed him to a wood gate, where we butted through and stepped into a small grassy area enclosed by a barbed-wire fence. The wire was wrapped and tied at six-foot intervals to knotted wood posts driven deeply into the earth. We continued toward the cinder-block structure to an opening cut to accommodate an average-sized man. The structure was topped unevenly by a corrugated tin roof laid over asbestos sheeting. A thin periscopic chimney rose out of the roof, and gray smoke drifted out through the chimney. The wheezy animal sounds grew heavier as we approached the gate that was hinged to the opening.

Crane pushed on the gate and strode in, lowering his head to clear the top-frame of the entrance. I followed him into a dark, concrete-floored area of roughly eight hundred square feet. The entire structure was elevated to provide for a concrete feeding trough that ran around the sty and was accessible from the outside. On the left wall two farrowing pens were lit and warmed by infrared lamps, and in those pens two sows lay on their sides. Several piglets suckled the sows' teats from behind a set of steel rails. On the right wall were sleeping compartments where slats of timber had been cross-nailed inches above the cold concrete. In the rear of the sty a copper circular trough was mounted on a brick base. A fire burned in the center of the base and the putrid steam that rose from the liquid boiling in the trough entered a hole that led through the chimney. Next to the cooker was an iron drinking trough. Next to that a black hose lay dripping and coiled on the concrete. On the wall behind the troughs several butchering knives rested in the hooks of a punch-board. Beside the punchboard was an exit, exactly the size of the opening through which we had entered. The ropes of a pulley dangled from the rafters, above it all.

Crane kept walking. He lowered his head once more and stepped outside through the rear opening. I followed. Now we were in another fenced enclosure with twice the area of the yard in front. Bales of hay were lined end-to-end around the bottom of this fence, and a few dozen pigs and weaners of varying litters were lying on their sides on the worn grass, butted up against the hay. It was colder in the yard than it had been in the sty, but the sun was bright and the air was bracing and clean.

Some of the pigs had risen at the arrival of Crane, and they began to move about the yard. They alternately snorted and squealed. A white pig larger than the others moved slowly in our direction. The rest remained against the bales. I nodded toward them. 'They like the feel of that hay?'

'Not really,' Crane said. 'Pigs like the sunshine, but they hate the wind. Hate it damn near worse than they hate anything. So they come outside for the sun and get behind the bales. Now one of those sows – that one over there' – Crane pointed to a large Middle White in the corner of the yard – 'she's lyin' back because she senses it's her time to die. I haven't fed her for twenty-four hours, for the reason of the mess the killin' makes if there's food in her belly, and that just adds to her confusion. But she knows, boy. She knows.'

A huge white pig came within ten feet of us and then turned and waddled off back toward the others. He had long deep sides and a strongly curled tail, and he appeared to be smiling. His huge balls hung low and nearly touched the ground.

'That must be the king,' I said.

Crane snorted and smiled. His capped teeth were even and gray. 'Yeah, he's the cock star. You get a Large White boar with a set o' nuts like that, boy, it only comes once in a lifetime. You can cross him with anything – Blacks, Middle Whites – the whiteness of his meat transports, makes great butcherin' pig.' Crane looked lovingly at the boar. 'I imagine he services fifty, sixty sow a year. Eats like a sonofabitch too – seven, eight pounds a day – but he earns it.'

'Pig-keeping your only business, Tommy?'

Crane squinted. 'Askin' questions yours?'

'No. I work in a bar in D.C.'

'Then there's your answer. Man does different things to get by – hustlin' drinks is just one, I guess. I do some hauling, small-engine repair – lawn mowers, go-carts. Stuff like that.' Crane ran his hand back through his hair once more and looked me over. 'Like I told you, I got work to do. What do you say we cut all this in half?'

'I'm for it.' I looked quickly past Crane to the car. I could only see half of it from that vantage point, but the half I could see included the driver's seat. Billy wasn't in it. I returned my attention to Crane. 'Talk about April.'

'The truth?' Crane grinned like a disease. 'April and me been doin' the crawl for years now,' he said. 'She didn't love me, and she didn't love her husband. But she liked what she got here more than she liked what she was gettin' at home. You see what I'm sayin'?' I shifted my feet. 'Anyway, she finally had enough of your friend Slick, and she split. On her way out she came to say good-bye.'

'When was that?'

'Early last week. I don't remember the day.'

'How long did she stay?'

'One night.'

'She say where she was going?'

'West.'

'That's pretty vague, Tommy.'

'It's the way she wanted it, friend.'

'Would you tell me where she was if you knew?'

Crane rolled his tongue around the inside of his cheek and slowly shook his head. 'No.'

That finished it for now. We stared each other down to no effect amid the mass of pigs that had by now closed in around us. Then Billy appeared from inside the sty and walked out into the yard.

'Hello, Tommy,' he said.

'Goodrich.'

Billy turned to me. 'You getting anywhere?'

'No.' I shoved my hands in my jeans and looked around the yard with studied indifference. 'Look,' I said. 'You guys talk it out, all right? I gotta take a leak.'

Before Crane could stop me I had negotiated myself through a mobile maze of pigs and had entered the sty. I moved quickly out and into the front yard. Maybelle was barking inside the car – her nose had made wormlike marks on the window as she pressed against it – but I ignored her and jumped up the steps and onto the porch. I looked behind me to see if Crane had followed – he hadn't bothered, or Billy hadn't let him – and turned the handle of the front door. The door opened and I walked inside.

The first thing I saw was a small living room. There was a battered couch upholstered in faded blue and a heavily varnished table fashioned from the cross section of an oak. On the table was a blue bong, and next to that lay a small mound of green piled in the inverted top of a shoe box. Behind the couch a Roger Dean print was mounted and framed on a yellow wall. On the opposite wall a nineteen-inch Zenith was elevated on a particle-board cart, and next to that stood a rack stereo. The tall black speakers of the system bookended the Zenith. I walked through.

At the end of a narrow hall were three doors. One was opened to Crane's bedroom. Through the crack of the second I could make out a bathroom. The third door was locked. I entered Crane's bedroom.

The bedroom window gave a view of the entrance to the compound. Crane and Billy had moved back from the yard and were in the sty now. Billy's royal blue jacket was visible through the gate, and next to that the duller blue of Crane's shirt. Only their torsos showed in the darkness of the sty. They appeared to be standing very close to each other. I moved quickly past the window and to the dresser.

Crane's dresser was topped with loose change, an eel-skin wallet, some odd porcelain figures of black birds, and a porno mag. The cover of the porno mag – *Bang-Cock Blossoms in Tie-Land* – featured a smiling Asian woman with pink lipstick. I glanced back through the window, then checked Crane's wallet. Slid between the wallet's stained plastic covers were two photographs of two different women, neither of whom I recognized. In the billfold was a ten and three ones. I closed the wallet and placed it back on the dresser.

The dresser drawers contained Crane's underwear, T-shirts, and socks, and in one there was an assortment of lingerie. I went through each drawer quickly, running my hand beneath the clothing, finding nothing. When I was done with that I looked back out through the window. Billy was out of the compound and walking heavily toward the car. There was a particular anger on his face, a genuine anger that I had seen on him only once.

I ducked the window and moved back out into the hall. The locked door was still locked. I entered the bathroom and flushed the head. Then I ran cold water into my cupped hands and splashed it on my face. There was a towel rack next to the sink but no towel. I opened a wall cabinet and pulled a white washcloth off the top of the stack. Small silver objects came out with the washcloth and fell to the tiled floor. They made a metallic sound as they hit. I bent down and scooped three pieces of jewelry – a ring and two earrings – up into my hand. I put those in the pocket of my jeans. Then I replaced the washcloth, stepped quickly out into the hall, walked through the living room, and bolted out the front door and onto the porch. The frantic cry of an animal mingled with the whir of the wind.

Billy was in the driver's seat of the Maxima, staring straight ahead. I moved to his window and made a roll-down motion with my hand. He pressed his thumb to a togglelike switch, and the window slid down.

'Gimme a smoke,' he said. Some red had bled into the azure blue of his wide eyes.

'Sure.' I shook one from my pack. Billy took it by the filter and pushed the lighter into the dash. 'Crane tell you anything, Billy?'

Billy bit down on the cigarette as he lit it and spit some smoke out the window. He shook his head. 'That son of a bitch knows where she is, Nick.'

'I know.'

'Well?'

'Stay here. I'll give it one more shot.'

The crippled black shadows of the oak pointed toward the compound. I followed their direction. The frenzied animal scream increased as I pushed past the gate, walked across the yard, and entered the sty.

Crane was by the back door. He had tied the ropes of the pulley to the hind legs of the white sow. She hung suspended above an empty trough, her head jerking as she wheezed and screamed. I stood before Crane.

'We're taking off,' I said.

Crane jerked his hand inside his black vest and pulled out a .38 snubnosed revolver with a nickel finish. He passed the short barrel across my chest as he moved it to his right hand. I felt the blood drain from my face and then a flush of raw anger as I watched Crane smile. He rested the muzzle of the .38 between the sow's eyes.

'You look a little shook, Stefanos. Ain't you never seen an animal slaughtered?'

'I've never seen a man like it so much,' I said.

Crane's smile turned down. He looked toward the sow and back at me. Then he ran his left hand down the sheath strapped to his leg.

'What I like is the efficiency, friend. Only takes one shot. Then this stickin' knife, straight in ahead of the breast bone, six inches deep. They die quick, believe me, and they bleed right out into the trough. No mess.'

I said, 'If April doesn't show up in a few days, I'm coming back down here to talk to you, Crane. Got it?'

Crane lowered the .38 and held it by his side. He looked me over slowly. 'I don't see a man who can back that up. All's I see is a two-day drunk. It's over, pal. April's gone. Now, you get gone too.'

He began to raise the pistol. I backed up and walked away and didn't look back. Out in the air, I breathed deeply as I headed for the car. Billy reached across and opened the passenger door. I slid into the cold leather seat and stared ahead.

'Well?' Billy said.

'Nothing,' I said as the sow's scream ripped the air. 'Close your window, okay?'

Billy hit the toggle and the window closed tight, sealing out the death cry from the sty. 'What about in the house? You find anything?'

'Nothing,' I said, touching the jewelry through the pocket of my jeans. 'Come on, man, let's get out of here. Let's go.'

Billy started the engine. As we neared the trees I heard the dull thump of a pistol shot, then tasted the bilious remains of alcohol and breakfast surge up in my throat. I swallowed it and shut my eyes. There was only the hum of the engine then, and the steady sob of Maybelle from the backseat. I pushed the lighter into the dash and fumbled in my jacket for a smoke. We followed the gravel road back through the trees, heading west for the highway.

16

High gray clouds chased us into D.C. Billy and I didn't speak much on the way in. An hour and a half after we left Crane's property, we parked the Maxima in front of my apartment in Shepherd Park and cut the engine.

Billy looked out at my yard and exhaled with control. 'So what's next?'

'You tell me. You want me to keep going, I'll do it.'

Billy's said, 'You gotta push Crane, is what you gotta do. You know that, don't you?'

I shifted in my seat. 'Maybe just pushing a guy like him won't do much. I need something on him.'

'You see anything in his house?'

'I saw a lot of things. But I didn't know what I was looking for.'

'What did you see?' When I didn't answer, Billy raised his voice. 'Come on, man, I'm paying you . . . I'm paying you to tell me.'

'All right, Billy,' I said evenly. 'Here it is. Crane's a green-head. He's also into porn – rough trade. April's doctor told me there was evidence she'd been tied up – that wasn't you, right?' Billy shook his head and opened his mouth stupidly. 'So it was Crane that was giving it to her the hard way. Want me to keep going?'

He nodded. 'Yeah.'

'I found some clothing in his dresser, maybe all belonging to the same woman. And I saw some jewelry. April wear much?'

'Jewelry?' Billy pushed some blond hair off his forehead and thought it over. 'Well, her wedding ring.'

'What else?'

'A cross. A gold cross on a gold chain, with a small diamond in the center of it.' He paused. 'And a ring on her other hand, on her pinky finger. A ruby in a silver antique setting.'

'She wear that stuff all the time?' I said.

'Most of the time, yeah.' Billy looked in my eyes. 'You find any of that at Crane's?'

I shook my head and looked away as I did it. 'No.'

Billy put his hand on my shoulder. 'Listen, Nicky . . .'

I pulled away from him, opened my door, and put a foot to the kerb. 'Don't worry,' I said. 'I won't drop it.'

'Call me,' he said.

'I will.'

I watched his car turn off my street. Then I walked around the side of my landlord's house and picked up the mail off the stoop that was my entrance. I called for my cat as I unlocked the door and stepped inside.

The red light on the answering machine blinked next to the phone on the table that end-capped my sofa. I moved to the machine and pushed down on the bar, then listened to my messages as I looked over the general solicitation that was my mail.

The first message was from Jackie Kahn. She called to remind me about Sunday night, and to 'bring a bottle of red, and not that cheap Spanish shit.' Dinner was at 7:30, she said, adding, 'Be here by seven.' The second message was from a collection agency. I finished glancing at the mail during that. The third message was from the security guard, James Thomas.

Thomas's confession was rambling, soaked in the moaning self-pity that comes only at the final inch of a deep night of whiskey. I got what I could from the quiet pauses and the long, low sobs that followed. The sound of a man gone to the bottom is more frightening than the tears of any woman, and I was only thankful that I wasn't there to see it, to see his cubbish head lowered into his thick hands and the spasmodic, infantile shake of his broad, round shoulders. 'I did what you said I did . . . I took the money, and . . . now I'm fixin' to take more . . . I'll be gone after that . . . I want you to know I didn't kill that boy . . . That boy sure didn't deserve to die . . . The man from the orange and red—'

The tape ran out. When it did, my apartment went silent. Then, through the silence, I heard the faint cry of my cat.

I followed the sound out into the backyard. She called out weakly once more when she felt me near, and that's when I saw her. She was caught in the latticework, where I had found her years before, after the cat fight that had taken her right eye. This time some thick wire my landlord had used as patch had done it; a piece of it had entered her paw and gone deeper as she had moved into it, trying to get away. Now she was lying in the dirt next to the lattice, breathing rapidly and staring ahead glassily. I bent down and tickled the scar tissue of her lost eye and stroked behind her ear. As I did that I pulled the wire from her paw. She stiffened and stopped breathing as one rooted yellow toenail came out with it.

I tore a piece off the tail of my shirt with one hand while I stroked her with the other. Then I wrapped that around her paw and cradled her up into my arms. I ran with her to my Dart and got behind the driver's seat and cursed the engine when it failed to start. When it did start I gunned it to the animal hospital at the District line on Georgia Avenue, landing on my horn several times to clear traffic along the way. My cat felt cool and hard in my arms. I talked to her all the way in, but she never once looked up in my direction.

Two hours later a young attendant wearing jodhpurs and a flannel shirt brought her out. I signed some papers and then the young woman put my cat into my arms. She was limp but warm now. Her paw was bandaged and her head drooped off my forearm.

'What do I do?' I asked the young woman.

'Just take care of her,' she said coldly. She stared me down and I let her do it.

'For the paw, I mean.'

'Change the bandage and put Neosporin on the puncture before you do it.' She gave me the long face again. 'The paw's not the problem. How long was she out there, without food or water?'

I looked away. A row of animal lovers sat against the wall and stared collectively with pursed lips in my direction. 'About a day, I guess,' I mumbled.

'She was dehydrated, and near frozen. You're lucky her heart didn't burst.'

I felt my own heart jump. 'Sorry,' I whispered to the young attendant, then put an edge on it. 'Want to spank me?'

She blinked and sighed. 'Just take care of your cat, okay?'

I thanked her and turned. Someone called me a dick as I slinked out the front door.

That night I had a slow bourbon and listened to the message from James Thomas. Occasionally I checked on my cat – I had placed her in a cardboard box, on a white blanket next to her blue foam ball – who remained awake and calm but pointedly uninterested in my presence. Later I laid Gil Scott Heron's *Winter in America* on the turntable and had another bourbon. 'A Very Precious Time' came on, and with it a heavy melancholic buzz. A third bourbon didn't change that. I picked up the cardboard box that held my cat, put it at the foot of my bed, and went to sleep.

On Saturday afternoon I drove out to Laurel with the heater of my Dart blowing cool air toward my numb face. The temperature had dropped severely overnight and remained somewhere in the high teens. I passed through a studentless College Park and then into the warehouse district of Beltsville. As I neared Laurel, the thick traffic reflected the last shopping weekend before Christmas. At a tree stand, a fire burned in an iron barrel. Near that a father tied a Douglas fir to the roof of his station wagon while his kids chased each other around the car. Loudspeakers were lashed to poles, and through the speakers came the echo of canned carols.

I parked the Dart near Laurel Mall and walked to a place called Bernardo O'Reilly's that stood in the mall's lot. Once inside I was greeted by a young brunette hostess. She was wearing shorts and a white oxford with green suspenders over the oxford. The suspenders had buttons pinned on them from top to bottom, and on the buttons were 'wacky' sayings redundantly punctuated with exclamation points.

'Welcome to Bernardo O'Reilly's,' the hostess said with a cheerfully glued-up smile, but her eyes had no depth. 'One for lunch?'

'One for the bar.'

'All righty,' she said.

'Okeydokey,' I said.

'Right this way.'

I followed her, dodging baby carriages, shopping bags, and perky waiters and waitresses dressed the same way as the hostess. There was the hood of a '50 Chevy mounted on the wall and next to that antique Coca-Cola ads and Moxie signs, and the mounted heads of wooden Indians. Bernardo O'Reilly's looked less like a bar than it did a garage sale run by Keebler elves.

I nodded my hostess off as I removed my overcoat, but she was already skipping toward a table where the entire wait staff had gathered to sing 'Happy Birthday' to a woman in a pink jogging suit. I had a seat at the empty bar.

There were two young bartenders. Both wore green suspenders, and both had green bow ties to match. The larger of the two stood in front of me. He was heavyset, leaning to fat, and he had a modified crew cut that seemed to be the Laurel rage. The little tuft of hair that remained on the top of his head had been gelled up.

'What can I get you?' he said. A button on his suspender said HAVE A REAL COOL YULE.

'Just a Coke, please.'

'Would you like to see a menu?'

'No, thanks.'

He pointed to a machine behind him that had a tap protruding from the front of a clear plastic plate. Behind the plate something swirled like a brown and white pinwheel. 'How 'bout a Coke-a-Doke?' the bartender said.

'What the hell's that?'

He looked at me through a sour smile. 'Rum and Coke. You know, frozen.'

'A regular Coke'll do it,' I said. 'And don't do anything cute to it, hear?'

He nodded and came back with my drink. I placed my car next to the coaster (which advertised COKE-A-DOKE) where he set the glass. He picked up the card and looked it over. His mouth dropped open and his lips moved as he did it.

'You wanna talk to the manager?' he said. 'Is that it?'

'No. I can talk to you if it's all right.'

'What about?'

I reached inside my overcoat and pulled out the photo of April that Billy had sent me and placed it on the bar. The bartender glanced down but didn't touch the photo. 'She was in here about a week and a half ago,' I said, 'on a Tuesday night. Drinking at this bar, I think.'

'I don't work Tuesday nights.'

'Who does?'

The bartender jerked his thumb toward the service area, where his partner was garnishing some frozen drinks on a tray. 'He does. He works the main bar at night and service bar on the weekends.'

'Ask him to come over here for a second, will you?' I pulled my wallet and from that a five. I placed the five on the bar and pushed it into my friend's hand. 'Thanks.'

'Sure thing.'

Bartender Number One walked over to Bartender Number Two to talk things over. As they talked, Bartender Number One dropped the five into an empty pitcher that was their mutual tip jar. I listened to the Beach Boys' pathetic 'Little Saint Nick' on the house stereo while some whistles screamed and boingers boinged in the background, probably signaling someone else's birthday. The place made me want to puke something, preferably Coke-a-Doke, directly on the bar.

Bartender Number Two walked my way. He puffed out his narrow chest and lowered his voice. 'How's it goin?'

'Good.' I tapped the photo once on the bar. 'She was in here Tuesday night last week, with a friend of mine.'

'What's this all about?'

'It's about another five, for you and your buddy.'

Number Two looked around and leaned over the bar. 'You're talkin' about a ten then, am I not right?'

'If ten can make you remember.'

He looked over the photo and back at me. 'What'd your friend look like?'

'My age and size. Blond hair.'

'Drinkers, right?'

'You tell me.' I put the ten on the bar and kept my hand on it. He studied the photograph.

'Okay. They were in that night. The reason I remember is 'cause Tuesday's rum night. You know, we do a special on it, get a premium back from the local distributor. Anyway, it doesn't draw much of a crowd, but this particular lady' – he touched his finger to the photo – 'she put away almost a liter of Bacardi Dark herself that night. Man, she could really pound it.'

I took my hand off the bill. Number Two pulled it off the bar, folded it, and slipped it into the breast pocket of his oxford shirt. 'How much for the Coke?' I said.

'On the house,' he said, and winked as I put on my overcoat. 'If you don't mind my asking, why are you after those two? They done anything wrong?'

'No,' I said. 'Nothing wrong. Just a man and his wife, gettin' a load on for the holidays. Thanks for the information.'

'No problem. Have a real cool yule.'

'Right.'

On the way home I stopped at Town Hall in College Park for one beer that turned into four and two hours' worth of pool with a biker named Robert. The sky was dark when I walked out. I drove down Rhode Island Avenue and cut across Northeast to my apartment in Shepherd Park.

My cat was lapping water from her dish when I entered my apartment. I spooned some salmon into her food dish and tapped the can with the spoon. She abandoned the water for the salmon. In my bedroom I hit the power button on my stereo – Weasel was still on, moving from the Kinks' 'Father Christmas' to the Pogues/Kirsty MacColl duet, 'Fairytale of New York' – and I let it play. Out in the

342

hall I opened the closet door and searched until I found a two-foot-high plastic Christmas tree with retractable arms, buried in the clutter. I dusted off the tree and set it up on the small table in my living room.

After that I made coffee and poured some whiskey in it and took it out to my couch. I drank it to the fade-in of the Pretenders' '2000 Miles.' When I woke up, my cat was sleeping in my lap. I talked to her for a long while as I scratched behind her ears. Then I picked her up and carried her into my bedroom, where I put her in the cardboard box. The clock on my nightstand said 2:14 A.M.

I undressed and removed my wristwatch and laid it on my dresser. Next to the watch were the earrings and the ring from Tommy Crane's cottage. I picked up the ring and looked closely at the silver antique setting. Then I absently rubbed the tiny ruby that was set like a spot of blood in the middle of the ring.

I switched off the light and got into bed. I thought of April and Billy, and of Tommy Crane. The next time I looked at the clock it read 4:05. I sat up in bed, reached for my cigarettes, and lighted one off a match. A half-hour later I sat up again and put fire to another one in the dark.

17

Jackie Kahn's accordion-gated elevator rose through the center of the marble staircase and stopped with pneumatic ease. My footsteps echoed on the marble floor that led to her door. I knocked once on the door. It opened and Jackie leaned in the frame.

She was wearing a mustard-colored bathrobe. Something black and lacy showed from beneath the collar of the bathrobe. She smiled. 'Nicky.'

'Hey, Jackie.'

'You're mighty punctual tonight.'

'That's me. Johnny-on-the-Spot. Here.' I handed her a bottle of Chilean cabernet. She inspected the label.

'Looks fine,' she said with a nod.

'Gran Torres, 1982.'

'Come on in.'

I stepped into the condo and removed my overcoat in the marble foyer. Jackie hung it in a hall closet, and then I followed her into the living room. A Yule log burned in the fireplace set in the lavender west wall, and in the dining room a beveled glass table was set for two. On the center of the table one lavender candle was lit. Jackie kept walking and I followed as I talked to her back and watched the shimmer of her thin calves.

'Where we going?'

'To the bedroom, pal. We've got a date, remember?'

'Sure, I do. But this is all happening so fast.' Jackie stopped walking, turned, and rolled her eyes.

'Dinner's almost ready. Let's do it, okay?'

'Do it?'

'Yeah.'

'How about a drink first?'

'Nope.'

'Hinders the sample, right?' Jackie didn't answer.

We moved into her bedroom. It was a futon-and-halogen-lamp affair with a fireplace on the wall adjacent to the bed. She had built a small fire, and the halogen lamp was dimmed to its lowest degree. Two Bose 301s were mounted in a teak wall unit behind the bed. Chaka Khan was doing 'Everlasting Love' through the speakers. I nodded to the speakers.

'Chaka a relative of yours?'

'She spells it differently,' Jackie Kahn said. 'Quit stalling, Nick. Let's make a baby.'

Jackie undid her robe and sat facing out on a sky blue towel that she had spread on the edge of the futon. She spread her knees and leaned back, resting her palms on the futon. The black lace teddy she was wearing ended at her midriff. Below that was her flat abdomen and below that faint tan lines where her panties would have been. The muscles of her inner thighs rippled and then met in one beautifully manicured vee of cleanly shaved pudendum. I felt slightly dizzy as the blood in my head quickly headed south.

'You plan on doing this through osmosis?' Jackie said.

I shook my head, closed my mouth, gulped, and removed my shirt. I tripped climbing out of my slacks, then did the one-legged hop as I pulled off my socks. Chaka Khan screamed as I took off my underwear and dropped it in the pile with the rest of my clothes.

'Okay, I'm ready.'

Jackie smirked. 'You only look half-ready.'

'It would help if you'd say something romantic.'

'How about grabbing that Vaseline off the nightstand?'

'That's a start,' I said.

I retrieved the blue-and-gold jar from the nightstand, removed the top, and dipped two fingers into the petroleum jelly. I walked toward Jackie with a cupped hand and a smile of crocodilian sensitivity.

Jackie said, 'Hold it right there, soldier. I'll do that.'

I nodded bashfully and handed her the jar. Jackie scooped out some Vaseline and massaged it into her vulva with two index fingers. When one of the fingers disappeared knuckle-deep into her vagina, the dizziness returned, and I glanced down to see my dick jumping about like some rude marionette.

'I think I'm about ready now,' I said.

'Well, you look it. Come on.'

I moved forward, and we did the dance. Except at the moment of entry, when she grudgingly let a parted-lip wince cross her face, Jackie remained quite expressionless throughout. Twice during our 'lovemaking' I greedily reached inside her negligee to feel her breasts, and both times she mechanically slapped my hand away. That slowed things down a bit, as did my lame attempts at humor ('Jackieee,' I shouted at one point, 'oh, Jackie, oh, Jackie, uh-Ooooh!'), but when I finally closed my eyes and began to enjoy the great pureness of sensation, the shortness of breath, and the last tongue-biting, eyes-rolled-up-into-the-head preejaculatory seconds, then everything in the room, everything in the world in fact, was better than fine.

When it was over I removed my sweaty forehead from Jackie's dry shoulder. The edges of Jackie's deep brown eyes crinkled as her smirk twisted up on one side. She brushed a hand back through her short black hair and leaned back on the futon.

'Well?'

'Well, I can't tell for certain, of course,' I said. 'But it sure *felt* like the mother load.' Then I cocked my head thoughtfully to one side. 'Was it beautiful for you?'

'Nicky,' she said. 'You are *such* an asshole.'

Jackie had grilled swordfish steaks on the Jenn-Air and served them topped with mustard, butter, and dill sauce. We ate them with grilled new potatoes and a green salad lightly seasoned with oregano and pepper and garlic vinegar. I had a sip of the cabernet and Jackie did the same.

'Nice wine,' she said.

'I'm a hero, then. I thought the red might not go with the fish.'

'A myth. The red goes fine. As for being a hero, I'll tell you in a couple weeks.'

'That when you find out?'

'Uh-huh.'

'Well, if it doesn't happen this time – you know, I'll always be there for you.' I slid an oil nod toward her bedroom, and Jackie laughed.

'If it doesn't work out, I'll try the insemination route next time, thanks.'

I put my wineglass on the table. 'It wasn't all that awful, was it?'

'No, it wasn't all that awful. But I didn't enjoy it, if that's what you mean. I went through my entire youth and my twenties not *enjoying* it, as a matter of fact.' Jackie had a taste of fish and closed her eyes briefly as she chewed and swallowed. 'When I finally did admit to myself what I really wanted, there was a long period of curiosity, and then some guilt, and after that acceptance. And now I just feel right. And happy.'

'Well, then I am too,' I said. 'Happy for you. We're friends, right?'

346

Jackie smiled radiantly in the light of the single candle that stood between us on the beveled glass table. 'You are a good friend.' She leaned in on her forearms. 'So I was wondering if you could scare up the energy to give it another shot after dinner. For insurance. I know I'm ovulating – I've been on Pergonal to stimulate it, and I can feel it, like a little tickle down there.' She looked toward her lap and back at me.

'What do you think?'

'It's been a while since I've Done the Deuce.'

'Is that a yes?'

'It is.'

I left Jackie's around midnight and drove out of Kalorama, up Connecticut and west to Wisconsin, where I turned right and headed uptown. Christmas lights were strung in the windows of the bars and in the pizza parlors that served AU students in that part of town. I listened to the Cure's 'Pictures of You' and kept listening after I had cut the engine of my Dart in front of Lee's apartment. When the song was done I climbed out of my car and turned the collar up on my overcoat as I took the stairs to Lee's.

She answered on the third knock after a check through her peephole. I straightened up as the door opened. Lee wore black jeans and a hip-length, army green sweater. The sweater picked up the green from her eyes.

'Hi, Nick.' She smiled weakly and looked behind her toward the living room, then back at me.

'Hi. Can I come in?'

'I don't think it's such a good idea,' she said.

'Got company?'

Her features softened. 'Yes.'

'Talk to me for a minute?'

Lee looked behind her once more and nodded. She checked the lock and closed the door, and stepped out with me into the yellow light of the stairwell. Her arms folded up and she began to shiver. I took off my overcoat and draped it over her shoulders. The hem of the coat nearly touched the ground. Lee looked up.

'How'd it go tonight?' she said.

'It went okay.'

'I'm sure you found a way to make it interesting. Anyway, I didn't expect to see you tonight.' She turned her head and nodded at the door. 'Obviously.'

I shuffled my feet. 'Listen, Lee. I'm not drunk . . . I didn't come over

347

here tonight to bother you. I just wanted to talk, maybe spend the night. Just sleep with you.'

Lee looked down at the overcoat that was billowing at her slippered feet. 'Sorry, Nick. About my friend in there' – Lee motioned her chin – 'it's nothing serious really, he's just a friend.'

'You don't have to tell me anything.'

'Well, I want to. And I want to talk. I've been meaning to call, to tell you.'

'Tell me what?'

Lee looked down again and then raised her head. She brushed some of her brown hair off her face. 'This isn't a good time, I know. But I'm graduating in January, in a couple of weeks. And after that . . . I've decided to leave town, Nick.'

'For how long?'

'I don't know. My parents have been bugging me all year, 'What are you going to do after graduation?' I guess they're probably right. My father wants me to do some paralegal work, he's got a job lined up for me. I'm going back up to Long Island. It's not like I'll never be back. Who knows, right?'

'You'll figure it out,' I said. 'You'll do fine.'

'Thanks.' Lee put her arms under mine and locked her hands behind my back. She kissed me lightly on the base of my ear. 'How's it going for you?'

'Things are moving.'

'Yeah?' She smiled. 'What about your friend's wife? You find her?'

'I'm close, I think.'

'Anything on your friend Henry?'

'I'm getting close on that too.'

'What happens to you after that?'

I chuckled unconvincingly. 'Short-term goals for me, Lee. You know that.'

Lee kissed me on the lips for a long while. I didn't want her to pull away. I didn't want to lose the warmth of her face, or her smell. When she backed up, her eyes were wet. It could have been the bitter air, but I wanted it to be the loss.

Lee handed me my overcoat and smiled. 'Bye, Nicky. I'll call you. Soon.'

'So long, Lee.' I turned and walked down the stairs to my car.

I stopped once more that night around the corner at May's, for a bourbon and a glass of beer. Steve Maroulis was behind the bar. Before I left I placed a ten-dollar bet with Maroulis on a horse named Miss

Emmy and then drove back by Lee's. The windows of her second-story apartment were dark now. I headed for Military Road and drove home through empty streets.

18

The next day I replaced Mai behind the bar at three o'clock. Monday night was the worst shift of the week, and it was traditionally hers, but Mai was making me do penance for my trip to southern Maryland. I stuffed my blue bar rag into the waistband of my jeans, smoothed it out on the side of my hip, and passed through the service entrance to the bar.

Happy sat on his favorite stool, staring straight ahead into the bar mirror, one hand around an up glass, the other holding a lit Chesterfield. Mai stood at the service bar and drank a shift Heineken while she talked to me about some unfortunate young marine she was dating. I stocked the backup liquor beneath the rack and nodded occasionally as she talked.

A guy named Dave drank coffee and sat alone at the end of the bar, reading a pulp novel called *Violent Saturday*, by W. L. Heath. Dave was the Spot's reader – every joint had one – who never drank anything stronger than black coffee. I suspected he was an on-the-wagon alkie who simple liked the nostalgia of sitting in a bar, but I never confirmed it. The only time he ever spoke to me was when I tried to empty and clean his overflowed ashtray. 'Don't do that,' he had said quietly, gripping the side of it. 'Dirty's the way I like it.'

When Mai left I put Bob Marley's *Kaya* on the house deck and turned up the volume. I poured myself a cup of coffee, lit a Camel, and folded my arms. In the rectangular cutout of the reach-through I could see Ramon in a boxer's stance, toe-to-toe with Darnell, who had raised his long arms, exposing his midsection. Ramon punched Darnell's abdomen with a left and then a right. Darnell smiled and slowly shook his head.

That was how the afternoon and early evening passed. Buddy and Bubba came in, whispered quietly to each other, and split one pitcher before leaving with a sneer in my direction. Len Dorfman stopped by for a late Grand Marnier and talked loudly about a 'savage' he had locked up that day, until a hard stare from Darnell sent him out the door. And Boyle came by for a draught beer and a shot of Jack.

Boyle mumbled about 'the fucking streets' and his 'fucking kids' throughout his round. I left him, and when I stumbled back from the walk-in with two cases of Bud in my arms, he was gone. A damp five-dollar bill lay across the Cuervo Gold coaster next to his empty shot glass. I restocked the cooler to Let's Active's *Cypress* while Darnell mopped the kitchen and hosed off its rubber mats. When I was done I slid a worn copy of *London Calling* into the tape deck and hung the dripping clean glasses upside down in the rack above the bar. Then I drained the sinks and wiped everything down and poured two inches of Grand-Dad into a heavy shot glass. I opened a bottle of Bud, stood it next to the shot, had a taste of both, and lit a smoke. An unlatching sound came from the direction of the front door.

A man and a woman walked in and took the two steps down into the bar area of the Spot. A stream of cold air flowed in with them. The man walked slowly and deliberately, and stopped in front of the bar, running his hands through the waistband of his tan polyester slacks. The woman stopped two feet behind him and stared. The heavy drama of cops was present in each choreographed movement.

'You Stefanos?' the man said.

'That's right.'

'Too late for a drink?'

'As a matter of fact, it is,' I said genially, keeping my arms folded. 'I'm about closed. Just waiting for my friend in the kitchen to finish up.'

The woman spoke in a low dull voice. 'He's finished now. Tell him that, and tell him we want to be alone.' She had military-short brown hair and round Kewpie-doll lips. Her pocked cheeks had been camouflaged with rouge.

'Detectives, Metropolitan Police,' the man said, and quickly opened his coat to reveal a badge suspended from his breast pocket. 'I'm Goloria, and this is Wallace.'

'Detectives?' I said, feigning surprise, looking them over. Goloria wore a stained London Fog raincoat over a brown plaid sport jacket. Wallace had on a gray wool skirt with a cotton oxford and a vinyl Members Only jacket worn over that.

'Just tell your friend to leave,' Goloria said, 'so we can talk.'

'Now?'

'Tell him.'

I walked back to the kitchen. Darnell was finished and dressed for the weather, his brown overcoat buttoned and his leather kufi tight on his head. He had been standing in the dark, looking at us from the reach-through.

'Better get going,' I said.

'You sure, man?'

'It's all right. They're cops.'

'That don't mean a *fuckin'* thing. You ought to know that.'

'Go on, Darnell. It's all right.'

Darnell walked out and passed without looking either of them in the eye. He closed the front door tightly as he left the Spot. I emerged from the darkness of the kitchen and took my place behind the bar. 'The Guns of Brixton' 's thick bass came from the house speakers. Goloria and Wallace had taken seats at two adjacent stools. Wallace lit a smoke and put her black vinyl handbag next to the ashtray in front of her. Sitting there, her shoulders appeared to be broader than Goloria's.

Goloria said, 'What are we listening to?'

'The Clash,' I said.

He turned to Wallace and raised his thin eyebrows mockingly. Then he turned back to me. 'Turn that shit off and fix us a couple of drinks. When you're finished, come around the bar and let's have a talk.'

'Sure. What'll it be?'

Goloria looked up at top call and squinted. 'Crown Royal on the rocks, with a splash. Wallace'll have the same. Okay, Wallace?' Wallace nodded.

I moved to the stereo and hit the STOP button on the deck. After that I filled two rocks glasses with ice and free-poured the whiskey. I topped it with a spurt of water from the gun, and set both glasses down in front of the cops. Then I drained my Grand-Dad and kept my eyes on Wallace as I did it. I grabbed my bottle of Bud off the bar, walked around to their side, and stood behind them. They swivelled their stools around to face me.

'What can I do for you?' I said.

Wallace blew some smoke in my direction, and Goloria sipped whiskey while we looked each other over. He was on the low side of forty, but his long narrow face had a cancerous gauntness. His mouth hung open and his lids drooped as he studied me. He looked somewhat like a hound.

'Ste-fa-nos.'

'That's right.'

'Greek?'

'Yeah.'

Goloria rubbed a bony finger along his ten o'clock shadow and grinned. The rubbing made a scraping noise in the bar. He looked at Wallace. 'Wallace, I've known a few Greeks in my years on the force. Hardworking people. Restaurant people, mostly. A few professionals, here and there. But never a Greek detective. That's strange, isn't it?'

'That's right,' Wallace deadpanned. 'It's strange.'

'Well, maybe not so strange,' Goloria said quickly, 'when you think about it. I mean, the Greeks never did mind taking on the dirtiest jobs – not if there was a buck in it for 'em. Hell, you can't even get niggers to do restaurant work anymore.'

'What's your point?' I said.

'My point is, being a detective – a private detective that is – it's dirty work. And it's usually work where you can pick up a quick dirty buck. So I figure it's not too different for a guy like you to be in the private detective business.'

''Cause it's dirty,' Wallace said.

'I figured that out,' I said. 'You two practice this before you walked in?'

'Shut up,' Goloria said, and then flashed me a smile of sharp carnivorous teeth. 'Okay?'

I swigged from the neck of my beer, swallowed, and sighed. 'What do you want?'

Goloria said, 'You've been out in my district asking questions about a woman named April Goodrich.'

'What district is that?'

'The Third.'

'I'm looking for her,' I admitted.

'Well, now you can stop. I've got that covered, understand?'

I said, 'Let's skip all the bullshit. What we're really talking about here is the reward money that Joey DiGeordano put out on the street. Am I right?'

Goloria said, 'Say that again?'

Wallace eased herself down off the stool and stood on the wooden floor under the smoky light of the conical lamp. She opened the clasp of her vinyl handbag. Goloria set down his drink, rose, and slowly straightened out his raincoat against his chest with both hands. I backed up a step. The Spot was quiet and suddenly very small.

I looked at Goloria. 'I'm not in it for the reward money. So I'm saying that I'm not in your way. That solve our problem?'

'I don't know a Joey DiGeordano,' Goloria said.

'I thought maybe you did,' I said, watching Wallace knead something inside her handbag.

'What else you think?' Goloria said.

'I thought for a second, maybe you were just a little bit Greek.' My eyes narrowed as I felt the warmth of the Grand-Dad. 'You know. Dirty.'

'He told you to shut up,' Wallace said unemotionally.

'Sorry,' I said. 'Detective Gloria?'

'It's Go-loria,' he said, taking a step toward me.

'Right. Anyway, I apologize. But you two have just got me a little confused. Being with you here, see, I just can't figure out' – I scratched my forehead – 'I just can't figure out which one of you two's got the swingin' dick.'

'I do,' Wallace said, and there was a metallic flash as her brass-knuckled fist swung and connected across my jaw. On the slow trip down I felt a dull ache and after that a jolt of pain. I landed on my elbows as cold beer emptied out across my chest, and I looked up. The two of them stood there, silhouetted against the light of the conical lamp. Their figures glided across a back-drop of smoke and white stars. I rubbed my jaw and squinted up in their direction. A small puddle of blood washed around in my mouth. I swallowed it and coughed.

'Now I think you get it, right, Stefanos?' It was Goloria's calm voice. I kept my mouth shut. He waited and spoke again. 'Well, here it is anyway, for the record: I don't want you playing detective anymore in my district. You got nothing to do with the Goodrich girl anymore. You got nothing to do with *anything* in my district anymore, understand?'

Wallace chuckled and kicked my foot. 'He understands. Sure, he does.'

Goloria made a head movement toward the door. 'Let's go, Wallace.' They began to turn.

I stopped them with my voice. 'Hey,' I said weakly. 'You forgot to pay for your drinks.'

Goloria withdrew a wallet from the seat of his polyester slacks and balled up a few one-dollar bills. Then he walked back and stood over me and dropped them on my chest. They bounced off and fell beside me to the floor.

'Merry Christmas,' he said.

I stayed on the wooden floor and listened to their shuffling footsteps and to the opening and closing of the front door. I remained there in that position for another ten minutes of silence. When I stopped feeling dizzy I got up on one knee and jiggled my jaw and wiped nausea-sweat from my forehead.

Five minutes later I was in Darnell's kitchen with my head in the washbasin, a steady stream of water running down my face. I stared into the blackness of the drain and thought things over for a long while.

Afterward I dried off with a towel and walked back to the service bar. I poured a shot of whiskey and threw it back, then picked up the telephone and got Mai's number from information. I dialed that number and Mai picked up on the fourth ring.

'Hallo.'

'Mai, it's Nick.'

'Nick that you? It doesn't sound like you. You drunk?'

'Drunk? Yeah, just a little.' I coughed and cleared my throat. 'Listen, Mai, I need you to do me a favor.'

'A favor. Shit, Nicky, don't ask me to take your shift tomorrow. It's Christmas Eve.' Mai whispered into the phone. 'I promised my soldier boy we'd spend all day together. He's here right now.'

'This is the last time, Mai, I promise. I've got to go out of town for the day. Believe me, it can't wait.'

'You don't sound so good, Nicky, honest to God.' She thought things over. 'If it's really important—'

'It is. Listen, I owe you.'

'You're damn right you do,' she said rapidly, but the edge was out of her voice. 'Anyway, maybe if I come in tomorrow, Phil will remember to hand me my Christmas bonus. Fat chance, huh?' She laughed broadly. 'By the way, where you going, back down to the country?'

'Southern Maryland.' I dabbed blood off the side of my mouth with a bar rag.

'Got a girl down there?' she said demurely.

'A girl?' I said, lighting a cigarette. 'I'll find out. Tomorrow.'

19

The next morning I packed my nine-millimeter Browning and a full clip into the trunk of my Dart and drove south on 301 in the direction of Cobb Island. The temperature was in the teens, but there was no wind and my Dart cruised effortlessly down the highway beneath a steel sheet of clouds. At Waldorf I cracked a window and huffed a Camel, and in La Plata I stopped for a burger and a Coke. A half hour later I was on the Island and sitting on a brown Leatherette stool in a nearly empty Formica-floored room that doubled as the dining area and bar of Polanski's.

The bartender's name was Andy. Andy had a brush cut and wore a green V-necked sweater over a white T-shirt that was exposed both at the neck and at the base of his great belly. His double-knit pants were chocolate brown and cinched with a wide black belt. Black work boots covered his long feet.

Andy shook my hand and said, 'Now we've been introduced. What can I get you?'

'A draught beer,' I said.

Andy plunged his thick knotted hand into the cooler and withdrew two glass mugs. He gripped the handles of both with one hand as he tapped out the beer and put a head on it without wasting more than a few drops. I looked at the two beers and then around the empty Polanski's. Andy placed both beers in front of me.

'There you go.' He leaned a scabbed elbow on the bar and studied the crescent-shaped bruise on my jaw.

'Maybe I have that look,' I said with a crooked smile. 'But one beer'll do it for me today. Thanks.'

Andy frowned and looked a bit hurt. 'It's Tuesday, man!' He pointed behind him to a glitter-drawn sign that itemized the daily specials. 'Two-for-one beers every Tuesday – best damn day of the week around here, 'cept for the weekends.'

'Just one for me today, Andy, thanks.' I pushed one of the mugs and slid it in front of his arm. 'You have it.'

He shook his head. 'Too early for me, pardner.' Andy took the mug by the handle and poured it out into the last of three sinks behind the bar. He walked down to the service end and began building a pyramid of shot glasses that he stacked on a piece of green bar netting.

I nursed the draught through a cigarette and stared into the bar mirror. Andy played a Tammy Wynette Christmas tape and stayed on his end of the bar. When my mug was empty I walked across the room to a pay phone near the men's room. In a worn directory I found the number to the Pony Point. I dropped a quarter in the slot and punched in the number and when Wanda picked up I asked to speak to Russel. She put the receiver down. I listened to Tammy Wynette on my end and Randy Travis on theirs until Russel picked up.

'Yeah,' he said.

'Russel, it's Nick Stefanos.' There was a silence. 'The detective from D.C., looking for April Goodrich.'

'I remember you,' he said. 'What you want?'

'You know how to get in touch with Hendricks?'

'Sure,' he said. 'Same way you would – dial nine-one-one.'

'Come on, man,' I said impatiently. 'You know how to get him direct, don't you?'

Russel said, 'What's up with you, man? You don't sound too cool.'

'I'm fine,' I said. 'Listen, Russel. Call Hendricks – this isn't for me, it's for April – and tell him to get over to Tommy Crane's place' – I looked at my watch – 'in about a half hour.'

'I can get him,' Russel said carefully.

'You going to do it?'

Russel paused. 'Sure, Stefanos. I'll do it.'

'Thanks.' I hung up the phone.

I walked back to the bar and dropped a five on it and thanked Andy as I put on my overcoat and slipped my smokes into the side pocket. Then I left Polanski's and stepped across the asphalt lot. The air was cooler now and there was a wind, and the steel clouds had deepened to slate. I climbed into my Dart and fired the ignition.

20

I followed 257 to the steepled church and hung a right onto the road that led to Crane's property. At the gravel entrance I cut left into the break of the oak forest. The trees were leafless but the overhang of their heavy branches darkened the road. In the clearing I stopped my car beneath the single oak that stood near Crane's cottage. Crane's F-150 wasn't there. I cut the engine.

Outside the car, I removed my overcoat, folded it on the driver's seat, and closed the door. I fastened the top button on my wool shirt and called out Crane's name twice. For several minutes I listened to the sound of animal movement in the compound and waited for a human response. When there wasn't one, I walked across the hard earth and hopped up onto the porch of Crane's cottage.

I opened the screen door and knocked on the solid door behind it. From behind the door I heard nothing. I stood there in the cold and stamped the porch with my work boots to circulate blood into my feet. Five minutes later there were still no signs of life, and I tried the knob on the door. It turned and I looked behind me, and then I stepped into Crane's cottage.

I yelled his name. With the door closed, there was only the occasional creak of the old house conceding to the rush of the wind. The smell of bong water and sulfur cut the living room. I walked to the oak-trunk table and touched my finger to the resin in the bowl of the bong. It was cool, as were the butts in the ashtray next to it. I wiped sweat and ash off my hands and onto the thighs of my jeans, and crossed the living room to the narrow hall. I passed the open bathroom door and stood in the doorway to Crane's bedroom. A Westclox alarm ticked loudly from his night table. From the doorway I looked out one window to the compound and out the other to my car beneath the oak. No sign of Crane. I called out his name once more and stood there, listening to the clock. Then I turned and walked back down the hall to the door that had been locked four days earlier.

I tried the knob. The door was still locked.

I jiggled the knob and quickly put a shoulder to the door's body. The frame cracked and split in the right corner, but the door didn't open. I said Crane's name again, but now it was only habit, and this time I didn't wait. I moved one step back and jammed the sole of my work boot into the area just below the knob, and the door kicked open.

I stood at the top of a dusty flight of irregular wooden stairs. The bottom of the stairs ended in darkness. I grabbed a loose banister and skimmed it as I walked down toward the cellar. A moldy, botanical smell rose up as I descended. At the last step I searched for a switch, rubbing my hand across a cold cinder-block wall clodded with dirt. I looked back once and saw colorless light at the top of the stairs. I felt no switch, but I kept inching forward.

A string brushed my face. I found it with my hand and pulled down. It clicked without result. I ran my hand up the string and touched a bulb caked with dirt. I wrapped my hand around the bulb and turned it clockwise until there was light.

I stood on a dirt floor in a root cellar that ran the length of the cottage. Rusted farm implements – wooden rakes, a fencepost digger, and a sledgehammer – leaned against the east wall. In the far corner several open-topped brown paper bags sat in rows, where bulbous plants had begun to sprout stalks like emaciated, grasping hands.

Two thick black snakes were stretched out sleeping next to the bags, their heads resting like rubber fists against the cinder-block wall.

My heart rate accelerated, and I looked back up the stairs. When I turned my head back I saw another door set in the third wall. The snakes appeared to be sleeping. I eyed them as I walked over to the door.

The door had been secured with a padlock fastened through a hasp. I put my ear to the cool wood and heard the steady hum of an appliance through the door. I stepped back and listened. There was still no movement above in the cottage. I walked to the east wall and grabbed the sledgehammer by the wood handle and returned quickly to the door. I swung the hammer once and tore the hasp off its hinges. Then I kicked open the door.

Inside, a carefully arranged room was carpeted in red. A mattress lay in one corner and a camera set on a tripod pointed down at the mattress. The walls of the room had been paneled in sound-treated tile. On one wall hung oak shelves filled with black videocassette cases. In one of the shelves a television rested beside a VCR. On another wall several mounted photographs depicted acts of sodomy and rape. Many of the photographs were simply closely cropped shots of women's faces. The faces reflected fear and pain.

A portable humidifier sat on a table and hissed steam into the room. Next to the table the coils of an oil heater glowed red. The room smelled of oil and incense.

I scanned the videotape selection. The cases were unlabeled, as were the tapes within. I walked back to the doorway and looked up the stairs, then returned to the bed and threw back the sheets. The mattress cover was clean. I felt the mattress and then lifted it. A brown leather briefcase lay beneath it on the red carpet.

I grabbed the briefcase by the handle and pulled it free from the bed's frame and dropped it on the floor at my feet. I fumbled with the catch – it wasn't locked – and opened the hinged top. I looked inside and ran my hand along its contents. Then I closed the briefcase and got up off my knees and walked quickly from the room, past the snakes on the cinder-block wall and the tools and the bags containing rooted plants, and up the stairs to the landing, through the narrow hallway to the living room, where I ran now, out the front door and off the porch and across the hard earth to my Dart parked beneath the oak.

I jangled my keys and fit one into the trunk and raised its lid. Inside, my nine-millimeter sat loaded and wrapped in oilskin. I set the briefcase next to it and slammed the trunk shut. Then I looked for my ignition key as I moved to the driver's side of my Dart. I had opened the door of it when I noticed a tall man leaning in the entranceway of the sty, fifty yards away.

His arms were folded and he was staring at me with a grin. Some of his thick black hair had fallen in front of his eyes. Tommy Crane pulled the hair back behind his ears.

He said, 'Can I help you, friend?'

I looked into the car and fingered the ignition key. I might have made it, though maybe not – Crane was quick, I had seen it in his walk – but it didn't matter, because by then I had already decided to push it. Billy Goodrich had hired me to find his wife; I had only found the money, so for me it wasn't over. I closed the door and stepped away from the car.

'I didn't see your truck,' I said with what I knew was an unnatural smile.

'I can't hear you,' Crane said.

'I said, I didn't see your truck.'

'I lent it to a friend.' Crane was wearing his black down vest over a red chamois shirt. He made a sweeping gesture with his hand. 'If you want to talk, come on. We can do it in the sty, but I don't have time to fuck around. I got work to do.'

I looked behind me to the empty gravel road that led into the dimness of the woods. Then I looked back at Crane. 'Okay. Let's talk.'

I walked toward the sty. By the time I reached the hinged gate, Crane had ducked inside. I cleared the lip of the entrance without lowering my head and stepped into the cinder-block structure. The concrete floor was freezing, and the cold traveled up and numbed my calves.

Crane was by the back exit, standing in front of the punch-board that held the butchering knives. He had picked up the black hose that had been coiled beside the copper trough. Liquid boiled inside the trough, and beneath it burned an orange pile of embers. The rank smell of swill filled the sty.

I moved toward Crane and passed a litter of piglets feeding from a sow beneath the warmth of an infrared lamp. Another sow lay alone in a farrowing pen. I could see the balance of the pigs through the exit in the yard out back. Some were down behind the bales of hay. The rest were moving slowly about, wheezing and snorting as they bumped one another with their snouts.

Crane fingered the brass nozzle of the hose and tightened it with a white-knuckled turn. 'So,' he said, looking at the nozzle. 'You came back.'

'I said I would.'

Crane slid his hand down off the nozzle and wrapped his fingers around the black rubber. 'Sayin' it's one thing. The other day, you didn't look like you had the stones.' He squinted. What changed your mind?'

'A dirty cop, back in D.C..'

Crane studied my discolored jaw. 'A cop, huh?'

'That's right. He told me to stay off the case. But it didn't really matter that he was a cop. He was just another guy, looking to get a piece of April Goodrich. It happened like that her whole dumb life. And I think the last time it happened, it happened here.'

Crane said, 'How you figure, friend?'

'It wasn't too tough.' I walked around Crane and leaned my back against the punchboard. It gave me a view through the entrance to the yard outside. I could see most of my car, and beyond that the empty gravel road that ran into the woods. My car sat alone beneath the oak. I thought of Russel and the warmth of his kitchen, and the care he gave to his animals. I wondered if he had picked up the phone and made the call.

'April headed west,' Crane said.

'No,' I said, 'she didn't.' Two large black pigs stood blocking the exit to my left, and Crane had squared off in front of me.

'Then where is she?'

I shifted my weight. 'Here, somewhere. She came down with a briefcase full of money she stole, from back in town. You killed her for the money. Or maybe you killed her for the kick. Either way, Crane, you killed her.'

Crane said, 'You crossed the line now. You better be able to prove what you're sayin'.'

I reached into my pocket of my jeans, pulled out the silver antique ring with the ruby stone, and held it out. Crane's black eyes widened. I said, 'Here's my proof.'

'That's a stupid trick,' Crane said. 'And it's one you're gonna die for.'

He swung the hose. The brass nozzle clipped my shoulder. I felt the sting and tucked my chin into my chest and pulled my elbows in, my balled fists in front of my face. I backed up and Crane swung again, making contact across my forearm. I grunted as the nozzle broke the cushion of muscle and reached the bone.

The black pigs screamed from the doorway. Crane made an animal sound and bared his clenched gray teeth as he brought the hose up over my head. It came down with force, but I moved to the side, and the nozzle chinked the concrete. Before he could bring it back up I pushed him off balance with an open palm, then came quickly out of my stance and fired off a left to his lower back and then a hard right into his kidneys, aiming two feet deep. Crane dropped the hose and doubled down to catch his breath, and when he did I moved in front of him again. I had time to rear back on this one, and Crane didn't even blink as he watched my punch come straight in and connect square on the bridge of his thick nose. The nose gave like dry sponge, but it only moved Crane back one step. He straightened up and walked toward me, blood inching down over his lip.

I stumbled and fell back. Crane grabbed me by the shirt and pulled me back up. There was blood now streaked across his teeth, and in his eyes a mechanical rage. He shook me and then without releasing his grip quickly moved me backward with a shove that sent me into the punchboard. Knives loosened and fell to the concrete. I groped for the handle of the largest one as it bounced but got my hand around its steel blade instead. I heard pigs wheezing and I heard Crane laugh as he kicked my hand and pinned it against the punchboard. I felt the edge of the blade bite the skin of my fingers, and I watched my

362

hand release the knife, and I saw the clean, even slice and then the blood.

Adrenaline brought my knee violently up into Crane's balls. He grunted and his eyes jerked skyward, and I shot my hands up between his and broke out of his grip. He threw a wild round-house. I ducked it, then shifted to the left and came up in a boxer's stance and combinated again with a left and then a right to his back. Crane screamed and spun with a hammer fist that hit my ear like a club and knocked me to the ground. I was up quickly and shaking my head clear when he grabbed me and ran me into the punchboard again. My forehead hit first, and as he pulled me back the sty was spinning and the sounds of Crane and the pigs were in the distance. I was pushed out the exit then, and I fell to my knees in the hard mud, and Crane put a boot to my back. I rolled over and stared at the moving gray sky as squealing pigs brushed my arms and walked with manic clumsiness across my chest. I was still trying to make the sky stop moving when everything suddenly turned to night.

It was day again. I raised myself up on one elbow. The pigs were now back along the fence. I moved my arms at the joint and then my legs. Nothing was broken, and nothing felt right. I wiped blood from my palm onto the leg of my jeans and stared at the ground until I could focus on the ridged mud. When I looked up I saw Crane taking long strides through the sty in my direction. The snub-nosed .38 was in his hand.

'I should have killed you straight up,' he shouted, still walking with purpose. 'Makes no difference now.'

I didn't try to move. I took a deep breath and smelled the air, and I remembered that it was Christmas Eve. Crane ducked his head and exited the sty. I thought of my grandfather, and of his hand around mine, the two of us, walking at night through the snow. Crane stood over me and cocked the pistol's hammer and pointed the .38 at my head.

He said, 'No mess, friend.'

There was a roar. Crane's red shirt ripped apart in the middle of his chest, and his black vest waved out as if it had been blown by a sudden gust of wind. Blood and bone jetted out and rained down. Crane threw the .38 aside and did an airy two-step dance. His eyes rolled as he fell to the ground and landed at my side, his arm draped across my chest. The arm jerked in spasm. I pushed it off me. Then I looked in the direction of the sty.

Hendricks was standing in the exit. Smoke curled out of the barrel of the .357 that he held at his side.

I wiped chunks of Crane off my face with a shaking hand. I looked at what was left of him. His mouth was open and his gray teeth were sunk into the mud. The large white boar hobbled by and stopped and inspected Crane's inert body. Something like a smile was on the boar's snout. I looked at Hendricks and nodded. Hendricks nodded back.

'April's dead,' I said.

'Then Crane had it comin'.'

'Maybe so,' I said. 'But you didn't have to kill him.'

Hendricks smoothed out the brim of his hat as he holstered the .357. 'I was aiming for his legs,' he said, with a shrug. 'Sight's way off on this goddamn Smith and Wesson.' A slight gleam appeared in his eye. 'Gotta get that son of a bitch fixed. Know what I mean?'

21

Hendricks walked slowly back to his car and radioed for an ambulance. While we waited for it he had a seat beside me in the mud and asked for the details. I handed him April's ring and described everything I had seen in the cottage, with the exception of the brown leather briefcase. Hendricks listened closely. He never once looked at Crane or touched the corpse.

When the ambulance arrived I left the keys to my car with Hendricks and was gurneyed and rushed north to La Plata General. I spent the next three hours in the emergency room, mostly next to a moaning, liver-spotted old woman who had stumbled and broken both wrists on what was probably her last Christmas Eve. She complained about her daughters who lived in Pittsburgh and never called, even at Christmas, and I sat there and let her complain. I had eaten a couple of Tylenol 3s, and I wasn't feeling all that bad. But a taste of whiskey would have made things a whole lot better.

The bearded doctor who finally saw me had the look of a lawn and garden department manager. He cleaned out the cut across the inside of my hand and wrapped my fingers together with tape over a gauze bandage. After that I was ushered off into a busy room and laid on a cold table, where an unsmiling brunette with shapely but occupationally cumbersome breasts took several X-rays of my bruised arms and shoulders. Everything turned up negative.

I asked for 'something stronger,' but the good doctor ignored me as he pushed his wire-rimmed glasses back up over the bridge of his nose and wrote out a prescription for more Tylenols. When I was released I walked out to the parking lot alone. Hendricks leaned on the trunk of my Dart. His white car sat idling next to mine.

I followed him to the station in La Plata and sat at a nondescript metal desk in a room that had a gated chain fence run along its interior. Hendricks asked me the same questions he had asked earlier, and I tried to duplicate my answers exactly. When it was over I asked if I was to be charged with anything, and I asked if my name would be released to any of the local media. He answered no to both questions, and I thanked him again and wished him a good Christmas. He did the same, and as he handed me the keys to my car I shook his hand and said good-bye.

Two miles up the road I pulled off onto the shoulder, got out of the car, and walked back and unlocked my trunk. Inside was my automatic, and next to that the leather briefcase. I closed the trunk and got back into my car and stopped at the next open bar and had a beer and two shots of Jim Beam, then drove back to my apartment in Shepherd Park.

My landlord was waiting for me at the door with my annual Christmas present, a fifty of green-seal Grand-Dad. I gave him a hug and a kiss on his dark brown cheek, and picked up my cat on the way in, rubbing the scar tissue in the socket of her right eye as I carried her. My landlord followed me. I poured two slugs of Grand-Dad into juice glasses and shook two Tylenol 3s into his palm, and two into mine, and we washed those down with the bourbon. Two hours later the bottle was nearly empty, and I had the English Beat's *I Just Can't Stop It* on the stereo, full blown, and my landlord and I were dancing wildly around my living room while my cat watched calmly from her roost on top of the radiator. It was Christmas Eve, and I guess I had a right to celebrate, but I wasn't thinking about the holiday. I was thinking that I had come close this time, that I had seen the empty black eye, and I had walked away. I was thinking how good it felt to be alive.

Hendricks phoned me from southern Maryland two days later. A dog search of Crane's property had failed to turn up any sign of April Goodrich. The cottage had been combed as well, with no result. Only when Hendricks screened the tapes from the root cellar did he find the evidence.

The collection had consisted of the standard rough trade pornography, with a few snuff films in the bunch. On the tail end of one, some home video footage had been cut in.

'You sure it was her?' I said carefully to Hendricks.

'Yeah,' he mumbled. 'You don't want to know the details, Stefanos. Let's just say he did her like one of his pigs. Tied up, with one bullet to the head.'

I thought about it and closed my eyes. Hendricks coughed once on the other end of the line. I said, 'That kind of thing can be faked, Hendricks. Any reason to think . . .'

'No reason. Listen, Stefanos – I've seen the tape, you haven't. What I saw can't be done with trickery, or special effects. April Goodrich is dead. Now, I don't know the motive, except that Crane surely was one sick son of a bitch. But it doesn't matter now, does it?'

'I guess not,' I said, thinking of the money.

'I called her husband,' Hendricks said.

'I know. I spoke to him myself.'

'How's he doin'?'

'How would you be?' I said.

'Right,' Hendricks said.

'There's a service for her tomorrow, outside of town.'

'I never get that close to D.C..'

'Bad things happen in the country too, Hendricks.'

'Bad things happen everywhere,' he said tiredly. 'You take care.'

The memorial service for April Goodrich was held in a small Baptist church in Beltsville, just south of Laurel. April had no family, and none of her former friends were in attendance. The group consisted of Billy, his parents, me, and a pale, anemic minister. I kept three pews back from Billy and his family and watched Billy the entire time. He stood with his hands folded, expressionless throughout.

Outside the church I shook Billy's hand and began to walk away. Billy told his parents to wait on the front steps and followed me across the gravel lot to my Dart. He caught me as I was putting the key to the driver's side lock.

Billy thanked me for coming, and for seeing everything through to the end. Then he asked if I had 'found anything' that day at Crane's.

I shoved him back with both hands. Billy fell onto the gravel. He sat there looking up at me, and we stared at each other for what seemed to be a very long time. Finally I got into my Dart, started it, and pulled out of the lot.

In the rearview I saw him stand and brush the dirt from his billowing cashmere overcoat as he watched me drive away. Billy's parents were behind him, staring at us both. They held each other on the steps of the church, wondering what kind of horrible thing had finally happened, just then, to end it between their son and his old friend.

22

The day after April's service I took the Metro to Gallery Place and had lunch at the District Seen. A bartender in combat fatigues served me a club sandwich and a cup of vegetable beef to go with it. I washed that down with a Guinness, and then another while I read that week's *City Paper* and listened to De La Soul on the house deck. When bicycle messengers started to crowd the place, and Jaegermeisters were served, I settled up my tab.

Out on the street I walked down Seventh, opened a common-entrance glass door, and took the stairs that led to both a portrait gallery and the offices of *DC This Week*, the alternative weekly that was itself a more hard-news alternative to *City Paper*. I entered the door marked DC THIS WEEK.

A young woman in rimless glasses was sitting at a desk, talking into a headset as she clipped art on a rubber mat. She looked up as I walked in, and raised one finger in the air to hold me off. I waited until she had released her call.

'Yes?' she said.

I placed my business card in front of her on the mat. As she looked it over I said, 'I'd like to speak to your editor, if he has a minute.'

'Do you have an appointment with Jack?'

'Nope.' I smiled. She didn't.

'What's this abou – what's this in reference to?'

'It's about my friend, William Henry.'

She relaxed took off her glasses, and rubbed her eyes. 'You knew William?'

'Yes.'

The woman slid her glasses back on and punched a finger at the switchboard. 'I'll see if he's in.'

I stood with my hands in my overcoat pockets and listened to her mumble into the phone. Other phones rang from beyond the makeshift barrier that nearly encircled her desk, and in between their rings the tapping sounds of several keyboards meshed with a dublike bass. The multitalented receptionist removed her headset and stood up.

'Follow me,' she said with a come-hither gesture.

I walked behind her through a room where several tieless young men and young women typed on word processors. In the corner of the room a man with no hair on the sides of his head but plenty on top leaned over a drawing table and drew a line down a straightedge. A small boom box sat on a makeshift ledge above the drawing table, and out of the box Linton Kwesi Johnson spoke over a throbbing bass and one scratchy guitar. None of the people in the room looked up as I passed.

The receptionist stopped at the first door on a row of small offices and opened her palm in direction. I thanked her and stepped into the office. A woman stood up from behind an oak desk.

She was my height, with full-bodied, shoulder-length red hair that had fine threads of silver running through it in several key places. Her cream satin blouse was open three-buttons down and tucked into a short olive green skirt. A wide black belt was wrapped around her waist. Black stockings covered her legs, and on her feet were a pair of olive green pumps. Her thin face was lightly freckled, and the freckles were the same shade of those that were liberally sprinkled across the top of her chest. Lipstick the color of her hair was drawn across her wide mouth. Her eyes were pale green. She extended her hand. I shook it and held it until she pulled it gently back.

'You're Jack?' I said.

'Jack can't see you,' she said. 'My name's Lyla. Lyla McCubbin. I'm the managing editor.'

'Nick Stefanos.'

I handed her the same card I had given the receptionist, removed my overcoat, and had a set in a high-backed chair across from her desk. Lyla sat back down and studied the card.

Her office was a clutter of newspaper and computer paper. Beside her desk was a word processor with green characters on the screen. A section of an article she was editing on the computer had been blocked off in black. Three Rolodexes, a black phone, and a blotter-style desk calendar crowded the top of her desk. Behind her on the white wall hung the office's sole photograph, a picture of a fair-haired child standing between her parents, a young hippie family at a Dupont Circle rally, circa 1969. The child had freckles across her face, and she was holding her father's hand. A Walkman rigged to an external speaker sat next to the computer, softly playing King Crimson's 'Matte Kudasai.'

369

Lyla folded her hands in front of her on the desk. 'Rolanda said you wanted to speak to someone about William Henry.'

'That's right.'

'What about?'

'His murder.'

'What have you got to do with it?'

'I'm looking into it.'

Lyla took a pencil out of a leather cup and tapped the sharp end on her blotter. 'Who are you working for?'

'Myself,' I said. 'And Henry.'

Lyla's phone rang. She kept her eyes on mine and let it ring a few times before she picked it up. 'Tell him I'll call him back.' She replaced the receiver and studied my face. 'So,' she said finally.' You're a private dick.'

' "A black private dick. With a sex machine for all the chicks." '

' "Shaft"?'

' "You damn right." '

Lyla threw her head back and laughed. It was an easy laugh, from way down in her throat. I liked the way it sounded and the unconscious way her mouth opened wide when she did it.

'Well,' she said, 'at least I know that we're from the same generation.'

'Yeah,' I said. 'I saw *Shaft*, first run, at the Town Theatre, on Thirteenth Street. 1971. My grandfather took me – against his better judgment.'

'The Loews Palace on F Street,' she said. 'That was my first downtown film experience. A Liz Taylor double bill, no less. *Butterfield Eight*, and *Cat on a Hot Tin Roof.*'

'So you're a real Washingtonian.'

'All my life.'

'Me too,' I said.

Lyla replaced the pencil in the cup, smiled, and leaned back in her chair. The movement made her camisole shift beneath her satin blouse, and I watched the rise of her freckled breasts. She crossed her left leg over her right. The muscles in her thighs became defined with the action. I shifted in my chair to get a better look. She watched me do it, and neither of us flinched.

'You came here to talk about William Henry,' she said.

'Right.'

'Any progress on the case?'

'Not with the police. Apparently things got cold, real quick. I managed to dig up some stuff on my own.'

'What kind of stuff?'

'You asking questions now?'

'Sorry,' Lyla said. She brushed some lint off the side of her skirt. 'It's a habit. You and I are basically in the same business, right?'

I nodded. 'I used to read your bylines when you were still doing investigative. Before they hired Henry and bumped you up to managing editor.'

'William Henry improved on my work,' she said. 'He was a damn good reporter.'

'He was a good friend too.'

'Yes, he was.' Lyla stared off toward the blank white wall to her left. 'Jack had hired him, in a private interview. So on his first day of work, when he walked in, none of us knew what to expect. Anyway, he comes in, and here's this trim, compact guy, on the short side, with long sideburns – they weren't stylish then – and one of those Ben Bradlee striped shirts, with a rep tie. His hair was receding too, remember, and he wore wire-rims, which only added to that Ivy League schoolboy look.' Lyla ran a finger along the top of her lip. 'So you can imagine that all of us so-called alternative types here didn't trust him at first. But right away he had us all loosened up – that little son of a bitch had the driest sense of humor, and the finest heart, of anyone ever walked through that front door.'

'His death,' I said. 'It wasn't a random murder. That lead, about the light-skinned guy with the bloody shirt, seen leaving his apartment – I think that was basically bullshit, a plant of some kind.'

Lyla leaned in and said, 'Tell me about it.'

'The information I got was that the murderer was let up into Henry's apartment, by the security guard who was on duty that night.'

'Who gave you the information?'

'The security guard.'

'Then you should be talking to him.'

I shook my head. 'He's gone. He's been gone, since he left the message and admitted that he was bought. I finally got hold of his mother – she says he left home a few days ago and hasn't been back since.' I winced inadvertently at the memory of her broken voice as she said it, knowing full well that he'd never be back.

Lyla settled in her chair. 'So that brings it back to us. How can I help you?'

'What was Henry working on here when he died?'

'Nothing,' she said. 'The funny thing is, he had just filed his last story, a week before his death. That week, he took a few days off, though he was in and out of the office, every day. But the cops asked Jack about all that. They took all his notes, and his diskettes.'

'The cops?'

'The two investigators that were assigned his case.'

'They talk to you?'

Lyla nodded. 'I didn't have anything to tell 'em professionally. As for their personal questions, I just didn't answer. I had the impression they weren't going to follow up on the murder anyway.'

Lyla watched me think things over. When I looked up, she was looking into my eyes, and her mouth was open, just a little. I felt something happen between us then, but I moved on.

'It's possible Henry was working on something you didn't know about, isn't it?'

'Sure. He played his cards close to the vest, when he wasn't on a specific assignment.'

'He keep backup diskettes on his notes?'

Lyla said, 'Yep.'

I said, 'You give those to the cops too?'

'Uh-uh.'

'Any chance you'd print out those disks for me?'

'A real good chance,' she said.

'I'd appreciate it.'

Lyla rang Rolanda and had her retrieve Henry's diskettes from the file room. Rolanda entered with a container, and Lyla instructed her to use the laser to print out the last two months' worth of work. Rolanda, who seemed a bit overworked, sighed a bit during the instructions. When she left, Lyla said, 'It'll be a few minutes.'

I nodded to the photograph on the wall. 'That's you, right?'

'Yeah. My parents were beatniks, and then they were hippies. They were a little old for it, even then. But for them it wasn't a fad. I was raised to believe that if you had to go against the grain and suffer a little bit to change things, it was worth it, if it made a difference. Even a small difference.'

'You're doing it.'

'I'm trying.'

I said, 'How close were you with Henry?'

Lyla's pale eyes widened a bit. Off guard, but only for a second. 'You mean,' she said, 'was I sleeping with him?'

'Approximately.'

'Well, it's none of your business, Stefanos. But just to get things on the table – no, I wasn't.' She smiled, but not at me. She was thinking about Henry. 'But hell, I would have, in a heartbeat. And it's not as if I didn't try. Once, when I got him drunk, I even asked him.'

'He was gay.'

'Sure, he was. But he didn't wear it on his sleeve. It was only one part of what he was. And since he didn't talk about it much, I mean, I didn't know if he was . . . exclusive about his gayness or not. Straight people are pretty naive about that kind of shit, aren't they? Anyway, I liked him, and at the very least, I thought it was worth a shot.'

'The cops thought his murder might have been a crime of passion, at first. You know any of his lovers?'

Lyla shook her head. 'Not personally. I did meet this guy once, a bartender, when William and I were drinking at the Occidental, in the Willard. The bartender's name was Michael – a gorgeous guy, but stiff. I didn't like him. William was a bit in the bag that night, and he told me that the two of them had dated.'

'Anything worth checking out?'

'I would say no. but I don't know how your business works. How you get your information, how things shake out.'

I shrugged. 'I talk to a lot of people and things happen.'

Lyla looked at my bandaged hand and then up at the deep purple crescent on my jaw. 'They certainly do.'

'Not as often as you'd think.'

'You a drinker, Stefanos?'

'Now it's your turn to get personal.'

'You look like a drinker.'

'I know what it tastes like.'

'No need to be defensive,' she said. 'I like a man who can take a drink.'

After that we sat without speaking. Her homemade tape was playing Richard Thompson's *Gypsy Love Songs*. The time went by like that, and the silence wasn't uncomfortable. I liked her looks, and her honesty, and her intelligence. I liked everything about her.

Rolanda entered the office with a manila folder filled with papers. I took the folder and thanked her, and stood to put on my overcoat. Lyla McCubbin wrote a phone number on the back of her business card and pushed it across the desk. I slipped the card into the cellophane cover of my cigarette pack. She took my card and placed it in the front compartment of her desk drawer. Then she stood and shook my hand.

'I hope this helps.'

'I'll let you know what happens. Thanks.'

Lyla leaned on one foot. She let her other foot out of her olive green pump and ran her stockinged toe around the shoe's instep. Then she crossed her arms and twisted her lovely mouth up into a lopsided smirk.

'Call me. Okay, Stefanos?'

I said, 'I will.'

23

I walked east on Pennsylvania Avenue. The temperature had fallen with evening, but I was warm with the buzz of new energy against the night. At the National, older couples were exiting cabs, dressed and eager for Andrew Lloyd Webber's latest scam on the theatre-going public. In Freedom Plaza tourists walked hurriedly past a man playing flute. The man stood coatless in front of an empty wax cup.

At Fourteenth and Penn I entered the leaded glass doors of the Occidental Restaurant in the Willard Hotel. I walked through a long hall, past black-and-white portrait photographs – Pat Schroeder and Carole Thompson on my right, George Bush and Harry Truman on my left – and down a flight of stairs into the bar area of the restaurant. Cole Porter played as I descended the stairs. I felt like Fred Astaire, with a two-day beard covering a bruised face.

I took off my black overcoat and hung it on a rack, transferred my smokes to the inside pocket of my Robert Hall sport coat, and had a seat at the bar. The seat I took was next to a black-haired Jewess who was picking at an appetizer plate of peppered scallops and squid on a bed of romaine lettuce. She held her fork as if it were hot. Next to her sat another young woman with large, expensive jewelry and a tiny nose that cost more than the jewelry. They were probably grabbing a bite to eat before heading a few blocks uptown to the Spy Club, where rich boys would buy them drinks from the proceeds of their trust funds. I gave the Occidental a look.

The room was all dark wood and candles, deuces primarily, young affluent couples with pale skin who looked pleasant in the light. In the bar area, three businessmen were hitting on a rather plain-looking woman who was wearing a dress that appeared to be decorated with a doily. On the far side of the bar, a distinguished elderly couple sipped their martinis and stared straight ahead. At the service bar, the manager fingered his Brooks Brother's tie with one hand and his brush mustache with the other. I signaled for the bartender.

The bartender walked over and stood square. He buffed the spot in front of me with a clean white cloth, though the spot was already dry. His name tag said MICHAEL, my first bingo in a very long while.

'Welcome to the Occidental,' he said with a white-toothed smile. He had the handsome but vacuous blue-eyed look of a military cadet, and he was built low to the ground, broad-shouldered and thick. 'How can I serve you?'

I had seen him pour a half ounce of scotch into a rocks glass overflowed with cubes and serve it to an unfortunate man on the other end of the bar. I said, 'You can serve me an Old Grand-Dad. Neat. And put a cold bottle of Budweiser next to it.'

Michael's smile went away but not his chipper tone of voice. 'It would be my pleasure,' he said, and drifted.

By the time he returned I had lit a cigarette. Michael placed my drink on the bar with a thud. About a dollar's worth of bourbon splashed out over the lip of the glass.

'Thanks' I said.

'Cheers!' Michael said, and walked away.

I drank my Grand-Dad and chased it with beer. From the corner of my eye I saw the black-haired young woman fan away the smoke of my cigarette. I had one more deep drag, crushed the butt in a clean ashtray, and had a look at the bar.

The bar blended mahogany and oak with an inlay of brass. The runoff board was shiny copper, and free of bar netting. The liquor wall was subtly lit and backed by an immaculately beveled mirror framed by miniature marble columns. 'Stardust' played on the house stereo. I signaled Michael for another round.

Michael returned with my bourbon and beer. 'Cheers,' he said tiredly.

'And to you,' I said as I slid my business card along the top of the bar until it touched his fingers.

He looked it over. His eyes shifted toward his manager, then back at me. He was still smiling, but the smile was tight. 'So what?' he said in a low, calm voice.

'Remember William Henry?'

Some color drained from his face, but he held on to the smile. 'It's my business if I do,' he said.

The woman next to me slipped down off her stool and ripped the receipt from the body of her credit card voucher. 'Thanks, Michael,' she said, stealing a contemptuous glance at me before winking in conspiracy at Michael.

'It's been my pleasure,' Michael said. The woman and her bobbed friend left the bar. Michael watched them until they had vanished at the top of the stairs.

I sipped bourbon. 'Can we talk?'

'No.'

'Why not?'

'I'm busy.'

'I'm busy too. Answer a couple of quick questions. After that you won't see me again.'

'What kind of questions?'

'About William Henry.'

Michael shifted his shoulders. 'I don't know anything about him.'

'You were his lover.'

Michael frowned. 'I went out with him, one time. Like I told you – that's my business.'

'Sure, it is. And you can bury it, or go tell it on the mountain, for all I care. It makes no difference to me. But the cops are following up on that angle. I can give them your name, if you'd like. Or you can tell me what you know.'

Michael made a head motion that encompassed the entire bar. 'Listen, pal,' he said softly. 'If I didn't' need this gig, I'd tell you to fuck off, right now.'

'I don't think so,' I said, looking him over. 'Anyway, you do need it.'

He loosened his shoulders. 'I'll give you one minute.'

'Fine. What was your relationship with Henry, the night he died?'

'It was over, way before that.'

'How long before?'

'Months.'

'He have many friends, besides you?'

'No idea.'

'He ever talk about anything, about being in any danger, while you knew him?'

'No.'

I sighed. 'You're not thinking too hard.'

'I'm answering your questions,' he said behind a smirk.

'And I'm trying to find my friend's killer.'

'What happened to William was a shame,' Michael said without a trace of sincerity. 'He was a nice guy, but that's all he was. I'm telling you, you're going down the wrong street. Our relationship – it didn't mean anything, understand?'

'I'm beginning to.'

Michael gave me his hard look. 'So why don't you just pick your things up and leave?'

I dropped fifteen on the bar, rose, and put on my overcoat. 'You're real tough,' I said. 'You know it?'

Michael looked around for his manager, who had gone into the kitchen. He leaned over the bar and whispered through a clenched jaw. 'Maybe I'll see you sometime, out on the street.'

I smiled and said, 'It would be my pleasure.'

I poured a cup of coffee, walked it into my bedroom, and had a seat at my desk. My cat followed me in and dropped on her belly, just resting against my feet. I turned on the gooseneck lamp that was clamped to the side of my desk and opened the manila folder that contained William Henry's notes. The notes were entered by date. I read them chronologically over the next two hours, then read them again, this time highlighting several names and passages that recurred throughout.

When I was done, I removed the third of the notes that were related exclusively to Henry's last filed story and placed them back in the folder. What remained was cryptic and, in several spots, frustratingly coded. But seemingly at random, two genderless names continued to appear: Pyshak and Bonanno.

I had one more cigarette and butted it halfway down. I washed up, undressed, and read a little until my eyes began to get heavy. My cat dozed on the blanket at my feet.

The words *Pyshak* and *Bonanno* drifted through my head as I fell into the dark arms of sleep.

24

The next afternoon I sat at the bar of the Spot with William Henry's notes spread before me. A telephone and the area white-page directories rested on the bar, near the notes. The Spot's reader, Dave, sat at the other end of the bar, his head buried in a slim novel. A coffee cup sat in front of him, and a lit cigarette burned in an ashtray next to the cup. Mai was on the long shift. She tried to talk to me about her latest military conquest while I looked over the notes. I kept my attention on my work.

There were no Pyshaks in any of the three metropolitan directories, but there were several Bonannos. I spent two hours placing calls to every one of them. Many had answering machines, on which I left no message. To the ones I reached I took the long shot of asking to speak to William Henry. I was hoping for a fumble, or a hang-up, or some sign of recognition. What I got was bewilderment, and a dead end.

Happy hour – a colossal misnomer at the Spot – soon came, and the regulars began to file in. Buddy and Bubba swaggered to the sports section and were followed shortly by Richard, who was immediately in their collective face over an '86 Super Bowl point-spread dispute. Melvin Jeffers had a seat alone and ordered a gin martini ('extra dry, darlin''), and asked Mai to change the music over to something more 'upbeat.' Mai slid an old Michael Henderson tape into the deck and served Melvin's drink. Henderson's 'Be My Girl' began to croon from the speakers.

After two verses of that, Dave collected his paraphernalia and got off his stool. On the way out he stopped behind my back and tapped me on the shoulder. His reading glasses hung on a leash across his broad chest. He placed the glasses back on his nose and scratched his gray-and-black beard as he looked over my notes.

'Workin' on a puzzle?' he said with the deep rasp of a heavy smoker.

'In a way.' I leaned back and rolled my head to loosen my neck. When

379

I turned around, Dave was still standing behind me. I didn't know what he wanted, or why he was waiting there with a fixed, dogged stare. But Dave read books, and he hadn't had a drink in years. That put him miles ahead of everyone else in the joint, including me. 'Have a seat,' I said.

Dave touched the right stem of his glasses and bellied up. I signaled Mai for Dave's dirty ashtray, and she retrieved it from his favorite spot and placed it in front of him. Dave lit a smoke and fitted it into the groove of the tray.

'What's got you stumped?' he said.

I told him about the case, and about the two names, and about the calls I had made. Dave stared at the names for a few minutes. Then he turned over one of the sheets of notepaper, withdrew a pen from the plastic holder in his breast pocket, and began writing down words in two parallel columns. Afterward he let the glasses off his nose and set the pen down on the notepaper. He pushed the paper along the bar until it rested in front of me.

I looked the words over and said, 'What'd you do?'

'You said the notes appeared to be in code, partially at least.'

'I said I didn't understand them – it's not the same thing.'

Dave said, 'So you're sure *Pyshak* and *Bonanno* are persons' names.'

'Not entirely. What do you think?'

Dave tapped the filter on the cigarette that was wedged in the ashtray. He let it burn there and looked at me. 'I think *Bonanno*'s a name. It's common enough. And when you break it out phonetically, and syllabically, screw around with it a little' – he pointed to the column of words on the right – 'you come up with nothing.'

My eyes traveled to the column on the left. 'Go on.'

'Now do the same thing with *Pyshak*,' Dave said, twitching excitedly, putting his glasses on again and adjusting them on the tip of his nose. 'Look what you get.' He ran his finger down the column of jumbled *Pyshak* mutations – *Piss Hack, Pishe Ak* – and stopped at the last two words. The words read *Pie Shack*.

'It's a business,' I said.

'It's a possibility,' Dave said, smiling.

I smiled back, getting ahead of things. 'A bakery?'

Dave shook his head and watched me from the corner of his eye. 'Think, Nick – the relationship to Bonanno. How many Italian bakers you know?'

I thumped my fist on the bar until it hit me like a stone. 'Pie Shack,' I said quietly. 'As in pizza pie.'

'If I was you,' Dave said, 'that's where I'd start.'

Three Pie Shacks were listed under Pizza in the Spot's year-old, tattered copy of the yellow pages. I wrote down the addresses and phone numbers and then had Mai place the bar's sticky black Rolodex in front of me. I withdrew the cleanest business cards of several food and beverage distributors, put them in my wallet, and grabbed some related price books that had been left behind by various salesmen. Then I lifted my overcoat off the hall rack and exited the Spot.

I stopped uptown at my apartment for a shower and a shave, and to feed my cat. Out of the shower, I dressed the cut on the inside of my hand and left the bandage off. I put on jeans and a black V-necked sweater over a white T-shirt, and slipped my Doc Martens oxfords onto my feet. Before I left I stroked my cat's head until her eye closed. She slinked across the room to her dish. Her eye was still closed as her pink tongue lapped water from the dish. I closed the door silently and walked out into the night.

The air was misty and cold. Halos ringed the streetlights on Sixteenth as I drove south. I hung a right at U Street and parked my Dart near the firehouse. The engine coughed a bit as I cut it. I locked up and crossed over to the south side of the street, where several bars and carryouts were grouped on this farthest corner of Adams-Morgan.

I checked the address from the list in my overcoat pocket and walked west. I passed Rio Loco's, the Tex-Mex bar that Jackie and I patronized with frequency. I passed an open but empty frozen-yogurt parlor and a pizza-and-sub shop named the Olde World. Just past that stood a bankrupt 'art bar,' and next to that the Pie Shack. Or, as I realized as I neared its boarded entrance, the Pie Shack's burnt remains.

A red condemnation sticker from the fire department hung crookedly on the front door. The plate-glass window that fronted the store had been busted out, replaced by iron bars. Cupping my hands around my eyes, I looked through the bars. The interior had been swept out, with remaining equipment, booths and counters pushed irregularly into one far corner. The ceiling had fallen through, leaving wires and fixtures dangling into the space. The interior walls were sooty and charred black. Nothing but a burnt shell. I backed away and retraced my steps, walking east on U.

A few doors down stood the Olde World, fluorescently lit and open for business. I entered and leaned my elbows on the Formica counter. Next to me at the counter was a long-haired man wearing a fringed leather jacket. He held in his hand a slice of pepperoni with extra cheese, and he studied it with interest between bites. There were no employees behind the counter, but through the door that led to the kitchen I heard the laughter of two young men over an LL Cool J single. I tapped my palm on the knob of a bell that sat next to the electronic register.

One of the young men emerged from the kitchen, still laughing as he downstepped out, yelling back to his partner about some 'serious bitch' that had been in earlier that evening. He stopped at the counter, looked over my shoulder onto U Street, and said, 'Yeah.'

'Let me get a slice of cheese.'

'Anything to drink?' Still looking past me.

'Just the pizza.'

The young man turned his head back to the kitchen and yelled, 'One slice o' plain, Dopey.' He turned back to me. 'Dolla-fifty.'

I handed him two ones. He bobbed his head to 'Round the Way Girl' and mouthed the chorus, shutting his eyes soulfully as he rang me up and slapped the change onto the counter. 'What happened to that place two doors down, the Pie Shack?'

The young man shook his head, stopped mouthing LL Cool J, and shrugged. 'Motherfucker burned, man.'

'When was that?'

He shrugged again. 'Don't know. Before I came to work here.'

'When was that?' I repeated.

'Near six months,' he said, and spun back into the kitchen. There was more laughter, then he bounded back out with my slice and dropped it on the counter in front of me. I thanked him, but by the time I got the words out he had disappeared into the back. I ate the pizza in silence, standing at the counter, next to the man in the fringed leather jacket.

Out on the street a Ford Escort came to a screaming halt in front of the Olde World. An orange-and-red cardboard sign logoed identically to the sign that hung above the Olde World's entrance was fastened to the roof of the Escort. The baseball-capped driver double-parked and jumped out of the car, a black thermal cover cradled in his arms. He ran past me and dashed into the entrance of the shop.

I stood on the street for a few minutes with my hands in my overcoat pockets and watched the activity. Outside Rio Loco's, a shirtsleeved man in his twenties wearing a fraternity cap leaned against the brick facade and vomited at his feet. I walked around him and entered the bar. The place was packed with college kids and neighborhood regulars. Some of the college kids were grouped near the back of the bar, loudly singing 'New York, New York,' drowning out the juke. My regular waitress saw me from across the room and fetched me a Bud from the service area near the kitchen. I leaned against the wall and drank it standing up, then placed the empty on the bar with a five spot pinned underneath. Fifteen minutes later I was in bed in my apartment, making plans to visit Pie Shack Number Two early the next day.

The second Pie Shack listed in the yellow pages was located on Sligo Avenue in Silver Spring. I drove up Georgia the following morning, passed under the railroad bridge, and turned left on Sligo. Just beyond a used bookstore and a body garage, I parked my Dart in front of the address written in my notes.

The Pie Shack was there, but it was closed, with black bars on the front window and a red fire sticker attached to the door. One block down, near the corner of Sligo and Fenton, stood the Olde World carryout. I grabbed my price books off the seat beside me and climbed out of my Dart.

The wind blew my knit tie back over my shoulder as I walked. I smoothed it down when I reached the glass door of the Olde World, and stepped inside. The layout was the same as in Adams-Morgan – a small waiting area, two or three tables with red vinyl chairs, and a Formica counter.

A thin, young dark-skinned man in his early twenties sat on a stool behind the counter, reading what looked to be a textbook. The man had sharply defined cheekbones and a small, pinched nose. Some Caribbean music played softly from a trebly speaker in the kitchen.

At my entrance the young man stood and closed the book. I put my own book on the counter and smiled.

'Can I help you?'

'I hope so,' I said in a chipper tone.

'What can I get you?'

I placed a business card in front of him. The business card was from Variety Foods, and the name on it was Ron Wilson. 'Ron Wilson,' I said, still smiling as I shook his hand. 'Variety Foods. And you are?'

'My name's Elliot,' he said with an island lilt, putting a palm up in front of my face in a halting gesture. 'Before you get into your pitch, man, let me tell you that you're talking to the wrong guy.'

'Who should I be talking to?'

'The main office is out of our store in Northwest. They do all the buying from there.'

'Write that address down for me, will you?' I handed him my pen and a torn piece of paper out of the notebook. While he wrote it, I said,

'What happened to the Pie Shack, down the street? I was supposed to make a call on them today.'

Elliot passed me the notepaper. 'You got some old information man. The Pie Shack's been closed for a long time, since right before we opened. Electrical fire is what I heard.'

'Who did I talk to in your main office?'

'Guy named Francis. Frank. Runs the operation.'

'Thanks,' I said as I shook his hand once again. 'By the way' – I nodded toward the kitchen – 'who are we listening to?'

'The Mighty Sparrow, man.' Elliot smiled. 'The Sparrow rocks.'

'He does. Thanks again.' I walked toward the door.

'Hey,' Elliot said from behind my back. 'Don't work so hard, man – it's New Year's Eve.'

I waved back at him and walked out onto the sidewalk. Back in my Dart, I cracked a window and lit a smoke. Across from the pizza shop, two Ford Escorts sat parked, signs strung to their roofs. I studied the delivery cars. The orange-and-red lettering of the signs' logos matched the orange-and-red logo on the Olde World's facade.

James Thomas's voice filled my head: 'I want you to know I didn't kill that boy . . . That boy sure didn't deserve to die . . . The man from the orange and the red . . .'

The orange and the red.

I pitched my cigarette out the window and spit smoke as I retrieved the address that Elliot had written out for the Olde World's office. Then I checked it against the address of the third Pie Shack. By then it was an exercise. I knew that they would be on the same block, and I knew without question that the last Pie shack would be empty, burnt, and abandoned.

I pumped the gas once and turned the ignition key. Six cylinders fired and I pulled away from the kerb.

25

The Olde World headquarters stood in the street-level space of an office building at the southeastern corner of Twenty-first and M. I parked my Dart in the lot behind a movie theater and restaurant at Twenty-third and slid the white-shirted attendant a couple of bucks for the privilege. At the restaurant's back door a Latino busboy sat on a black railing, smoking a joint. He took a hit, held it in, and followed my path with his gaze as I crossed the lot.

I walked east on M Street. Downtown had begun to empty out for the holiday. An early rush hour thickened the streets, leaving few pedestrians afoot. Underdressed homeless men shared the sidewalks with blue-blooded attorneys in plain charcoal suits and with women dressed unimaginatively and mannishly in their pursuit of success. The West End balanced poverty and ambition, granite and spit, money as new as the morning paper and glass-eyed hopelessness older than slavery.

At Twenty-second I checked the location of the third Pie Shack. A synthetic-diamond store now stood at the address. If there had been a Pie Shack, and it had burned, it had burned a long time ago.

I kept walking until I reached the door of the Olde World. When I got to it, I stepped inside.

The layout was the same as all the others. This time a man in his thirties with Mediterranean features stood behind the counter. He was writing something in a spiral notebook when I walked in, and as the entrance bell above the door sounded he slipped the notebook into a space below the register. I smiled and placed my Variety Foods business card on the counter.

'Afternoon,' I said. 'Ron Wilson, Variety Foods. And your name?'

'Cheek.'

'Cold enough out there for ya today?'

'Yeah,' he said.

'Colder than a brass monkey's balls, right?'

Cheek rolled his eyes in exasperation and sighed. 'What can I do for you?'

'Is the owner or manager in?'

'He's in,' he said in a high voice, and touched the paper hat that was stained at the rim with the oil of his hair. He wiped a smudge of grease off one thick eyebrow that ran unbroken over his deeply set brown eyes. 'But he don't see salesmen without an appointment.'

'What's his name?'

'Frank.'

'Do me a favor.' I leaned on the counter, buddying up. 'It's New Year's Eve, and this is my last call of the day. Hell, it's my last call of the year, and I've got to make my numbers.' I winked. 'Go back there and tell Frank that there's a guy out here, he's willing to sell anything on his price sheet for fifty percent better than what he's buying it for anywhere else.'

'Fifty off?'

'Five-oh.'

'He still won't see you,' Cheek said.

I said, 'Give it a shot, huh?'

Cheek moved into the kitchen and stayed there for quite some time. I waited with my price book under my arm. When a customer entered and the door chime sounded, Cheek returned from the kitchen. He licked the graphite tip of his pencil before he wrote the customer's order on a green guest check pad, then he turned and walked back into the kitchen. I stayed put and five minutes later Cheek was back with a square, flat box of pizza. He rang the customer up and slammed the drawer closed as the customer headed out the front door. Cheek began to reenter the kitchen when I stopped him.

'What about Frank?' I said cheerfully.

Cheek turned around and pushed the paper hat back on his damp head. 'He says he'll see you for a minute, if what you got's legit. But only for a minute. He's busy.'

'A minute's all it will take. Thanks.'

Cheek waved me back. 'Come on,' he said.

I followed him behind the counter, through a doorless frame, and into the kitchen. The kitchen was open and bright with a track of fluorescent tubes that lighted it from front to back. On the north wall stood a large baker's oven, its door down. A thick young expediter with curly brown hair, long in the back and shaven on the sides, peered into the oven. He checked the pies inside and then flung the door up and shut. Beside the oven, warming lights glowed red over a two-level steel

386

table, and on the shelf above the lights sat an institutional microwave oven. Next to the microwave a Sony box with removable speakers was set on DC101. The righteous freak-out of Van Halen's guitar careened throughout the room.

A large stainless-steel prep table was situated in the middle of the room, and on the opposite wall a cold salad bar abutted a sandwich block, both refrigerated underneath. Several black-handled knives of various sizes were racked above the sandwich block. Next to the block a four-foot-wide stainless-steel refrigerator stood upright and stopped inches from the ceiling. On the third wall sat two deep stainless-steel sinks, with a rinse hose suspended above. A tall, wiry man with slick black hair and a severely pocked face stood before the prep table in the middle of the room, ladling sauce into a pie shell. Neither he nor the expediter looked up as I passed into the kitchen.

Cheek raised his hand and said, 'Wait here.'

I stopped walking and cradled my book. The thick young expediter moved quickly behind me to the sandwich block and pulled a knife off the rack. He retrieved some onions from a plastic container below and deftly began to peel and slice them on the board with the knife's serrated edge. The pock-faced man pushed tomato sauce around the pie shell with the bottom of his ladle in slow, careful circles. Cheek entered a small office in the back of the kitchen. I watched him do it.

Two men sat in chairs in the office. I could see their pants legs – one wore black twills, the other khakis – and the wooden legs of the chairs in which they sat. Some smoke drifted out of the office door. I listened to Cheek's high voice, and a deeper one after that, and then the khaki legs unwound and the man inside them stepped out of the office with Cheek.

He was an average man of average-to-heavy build, with a blue work shirt tucked into the khakis and a dirty apron tied over half of both. There was a plastic foam cup in his right hand and the ass end of a cigar in the fingers of his left. He plugged the cigar in the side of his saliva-caked mouth and stopped walking a foot shy of my face.

'What ya got,' he said. Booze was heavy on his breath.

'Deals,' I said, my salesman's smile glued ridiculously high. 'Unbelievable deals, Frank.' I extended my hand. 'Ron Wilson, Variety Foods.'

Frank put his hand to his mouth, unplugged the cigar, and had a gulp of scotch from the plastic foam cup. 'Let's skip all the bullshit, okay? Cheek said you had something good, and it's New Year's Eve, and to tell you the truth I'm already half in the bag. So let's see what you got, quick, before my mood changes and I make you come in on order day like every other slob.'

'Sounds good to me,' I said. 'Where should we go? In your office?'

'Uh-uh.' Frank's head tipped like a bell in the direction of the sinks. 'Over there.'

I followed him and watched the office as I walked. Smoke still leaked out from behind the door. At the sink I set my black book on the drain platform and opened to a random page. Black-and-white photographs of canned goods ran top to bottom on the left quarter of the page, and corresponding price columns took up the balance.

'I assume you use all of these goods,' I said, lightly running the tip of my forefinger down the column of photographs, studying the gimmick as I spoke. The dollar amounts lessened as the purchase quantities increased.

'We use a lotta shit,' Frank said as he pulled the scotch cup away from his lips. He had chewed small crescents of plastic foam off the rim. 'What's the deal?'

'Like I told Mr Cheek, fifty off.' I looked around for Cheek's support, but he was back out front.

'Fifty off what?'

'Our best price on the sheet.' I stuttered through the smile. The smile had atrophied now to a twitch.

'Bullshit,' Frank said. A cloud of cheap cigar smoke hung between our faces. 'What's the catch?'

'No catch,' I said with wide eyes. 'New Year's special, onetime order. No limit. You get acquainted with our business, we make a new friend.'

The bluesy intro to Jethro Tull's 'Locomotive Breath' played through the Sony. Frank had another slug and belched. The belch watered his eyes and caused his lips to part like two pink slugs.

'One thing I always say, Winston.'

'Wilson. Ron Wilson.'

'One thing I always say. If it's on sale today, it can be on sale tomorrow. Right?'

'Maybe so,' I said. 'But I sure would like to write an order before the clock strikes twelve.'

'Never happen,' Frank said. 'I'm not that kind of sucker. Nice try, though. Always ask for the sale.' He rocked back on his heels. 'Look me up after the New Year, hear?'

'I will. Thanks.' I extended my hand again, and again Frank ignored it. Instead he turned his head back toward the young expediter.

'Turn that shit down!' he yelled, pointing at the boom box. Then he waddled back like a man carrying something odious in the seat of his pants and shut the door behind him.

The thick young expediter moved to the Sony and reduced the volume by a hair. I closed my book, put it under my arm, and walked through the kitchen toward the lobby. The tall, wiry, pock-faced man glanced up and looked me over as I passed. His eyes were small and heavily hooded, all black pupil, whiteless as a snake's. I felt them on me as I exited the kitchen.

26

Out on the street I walked quickly back to my Dart. I put the price book in the car and retrieved a heavy wool sweater from the trunk. I removed my tie and put the sweater over my shirt, and my overcoat on top of them both.

On my way back I stopped in a deli named Costaki's and bought the largest go-cup of coffee they sold. I tore a hole in the plastic lid and sipped the contents as I walked south on Twenty-first. I kept low passing the Olde World and just beyond it cut left down a narrow alley.

The alley ran between Twentieth and Twenty-first. A tan building stood east to west on the south side of the alley, with two green dumpsters positioned and spaced against its side. A doorway cut into the building next to the dumpster closest to Twentieth. I walked down the alley and stepped up onto the kerb and stood in the doorway. I could see the Olde World's back entrance from the doorway, on the north side of the alley.

Nothing much happened after that. Steam rose from the hole in the coffee lid, and the traffic sounds from the right and the left began to soften. I had a cigarette and smoked it down to the filter. A couple of women walked across the alley and quickened their pace when they saw me in the doorway. A bundled bicycle courier rode by, and then a gray Step-Van, both without incident. An hour passed and dusk darkened the alley.

At 7:25 a brown Mercury Marquis drove by slowly and stopped in the alley at the Olde World's door. From the shadow of my doorway I watched an obese man in a brown coat get out of the Marquis and open the trunk. He removed what looked to be two filled pillowcases and carried them up to the door, where he rang the buzzer. Hands appeared shortly thereafter from behind the door. The hands grabbed the pillowcases, pulling them inside. The obese man in the brown suit

390

walked back to the trunk and closed it, then reentered the driver's side and drove out of the alley.

I lit another cigarette. By eight o'clock no one else had driven in or out of the alley. There was little sound now, except for the rustle of paper and debris that the wind blew and lifted in tight, violent circles.

I jogged back to my Dart, started it, and drove over to Twenty-first, where I parked facing south on the street, in sight of the Olde World's window. I turned the radio on and switched it to WDCU. I listened to a Coltrane set, and one by Stan Getz. In the middle of the Getz set, the lights in the Olde World's window went out. I turned the ignition key on my Dart.

A black Lincoln passed my car and stopped in front of the Olde World. The young expediter who had retrieved the car got out of the driver's seat and left the engine running. A heavy man in his fifties with bushy gray sideburns walked out of the Olde World and moved toward the car. A live cigarette in an alabaster holder dangled between his fingers as he walked. Black twill pants legs showed beneath his double-breasted black overcoat. The heavy man climbed into the Lincoln and drove away. Before he did it I wrote his D.C. license plate number in my notebook and checked my wristwatch. The time was 8:35.

The expediter zipped his green army jacket and walked north on Twenty-first, toward Ward Park. Frank and the tall pock-faced man emerged from the Olde World right after that. Frank had an inch of cigar in his mouth and a plastic foam cup in his hand, and he wore a corduroy car coat. The tall man had changed into gray slacks and a long gray overcoat a shade darker than the slacks. The two of them walked to a silver blue Lincoln parked three car lengths ahead. Frank unlocked the door and got behind the wheel. The tall man waited in the street until his side unlocked, then climbed into the shotgun seat. They pulled away from the kerb. I yanked the column shift down out of neutral and felt it engage.

The Lincoln turned down the alley and at the end of it made a left onto Twentieth. When the taillights disappeared around the corner of the building, I followed. At New Hampshire Avenue the Lincoln cut right and headed northeast. At Georgia it turned left and shot straight north, and at Kansas Avenue it turned right again and resumed its northeastern path.

Kansas was wide and clean and residential, and free of cops. The Lincoln accelerated and stayed at fifty. I kept back two hundred yards the entire trip, running three reds along the way.

391

The Lincoln cut right at Missouri, crossed New Hampshire, and continued on at the top of North Capitol. Missouri became Riggs, and the Lincoln veered right down a slope that began South Dakota Avenue. We headed southeast then, paralleling Eastern Avenue at the Maryland line. At an arm of Fort Totten Park in Northeast, as the garden apartment complexes decreased, near an industrial section of concrete yards and waste-disposal sights, the Lincoln turned right on Gallatin, along a grove of widely spaced trees. I kept on, easing my foot off the gas.

A quarter-mile past a home for unwed mothers, the Lincoln turned left onto an unmarked, unpaved road and slowly drove into a break of trees. I continued past and in my rearview watched the taillights fade. I stopped the Dart in front of an isolated row of brick colonials on Gallatin and killed the engine.

I pulled my arms out of my overcoat, put lined leather gloves over my hands, and left the coat behind me on the seat. Out of the car, I ran quickly across the road, through a hard field, and into the grove of evergreens and willows. A dim yellow light glowed in the direction of the Lincoln's path, and I cut toward it diagonally through the trees, with slow, careful steps. As I neared a wide clearing, I stopped and crouched down behind the trunk of a scrub pine. My breath was visible in the yellow light ahead. Through it, I watched the Lincoln come to a slow stop.

The light topped a leaning lamppost. Next to the lamppost a bungalow stood far back at the edge of the clearing. The woods continued on behind the bungalow. The silver blue Lincoln sat parked next to the black Lincoln that had been driven by the man in black twills. Lights glowed from inside the bungalow.

Frank and the pock-faced man climbed out of the silver blue Lincoln. Frank walked over to the black Lincoln and unlocked the trunk while his partner, tall and unmoving, stood by. Then Frank pulled the two pillowcases out – the pillowcases the expediter had transferred earlier to the trunk when he had retrieved his boss's car – and shut the lid. They crossed the yard and stepped up onto the bungalow's porch. The wooden porch gave and creaked beneath their weight.

The two of them entered with the turn of Frank's key. A square of light spilled out as the door opened. After it closed, the porch darkened, and then there was only my breath against the light of the lamppost, and the headstone cold of the woods around me. I waited awhile to let some nerve seep in. When I thought I had it, I looked behind me once, and again. I swallowed spit and crept low, like a prowler, away from the pine and out into the clearing.

I stopped behind the trunk of the black Lincoln. Soft music hopped with the intermittent surge of horns played from inside the bungalow, but the clearing was quiet. I could hear my own breathing and feel the rubbery thump of my heart against my ribs. I pushed away from the car, staying low, and stepped up onto the porch, crawling heels-to-ass to a spot below the front bay window.

I raised my head until my eyes cleared the bottom of the window's frame.

It was a Sears bungalow from the 1920s, modified into some sort of private casino. The walls of the first floor had been removed, leaving one large room with a door leading back to the kitchen. Two twenty-five-inch televisions sat on the left wall, and two different basketball games were being broadcast on the sets. A round card table covered with dirty green felt stood in the center of the room, with six wooden swivel chairs placed around it. Red, white, and blue chips were strewn about the table's green top.

On the back wall an oak bar ran between the kitchen door and a wood staircase. The kitchen door was open, and the staircase led to a dark landing. Two closed doors were outlined in the shadows of the landing.

One high-backed stool stood at the far end of the bar. Behind the bar Frank poured scotch into a rocks glass filled with ice. The checkered walnut stock of a .38 Airweight showed above the waistband of his khakis, where it was secured by a snap in a nylon holster. Frank replaced the scotch in a small group of medium call bottles illuminated by a naked-drop light from above. A small dirty mirror hung on the cedar panelling behind the bottles. A compact stereo with squat black speakers stood next to the bottles.

The heavy man in black twills stood with a drink in his hand in front of the two television sets, shifting his head slowly between the two games. The blue light from the sets danced across his unemotional, heavy-lidded eyes. The tall, pock-faced man was bent over one of the pillowcases, with his hand inside. He withdrew a fistful of small white slips of paper, and he turned and said something to Frank, and both of them laughed. A mangled smile turned up on the heavy man's face as well, but he kept his eyes on the games.

The pock-faced man turned his head back down toward the pillow-case on the floor. It was then that I studied his face for the first time. The scars only covered the right side, and they were chunked deep, and red. The left side of his face was tightly smooth, with street-pretty definition. I lowered my head and crawled away from the window, off the porch.

A small, curtained window was positioned on the right side of the bungalow. I walked lightly past it, to the rear of the house. A narrow set of painted wood stairs led to the back entrance of the kitchen. From the bottom of the stairs I could see a tubular fluorescent light hung on the white plaster ceiling. A string switch dangled from the light. I walked up the stairs, my hand sliding up a loose splintered rail, and looked through a sheer lacy curtain.

Through the tiny kitchen, past the main room, and out the front bay window to the yard, a set of headlights approached from up the road.

I jumped off the steps and hit the ground running. I saw the headlights pass across the house and traverse the ground at my feet, and I heard myself grunt as I sprinted blindly into the woods. Willow sticks lashed my face, and there was the sound of branches snapping at my feet, and the sound of the branches adrenalized my legs, and I turned right and ran harder and faster, as if a fire were chasing me up a flight of stairs. I kept running until I reached the broken grove of willow and pine.

I stopped for breath, looked behind me once more, and ran out of the grove, across the hard field and the road, back to my Dart. I gunned it and drove up Gallatin to the Maryland line at Chillum, where I cracked the window and lit a smoke, hanging a left and then another just after that, back into the District.

The streets were shining and noisy, filled with loud, swerving vehicles and juiced-up, hard-luck cops on the worst beat of the year. I dodged them all, driving beneath a pearl moon, my fingers tight around the steering wheel, all the way back to my apartment in Shepherd Park.

I turned on the lamp switch next to my couch on the way to the liquor cabinet in my kitchen, where I withdrew what was left of my green-seal Grand-Dad. My cat circled my feet as I poured the bourbon into a juice glass, and kept circling as I tossed it back. I swallowed the whiskey, leaned over the chipped porcelain drain board, felt the burn, and waited for the warmth to wash over my face. I poured another shot and let the liquor slop out of the bottle's neck. Some of it spilled out onto the porcelain. The rest filled half the glass. I had a sip this time and walked out of the kitchen with the glass in my hand to the couch in my tiny living room.

I balanced the glass on the arm of the couch, picked the telephone up off the rug, and placed it in my lap. My cat jumped up on the couch and touched her nose to my arm, then jumped down and walked off, tail up, to the bedroom. I dialed Winnie Luzon.

Winnie picked up on the third ring. 'Talk about it,' he said.

'Winnie.'

'Yeah?'

'Nick Stefanos.'

'Nicky! Happy New Year, Holmes.'

'And to you, man.' There was some sort of tinny disco in the background, and the laughter of a woman.

'So what's up, Nick?'

'Partying tonight?'

'You know me, man, tonight the shit is *serious*.'

'I won't keep you, then. Got a couple of questions, though, if you can spare a minute.'

'Hold on.' Winnie put his hand over the mouthpiece and yelled something I couldn't make out. When he got back on the line the music had been cut, and the woman was talking rapidly in Spanish, her voice fading as she walked away. I heard a match strike and the crackle of lit paper, and Winnie's exhale.

'We talk now?'

Winnie said, 'Sure.'

'Listen – you ever hear of a place called the Olde World? Pizza and subs, down in your neighborhood, Sixteenth and U?'

'Down near Rio Loco's, right?'

'The same.'

'Yeah, sure. Good pizza, man.'

'You know the owners, anything about 'em?'

Winnie took in some smoke and held it. I could envision the glaze in his eyes, and the shrug. 'Uh-uh.'

'There was a place near the Olde World, another pizza joint, called the Pie Shack.'

'The Pie Shack – that's that place burned.'

'Arson?' I said.

'That was the rumor.'

'Any real word on that?'

'Nothing in stone.'

'How about the name *Bonanno*, that mean anything?'

'Bonanno?' Winnie said. 'It's a Guinea name, Nick, common as Smith.'

'So it doesn't click.'

'Uh-uh. This about that Goodrich thing, the thing with Joey DiGeordano?'

'That's taken care of,' I said.

Winnie went silent for a minute or so, then snapped his finger into the receiver. 'Hey, Nicky, that reminds me, man. You had some heat come around, asking questions about you, in Malcolm X.'

'What kind of heat?'

'Two cops. Detectives I do business with, now and again.'

'You sell them information?'

'When I have to, yeah. But this one, I don't like the way he looks, or the way he talks. I don't sell him nothin'.'

'What was he asking?'

'About your friend, the one got slashed in the Piedmont.'

'William Henry.'

'Right. This joker wanted to know if you been around, askin' about your friend.'

'You tell him anything?'

Winnie paused. 'Don't embarrass yourself, Nick.'

'Thanks, Winnie.' I had sip of bourbon and let it settle while I thought things over. 'What'd this cop look like?'

'Skinny and mean. Like a wet dog.'

'He give his name?'

'Goloria.'

I put fire to a Camel and rolled the bourbon around in the glass. 'And his partner?'

'Lady cop, with nuts.'

'Wallace, right?'

'That's right. Ring a bell, Nick?'

'It's beginning to,' I said.

'Listen, man, I gotta go.' Winnie's voice lowered to a whisper. 'Don't want to piss off the pussy, Holmes. Know what I'm sayin'?'

'Go on, Winnie. Have a good time, man.'

'Stay safe, Nick.' The phone clicked dead.

My landlord was having a small party upstairs. I listened to the thump of bass and the sound of feet moving on hardwood floors. My cat emerged from the darkness of the bedroom and hopped back up onto the couch. She waited for me to move the telephone aside, then crawled onto my lap and kneaded it until she tucked her paws in and dropped down on her belly.

I lit another smoke and finished my bourbon. A blanket of gray had settled in the center of the room. I butted the cigarette and turned off the lamp next to the couch, letting my head ease back as I ran my fingers through the fur of my sleeping cat. The last thing I heard was an ebb of laughter from above, the swell of music, and the muffled screams of old friends and lovers.

27

'Hello?'

'Mr DiGeordano?'

'Yes.'

'Nick Stefanos.'

'Nick, how are you? Happy New Year.'

'Thanks, same to you.'

'What can I do for you?'

'I apologize for calling you at home on the holiday, but I need to ask a favor.'

'You want to speak to Joey?'

'No, sir, it's you I'd like to speak to.'

Louis DiGeordano cleared his throat. 'Go ahead,' he said in his high rasp.

'Not over the phone, if you don't mind.'

'Is this about the Goodrich girl?'

'Some of it is,' I said. 'Most of it's about something else.'

DiGeordano's voice went in and out as he mumbled for a bit. I sat on the couch at my apartment, sipping coffee. He put his mouth closer to the line. 'The family's coming over for New Year's dinner,' he said, 'at five. I suppose I can meet you this morning, for a short while.'

'How about in about an hour? Say, eleven o'clock?'

'Fine.'

'Hains Point, is that okay? Parking Area Six. You know where that is?'

'Do I know it? Nick, it was me that took you to Hains Point for your first time, nearly thirty years ago.'

'Can I pick you up?'

'No, I'll have Bobby drive me. See you at eleven.'

I waited for another dial tone, then rang Darnell. He lived alone in the Shaw area of Northwest, with only a mattress on the floor and a small table and chair set in a bare-walled efficiency. The holidays were rough on guys like me, rougher on guys like Darnell.

Darnell said, 'Yeah.'

'Darnell, it's Nick.'

'Nick, what you doin', man?'

'Headin' down to Hains Point. Want to come along?'

'Hains Point? While the hawk flies? Shit.'

'I've got to meet a man. It won't take long. But it's a nice day, thought you might want to take a drive. Matter of fact, thought you might want to drive.'

'You know I ain't driven a car since I checked outta Lorton. Don't even have a license, Nick.'

'Come on, Darnell – what're you going to do today, sit around, watch beer commercials in black and white? You don't even drink.'

Darnell thought it over. 'I can drive?'

'Yeah.'

'You swing by my way?'

'In a half hour.'

Darnell said, 'Right.'

We caught the park off Thirteenth at Arkansas and took the express route downtown. Heavily clothed joggers bounded coltishly through blocks of sunlight on the path to our right, the wind at their backs.

Darnell wore his brown overcoat, his matching brown leather kufi tight on his head. He drove my Dart with one hand on the wheel, his left elbow resting on the window's edge. Darnell had brought his own tape – Sly Stone's *There's a Riot Goin' On* – for the ride, and he slipped it in as soon as he had slid gleefully into the driver's seat. He had rolled down the window right after that, and I had let him do it without objection, seeing the involuntary, childlike grin on his face, though it wasn't a day for open windows. The bright sun barely dented the cold front that had fallen into town overnight.

We passed the Kennedy Center and drove along the river to East Potomac Park, winding finally into Ohio Drive. Darnell eased off the gas as the road went one-way, a line of naked-branched cherry trees to our left, the golf course to our right. After another quarter-mile, at Parking Area Six, Darnell pulled the Dart into a small lot that faced Washington Channel.

There were few cars circling the park, and only one – a red Mercedes coupe with gold alloy wheels – in the lot. In the light I could make out the outline of a shaven head behind the tinted glass of the coupe's driver's side. I rolled my own window down and pushed the lighter into the dash. When the lighter popped out thirty seconds later, I used it to burn a Camel.

Darnell rocked his head and softly sang the chorus to 'Thank You for Talkin' to Me Africa.' He turned the volume up a notch and looked across the channel to the restaurants and fish stands that lined Maine Avenue. I blew a jet of smoke out the window and watched it vanish in the wind.

'Nice day,' Darnell said, breaking away from his own song. 'Thanks for askin' me out. You been decent to me, man, and I appreciate it. To most people, it's like I'm invisible.'

'Thought you might like to drive.'

'Been a while,' he said, staring toward the water. The sun made sailing shards of glass on the channel. 'Funny how a simple-ass thing like a drive down the park' – he stopped, shook his head, and smiled weakly. 'Drivin's what got me my bid in Lorton in the first place, you know that.'

'I heard you got caught up in something.'

Darnell laughed shortly and without pleasure, then shook his head. 'More than caught up, Nick. I knew what I was doin', in the way that any kid knows he's gettin' into somethin' wrong, knows it but can't stay away.'

'What happened?'

Darnell rubbed a skeletal finger down the bridge of his long, thin nose. 'Round about the mid seventies, I was runnin' with this Southeast boy. I knew he owned an army forty-five, used to brag how he brought it off some vet in the street. One day, he asked me to drive him down to see this girl he knew, down his way. I was known in the neighborhood as a guy who knew cars, see, knew how to make 'em move. I did it, even knowin' he was on somethin', talkin' more bullshit than usual that day, actin' strange. Anyway, on the way down he told me to pull over in front of some market, down off Minnesota Avenue. I parked out front, left the motor run – he said he'd be back right quick – and then this stickup boy I was runnin' with, he started shootin' that forty-five of his inside, shootin' that motherfucker all to hell.'

I dragged off my smoke and flicked ash. Darnell stopped, took a long breath, and continued. 'The way it ended, somebody died, and the police were all over the joint straight away, and they ran in and killed that boy too. I stayed in the car, didn't even try to run, knew it was over then, let them pull me out, my hands up, let them push my face right into the street.' He glanced in my direction but averted his eyes. 'Later on, they told me that boy was hard on the Boat. Had enough green in him to knock down a horse.'

'You paid up,' I said.

'I did, man. More than you know.'

A black BMW pulled into the lot and stopped alongside the Mercedes. The driver, a young man wearing a black jacket with a large eight ball embroidered across the back, stepped out and gave the world a tough glance. The Mercedes' door opened and a man not yet twenty wearing a parka with a fur collar put his foot out onto the asphalt. They shook hands elaborately, and then the driver of the BMW walked around the passenger side of the Mercedes and got in. Both doors closed, leaving only an armor of tinted glass.

Darnell said, 'What do you think that's about?'

'Couple of young professionals. Doctors, maybe, or lawyers. Right?'

'Nick, man, what the fuck *happened* to this town?'

'I can't tell you what happened. Only that it did.'

Darnell leaned closer to me on the seat. His eyebrows veed up and wrinkles crossed his forehead. 'Remember 1976, man? The way people acted to each other, everything – the shit was so *positive*. Groups of kids on bicycles, blowin' whistles, ridin' in Rock Creek Park. The message in the music – Earth, Wind and Fire, "Keep your Head to the Sky." Even that herb-smokin' motherfucker George Clinton, Parliament, "Choco-late City" – "You don't need the bullets, if you got the ballots, C. C." – you remember that, Nick?'

'I remember.'

Darnell sat back and spoke softly. 'When I got out, in '88, it was a new world, man. There wasn't no hope, not anymore – not on the street, not on the radio, nothin'. Nothin' but gangster romance.'

I looked in the rearview and said, 'Here comes our man.'

A black 1974 Eldorado turned in to the lot and pulled three spaces down from our car. The engine cut, the passenger door opened, and Louis DiGeordano slowly climbed out. He looked in my direction and tilted his head toward the concrete walk that ran around the park at the water's edge. I nodded and stepped out of the Dart.

'I'll be back in a few minutes, Darnell,' I said before I closed the door.

'I'll be waitin' on you right here,' he said.

I buttoned my overcoat. DiGeordano was down on the walkway, facing southeast toward the brick edifice of Fort McNair. I walked to the driver's side of the Caddy and watched the window roll down. Bobby Caruso sat behind the wheel.

He filled a shiny suit, the French cuffs of his shirt four inches ahead of the sleeves on his jacket. His hair was gelled and spiked, and the fleshy rolls of his neck folded down over the collar of his starched shirt.

'What is it?' he said, his face stretched in a constipatory grimace.

I leaned on the door. 'That day in the market, when we went at it.'

'I remember. What about it?'

'I called you a name that day. I want to apologize for that.'

Caruso relaxed, letting the boyishness ease into his face. He looked then like the kid he was, dressed for the P.G. County prom. 'Forget about it,' he said.

I shook his hand and walked away. Caruso yelled, 'Hey, Stefano,' and I turned. 'That shit you pulled on me that day, with your hands – where'd you learn it?'

I smiled. 'From my doctor.'

Caruso smiled back, showing his beaver teeth. 'I thought doctors were supposed to help people, not hurt 'em.'

'Take care of yourself,' I said, and walked across the grass, through the thin branches of a willow to the concrete walkway, where I stood beside Louis DiGeordano.

'Let's walk,' DiGeordano said. 'Shall we?'

DiGeordano put his hand on the two-tiered rail that ran along the channel, and began to move. I walked beside him, taking a last pull off my smoke.

He was wearing a gray lamb's-wool overcoat with a black scarf over a suit and tie, and a matching felt fedora. The brim of the fedora was turned down, with a slight crease running back to front in the crown. A small red feather was in the band, the same shade of red as the handkerchief folded in the breast pocket of his suit. A liquid wave of silver hair flowed under the hat, swept back behind his ears.

DiGeordano smoothed the black scarf down across his suit and pulled together the collars of the overcoat, against the wind. 'Those two in the parking lot,' he said. 'You see them?'

'Yes.'

'*Titsunes,*' he said. 'Drugs, guns, and *titsunes.* That's what this park is now. That's what this whole city is.'

'I don't know. I come down here in the summer, ride my bike down here quite a bit. I see a little of that. But what I mostly see is families having picnics, getting out of the heat. Old men fishing, couples holding each other, sitting under the trees.'

'It's not like it was.'

'It's exactly like it was. It's people, enjoying their city.'

DiGeordano looked across the channel and shook his hand in the air as he walked, the wag of his fingers meant for me. 'You don't know what I'm talking about, Nicky,' he said. 'You're not old enough to remember.'

'I guess not,' I said, deferring to his age, though in one sense he was right. We lived in the same city, but a million miles apart.

He put his hand back in his side pocket, his brown eyes squinting now in the wind. 'We always walked this side of the park, in the old days, every Sunday. The Potomac side, looking toward Virginia; it gets too much wind, and too much spray from the chop.'

'You said you were with me and my grandfather the first day I came down here.'

DiGeordano's pink lips turned to a smile beneath his gray mustache. 'Yes. This was very early in the sixties, you were maybe five years old. Nick had bought a cheap fishing pole for you and baited it with a bloodworm. You were holding the pole – he was holding it, really, standing over your shoulder – and a perch hit the line. Nick yanked it from the channel and removed the hook, and this little perch, it was no bigger than the palm of your hand, it flipped off the walkway and back into the channel.' DiGeordano laughed deeply. 'You were wearing a pair of denim overalls with a red flannel shirt underneath, and I'll never forget you chasing after that fish, trying to scoot under the railing. Nick grabbed you by the straps of your overalls and pulled you back – he laughed the rest of the day about it, talked about it at our card games, how you tried to go in after that fish. He talked about it for years.'

I stopped walking and put my hand on his arm. 'I need your help, Mr DiGeordano.'

He looked me in the eyes, shrugged, and made a salutatory motion with his hand. 'Anything.'

We walked on. A low, thick cloud passed beneath the sun. Its slow shadow crossed the channel in our direction. 'Do you remember a murder last year, a young white man in his apartment on Sixteenth Street, a reporter for a small newspaper in town?'

DiGeordano withdrew a lozenge from his overcoat pocket, unwrapped it, and popped the lozenge into his mouth. He clucked his tongue, staring ahead. 'Yes, I remember it. It was in the papers, every day. Then nothing.'

'That young man was a friend of mine,' I said.

'Go on.'

'He was researching a story on a pizza place called the Olde World and a man named Bonanno at the time that he was killed. I think the people that run the Olde World have an arson business and gambling operation as well, and I think my friend was murdered because he got too close.'

'Bonanno's a filthy pig,' DiGeordano said.

'You know him?'

'Of course.'

I stopped and struck a match, cupping one hand around it, lighting another cigarette. Then I blew out the first sulfurous hit and ran a hand through my tangled, uncombed hair. DiGeordano leaned his back against the rail and looked at my unshaven face. 'You're deep into this,' he said, 'aren't you?'

I took a fresh drag off the smoke. 'Bonanno's a fat man, bushy gray sideburns, right?' – DiGeordano nodded – 'and there's two more with him, a guy named Frank and a tall man with bad skin. Who else?'

'No one else,' he said tiredly. 'Bonanno and Frank are small-time hoods out of Jersey. The tall man goes by the name of Solanis. Contract mechanic, from Miami. They say he killed a cop and drifted north. Caught some buckshot in the face while he was drifting. Bad business, that – killing cops, and outsiders – it isn't done. Very sloppy. They're not going to last.'

'What are they into? Organized gambling?'

DiGeordano chuckled. 'Not too organized, from what I hear. As far as bookmaking goes, they don't know shit from apple butter. They still work from chits, for Christ's sake, and note-books.'

'So what's their game? Arson?'

'Their game?'

'They moved their shops near a string of pizza parlors called the Pie Shack, and every one of the Pie Shacks got burned out. That can't be a coincidence.'

'It's not,' he said. 'But arson's not their source of income. Neither is gambling.'

'What is, then?'

DiGeordano said, 'Pizza.'

I dragged off my cigarette and looked out into the water. The cloud had passed, leaving the channel shiny and brilliant in the noon sun. 'Tell me about it.'

'It's simple,' he said. 'The pizza business is very profitable. Bonanno moved into proven, established neighborhoods and burned out the competition. Solanis was there to make sure there weren't any belches. The guy who owned the Pie Shack simply left town, and felt lucky to leave alive. Bonanno puts a couple hundred thousand in non-taxable income in his pocket every year. The gambling is their kick, and the business end of it just covers their losses. No drugs, prostitution, nothing like that – just a bunch of hoods, selling pizzas.'

'What about the law, the fire people?'

DiGeordano shrugged. 'Bought.'

I flipped the remainder of my cigarette out into the channel. 'A cop by the name of Goloria, and his partner, a woman named Wallace, they paid me a visit a while back.'

'Goloria,' DiGeordano said.

'That's right. Things got rough – he said it was about April Goodrich, but something wasn't right. Is Goloria connected to your son Joey?'

'No. My ties with the law in this town go farther back, and higher than that. We don't have to get down in the shit with cops like him. He tried to approach us, once. I sent him on his way.'

'He's been talking to people I know about the young reporter's murder.'

'That's not a surprise – I would think he'd be a little nervous that you're looking into it.'

'Why's that?'

DiGeordano ran his fingers along the brim of his hat. 'Goloria's in with Bonanno.'

I leaned on the railing and looked down into the gray channel. A dead catfish floated on the surface, near a large sheet of packaging paper. I felt feverish and dizzy in the cold wind, and I unfastened the top buttons of my overcoat as I turned to DiGeordano. 'Who killed the reporter?' I said.

'You should have talked to me from the beginning,' he said. 'There's still very little going on in this town that gets by me. I know you disapprove of me, and my son. I can only tell you that in all my years, I never shed any innocent blood, in anything I did. In fact, there was very little violence at all. That's why I can't stomach what's happened to this city. People like Bonanno – they're vampires, but fragile as dust. Their own ignorance exterminates them. Do you understand?'

'Who killed the reporter?' I said again. The wind whistled through our silence, and water slapped the concrete.

'The knife job,' DiGeordano said. 'That's the signature of Solanis.'

'That's what I needed to know.'

'Before you act on this,' he said, 'you'd better think things over.'

'I'm fine,' I said. The cold wind stung my face.

DiGeordano studied me. 'There's something else?'

I nodded. 'There's one more piece of business.'

'You're talking about my son's problem, with April Goodrich.'

DiGeordano waved his hand slowly in front of his face. 'Like I said, nothing gets by me. You found the girl, and she's dead. Isn't that right?'

'Yes. But there's more to it.'

'Such as?'

'Have Caruso pull the Caddy next to my Dart,' I said, pushing away from the rail. 'I've got something to show you.'

I worked early shift at the Spot for the next four days. At the end of each shift I changed clothes, drove out to Gallatin in North-east, and parked my car in front of the row of brick colonials. Then I walked into the woods and waited for them to arrive at the Sears bungalow, and on each of the four nights, they showed with the pillowcases filled with gambling chits, at roughly the same time. Occasionally there were visitors, interchangeable ruddy-faced men in dark clothing who drove through the woods in Buick Electras and Pontiac Bonnevilles and stayed for a few quick, stiff drinks. But always at the end of the night there were the three of them – Bonanno, Frank, and Solaris.

On the fourth night, a Wednesday, I returned to my apartment, poured a drink, phoned Dan Boyle, and told him everything I knew.

On Thursday afternoon Boyle walked into the Spot with a gym bag in his hand and took a seat at the bar. He put the bag at his feet, ordered a draught, and asked for it in an icy mug.

'What's in the bag, Boyle?' I said as I wiped down the bar.

'You'll find out soon enough.' Boyle put a Marlboro to his lips and pointed a thick finger past my shoulder. 'This beer's gettin' lonesome,' he said. 'How 'bout a hit of that Jack?'

28

Boyle drank slowly and silently through happy hour. Buddy, Bubba, and Richard sat at the far end of the bar and drained a pitcher, their shoulders touching. Melvin Jeffers sang ballads softly through two gin martinis before walking out with a cheerful wave, and Happy knocked back several Manhattans as he dented a deck of Chesterfields. Ramon and Darnell stood in the kitchen, Ramon demonstrating his proficiency with a switchblade knife. I leaned against the call rack, my arms folded across my chest, moving occasionally to empty an ashtray or fill a pitcher. John Hiatt's *Bring the Family* played through the house speakers.

By eight o'clock, Buddy, Bubba, and Richard were gone. Buddy had sneered on his way out, doing his Tasmanian-devil-with-stretch-marks walk, and Bubba had followed, scratching his head. Happy had fallen asleep at the bar, a half-inch of hot Chesterfield wedged between his yellowed fingers. I phoned him a cab and walked him outside, and put the cab on his weekly tab.

When I returned, Boyle had gone to the head. I retrieved two bottles of Bud from the cooler and buried them in the ice chest. Darnell was in the kitchen placing dishes in the soak sink, his back to Ramon. Ramon touched his knife to Darnell's back and pushed on the blade. Darnell turned with a balled fist. Ramon laughed and pursed his lips in a kiss, but stepped back. I poked my head in and asked them to keep an eye on the bar while I shot down to the basement for some beer.

The Spot's dirt-floored basement was long and dusty and lit by a single naked bulb. I went down a narrow set of wooden stairs and walked through powdered poison. Rat tracks were etched in the powder, and the smell of death hovered in the room like a heat. I set up two cases of Bud and a case of Heineken on top of that and got under all of them, lifting with my knees. By the time I reached the top of the stairs and reentered the bar, a line of sweat had formed across my forehead.

Boyle was back on his stool, his hand around a mug of fresh draught. A Marlboro burned in the ashtray, next to the draught. I set the beer at the foot of the cooler and locked the front door.

I returned to the cooler and pulled out all the cold Buds and Heinekens. Then I ripped open the cardboard cases and stocked the warm beer on the bottom of the cooler, placing the cold beer back on top. I slid the cooler lid to the left, closing it. Boyle asked for another shot of Jack. I poured it, replaced the bottle on the shelf, walked back down to the deck, and slipped in Winter Hours' EP, *Wait till the Morning*. The rumble of 'Hyacinth Girl' came forward.

On the walk back toward Boyle I dimmed the rheostat and took the lights down in the bar. I pulled a Bud out of the ice by its neck and popped the cap. I set it on the bar next to a heavy shot glass and poured Grand-Dad. Boyle raised his glass and tapped it against mine.

'Here's to you, Boyle.'

'And to you.'

I closed my eyes and felt the bourbon numb my lips and gums and the back of my throat. I waited for the warmth to fill my chest and followed it then with a deep pull of beer. The beer was cold and good, and a chip of ice slid down the neck and touched my hand as I drank. I placed the bottle back on the bar and bent down over the three sinks and began to wash the last of the night's glasses.

Boyle said, 'You ready to talk?'

I looked into the foamy wash sink as I plunged a collins glass over a black-bristled brush. 'Go ahead.'

Boyle lit a cigarette and dropped the match into the ashtray. A wisp of smoke climbed off the match. 'What you told me last night,' he said. 'It was an awful lot to swallow. So I did some checking today, called in some favors, ran plates – the whole shooting match.'

'And?'

'Goloria was on the William Henry case from day one. He collected the evidence from the newspaper where Henry worked, and he buried it, and he probably bought or threatened a phony witness to testify to that "light-skinned man in a blue shirt" crap. The Pie Shack arsons are all listed as electrical fires. Somebody got bought there too.'

'What about Wallace. She in on it?'

'I don't think so. Goloria's her hero, and they're fuckin' the hell out of each other – that's no secret – but aside from her being a strange bird on the edge, that's as far as it goes. Believe it or not, I think she's an honest cop. She just happens to be in love with a disease.'

I finished grouping the clean glasses on the ridged drain area of the sink. Then I hung them upside down by their stems in the glass rack above the bar. I watched Boyle as I worked. He sipped his mash, and as he lifted his glass to his lips the lapels of his Harris tweed jacket spread apart. The stock of his Colt Python angled out from the shoulder holster lashed to his chest. A second holster hung empty below the opposite arm.

'Anything on Bonanno?'

Boyle put his glass down on the bar and switched his hand to the beer mug's handle. 'The plate numbers you gave me checked out. Both Lincolns are registered to the Olde World. Bonanno's down as the owner. No criminal record on Bonanno locally, or on Frank Martin.'

'And Solanis?'

'He's what you think he is. I called a DEA buddy of mine, on a hunch. Solanis was an enforcer in the Miami drug trade, and he's on the Fed's hot list. Took out an undercover cop.' Boyle's skittish blue eyes settled on mine. 'Knife job.'

I shook a cigarette out of Boyle's pack. Boyle produced a Zippo from his jacket pocket and thumbed open its lid. I leaned toward the flame, hit it, and took in a drag that burned deeply into my chest. My smoke found his and drifted up through the misty cones of light that opened out from the lamps above.

'You tell your DEA buddy that Solanis was in town?'

'No.'

'How about the Metro cops?' Boyle shook his head and gave me a twisted smile. 'Why not?' I said.

Boyle said, 'You called *me*. Thought you might have something else in mind.'

I turned to the left and saw Darnell and Ramon, their heads framed in the reach-through, looking at Boyle. Ramon stepped away, and I watched him hand Darnell his closed knife, passing it palm to palm. Darnell slid the knife into his back pocket.

Ramon walked out of the kitchen, his coat in his hand. He nodded to me with his chin and walked to the front door. I let him out, locked the door behind him, and returned to the bar. I pointed to Boyle's glass.

'You ready?'

'Yeah.'

I topped him off, then had a pull of Bud. 'Island of Jewels' 's clean guitar filled the room. Boyle ran a hand through his short dirty blond hair.

'What you got in mind, Boyle?'

Boyle smiled. 'What *you* got in mind?'

409

'I'm not sure.' I looked at him carefully. 'You said you'd help, and now I need it. I think you're honest, and I think you've got a cast-iron set of nuts. And I think you're a little bit crazy, Boyle.'

'Sure I am,' he said. 'But how crazy are you?'

'I'm here,' I said, 'and I'm listening.'

Darnell shut the kitchen light down and stepped out into the room. His kufi was tilted crookedly on his head, and he had folded his brown overcoat over his arm. He placed the overcoat on a stool and leaned his mantis arms on the service bar.

Boyle's eyes shifted to Darnell, then to me. 'Just you and me on this.'

'I want him to stay,' I said.

'He's a con,' Boyle said.

Darnell said, 'You got a problem with that, redneck?'

'*Do* you?' I said.

Boyle smiled as he looked Darnell over. 'He's all right, you know it? I like this guy.'

I sipped bourbon and placed the shot glass on the bar. 'Then let's get to it.'

'Okay,' Boyle said. 'Here it is. I can turn all this information over to the proper channels, and maybe something will shake out. Maybe they'll bust Bonanno on a tax rap or even the arsons. Maybe Solanis will go down on the murder charge, but that's a long shot too – you can believe the knife he used is long gone. And without that security guard, maybe Goloria will go up on charges, and maybe he'll walk. A shitload of maybes.'

'You saying that's one way of doing it?'

'That's the straight way.'

'What's the other way?'

'It depends on what you want, Nick.'

I pulled another beer from the ice, uncapped the neck, and glanced into the amber bottle. 'I figure Solanis is going to burn, sooner or later. But there's something wrong when outsiders can come into this town and get rid of an innocent man, and there's sure as hell something wrong when one rotten cop helps them do it.' I looked straight into Boyle. 'You know what I want.'

'I figured that,' Boyle said, leaning forward. 'So I set things up. I called Goloria this afternoon. I told him we wanted to meet.'

Drops of water fell from the glasses suspended in the rack above, darkening the mahogany of the bar. I finished the rest of my bourbon and dragged on my cigarette. Darnell pushed his hat back on his head. 'What'd you tell him, Boyle?' I said. 'Exactly.'

'That you knew about the arsons, and the murder. That you told me you knew. And that you wanted to see them and talk things over.'

'When?'

'I didn't say. Goloria got all quiet when I laid it out for him, didn't want to talk about it on the phone. But here's a bet – that crooked bastard will be at that house in the woods tonight to discuss it, and so will Bonanno. And the others.'

I tilted the beer bottle to my lips, drank deeply, and wiped the backwash from my chin. A lull came in the tape, and the Spot grew quiet. I looked at Boyle and Darnell, and I wondered how it had happened that I had ended up with them, wondered what had brought us together like thieves in the night, in a shitty little bar in the southeast part of town. The thought of Tommy Crane crossed my mind, and how close I had come. But that thought passed. I felt my buzz swell, and I smiled, knowing then that it was done.

'What's the plan, Boyle?'

Boyle butted his Marlboro. 'You and me walk right into that house, start a fire under their asses, and make the arrest. From what you tell me, there's enough there for a bookmaking charge straight away. But I think we got a shot at some confessions too. Once we get into it, let it develop.'

'How?' I said.

'You carry a gun, Stefanos?'

'I own a nine. I don't carry it.'

Boyle reached down and pulled the gym bag up and placed it on the bar. He yanked back the zipper and put his thick hand into the bag. 'A nine, huh?' Boyle dropped a nine-millimeter semiautomatic on the bar and spun it so the grip pointed toward me. 'Then this ought to do. Beretta, ninety-two. Fifteen in the clip.'

I picked it up, hefted it in my palm, and released the magazine. It slid out, into my hand. I heeled it back in, checked the safety, turned, and lined up the front and rear white-dotted sights on the stereo system at the end of the bar. Then I lowered the pistol and placed it back on the bar.

'Where'd you get this?'

'From a suspect,' he said.

I nodded in the direction of the bag. 'What about you?'

Boyle said, 'I'm already heeled.' He pulled back the collar of his Harris tweed jacket, showing me the Python. Then he reached into the bag and retrieved a five-shot .38 Special, slipping it into the empty holster below his left arm. 'Now I'm real good.'

Darnell pushed away from the service bar, stood up, and cleared his throat. 'You'll be needin' a driver,' he said.

I looked at Boyle. 'That okay with you?'

'Yeah.'

I finished my beer, left the empty on the bar, and shoved the Beretta barrel down against the small of my back, behind the waistband of my jeans. Darnell shifted his shoulders into his overcoat, and Boyle buttoned his raincoat over his tweed. I switched the lights off from behind the bar. The neon Schlitz logo cast a blue light in the room.

Boyle said, 'How 'bout grabbing a bottle, for the ride.'

I reached into the stock under the call shelf and pulled out a fresh bottle of Jack. Boyle raised his hand. I tossed the bottle over the bar, and he caught it by the neck. Then he broke the seal and had a drink.

Darnell gave me a sidelong look. 'You sure about this, man?'

'He knows what he's doing.'

'Goddamn right I do,' Boyle said. 'It's time for some fucking justice.' He ran a hand through his tight curly hair and slipped the bottle of Jack into his raincoat pocket.

I set the alarm and locked the door. The three of us walked out into the night.

29

We took the Dart northeast across town. Darnell kept the speedometer just over the limit and signaled at his turns. The radio stayed off. Boyle sat in the back, drinking steadily and asking me questions about the layout of the bungalow. I answered from the shotgun seat and drummed my fingers on the dash, staring straight ahead.

Darnell took Missouri to Riggs and dipped down onto South Dakota. After a few miles of that he cut left on Gallatin Street and drove along the edge of Fort Totten Park. We passed the break in the grove of trees and slowed a few hundred yards down the street, stopping in front of the row of brick colonials. Darnell cut the engine.

Few lights were on in the windows of the houses to our right. The street was dark and quiet, tucked in for the night. I heard the chamber spin and shut on Boyle's Python, and the sound of gunmetal scraping against leather.

Boyle said, 'We walk in, Nick, straight up the road and to the house. Okay?'

'Then what?'

'This isn't going to be a surprise. They're expecting us, though maybe not so soon.'

'How do we play it?'

'Like a shakedown, at first. Like we want a piece of what's going on.'

'You start it off, Boyle.'

'Right.' I could hear the plastic cap unthread and the slosh of liquid as Boyle tipped the bottle to his lips. 'You'll catch the rhythm, as it goes. When I get a confession out of Solanis, I'll draw down on 'em, make the arrest.'

'You deputizing me?'

'Fuck, no. You're a witness. Don't be afraid to pull that Beretta, though, if the shit starts raining down.'

I could see Darnell to my left, staring at me, trying to get my

413

attention. I drew the Beretta, eased a cartridge into the chamber, and replaced the pistol behind the waistband of my jeans. Then I unlocked my door and spoke to him, looking away. 'If you hear it start to fly apart, Darnell, pull the car around at the break in the trees. Got it?'

Darnell nodded. Boyle had another long drink, capped the neck, and dropped the bottle on the seat. He and I stepped out of the car and shut the doors. We walked down Gallatin toward the unmarked road, the wind blowing back our coats.

At the gravelly break in the trees, we turned right. I heard the slam of a car door, recognized the sound of it, and turned my head. Darnell's reedy silhouette stepped across the field and vanished into the woods. I nudged Boyle, but he stared straight ahead. We continued down the road, toward the light of the house. The liquor still warmed me like an ember; it took the edge off the fear that was churning in my gut.

The Lincolns were parked out in the clearing, cast yellow under the light of the lamppost. On the porch of the house a figure moved toward the door. The door opened and a square of light spilled out onto the porch, and then the door closed again and the light vanished. The figure remained on the porch.

'You see that?' Boyle said.

'Yeah.'

'Whoever it is, he just put his head in and told them they had company.'

I adjusted my eyes to the light as we neared the house, gravel splitting beneath my feet. 'It's Frank Martin,' I said.

'Martino,' Boyle said. He chuckled and shook his head. 'Martin. Fuckin' goombahs and their names.'

We brushed past the Lincolns and moved toward the porch. I left my hands in the pockets of my overcoat as we walked up the steps. Frank's arms hung loosely at his sides. His corduroy car coat was open, exposing the khakis and a dark blue shirt. The Airweight was in the nylon holster, unsnapped, tucked into the side of his khakis, and Frank made no effort to hide it. He touched his fingers to the grip, then let his hand fall back at his side. We stopped on the porch in front of him. Frank looked at me.

'Salesman, huh? I knew you weren't no fuckin' salesman. No such thing as fifty off.' A big band sound with a vocalist came softly through the front door.

'Can we go in?' I said.

Frank looked at Boyle for the first time. 'You've got heat under your coat – I can see it. Take the guns off and leave 'em at the door.'

'I'm a cop,' Boyle said, his voice deepening a note. 'I wear a gun, and it doesn't come off. We came to talk to your boss. You want to start somethin' before we get into that, start it now.'

Frank swung both hands nervously, careful not to swing them near the Airweight. He looked away from Boyle and put his hand on the knob of the front door. Frank turned the knob and opened the door. 'Go on.'

Boyle stepped first, and I followed. Sinatra was the vocalist, and he was singing 'It Happened in Monterey' at a low volume through the Sony's black speakers on the bar. Goloria was sitting on one of the chairs near the two blank television screens, his bones etching their angles on a cheap brown suit. A tan shirt and a yellow-and-brown rep tie hung beneath the suit. The tie was crooked at the knot.

Solanis stood behind the bar, wearing a black sport jacket and a tieless deep red shirt, buttoned to the neck. His buckshot scars matched the redness of the shirt, but the rest of his face was finely lined and almost serene, his black hair damp with gel and lazily combed back. He moved the swizzle stick around slowly in a rocks glass filled with scotch whiskey and watched Boyle move into the room. I closed the door behind me and withdrew my hands from the pockets of my overcoat.

Goloria stood quickly, touched the knot of his tie, and slid four fingers of the other hand behind his belt. 'Boyle,' he said nodding. 'We didn't expect you so soon. You should have called. We could've set a time, when we could all talk together.'

'Where's Bonanno?' Boyle said.

'Not here.'

'I can see that. His car's out front.'

'He got picked up by friends,' Goloria said. 'What can we do for you?'

Boyle moved toward Goloria and stopped a few feet away. I walked over to the card table. Solanis watched me do it, a restful smile growing on his face. I picked some red chips up off the table and ran them around in my fingers, glancing up the stairs to the landing. The lights were out and the landing was deep in shadow.

'How's the wife and kids, Goloria?' Boyle said.

'Same as yours, I guess. Same as anybody's.'

'And Wallace?'

Goloria paused to narrow his eyes. 'You want a drink, Boyle? You look to me like you could use a drink. Jack's your pleasure, isn't it?' He glanced over toward the bar and grinned with effort. 'Solanis, fix Detective Boyle here a Jack Daniels.'

Boyle said, 'Keep your hands on the bar. I drink with my friends. This is business.' Solanis's face remained expressionless as a stone.

Goloria rubbed the heel of one brown shoe against the instep of the other. 'Tell us what you two want.'

'Stefanos wants what I want,' Boyle said. I didn't know where he was going with it, and I don't think he did either, but he had their attention. Standing there, a head taller than Goloria, his feet spread wide and firm on the wood floor, Boyle was like a bull, staring them down on their own turf.

'You've got to get clearer than that,' Goloria said.

'All right,' Boyle said. 'Stefanos came to me with the details of your operation. He knew the reporter that was looking into it, and he got curious. Pretty soon the Pie Shack arsons and the bookmaking came to the surface.'

'So?'

'You always were a piece of shit, Goloria.' Boyle took a step forward but kept his voice low and even. 'Shaking down bartenders, threatening informants, that's one thing. Making book and setting fires, that's another. It depends on where you draw the line. I draw the line at all of it. You got no problem with turning your head and getting your palm greased, that's up to you I guess – as long as nobody gets hurt.'

'Keep talking.'

'Solanis over there – murder one on the reporter. You buried the evidence, and you planted some that was phony.'

Goloria sighed and ran one finger down a crease in his gaunt face. 'You still haven't told me a fuckin' thing, Boyle. Now I'm going to ask you again – what do you want?'

Boyle said, 'Low as you are, Goloria, you're still a cop. I'm not about to turn you in, if there's any other way.'

'You talking about a payoff?'

'I'm talking about options.'

A heavy dull sound pushed in from beyond the front door. Goloria and I turned our heads in the direction of the sound; Boyle stared ahead. The song from the box ended and another one began, Sinatra's 'I've Got You under My Skin.' Goloria grinned and turned his attention to the bar. 'Turn it up, Solanis,' he said, snapping his fingers. 'This one really jumps.'

Solanis walked slowly to the Sony and hiked up the volume. I heard movement from the second floor and looked up, but there was nothing, and then the sound of the movement was drowned out by the music.

When I looked back Solanis was walking back to his spot behind the bar, staring at me.

I stared back and said, 'We've got a problem here.'

Goloria said, 'We don't need a private cop in this, Boyle. It's between you and me.'

'What kind of problem you got, Stefanos?' Boyle said, smiling a little now, ignoring Goloria, getting into the rhythm he had talked about.

'The security guard,' I said, feeling that rhythm, and a warmth in my face.

'What about him?' Solanis said, his voice dry as a December leaf.

'Shut up,' Goloria said, turning his head to the bar. The Nelson Riddle arrangement swelled in the room, horns rising, Sinatra bending his vowels as he jumped back into the verse. I put my hands on the belt loops of my jeans, hiked them up, and ran my right hand around the waistband to the back, feeling the checkered points of the Beretta's serrated grip. I rested my thumb on the grooved hammer.

'If I'm going to get involved in this,' I said, 'there better not be any loose ends. I talked to that security guard myself. He's a broken-down drunk. He'll talk, eventually.' In my peripheral vision I saw motion from above. I kept my eyes on Solanis.

Solanis smiled. 'He won't talk.'

'I told you to shut up,' Goloria said.

'Maybe you better let me handle it,' I said.

'No need,' Solanis said, the smile gone now, a sudden emptiness in his black eyes. 'I took care of him, the same way I did that reporter.' The black eyes narrowed. 'That nigger screamed when I gave him the knife. He screamed like a girl.'

'Goddamn it, Solanis, shut up!' Goloria said.

Boyle crossed his arms and reached into his coat. Then he drew his guns, pointing them at Goloria. Solanis's hand slid under the bar, and he began to crouch down.

I pulled the Beretta and thumbed back the hammer.

Goloria whitened and said, 'Take it easy, Boyle,' and as he said it his own hand jerked toward the inside of his brown suit.

Boyle said, 'I'll see to your wife and kids, Goloria,' and he turned one gun on Solanis, and that's when everything blew up at once.

Solanis dropped just as Boyle fired the Python. A strip of oak splintered off the bar and bottles exploded from the shelf.

I saw the movement again from above on the landing, and I looked up. A man stepped out of the shadows and swung a sawed-off in my direction.

I dived, and then there was thunder, and the card table heaved up at my side and seemed to come apart. Something tore away at my cheek. I squeezed the trigger on the nine as I fell, aiming in the direction of the landing, the Beretta jumping in my hand, my knuckles white-hard on the grip. I saw a figure tumble and fall through the smoke of the muzzle and the ejecting shells, and then I saw a man in black twills convulsing at the base of the stairs.

Boyle walked across the room, firing both guns into Goloria, alternating shots from the Python to the .38. Goloria was covering his face with his hands, and one of his hands was without fingers now, and he was dancing backward, shaking his head furiously like he was coming out of water, fighting for breath. Goloria's knees buckled and he toppled onto his back, his hands crossed now as if tied at the wrist. The heels of his brown shoes kicked at the floor.

Boyle dropped the .38, turned toward the bar, and switched the Python to his right hand. He yelled, 'He's coming up, Stefanos!' and Solanis stood straight behind the bar, the dreamy smile on his face, his eyes wet and black, a .45 in his hand.

Solanis howled and fired blindly in my direction, the round fragmenting the arm of a wooden chair beside me. Boyle shot Solanis once in the chest. The slug threw him hard against the liquor shelf and the mirror, and Solanis's back was blown out, his blood and cartilage spraying the mirror. Pieces of the stained mirror shattered and flew off, and Solanis fell to the floor.

Sinatra sang from the box.

Boyle said, 'Cover the front door.'

I pointed the Beretta there, keeping both shaking hands on the grip. I looked down at the blood on my shirt. The blood seemed to run from my cheek.

Boyle moved through the gun smoke, his arm extended, the Python at the end of it, and walked behind the bar. He pointed the barrel down at Solanis and clicked off an empty round.

Boyle turned, switched the radio off, and went to Bonanno at the foot of the stairs, kicking the shotgun across the room. He bent at the knees, pressed a finger to Bonanno's neck, then holstered the Python inside his jacket as he stood. He didn't bother to check Goloria.

'Dead,' Boyle said. 'All of 'em.'

'I took one in the face,' I said.

Boyle rubbed his nose as he walked to my side. I sat on the floor and held the Beretta at the door. Boyle crouched down and looked me over. He put two thick fingers to my cheek, and pulled something away.

There was raw pain, and the pain blinded me for a short second, and then it went away. Boyle focused his pinball eyes on the fragment of red poker chip he held in his hand.

'You'll live,' he said.

I rubbed my cheek and surveyed the ruins. 'Jesus Christ, Boyle.'

'You can lower that gun. Martin's long gone. You better get going too.'

'What are you going to do?'

Boyle said, 'Fix it.'

I dropped the Beretta to the hardwood floor. Boyle drew a handkerchief from his jacket and rubbed my prints from the gun as I stood. He moved to Goloria and placed the automatic in the hand that still had fingers, and he wrapped the fingers of that hand around the grip. Then he drew the Python and the .38 and walked around the bar to Solanis. Boyle bent down, and when he came back up the guns were no longer in his hands. I knew then what he was going to do. Boyle looked at me with impatience

'Get going,' he said, turning to put his hand around a bottle of Jack Daniels that stood with a few remaining bottles on the liquor shelf. He undid the cap.

I nodded, said nothing, and walked out the front door. Standing on the porch, I saw a set of headlights pointed in the direction of the Maryland line on Gallatin Street, and I heard the faint wail of sirens. I looked down at the base of the porch. In shadow, Frank Martin's body lay like a large crumpled bird, the head twisted at an odd angle to the shoulders. A vague black line ran open beneath his chin.

I looked back through the lace curtains of the porch window, to the heavy figure with the bushy gray sideburns heaped at the foot of the stairs. Boyle was standing over Bonanno, the sole of one shoe resting on the dead man's chest, the bottle of Jack tilted back to his lips.

I stepped off the porch and walked through the trees, toward the lights that burned at the end of the gravel road.

30

Boyle fixed it.

In the three days that followed, an article ran daily on the front page of the *Post*'s Metro section, detailing the violent events that transpired in the house near Fort Totten Park. Every day that week, when I arrived for my shift at the Spot, a newspaper was left for me by Darnell, folded behind the register to the story's page.

Darnell had not spoken one word on the ride back that night, had never mentioned the name Frank Martin, and he would never speak about any of it again. With Boyle it was the same, though he could not enjoy Darnell's anonymity. Boyle's daily entrance at the Spot invariably created a nervous flurry of whispers from the regulars. The papers had made him out to be the city's premier badass, a Wyatt Earp-style lawman in a town whose initials had come to stand for Dodge City. No one took a stool next to Boyle at the bar again.

By the time of the last article, some basic facts had been embedded in the public's mind: Two detectives, Boyle and Goloria, had gone into a house without backup and had attempted to arrest a group of low-level bookmakers headed by a man named Bonanno. After the gun battle, in which Bonanno, his cohorts, and Goloria were killed, Boyle came upon evidence, through the notes of a young reporter killed months earlier, linking the group to a series of arsons, which in turn connected them to the reporter's own murder. The murderer turned out to be a cop killer named Solanis, wanted in several states by the FBI.

As for Goloria, he had died a hero, and he was given a hero's burial, with separate features on his career in the *Post* and on the local TV news. His family was the recipient of a full pension, along with several remunerative gifts from local police associations and booster clubs. In one of the pictures that ran in the newspaper, Goloria's wife and children stood graveside, the veiled wife holding a handkerchief to her grimacing face. Behind her in the picture, posture-straight and stone-faced, her badge clipped to her breast pocket, stood a stoic Detective Wallace.

A card arrived at my apartment a few days later. The envelope was postmarked D.C., without a return address, and the card was plain white. Inside the card was a short note, in handwriting I didn't recognize. The note read, 'Nice work, Stefanos. And thanks.' It was signed, 'A Fan.'

I threw away the newspaper clippings on the case shortly thereafter and kept the card.

A couple of weeks passed. February announced itself with a sunny, seventy-degree day. Two days after that a front traveled down from Canada and dropped a foot of snow on the area, and the cold air that hovered above for the next week kept the snow in place. Temperatures inched back up into the forties, and after another week the snow was gone.

On one of those dull gray days in late February, as I was sifting through the mail at the Spot, I opened an envelope addressed to me from Billy Goodrich. Inside the envelope a check had been made out in my name for services rendered.

The bar was slow that day, and it gave me time to sit next to the register and consider the check. As I did, I looked into the bar mirror, stared at my reflection between the bottles of Captain Morgan's and Bacardi Dark, and I thought about the night that Billy Goodrich had walked into the Spot, and how I had been staring into that same mirror, between those very bottles, that night.

The moment gave me the feeling that there was something dangling, something left to do. I stared harder, and my eyes began to burn from it, and I heard someone ordering a drink from far away, but now I wasn't listening.

I turned the bar phone toward me and punched Billy's number into the grid.

'Hello.'

'Billy, it's Nick.'

Billy paused. 'Nick, how you doin'?'

'Good.'

'You get my check? I sent it—'

'I got it.'

'It's okay, isn't it?'

'It's fine.'

Billy cleared his throat. 'What's up, Nick?'

'We got some unfinished business, Billy.'

There was another pause, longer this time. I listened to the sounds of the Spot. 'I've been waiting for your call,' he said.

I said, 'It's time we settled up.'

'That's what I want too.'

'Where and when?'

Billy thought things over. 'Down at April's property, at Cobb Island. That's where it is, right?'

'That's right, Billy. That's where it is.'

'You working tomorrow?'

'I'm off.'

'I'll pick you up, then, at your place. About eleven?'

'Eleven's fine.'

'See you at eleven.'

'All right.'

I hung the receiver in its cradle, waited for a dial tone, and phoned Hendricks at the station in La Plata. When he told me what I needed to know, I said good-bye, and stood there for a long while, running my finger along the thin scar on my cheek, a permanent reminder of the bungalow on Gallatin Street.

I went to the men's room to wash my face. When I was done I stood outside the bathroom door, rubbing my hands dry on the blue rag that hung on one side of my jeans. I walked back into the bar and finished off the remainder of my shift.

31

Billy's white Maxima pulled up in front of my apartment the next morning at eleven sharp. On the way out the door I scratched the soft area behind my cat's gnarled ear, felt her head push into my hand, and watched her eye slowly shut. I left her outside on the stoop with a dish of salmon mixed with dry meal and locked the door behind me.

The sun that day was weak, high above an unbroken sheet of gray clouds, and I zipped my jacket to the neck. I walked to the Maxima and opened the passenger door, sliding onto the leather seat. Billy offered his hand, and I shook it.

'Where's Maybelle?'

'I took her back to the pound,' Billy said. 'I'm not a dog lover to begin with, you know that. Anyway, she was never mine.'

Billy wore his logoed royal blue jacket with blue jeans and Timberland boots. His hair was long now, blond and disheveled, almost exactly as it had been fifteen years earlier. But there was a stretched quality to his smooth face, a painted tightness around his azure eyes.

'Let's stop for some coffee, Billy, on the way out.'

'Sure,' Billy said, looking me over. 'You can take that jacket off, man. I've got this heat workin' pretty good.'

'I'm fine,' I said. 'Let's get going.'

We drove down North Capitol, cutting east around Union Station, following Pennsylvania to Branch Avenue, past car dealership row at the commercial hub of Marlow Heights, then down Route 5 through the ruin that was Waldorf. The road flattened as 5 became 301, the strip malls and antique dealers breaking the brown, leafless countryside.

Billy pulled over in La Plata for a couple of burgers, and a few miles farther on we stopped again at the unmarked pool hall that advertised on/off sale. I bought a pint of Jim Beam from the woman with the raspberry birthmark and made a phone call from inside the bar and then returned to the Maxima. Billy gunned it back onto 301, and we continued south.

At 257 Billy turned left across the highway, passing the hardware-and-bait store with the John Deere sign in the window. We stayed on the highway this time, Billy keeping the Maxima at sixty-five. He hadn't spoken much on the ride down, though the silence was not uncomfortable; there was little between us left to damage. I pulled the pint of Jim Beam from my jacket, cracked the seal, and had a taste. I offered the same to Billy.

'Too early,' Billy said.

'Suit yourself.' I looked out the window at a row of evergreens blurred against a brown stretch of tobacco land and pasture. I had another drink and tightened the white cap onto the neck of the bottle.

Billy downshifted at the gravel road that marked the entrance to April Goodrich's property and turned left. We took the road into the woods and out through the open field, toward the creek. Billy coasted and came to a stop beneath the hickory tree that stood next to the trailer.

'We can walk from here,' he said.

'Walk where?'

'Into the woods, right?'

I looked out toward the creek. 'Whatever you want, Billy.'

Billy said, 'Wait here. I'll be right out.'

Billy got out of the car and went to the door of the trailer, where he used his key to enter. I watched him step inside, and after a while I got out of the Maxima and closed the passenger door.

I stood with my hands in my jacket, facing the creek. A circle had opened in the sheet of clouds, and a tubular shaft of sunlight shot through the circle, illuminating a section of the creek. Some barn swallows darted through the light, just off the dock. The clouds closed and the light was wiped away. I heard the trailer door shut, and I turned.

Billy stepped across the concrete patio, the old Remington shotgun from the trailer cradled in his arms. He stopped, reached into his pocket, and withdrew two shells. He shook the shells next to his ear, heard the rattle of buckshot, and thumbed the shells into the shotgun's broken breach.

'We going hunting, Billy?'

'No,' Billy said. 'Guy got killed on this property, two years back, in those woods. Fuckin' rednecks get drunk, shoot at anything. I don't walk back in there without this shotgun, not anymore.' He nodded toward the line of trees, three hundred yards west across the field. 'We'll go in over there.'

'I'm with you. Let's go.'

We walked over the winter wheat ground cover, through pockets of mud spotted in the hard earth. The sun broke through again and retreated. In the open field the wind was damp and cold, and it blew Billy's hair back on his scalp.

At the end of the field we cut right and walked along the tree line, passing a matted deer carcass in a ditch at the edge of the woods. Fifty yards later there was a break in the brush and trees, and we took it. I looked behind to get my bearings; the trailer, the hickory tree, and the car sat dwarfed on the open land, very far away.

The trail narrowed and dipped, and ended at a thin stream that ran down toward the creek. We followed the stream north-west, deeper in the woods, to a marshy area, where tadpoles swam through leaves beneath the last of the winter's ice, and then on through a section of high grass that had been flattened by sleeping deer. After that the ground became a bed of soft needles, and we were in a forest of oak and tall pine, the thickness of the pine trees broken by the occasional holly that grew underneath. We walked through the forest for nearly a mile, until it seemed as if we were deep inside of it, and we reached a small clearing near another marsh. Billy said then that we should stop, and I had a seat on the trunk of a fallen oak that had begun to rot before the freeze.

I pulled the bottle from my jacket and took a slug of warm bourbon. I swallowed it, breathed deeply, and smelled the air. 'Where to now?' I said.

Billy said, 'You tell me.' He was standing in front of me, fifteen feet away, his legs wide, his boots planted in the damp leaves and pine needles, the shotgun across his arms. 'You said it was down here.'

'It?'

He frowned. 'Don't fuck with me, Greek. Not today. I lost my wife because of some cockeyed scheme that went all wrong. I can't bring her back. But I have to be real now.' Billy looked a little past my eyes. 'If I let this go, then it *was* for nothing. I'm talking about the money, Nick. It's out here in these woods, isn't it?'

'Who told you that? Tommy Crane?'

Billy's face became tight with anger. 'What's that supposed to mean?'

I stood and slid the pint into my side pocket, unzipping my jacket halfway down. A flock of crows glided in over the trees and landed in the clearing. 'Settle down, Billy. We'll get back to that. You want to talk about the money, fine. Let's get that out of the way.'

'Go ahead.'

'You were right about one thing. I found the suitcase in Crane's root cellar, the day Hendricks took him out.'

Billy squinted. 'Where is it?'

'I used it,' I said.

'Used it how?'

I pushed some hair off my eyes and shifted my weight. 'To save your ass, Billy. I met Louis DiGeordano at Hains Point a few weeks ago, and I gave him the money. He owed me a favor, going back a long time ago. I asked that there wouldn't be any retribution against you, for what you tried to pull on his son. He agreed.'

Billy's shoulders hunched and shadows fell beneath his eyes. He rubbed his hand over the barrels of the shotgun. 'I didn't need that kind of help from you,' he said, looking at the ground, moving his head slowly from side to side. 'That money was dirty. It didn't *belong* to anybody. I didn't hire you to give that money away.'

'I know that, Billy. I know exactly what you hired me for.'

'I hired you to find my wife, and that's it.'

'You knew where your wife was,' I said. 'You knew it all along. You knew it the night you came to me in the Spot, the night you asked for my help. She was already dead, Billy. She's buried in these woods right now.'

'What's that?' Billy said softly. 'You sayin' I killed my wife?'

'No. Tommy Crane killed April. You didn't put the gun to her head. But you were part of it.'

Billy's finger curled around the trigger of the shotgun. 'You got everything all wrong, Nick.'

'I don't think so,' I said. 'I should have seen it when I woke up in the trailer. You were down by the creek, washing Maybelle with a brush. She had gone off and spent the night in the woods, and she had found April.' I moved to the side, away from a branch that partially blocked my view of Billy. 'April had taken the money and left town – that part of what you told me was true. You knew she'd head right down here and see Crane. I think you phoned Crane and tipped him off about the cash. You probably told him to get it from her, and then there'd be some sort of split between the two of you. But Crane killed April – maybe because she resisted, or maybe just because he wanted to watch her die. When it was over, Crane decided to keep it all himself – he didn't need you anymore, and he could always use blackmail if you tried to get rough.'

A forced, sickly smile spread across Billy's face. 'You're way off,' he said.

'No,' I said. 'I'm not. You didn't hire me to find your wife. You hired me to shake down Crane for the money. You knew I wouldn't give up on it. You knew it because we were friends, and our being friends meant something.' I looked him over. 'You were really slick, Billy. Those photographs you sent me, of April. They weren't pictures of April at all. It wasn't much of a risk on your part – I wouldn't have shown them to anyone who knew her, there wouldn't have been any need. And April's jewelry – you planted it in the bathroom of Crane's cottage while I was with him in the sty. The bathroom was the one room of his house I had told you I'd be in. When I confronted Crane with the ring, he told me that it was a stupid trick. It didn't hit me at the time, but that's exactly what it was – a trick you used, with a duplicate ring, to get me back down to Crane's. If it worked, fine. If it didn't, and Crane took me out, then there was no loss there either, right, Billy? I'm willing to bet that when the cops dig April up, that ruby ring will still be on her finger.'

'This is bullshit,' Billy said. 'You've got no proof of any of this. None.'

'I've got proof. April was killed on Tuesday night – I confirmed it with Hendricks. The date and time of her death were displayed right on the videotape. And Crane was seen with April, earlier that night, at Polanski's. Crane had two beers in front of him on the bar, and Tuesday's two-for-one night. But you told me you went drinking with your wife on Tuesday night, at Bernardo O'Reilly's.'

'You confirmed it yourself. You went there and—'

'Shut up, Billy. Shut up and let me finish. The bartender at Bernardo O'Reilly's said you were with a woman that night who polished off nearly a fifth of rum, all by herself.'

'That's right,' Billy said. 'Rum was April's drink. It's all she could keep down.'

'April was grape-sensitive. That means she could only drink rum that was bottled in Jamaica. The woman you were with in O'Reilly's was drinking Bacardi Dark.' I spoke slowly. 'That's Puerto Rican rum, Billy.'

Billy swung the shotgun in my direction. I reached into my jacket and drew the Browning from its holster, locking back the hammer. I pointed the gun at Billy's chest.

'Break that Remington,' I said. 'Break it and throw the shells to the right. Then toss the shotgun to the left.'

A watery redness had seeped into Billy's azure eyes. 'Nick, you don't think—'

'Do it,' I said, my voice rising. Billy separated the shotgun from the shells and threw them onto the leafy earth. Behind him the crows lifted out of the clearing and flew over the trees.

'So,' Billy said. 'This is how we end it.'

'That's right.'

Billy dug his feet into the leaves and looked up at the tops of the trees, then back at me. 'I would have been square with you from the beginning, Nick. That was my intention – to get your help in getting my money back from Crane, with a piece of it going back to you. But from the first minute I hooked up with you, I could see it wasn't going to be like that.' He stared down at his boots. 'The world isn't all good or all bad, like you think. It's somewhere in between. The ones who come out of it all right are the ones who pull from both ways.'

'Skip the bullshit,' I said, my knuckles bloodless on the automatic's grip. 'Our friendship – any friendship – it's the only thing that sticks. Everything rots, but that's always supposed to be there. You used it, man. You ruined it.'

Billy looked me over and shook his head. 'You better wake up,' he said. 'You think anything I did when I was nineteen means anything to me? You talked about that time in the park when we tripped, when I gave you my shoes. You talked about it like it was important. Shit, Nick, I barely even remember it. That might as well have been two different people that day. It's got nothing to do with this.'

'It's got everything to do with this.'

Billy buried his hands in the pockets of his jeans. 'Then that brings us back to now.'

I straightened my gun arm. 'I'm not letting you walk, Billy.'

Billy said, 'I'm walkin'.'

'Don't try it, Billy. I'll shoot you in the back.'

'No, you won't.' Billy smiled. 'I'm walkin', Greek. I'm walkin' back to my car. You're going to let me, and you're going to give me some time to do it. After that, everything's fair.'

'Don't, Billy,' I said, my voice shaking.

'So long, Nick.'

He turned. I shouted his name once, keeping the gun pointed at his back. I held it there until his royal blue jacket faded in the thickness of the forest. Then I lowered the gun to my side. A few minutes later the crows returned to the clearing. I holstered the Browning, sat on the trunk of the oak, and pulled the Jim Beam from my jacket.

Billy was right – I couldn't have squeezed that trigger on him, ever – but he was only half right. He wasn't going to walk. I had called Hendricks earlier that day, from the pool hall on 301.

There are only two ways off the peninsula that ends at Cobb Island – by highway or by water. Billy didn't own a boat. Hendricks was waiting for him, the big cop-car engine idling out front of the hardware store, where 257 meets 301.

The woods grew darker as I finished the pint. I rose off the trunk and walked toward the deep gray light, through another stretch of woods to the highway. A long-haired young man in a Chevy truck stopped as soon as my thumb went out, and he drove me onto the island, letting me out at the Pony Point.

For the next three hours Russel and I sat together, drinking with slow and steady intent. Hendricks showed at dusk and joined us at the bar until closing time. At the end of the night the three of us made a wordless toast, and after that Hendricks drove me all the way back to my place in D.C.

I offered him my couch, but he declined. I said good-bye, moved across the yard, and walked around the side of the house. At the stoop, I reached down to stroke the ball of black fur that was lying on the cold concrete and felt the push of a tiny nose against my hand. I put the key to the lock and turned the knob. The two of us crossed the threshold and stepped into the darkness of my apartment.

32

I took on no new cases in the months that followed. At Billy's trial, sometime in April, I was asked to testify as to the deceptions he had initiated relative to the cover-up of April Goodrich's murder.

The state went for conspiracy to commit murder, hoping to ensure a conviction on a lesser charge, and I answered their questions. Billy wisely claimed that the money in question had been gotten through gambling, eliminating the involvement of the DiGeordano family in court. I went along with that part of it, allowing Billy to play that particular string out to the end.

On the final day of my testimony, I walked from the courthouse and did not return. Hendricks phoned a few days later and told me that Billy had been given a two-year sentence for conspiracy after the fact. Billy and I had not made eye contact once during the hearing; he was gone from my life.

Two days later, on a Saturday afternoon, I was driving my Dart down the Dulles Access Road, the windows rolled down, the spring sun whitening the road. Jackie Kahn was beside me on the passenger seat, and Sherron was seated in the rear. Their luggage had been shoehorned into the trunk. The Smithereens' 'Behind a Wall of Sleep' played loudly from the radio, just covering the sputter of the engine beneath the hood. I lit a cigarette and watched Sherron's face in the rearview.

She frowned. 'You sure this piece of junk's going to make it, Stefanos?'

'Mopar engine,' I said. 'You can bet on it. What time's your flight?'

'In about twenty minutes,' Jackie said.

I goosed the accelerator and swerved into the left lane.

We reached Dulles International Airport ten minutes later. I dropped Sherron and Jackie at the terminal and told Jackie to meet me at the gate.

I parked the Dart and walked across the lot, toward the main terminal's great arced wall of glass. Inside, I checked the arrival/departure board, then made my way to the gate through a block of servicemen and European tourists. The steward had made the final call for boarding, and the line had dwindled to three. Jackie and Sherron were standing at the end of the line, the tickets in Jackie's hand.

'Think we cut it close enough?' I asked as I reached them.

'Didn't know that Dodge could break eighty,' Sherron said. She wore a double-breasted designer suit, and her lips were painted a lovely pale pink.

Jackie looked at Sherron and made a gentle nod toward the gate. 'I'll be right along. Here.' She handed Sherron her boarding pass.

Sherron put a hand to Jackie's shoulder and gave me a kiss on the cheek. 'Take it easy, Stefanos. You come visit, okay?'

'I will.'

Sherron walked stylishly through the gate. She looked back once and smiled in my direction, and capped the smile with a wink. When she rounded the corner, I turned to Jackie.

Jackie wore a smock-and-pants arrangement that day, a colorful handbag draped over her shoulder. Her short black hair was combed forward at the sides, flapper style. Small gold coins hung from her ears, and her brown eyes seemed transluscent in the light.

'I'd better go,' she said.

'You'd better.'

'Got a lot to do when I get there.'

'I'll bet. You've got, what, two or three weeks before you start your new job?'

'Something like that. It'll give me a chance to explore, get comfortable.'

'San Fran's a nice town, what I hear.'

'I couldn't turn down the offer,' she said. 'And, with what's coming up' – Jackie stopped to run a hand across her stomach – 'I thought a new start was in order, all the way around.'

I dug my hands into my pockets. 'You know I don't want you to go.'

'Sherron wasn't just being polite,' Jackie said. 'We want you out there, Nick. You're welcome anytime.'

'I plan on it,' I said. 'In the meantime, write. And send pictures.'

The steward began to attach a rope at the gate. Jackie stood on her toes and kissed my mouth. She pulled away and touched a finger to my cheek.

'I trust you,' I said. 'You know that?'

Jackie smiled. 'You did good, soldier.'

She squeezed my hand and walked away.

Later I stood at the window and watched her plane lift off. It gained altitude, made a wide arc, and flew west. When the plane was only a dot of black entering the clouds, I walked back through the main terminal, out into the parking lot. I found my car and sat in it for a while, watching the sunset, and the flow of foot traffic and cars. A chill cut the air. I started the Dart, pulled out of the lot, and headed back downtown.

Mai placed a cold bottle of Budweiser on the bar when I entered the Spot. I walked to the stool that was centered beneath the blue neon Schlitz logo. I bellied up and wrapped my hand around the bottle. The joint was empty.

Mai stocked beer in the cooler while Darnell washed the last of the night's dishes. I could hear the clatter of china and see his long brown arms against his stained apron through the reach-through as he worked.

'Slow night?' I said to Mai.

'Yep,' she said, her plump little hand buried in the cooler, her blonde hair pinned up in a pretzel-shaped bun. 'A long night watching Happy stare at the cigarette burning in his fingers.'

'Sounds thrilling.'

'I did get a seventy-five-cent tip out of it, though.'

'Then it was worth it.' I saw some sweat roll down the back of her neck and felt the guilt. 'You got plans tonight, Mai?'

Mai pulled her arm out of the cooler and faced me. She wound a twist of blonde back behind her ear and showed me some teeth. 'Got me a new soldier boy, Nicky.'

'Why don't you take off, then, take a hot bath, get ready. I'll close up.'

She smiled and straightened her posture. 'You mean it?'

'Go on, get out of here.'

Mai untied her tip apron dexterously and tossed it behind the register. She kissed me on the cheek, yelled good-bye into the kitchen, and skipped out the front door. I followed her, locked up, and walked back in.

I slid an old wave mix – Squeeze, Graham Parker, and Costello – into the tape deck. I listened to that while I finished restocking the cooler. When I was done I wiped down the bar, drained the sinks, and laid the green bar netting out in the service area to dry. I put most of the cash in a metal box and placed it underneath the floorboards, and left the register drawer open with a few ones and a five in the till. Then I grabbed an empty shot glass, the bottle of Grand-Dad off the call shelf, and a fresh Bud, and set them all up on the bar next to a clean ashtray. I placed the deck of Camels and a pack of matches beside the ashtray, had a seat, and settled in.

Darnell came out of the kitchen an hour later, tucking the tails of his beige shirt into his work pants as he walked. He stood next to me, leaned one foot on the rail, and unwound his long arms, resting them on the bar. I finished my fourth shot of bourbon and poured another to the lip of the glass.

'Private party?' Darnell said.

'Uh-uh.'

'Mind if I hang?'

I gestured toward the empty stool to my right. 'Have a seat.'

Darnell sat and picked up my bottle of beer. He looked at the label, studied it, and placed the bottle back with the shot glass. I cupped my hand around both, a low, even tone encircling my head, entering my ears.

Darnell said, 'You look pretty far away, man.'

'I guess I am.'

'Trouble with the ladies?'

I concentrated, looking at myself in the bar mirror. I had been thinking about Jackie at the beginning of the night, and then Billy Goodrich. But afterward my thoughts had gone much further back, long before the day I had met Billy on the bench in Sligo Creek Park. More skeletons, come to life.

'No,' I said. 'I was thinking about this Greek boy I knew way back. A kid named Dimitri.'

'Never heard you mention him.'

'He's been gone,' I said, 'a long time.' I had a drink of bourbon, rolled it around the glass, and followed it with another swallow. I chased that with beer and rested the bottle on the bar, keeping my fingers on the neck. Costello's beautiful country import, 'Shoes without Heels,' flowed through the speakers.

Darnell said, 'Talk about it, man.'

I looked into my shot glass. 'I met this kid Dimitri, playing basketball in the church league, when I was seventeen. He was from Highlandtown – Greektown – up in Baltimore. We came from different places, but our friendship clicked for some reason, real fast. We started hanging out together, I'd drive up to Baltimore to see him, he'd take the bus to D.C. This kid was tough, big shoulders, but he had this smile . . . He had a lot of life, you know what I'm saying?' Darnell nodded, watching my eyes in the mirror. 'That summer, we used to crank up J. Geils's

Bloodshot, dance out front of his row house, the tape deck set up right on his stoop. So when Geils came to the Baltimore Civic Center, you know we were the first ones with tickets, the first ones at the show.' I paused. 'Dimitri was wearing this hat that night, sort of like a Panama hat, but gangster style. And J. Geils came on – this was the *Ladies Invited* tour, they opened with the first track off the LP, "The Lady Makes Demands" – and turned the place out.' I poured another inch of Grand-Dad into the shot glass, downed it, and exhaled. The glass left a ring of water on the mahogany bar. 'Somehow I lost Dimitri in the crowd. But later, from my seat above, I recognized him by his hat, pushing his way up to the front of the stage. That show was bumpin', man.' I paused, picturing the crowd, girls in halter tops, a cloud of marijuana hovering in the arena. 'Anyway, when Dimitri finally came back to the seats, he wasn't wearing the hat – when I asked him where it was, he said he had handed it to Peter Wolf, on the stage. I told him he was full of shit, and Dimitri didn't argue about it – that wasn't his style. He just smiled.'

Darnell said, 'What happened to that boy?'

I moved my face around with my hand and pushed hair away from my eyes. 'A couple weeks later he got into a car with a couple of Polish boys from the neighborhood. He didn't know the car was stolen. They were driving down the Patterson Parkway, and a cop made the car, and the driver tried to outrun the cop. He flipped it doing seventy. Dimitri went through the windshield. He was in a coma for a week, and then he died. The boys who stole the car walked away with scratches.'

Darnell said, 'You don't need to be thinkin' about that tonight, Nick.'

'Listen' – I smiled and shook my head – 'that's not the end of the story. Six months later I pick up an issue of *Creem* magazine, off the newsstand. Inside, there's a story on the J. Geils Band, and on the facing page there's a photograph of Peter Wolf. He's wearing Dimitri's hat, Darnell. And the caption underneath says, "Lead singer Peter Wolf wears a hat given to him by a fan at a Baltimore concert".'

'That must've tripped you out.'

I had a sip of bourbon, put it down, and drank deeply of the beer. 'Dimitri went out like a fuckin' champ.'

Darnell frowned. 'You don't believe that, Nick.'

'You're wrong,' I said. 'Dimitri checked out at the top of his game. The way everybody should.' I lit a cigarette, blew smoke over the bar, and let it settle. 'He never had to watch himself get old in the mirror. He never had to hold a fucking gun on his friends.'

Darnell looked at the drink in front of me and straight back in my eyes. 'Man, you're the one that's wrong. That shit you're drinkin, it's got you all twisted up inside.' He put a hand to my arm. 'I'll tell you what that boy never got to do. He never got to walk his woman down the aisle. He never got to hold his baby up to the sky. He never got a chance to taste the good *or* the bad. You better see that, man. If you don't, you're lost.'

I reached for my drink. Darnell pushed the glass away, out of my reach.

'I'm all right,' I said.

'I'm drivin' you home.'

'Let me sit here for a little bit.'

'I'm drivin' you home,' Darnell said. 'Come on.'

I steadied myself, my hand on the bar. 'I'm all right.'

'Let's go, man.'

I focused on Darnell's eyes. 'You lock the place up. Okay?'

'I'll take care of it,' he said, getting under my arm.

We walked together to the front door. A cool blue light burned behind us in the room, and smoke rose off the ashtray on the bar.

I stood in the shower and slept on my feet. The water temperature fell, and when it did, the coolness of it woke me. I exited the stall, dried off, combed out my hair, and dressed in a black sweatshirt and jeans. My cat followed me into the kitchen, circling my feet as I brewed a cup of coffee.

I took the coffee out into the living room and had a seat on the couch, resting the cup on the couch's arm. I sat there and drank the coffee, stroking the cat on my lap. I did that for a while, and then the phone rang. The cat jumped off as I picked the phone up from the floor and placed it in my lap. I put the receiver to my ear.

'Hello.'

'Stefanos?' It was a woman's voice, unidentifiable but familiar.

'Yes.'

'You never called me.'

'Who is this?'

'A fan,' she said.

I thought about that, and I remembered the note. Then I thought some more about the voice. 'How's it going?' I said.

'It's goin' good. Why didn't you call?'

'I'm not the aggressive type.'

'You got aggressive pretty quick on the William Henry case.'

'What's that?'

'I read the *Post*,' she said. 'I figured you were behind it somehow,

435

though I don't know how you finessed it.' I let her talk. I liked the sound of her voice. 'Don't want to discuss it, huh?'

'Uh-uh.'

'You drunk Stefanos? You sound a little drunk.'

'Tired,' I said.

'Well, it is late. So I'll get right to the point. Listen, I was wondering – you didn't call, so I thought I'd take the initiative here – I was wondering if maybe you wanted to take in a double feature tomorrow night, down at the AFI.'

My cat sat on the radiator, watching me twist the phone cord around my hand. 'What's on the bill?' I said.

'Some shoot-em-up out of Hong Kong, and a Douglas Sirk melodrama. *Magnificent Obsession.* Something for you, something for me.'

'No Liz Taylor?'

'Nope,' she said. 'And no Isaac Hayes.'

I grinned. 'Sounds good to me. You buy the tickets, I'll spring for whatever comes up next. Okay?'

'Okay. I'll pick you up at your place,' she said. 'About six-thirty.'

'You know where I live?'

'Your number's on the card. I cross-referenced it to your address in the Hanes Directory.'

'You're a hell of an investigative reporter.'

'See you tomorrow night, Stefanos.'

'Right.'

I got off the couch with the phone in my hand, and I stood in the center of the room. A Dinah Washington number played from my landlord's apartment above. I danced a few steps and put the phone down. My cat watched me and blinked her eye.

I took the coffee cup to the kitchen and found the note that had been signed 'A Fan' on the plain white card, in the basket where I dumped my overdue bills. I walked with the note to my bedroom, and I opened the top dresser drawer.

I wasn't certain that night as to why I kept the note. Call it a feeling, listening to the woman's voice on the phone, that something right would happen next. But as spring became summer, I began to understand.

That was the summer that I first noticed the texture of the crepe myrtle that grew beside my stoop, the summer I woke each morning to the sweet smell of hibiscus that flowered outside my bedroom window. That was the summer that a tape called *The La's* played continuously from my deck, the summer that a Rare Essence go-go single called 'Lock It' raged from every young D.C. driver's sound system on the street. And that was the summer that I held hands in the dark with a freckly, pale-eyed redhead with the perfectly musical name of Lyla McCubbin.

Under a shoe box filled with trinkets from my youth, in the bottom of the dresser drawer, lay the envelope that held the few memories I had chosen to hold on to through the years. I placed the white card into the envelope, behind the photograph of me and Billy Goodrich sitting high on the fire escape in New Orleans. I slipped the envelope back under the shoe box and closed the drawer. My cat walked slowly into the room and settled at my feet.

Down by the River
where the
Dead Men Go

For Peter

1

Like most of the trouble that's happened in my life or that I've caused to happen, the trouble that happened that night started with a drink. Nobody forced my hand; I poured it myself, two fingers of bourbon into a heavy, beveled shot glass. There were many more after that, more bourbons and more bottles of beer, too many more to count. But it was that first one that led me down to the river that night, where they killed a boy named Calvin Jeter.

This one started at the Spot, on 8th and G in Southeast, where I tended bar three or four shifts a week. It had been a hot day, hazy and soup-hot, like most midsummer days in D.C. The compressor on our ancient air conditioner had gone down after the lunch rush, and though most of our regulars had tried to drink their way through it, the heat had won out. So by ten o'clock it was just me behind the stick, lording over a row of empty bar stools, with Ramon in the cellar and Darnell in the kitchen, cleaning up. I phoned Phil Saylor, the owner of the establishment, and with his okay shut the place down.

Ramon came up the wooden stairs carrying three cases of beer, his head just clearing the top carton. He was smiling stupidly – he had just smoked a joint in the cellar – but the smile was stretched tight, and it looked as if he were about to bust a nut. Ramon in his cowboy boots stood five two and weighed in at 129, so seventy-two beers was pushing it. He dropped the cases at my feet and stood before me, wiping the sweat off his forehead with a red bandanna. I thanked him and tipped him out.

For the next fifteen minutes, I rotated the beer into the cooler, making sure to leave some cold ones on the top, while I listened to Ramon and Darnell cut on each other back in the kitchen. Through the reach-through, I could see Ramon gut-punching the tall and razorish Darnell, Darnell taking it and loving it and laughing the whole time. Then there were loud air kisses from Ramon, and Darnell saying, 'Later, amigo,' and Ramon motoring out of the kitchen, through the bar area, toward the door.

I finished with the beer and wiped down the bar and rinsed out the green netting and put the ashtrays in the soak sink, leaving one out, and then I washed up and changed into shorts and a T-shirt and high-top sneakers. Darnell shut off the light in the kitchen and came out as I tightened the laces on my Chucks.

'Whas'up, Nick?'

''Bout done.'

'Any business today?'

'Yeah. The catfish went pretty good.'

'Used a little Old Bay. Think anybody noticed?'

'Uh-uh.'

Darnell pushed his leather kufi back off his sweat-beaded forehead. 'You headin' uptown? Thought maybe I'd catch a ride.'

'Not yet. I'm gonna call Lyla, see what she's doing.'

'All right, then. Let me get on out of here.'

On the nights we closed together, this was our routine. Darnell knew I would stick around, usually alone, and have a drink; he'd always try and get me out of there before I did. A stretch in Lorton had straightened him all the way out, though no one mistook his clean lifestyle for the lifestyle of a pushover, least of all me; I had seen what he could do with a knife. Darnell went out the door. I locked it behind him.

Back in the main room, I counterclockwised the rheostat. The lamps dimmed, leaving the room washed in blue neon light from the Schlitz logo centered over the bar. I found WDCU on the house stereo and notched up the volume on the hard bop. I lit a cigarette, hit it, and fitted it in the V of the last remaining ashtray. Then I pulled a nearly full bottle of Old Grand-Dad off the call shelf, poured a shot, and had a taste. I opened a cold bottle of Bud, drank off an inch or two of that, and placed the bottle next to the shot. My shoulders unstiffened, and everything began to soften and flow down.

I looked around the room: a long, railed mahogany bar, mottled and pocked; several conical lamps spaced above, my own smoke swirling in the low-watt light; a rack behind the lamps, where pilsner and rocks and up glasses hung suspended, dripping water on the bar; some bar stools, a few high-backed, the rest not; a couple of vinyl-cushioned booths; a pair of well-used speakers mounted on either side of the wall, minus the grills; and some 'artwork,' a Redskins poster furnished by the local beer distributor (1989's schedule – we had never bothered to take it down) and a framed print of the Declaration of Independence, the signatures of our forefathers joined in various places by the drunken signatures of several of our regulars. My own signature was scrawled somewhere on there, too.

I finished my bourbon and poured another as I dialed Lyla's number. Next to the phone was a photograph, taped to the yellowed wall, of a uniformed Phil Saylor, circa his brief stint as a cop on the Metropolitan Police force. I looked at his round face while listening to Lyla's answering machine. I hung the receiver in its cradle without leaving a message.

The next round went down smoothly and more quickly than the first. During that one, I tried phoning my old buddy Johnny McGinnes, who had gone from electronics sales to mattresses and now to major appliances, but the chipper guy who answered the call – 'Goode's White Goods. My name is Donny. How may I help you?' – told me that McGinnes had left for the evening. I told him to tell McGinnes that his friend Nick had called, and he said, 'Sure will,' adding, 'and if you're ever in need of a major appliance, the name is Donny.' I hung up before he could pry his name in again, then dialed Lyla's number. Still no answer.

So I had another round, slopping bourbon off the side of the glass as I poured. Cracking a beer I had buried earlier in the ice bin, I went to the stereo and cranked up the volume: a honking session from some quintet, really wild shit, the Dexedrined drummer all over the map. By the time the set was over, I had finished my shot. Then I decided to leave; the Spot had grown hellishly hot, and I had sweat right into my clothes. Besides, my buzz was too good now, way too good to waste alone. I killed the lights and set the alarm, locked the front door, and stepped out onto 8th with a beer in my hand.

I walked by an athletic-shoe store, closed and protected by a riot gate. I passed an alley fringely lit at the head by a nearby streetlamp. I heard voices in its depths, where an ember flared, then faded. Just past the alley sat Athena's, the last women's club in my part of town. Behind its windowless brick walls came the steady throb of bass. I pushed open the door and stepped inside.

I heard my name called out over a Donna Summer tune and the general noise of the place. I edged myself around a couple of women on the dance floor and stepped up to the bar. Stella, the stocky, black-haired tender, had poured me a shot when she saw me come through the front door. I thanked her and put my hand around the glass and knocked it back all at once. Someone kissed me on the back of my neck and laughed.

I found Mattie, my transplanted Brooklyn friend, by the pool table in a smoky corner of the room. We shot our usual game of eight ball, and I lost a five. Then I bought us a round of beers and played another game, with the same result. Mattie had the whole table mapped out before her first stroke, while I was a power shooter who never played for shape. Some nights I won, anyway – but not that night.

I went back to the bar and settled my tab and left too much for Stella. In the bar mirror, I saw my reflection, bright-eyed and ugly and streaked with sweat. Near the register hung a framed photograph of Jackie Kahn, former Athena's bartender and the mother of my child, a boy named Kent, now nine months old. I said something loudly to Stella then, my voice sounding garbled and harsh. She began to smile but then abruptly stopped, looking in my eyes. I pushed away from the bar and made it out the front door, to the fresh air and the street.

I unlocked the Spot's front door, deactivated the alarm by punching in a four-digit number on a grid, and went back behind the bar. I cracked a cold beer and drank deeply. Then I poured Old Grand-Dad to the lip of a shot glass and bent over, putting my lips directly to the whiskey, drinking off an inch of it without touching the glass. I shook a Camel filter out of my pack and lit it. The phone began to ring. I let it ring, and walked down toward the stereo, stumbling on a rubber mat along the way. I found a tape by Lungfish, a ranging guitar-based band out of Baltimore, and slid that in the deck. I hit the play button and gave it some bass.

Black.

I sat on a stool at the bar, tried to strike a match. A cigarette had burned down, dead-cold in the ashtray. I lit a fresh one, tossed the match toward the ashtray, missed. I reached for my shot glass and saw the half-filled bottle of Grand-Dad in the middle of a cluster of empty beer bottles. I tasted whiskey. The tape had ended. There was not a sound in the bar.

Black.

I stepped off the kerb outside the Spot. A whooping alarm screamed in the night. Stella walked by me, said, 'Nicky, Nicky,' went through the open front door of the Spot, reset the alarm. She asked for and took my keys, then locked the front door. A few women had spilled out of Athena's onto the sidewalk. Stella returned, held my keys out, then drew them back as I reached for them.

'Come on, Nicky. Come on and sleep it off in the back.'

'I'm all right. Gimme my keys.'

'Forget it.'

'Gimme my keys. I can sleep in my car. What the fuck, Stella, it's ninety degrees out here. You think I'm gonna freeze? Gimme my fuckin' keys.'

Stella tossed me the keys. I tried to catch them, but there was an open beer in one of my hands and the bottle of Grand-Dad in the other. I went to one knee to pick my keys up off the street. I looked up, tried to thank Stella, She had already walked away.

Black.

Driving down Independence Avenue, a Minor Threat tune at maximum volume, blowing through the speakers of my Dodge. I stopped my car in the middle of the street, let the motor run, got out of the car, urinated on the asphalt. To my left, the Mall, the Washington Monument lit up and looming, leaning a little toward the sky. Tourists walked hurriedly by on the sidewalk, fathers watching me from the corner of their eyes, pushing their children along, the singer screaming from the open windows of my car: 'What the fuck have *you* done?' Me, laughing.

Black.

I drove down M Street in Southeast, the Navy Yard on my right. My first car, a '64 Plymouth Valiant, bought there at a government auction, accompanied by my grandfather. Must have tried to get back to the Spot, made a wrong turn. Lights everywhere, streetlights and taillights, crossing. I hit my beer, chased it with bourbon. The bourbon spilled off my chin. A blaring horn, an angry voice yelling from the car at my side. The beer bottle tipped over between my legs, foam undulating from the neck. My shorts, soaked; pulled my wallet from my back pocket and tossed it on the bucket seat to my right. Music, loud and distorted in the car.

Black.

The car went slowly down a single lane, asphalt road. Trees on both sides of the road. To the right, through the trees, colored lights reflected off water. No music now in the car. The surge of laughter far away, and trebly slide guitar from a radio. Blurry yellow lights ahead, suspended above the water, shooting straight out into the sky. Had to pee, had to stop the car, had to stop the lights from moving. Heard gravel spit beneath the wheels, felt the car come to rest. Killed the ignition. Opened my door, stumbled out onto the gravel, heard the sound of a bottle hit the ground behind me. Started to fall, then gained my footing, stumbling, running now to the support of a tree. Needed to lie down, but not there. Pushed off the tree, bounced off another, felt something lash across my cheek. Shut my eyes, opened them, began to float into a fall.

445

Nothing beneath me, no legs, a rush of lights and water and trees, spinning. The jolt of contact as I hit the ground, no pain. On my back, looking up at the branches, through the branches the stars, moving, all of it moving. Sick. The night coming up, no energy to turn over, just enough to tilt my head. A surge of warm liquid spilling out of my mouth and running down my neck, the stench of my own flowing puke, the steam of it passing before my eyes.

Black.

A sting on my cheek. Something crawling on my face, my hands dead at my sides. Let it crawl. The branches, the stars, still moving. My stomach convulsed. I turn my head and vomit.

Black.

The slam of a car door. The sound of something dragged through gravel and dirt. A steady, frantic moan.

The voice of a black man: 'All right now. You already been a punk, and shit. Least you can do is go out a man.'

The moan now a muffled scream. Can't move, can't even raise my head. A dull plopping sound, then a quiet splash.

The black man's voice: 'Just leave him?'

Another voice, different inflection: 'Kill a coon in this time and it barely makes the papers – no offense, *you* know what I mean. C'mon, let's get outta here. Let's go home.'

Black.

I opened my eyes to a gray sky. I ran my hand through dirt and paper and grass, and something plastic and wet. I stayed there for a while, looking at the leafy branches and the sky. My back ached and I felt stiff behind the neck. I could smell the odor of garbage, my own bile and sweat.

I sighed slowly, got up on one elbow. I looked across the water at the sun, large and dirty orange, coming up in the east. I sat up all the way, rubbed a fleck of crust off my chin, ran my fingers through my hair.

I was down by the Anacostia River – in the marina district, where M Street continues unmarked. I recognized it straight away. My grandfather and I had fished here when I was a kid. He had always thrown back the perch and occasional catfish he had reeled in. The river had been virtually dead, even then.

I was sitting in a wooded area, the grass worn down to weeds and dirt, littered with plastic bags and fast-food wrappers, empty beer cans, malt liquor bottles, peach brandy pints, used rubbers, the odd shoe. I turned to the right and saw my car, nearly hidden in the start of the woods, parked neatly and without a scratch between two trees, all dumb luck. Beyond that, I could see the moored runabouts and powerboats of a marina, and past the marina the 11th Street Bridge, leading to Anacostia. Behind me was the road, cracked and potholed, and behind the road a denser block of trees, then railroad tracks, and then more trees. To my left, the woods gave to a clearing, where a rusted houseboat sat half-sunk in the water. After that, another hundred yards down the shoreline, the Sousa Bridge spanned the river, the lights of which I had noticed but not recognized the night before.

The night before. My memory flashed on something very wrong.

I got up on my feet and walked unsteadily through the trees to the clearing, continued on to the waterline. Wooden pilings came up out of the brown river, spaced erratically around the sunken houseboat. Something appeared to be draped around one of the pilings. The sun nearly blinded me, sent a pounding into my head. I shaded my eyes, went to where the scum of the river lapped at the concrete bulkhead, stood there on the edge.

A young black man lay in the water, his head and shoulders submerged, the shirtsleeve of one bound arm caught on a cleat in the piling. Duct tape had been wound around his gray face, covering his mouth. I could see an entry wound, small and purple, rimmed and burned black, below his chin. The bullet had traveled up and blown out the back of his head; brain stew, pink and chunked, had splashed out onto the piling. The gas jolt had bugged his eyes.

I fell to my knees and retched. The dry heave came up empty. I stayed there, caught air, stared at the garbage and debris floating stagnant in the river. I pushed off with my hands, stood and turned, stumbled a few steps, then went into a quick walk toward the trees. I didn't look back.

I picked up the empty bottle of bourbon at the side of my Dodge and opened the door. I dropped the bottle inside and fell into the driver's seat. My keys still hung in the ignition. I looked in the rearview at my eyes, unrecognizable. I checked my watch, rubbed dirt off its face: 6:30 A.M., Wednesday.

My wallet lay flat and open on the shotgun bucket. I picked it up, looked at my own face staring out at me from my District of Columbia license: 'Nicholas J. Stefanos, Private Investigator.'

So *that's* what I was.

I turned the key in the ignition.

2

My girlfriend, Lyla McCubbin, stopped by my apartment early that evening. She found me sitting naked on the edge of the bed, just up from a nap, the blinds drawn in the room. I had thrown away my clothes from the night before and taken two showers during the course of the day. But I had begun to sweat again, and the room smelled of booze. Lyla had a seat next to me and rubbed my back, then pulled my face out of my hands.

'I talked to Mai at the Spot. She told me she picked up your shift tonight. You had a rough one, huh?'

'Yeah, pretty rough.'

'What's all over your face?'

'Bites. Some kind of roaches, I guess. I woke up – I was layin' in garbage.'

'Shit, Nicky.'

'Yeah.'

'I called you last night,' she said.

'I called *you*.'

She looked in my eyes. 'You been crying or something, Nick?'

' I don't know,' I said, looking away.

'You got the depression,' she said quietly. 'You went and got yourself real good and drunk. You did some stupid things, and then you fell out. The only thing you can do now is apologize to the people you dealt with, maybe try and be more sensible next time. But you shouldn't beat yourself up about it. I mean, it happens, right?'

I didn't answer. Lyla's fingers brushed my hair back off my face. After awhile, she got up off the bed.

'I'm going to make you something to eat,' she said.

'Sit back down a minute,' I said, taking her hand. She did, and everything poured out.

Later, I sat on my stoop as Lyla grilled burgers on a hibachi she had set up on the brick patio outside my apartment. Lyla's long red hair switched across her back as she drank from a goblet of Chablis and prodded the burgers with a short-handled spatula. My black cat circled her feet, then dashed across the patio and batted at an errant moth. I watched Lyla move against a starry backdrop of fireflies that blinked beyond the light of the patio, and I smelled the deep-summer hibiscus that bloomed in the yard.

After dinner, Lyla drove up to Morris Miller's, the liquor store in my Shepherd Park neighborhood, for more wine. My landlord, who owned the house and lived in its two top floors, came out and sat with me on the stoop. I had my first cigarette of the day while he drank from a can of beer and told me a story of a woman he had met in the choir, who he said sang like an angel in church but had 'the devil in her hips outside those walls.' He laughed while I dragged on my cigarette, and pointed to my cat, still running in circles, chasing that moth.

'Maybe if that old cat had two eyes, she'd catch that thing.'

'She might catch it yet,' I said. 'Nailed a sparrow and dropped it on my doorstep the other day.'

'Whyn't you get a *real* animal, man? I know this boy, lives down around 14th and Webster? Got some alley cats would fuck up a dog.'

'I don't know. I bring a cat around here like your boy's got, might scare away some of your lady friends.'

'Wouldn't want that.' My landlord hissed a laugh. ''Cause that woman I got now, that church woman? She's a keeper.'

Lyla returned, uncorked her wine, and poured another glass. My landlord gave her a kiss and went back in the house to his easy chair and TV. Lyla sat next to me and dropped her hand on the inside of my thigh, rubbing it there.

'How you feeling?'

'Better.'

'You'll be better still tomorrow.'

'I guess.'

She bent toward me, and I turned my head away. Lyla took my chin in her hand and forced me to meet her gaze. I looked into her pale green eyes. She kissed me then and held the kiss, her breath warm and sour from the wine.

After awhile, we went inside. I dropped a Curtis Mayfield tape into the deck while Lyla lit some votive candles in my room. I undressed her from behind, kissing the pulsing blue vein of her neck. We fell onto my bed, where we made out slowly in the flickering light. Lyla rolled on top of me and put my hands to her breasts. The candlelight reflected off her damp hair, the sweat on her chest like glass.

I shut my eyes and let her work it, let myself go with the sensations, the sounds of her open-mouthed gasps, the rising promise of my own release, the sweet voice of Curtis singing 'Do Be Down' in the room. She knew what she was doing, and it worked; for a few minutes. I forgot all about the man I had become. Or maybe I had gone to another place, where I could let myself believe that I was someone else.

Lyla had placed my coffee next to the *Post* on the living room table the following morning. I picked up my mug and sipped from it while I stood over the newspaper and stared blankly at its front page. Lyla walked into the room, tucking a cream-colored blouse into an apple green skirt.

'It made the final edition,' she said. 'Deep in Metro. The Roundup.'

The *Post* grouped the violent deaths of D.C.'s underclass into a subhead called 'Around the Region'; local journalists sarcastically dubbed this daily feature 'the Roundup.' As the managing editor of the city's hard-news alternative weekly, *D.C. This Week*, Lyla was not immune to criticism of local media herself. But her competitive spirit couldn't stop her from taking the occasional shot at the *Washington Post.*

'What'd it say?'

'You know,' she said. ' "Unidentified man found in the Anacostia River. Fatal gunshot wounds. Police are withholding the name until notification of relatives, no suspects at this time" – the usual. When you read it, you automatically think, Another drug execution. Retribution kill, whatever. I mean, that's what it was, right?'

I had a seat on the couch and ran my finger along the edge of the table. Lyla kept her eyes on me as she pulled her hair back and tied it off with a black band.

I looked up. 'You still got that friend over at the city desk at Metro?'

Lyla moved my way and stood over me. She rested her hands on her hips, spoke tiredly. 'Sure, and I've got my own sources in the department. Why?'

'Just, you know. I thought you could see what else they got on this so far.'

'So, what, you could get involved?'

'Just curious, that's all. Anyway, it's been awhile. I wouldn't know where to start.' I thought of my last case, a year and a half earlier:

William Henry and April Goodrich, the house on Gallatin Street – a bloodbath, and way too much loss.

Lyla leaned over and kissed me on the lips. 'Get some rest today, Nick. Okay?'

'I'm workin' a shift,' I said.

'Good,' she said. 'That's good.'

She gave me one more knowing look and walked from the room. I listened to the slam of the screen door and slowly drank the rest of my coffee. Then I showered and dressed and left the apartment. The newspaper remained on my living room table, untouched, unread.

The Spot cooked during the lunch rush that day. Darnell's special, a thick slice of meat loaf with mashed potatoes and gravy, moved quickly, and he was sliding them onto the reach-through with fluid grace. Ramon bused the tables and kept just enough dishes and silverware washed to handle the turns. Our new lunch waitress, Anna Wang, a tough little Chinese-American college student, worked the small dining room adjacent to the bar.

Anna stepped up to the service bar, called, 'Ordering!' She pulled a check from her apron, blew a strand of straight black hair out of her eyes while she made some hash marks on the check. I free-poured vodka into a rocks glass and cranberry-juiced it for color. Then I poured a draft and carried the mug and the glass down to Anna, a lit Camel in my mouth. I placed the drinks on her cocktail tray just as she speared a swizzle stick into the vodka.

Anna said, 'How about some of that, Nick?'

I took the cigarette out of my mouth and put it between her lips. She drew on it once, let smoke pour from her nostrils, and hit it again as I plucked it out. She nodded and carried off the tray. I watched Ramon go out of his way to brush her leg with his as he passed with a bus tray of dirty dishes. Anna ignored him and kept moving.

'Another martini for me, Nick,' said Melvin, the house crooner, whose stool was by the service bar. I poured some rail gin into an up glass and let a drop or two of dry vermouth fall into the glass. I served it neatly on a bev nap, watching Melvin's lips move to the Shirley Horn vocals coming from the Spot's deck, and then I heard Darnell's voice boom from the kitchen over the rattle of china and the gospel music of his own radio: 'Food up!'

I snatched it off the reach-through and walked down the bar toward Happy, our resident angry alki, seated alone, always alone. On my trip, I stopped to empty the ashtray of a gray beard named Dave, who was quietly reading a pulp novel and drinking coffee at the bar, his spectacles low-riding his nose, doing his solitary, on-the-wagon thing. Some ashes floated down into Happy's plate, and I blew them off before I placed the plate down in front of him. Happy looked down mournfully at the slab of meat garnished with the anemic sprig of wilted parsley and the gravy pooled in the gluey mashed potatoes. His hand almost but not quite fell away from the glass in his grip.

'This looks like *dog* shit,' he muttered.

'You want another drink, Happy?'

'Yeah,' he said with a one o'clock slur. 'And this time, put a little liquor in it.'

I prepared his manhattan (an ounce of rail bourbon with a cherry dropped in it, no vermouth) and placed it on a moldy coaster advertising some sort of black Sambuca we did not stock. Then I heard Anna's tired voice from down the bar: 'Ordering!' I moved to the rail and fixed her drinks.

That's the way it went for the rest of the afternoon. Buddy and Bubba, two GS-9 rednecks, came in at the downslope of the rush and split a couple of pitchers. They argued over sports trivia the entire time with a pompadoued dude named Richard, though none of them had picked up a ball of any kind since high school. Before they left, they poked their heads in the kitchen and congratulated Darnell on the 'presentation' of the meat loaf. Darnell went about his work, and Buddy sneered in my direction as he and Bubba headed out the door.

After lunch, I put some PJ Harvey in the deck for Anna while she leaned and reset her station. Phil Saylor had instructed me to keep blues and jazz playing on the stereo during the rush, but Happy, dashing in his dandruff-specked, plum-colored sport jacket, was now the only customer in the bar. Sitting there in a stagnant cloud of his own cigarette smoke, he didn't ever seem to respond to the musical selection either way.

Anna split for the day after bumming a smoke, and Ramon retreated to the kitchen, where he practiced some bullshit karate moves on an amused Darnell while I began to cut limes for Mai's evening shift. I had just finished filling the fruit tray when Dan Boyle walked through the front door.

Boyle parked his wide ass on the stool directly in front of me and ran fingers like pale cigars through his wiry, dirty blond hair.

'Nick.'

'Boyle.'

His lazy, bleached-out eyes traveled up to the call rack, then settled

452

back down on the bar. I turned and pulled the black-labeled bottle of Jack Daniel's off the call shelf. I poured some sour mash into a shot glass and slid it in front of him.

'A beer with that?'

'Not just yet.'

He put the glass to his lips and tilted his head back for a slow taste. The action opened his jacket a bit, the grip of his Python edging out.

On any given night, the Spot could be heavy with guns, as the place had become a favorite watering hole for D.C.'s plainclothes cops and detectives, the connection going back to Saylor. Guns or no, Boyle had earned a different kind of rep, topped by his much-publicized role in the Gallatin Street shoot-out. I had been there with him, right next to him, in fact, but my participation had remained anonymous. I was reminded of it, though, every time I passed a mirror: a two-inch-long scar, running down my cheek.

'Goddamn it, that's good,' Boyle said, wiping his mouth with the back of his hand. 'I'll take that beer now.'

I tapped him one and set the mug next to the shot. Boyle pulled a Marlboro hard pack from his jacket, drew a cigarette, and tamped it on the pack. He put it to his lips and I gave him a light.

'Thanks.' Boyle spit smoke and reached for the mug. I bent over the soak sink and ran a glass over the brush.

'Good day out there?' I said, looking into the dirty gray suds.

'Not bad today, if you really want to know. Picked up the shooter that fired off that Glock on school grounds over at Duval two weeks ago.'

'The one where the bullet hit the wrong kid?'

'The wrong kid? If you say so. The kid that got shot, he had a roll of twenties in his pocket, and a gold chain around his neck thicker than my wrist. So maybe he didn't hit the kid he was going for, but he damn sure hit a kid that was in the life. Shit, Nick, you throw a fuckin' rock in the hall of that high school, you're gonna hit someone guilty of something.'

'You're a real optimist, Boyle. You know it?'

'Like now I need a lecture. Anyway, you want to talk about sociology and shit from behind that bar, go ahead. In the meantime, I'm out there—'

'In that concrete jungle?'

'What?'

' "Concrete Jungle," ' I said. 'The Specials.'

'Gimme another drink,' Boyle mumbled, and finished off what was in his glass. He chased it with a swig of beer and wiped his chin dry with the back of his hand.

Happy said something, either to himself or to me, from the other end of the bar. I ignored him, poured Boyle another shot. I leaned one elbow on the mahogany and put my foot up on the ice chest.

'So, Boyle. How about that kid, the one that got it two nights ago—'

'The one they found in the river?'

'Yeah. I guess that was a drug thing, too.'

'Bet it,' Boyle said. 'But it's not my district. So that's one I don't have to worry about.'

'Let me ask you something. You know what the weapons of choice are on the street this month, right? I mean, it changes all the time, but you're pretty much on top of it. Right?'

'So?'

'These enforcers. They in the habit of using silencers these days?'

Boyle thought for a moment, then shook his head. He watched me out the corner of his eye as he butted his cigarette. Happy called again and I went down his way and fixed him a drink. When I came back, Boyle was firing down the remainder of his Jack and draining off the rest of his beer. He left some money on the bar, stashed his cigarettes in his jacket, and slid clumsily off his stool.

'Take it easy, Nick.'

'You, too.'

I took his bills and rang on the register, dropping what was left into my tip jar. In the bar mirror, I saw Dan Boyle moving toward the front door. He turned once and stared at my back, his mouth open, his eyes blank. Then he turned again and walked heavily from the bar.

I worked another shift on Friday, and in the evening Lyla and I caught a movie at the Dupont and had some appetizers after the show at Aleko's, the best Greek food in town for my money, on Connecticut, above the Circle. Lyla had a few glasses of retsina at the restaurant and a couple more glasses of white before we went to bed. I didn't drink that night – three days now without a drop, the longest downtime in a long, long while. I had some trouble going to sleep, though, and when I did, my dreams were crowded, filled with confusing detail, unfamiliar places, blue-black starlings rising in the corners of the frame.

On Saturday, Lyla went into the office to put the finishing touches on a cover story, and I rode my ten-speed down to the Mall to catch a free Fugazi show at the Sylvan Theater. A go-go act opened to a polite crowd, and then the band came out and tore it up. I saw Joe Martinson, a friend and contemporary of mine from the old postpunk days, and we hung together in the late-teen crowd that was getting off – clean off – on the music.

That night, Lyla and I stayed at my place and listened to a few records. Lyla drank a gin and tonic and switched over to wine, and around midnight she called me outside, where I found her sitting on a blanket she had spread in the yard. She smirked as I approached her, and as she opened her legs, her skirt rode up her thighs, and I saw what that smile was all about. It was a good night, and another day gone by without a drink. But my dreams were no better than those of the night before.

On Sunday, we drove down to Sandy Point and buried our toes in the hot orange sand, then cooled off in the bay, dodging the few nettles, which were late that year due to the heavy spring rains. In the evening, I drove over to Alice Deal Junior High and worked out with my physician. Rodney White, who ran a karate school in the gym. Though I had resisted 'learning' tae kwon do – I had boxed coming up in the Boys Club and was convinced that hand technique was all I needed to know – I had been doing this with Rodney for years now, and he had managed to teach me some street moves as well as the first four forms of his art. I finished the last of those forms, and Rodney and I got into some one-step sparring.

'All right, man,' Rodney said.

We bowed in, and then I threw a punch. Rodney moved simultaneously to the side and down into a horse stance, where he sprang up and whipped a straight, open hand to within an inch of my throat. I heard the snap of his black gi and the yell from deep in his chest.

'What the hell was that?'

'Ridge hand,' Rodney said. 'Keep the first joints of your fingers bent. You'll be striking with the whole side of your hand. And the kicker's in the snap of the wrist, right before the strike. Step aside, and use the momentum coming up to drive it right into the Adam's apple. You do it right, man, you'll ruin somebody's day.'

I tried it, then tried it again. 'Like that?'

Rodney gave a quick nod. 'Something like that. More snap, though, at the end. Like everything else, it'll come.'

'What now?'

'Get your gloves, man,' Rodney said. 'Let's go a few.'

After we sparred, I drove back to my place and grabbed a beer out of the refrigerator and took it with me into the shower. I didn't think about it one way or the other, as this was something I did every time I returned from Rodney White's dojo. No bells went off and I felt no guilt. The beer was cold and good.

I stood in the spray of the shower, leaned against the tiles, and drank. I thought about what had happened at the river, and what I had heard: the inflection of the voices, the words themselves, the animal fear of the boy. The memory had resonance, like a cold finger on my shoulder. Everyone else had this wrapped up and tied off as a drug kill, another black kid born in a bad place, gone down a bad road. But I had been there that night. And the more I went back to it, the more I suspected that they were wrong.

I got out of the shower and wrapped a towel around my middle, then got myself another beer. I cracked the beer and went to the living room, where I phoned Dan Boyle.

'Yeah,' he said, over the screams and laughter of several children.

'Boyle, it's Nick Stefanos. What's goin' on?'

'These fuckin' kids,' he said, letting out a long, tired breath into the phone. 'What can I do for you?'

I told him, and then we went back and forth on it for the next half hour. In the end, against his better judgment, he agreed to do what I asked, maybe because he knew that we both wanted the same thing. I set a time and thanked him, then hung the receiver in its cradle. Then I tilted my head back and killed the rest of my beer.

I could have called Boyle back and ended it right then. If I had just called him back, things might not have gone the way they did between Lyla and me, and I never would have met Jack LaDuke. But the thirst for knowledge is like a piece of ass you know you shouldn't chase; in the end, you chase it just the same.

3

After my Monday shift, I walked out of the Spot and headed for my car, with Anna Wang at my side, a colorful day pack strung across his back. She wore black bike shorts and a white T-shirt that fell off one muscled shoulder, leaving exposed the lacy black strap of a bra. I let her into the passenger side and then went around and got myself behind the wheel.

'Boss car,' Anna said as she had a seat in the shotgun bucket of my latest ride.

'I like it,' I said with deliberate understatement. Actually, I thought it was one of the coolest cars in D.C.: a '66 Dodge Coronet 500, white, with a red interior, full chrome center console, and a 318 under the hood. After my Dart blew a head gasket a year earlier, I had gone into the Shenandoah Valley and paid cash – two grand, roughly – to the car's owner in Winchester, and I hadn't regretted it one day since.

Anna snagged a cigarette from the pack wedged in my visor and pushed in the dash lighter. I hit the ignition, and the dual exhaust rumbled in the air. Anna glanced over as she lit her smoke.

'What are you, some kind of gearhead, Nick?'

'Not really. I just like these old Chrysler products. My first car was a Valiant with a push-button trans on the dash. After that, I had a '67 Polara, white on red, the extralong model, a motel on wheels. My buddy Johnny McGinnes called it my 'Puerto Rican Cadillac.' It had the cat-eye taillights, too. A real beauty. Then I had a '67 Belvedere, clean lines, man, and the best-handling car I ever owned. I guess because of the posi rear. Then my old Dart, and now this. I'll tell you something, these Mopar engines were the strongest this country ever produced. As long as there's no body cancer, I'll keep buying them.'

Anna took a drag off her cigarette and smirked. ' "Posi rear"? Nick, you *are* a gearhead, man.'

'Yeah, well, I guess you got me nailed.' I looked her over and caught her eye. 'Speaking of which, there's this tractor pull, next Saturday

457

night? I was wonderin' . . . if you're not doing anything, I'd be right proud if you'd care to accompany me—'

'Very funny. Anyway, you can just take your girlfriend to that tractor pull, buster.'

At the top of 8th, we passed an old haunt of mine, a club where you used to be able to catch a good local band and where you could always cop something from the bartender, something to smoke or snort or swallow in the bathroom or on the patio out back. I had met my ex-wife Karen there for the first time one night. The original club had closed years ago, shut down at about the same time as my marriage.

Anna looked out the window. 'You ever go in that place?'

'Not anymore.'

'I thought 'cause, you know, they cater to that thirty-plus crowd.'

'Thanks a lot.' I could have backhanded her one, but she was so damn cute. 'Where you headed, anyway?'

'Drop me at the Eastern Market Metro, okay?'

I did it and then got on my way.

I drove down M Street, past the Navy Yard and the projects and the gay nightclubs and the warehouses, and kept straight on past the 11th Street Bridge ramp as M continued unmarked, past Steuart Petroleum, down through the trees toward the water, past a couple of marinas and the Water Street turnoff, to the wooded area where the rusted houseboat sat submerged in the river amid the wooden pilings. I pulled off in the clearing and parked my car next to Boyle's.

An old man with closely cropped salt-and-pepper hair sat in a metal folding chair, holding a cheap Zebco rod, a red plastic bucket and green tackle box by his side, a sixteen-ounce can of beer between his feet. Two young men leaned against a brilliantly waxed late-model Legend parked beneath the trees and looked out toward the carpet green of Anacostia Park across the river. Boyle stood on the edge of the concrete bulkhead, his shirtsleeves rolled above his elbows, his beefy hands at his side, a manila envelope wedged under one arm, a hot cigarette drooping lazily from his mouth. I walked across the gravel and joined him.

'You're a little late,' Boyle said, glancing at his watch.

'Had to wait for Anna to clean her station. Gave her a lift to the subway.'

'What're you, sniffin' after that Chinee heinie now?'

'Just gave her a ride, Boyle.'

'Like to have me some of that. Never did have a Chinese broad when I was single. Any suggestions how to get one?'

'You might start by not calling them "broads." Women don't seem to like that very much these days. They haven't for, like, forty years.'

'Thanks for the tip. I'll work it into my next sensitivity discussion. The department's very big on that now, since those uniforms hand-cuffed that drunk broad – I mean, *inebriated woman* – to that mailbox last winter. Maybe I could get you to come down and lecture.'

I looked at the envelope under Boyle's arm. 'So what you got?'

'Not yet,' Boyle said. He transferred the envelope to his hand and dragged deeply on his cigarette. A large drop of sweat ran down his neck and disappeared below his collar. 'Where were you that night?'

I pointed to a dirt area of paper and cans and garbage just inside the tree line, behind the fisherman. 'Right about in three.' One of the young men leaning on the Legend gave a brief, tough glance my way, and the other stared straight ahead.

'If they were parked where we are—'

'I don't know where they were parked. I didn't see anything. I couldn't even lift my head.'

'Well, the freshest tire prints we got were there. We were lucky to get those – someone called in an anonymous on the murder pretty soon after it happened. That was you, right?'

'Yeah.'

Boyle moved his head in the direction of our cars. 'So if that's where they were parked, and they took the kid straight down to the water and did him, then went right back to their vehicle, it's possible they didn't see you layin' back there in the trees.'

'What, you don't believe me?'

'Sure, I believe you all right.' Boyle took a last hit off his smoke and ground it under his shoe. 'Just tryin' to figure things out. C'mon, let's take a walk, get away from those two entrepreneurs.'

'Those guys dealers?'

Boyle shrugged. 'That's a thirty-thousand-dollar car, and they ain't real estate developers. Anyway, I'm Homicide, not Narcotics, so I couldn't give a rat's ass. But it's a bet that they aren't holdin' right now. This road dead-ends up ahead, past the bridge at the last marina. The locals know not to do business down here – no place to run to. Those guys are probably just relaxing before going to work later tonight. But I don't need any witnesses to what I'm about to do. Come on.'

We went back to the road and walked north toward the Sousa Bridge. A mosquito caught me on the neck. I stopped and slapped at it, looked at the smudge of blood on my fingers. Boyle kept walking. I quickened my step and caught up with him.

Boyle said, 'That thing you pulled with the silencer. That was pretty cute. It didn't hit me until I got off my bar stool. 'Course I phoned the detective in charge of the case soon as I left the Spot. Ballistics report had come in earlier that day.'

'And?'

'You were right. A silenced twenty-two. A Colt Woodsman, I'd guess, if it was some kind of hit.'

'A twenty-two. That proves it wasn't a gang thing, right?'

'It doesn't prove anything. A kid on the street can get his hands on any piece he wants, same as a pro, and for all I know, a twenty-two is the latest prestige weapon. Don't get ahead of yourself, Nick.'

We went beneath the bridge and moved to the last set of legs before the river. A gull glided by and veered off toward the water. The metallic rush of cars above us echoed in the air.

Boyle leaned against a block of concrete, one of many that sat piled near the legs. 'Tell me why else you think this isn't a drug kill.'

'Let me ask you something, Boyle. You ever know whites and blacks to crew together in this town?'

''Course no. Not in this town or any other town I ever heard of.'

'It was a white man and a black man killed that kid. I heard their voices. And I'll tell you something else. You might want to check up in Baltimore, see if some similar shit has gone down. The white guy, he talked about going "home," used that extra long *o* the way they do up in South Baltimore. The guy was definitely out of BA.'

'You got it all figured out. A pro hit, out-of-town talent. Come on, Nick, you're puttin' an awful lot together with nothin'.'

'I'm telling you what I heard.'

Boyle looked down at the manila envelope in his hand, then back at me. 'I give you what we got, what are you gonna do with it?'

'I know what's going to happen to this if the shooters aren't found in a few more days. Not that it's the fault of you guys. They got you working two, maybe three homicides at a time, and I know it doesn't stop.' I shrugged. 'I'm just going to get out there, ask around like I always do. I find anything you can use, I'll head it in the direction of the guy who's assigned to the case.'

'Through me.'

'Whatever. Who's on it?'

'Guy named Johnson's got it. He doesn't come in the Spot, so you don't know him. He's a competent cop, a little on the quiet side. But he is straight up.'

'If I find out anything, it'll come to you.' I pointed my chin at the envelope.

Boyle breathed out slowly. 'Well, we got nothing, really. Nothing yet. The kid's name was Calvin Jeter. Seventeen years of age. Dropout at sixteen, high truancy rate before that, no record except for a couple of f.i.'s, not even misdemeanors. Johnson interviewed the mother, nothing there. Said he was a good boy, no drugs. It's like a broken fuckin' record. Jeter didn't run with a crowd, but he hung real tight, all his life, with a kid named Roland Lewis. Haven't been able to locate Lewis yet.'

'Lewis is missing?'

'Not officially, no.'

'What about forensics, the crime scene?'

'The slug was fired at close range. You saw the burn marks yourself. A twenty-two'll do the job when the barrel's pressed right up there against the chin.' Boyle's eyes moved to the river. 'The tire tracks indicate the doers drove some kind of off-road vehicle. Similar tracks were found in a turnaround area at the end of the road, past the last marina. Which tells me that when they left, they headed right for the dead end, had to backtrack – so maybe they weren't local guys after all.' Boyle looked at me briefly, then away. 'Like you said.'

'What else?'

'One important thing, maybe the only real lead we got. There's a potential witness, someone who actually might have seen something. A worker down at the boatyard says there's this guy, some crazy boothead, sits under this bridge' – Boyle patted the concrete – 'sits right on these blocks, wearing a winter coat, every morning just before dawn, reading books, singing songs, shit like that. And the estimated time of death was just around dawn.'

'That's about right,' I said.

'And if your friends drove under the bridge, then turned around and drove back, and if this mental deficient was here, there's a very good chance he got a good look at the car. Maybe he noticed the license plates. Maybe he can ID the shooters themselves.'

'So who's the guy?'

'The guys at the boatyard, they don't know him. They never introduced themselves, on account of the guy was stone-crazy.'

'Anybody interview him since?'

Boyle flicked a speck of tobacco off his chin. 'He hasn't been *back* since. We don't even know if he was here that particular morning. Johnson's checked it out a couple of times, and we've got a couple of uniforms sitting down here at dawn for as long as we can spare 'em. But so far, nothing.'

'All this stuff in the reports?'

'Yeah.' Boyle pushed the envelope my way but did not hand it over.

'What's the problem?'

'I know what's going with you, that's all. You think because you got polluted and happened to fall down near where a kid got shot, that makes you responsible in some way for his death. But you ought to be smart enough to know that you had nothin' to do with it – that kid woulda died whether you had been laying there or not. And consider your being drunk some kind of blessing, brother. If you coulda got up off your ass, most likely they woulda killed you, too.'

'I know all that.'

'But you're still gonna go out and ask around.'

'Yes.'

Boyle sighed. 'You got no idea what kind of trouble I could get into.' He pointed one thick finger at my face. 'Anything you find, you come to me, hear?'

'I will.'

Boyle tossed me the envelope. 'Don't fuck me, Nick.'

He walked away and left me standing under the bridge.

4

That evening I categorized and studied the Xeroxed police file on the Jeter case, and in the morning I sat at the desk of the small office area in my apartment and studied it all over again. I showered and dressed, grabbed some of the pertinent material, and took a few legitimate business cards and some phony ones and slid them in my wallet. Then I took a dish of dry cat food and a bowl of water, placed them out on the stoop, and got into my Dodge and headed downtown.

I stopped for some breakfast at Sherrill's, the Capitol Hill bakery and restaurant that is the last remnant of old Southeast D.C., and had a seat at the chrome-edged lunch counter. My regular waitress, Alva, poured me an unsolicited coffee as I settled on my stool, and though the day was already hot, I drank the coffee, because you have to drink coffee when you're sitting at the counter at Sherrill's. Alva took my order, watching me over the rims of her eyeglasses as she wrote, and five minutes later I was sweating over a plate of eggs easy with a side of hash browns and sausage and toast. After the food, I had a second cup of coffee and a cigarette while I listened to a nearby conversation – the uninitiated might have called it an argument – between the owner, Lola, and her daughter, Dorothy. I kept my eyes on the Abbott's ice cream sign hung behind the counter and grinned with fondness at the sound of their voices.

Out on the street, I fed the meter and walked the four blocks down to the Spot. Darnell was in the kitchen prepping lunch and Mai sat at the bar, drinking coffee and reading the *Post*. The sandled feet at the end of Mai's stout wheels barely reached the rail of the stool, and her blonde hair was twisted and bound onto her head in some sort of pretzelized configuration. Phil stood at the register, his back to me, his lips moving – I could see them in the bar mirror – as he counted out from the night before.

'What's going on, Mai?' I said, walking toward the phone.

'Jerome,' she said happily. Jerome had to be her latest Marine from the nearby barracks, but I didn't ask.

I placed the list of numbers and addresses in front of me on the service bar and picked up the phone. I began to dial Calvin Jeter's mother, then lost my nerve. Instead, I dialed the number for the Roland Lewis residence. Ramon walked from the kitchen, smiled a foolish gold-toothed grin, and sucker punched me in the gut as he passed. I was coughing it out when a girl's voice came on the other end.

'Yeah.'

'Is Roland there?'

'Uh-uh.'

'How about Mrs Lewis? Is she in?'

'Nope.' Some giggling by two other females in the background over some recorded go-go. I listened to that and watched Mai send Ramon down to the basement for some liquor.

'You expect her in?'

'She's workin', fool.' A loud explosion of laughter. 'Bah.'

I heard the click of the receiver on the other end. I hung up the phone and checked the list for Mrs Lewis's work number, saw that I had it, and decided, Not yet. Phil walked by me without a glance or a word, took his keys off the bar, and split.

I went into the kitchen. Darnell stood over a butcher block, chopping white onions, a piece of bread wedged inside his cheek to staunch the tears.

'Goin' on, Nick?'

'Just stopped in to make a couple of calls.'

'You see Phil?'

'Yeah. He's still punishing me over last Tuesday night.'

'You got all liquored up, left his place wide open, and walked out into the street. You can't really blame the man, can you?'

'I know.'

'Yeah,' Darnell said. 'You know. But do you *really* know?'

'Thanks, Father. Light a candle for me the next time you're in church.'

'Go on, man, if you're gonna be actin' funny.' Darnell cocked his head but did not look up. He said quietly, 'I got work to do.'

I left the kitchen and walked through the bar. Ramon came up from the cellar, both hands under a bus tray filled with liquor bottles and cans of juice. I slapped him sharply on the cheek as he passed. He called me a *maricón* and we both kept walking. He was cackling as I went out the door.

464

The Lewis residence, a nondescript brick row house with a corrugated green aluminum awning extended out past its front porch, was on an H-lettered street off Division Avenue in the Lincoln Heights area of Northeast. I had taken East Capitol around the stadium, over the river, past countless liquor stores, fried-chicken houses, and burger pits, and into the residential district of a largely unheralded section of town, where mostly hardworking middle-class people lived day to day among some of the highest drug and crime activity of the city.

I parked my Dodge on Division, locked it, and walked west on the nearest cross street. I passed a huge, sad-eyed guy – a bondsman, from the looks of him – retrieving a crowbar and flashlight from the trunk of his car. Three more addresses down the block and I took the steps up the steeply pitched front lawn of the Lewis house to its concrete porch, where I knocked on the front door. No one responded and no sounds emanated from the house. The girl who had answered the phone earlier and her friends were obviously gone. I stood there, listening to a window-unit air conditioner work hard in the midday heat.

I waited a few minutes, looked over my shoulder. The bondsman had gone off somewhere, leaving an empty street. I went to the bay window, stepped around a rocker sofa mounted on rails and springs, and looked through an opening in the venetian blinds: an orderly living room, tastefully but not extravagantly furnished, with African-influenced art hung on whitewashed walls.

I dropped my card through the mail slot in the door and walked back down to the street.

Division Liquors stood on a corner a couple of blocks south of the Lewis house, between an empty lot and the charred shell of something once called the Strand Supper Club. Two other businesses on the block had burned or been burned out as well, leaving only the liquor store and a Laundromat open on the commercial strip. I parked in front of the Laundromat and walked towards Division Liquors.

Several groups of oldish men stood in front of the store, gesturing broadly with their hands and arguing dispassionately, while a young man stood next to his idling Supra and talked into a pay phone mounted on the side of the building that faced the lot. The young man wore a beeper clipped to his shorts – some sort of statement, most likely meaning nothing – and swore repeatedly into the phone, punctuating each tirade with the words *my money*. I passed a double amputee sitting in a wheelchair outside the front door. His chair had been decorated

465

with stickers from various veteran's groups and a small American flag had been taped to one of its arms. The man sitting in it had matted dreadlocks tucked under a knit cap, with sweat beaded on the ends of the dreads.

'Say, man,' he said.

'I'll get you on the way out,' I said, and entered the store.

I grabbed two cans of beer and a pack of Camels, paid a white man through an opening at the bottom of a Plexiglass shield, and left the store. Out on the sidewalk, I slipped a couple of ones and some coin into Knit Cap's cup, checked to see if the young man was still using the phone, saw that he was, and walked back to my car. Sometime later, as I finished off my first can of beer, the young man dropped into the bucket of his Supra and drove off. I got out of my car and walked to the pay phone, where I sunk a quarter in the slot and punched in a number that was written on the notepad in my hand.

'Mrs Jeter, please.'

A bored young female said, 'Hold on.' A television set blared in the background, competing against the sounds of young children yelling and playing in the room. A woman's voice screamed out, silencing the children. She breathed heavily into the phone.

'Yes?'

'Mrs Jeter?'

'Y-y-yes?'

'My name is Nick Stefanos. I'm working with the Metropolitan Police on your son Calvin's murder,' I said, breaking some kind of law with the lie.

'I've done talked to the p-p-police three times.'

'I know. But I'd like to see you if possible. I'm in your neighborhood right now.' I gave her the name of the liquor store.

'You're in the neighborhood all right. Fact, you're just around the corner.' I listened to the TV set and the kids, who had started up again, as she thought things over. She told me how to get to her place.

'Thanks very much. I'll be right there.' After I shotgun another beer, I thought, hanging the phone in its cradle.

The Jeter apartment was in a squat square structure housing five other units, oddly situated on a slight rise in the middle of a block of duplex homes. I parked in a six-car lot to the right of the building, beside a green Dumpster filled to overflowing with garbage. Bees swarmed around a tub-sized cup of cola abandoned on top of the Dumpster, and two boys stood nearby on brown grass and swung sticks at each other in the direct sun. I finished my beer, popped a stick of gum in my mouth, locked my car, and walked across the grass. One of the boys, no older than eight, lunged at me with his stick. I stepped away from it and smiled. He didn't smile back. I walked around to the front of the apartment.

A woman sat in a folding chair outside the entrance, her huge legs spread, the inside of each wrinkled thigh touching the other, fanning herself with a magazine. Some kids stood out on the street, grouped around an expensive black coupe, the name MERCEDES scripted along the driver's side rocker panel. Bass boosted and volumed to distortion thumped from the sound system, burying the rap. A kid looked my way and spread his fingers across his middle, and one of his friends smiled. I approached the woman and asked her the number of the Jeter apartment. A wave of the magazine directed me to a dark opening centered in the front of the building.

The Jeter apartment was one of two situated down the stairs. The stairwell smelled of urine and nicotine, but in the depth and insulation of the cinder block, things were cooler and there was less noise. I wiped sweat off my face and knocked on a door marked 01.

The door opened, and a woman who could have been forty or sixty-five stood in the frame. She wore turquoise stretch pants and a T-shirt commemorating the reunion of a family name I did not recognize. Her breasts hung to her belly and stretched out on the fabric of the T-shirt. Her face was round as a dinner plate and her hair was doing different things all at once on different parts of her head. By anyone's standard, she was an unattractive woman.

'Mrs Jeter? Nick Stefanos.' I put out my hand.

She took it and said, 'C-c-come on in.'

I walked into a living room crowded with a plastic-covered sectional sofa and two nonmatching reclining chairs. Over the sofa, on a pale yellow wall, hung a black blanket embroidered with a fluorescent wild pony. A rather ornate sideboard of cheap material stood against the next wall, with just about a foot of space between it and the sofa. Except for one dusty teacup, the shelves of the sideboard were empty. A big-screen television sat flush on a stand against the next wall, with wires extended from the Sega beneath it, the wires leading to the hands of a young man sitting on the sofa next to a young woman. Around them both, and on the table where the young man's feet rested, were scattered junkfood wrappers and plastic cups. The young man played the game with intensity, his features twitching with each explosion and laser simulation from the set. As I entered, he glanced up briefly in my direction with a look that managed to combine aloofness with contempt. The young woman, who I guessed had answered the phone when I called, did not acknowledge me at all.

I followed Mrs Jeter toward the kitchen, looking once into a deep unlit hallway where a little boy and a toddler of indeterminate sex jostled over a rideable plastic fire engine. In the shadows, I saw another young man move from one room to the next.

The kitchen, lit with one circular fluorescent light and a bit of natural light from a small rectangular window, was through an open doorway to the right of the television. Mrs Jeter leaned against an efficiency-size refrigerator and folded her arms.

'Can I get you somethin', Mr Stefanos?'

The heat, oppressive in the living room, was stifling in the kitchen; I rolled my sleeves up over damp forearms to the elbow. 'Water. A little water would be great, thanks.'

'H-h-have a seat.'

She gestured to one of four chairs set tightly around a small folding table with a marbleized red Formica top. I sat in one, under a clock whose face featured a Last Supper depiction of white disciples grouped around a white Jesus. Mrs Jeter turned her back to me, withdrew a glass from a sinkful of dirty dishes, rinsed the glass out, and filled it from the spigot. She placed the glass in front of me and took a seat in a chair on the other side of the table.

Mrs Jeter watched my face as I looked at the grayish water in the glass, the lip of which was caked yellow. I turned the glass inconspicuously in my hand and had a sip from the cleanest side. The water was piss-warm and tasted faintly of bleach. I put the glass down on the table.

'Mrs Jeter—'

'Call me Vonda, if you don't mind. I ain't all t-t-that much older than you.'

I nodded. 'My sympathies on your son's death, Vonda.'

'Your sympathies,' she said quietly and without malice. 'Your sympathies gon' bring my baby back?'

'No,' I said. 'It's just that . . . I'd like to help, if I can.' I rotated the glass in the ring of water that had formed beneath it and listened to the sounds of the toddler crying in the hallway and the explosions coming from the game on the television set in the other room.

'You say you're with the p-p-police?' She closed her eyes tightly on the stutter, as if she could concentrate her way through it.

'Unofficially, yes. I'm working with them on this,' I said, repeating my lie. 'I know what you've told them already. I need to know if there's anything else.'

'Like?'

'Things the police may not have asked. Like where Calvin usually went when he went out. What he did for money. That sort of thing.'

'You mean, was he druggin'? Ain't t-t-that what you mean to say?' Her eyes flared momentarily, then relaxed. 'Calvin wasn't in the life. He was just a boy. Just a boy.'

I looked away from her. The crying from the toddler in the hallway intensified. I wondered, Why doesn't someone pick that god-damned baby *up*?

'Those your children out there?' I said, hoping to loosen what had fallen between us.

'The girl is my oldest. The babies, m-m-my grandchildren, are hers. That boy out there, on the couch? That's Barry. He's the father to the youngest child. His little brother, the one back in the bedrooms, he's stayin' with us awhile. Got put out, up his way.'

'Mind if I talk to your daughter?'

'She don't know nothin' more than what I told you. What I already told the police.'

The television set clicked off and the sound from it died. The front door opened and shut, and soon after that the toddler stopped crying. The older child came into the kitchen then and stood by his grandmother's side, patting his hand against her thigh. She picked him up and sat him in her lap, rubbed her palm over his bald head.

'Have the police been back in touch with you?'

''Posed to be,' she said, brushing some crumbs off the child's lips.

'They're trying to find Calvin's friend Roland,' I said. 'Know if they had any luck?'

'Roland? If they did, n-n-nobody said nothin' to me.'

I rubbed a finger down the scar on my cheek. 'Mind if I have a look in Calvin's room?'

'You can look,' she said, with a shrug and a grunt as she picked up her grandson and rose from the chair. 'Come on, Mr Stefanos.'

We walked out and through the living room, where the girl sat on the sectional couch, giving the toddler a short bottle of juice. I followed Vonda Jeter into the hallway, past a bathroom and then four bedrooms, which were really two rooms divided by particle-board in one and a shower curtain hung on laundry cord in the other. Three of the rooms contained single beds and scuffed dressers and small television sets on nightstands or chairs. In one of the rooms, the younger brother of the

469

toddler's father slept on his back, bare-chested in his shorts, with one forearm draped over his eyes. Vonda Jeter directed me into the last room, which she said was Calvin's. She pulled on a string that hung from the ceiling and switched on a light.

The room was windowless, paneled in mock birch, separated from its other half by a chair-supported board running floor to ceiling. An unfinished dresser stood flush against the paneling, and next to that an army-issue footlocker. Some change lay on the top of the dresser, along with a set of house keys on a rabbit's foot chain and a knit cap with the word TIMBERLAND stitched in gold across the front.

'The detective, that Mr Johnson? He went through C-C-Calvin's stuff.'

I looked back at Vonda Jeter. Her eyes, yellow and lifeless before, had moistened now and pinkened at the rims.

'Do you have a photograph of Calvin that I could borrow? In the meantime, I'd just like to have a quick look around. I won't disturb anything.'

'Go on ahead,' she said, and walked from the room without another word.

I went through the dresser drawers, found nothing to study or keep. As a teenager, I had always kept a shoe box in my dresser filled with those things most important to me, and in fact, I still had it; Calvin's drawers were filled with clothing, nothing more, almost obsessively arranged, as if he had no personal connection to his own life.

In the footlocker, a basketball sat in the corner on a folded, yellowed copy of *D.C. This Week*. Several shirts hung on wire, along with a couple of pairs of neatly pressed trousers. I ran the back of my hand along the print rayon shirts, my knuckle tapping something in one of the breast pockets. I reached into the pocket and withdrew a pack of matches: the Fire House, a bar on 22nd and P in Northwest. Across town, and in more ways than one a long distance from home. I slipped the match-book into my shirt pocket, switched off the light, and left the room.

Vonda Jeter stood in the living room, by the door. I stepped around the couch and met her there. She handed me a photograph of a tough, unsmiling Calvin wearing a suit jacket and tie. He looked nothing like the boy I had seen lying in the river.

'Thank you,' I said. 'I'll be in touch.'

'Whatever you can do,' she said, looking away.

She opened the door. I stepped out, quickly took the concrete steps up the stairwell, and walked out into the white sunlight. I heard her door close behind me as I moved across the grass.

I went to my car, unlocked it, and rolled the windows down. The father of the toddler, the game player from the couch, stood looking under the hood of a burnt orange 240Z parked beside my Dodge. He wore shorts that fell below his knees and a black T-shirt showing Marley hitting a blunt. Like most of the young men I had seen that day, he was narrow-waisted, thin, and muscled, with hair shaved to the scalp, broken by a short part. I put him somewhere at the tail end of his teens.

'Is it burnin' a lot of oil?' I said, walking up beside him.

He pulled the dipstick, read it, wiped it off with a cranberry red rag, and pushed it back down into the crankcase.

'Nick Stefanos,' I said, extending my hand. 'It's Barry, isn't it?' He ignored the question and my gesture. 'These old Zs, they're trouble. But they do have style. The two-forties have those headlights—'

'Somethin' I can do for you? 'Cause if not, whyn't you just go on about your business.' He closed the hood, wiped his hands off on the rag.

I placed my card on top of the hood. He read it from where he stood without picking it up.

'I'm looking for Roland Lewis,' I said. 'Thought maybe he could tell me something about Calvin's death.'

'That punk,' he muttered heavily, staring at the asphalt. He went around to the driver's side and began to fold himself into the bucket. I could see some sort of garishly colored uniform thrown on the floor behind the seat.

'Let me ask you something, Barry,' I said, stopping him. 'What do *you* think happened to Calvin? At least you can tell me that.'

He stopped, chuckled cynically, and looked me in the eyes for the first time. 'What do *I* think happened? Whyn't you just take a look around you, chief, check out what we got goin' on down here.' Barry made a sweeping gesture with his hand and lowered his voice. 'Calvin *died*, man. He died.'

He got into his car, started it, and backed out of the lot. My card blew off the hood, fluttered to the asphalt. It landed next to a fast-food wrapper dark with grease. I left it there, climbed into my Dodge, and steered it back onto the street.

I stopped for another can of beer at Division Liquors and went back to my car, where I found some dope in the glove box and rolled a joint. I smoked half the number driving across town, slid an English Beat into the deck. By the time I hit my part of the world, upper 14th around Hamilton, 'Monkey Murders' poured out of the rear-deck speakers of my Dodge, and I was tapping out the rhythms on my steering wheel, and singing, too, and many of the things I had seen that day seemed washed away.

I stopped at Slim's, near Colorado Avenue, for a beer, drank it while I listened to some recorded jazz, then hit the Good Times Lunch on Georgia for an early dinner. Kim, my Korean friend who owned the place, put a can of beer on the counter when I walked in, then went off to fix me a platter of fried cod and greens and potatoes. I took the beer to a pay phone near the front register, stood beneath a malt-liquor poster featuring a washed-up black actor embracing a light-skinned woman with Caucasian features, and dialed the number once again to the Lewis residence.

This time, the mother of Roland Lewis answered the phone. She had just gotten in from work and had found my card in the pile of mail inside her door. Her tone was cool, even, and clear. I explained to her that I needed to speak with her son, adding for the third time that day that I was 'with' the police on the Calvin Jeter case. I listened to my own voice, caught the slur in it from the alcohol and the pot, wished then that I had waited to straighten up before I called. But after a moment or two, she agreed to meet me, and I set something up for the next day at her place of business, on M Street in the West End.

I returned to my stool at the counter and ate my food. A man came into the restaurant and ordered a beer, talked to himself as he drank it. I pushed the empty plate of food away and smoked a cigarette while I watched rush hour dissipate through the plate-glass window of the Good Times Lunch. I butted the smoke and went to the register to get my check from Kim.

'Any trouble down this way lately?' I asked as he ripped a green sheet of paper off a pad. There had been two gun deaths, merchant robberies on the strip, in the last six months.

Kim produced a snub-nosed .38 from somewhere under the counter. He waved it briefly, then replaced it as quickly as he had drawn it. Kim blinked, wiped a forearm hard as pine across his brow.

'Take care,' I said. I went back down to my spot, left ten on seven, and walked out under the damp veil of dusk.

When I got back to my apartment, I fed the cat and phoned Lyla. Her recorded message told me that she had gone out for happy hour with a friend and that she'd check the machine later that night. I left my own message, asking her to come by, adding, 'I could use some company.'

But Lyla did not call back or drop in on me. I ended the night sitting on a bench in the back of my yard, another beer in my hand, listening to the crickets sounding out against the flat whir of air conditioners from the windows of the neighboring houses. My cat slinked out from the darkness and brushed against my ankles. I scratched behind her ears. After awhile, I walked back inside and fell to alcohol sleep.

5

The police report had the only potential witness to the Jeter murder as a black male, mid-forties, average height and build, with no distinguishing characteristics, a typically blank cross-racial description. It wasn't much to go on, not anything at all, in fact, but the boatyard worker had mentioned that the man wore a brilliant blue winter coat year round. Everyone concerned had accepted the worker's opinion that the man who sat singing under the bridge every morning at dawn was crazy. Crazy, maybe, but not necessarily stupid. If he knew that he had witnessed a killing and understood the implications, then he had probably disposed of the coat by now, or, at the very least, quit wearing it. I was reminded of the time when, as kids, my friends and I had stood on a hill and thrown hard-packed snowballs at cars driving south on 16th Street. One of my buddies had winged a smoker that shattered the side window of a green Rambler Ambassador, bloodying the driver's lip. We all scattered and ran; the cops nailed me at the end of a nearby alley, identified me by my neon orange knit cap, which I had neglected to remove from my head. The hat had been the only thing the driver had remembered from his brief look at us on the hill. I figured that nobody, even a straitjacket candidate, is as mindless as a kid who is running from the cops for the first time. But I hoped that I was wrong.

So the next morning, I woke up in the dark and headed downtown and into Southeast, down M Street to the waterline, in search of the man in the brilliant blue coat. By the time I got there, the sky had lightened and a line of orange had broken the green plane of Anacostia Park across the river. A blue-and-white sat parked beneath the Sousa Bridge, with two uniforms in the front seat. They noted me without incident as I went by. I turned the car around at the end of the road and passed them again on my way back out. No man sat singing or reading on the concrete pilings beneath the bridge, blue coat or otherwise. I moved on.

I drove all the way across town, bought a go-cup of coffee at a market on Wisconsin and P in Georgetown, then went up to R and parked near Dumbarton Oaks. I walked through open grounds, down into the woods of Rock Creek Park, and found my seat on a large gray rock at the crest of a winding bridal trail overlooking the creek and Beach Drive. I watched the cars and their occupants, making their morning rush to wherever it is that people who wear ties and business suits go, and I listened to the serpentine creek running to the Georgetown Channel and the songbirds in the trees above. Everyone has their own spot in their hometown, and this was mine.

Afterward, I walked to the iron fence surrounding Oak Hill, wrapped my hands around the rungs, and admired the most beautiful cemetery grounds in D.C. Privileged people lead privileged lives, and even find privileged places to rest. I wondered idly about the final whereabouts of Calvin Jeter's body. Then for a while I thought of nothing earthbound at all. I noticed an old man in a physical-plant uniform sitting atop a small tractor in the cemetery, and for a moment our eyes met. Then he looked away, and we both went back to what we had been doing for the last half hour: trying to find a kernel of spirituality before returning to the cold reality of our day.

I spent that morning reading local history in the Washingtonian room of the Martin Luther King Memorial Library, then walked into Chinatown and met Lyla for lunch at a nondescript restaurant packed with locals at the corner of 7th and H. I crossed the dining room with a bag in my hand and had a seat next to Lyla.

'Hey,' I said, kissing her mouth.

'Hey, you.' She looked me over. 'Why so sporty?'

I wore an open-necked denim, sleeves up, and a pair of khakis, with monk-straps on my feet. 'You think this is sporty?'

'Well, you ran an iron over the shirt.'

'Just for you, baby. And, I'm meeting a woman this afternoon.'

'What, I'm not a woman?'

'Sweetheart, you're all woman. But I'm talking about a business appointment. Over at Ardwick, Morris and Baker, in the West End.'

'That's the firm that defended those S and L boys.'

'I don't know anything about that. I'm meeting one of their secretaries.'

'Uh-huh.' She smiled maternally. 'You're poking around on the Jeter murder, aren't you? I can see it on you, Nick. The only time you get wired during the daylight like this is when you're juiced on some kind of case. Am I right?'

'I'm asking around, that's all. Maybe I'll kick something up.'

'Yeah,' she said.

Our waitress, an angular woman with coal black hair and bad teeth, arrived at the table. I ordered steamed dumplings with a main of squid sautéed in garlic, and Lyla ordered the special, asking only if it contained chicken. We avoided anything in the way of chicken here, as several of them hung plucked in the midday heat of the window. Lyla asked for white wine, and I took ice water.

'What do you suppose is in the special?' Lyla said.

'I'm not sure,' I said. 'But it's probably better you didn't ask.'

The waitress came back momentarily with our drinks.

Lyla lifted her wineglass. 'Takes the edge off,' she said, and had a sip. 'Yeah, that'll do it.'

'I thought you looked a little thick today,' I said. And I had noticed her hand shaking as she picked up her glass.

She shrugged apologetically. 'Happy hour stretched to last call. Sorry I didn't make it over last night.'

'That's okay.'

She flicked the brown paper on the table. 'So, what's in the bag?'

'Some stuff I picked up at the Chinese store on H. Something for you.'

I withdrew a small ceramic incense burner, hand-painted lilacs on a black background, and put it in front of her.

'Love it.' She smiled, turned the burner in her hand. 'What else?'

'Something for me.' I took a videotape from the bag and waved it in front of her. 'A Ringo Lam flick, for the collection.'

'Okay. What else?'

'Something for us.' I pulled out a tub of cream, labeled completely in Mandarin characters. 'The lady at the counter said it was "very special lotion for lovers." '

'What's so special about it?'

'I don't know. But we've got a date, tomorrow night, right?'

'Yeah?'

'So I was thinkin'—'

'Oh boy,' she said.

'That, at the end of the night, maybe you'd care to dip your fingers in this jar and give me a back rub. And maybe after that, I could return the favor and give you a front rub.'

'Here it comes.'

'And then we could rub it all over us and get some kind of friction going.'

'You could get a burn like that.'

'And maybe we'd get so much friction going, that, I don't know, the two of us could just explode.'

'At the same time?'

'Well, we could try.'

'Nick, why are you such a dog?'

'Speaking of dog,' I said, 'here comes your food.'

Lyla and I spent a couple of hours in the restaurant, enjoying the food and talking and having a few more laughs. There was a sign over the kitchen door that read MANAGEMENT NOT RESPONSIBLE, and Lyla commented dryly on that. I stuck with water and she had another wine. Lyla paid the check and I left the tip, and we kissed outside on the street. I stood there and watched her walk in the direction of the subway stop, moving in that clipped, confident way of hers in her short peasant dress, her red hair brilliant in the sun and long on her back. You're a lucky bastard, I thought, and then I added, Nick, just try not to fuck this up.

The offices of Ardwick, Morris and Baker occupied the top floors of an Oliver Carr building on M Street at 24th. I have to laugh now when I hear any law firm's name; a guy by the name of Rick Bender comes in the Spot for a vodka gimlet once a week – I don't know what Bender does, but he's a profoundly silly guy, and I know he's not an attorney – and always leaves a business card on the bar with his tab: 'Rick Bender, Esquire.' Printed below his name is the name of his 'firm': 'Bender, Over, and Doer.'

I passed through the marble-floored lobby and made an elevator where a couple of secretaries stood huddled in the back. I was of the tieless variety, and after a quick appraisal, the two of them went right on complaining about their respective attorneys. A few floors up, a paralegal joined us, a guy in his twenties who was struggling mightily in his attire and haircut to look fifteen years older. Then on the next floor, we picked up a real attorney, wearing a real charcoal suit with chalk stripes and a really powerful tie. I said hello to him and he looked both confused and scared to death. Finally, we made it to the top floor of the building, where I put my back to the door to let the ladies out first, which seemed to perplex everyone further. My grandfather taught me to do that, and it isn't done much in D.C. anymore. I'm almost never thanked for it, but that doesn't mean that I'm going to stop.

I announced myself to the receptionist, had a seat in a very comfortable chair, and leafed through a *Regardie's* magazine set on a round glass table. I wasn't far into it when Mrs Lewis walked into the lobby on two nice cocoa-colored legs and stood over my chair. I got up and shook her hand.

She wore a tan business suit and a brown blouse with an apricot scarf tied loosely around her neck. Her face was long and faintly elastic, with large brown eyes and a large mouth lipsticked apricot like the scarf. She was younger than the voice on the phone, and I bet she had a good smile, but she wasn't using those muscles just yet. I looked at the fingernails on the spidery fingers that rested in my hand; the polish on the nails was apricot, too. Neat.

'Nick Stefanos. Thanks for seeing me.'

'Shareen Lewis. We can use one of the conference rooms. Follow me.'

I did it, walked behind her, passing open-doored offices where men stood reading briefs or sat talking on telephones. They wore British-cut suits with suspenders beneath the jackets and orderly geometric-paterned ties. I thought, Why the suspenders? Did these guys collectively buy their pants in the wrong size?

Shareen Lewis directed me into a conference room whose center held a long, shiny table with gray high-backed swivel chairs grouped around it. The shades had been drawn, and when she closed the door the room became cool and quiet as a tomb. We sat next to each other by the windows. She turned her chair in my direction, folded her hands on the table in front of her, and faced me.

'Are we being recorded?' I said, kidding only by half, trying to break things down.

'Should we be? You look a little uncomfortable.'

'Well, I'm playing an away game here. This isn't my usual arena.'

'That much I can see.' Her enunciation was careful, slightly forced.

'So I'll be brief. I've got to get to work myself.'

'What do you do, Mr Stefanos? Besides . . . this.'

'I work in a bar, a place called the Spot. Over on 8th in Southeast.'

'I don't know it.'

'You wouldn't,' I said, intending it as a compliment. But she didn't know what I meant by the remark, and the muscles of her jaw ratcheted up a notch.

'What can I do for you?' she said.

'Like I told you on the phone, I'd like to have the opportunity to speak with your son, Roland. Everything I've been able to uncover tells me that he was the closest friend that Calvin Jeter had. I'm assisting the police on the Jeter murder.'

'I don't believe that I can help you.'

'Maybe Roland might like to help.'

'I don't think so.'

'Could you tell me where to contact him?'

'No.'

'Is that because you don't know where he is?'

'Roland is seventeen years old. Almost a man. He comes and goes as he pleases.'

'So he's not missing.'

'No.'

'But he didn't attend Calvin's funeral, did he?'

'How do you know that?'

'The police haven't talked with Roland since the murder. Don't you think it's odd that Roland didn't attend Calvin's funeral, seeing that the two of them were best friends?'

She spoke quietly, but for the first time her voice registered emotion. 'I would hardly say, Mr Stefanos, that Roland and Calvin were best friends. Roland might have felt sorry for that boy, but nothing in the way of real friendship. After all, the Jeter boy lived in a welfare setup, down in those . . . apartments.'

So she was about that. I didn't like it, and stupidly, I've never been one to hide it. I leaned forward. 'I've been to your house, remember? And those apartments are just a few blocks away from you. The people who live in them are your neighbors. And I've got to tell you, Calvin's mother – that welfare mother you're talking about – treated me with more dignity and grace than you're showing me here.' I relaxed in my chair, then tried to throw some water on the fire. 'I'm only trying to help.'

But it didn't move her. If anything, she sat up straighter, eyeing me coldly. She tapped her fingernail on the lacquered table – the only sound in the room.

'All right,' she said. 'Let me tell you why I agreed to see you today. It's not to talk about my son, I can assure you of that. You just told me that you were "assisting" the police on the Jeter case. It's the second time you've told me that. And not only is what you're telling me a straight-up lie; it happens to be a criminal offense. I work in a law firm, Mr Stefanos. I'm not an attorney, but I'm not just a message-taker, either, and I've had this checked out. I could turn your ass in to*day*, my friend, bust you right out of your license. I don't know what your business is with this, but I'm telling you, I don't want to know. I don't ever want to see you or hear from you or have you around my house or near my children again. Understood?'

'Yes.'

'This conversation is over.' She stood from her chair and left the room.

I waited a couple of minutes to let the heat dissipate. I found my way out.

I first noticed the white sedan as I drove east on Constitution toward the Spot. The driver had tried to catch up by running a red, and the horns from the cars starting through the cross street caught my attention. It wasn't until I got stuck in a bus lane and saw the white sedan deliberately pull into that same stalled lane that I knew I was being tailed. I made a couple of false turn signals after that, saw the tail make the amateur's mistake and do the same. I hit the gas at the next intersection and hooked a wild right into the 9th Street tunnel. I lost him in the Southwest traffic and went on my way.

The Spot was empty of customers when I arrived. Mai untied her change apron as I entered and tossed it behind the cooler. She wore her angry face, splotched pink, and she left without a word. An argument with Jeremy, most likely – or had she said Jerome? Anna Wang had hung out past her shift and now stood in the kitchen, talking with Darnell, showing him some crystals she had bought in Georgetown. The week my son was born, when I flew out to San Francisco to visit Jackie and her lover, Sherron, Anna had given me four crystals wrapped and tied in a square of yellow cloth, crystals specifically selected to protect me on my journey. The crystals hung now in their cloth sack from the rearview of my Dodge, along with a string of worry beads given to me by my uncle Costa, the two elements forming some hoodoo version, I suppose, of a St Christopher's medal.

I changed into shorts and a T-shirt, poured myself a mug of coffee, put some music on the deck, and began to slice fruit for the tray. After that, I washed the dirty dishes from lunch, soaked the ashtrays, and wiped down the bar. Mai should have prepped all that, but I didn't mind. The dead time between lunch and happy hour, standing idly in front of the sexy, backlit pyramid of liquor with nothing much to do, was just plain dangerous for a guy like me.

Mel came through the door as I finished the prep. He found his stool, ordered a gin martini, and requested 'a little Black Moses.' I managed to find our sole Isaac Hayes tape buried in a pile of seventies disco and funk and slipped it into the stereo. Mel closed his eyes soulfully, began to sing off-key: 'You're my joy; you're everything to me-ee-eee.' Happy entered at about that time, sat at the other end of the bar, complained about the speed of my service as I placed his manhattan down in front of him, stopped complaining as he hurriedly tipped the up glass to his lips. Then it was Buddy and Bubba taking up the middle of the place, two pitchers deep, and later a gentleman I'd never seen before, who started off fine but degenerated spectacularly after his first drink, and an obnoxious judge named Len Dorfman, who spouted off to a dead-eared audience, and Dave, reading a paperback Harry Whittington, and a couple of plainclothes detectives talking bitterly about the criminal-justice system, cross-eyed drunk and armed to the teeth Finally, after all of them had gone or been asked to leave, it was just Darnell and I, closing up.

'You about ready?' Darnell said, leaning one long arm on the service bar.

'Yeah, but—'

'I know. You're gonna have yourself a drink.'

'Just one tonight. If you want to stick around, I'll give you a lift uptown.'

'That's all right.' Darnell tipped two fingers to his forehead. 'Do me good to catch some air, anyhow. See you tomorrow, hear?'

'Right, Darnell. You take care.'

He went through the door and I locked up behind him. I dimmed the lights and had a shot and a beer in the solitary coolness of the bar. I smoked a cigarette to the filter, butted it, and removed my shirt. I washed up in the basin in Darnell's kitchen, changing back to my clothes from the afternoon. Then I set the alarm and walked out onto 8th.

Parked out front beneath the streetlamp was a white sedan, a big old piece-of-shit Ford. I recognized the grille as belonging to the car that had tailed me earlier in the day. No one sat inside the car. I looked around and saw nothing and began to walk. A voice from the mouth of a nearby alley stopped me.

'Stevonus?'

'Yes?'

I turned around and faced him. He walked from the shadows and moved into the light of the streetlamp. He had a revolver in his hand and the revolver was pointed at my chest.

'Who are you?' I said.

'Jack LaDuke,' he said. He jerked the gun in the direction of the Ford. 'Get in.'

6

I stood there staring at him. He had a boyishly handsome face, clean-shaven and straight-featured, almost delicate, with a long, lanky body beneath it. His light brown hair was full and wavy on top, shaved short in the back and on the sides, a *High Sierra* cut. His manner was tough, but his wide brown eyes were curiously flat; I couldn't tell what, if anything, lived behind them. He tightened his grip on the short-barreled .357.

'Why aren't you moving?' he said.

'I don't think I have to,' I said. 'You're not going to mug me, or you'd already have me in that alley. And you're not going to shoot me – not with your finger on the outside of that trigger guard. Anyway, you're not throwing off that kind of energy.'

'That a fact.'

'I think so, yeah.'

He shifted his feet, tensed his jaw, and tilted his head toward his car. 'I'm not going to ask you again, Stevonus.'

'All right.' I moved to the passenger side and put my hand to the door.

'Uh-uh,' he said, and tossed me his keys. 'You drive.'

I walked around to the front of the car and got into the driver's seat. LaDuke settled into the shotgun side of the bench. I fitted his key in the ignition and turned the engine over.

'Where to?'

'It doesn't matter,' he said, the gun still pointed at my middle. He wore a long-sleeved white shirt and a plain black tie tightly knotted to the neck. His slacks were no-nonsense, plain front, and he wore a pair of thick-soled oxfords on his feet. A line of sweat had snaked down his cheek and darkened the collar of the shirt. 'Drive around.'

I pulled the boat out of the space and swung a U in the middle of 8th.

I headed toward Pennsylvania Avenue, and when I got there, I took a right and kept the car in traffic.

'You gonna tell me what this is about?'

'I'll tell you when I'm ready to tell you.'

'That's a good line,' I said. 'But you're in the wrong movie. Let me help you out here. This is the part where you're supposed to say, "I'm asking the questions here, Stevonus."'

'Shut up.'

'You're making a mistake,' I said, speeding up next to a Mustang ahead of me and in the lane to my left. 'You've been making mistakes all day. Your shadow job was a joke. Stevie Wonder could have made your tail.'

'I said, shut up.'

'Then you sit out front of where I work for I don't know how long. How many people you figure walked down 8th in that time happened to see you? Those are all people that could ID you later on.'

'Just keep pushing it,' he said.

'And now this. "You drive" – that's some real stupid shit, pal. You let me drive, and who do you think's got the power? Yeah, you're holding the gun, but I've got both our lives in my hands. I can drive this shitwagon into a wall, or into a cop car, or I can drive it right into the fucking river if I want to. Or I can do this.'

I stuck my head out the window and yelled something at the driver of the Mustang. The man turned his head, startled. I yelled again and flipped him the bird. The driver was alone, but he was a Southeast local, and he wasn't going to take it. He screamed something back at me and swerved into my lane.

'Now he'll remember us,' I said, talking calmly over the man's angry shouts. 'And he'll remember the car. In case you got any ideas of doing me and dumping me out somewhere. I guess I better make sure he's got our plate numbers, too.'

I accelerated and cut in front of the Mustang, then jammed on the brakes. The Mustang missed us, but not by much. I floored it, leaving some rubber on the street.

LaDuke's fingers dug into the armrest on the door. 'What the fuck are you doing, man!'

'Put that gun away,' I said, and cut across two lanes of traffic. The oncoming headlights passed across LaDuke's stretched-back face. I jetted into a gas station without braking. The underside of the Ford scraped asphalt, and as the shocks gave it up, the top of LaDuke's head hit the roof. I continued straight out of the station lot, tires screaming as I hit the side street.

'Put it away!' I said.

'Fuck,' he muttered, shaking his head. He opened the glove box in front of him, dropped the revolver inside, and shut it. I pulled the car over in front of some row houses and cut the engine.

LaDuke wiped his face dry with his shirtsleeve and looked across the seat. 'Fuck,' he said again, more pissed off at himself than at me.

'Just sit there and cool down.'

'You know,' he said, 'she told me she had the feeling you were some kind of headcase.'

'Who told you?'

He turned his head and stared out the window. 'Shareen Lewis.'

'What is she to you?'

He withdrew his wallet from the seat of his pants and slid out a business card. I took it and read it: 'Jack LaDuke, Private Investigations.' His logo – I'm not kidding – was one large eye. I stifled a grin and slipped the card into my shirt pocket.

'You know,' I said, 'you didn't need to pull that gun.'

'Just wanted to see how you'd handle it.'

'Am I auditioning for something?'

'You might be,' he said, giving the mysterious routine one last try.

I shrugged and fished a smoke out of my pack and pushed in the dash lighter. 'Cigarette?'

'I don't smoke.'

'Okay.' I lit the Camel and drew some tobacco into my lungs. I noticed that my hand was shaking, and I put it by my side. On the corner up ahead, a neighborhood market stood open for business, moths swarming in the spotlight mounted above the door. Young people walked in and out carrying small packages and forties in brown paper bags wrapped to the neck. An older man leaned against the store's plate glass and listlessly begged for change, barely raising his head. I sat there calmly and smoked my cigarette and waited for Jack LaDuke to regain his composure and enough of his pride to the point where he could talk. After awhile, he did.

'Shareen Lewis hired me to find her son,' he said.

'So she *is* worried about him.'

'Yes.'

'Why'd she call you?'

'She didn't,' he said. 'at first. She called a bondsman she knew named William Blackmon.'

'I've heard of him.'

'Yeah, they tell me he's been around forever. But he farms out a lot of his work now. First thing I did when I came to town, I went to all the skip tracers and bondsmen, went to see if I couldn't work something out.'

'Blackmon recommended you to Shareen Lewis.'

'They go to the same church. Blackmon took me for a flat referral fee.'

'And when I dropped my card in the Lewis's door, she wanted to know what was going on.' LaDuke nodded. 'She agreed to meet with me just so you could set up the tail, check me out.'

'That's right,' LaDuke said. 'Now I've been straight with you. What *is* going on, Stevonus?'

'I'm working on the Calvin Jeter murder,' I said, 'just like I told her. Roland Lewis seems to be the key.'

'Working for who? And don't kid me with that "police assistant" crap, okay?'

I considered how much I wanted him to know. 'I was the first one to find Jeter's body. I came on it by accident. I called it in anonymously to the cops. The cops have gone as far as they're going to go on it. I'm doing some digging on my own.'

'For who?' he repeated.

'Jeter's mother. And me.'

LaDuke eyed me suspiciously. 'There's more to it than what you're telling me. But I guess that's good enough for now, Stevonus.'

'The name's *Stefanos*. What have you got, a speech impediment or something?'

'I've got trouble with names,' he said with a touch of embarrassment. 'That's all.'

'Call me Nick, then. You can remember that, can't you?'

'Sure.'

I flicked my cigarette out the window and watched its trail. LaDuke shifted nervously in his seat, tapped his fingers on the vent window.

'So what are we going to do now?' I said.

'Well,' LaDuke said, 'I could use a little help on my end.'

'I bet you could.' I looked him over. 'How long you been in D.C.?'

'Does it show?'

'A little.'

'I don't know. Six, maybe seven months.'

'Six months. Shit, LaDuke, you don't even know your way around yet. You're never gonna find that kid.'

'It's beginning to look like that.' He rubbed the top of his head. 'How much have you got on the Jeter case?'

'A few things,' I said.

'I was thinking . . . maybe you and me, we ought to work together on this. You know, feed each other information. I mean, you're not getting paid right now, isn't that right? We could cut it straight down the middle.'

'Cut what? After Blackmon's piece, that doesn't leave enough for two.'

'I've got a couple of other cases I'm working on,' he said. 'I'm after a deadbeat husband, for one. Maybe you could help me out there, too.'

'I don't think so,' I said.

'Sleep on it,' he said. 'Because, the thing is, if you're set on talking to Roland Lewis about Jeter, you're going to have to go through me. Shareen Lewis isn't going to let you near her house, that's for sure. I don't think she cares too much for you.'

'She must prefer them on the clean-cut side,' I said, scanning his shirt-and-tie arrangement, damp and limp now in the evening heat.

'Yeah, well, this is a business. If you're going to make it, you've got to treat it like a business, act in a businesslike manner, and be presentable.'

'And brush your teeth after every meal.'

'What's that?'

'Forget it. We about done?'

'Yeah,' he said, 'let's go. But move over, will you? This time, I'm gonna drive.'

He parked the Ford in front of the Spot and let it idle. I got out, went around to the driver's side, and leaned my arms on the lips of the open window.

'Think about my proposition,' he said.

I nodded and said, 'I will.'

He looked at me curiously. 'Something else?'

'There's one thing I wanted to tell you.'

'What's that?'

'Don't ever pull a gun on a man unless you intend to use it. And even then, don't pull it. Do you understand?'

'I know all about guns,' he said. 'I grew up in the country. 'I've known how to shoot since I was a kid.'

'Congratulations. But it's not the same thing. An animal's not a man.'

'No shit,' he said with a cocky grin.

I pushed off from the car and stood straight. 'Well, I guess you already know everything there is to know. So you might as well get on home.'

'Right. I'll call you tomorrow.'

'Take care, hear?'

I walked across the street to my car. LaDuke drove away.

7

I woke up early the next morning, fed my cat, went outside and picked my *Post* up off the stoop, then went back in and read it over a couple of cups of coffee. After a week, there had still been no follow-up on Calvin Jeter's murder. Nothing in the *Post* or in the *Washington Times*, and nothing on the TV news.

I phoned Boyle, and when he phoned me back he confirmed it: 'This one's already cold, Nick.'

He asked me what I had. I said, 'I've got nothing.' It wasn't exactly the truth, but it was close enough. Boyle told me to keep in touch before he cut the line.

I paced around some after that, did a few sets of sit-ups and push-ups in my room, showered, dressed for work, and paced around some more. I found Jack LaDuke's business card on my dresser and rubbed my finger across its face. I put it down and walked to another room. A little while later, I returned to my bedroom and picked the business card up off the dresser once again. I went to the phone and dialed LaDuke's answering service. He phoned me back right away.

'Glad you called,' he said.

'Just wanted to make sure you were all right after last night.'

'I've got a hell of a stiff neck. All that bouncing around and shit. Where'd you get your license, anyway? Sears?'

'You were holding a gun on me, remember?'

'Yeah, well . . .'

'Listen, last night's over, as far as I'm concerned. You say you can get me into the Lewis house.'

'Sure I can.'

'Well, let's do it. Today.'

'It'll have to wait until after Shareen gets off work.'

'That's fine. I've got a day shift at the Spot. I can swing by afterward, pick you up. Where's your crib?'

'Never mind that,' he said. 'I'll pick you up at the bar. You tellin' me we got a deal?'

'Not so fast. Let's take this a little bit at a time, okay?'

'Just don't want to give everything away and get nothing back.'

'I don't blame you. But let's see if we can work together first. And LaDuke?'

'Yeah?'

'Don't forget your tie.'

He didn't forget it. He was wearing it, a solid blue number on a white shirt, knotted tightly despite the heat, when he walked into the Spot at half past four that afternoon. LaDuke had a seat next to Mel, who had stretched a lunch hour into three and was working on his fifth martini of the day. Anna stood by the service bar, counting the sequence of her checks. She glanced at LaDuke when he entered, then gave him a second look as he settled onto his bar stool.

'Nice place,' LaDuke said. 'Really uptown.' He wiped his hands off on a bev nap and left the crumpled napkin on the bar.

'Thanks,' I said. 'Get you something?'

'I'll just have a Coke, please.'

'So you don't drink either.'

'Not really, no.'

'Okay, Boy Scout. One Coke, coming up.' I shot a glassful from the soda gun and placed it in front of him. 'Want a cherry in it?'

'No. But do you have a place mat I can color on?'

I heard Anna laugh from the service end of the bar. Ramon walked behind her on his way to the kitchen and patted her ass. She slapped his hand away. Mel continued to croon along to the Staple Singers coming from the system, doing a Mavis thing with his pursed-out mouth. Happy sat in the shadows, his hand curled listlessly around a manhattan.

'I'll be ready to go,' I said, 'soon as my replacement shows up.'

'I'll just sit here and soak up the atmosphere,' said LaDuke.

'Cash in!' Anna yelled.

I went to her and took her tip change, all lined up in neat little rows, and turned it into bills. I handed it over to her and she put her hand into my breast pocket and withdrew a smoke. I lit it for her and she blew the exhale away from my face.

'Who's the guy?' she said.

'Name's Jack LaDuke.'

'I like it,' she said.

'The name?'

489

'The whole package.'

'You go for the puppy-dog type?'

'Not usually,' she said. 'But he's cute as shit, man. What's he do?'

I winked broadly. 'Private dick.'

'Why's he keeping it private?'

'I don't know. Why don't you ask him?'

She did, but it didn't work out. She started by getting herself a beer and having a seat next to LaDuke and initiating some conversation. LaDuke was polite, but clearly uncomfortable. Anna took his manner for disinterest; she downed her beer quickly and drifted away. Darnell came out of the kitchen and introduced himself, and soon after that Mai arrived in a chipper mood and relieved me of my position behind the stick. I changed into something presentable and told LaDuke that it was time to go.

We headed into Northeast in LaDuke's Ford. He stared ahead as he drove, his hands tight on the wheel, ten and two o'clock, right out of driver's ed. I tried to get a station on his radio, but he reached across the bench and switched it off. I wondered, What does this guy do to get off?

'Anna thought you were interesting,' I said.

'You know that little guy? The busboy, the guy with the gold tooth?'

'You mean Ramon?'

'Yeah,' LaDuke said. 'Him. Does he like her or something?'

I laughed. 'Ramon likes anything that has to sit down to take a piss. But no, they got nothin' going on.'

'Well, she's really cute.'

'That's what she said about you. So why'd you blow her off?'

LaDuke blinked nervously. 'I didn't mean to, exactly. I'm not very good with women, to tell you the truth.'

'I'm not very good with them, either. But when I find one I like and I think she likes me back, I give it a better shot than you did. Anyhow, a pretty motherfucker like you shouldn't have any problems.'

'I'm not pretty,' he said, a touch of anger entering his voice.

'Relax, man, I'm only kidding around.'

'Look,' he said, 'just forget it, okay?'

'Sure.'

We drove for a couple of miles in silence. LaDuke looked out the window.

'Maybe I'll give her a call,' he said.

Shareen Lewis was sitting on the rocker sofa on her porch when we reached the top of the steps leading to her house. She stood and took

LaDuke's hand, then briefly shook mine without looking in my eyes. She wore linen shorts and a short-sleeved blouse, with a masklike brooch pinned beneath the collar. As on the day before, the makeup somehow managed to match the clothes. She was a handsome woman, nicely built; she might have been lovely had she simply smiled.

We followed Shareen through the front door and found seats in her comfortably appointed living room. For my benefit, LaDuke repeated to Shareen what they had obviously discussed earlier over the phone: that I would team up with him in trying to locate her son, and that the teaming could only double our chances of finding him. Her eyes told me that she doubted his reasoning, but she nodded shortly in agreement. I asked her for a recent photograph of Roland. Shareen Lewis nodded with the same degree of enthusiasm. I asked her if she had heard from her son either directly or by message and she said, 'No.' I asked her if she had any idea at all as to his whereabouts. To that one, she also said, 'No.' We sat around and listened to the clock tick away on her mantelpiece. After some of that, I asked to see Roland's room.

We took the carpeted stairs to the second floor – three small bedrooms and a bath. We passed the largest room, which I guessed to be Shareen's. Its absolute cleanliness and frilly decor told me that, under this roof at least, Shareen Lewis slept alone. The next room belonged to the teenaged daughter, Roland's sister, who had blown me off two days earlier on the phone. She was in there, sitting at a desk, listening to music through a set of headphones. She was already heavier than her mother, and she had chunkier features, or it could have been that she was at an awkward age. We made eye contact, and for some reason, I dumbed up my face. She laughed a little and closed her eyes and went back to her groove. Then we were in Roland's room at the end of the hall.

Shareen pulled the blinds open and let some light into the space. LaDuke leaned against a wall and folded his arms while I took it in: another clean room, too clean, I thought, for a boy his age. Maybe Shareen had tidied it up. But even so, there was something off about it, from the rather feminine color scheme to the schmaltzy souvenir trinkets on the dresser. A large dollar sign had been cut out and tacked to the wall. On an opposite wall, a poster of the group PM Dawn. No pictures of fat-bottomed women, no basketball stars, no hard rappers, no gun-culture or drug-culture symbolism, nothing representative of the mindless, raging testosterone of a seventeen-year-old city boy trying to push his manhood in the 1990s. Nothing like my own bedroom at seventeen, for that matter, or the bedrooms of any of my friends.

'Mind if I look in the closet?' I said.

'Go ahead,' Shareen said.

I went to it, opened it. I scanned a neat row of clothing, shirts of various designs and several pairs of slacks, the slacks pressed and hung upside down from wooden clamps. I put my hand on the shelf above the closet rod, ran it along the dustless surface. I found a back issue of *D.C. This Week* and took it down. I looked at it with deliberate disinterest, folded it, and put it under my arm.

'Anything?' LaDuke said, nodding at the newspaper.

'No,' I said, and forced a smile at Shareen. 'You don't mind if I take this, do you?'

'I don't mind,' she said, looking very small, hugging herself with her arms as if she was chilled.

'Thanks. By the way, did you clean this room recently?'

'I haven't touched a thing. Roland always kept it this way.'

'Have you noticed anything missing? Did he take any clothes with him, pack anything before . . . the last time you saw him?'

'I don't think so,' she said, a catch in her voice.

'You keep a nice house,' I said, trying to keep things light.

'Thank you. It's not easy with these kids, believe me.'

'I can imagine,' I said, but it was too much.

'You can?'

'Well, no. Actually, not really.'

'Then don't patronize me.' The resentment crept back in her tone. 'Let me tell you how it is. When I inherited this house from my mother, I also inherited the balance of the mortgage. That, and everything else it takes to be a single working mother – car, clothing, new stuff for the kids all the time. You come into this part of town, see what it is over here, and maybe you make a judgment about where I prioritize my family in the scheme of my life. What you don't know is, I'd like to get my children out of this neighborhood, too, understand? But the way it is out here, in this economy, me and everyone I know, we're all one paycheck away from the street. So, no, it's not easy. But I've done pretty good for them, I think. Anyway, I've tried.'

I didn't ask for that, but I allowed it. LaDuke cleared his throat and pushed off from the wall.

'I'll take that photograph of Roland now,' I said, 'if you don't mind. Then we'll be on our way.'

She left the room. I walked out with LaDuke and told him to meet me at the front door. After some hesitation, he followed Shareen downstairs. I went to the daughter's room, knocked on her open door. She pulled one earphone away from her head and looked up.

'Yeah.'

'I'm Nick Stefanos.'

'So?'

'What's your name?'

'Danitra.'

'So how's it going?'

'It's goin' all right.'

'Listen, Danitra, I'm here because your mom hired me and my friend to find your brother, Roland.'

'So?'

'Just wanted to introduce myself, that's all. What are you listening to?'

'Little bit of this and that. Nothin' you'd know.'

'Yeah, you're probably right. But I recognized that Trouble Funk you and your friends had on the other day when I called.'

'That was you?'

'Yep.'

For a second, she looked like she might apologize for her attitude that day, but she didn't. Instead, she shrugged and began to replace the earphone over her ear.

'Hold on a second,' I said.

'What?'

'You got any idea where your brother went off to?'

'Uh-uh.'

'You think he's okay?'

'That fool's all right,' she said.

'Why are you so sure?'

' 'Cause if he wasn't, he would've called. Listen, most likely he's off on one of his money things. That boy just wants to be large, know what I'm sayin'? Always wantin' to be like some movie star, ride around in a limousine. When he finds out it ain't like that, he's gonna come home.'

'You think so, huh?'

I stood there and waited for a reply. But she turned away from me then and went back into herself. I left her alone and headed back down the stairs.

'Mrs Lewis really digs you, man,' LaDuke said with a laugh as he negotiated the Ford around RFK, then got it on to East Capitol. 'Every time you open your mouth, she'd like to bite your head off.'

'Yeah, thanks for all your support back there.'

'Kinda liked watchin' you bury yourself.'

I fired a smoke off the dash lighter. 'Well, the funny thing is, in some ways I agree with what she's saying. She's out there working for a big firm, and she probably knows just about as much law now as the people she's working for. You know how that goes, Xeroxing and taking messages for people who really have no more intelligence than you. I mean, lawyers, they've got the degree, and they worked for it, but that doesn't necessarily make them geniuses, right? But I'm sure that doesn't stop them from condescending to her all day long. Then she's trying to raise those kids in a bad environment, with no way to get out . . . I don't know . . . I guess I can see why she's so angry. 'Course, that doesn't explain why she's so angry at me.'

'Maybe you remind her of the type of guy that left her with those kids,' he said.

'Yeah, maybe.' The thought of my failed marriage crossed my mind. The thought must have transferred to my face.

'Hey look, Nick, I didn't mean anything.'

'Forget it.'

LaDuke punched the gas and passed a Chevy that was crawling up ahead. He drove for a couple of miles, then said, 'You get anything from the sister?'

'Uh-uh. Typical teenager with no time for me, and nothing good to say about her brother. She thinks he's just out there being an entrepreneur, trying to make some kind of score.'

'You saw the dollar sign plastered on his bedroom wall. Maybe that *is* all he's into. Maybe he's running some kind of game.'

'What else you see in that room?'

'I saw what you saw,' he said.

'No, I mean the details.'

LaDuke rubbed the top of his head, something I had seen him do over the last couple of days when he was trying to think. 'Well, it's kind of a funny room for a seventeen-year-old boy. It looked like it could have been his sister's room.'

'Right. How about that PM Dawn poster?'

'PM Dawn? What the hell is that?'

'It's a rap group – but soft, man, all the way soft. Not what anyone down here would call "street authentic." Like what U2 is to rock and roll.'

'U2?'

'Yeah. The Eagles, in black leather.'

'What?'

'Never mind. It's just not the kind of music a kid in that neighborhood would want to advertise that he was into. That and the room, you know, it if got around, it's something that could get your ass kicked for you.'

LaDuke breathed out through his mouth. 'You sayin' that maybe him and the Jeter kid were boyfriends?'

'No, not exactly.'

But I thought of Barry called Roland a 'punk.' And the killer had called Calvin one, too. And then there was the Fire House matchbook from Calvin's room. I dragged on my cigarette, blew the exhale out the open window.

'What, then?'

'It's just that this Lewis kid is different, that's all, at an age when being different from your peers is the last thing you want to be. It might not mean anything. I don't know if it does, not yet.'

I picked up Roland Lewis's photograph: unsmiling, like Calvin's, but with a certain vulnerability. Unlike the sister, Roland looked very much like his mother. I slipped the photograph in the folded-up newspaper. LaDuke watched me do it.

'What's with the paper, anyway?' he said.

'Nothing.'

'Bullshit. Don't hold out on me, Nick.'

I hot-boxed my cigarette and pitched it out the window. 'I'm not.'

'Yes you are,' he said. 'But you won't keep holdin' out, not for long. 'Cause we're gonna do this thing, you and me. You hear me?' He was pumped, his face lit and animated. A horn blew out as he lost his attention and swerved into another lane.

'Okay,' I said. 'We'll find the kid, LaDuke. But do me a favor.'

'What?'

'Keep your eyes on the road.'

He dropped me in front of the Spot. I thanked him for the lift, picked up the newspaper, and started to get out.

'What are we done already?'

'I am. I've got a date tonight.' He looked a little deflated. 'Listen, man, we'll get on this again, first thing tomorrow. Hear?'

'Sure, Nick. I'll see you later.'

He pulled away from the kerb and drove down 8th. I went to my Dodge and fumbled with my keys. When LaDuke was out of sight, I walked into the Spot, phoned Lyla, and told her I'd be a little late. Then I returned to my car, ignitioned it, and headed back into Northeast.

8

The heavy woman with the elephantine thighs sat out front of the Jeter apartment, her folding chair in the same position as it had been two days before. I turned into the lot and parked beside Barry's Z, walked across the worn brown grass, into the cool concrete stairwell, and down the steps to the Jeter's door. I knocked on it, listening to the noises behind it, television and laughter and the cry of a baby, until the peephole darkened and the door swung open. Calvin's sister stood in the frame, her baby resting on her hip.

'Yes?'

'Nick Stefanos. I was here the day before yesterday, talking to your mom.'

'I remember.'

'Is she in?'

The girl looked behind her. Barry's younger brother and another shirtless young man about his age sat on the couch, describing a movie they had both seen, talking loudly over the minstrel-like characters acting broadly on the television.

'Uh-uh,' the girl said. 'She's at the store.'

'Can I talk to Barry for a minute?'

She thought about it while I listened to the shirtless young man talking about the movie: 'Carlito' did this and 'Carlito' did that, and 'Carlito, he was badder than a motherfucker, boy.' Then the young man was on his feet, his hand figured in the shape of a pistol, and he was jabbing the hand back and forth, going, 'Carlito said, bap-bap-bap-bap-bap.'

'Come on in,' the girl said, her lips barely moving.

I followed her into the room and back through the hall. The young men stopped talking as I passed, and when my back was to them, they broke into raucous laughter. I supposed that they were laughing at me. Calvin's sister gestured me toward a bedroom. I stepped aside to let her pass back through the hall.

I went to the bedroom and knocked on the frame. Barry stood next to an unmade double bed in a room as unadorned as the rest. He read from a book, one long finger on the page. He looked up at my knock, gave me an eye sweep, then returned his gaze to the book.

'Wha'sup?'

'I need to get something out of Calvin's room. It's nothing personal of his. Would that be all right?'

Barry closed the book and sighed. 'Come on.'

He walked with me to Calvin's bedroom. Barry folded his arms, watched me go to the footlocker and get the folded copy of *D.C. This Week* that sat beneath the basketball. When I turned around, he was looking at the paper. I thought I saw some kind of light come into his eyes.

'What am I, getting warm or something?'

Barry said, 'You're really into this shit, aren't you?'

'I'm going to find out who killed Calvin, if that's what you mean.'

'And if you do? What's that, gon' bring Calvin up from the dead?'

'No. But maybe his mother might rest a little easier if she knew what happened to her son. You ever think about that?'

Barry breathed out heavily through his nose. 'Moms ain't worried about no justice. She thinks Calvin's up there, sittin' by the right hand of Jesus and shit, right now. Anyhow, who *asked* you to get on this?'

'That doesn't matter. The point is, I'm being paid now, and that makes it work. And when someone pays you to do something, you do it. Once you accept that, you don't think about why, and you finish whatever it is you started.'

'I wouldn't understand about all that.'

'The thing is, I think you do understand. See, I noticed that uniform in the back of your car. You got that fast-food job of yours – what do you make, five and a quarter an hour, maybe five-fifty?'

Barry's eyes narrowed. 'So?'

'So, you could be like all those other knuckleheads out there, making ten times that a week on the street. But instead, you're being a man, trying to be right for your family.'

'Listen, man, I ain't got time for all this bullshit, understand? Matter of fact, I got to get into work, right now.'

I withdrew my wallet, slipped out a card, and handed it to Barry.

'Here,' I said. 'You dropped this the first time around.'

'I got to go to work,' he said softly, slipping the card into his shorts. 'Come on, I'll let you out.'

We walked back into the living room. Barry stopped by the TV set and I headed for the front door.

The shirtless young man said, 'Hey, Barry, who's your boy?'

'Man's a private detective,' Barry said mockingly. 'He *finds* things.'

Barry's younger brother said, 'Maybe he could find Roger some onion, know what I'm sayin'? 'Cause Roger ain't *had* none in a long time.'

'Go on, man,' Roger said. 'I forgot about more pussy than you ever had, boy.' Barry's brother and Roger touched hands and began to laugh.

I looked at Barry. He wasn't laughing, and neither was I. I tucked the newspaper under my arm and left the room.

On the way to my place, I stopped at Athena's and had a seat at the bar. I lit a cigarette, drew on it, and laid it in the ashtray. It was early yet for any kind of crowd, but I recognized a couple of regulars in quiet conversation, along with an Ultimate solo drinker who was as beautiful as a model and an intense woman I knew who was running the pool table on a youngish woman I had never met. Stella came over and wiped the area in front of me with a damp rag. She cocked her head and raised her eyebrows. I nodded my head one time. She reached into the cooler and pulled a bottle of beer. She popped the cap and set it down on a dry coaster. I thanked her and had a swig.

'So you're back to it,' she said.

'Never had any intention of getting off it. I've never kidded myself about what I am. I've just got to try and not be so stupid about it, that's all. Like I was that night.'

Stella adjusted her eyeglasses, put her fist on her hip. 'That some kind of back-door apology?'

'Yeah, and a thank-you at the same time. I was probably rude about you stepping in – you know how I get. I know you were just trying to look out for me.'

'Don't worry about it,' she said. 'You'd do the same for me, right?'

'You bet.'

'Anyway, nobody got hurt.'

I left that alone and reached across the bar and shook her hand.

'So what're you up to tonight, Nick?'

'Date with Lyla. But I wanted to ask you something.'

'Go ahead.'

'You still play in that gay and lesbian bartenders' softball league?'

'Every Monday night.'

'You know anybody from over at the Fire House, on P?'

Stella rubbed a finger under her nose. 'There was this guy, Paul Ritchie, played for a long time on our team. Knees went out on him a couple of years back. Good guy. Good ballplayer, too. Ritchie, he could really hit.'

'You ever in touch with him anymore?'

'He still comes to the games. It's more a chance to see old friends now than it is a competition. So, yeah, he stays up with us.'

'He still tends at the Fire House?'

'He's been there, like, a hundred years. Where's he gonna go?'

I drank off some of my beer. 'I need to talk with him, if I can. I'm working on something that might involve that place.'

'Something that could get him into trouble?'

'Not unless he's directly involved. The truth is, I don't know yet. But I'll do my best to keep him out of it. Could you hook me up?'

Stella took her hand off her hip, pointed a stubby finger at my face. 'I thought you came in here to apologize, Nick.'

'I did, Stella.'

'Uh-huh. Well, I'll give Paul a call, see what he says.'

'Tomorrow would be good for me,' I said.

'Don't push it,' Stella said sternly. 'I'll call him.'

I told her to leave a message about it on my machine. She nodded and went to fix a cocktail for a customer. I drank the rest of my beer and put my cigarette between my teeth. Stella winked and gave me a little wave. I left ten on three and went out the front door. I walked to my car in the gathering darkness.

The two copies of *D.C. This Week* were identical, the last ones printed before Calvin Jeter's murder. That the issues were the same couldn't have been a coincidence, but as I looked through them, sitting at the desk of my makeshift office in my apartment, I saw no connection to either Calvin's death or Roland's disappearance. I skimmed every article, weekly feature, arts review, and column and came up empty. So I showered, changed into slacks and a blue cotton shirt, and went to pick up Lyla.

'Wow,' I said as she opened her door.

She wore a gauzy green-and-rust sundress cut high above her knees. Her hair was pulled back, with some of it left to fall around her lovely face, the light catching threads of silver in the red.

'You're late, Nick.'

'I know. I'm sorry, I just got hung up in what I've been working on.'

'That's okay.' She held up her goblet of wine. 'But I got started without you.'

'I'll catch up,' I said. 'Let's go.'

We drove across town in my Coronet 500, all four windows down, some Massive Attack pumping from the deck. Lyla was moving her head, digging on the music and the night, and I reached across the buckets and put my hand in her hair. At the next stoplight, we kissed and held it until the green. The air felt clean, with a crispness running through it, a rarity for that time of year; it was a fine summer night in D.C.

We ate at a Thai place on Massachusetts Avenue, in a row of restaurants east of Union Station. We talked about our respective days over satay and spring rolls and a barbecued beef salad; Lyla stayed with white wine while I worked on a couple of Singhas. By the time the waitress served our main course, a whole crispy fish with hot chilli and garlic, the subject turned to Lyla's newspaper and what I had found that day.

'Any thoughts?' I said.

'If you think something criminal is going on in relation to the newspaper, a good bet would be the personals.'

'What do you mean?'

'There's all sort of things happening in there – messages for meeting places that are really drop locations, model searches looking for porno candidates, stuff like that. Nick, you wouldn't believe how many of the entries are just ads for prostitution, or for some other scam that's even worse.'

'And you guys know about it?'

'We don't knowingly take any ads or personals that are criminal. But we're running a business. The *Post* and *City Paper* are doing it and making good money at it, and we have to do it, too. With the personals – it's a nine hundred number – we get ninety-five cents a minute. There're a couple hundred of those in each issue. When you annualize the revenue – well, you figure it out.'

'Yeah, I see what you're saying. I'll go back to it, check it out.' I cut a piece of fish off and dished it onto Lyla's plate. 'Here.'

'Thanks.' Lyla had a bite and signaled the waitress for another wine.

'You're hittin' it pretty good tonight,' I said.

'It's all this hot stuff,' she said. 'This fish is making me thirsty.'

'It's making me thirsty, too. Next time that waitress goes by, get me a beer, as well.'

After dinner, we walked across Mass to a nice quiet bar in a fancy restaurant run by friends of Lyla's. We ordered a couple of drinks – a bourbon rocks for me and a vodka tonic for Lyla – and had them slowly, listening to the recorded jazz that was a particular trademark of the house. A local politician whom Lyla had once interviewed and buried in print stopped on his way to the men's room and talked with her for a while, leaning in close to her ear, a toothy smile on his blandly handsome face. I sat on my stool and drank quietly and allowed myself to grow jealous. On the way out of the place, Lyla tripped on the steps and fell and scraped her knee on the concrete. We got into my car and I leaned forward and kissed the scrape, tasting her blood with my tongue. From that fortuitous position, I tried to work my head up under her dress. She laughed generously and pushed me away.

'Patience,' she said. I mumbled something and put the car in gear.

We stopped once more that night, to have a drink on the roof of the Hotel Washington at 15th and F, a corny thing to do, for sure, but lovely nonetheless, when the city is lit up at night and the view is as on time as anything ever gets. We managed to snag a deuce by the railing, and I ordered a five-dollar beer and a wine for Lyla. We caught a breeze there, and our table looked out over rooftops to the monuments and the Mall. A television personality – a smirky young man who played on a sitcom called *My Two Dads* (a show that Johnny McGinnes called *My Doo-Dads*) – and his entourage took a large table near ours, and on their way out, Lyla winged a peanut at the back of the actor's head. The missile missed its target, but we got a round of applause from some people at the other tables who had obviously been subjected to the show. I could have easily had a few more beers when I was done with the first, could have sat in that chair for the rest of the night, but Lyla's eyes began to look a little filmy and unfocused, and her ears had turned a brilliant shade of red. We decided to go.

We drove to Lyla's apartment off Calvert Street, near the park, and made out like teenagers in her elevator on the way up to her floor. At her place, I goosed her while she tried to fit her keys to the lock and then we did an intense tongue dance and dry-humped for a while against her door, until a neighbor came out into the hall to see what the noise was all about. Inside, she pulled a bottle of white from the refrigerator, and we went directly to the bedroom. Lyla turned on her bedside lamp and pulled her dress up over her head while I removed my shirt. The sight of her – her freckled breasts, the curve of her hips, her full red bush – shortened my breath; it never failed to. She draped the dress over the lamp shade, kicked her shoes off, and walked naked across the room, the bottle in her hand. She took a long pull from the neck.

'We don't need that,' I said.

Lyla pushed me onto my back on the bed and spit a mouthful of wine onto my chest. She straddled me, bent over, and began to slowly lick the wine off my nipples.

'You sure about that?' she said.

I could only grunt, and close my eyes.

Lyla's heavy breathing woke me in the darkness. I looked at the LED readout on her clock, laid there for a half hour with my eyes open, then got out of bed, ate a couple of aspirins, and took a shower. I dressed in my clothes from the night before, made coffee, and smoked a cigarette out on her balcony.

I came back into the apartment, checked on Lyla. In the first light of dawn, her face looked drawn and gray. Her mouth was frozen open, the way she always slept off a drunk, and there was a faint wheeze in her exhale. I kissed her on the cheek and then on her lips. Her breath was stale from the wine. I brushed some hair off her forehead and left the place, locking the door behind me.

I drove straight down to the river, passed under the Sousa Bridge, turned the car around, and parked it in the clearing. No sign of a crazy black man in a brilliant blue coat. No cops, either; I guessed that, by now, the uniforms had been pulled off that particular detail.

I got out of my car, sat on its hood, and lit a cigarette. A pleasure boat pulled out of its slip and ran toward the Potomac, leaving little wake. Some gulls crossed the sky, turned black against the rising sun. I took one last drag off my cigarette and pitched it into the river.

Back in Shepherd Park, my cat waited for me on my stoop. I sat next to her and rubbed the hard scar tissue of her one empty eye socket and scratched behind her ears.

'Miss me?' I said. She rolled onto her back.

I entered my apartment and saw the blinking red light of my answering machine. I hit the bar, listened to the message. I stripped naked, got into bed, and set the alarm for one o'clock. Stella had come through; I had an appointment with Paul Ritchie for 2:30 that afternoon at the Fire House on P.

9

The Fire House had changed hands several times in my lifetime, but as long I could remember, it had been a bar that catered primarily to homosexuals, in a neighborhood that had always been off center in every interesting way. This particular corner unofficially marked the end of Dupont Circle, where the P Street Bridge spanned the park and led to the edge of Georgetown. There were many hangouts down here, restaurants and a smattering of bars – the Brickskeller for beerheads, Badlands for the discophiles – but the Fire House had become something of a landmark for residents and commuters alike. For many years, gas logs burned day and night behind a glass window that fronted P at 22nd, the logs being the establishment's only signage. The building's facade had been redone now in red brick, and the window and the logs had been removed. But the fire imagery remained in the bar's name, a small nod to tradition.

I had taken the Metro down to Dupont, then walked down P. By afternoon, the day had become blazing-hot, with quartz reflecting off the sidewalk and an urban mirage of shimmering refraction teaming up off the asphalt of the street. My thrift-shop sport jacket was damp beneath the arms and on my back as I reached the entrance to the Fire House. I pushed on the door, removed my shades, and entered the cool darkness of the main room.

Several couples and a few solo drinkers sat in booths and at tables partitioned off from the empty bar. I went to the stick and slid onto a stool, dropping the manila folder I had been carrying on the seat to my right. The heat had sickened me a bit, that and my activities from the night before. I peeled a bev nap from a stack of them and wiped my face.

A thin young waiter stepped up to the service area and said in a whiny, very bored voice, 'Ooordering.' The bartender ignored him for the time being, walked down my way, and dropped a coaster in front of me on the bar.

'How's it going?' he said. He was large-boned, with some gut to go with it. His brown hair had streaks of red running through it, and there was a rogue patch of red splotched in the chin area of his beard.

'Hot.'

'Not in here, it isn't. Thank God for work, when it's air-conditioned. What can I get you?'

'A cold beer.'

'Any flavor?'

'A bottle of Bud. And a side of ice water, thanks. By the way, where's the head?'

'Top of the stairs. You'll see it.'

I took the stairs, passed an unlit room where a piano sat in the middle of a group of tables. The men's room was at the end of the hall. I went in and took a leak at one of two urinals. A mirror had been hung and angled down, centered above the urinals. I understood its purpose but didn't understand the attraction. Years ago, I had a date with a woman who at the end of the night asked me to come into her bathroom and watch her while she took a piss. I did it out of curiosity but found it to be entirely uninteresting. I never phoned her again.

I zipped up my fly, bought a pack of smokes outside the bathroom door, and went back down to the bar. The bartender had served my beer and was placing the ice water next to it.

'Nick Stefanos,' I said, extending my hand.

'Paul Ritchie.' He shook my hand and said, 'How do you know Stella?'

'I tend at the Spot. A couple times a week, I go into Athena's, shoot a little pool.'

'You that guy that used to hang out with Jackie Kahn?'

'You knew Jackie?'

'Sure. I heard she had a kid.'

'Yeah.'

'Heard she had some straight guy impregnate her.'

'I heard that, too.'

'You know, I think I met you, in fact, one night when I was in Athena's with a friend.' His eyes moved to the beer in my hand, then back to me. 'I guess you don't remember.'

'Must have been one of those nights,' I said. 'You probably know how that is.'

'Not anymore,' he said.

'Ooordering, Paul!' said the prematurely world-weary voice from down the bar.

Paul Ritchie said, 'Give me a minute,' and went to the rail to fix the waiter a drink. I gulped down the ice water and lit a cigarette. By the time Ritchie returned, I had finished half my beer; my stomach had neutralized, the quiver had gone out of my hand, and my head had become more clear.

'Thanks for seeing me.'

'No problem. What can I do for you?'

I put the manila folder on the bar, opened it, and slipped out the photographs of Calvin Jeter and Roland Lewis. I turned them around so that Ritchie could have a look.

'You recognize either of these guys?'

Ritchie studied the photos. 'Uh-uh. I don't think so.'

I searched his face for the hint of a lie, saw nothing irregular. I tapped my finger on Calvin's photo. 'This one here, I found a book of Fire House matches in one of his shirts.'

'What'd he do?'

'He got himself murdered.'

Ritchie breathed out slowly. 'I don't work every shift, obviously, so I can't say he's never come in here. But I know he's not a regular. And these two look like minors on top of that, and we make a pretty good effort not to serve minors. They *are* minors, right?'

'Yeah. What else?'

'To tell you the truth, neither of these kids look like my type of clientele.'

'You mean they don't look gay.'

'Look schmook, Stefanos. I don't have much of an idea what a gay person "looks" like anymore. Do you?'

'I guess not. But what *did* you mean? They're not your clientele – what, because they're black?'

'No,' he said tiredly, 'not because they're black. Turn your head and take a look around this place.'

I did. I saw some men getting on into their thirties and forties, some wearing ties, most of them with expensive haircuts and fine watches. The racial mix seemed to be about 80 percent white to 20 black; on the social and economic side, though, the group was homogenous. I turned back to Ritchie.

'So you run a nice place.'

'Exactly. These men that come in here, they're not just well-adjusted; they're well-connected. That guy's suit over there – no offense, Stefanos – it's probably worth more than your whole wardrobe. I know it's worth more than mine.'

'What about these kids?'

'Straight or gay,' Ritchie said, 'it's irrelevant. These two are street. This isn't their kind of place.'

'So how do you think this kid came to get a hold of your matchbook?'

Ritchie shrugged. 'Who knows? Maybe they were working the corner outside, working with all those other hustlers. The ones I'm talking about, they come in here, snag matches, bum smokes, sometimes try to hit on my customers. I'm telling you, my clientele's not interested. I know a couple of these hustlers, and some of them are all right. Most of them are country kids. You look at 'em, weight lifters, gym rats, with the sideburns and the pompadours, they all look like young Elvises. But usually, if they're not drinking – and most of the time they're not – I ask them to leave. There've been a couple of incidents, and I just don't want those guys in here.'

'What kind of incidents?'

'Where some people got hurt. See, the way it typically goes down, the way I understand it, these hustlers make the arrangement with the customer, usually some closeted businessman who works up around the Circle, and then they go down to the woods around P Street Beach. The money changes hands, and after that they do whatever it is they do – giving, receiving, whatever. But what happened last month, a couple of kids were leading those businessmen down there to the woods, then taking them for everything they had.'

I dragged on my cigarette. 'You know who these guys were?'

'No. 'Course, it never got reported to the cops. But it got around down here fast. What I heard, the other guys out on the street, they took care of the problem themselves. The whole thing was bad for their business.'

'Ooordering,' came the voice from down the bar.

Ritchie rolled his eyes. 'Be back in a minute,' he said.

I stood up and finished my beer, slid the photographs back in the folder. I took out my wallet and left money on the bar for the beer, and an extra twenty for Ritchie, with my business card on top of the twenty. Ritchie came back, wiping his hands with a damp rag.

'Thanks for your help,' I said.

'Wish I could have done more.'

'You did plenty. Any chance you could hook me up with one of those hustlers you were talking about? There's money in it for them – I'd pay for their time.'

'I could give it a try, yeah. I don't see why not, if you're talking about money. I don't know what an hour of their time is worth, though. I'm out of that scene, way out. Not that I didn't have my day in the sun. But I've had the same boyfriend for the last five years. When I'm not in here, I'm sitting at home on the couch, watching sports on the tube, like the old fart that I am.'

'Stella said you used to be pretty good with a bat.'

'Yeah,' he said. 'I blew out my fucking knees. Now about the only thing I can do is water sports.'

'Water sports, huh.'

'Don't be a wise guy, Stefanos. I'm talking about swimming laps, down at the Y.'

'Sorry.' I ran my hand down the lapel of my sport jacket. 'So you don't think too much of my threads, huh?'

A light came on in Ritchie's eyes. 'Hey, look, don't feel bad. I used to have a jacket just like that.'

'Yeah?'

'Yeah,' Ritchie said. 'Then my father got a job.'

'Lucky me. I get to talk to an ex-jock bartender who doesn't drink. And I get a comedian in the bargain.'

'I'm crackin' myself up here.'

'Take it easy, Ritchie.'

'Yeah, you, too. I'll let you know if I can set that thing up.'

'Gimme a call,' I said. 'The number's on the card.'

10

I heard from Paul Ritchie, and some others, early on Saturday morning at my apartment. Boyle called first, and he asked about my progress on the case. I told him that up to that point, my few leads had led only to blind alleys. I kept on that tack, and when I was done, I had managed to dig a big hole and fill it to the top with lies. I asked Boyle if the cops had anything new. He told me that an informant in a Southeast project had claimed that Jeter and Lewis were mules for a supplier down that way. I asked them if his people had any details on it and he said, 'Nothing yet.' We agreed to keep up with each other if something shook out on either end. I didn't like lying to him, and I wasn't exactly sure why I was doing it, but I had the vague feeling that I could see the beginning of some kind of light off in the distance. And it wasn't in me to give anything away.

Paul Ritchie called next. I thanked him and promised to buy him a beer the next time he was in my part of town. He reminded me that he didn't drink, and I suggested that instead I'd buy myself one and dedicate it to him. Ritchie laughed, but he couldn't help mentioning how good it felt each morning to wake up with a clean head and be able to remember all the details from the night before. I told him I appreciated the testimonial, thanked him once again, and said good-bye.

Later in the morning, the phone rang for the third time that day. I thought it might be Lyla, but instead I heard the excited voice of Jack LaDuke.

'Nick!' he said.

'LaDuke!'

'What do we got?'

'I don't know. Maybe something, maybe not.'

'I called you yesterday, Nick. Why you didn't call me back?'

'I was out during the day. And then I had a night shift, got home late.'

'Out doing what? Working on the case?'

'Well, yeah. LaDuke, you got to understand, I've got to ease into this, man. I'm used to working alone.' He didn't respond. I crushed the cigarette I had been working on in the ashtray. 'Listen, LaDuke, I've got an interview with this guy, later today. You want to come along?'

'Demn right I do.'

'Okay. I'll pick you up in an hour.'

'Uh-uh. I'll pick *you* up.'

'What's the big secret? You don't want me to know where you live?'

'I'll swing by in an hour, Stevonus.'

'It's Ste*fa*nos, you asshole.'

'One hour,' LaDuke said, and hung up the phone.

Paul Ritchie had set me up with one of the hustlers who worked the corner outside the Fire House, a guy who called himself Eddie Colorado. The name was a phony, but it sung, a canny cross of urban hood and westerner. Over the years, I had seen some of the men who stood around and worked that part of the street, and out of all the butch gimmicks that had passed through town – soldier of fortune, construction worker, lumberjack, and others – the cowboy thing seemed to have more staying power than the rest.

'What have you got goin' on this weekend?' LaDuke said. We were sitting in my Dodge, alongside a small park near the P Street Bridge.

'Dinner with Lyla's folks tomorrow, at their house. What about you?'

'I've got a date with Anna Wang tonight,' LaDuke grinned, proud of himself. 'I called her up.'

'Congratulations,' I said, then pointed through the windshield to the bridge. 'Here comes our boy.'

Eddie waited for the green at 23rd, crossed the street, and headed for my car. Ritchie had told me to look for an unnatural blond, a 'skinny rockabilly type with bad skin,' and Eddie fit the bill. His orangish moussed hair contrasted starkly with his red T-shirt, the sleeves of which had been turned up, the veins popping on his thin biceps. His jeans were pressed and tight, and he walked with an exaggerated swagger, a cigarette lodged above his ear, a cocky smile spread across his face.

'Look at this guy,' LaDuke said with naked disgust.

'Relax,' I said, 'and get in the backseat. Okay?'

LaDuke got out of the shotgun bucket, left the door open for Eddie, and climbed into the back. Eddie stepped up to the door, took a look around like he owned a piece of the park, pulled a wad of gum from his mouth, and chucked it onto the grass. He leaned a forearm on the frame and cocked his hip.

'You Stefanos?' he said.

'Yeah. Get in.'

'Sure thing,' Eddie said with a slow accent that had just crawled down off the Smokies. He dropped into the bucket and pulled the door closed.

I looked across the console at Eddie. 'Paul Ritchie said twenty-five would buy some of your time.'

'A little of it.'

'Here.' I passed him a folded twenty along with a five. Eddie Colorado pushed his pelvis out and jammed the bills into the pocket of his jeans. He hit my dash lighter, slid the cigarette off the top of his ear, and put the filtered end in his mouth.

'No,' LaDuke said from the backseat, 'we don't mind if you smoke.'

Eddie turned his head, gave LaDuke a quick appraisal, smiled, followed the smile with a tight giggle. 'Who's your friend?'

'His name's Jack.'

Eddie smiled again, raised his eyebrows, touched the hot end of the lighter to his smoke. He held the cigarette out the window, settled down in his seat, the sun coming directly in on his face. The acne on his cheek looked red as fire in the light.

Eddie stared straight ahead. 'Paul told me you wanted me to look at some pictures.'

I opened the chrome cover on the center console, took out the photographs of Calvin and Roland, gave them to Eddie. He dragged on his cigarette and blew smoke down at the images in his hand.

'You know them?' I said.

Eddie's mouth twitched a little. He nodded and said, 'Yes.'

'Were they workin' this area?'

'For a little while, yeah.'

'And you and your buddies kicked them out.'

'Right.'

'What'd they do to make you do that?' I said.

Eddie grinned. 'You're getting into somethin' here that might come back to me. It's gonna cost you another twenty-five.'

'Bullshit,' LaDuke said. 'This guy didn't kick anybody out of any-where, Nick. Look at him.'

'Your friend thinks I'm weak,' Eddie said. 'But I've been dealing with rednecks all my life, calling me this and that, beatin' me up on the way to and from school. Let me tell you somethin', it ain't no different here in Washington D.C. than in the country. First day I got into town, I went into this burger joint off New York Avenue. This guy says to me, "Hey, you fuckin' queer." You wanna know what I did about it? I broke his fuckin' jaw.'

I watched a man with matted hair carry a backpack past my car. 'So, what, you kicked these two off your turf because they called you a name?'

Eddie shook his head and said, 'The twenty-five.'

I said, 'Give it to him, Jack.'

LaDuke pulled his wallet, withdrew the money. He crumpled the bills and dropped them over Eddie's shoulder, into his lap. Eddie smoothed the bills out carefully, folded them, and slipped them into his pocket.

'You say you knew these two,' I said. 'What were their names?'

'I don't know. Ain't nobody uses his real name down here, anyhow.'

'They were doing prostitution down in those woods?'

'"Doing prostitution"?' Eddie laughed. 'If you want to call it that. They were *workin'*, Stefanos, that's what they was doin'.'

'Down in those woods?'

'On the edge of the beach,' Eddie said. 'At first, it didn't bother anybody, 'cause, you got to realize, there's a certain kind of man only goes for boys got dark meat.'

'Jesus Christ,' LaDuke muttered.

'So,' Eddie said, 'it wasn't no competition for the rest of us. But then this one here' – Eddie put one dirty finger on the face of Roland Lewis – 'he took some man's money. I mean all his money. Took more than they agreed to. Just took it.'

I said, 'You sure he wasn't provoked? Maybe one of these johns threatened him or something, tried to hurt him.'

Brown lines of tobacco stain ran between the gaps of Eddie's toothy grin. 'The *johns*, man, they don't hurt us. Most of the time, if there's anything like that to be done, they want us to do it to *them*. Just last week, I had this old man down in the woods, this lawyer works for some fancy firm, down around 19th? He had me slide this rod with little barbs on it right up into his dick. And right before he came, he had me rip it out. Man, you should have seen the blood in his jizz. With all his screamin' and shit, it was hard to tell the pleasure from the pain.'

'Goddamn it,' LaDuke said, 'stick to what we're talking about here.'

'Stick to it, Eddie,' I said. 'We don't need all the extra details.'

'All right,' Eddie looked in the rearview at LaDuke, back at me. 'So anyway, we find out from some of our regulars that this thing has been happening again and again. That these boys are rolling our businessmen on a regular basis, takin' the short road to big money. But there is no short road, see? This is work, like anything else. You don't treat your customers right, they're gonna go somewheres else. So we went and had a meeting with your boys one night, down in the woods.'

'You told them to get lost?' LaDuke said.

'It wasn't all that dramatic,' Eddie said. 'The one who started all the shit said that they were off to something better, that they didn't need this anymore.'

'Off to what?'

Eddie stabbed a finger at Roland's picture once more. 'He said they were going to get themselves into the movies. Said they met a man who was going to make them a whole lot of money. Big money, man, extra-large.'

LaDuke said, 'Porno?'

'What do *you* think?' Eddie said.

'This kid you keep pointing to,' I said. 'Did he seem to be the leader of the two?'

'Appeared to be.'

I took a cigarette from the pack on the dash, rolled it unlit between my fingers. 'Eddie, did these guys seem like they were into what they were doing?'

'They were into making money,' Eddie said. 'But what you really mean is, Were they faggots? If I had to make some kind of guess, I'd say the other kid was kinda, I don't know, not sure about anything he was doing. The leader, though, he was definitely into it.'

'Into it how?'

'His eyes.' Eddie looked in the rearview at LaDuke, held his gaze. 'Me and my friends, when things are slow out here, we play this game: Gay, Not Gay. We check out these suit-and-tie boys walking down the street and we make the call. Me, I look at their eyes. And when it comes to knowing what it really is that they're about, I believe I'm usually right.' Eddie smirked a little at LaDuke.

'Fuck this,' LaDuke said. 'I've had enough.'

'A couple more questions,' I said. 'You know anybody in this movie business you were talking about?'

'Uh-uh,' Eddie said. 'Not my thing. I like the fresh air, Stefanos. Can't stand being cooped up in a small space, under some hot light. I ain't got no ambition to be that kind of star.'

'Some of your friends might know something about it.'

'Maybe,' Eddie said. 'I'll ask around. I find out anything, I'll give you a call.'

I gave him my card. 'There's money in it for you if you come up with something.'

'That's the case,' Eddie said, 'you *know* I'll call.'

'We about done?' said LaDuke.

'Your friend needs to relax,' Eddie said. 'It's not good for him to be so angry.'

'See you later, Eddie,' I said.

Eddie turned to LaDuke. 'Take care of yourself, Stretch.'

He got out of the car, and shut the door behind him. I watched him strut across the street and disappear over the hill at the start of the bridge. He lived for money, but he was stupid and he was sloppy, and he had a short attention span. He'd lose my card, or forget my name; I knew I'd never hear from him again.

'*God*damn it,' LaDuke said softly from the backseat.

I lit the cigarette that I had been playing with for the last five minutes, took some smoke into my lungs. 'Listen, Jack. These kids out here, man, they're going to get into some shit. You didn't think Roland was totally innocent, did you? If you're going to do this kind of work, you've got to stop setting yourself up for disappointment.'

'It makes me sick, that's all. To think that Roland comes from a home where his mother raised him with love, and then he ends up down in some woods, having some middle-aged man suck his dick, maybe go butt-up in some porno movie. A kid is confused enough, Nick; he doesn't know shit yet about what he is. To have all these adults doing these things to him . . . I swear to God, it just makes me sick.'

'We're not done yet,' I said. 'And what we found out here, it could be nothing compared to what we're going to find. Earlier today, I talked to this cop I know. He told me that they've got some information – I don't know how reliable it is – that Calvin and Roland were moving drugs.'

'Who were the cops talking to?'

'An informant of theirs, out of Southeast.'

'Well, let's find this guy, talk to him ourselves!'

'There's things we can't do, LaDuke. The cops can go into those projects, ask around, because they're cops. We go in there, a couple of white-boy private cops, nobody's gonna talk to us. And it's a good way to get ourselves capped.'

'What now, then?'

'We keep doing what we're doing, work with what we know. Here's the thing: Calvin was killed because of something wrong he and his friend got themselves into – there's no doubt about that now. You're going to have to deal with it, Jack – Roland might be dead, too.'

'*God*damn it,' LaDuke said again, and shook his head.

We didn't say much after that. I sat there and smoked my cigarette and checked out the flow of traffic while the bike messengers and the homeless and the hustlers moved about in the park. LaDuke mumbled to himself occasionally, and once he slapped the back of my seat with his palm. Then he picked up a couple of empty beer cans that were at his feet and told me he was going to throw them away.

I watched him walk around the front of the car, moving heavily, shifting his shoulders awkwardly, a tall, gawky guy not entirely comfortable in his own skin, like an adolescent who has grown too fast. There was something else, too, something a little off center and soiled beneath Jack LaDuke's fresh-scrubbed looks. I couldn't put my finger on it that day, and when I did, it was way too late. Eventually, the snakes that were crawling around inside his head found their way out. By then, there was nothing I could do but stand beside him, and watch them strike.

11

Lyla McCubbin had grown up in a boxy brick house on a street named Bangor Drive, in an unremarkable but pleasant development called Garrett Park Estates in the Maryland suburb of Kensington. Her parents had raised three children there, and they had remained long after Lyla, the last child, had graduated from college and gone out on her own. Lyla said that the neighborhood had changed very little since her childhood: a mixture of starter homes and rentals, none too ostentatious, a comfortable kind of place, where you came to recognize the bark of every dog through the open window of your bedroom as you drifted off to sleep on summer nights.

Lyla's mother, Linda, had practically raised the children herself, as the father, Daniel McCubbin, was usually off at some meeting, organizing the unions or planning the demonstration for his latest cause. The first day I met Lyla, in her office at *D.C. This Week*, I had noticed the photograph of her as a child, standing between her bearded father and straight-haired mother, at a Dupont Circle rally circa 1969. Lyla said that the family never had a dime, but there was some pride in her voice as she said it, never regret. Her father, a fine trial lawyer by all accounts, had managed to resist the advances of the corporate firms in town throughout his career, preferring to use his talents to advance the causes of those individuals whom he considered to be on the side of 'right.' He wasn't your typical pompous windbag, though. I liked him and I admired him, despite the obvious fact that he was not awfully crazy about me.

We were greeted at the door by Linda McCubbin, who kissed Lyla and then me on the cheek. Linda was Lyla with thirty years added to the odometer, with more silver in the hair than red now and an organic heaviness around the waist and in the hips, Men were always told to look at the mothers, as if that was some kind of test; it never had been for me, but if it had been, then Lyla would have passed.

'Here, Ma,' Lyla said, handing Linda a bag containing two liter bottles of white wine. Lyla had insisted we stop for it, though both of us had once again consumed a little too much the night before.

Linda took it, said, 'Come on in.'

Daniel sat under an overextended air conditioner in the simply furnished living room, in a La-Z-Boy chair, the arms of which had been shredded by the McCubbin cat, a mean tom that someone had ironically named Peace. Lyla bent to her father and kissed him, and then he shook my hand without rising from the chair.

'Don't get up,' I said.

'Didn't plan to,' he said. 'Hot day like this, I'm going to expend as little energy as possible. How's it going, Nick?'

'Good. Good.'

Daniel smiled, studied me and kept the smile until it looked nothing like a smile at all. Maybe I had overdone the aftershave, or maybe it was the unironed khakis or the color of my shirt. Or maybe he liked me just fine, and it was just that I was dating his baby daughter.

'Linda,' Daniel said, watching my eyes. 'Get Nick here a drink. What'll it be, Nick?'

'Nothing just yet. Too early for me,' I said, rocking on my heels.

'Is it?' Daniel said, scratching beneath the white of his beard.

'Well,' Lyla said, '*I'll* have one. C'mon Mom, let's go in the kitchen. I'll help you get ready.'

Lyla winked, left me there with her dad. I gave her a brittle smile as she walked away. I had a seat on the sofa, crossed one leg over the other, nervously missed it on the first go-round.

'Where's the rest of the family?' I said.

'They'll be along,' Daniel said. 'How's the bar business going?'

'Good. Real good.'

'You know, I used to go into that place, in the old days, when I was working on the Hill.'

'Really.'

'Yes, it was called something else back then. You've been there awhile, haven't you? Thought you might own a piece of it by now.'

'No, not me, Tough business, that.' Real tough.

'And your investigative work?'

'Coming along,' I said as I watched my free foot wiggle in the air. 'How about you . . . how's retirement?'

Daniel raised his substantial eyebrows. 'Linda says I don't know how to spell the word *retirement*. I guess the difference is, now I don't get paid for what it is I do. Right now, I'm setting up group homes for

516

Haitian refugees. Our church owns these properties, so . . . I'm helping fix them up.'

'Why fix them up?' I said, my foot pinwheeling now, out of control. 'You could make more profit by, you know, leaving them the way they are. Crowd a bunch of people in the rooms, I mean – where they come from, they're used to it. Jack up the rents, too, while you're at it.'

A smile came into Daniel's eyes. 'Of course,' he said, 'you're ribbing me, aren't you?'

'Just a little.'

'You know, you don't always have to work so hard at being cynical around me, Nick. I know that, in your own way, you have a fairly clear idea of what's right and what's wrong. Not all the good that gets done in this world gets done in a church or a meeting hall, I realize that.'

'Yeah, well, we make due with what we have, and work with it, you know?'

'Yes, I do.'

He stopped giving me the business and picked up the Outlook section of the *Post* that was lying by his chair. I noticed a makeshift bar that had been set up on a mobile cart near a mirrored armoire in the corner of the room. There were bottles of gin and vodka, tonic and ginger ale, an ice bucket, and a sealed bottle of Old Grand-Dad. Apparently, that had been purchased just for me; I had never seen the old man take a drink, and Lyla's mother drank wine, and only with dinner. Something rushed out at the base of the curtains at the bay window and moved along behind them with a deliberate slink: That would be Peace, stalking me as he always did when I came to the McCubbin house for dinner.

I was watching the curtains, thinking of my possible defense against an attack from that lousy cat, when the front door opened and four people stepped inside: Lyla's brother, Mike, his wife, Donna, Lyla's older sister, Kimmy, and Kimmy's husband, Leo. This time, Daniel stood up from his chair, and we all did our back-slapping moves around the living room. A half hour later, we were seated at a cramped table in the dining room, with Daniel McCubbin leading a prayer. During the prayer, our hands were all joined underneath the table, a McCubbin tradition, and my index finger was wiggling around on the inside of Lyla's thigh. Lyla, seated to my right, dug a fingernail into my own thigh, leaving a crescent mark that I discovered an hour later in the bathroom.

'Amen,' everybody said, and then Leo, as usual, reached across the table for the first shot at the main course, and started pushing thick slices of roast beef onto his plate.

'Leave some for the rest of the family, Leo,' Kim said, only kidding by half.

'Sure, honey,' he said, then issued his trademark high cackle, a sound that was always surprising coming from a man as fat as Leo. 'You know I can't help it. The Irish love their liquor and us Greeks love to eat. Right, Nick?'

Daniel McCubbin's eyes flashed on Leo. I nodded weakly, not wanting to appear too anxious to admit to being a member of Leo Charles's ethnic tribe. Leo *was* a Greek – the Charles had been Charalambides before his grandfather stepped off the boat – but he was not a kid my friends or I had known growing up. Leo Charles was also a bigot, and like all bigots, black and white, he was a loser, and he directed his shortcomings and utter lack of self-confidence outwardly and onto the backs of others. Lyla said Kimmy had zero self-esteem and that was why she had married him. And all the time, I'd thought it was his 280-pound frame, all five foot eight inches of it.

'How about those Orioles?' Mike said in the too-gentle way of his that unfortunately suggested a weaker version of his father. Mike ran a volunteer soup kitchen operation out of Le Droit Park. He plopped a mound of mashed potatoes onto his plate and passed the platter to his wife, Donna, a shame-about-the-face public defender with just a killer body. All these do-goodniks at the table, and me. Well, there was Leo, too.

'Yeah, how about 'em, Nick?' Leo said. 'Think the bullpen's gonna take 'em through to the Series?' Leo loved to talk sports but couldn't do a push-up.

'Lookin' good,' I said, feeling not so good. I really could have used a drink. 'I'm going up to Camden Yards tomorrow with a buddy of mine, a guy named Johnny McGinnes,.'

'An Irishman,' Leo said, spitting a little ball of mashed potato across the table in the process.

'They love their liquor,' Daniel said, but it went over Leo's head, missed him by a mile. He kept right on chewing, breaking down the load that was in his mouth. Lyla's mother laughed a little, and she and Mike exchanged fond looks.

'You didn't tell me you were going to the game,' Lyla said.

'Yeah, Johnny won some tickets, sold a million refrigerators last month in some promotion, something like that.'

'*That* ought to be interesting,' Lyla said, killing the remainder of the wine in her glass. She picked up the bottle off the table and poured herself some more, clumsily trying to fill the glass to the top, spilling some in the process. Daniel looked at her and then at me. Lyla's ears were a little red, her cheeks flushed.

'Anybody want a little more cool in here?' Lyla's mother said. 'We could turn up that air conditioner.'

'Let me handle this,' I said with a wink. 'I used to be in electronics – I know how to operate the unit.'

I got out of my chair and walked to the window where the air conditioner had been set. As I got to it, I saw something black seem to rise out of nowhere from behind the curtains near my feet, and I heard a woman's voice cry out behind me just as the wail of an animal pierced the air. I felt a slash of pain, pulled my hand back as the crazy tomcat cartwheeled in the air, landed on his feet on the carpet, and took off back across the room, scurrying for his hiding place behind the drapes.

'Fuck!' I shouted, waving my hand, the blood already coming to the surface of the cut. That quieted the rest of them down.

Mike got up and found the cat, carried him back into the room. Lyla tossed me a napkin and went to get a Band-Aid. She returned with it, but by now the cut had stopped bleeding. I put the Band-Aid on anyway, a sympathy play to make my obscenity seem more justified.

'Peace, man,' Mike whined, stroking the cat.

'Peace, man,' I said, and made a V with my fingers, smiling stupidly at the McCubbin family. Nobody laughed.

'I guess that cat doesn't like you so good,' Leo said. 'Right, Nick?'

'Leo,' Kimmy said, 'you've got a piece of lettuce on your cheek.'

I sat back down. Lyla patted my thigh under the table. We finished our Sunday dinner.

A couple of hours later, when Lyla's siblings and their spouses had gone and Lyla went to the kitchen with her mother to wash and dry the dishes, I took a beer to the concrete patio out back and had a seat in one of four wrought-iron chairs grouped around a glass-topped table. I lit a cigarette and watched a young father play catch with his son in an adjacent yard. The man rubbed the top of his son's head when they were done, and the boy skipped off toward their house. Then the back door of the McCubbin house opened and Daniel came out and stepped down to the patio.

'Mind if I join you?'

'Of course not,' I said. 'Have a seat.'

He grunted as he settled into a chair across the table. I dropped my lit butt into the top of the beer can and heard it hiss as it hit the backwash. I put the can at my feet.

'How was it?' Daniel said.

'Cold beer on a Sunday in the summer, it's always pretty good.'

'Yes, I remember. Watching you today, it took me back to when I was first dating Linda, the times we'd go to her parents' house for dinner. I could have used a drink on those occasions, wanted one desperately, as a matter of fact. It really would have relaxed me, taken the edge off. There's nothing more humbling than dealing with the potential in-laws, no matter how much confidence you have. It's like, all of the sudden, you're a little boy again.'

'You guys aren't so bad,' I said, and a smile passed between us. 'Besides, it's Lyla, so it's worth it.'

'You love her, don't you?'

'Yes, sir. I believe I do.'

'How much do you love her? Do you love her enough to do what's right for her, even if it means losing her?'

'I don't follow you.'

Daniel sat back in his chair, looked into the depths of his own yard. 'I told you earlier today that I used to frequent that place your bartend in, when I was on the Hill. I don't know if Lyla's ever told you the . . . degree to which I frequented those types of establishments.'

'No,' I said, 'she hasn't.'

'Well, I was quite a regular in those days, in that place and plenty of others. I wish that I could give you the details, but I don't remember all that much of those years. If it wasn't for photographs, it would be difficult to recall even the faces of my children as they were growing up. All that wasted time. But I can't get it back now, so . . .' Daniel pulled at the errant edges of his beard. 'Anyway, things turned out all right, I think. I got myself into a program, managed to see my children become wonderful adults, with most of the credit for that going to Linda, of course, and I ended up doing a bit of good along the way. So I think you'll understand it when I say, maybe because of the fact that I wasn't always there for them, that I'm rather fiercely protective of my children to this day.'

'I understand.'

Daniel breathed out slowly, folded his hands on the table, bumped one thumb against the other. 'Lyla, she's always taken on my traits, even as a child. I know you think she looks like her mother, and certainly she does. But I'm talking about resemblances in less obvious ways.'

I didn't respond.

Daniel kept on: 'When Lyla was a teenager, when she used to come home late at night, I could always tell what she had been up to. Her own body, it betrayed her. When she drinks, you know, even now, her ears turn this blazing shade of red. That same thing used to happen to me – in fact, they used to call me "Red" in some of the bars where they knew me pretty well.' Daniel looked me in the eyes. 'She's got a problem with it, you know. It's hereditary, I suppose, in a gene I gave her. The researchers, they've been claiming that for quite some time now. She's got the same problem that I had when I was her age. And I see it . . . I see it only getting worse.'

Again, I didn't answer him or respond in any way. A drop of sweat moved slowly down my back. Daniel leaned in, rested his forearms on the table.

'You're an alcoholic, Nick,' he said. 'You would never admit to it, but that's what you are. You've probably done some binge drinking in your day, but I would say that in general you're what they call a controlled drinker. The worst kind, because it allows you to convince yourself that you don't have a problem, and now you've managed to bury the thought of doing something about it entirely. I've been around enough people like you; I just don't think you're ever going to give it up.'

'I know what I'm about.'

'Yes, I think you do. But I'm not responsible for you, so that's not good enough. Lyla needs someone strong to tell her what she is and to stand next to her and help her through it. You're just not that person.'

I pushed away from the table and stood slowly from my chair. 'It's getting late. I better be going.'

I began to walk past him, but he wrapped a hand around my forearm. I looked down on him, saw that his eyes had softened.

'I like you, Nick. I want you to know that. I think that you're a good man. You're just not good for *her*.'

'Thanks for dinner.'

I walked across the patio in the dying light.

'What were you and Dad doing out back?' Lyla said. We were driving south on Connecticut, to Lyla's apartment. 'What was he saying, asking about your intentions?'

'Something like that.'

'Dad's always been tough on my boyfriends.'

'He's only looking out for you,' I said.

'I know,' Lyla said, and touched the Band-Aid on my finger. 'Tough day, huh, Stefanos?'

'Tough day.'

I stopped at Lyla's apartment building off Calvert, let the engine idle.

'What, you're not coming up?'

'I better not,' I said. 'Got something going on early tomorrow on this Jeter thing.'

'I should chill out, too. My editor left a message on my machine yesterday. That story I've been working on, the one I finished and turned in after we had lunch the other day, in Chinatown? He wants to meet with me about it in the morning. Sounds ominous.'

'You've always been able to control him. You'll do fine.'

Lyla leaned across the seat, put her hand behind my head, and kissed me on the mouth. 'Love you, Nick.'

'I love you too, baby. Take care.'

12

In D.C., it's tough to find a good clean place to catch an art film anymore, and next to impossible to find consistency in repertory. The near-legendary Circle Theater on Pennsylvania Avenue, where many Washingtonians got their film education, is long gone, its 'ten tickets for ten dollars' deal a permanent fixture now in the local nostalgia file. Georgetown boasts the Key and Biograph theaters, but Georgetown has devolved into a slum-out for suburban teens, drunks, and tourists – a guy I know calls it a 'shopping mall without a roof' – and a lot of in-towners just don't care to bother. Out-of-town bookers place the rest of the films in their corporately designated 'art theaters,' their unfamiliarity with our city demographics resulting in sometimes laughably illogical bills. It's true that you can catch some cool stuff at the Hirshhorn or at other galleries or museums, but you have to know where to find the listings, and by the time you've gotten around to checking out the art calendars in *City Paper* and *D.C. This Week*, it's often too late.

I have a friend named Gerry Abromowitz, whom I've known since the club days in the early years of the New Wave – music, not film. Gerry owned his own club for a while, a place called the Crawlspace, a venue for harDCore bands and slammers. Off and on, Gerry went by the name of Gerry Louis, Jr., and even looked into having the legal change. But he stopped short of doing it about the time that the Crawlspace closed down after one steaming-hot summer. A personal-injury suit put a lock on the front door, but in truth, the place was a loser from the word go. Now, Gerry Louis, Jr., was back to Gerry Abromowitz and settling into the beginnings of middle age, working as the owner/operator of a movie theater called the Very Ritzy down on 9th.

The Very Ritzy had just been the Ritz, of course, in its original incarnation, but as usual, Gerry couldn't resist fucking around with the name. It started out as a burlesque house, and then it was the last of the burlesque houses, and then it was the last of the porno houses, and when Gerry took it out of mothballs on a short-term lease, his intention was to make it an art house. But he soon found out that it was difficult to outbid the more powerful competition for the bookings, and when he could get a decent film, nobody seemed to be interested in traveling to that part of town after working hours. So he quietly took it back to porno for the matinees and made it straight repertory at night, taking in the spillage and the last-call crowd from the Snake Pit and other clubs in the surrounding area. He seemed to make a living from this novel arrangement, though that was probably due to the fact that his skin-flick matinees were all profit; over the years, Gerry Abromowitz had amassed one of the most extensive privately owned sixteen-millimeter porno collections south of Jersey.

'Ge-roo,' I said, shaking his hand. He had agreed to meet me Monday noon at the theater. We stood in the red-carpeted lobby.

'Nick the Stick,' Gerry said. 'Lookin' good. How about me . . . I gain much weight?'

About forty, I thought. But I said, 'Nah.'

'C'mon up. I'm runnin' the projector. My kid's up there; I don't want to leave him alone.'

A man in a business suit walked into the lobby, his eyes straight ahead. An usher – long hair, wearing a black T-shirt and ripped black jeans – took the man's ticket, tore it in half, then returned to the paperback he was reading without moving from his stool. The business suit scurried quickly through the lobby to the darkness of the theater. I followed Gerry up a carpeted set of stairs.

We hit a landing and then an office area, where a boy just past toddler stage played with an action figure that looked to me like the Astro Boy of my youth. All four walls of this room had film cans racked and labeled on wooden shelves, with a large slotted area set aside for one-sheets and stills.

'Gerry junior,' Gerry said, tipping his head proudly at the boy.

'Gerry Louis, Jr.?' I said.

'Nick, Nick, Nick,' Gerry said.

I turned to his kid. 'What's that guy's name?' I said, nodding at his toy.

'Jason the Power Ranger!' the kid said, puffing out his chest and his cheeks. When he did that, the little fats looked a lot like his dad.

'Aw, man,' I said, 'I wish *I* had one of those.' That got Gerry junior excited, and he started running around the room, holding up Jason the

Power Ranger in the go-fly position. Gerry senior motioned me up another short set of stairs.

We took seats outside the shut door of the projection booth, close enough to hear if something mechanical went wrong. The air was stagnant and warm, but I was in shorts and a T-shirt, and Gerry was dressed approximately the same way. Gerry's kinky hair had plenty of gray in it, and he had one of those faces that always seemed to be smiling, even when it was not.

'So what's on the bill today?' I said. '*The Sorrow and the Pity?*'

'Not quite. *Crotchless in Seattle.* It's a big title for me this summer.'

'I'll bet. So the porno's keeping this place afloat.'

'So far. The associations, the exodus of the law firms moving east into the city, that's helped. These guys pay their seven bucks, come in for the first show, fifteen minutes, wack-adoo, wack-adoo' – Gerry contorted his face, made a fist, pumped out a two-stroke jack-off mime – 'they're in and out. It's cheaper than a prostie, Nick. And with the plague out there, it's damn sure safer. Everyone thought, with videotape rental, the theatrical was gonna go the way of quadrophonic sound. And that was true to some degree, especially with the pervs. But these married guys, for whatever reason – maybe they're not gettin' enough at home, whatever – they can't pop in a porno tape in their own house. What are they gonna tell junior? "Keep it down. Daddy's tryin' to watch Stormy Weathers give Ralph Rimrod some head"? Excuse me.' Gerry pulled balled Kleenex from his pocket, blew his nose loudly into the tissue. 'I'm telling you, this porno thing is a growth market, if you got the right location.'

'Yeah, but who cleans up the theater?'

Gerry smirked. 'That kid you saw in the lobby, he came to me, said he wanted to learn the exhibition business. I gave him a bucket and mop, said, "Here, go to school." Between shows, he does the honors. But it's not as bad as you think, Nick. These business types are very fastidious – they bring their own socks, *Wall Street Journals*, shit like that. They're better behaved than my nighttime repertory crowd, I'll tell you. But even that's beginning to pick up. Kids are smoking pot again, you know it?'

'Sure,' I said, thinking of the stash in my glove box.

'That helps. Helps the "appreciation of cinema." Helps music, and fucking, and everything else, too, right? Anyway, I'm gonna start adding psychotronic midnights on the weekends—'

'Listen, Ger—'

'I know, you don't have all day. You called because you needed some information.'

'That's right. I'm looking for a kid, got himself into some local porn action.'

'How old?'

'Seventeen.'

'What genre?'

'Man on boy, what I can make out. Maybe interracial, if that narrows it down. The kid is black.'

Gerry scratched behind his ear. 'I wouldn't know, directly. Everything I got here is classic, on celluloid, from the archives. The video business is wide open, man; anybody can do it. Let's say you want to make a movie with a school theme. All's you need is a camera, a couple of lights if you want it real clean, some props – a piece of chalk, maybe a blackboard – and you got yourself a real intricate story about a teacher disciplining his student.'

'Isn't there any risk? I mean, it's got to be illegal, right?'

'Yes and no. The situation you're describing, if the kid's a minor, yeah, that's illegal, but lookswise he's probably right on the cusp, so who's gonna check? Basically, as long as there're no penetration shots, you're in the clear.'

'The business is that scattered.'

'Sure. It's done all over the city. Like I say, I wouldn't have any idea where to tell you to start. I'm not in that business.'

'Somebody's got to distribute the stuff, though.'

Gerry shifted in his seat. 'In the man-boy arena? All the homo stuff, and the different varieties of it, everything comes out of this little warehouse around 2nd on K. This guy owns a storefront porno operation. I think it's called the Hot Plate.'

'What's his name?'

'Bernard Tobias. Bernie.'

'Think he'll talk to me?'

'Not *just* to you, no. Bernie, he's a weird bird. Well, maybe not so weird if you're an amateur psychiatrist. He's a little guy who always needs to be the big magilla. I've met him a few times; he's always bragging about how he only does business with "executive officers," never meets with anybody's assistant, like we're talking about Wharton graduates in the skin trade here. I think if you go in with a couple of guys, wear ties, do the dog and pony show, you'll be all right.'

'Thanks, Gerry. Appreciate the help.'

'Hey, Nick – how'd you end up in this, anyway? I ran into one of my old bartenders from the Crawlspace a few months ago—'

'Joe Martinson.'

'Joe, right. He told me what you were doing. The way I remember you, you were this music-crazy guy used to stand in the corner watching the bands, a beer in each hand. Fact, I used to call you "Nick Two-Beers," remember?'

'You said it was my Indian name. 'Course, I remember when you insisted everyone call you Gerry Louis, Jr. Things happen to people – you never know where they're going to end up.'

'You got that right. That guy in that back Big Black, Durango's his name, remember? He's a corporate lawyer now. I saw his picture in a magazine, little bald guy in a hot-shit suit like every guy you see walking out of Arnold and Porter. So yeah, you never know.' Gerry got out of his chair. 'Speaking of Jerry Lewis, I'm doing a retrospective next month, kicking it off with *The Nutty Professor*. I can get you a pass.'

'I don't think so.'

'It's an American classic!'

'So are you, Gerry.' I shook his hand. 'Listen, thanks again, man. Thanks a million.

I used Gerry's directory before I left, then found a pay phone out on 9th and called Bernie Tobias. I identified myself as Ron Roget – an appropriately lizardly name I had just seen in the directory – and bullshitted him about my production company out of Philadelphia, which I said did the 'man/boy discipline thing' better than anyone 'on the East Coast.' He said he couldn't meet with me that week, but when I told him that 'my associates' and I would be in D.C. tomorrow, and only for one day, he agreed. As Gerry had predicted, the 'associates' tag hit Bernie's hot button. We agreed on a time the next day.

I made it to the Spot after the lunch rush had subsided. Mai was behind the bar, bent into the soak sink with a glass load, and Phil Saylor stood at the register counting checks. Anna was by the service bar, arranging her tip change in dollar stacks on the green netting. I spoke to Mai briefly, thanked her for what we had arranged over the phone the day before.

'Hey, Phil,' I said, speaking to his back. 'I'm taking some time off. Mai and I set it up. That okay by you?'

'I need the shifts, Phil,' Mai interjected.

'She told me already,' Phil said without raising his head. He didn't add anything, so I went down to the service end of the bar and rubbed the top of Anna Wang's head.

'Hey, Nick.'

'Hey, what's up?'

'Got a cigarette?'

'Sure.'

I gave her one, lit it for her. She leaned her back against the wall, dragged sharply on the smoke, exhaled just as sharply. 'Some woman called you,' she said. 'Said your uncle wants to see you.'

'Costa,' I said. 'The woman would be his nurse.'

'He sick?'

'Cancer,' I said. Anna looked at the cigarette in her hand, thought about it, took another drag.

'That's rough.'

I nodded. 'How'd your date go with LaDuke?'

'Okay, I guess.'

I reached out and Anna passed me the cigarette. I took a puff, handed it back. 'Just okay?'

'It was fun.' Her eyes smiled. 'He took me to the Jefferson Memorial last night. We sat on the steps, split a bottle of wine. Or rather, I drank most of it. No guy's ever tried anything so obvious with me. I know it's a corny move, but I got the feeling he didn't think it was, if you know what I mean.'

'He's strictly from L-Seven, but genuine.'

'Exactly. Most of the guys I meet still in their twenties, they're so ironic, so cynical, you know. I just get tired of it sometimes. Jack's cute, and he's funny, and all those good things, but he's also really square. In some weird way, that's refreshing.'

'So why was the night "just okay"?'

'It always comes down to the big finish, doesn't it? Anna butted the smoke in an ashtray, looked up. 'Well, at the end of the night, I wanted to kiss him, you know? And I'm pretty sure he wanted to kiss me, too. So I took the initiative.' Anna grinned. 'I gave it to him pretty good, I think. But he was shaking, Nick. I mean, shaking real deep. It's like, I don't know, he was scared to death. And then he just pulled away, and it was like something just seemed to go out of him.'

'Maybe it's been awhile for him.'

'I guess.'

'You gonna see him again?'

'Maybe. I don't know. The guy's carrying something serious around on his back. I'm not sure if I need that right now.'

I touched her arm. 'Listen, I've got to go.'

'Take it easy,' she said.

I poked my head into the kitchen, hooked Darnell up as the driver for my appointment the next day. Then I phoned LaDuke from the bar, got him in on it, too. On the way out the door, Phil Saylor grabbed my arm.

'What's your hurry?' he said.

'I'm off to the ball game with a friend of mine. Got to pick him up where he works.'

'Don't stay away too long, hear? Mai, she's okay, but after she works a few days straight, she starts jumping all into the customers' shit.'

'I thought you were mad at me, Phil.'

'You made a mistake. You're allowed one or two.'

I moved to shake his hand, but he turned away. The two of us were square again, I guess.

When I walked into Goode's White Goods in Beltsville, the first thing I saw was Johnny McGinnes, bent into an open refrigerator, blowing pot smoke into the box. During working hours, McGinnes's pants pocket always contained a film canister and a one-hit pipe, which he lit at regular intervals right on the sales floor. After the exhale, he would tap the ashes out against his open palm and drop the pipe back into his pocket in one quick movement. I had worked with him for many years, and to my knowledge, no one, customer or management type, had ever caught him in the act of getting high.

McGinnes saw my entrance, pulled a six of Colt 45 tall boys from the fridge, held them up, winked, and put the back inside. He shut the door and goose-stepped down the aisle back to his customer, a middle-aged woman looking at a dishwasher. As usual, McGinnes was done up synthetic-crisp: navy blue slacks, poly/cotton oxford, and a plain red tie with a knot as pretty as a fist. His thinning black hair slashed down across his high forehead, with only his silver sideburns betraying his age. McGinnes managed to throw me a mental patient's grin as he spoke to the woman; even across the showroom, I could see that he was half-cooked.

Goode's White Goods, one of the few major appliance independents left in the D.C. area since brand-name retailing came to Sears, had managed to carve out a niche for itself as a full-service operation. *White goods* was the industry term for big-ticket appliances, and the company's owner, Nolan Goode – it was inevitable that McGinnes would dub him 'No Damn Good' – mistakenly overcalculated the public's comprehension of the wordplay in the store's name. Confusion notwithstanding, Goode's White Goods had managed to survive. And after McGinnes had joined the team, it had actually begun to thrive.

In contrast to the noise common on an electronics' floor, No Damn

Good's appliance shop seemed quiet as a museum, orderly rows of silent, shiny, inanimate porcelain aligned beneath wall-to-wall banners. In the center aisle, a young man used an unwieldy buffer to wax the floor, solemnly repeating the phrase 'Slippery, slippery,' though there were no customers anywhere near him. A man I pegged as the manager – prematurely bald, prematurely overweight – stood behind the counter, hiking his pants up sharply, as if that was the most aggressive act he would attempt all day. On the other side of the counter stood a young, square-jawed guy, smiling broadly, arranging point-of-purchase promotional materials. He had the too-handsome, dim-bulb look of a factory rep, *Triumph of the Will* in a navy blue suit. Out of the corner of my eye, I saw a little guy shoot out of the stockroom and head in my direction, his hand extended all the way out, his hip-on-the-cheap clothing drooping everywhere on his skinny frame.

'And how are we doin' today?' he said as he reached me, his hand still out.

I shook it and said, 'Waiting on McGinnes.'

'Anything I can do for you while you're waiting?'

'No thanks.'

'Well, if you have any questions about a major appliance—'

'The name is Donny,' I said.

Donny smiled a little strangely and I smiled back. He scratched his ratty 'fro and walked back down the aisle, slinking behind the counter. I checked McGinnes: He had removed the dishwasher's wash tower – it looked exactly like a vibrator – and was making little jabbing movements with it behind the customer's back, pitching the merits of the machine to her all the while. This was for my benefit, I supposed, or maybe he was just bored. Then a young couple came through the door with buy signs practically tattooed on their foreheads – any salesman worth his salt can tell – and McGinnes excused himself to greet them.

Donny yelled across the sales floor, 'Hey, Johnny, you got a call on line one. Guy wants to give you an order,' and he pointed to a wall-mounted phone where a yellow light blinked clear as a beacon. McGinnes hesitated, went to take the call. Donny racewalked toward his new customers. Even before I saw McGinnes pick up the phone and make a bitter face, I knew what Donny Boy had done: gotten a dial tone and put it on hold, then used the phony bait to draw McGinnes away from the live ones coming through the door. Johnny should have known; in fact, it was one of the very first tricks he had played on me years ago.

McGinnes closed his deal, though, and Donny did not. Afterward, when I had been introduced to the boys and stood with them around the counter, there seemed to be no residual animosity coming off Johnny. Just another way to grab an up, the memory to be filed away by McGinnes under 'payback,' to be retrieved the next time a *yom* came walking through the door.

'So, Tim,' a very serious Donny said to the factory rep. 'You read about Maytag in the paper today?'

'No,' Tim said, breathing through his mouth. 'What about Maytag?'

'Kelvinator!' Donny said. 'Get it? Kelvin . . . he ate 'er!' Donny cackled, slapped his own knee.

'Ha, ha, ha.' Tim's laughter and the brittle smile that went with it failed to mask his contempt.

''Course,' Donny continued, 'that ain't nothin', compared with what the general did.'

'What general?' Tim said, and I saw it coming.

'General Electric!' Donny said. 'He was Tappan Amana, dig? Put his Hotpoint right on her Coldspot. Know what I'm sayin'?'

Tim began to turn red. McGinnes walked up to the group, a brown paper bag in his hand. He looked at me and smiled.

'You ready, Jim?' he said.

'I'm ready.'

'Hold on a second,' the manager said.

'What?' McGinnes said.

'I got a belch a few minutes ago,' the manager said. 'That's what. Customer called, said you stepped him off an advertised single-speed washer to what you claimed was a two speed – an LA three-five-nine-five.'

'So?'

'An LA three-five-nine-five is a single-speed washer, too, McGinnes. You told him it had two speeds!'

'It does have two speeds,' McGinnes said. 'On . . . and off.'

'Off's not a speed, McGinnes!' the manager yelled, but Johnny had already pulled me away, and the two of us were headed for the front door.

McGinnes drew a malt liquor out of the bag and popped the top. He handed the open one to me, found one for himself.

'Off is not a speed! . . .' The manager's voice trailed off as we pushed through the store's double glass doors.

Out in the lot, McGinnes tensed up his face. 'All these complaints. I'm gonna get a sick stomach.'

'Had a lot lately?'

McGinnes nodded. 'This guy called this morning, all bent out of shape. Says when I sold him his refrigerator, I guaranteed him it was a nice box. And the thing's had three service calls in the last month.'

'So? Did you guarantee it?'

'Hell no! I never said it was a nice box. I said it was *an icebox!* The guy just misunderstood me.'

'I can't imagine how that happened, Johnny.'

'The guy was a putz,' McGinnes said. 'You know it?'

13

My first day as a stock boy at Nutty Nathan's on Connecticut Avenue, back in 1974, I checked out this pale, speeded-out looking Irishman named Johnny McGinnes and I thought, Who *is* this guy? It didn't take too long to find out. Shortly after meeting him, I watched him volunteer to microwave the frozen dinner of a visiting district manager, and I pegged him as a brownnose. That notion was dispelled a few minutes later when I walked around the display rack and caught him hawking a wad of spit into the DM's food, his chest heaving in suppressed laughter as he carefully mixed it in. By the end of the day, I had witnessed him hit his pipe repeatedly, knock down a steady succession of beers, and swallow two suspicious-looking pills, all the time maintaining his mastery of the floor. Then, at closing time, he laid 'Willie the Pimp' on the store's most expensive system, and eighty watts of Zappa were suddenly blowing through a pair of Bose 901s, and Johnny stood atop a vacuum cleaner display, playing air guitar, his bleeding red eyes closed as if in prayer. Even a sixteen-year-old stoner like me could see that Johnny McGinnes was one man who would never grow up.

'You're drinking too slow,' McGinnes said, as my Dodge pushed up 95.

'*You're* not,' I said. We were nearing Baltimore and the six of tall boys was almost done.

McGinnes gave the radio some volume. 'Hey,' he shouted, 'how you like being a parent?'

I turned the volume down a notch. 'I'm not a parent. A kid's parents are who raises them, and I've got nothing to do with that.'

'Yeah, but' – McGinnes wiggled his eyebrows foolishly – 'you gave her your seed, didn't you?'

'Yes, Johnny, I gave her my seed.'

'So, what did Jackie name the boy?'

'Kent,' I said, and waited for his comment.

'She named him after a cigarette?'

'It's British or something.'

'Her last name's Kahn, isn't it? I thought Kahn was a Jewish name—'

'Shit, Johnny, I don't know. She liked the name, that's all.'

I swigged my malt liquor. Some of it ran down my chin. I went to wipe it off and swerved a bit into another lane. Someone reprimanded me with a polite beep and I got the car back between the lines.

McGinnes said, 'I don't like it.'

'What?'

'The name.'

'Why not?'

He raised a finger in the air, like he imagined an academic might do. 'You know how kids are. I mean, the other boys, on the playground, they're gonna give him shit about it, twist it all around.'

'I don't follow.'

McGinnes sighed, exasperated. 'You say his name's Kent, right? Nick, the other kids – well, they're gonna call him "Cunt"!'

'Aw, come on, man . . .'

'Hey, look!' McGinnes said, pointing through the window excitedly. 'Baltimore!'

We stopped in a bar near the stadium, split a pitcher, and watched the first two innings from there. We would have made it for the third, but we got waylaid by the kick-ass food at the concession stands inside the Yards. McGinnes and I both had half smokes smothered in kraut and mustard and two more beers before we got to our seats. By then it was the fourth and the Birds were down by two to the White Sox.

Our seats were in section 330, to the right and way up from home plate. A deaf kid sat alone in front of us, and next to him sat a solid Korean man and his two sons. The Korean ate peanuts the entire game, a mountain of shells at his feet. Behind us a red-bearded, potbellied man loudly heckled the players, with most of his choice obscenities reserved for Sid Fernandez, who that night was truly getting rocked. Near him, a couple of D.C. attorneys in polo shirts talked about how 'quaint' the Bromo-Seltzer Tower looked against the open B-A skyline and how D.C. had nothing 'like that.' It was the kind of boneheaded conversation you heard from transient Washingtonians every time they went to Camden Yards, as if one old building set against a rather ordinary backdrop had any significance at all. Not that I had anything against this city – Baltimore was a fine town, with top-notch food and bars and good people. But Baltimore wasn't mine.

'Hey,' McGinnes said, pointing to a vendor. 'Let's get a pretzel, man.'

'I'd love to,' I said. 'The trouble is, you gotta put mustard on a pretzel, and I had too much mustard on my half smoke. I feel like it and I don't feel like it, you know what I mean?'

'A couple more beers, then.' McGinnes whistled at a guy coming up the steps with a tray of them.

We drank those, and another round, and then it was the sixth. The Sox were taking off behind their suddenly hot bats and the awesome heat coming from Jack McDowell on the mound. McDowell's goateed photograph was up on the telescreen, and McGinnes gestured to it with his head.

'What's with the goatee action?' McGinnes said, loud and a little drunk. 'McDowell looks like a Chink! Like he ought to be servin' us dinner and shit.'

The Korean looked at McGinnes out of the corner of his eyes and cracked a peanut shell between two thick fingers.

'Johnny, keep it down.'

'What,' McGinnes said, nodding to the deaf kid, 'am I bothering him or somethin'?'

'Listen,' I said, changing the subject. 'I've got something going on tomorrow, an acting job, for you and a buddy, if you're interested.'

'Oh yeah? What's it about?'

After I briefed him, I said, 'How about your boy Donny? Think he can handle it?'

'That guy *is* an actor. Sure, it gets on my nerves, I got to listen to him run his cocksucker all day long. But he's all right. Good salesman, too.'

'Set it up, then,' I said.

McGinnes nodded, then stared sadly at the hot-pretzel man, who was moving our way once again.

'If you want one,' I said, 'just get one.'

'No, that's okay.'

'Then what's the problem?'

McGinnes said, 'I put too much mustard on my half smoke, too.'

McDowell retired the side, three up, three down. We left in the eighth, when the stadium stopped selling booze.

At a liquor store outside the Yards, we stopped for another six, then drank it on the drive back to D.C. McGinnes talked about his girlfriend, Carmelita, and about his 'spot' of TB and how the doctors had treated it with INH, which he had taken every morning for a year. Then McGinnes told a very funny joke about an Indian named Two Dogs Fucking, and about that time we killed our last beer and crossed over into PG County. I dropped him at his car in Beltsville, then drove to my apartment, where I fed the cat and paced around listening to records, too drunk to have the sense to go to bed but not drunk enough to pass out. I called Lyla, but she wasn't in, so I left a message on her machine. I thought of Joe Martinson, rang him up.

'Hello.'

'Hey, Joe – "Where you goin' with that gun in your hand?"'

'Nick!'

'Thought you might be up for some music.'

'I might.'

'Snake Pit?'

'Sounds good.'

'Meet you in there in a half hour or so.'

'Who's playing?'

'What difference does it make, right?'

The Mekons were playing, and the place was jammed. The band had been around forever, but it had still managed to retain its indie status, so the crowd was a mixture of young introductees and veterans like Joe and I. I grabbed two Buds at the door bar and pushed my way back to the right corner of the stage, my usual spot. Joe found me in midset, guitars flailing against the saw of a fiddle, the band just pushing it all the way out, and that's where we stayed until the end of the first show. The Snake Pit can be a drag with its put-on attitude, but on hot summer nights, when the acts are really cooking and the place is drowned in music and sweat, there's still nothing better in D.C.

Out on F, I stumbled into the alley a few doors down from the club to urinate, Martinson filing in behind me, laughing. A lighted office building rose out of the darkness ahead, cutting the symmetry of the brick walls running at my side. I looked into the alley, where rats moved about in the shadows of several green Dumpsters. The picture was odd but strangely beautiful. A smile of relief spread across my face as I stood there, peeing on the stones, and I thought, You know, I really do love this fucking town.

Joe and I got into my Dodge and headed west. Joe found some pot in my glove box and dropped a bud onto the hot end of the lighter from my dash. We took turns snorting the smoke. I pushed a Stereolab tape into the deck and boosted the base, and we tripped on that as we made our way across town, drinking a couple of beers we had smuggled out of the club. I found a place to park on U at 16th – had to piss again. Did it right on the street.

'Hey, ladies,' Joe screamed at some women passing by. 'This here is my friend, Nick Stefanos.'

Black.

I sat at the full bar at Rio Loco's, Joe Martinson on the stool to my right. There was a bottle of beer in front of me, a shot of bourbon next to that, and a cigarette burning in the ashtray. I sampled all three. A floor waitress I knew, on the heavy side, real sweet, with missile tits and a plain-Elaine face, came by and smiled, and we exchanged a few smart sentences. She drifted, and Joe tapped his bottle against mine.

'I think she digs you, man,' Joe said.

'Yeah, sure.'

'I know she does. What's her name?'

'I think it's Lynn,' I said. Or was it Linda?

Joe swigged from his beer. 'One thing about you, Stefanos. I wanna get fucked up, I can hook up with you anytime. I know you're never gonna disappoint me, man. With you, it's like it's still 1980. One thing's for sure, I couldn't run with you all the time.'

'Yep.'

'Okay, so . . .' Martinson leaned in. 'Best tracks, 1990s.'

'Best tracks, huh?' I tried to concentrate against the bar noise and the zydeco jump coming from the juke.

'I'll start,' Martinson said. ' "Get Me" – Dinosaur Jr.'

I hit my cigarette. 'Dinosaur Jr.? Who does he think he is, Frank Marino or somethin'? You smoke too much weed, Joe.'

'Listen to it some time – the kid Mascis can really fuckin' play.'

'Okay,' I said. ' "Summer Babe." Pavement.'

Joe smiled. ' "Chapel Hill." Sonic Youth.'

' "Instrument," ' I said. 'Fugazi.' On that one, Martinson slapped me five.

'Desert island LP, said Joe. 'If you had to pick one, what would it be?'

' "Let it Be," ' I said without hesitation.

'The Beatles?' he said, screwing up his face.

'Fuck the Beatles!' I said. 'I'm talkin' 'bout the Replacements!'

Joe laughed. I reached for my drink. A lot of time passed, or maybe it did not. I looked to my right, and Martinson was gone. A couple of white boys wearing baseball caps were sitting a few stools down. One of them was looking at me and laughing.

Black.

I sat at a deuce under the harsh lights of last call. Lynn or was it Linda? sat in the chair across the table. She raised her shot glass, tapped it against mine, and smiled. I closed my eyes and drank my goddamned whiskey.

Black.

The sound of an engine turning over, streetlights and laughter and double white lines.

Black.

I was standing in an unfamiliar apartment.

'Where are we?' I said.

'My place,' said Lynn or was it Linda? 'Adams Morgan.'

'What about my car?'

'Out on Belmont,' she said with a laugh. 'And by the way, you drove great.'

I stood in a living room, where a long-haired girl and a long-haired guy were sitting on a couch, cleaning pot in the lid of a shoe box. A singer wailed over some very druggy guitar.

'So what are we listenin' to?' I said to the guy.

'Smashin' Pumpkins,' the guy said.

'I want to listen to this kinda shit, I'll dig out some old Sabbath albums. "Masters of Reality" maybe.'

'Yeah?' the guy said. 'Well, you had your day, didn't you? Anyhow, your girlfriend's waitin' for you, ace.' He and the long-haired girl laughed.

I found my girlfriend in the bedroom, lying on a floor mattress, nude above the waist, her hands locked behind her head. The room was lit by candles, and a stick of incense burned by the bed. I climbed out of my shorts clumsily and pulled my T-shirt over my head.

'I didn't bring anything,' I said.

'That's not what I had in mind,' she said, pushing her huge breasts together until there was a tight tunnel formed between them. 'Come here, Nick.'

I straddled her chest and gave her the pearl necklace she was looking for. Our shadows slashed across the wall in the dancing light.

Black.

The room was dark. Through the slots in the curtains, I could see that the sky had not yet begun to turn. I rose and sat naked on the edge of the bed, listened to the steady snore of the woman next to me, waited for my eyes to adjust to the absence of light. I made my way to the bathroom, put my mouth under the faucet, and drank water until I thought I would be sick. I took a shower, scrubbing my genitals and fingers until I was certain that her smell was gone, then dried off and found my clothes lying in a heap by the bed. I dressed in the light of the bathroom and left the room.

Out on the stoop of her apartment building, I looked down the slope of Belmont, saw my car parked at the bottom of the street. My stomach flipped and I took a seat on a step. I leaned my head against a black iron railing and closed my eyes. A woman and a man argued violently in Spanish not very far away.

Black.

I woke up behind the wheel of my car. My keys were in my hand. The windows were rolled up and the heat was hideous, my hair and clothing wet with the smell of alcohol and nicotine. I turned the ignition and drove Northeast into Shepherd Park.

I entered my apartment and looked into my room. Lyla slept in my bed. I fed my cat, took another cold shower, and got under the covers, turning onto my side. Lyla moved herself against me and draped a forearm over my shoulder, brushing her fingers across my chest.

'You okay?' she said drowsily.

'I'm fine.'

'I was worried about you.'

'I'm here now, baby. Relax.'

She drifted off, holding me. I fell to sleep knowing we were done.

14

I slept until noon and woke with a head full of dust and a stomach full of rocks. Lyla had gone, left some chocolate kisses on top of a note in the kitchen. The note said that she'd call me later and that she loved me.

I ate the chocolate out on my stoop, where I drank the day's first cup of coffee and sat with the worn copy of *D.C. This Week* spread open between my feet. My cat rolled on the grass in the high sun. The phone rang inside my apartment. I went back into the living room and picked it up.

'Nick!'

'LaDuke.'

'You sound like you just woke up.'

'I'm just sitting here, going through the classifieds in the newspaper. One of the two we found at Calvin's and Roland's.'

'Anything?'

'Uh-uh. A few ads, escort services specializing in young black males, that kind of thing. They could be solicitations for prostitution, but, I don't know, there's more than a few of them, and to me they look too organized, too legit.'

'Maybe you're looking in the wrong place,' LaDuke said.

'Say what?'

'You're assuming that Calvin and Roland were using the personals to sell themselves, maybe set up prospective johns for some sort of roll. Right?'

'That's what I was looking for, yeah.'

'Well, I've been thinking about it – maybe our boys were the buyers, not the sellers. Maybe they read an ad in there, got themselves hooked up as actors in this porno thing.'

I pushed my coffee cup around on the table. 'You know, Jack, you might not be as dim as you look.'

'If that's some kind of compliment, then I guess I better take it.'

'You pick me up at my place?'

'In an hour,' he said. 'Look presentable, okay?'

'Sure thing, Boy Scout. See you then.'

After several forced sets of push-ups and sit-ups, I took a long, cold shower. I didn't feel much better, but I felt human. LaDuke swung by right on the button, and I went out to meet him with one of the newspaper copies in my hand. I got into the passenger side of the big Ford and dropped the tabloid on the seat between us. LaDuke wore a starched white shirt with a solid black tie. He had shined his thick black oxfords, the only shoes I had ever seen on his feet. I nodded at the newspaper on the seat.

'Good call,' I said. 'I was looking in "Adult Services," when I should have been looking under "Wanted." I found a couple of items in there . . . could be something. One's a photographer looking for healthy young black males to pose nude. The other one's got a local filmmaker looking for young African-American males for his next production.'

'Might be a winner,' LaDuke said.

'We'll check it out later,' I said. 'Let's go.'

LaDuke looked me over. 'You look like hell, you know it?'

'Thanks for the observation.'

'You ought to slow it down a little, Nick.'

'Just turn this piece of shit over,' I said. 'We gotta go pick up Darnell.'

At the Spot, Darnell was finishing his load of lunch dishes, so LaDuke and I had a seat at the bar. Boyle sat alone, a beer and a Jack in front of him, two stools away from Mel, who softly sang along to the Stylistics coming from the deck. I ordered a quick beer from Mai, just to steady my hands. It worked. Mai put an ice water on the bar, and I chased the beer with that. LaDuke got up and went to talk to Anna, who was cleaning her tables in the other room. Boyle looked down the bar in my direction.

'Who's your friend?' he said.

'Guy's name is LaDuke,' I said.

'I knew that,' Boyle said. 'Johnson's been talking to Shareen Lewis. She told him all about him – and you.'

'So why'd you ask?'

'Just wanted to see how deep you'd go in your lies, Nick. You keep playing me, tellin' me you've got nothing on the case. But you and Boy Detective over there are working on some kind of angle, am I right?'

'I said I'd square it with you when I had something concrete.'

'Sure you will.'

'How about you? Johnson get any more evidence that Roland and Calvin were moving drugs?'

'I'm done feeding you information,' Boyle said. 'You're on your own.'

'Okay,' I said. 'Okay.'

Darnell came out of the kitchen, rubbing his hands dry on a rag. I left a few bucks for Mai and got LaDuke's attention. He said good-bye to Anna and tossed Darnell the keys to the Ford. The three of us went out the door.

Darnell parked near the entrance to Goode's White Goods, and soon afterward McGinnes came goose-stepping out into the lot. He got into the back with LaDuke, introduced himself, said hello to Darnell. Darnell, his hands on the wheel, gave McGinnes an amused smile.

'Where's Donny?' I said.

'He'll be along,' McGinnes said, and just as he got the words out, Donny came through the double glass doors. He was wearing some sort of green double-knit slacks and two-inch heeled shoes. It had green shirt and green tie combo to complete the hookup.

'I remember this movie,' Darnell said, 'when I was a kid. Had Sammy Davis, Jr., in it, playing some cavalry guy, like Sammy was supposed to be Gunga Din and shit.'

'*Sergeants Three*,' I said.

'With all this green this cat's wearin',' Darnell said, 'kind of reminds me of Sammy, tryin' to be Robin Hood.'

'Donny's all right,' McGinnes said.

Darnell said, 'Must be one of those Baltimore brothers, with those threads and shit.'

'Here,' McGinnes said, passing a few spansules over the front seat, pressing them into my hand. 'Eat one of these, man. It'll do you right.'

'What is it?'

'Make you go, Jim,' McGinnes said.

'Maybe later.' I stashed the speed in my pocket.

Donny got in the car, next to McGinnes in the backseat. He shook hands with everyone, gave Darnell a different shake than he gave everyone else. Darnell rolled his eyes and put the Ford in gear.

On the way to the Hot Plate, I gave everyone some background and general instructions. I wasn't worried about McGinnes – I knew he would pick up on the rhythms once we got started. LaDuke sat quietly next to the open window while McGinnes and Donny bantered verbally over who would play what roles when the time came.

'Listen,' I said, 'we're all supposed to be equal, managementwise – that's the whole point of this thing. This Bernie guy, he likes to feel like he's being courted by a bunch of execs, get it?'

'I get it,' Donny said. 'But I ain't never run down this kind of game before. Understand what I'm sayin'?'

'Hey, Donny, if you're not comfortable—'

'I'll be all right. It's just that, you know, I don't want anybody thinkin' I'm some kind of *punk*. See what I'm sayin'?'

'We're just businessmen selling this stuff,' I said. 'So relax.'

''Cause I ain't no punk,' Donny said, unable to give it up. 'I ain't never had nothin' back there didn't belong back there. Fact is, I'm so tight, it hurts me to fart.'

'Shit,' Darnell mumbled.

'Now, women?' Donny continued, moving forward and leaning his arms on the front seat. 'I *get* me some women. Had me this girl last night, this freak from Dundalk?'

'Told you he was from Baltimore,' Darnell said.

'Anyway,' Donny said, 'in the beginning, this freak didn't want to come over to my place, on account of I'm on the . . . slight side. Maybe she thought that meant I was light in other ways, too. See what I'm sayin'? But when I unspooled that motherfucker' – and here Donny imitated the sound of a line being cast – 'the freak says, "Goddamn, Donny, where'd a little man like you get so much dick?" '

'Step on it,' LaDuke said, 'will you, Darnell?' Darnell gave the Ford some gas.

The only sign outside the Hot Plate said NEWSPAPERS, MAGAZINES, BOOKS. The address, however, jibed with the one given to me by Gerry Abromowitz, so Darnell parked the car on K. We left him sitting behind the wheel, reading a paperback on the teachings of Islam, and went inside the shop.

The first section of the store featured racks of daily newspapers and magazines, weeklies and monthlies, all of the legitimate variety. The clerk behind the counter did not so much as look up when we entered. We went through another open door, into a considerably livelier and more populated section where the real business was being conducted.

A couple of employees – one skinny, one fat, there never seemed to be middle physical ground in places like these – were ringing up sales and keeping an eye on the display floor. Donny immediately went to a rack containing shrink-wrapped magazines whose covers almost exclusively featured women with extralarge lungs. McGinnes seemed more interested in the business aspect of things, wondering aloud how the 'profit pieces' were merchandised. LaDuke stood with his hands in his pockets, clearly disgusted at the sight of middle-aged men eye-searching the mags that specialized in man-boy action. Most of the activity seemed to be in that area of the store. I waited for one of the clerks to get free, the pock-faced, skinny one, and announced myself. The kid punched an in-house extension, spoke to someone on the other end, pointed to another open door, and told me we could 'go on.' I got everyone together and we went through to the back.

We entered a large warehouse arrangement where three men sat in an office area in front of computers, taking orders over the phone. I guessed that the mail-order end of things was Tobias's biggest number, the on-line factor a big element in the company's growth, a way for pedophiles and other pervs to home-shop and network coast to coast without fear of exposure. Progress.

Bernard Tobias stepped out from a row of shelves. He was short and dumpy, but clean, the kind of man who has a wife and kids and a house in Kemp Mill or Hillandale, complete with ashtrays stolen from Atlantic City hotels and clown prints hung on the bathroom walls. He would have told you that he was providing a service, a form of release for those 'poor slobs' who 'have a problem' with kids, and that maybe, just maybe, it was safer to sell a magazine to a guy who could take it home and jerk off on some boy's photograph, rather than have him out prowling the local video arcade, trying to hand quarters out to someone's son. I hadn't come here to judge him, though, only to get some information: I smiled warmly and shook his hand.

'Ron Roget,' I said.

'Bernie Tobias,' he said, and looked expectantly at the rest of my group.

'My associates,' I said, presenting them with an elaborate swing of my hand. 'Mr Franco, Mr Magid, and Mr Jefferson.'

The names were characters from the film *The Dirty Dozen*. After a pointless argument on the drive over – McGinnes wanted to be Jefferson, but Donny, of course, wouldn't let him – we had agreed on the aliases.

'I've heard of you guys,' Bernie said, scratching his head.

'Of course you have,' Donny said. 'We're large.'

'Follow me,' Bernie said, and we all walked through the warehouse aisles to an open area that looked like a small-timer's idea of a meeting room. We took seats around a shiny oval table, with Tobias in the sole chair with arms. There was a desk near the table. Plaques of some sort hung on cinder block. A wooden shelf over the desk contained a row of trophies.

'Thank you for seeing us,' I said. 'I can see you're very busy.'

'Business is good,' Bernie said, his fingers locked and resting on his ample belly. 'You say you guys are out of Philly?'

'South and Main,' Donny said.

'I'd give you a card,' I said, 'but the truth is, we didn't come prepared for this. We're on a kind of vacation here.'

'A retreat,' McGinnes said.

'Down south,' I said.

'Miami,' LaDuke said, probably just wanting to hear his own voice.

'*South* Miami,' Donny said, as if he had ever been out of the Baltimore-Washington corridor. 'South Beach.'

'We got a boat down there,' McGinnes said.

'A yacht,' said Donny.

'So,' I said, 'we were passing through town, heading south, and I thought I'd look you up, make an introduction.'

Bernie Tobias looked at Donny and McGinnes, back at me. 'What exactly is it that you and your associates do, Mr Roget?'

'Ron,' I said.

'What do you do, Ron?'

'Like I told you on the phone, we cater to the NAMBLA crowd – man-boy discipline, that sort of thing.'

'In what capacity?' Bernie said.

'We're producers,' I said. 'We specialize in the type of product you specialize in, on the distribution end.'

'And how do you know of me?'

'The network,' I said mysteriously, and with a wink.

'But we ain't no punks, now,' Donny said.

'It hurts him to fart,' McGinnes said, giving a quick head jerk toward Donny.

Bernie Tobias looked oddly at Donny, and then the phone rang on his desk. He excused himself, got up to answer it. LaDuke and I simultaneously shot killer looks at Donny and McGinnes. Tobias raised his voice into the phone, hung it up, and returned to his seat.

'I'm sorry,' he said. 'I really don't have much time today. There's a lot going on.'

'We won't keep you,' I said. 'But I just wanted to let you in on what we're doing. As far as production values go, we're doing the highest-quality videos for the broadest customer base of anyone else on this coast.'

'But I'm very satisfied with what I have,' Bernie said. 'I deal with only a couple of suppliers. They're local, so there's never any problem in getting merchandise quickly. And they know just what I want – this discipline thing is really taking off for me right now, I'm telling you. It's legal, too – no penetration shots, no actors who are obviously underage.'

'Not obviously underage,' LaDuke said.

'Well, you have to know how to straddle that line, don't you?'

'Of course,' LaDuke said, struggling to form a smile.

'Your suppliers,' I said, 'they wouldn't be the Brontman Brothers, out of Northwest, would they?' I had seen a sign for Brontman Bakers on a storefront on the way downtown.

'No,' Bernie said, distracted by Donny, who had gotten out of his chair and picked up one of Tobias's trophies off the shelf. 'I don't even know them. Look, Mr—'

'Jefferson,' Donny said.

'Mr Jefferson, please put that down, it's my son's—'

'Mr Tobias,' McGinnes said, warming to it now, 'you sure you're not getting your product from the Brontmans? Because I know – I *know* – that our product has ten times the value—'

'Sir,' Bernie said, 'I'm getting most of my product out of Southeast right now, the Buzzard Point area. Some of my stuff comes out of an apartment house in Silver Spring. I mean, I know where my product's coming from.'

'We wouldn't suggest otherwise,' LaDuke said. 'But aside from the fact that we offer the best value for the money, we also offer a steady supply of product. New titles every two weeks.'

'I've even got you there,' Bernie said. 'My suppliers, they shoot one night a week, deliver me new product each Saturday. I couldn't be happier with the situation I've got.'

'They shoot on what night?' I said, and saw from the exasperated look on Tobias's face that I had pushed it too far.

He breathed out slowly, let his composure creep back in. 'Gentlemen, I know what you're trying to do here. You're trying to pump me for information, gain some kind of competitive advantage so you can come back to me with a program. But that's not the way I do business.' Tobias smiled genially. 'Listen, the next time you're in town, bring some samples of your product. We'll have a look, sit down, work on some pricing. If I like what I see, who knows, maybe we'll make a deal. In the meantime, I've really got to get back to work.'

'Fair enough,' I said, and pushed myself up from my chair. My associates followed suit. I shook Tobias's hand.

'Thanks for your time, Mr Tobias,' I said. 'We'll be in touch.'

'I'm sure you will,' Bernie said. 'You fellows have an unusual style, by the way.'

'We try,' I said. 'Thanks again.'

LaDuke went to shake Tobias's hand. I heard a bone crack, and Tobias jerked his hand back.

'You've got a hell of a grip,' Bernie said with a nervous chuckle. 'That's my golf hand, you know.'

'Sorry,' LaDuke said. 'I'm stronger than I look, I guess.' He smiled, his teeth bared like a dog's. We walked from the room, leaving Tobias staring at his hand.

Darnell drove us back to the lot of Goode's White Goods. Donny and McGinnes got out of the car, and I got out with them. The heat rose off the black asphalt of the lot. I put fire to a smoke.

'How'd I do?' Donny said. He looked shrunken in his clothes, his mouth screwed up to one side.

'You did good,' I said. 'When I get paid on this one, I'll send you and Johnny a little piece of it.'

'At your service.' Donny looked at Darnell through the open window of the Ford and said, 'My brother.' Darnell smiled, and Donny stepped across the parking lot, toward the double glass doors.

McGinnes said, 'Told you he was all right.'

'Thanks, man. Thanks for everything.'

'Hey, you and me . . .' McGinnes shuffled his feet. 'Nothing to it.' He rubbed at the bridge of his nose. 'By the way, No Damn Good's got an opening on the floor. Any interest? You can't keep doing this sideline thing of yours forever.'

'It's not a sideline,' I said. 'It's what I do.'

'Right,' McGinnes said, unconvinced. 'Just thought I'd ask.'

'You wouldn't want me to take the food out of your mouth, would you?'

'Wouldn't want that.'

'Take it easy, Johnny.'

'You too, Jim.' McGinnes grinned. 'Better get my ass back inside. The little bastard's probably in there stealing all my ups.'

He put his hands in his pockets and walked away, whistling through his teeth. I hit my cigarette, dropped it, and ground it under my shoe.

We dropped Darnell back at the Spot, and afterward LaDuke took me back to my place. We sat out front, the Ford idling at the kerb.

'Wish we could have gotten more out of Tobias,' LaDuke said.

'We got everything we could,' I said. 'And anyway, I think we got plenty.'

'Like?'

'Just a feeling. This thing's getting ready to bust.'

'You think?'

'Yeah.' I put my hand on the door latch and lightly tapped his arm. 'You did all right back there, you know it?'

'I'm catching on.'

'I'll call you in the morning,' I said. 'We'll put it in gear.'

'Why not tonight?'

' 'Cause I got to go see somebody right now.'

'On the case?'

'No.'

'What, then?'

'Look, LaDuke, you don't have to worry. I'm not gonna leave you behind. We're partners, right?'

LaDuke smiled, sat a little straighter behind the wheel. I got out of the car, rapped the roof with my knuckles, and walked toward my apartment as he pulled out from the kerb. Some electric guitar and a screaming vocal cut the quiet of the early-evening air. If I hadn't known better, I would have sworn LaDuke had turned his car radio on, and was playing it loud as he drove away.

15

My uncle Costa is not my uncle. He is not my father's brother, or my grandfather's, or a distant cousin, and I'm fairly certain that there is none of his blood running through my veins. But to Greeks, this is a minor detail. Costa is as much a part of my family as any man can be.

Ten years younger than my grandfather, Big Nick Stefanos, Costa came to this country from a village outside Sparta. Though I've not confirmed it, it's been said that Costa killed his sister's groom over a dowry dispute the night after their wedding and then left Greece the following day. He worked for many years as a grille man in my grandfather's coffee shop downtown and lived above it in a small apartment with his wife, Toula. In the forties, my grandfather hit the number in a big way and staked Costa in his own store, a lunch counter on 8th and K.

Children tend to force assimilation in their immigrant parents, and as Costa and Toula were childless, Costa never fully embraced the American culture. But he loved his adopted country as much as any native-born, and he was especially enamored of the opportunities available for men who had the desire to work. Fiercely loyal to my grandfather, he remained friends with him until Big Nick's death. I saw Costa on holidays after that and spoke to him on the phone several times a year. The last time he phoned, it was to tell me that he had cancer and had only a short time to live.

The beer in my hand wouldn't help Costa, but it would make it easier for me to look at him. I sat in my car on Randolph Street, off 13th, in front of Costa's brick row house. When I had taken the last swig, I crushed the can and tossed it over my shoulder behind the seat. I locked my car and took the steps up to his concrete porch, where I rang the bell. The door opened, and a handsome, heavy-hipped woman stood in the frame.

'Nick Stefanos. I'm here to see my uncle.'

'Come on in.'

I entered the small foyer at the base of the stairs. The air was still, as it always was in Costa's house, but added to the stillness now was the distinct stench of human excrement. The nurse closed the door behind me and caught the look on my face.

'He's nearly incontinent,' she said. 'He has been for some time.'

'That smell.'

'I do the best I can.'

I could hear Costa's voice, calling from his bedroom up the stairs. He was speaking in Greek, saying that his stomach was upset, asking for some ginger ale to settle it.

'He wants some soda,' I said.

'I can't understand him,' she said, 'when he's talkin' Greek.'

'I'll get it for him,' I said, and moved around her.

I went to the kitchen, dark except for some gray light bleeding in from the screens of the back porch. Two cats scattered when I walked in, then one returned and rubbed against my shin as I found the ginger ale and poured it into a glass. There were probably a dozen cats around the house, on the porch or in the dining room or down in the basement. Generations of them had lived here and out in the alley; Costa collected them like children.

The nurse sat in a chair in the foyer as I walked out of the kitchen. She fumbled in her pack for a cigarette. I struck a match and gave her a light.

'Thanks.'

'I'll just go on up,' I said.

'There's a metal cup by the bed. He probably needs to urinate. You might want to help him out. He won't wear those panties from the hospital. You know I tried—'

'I'll take care of it.'

I went up the stairs, made an abrupt turn on the narrow landing, and entered his room. Several icons hung on florid, yellowed wallpaper and a candle burned in a red glass holder next to the door. A window-unit air conditioner set on low produced the only sound in the room. Costa was in his bed, underneath the sheets. Even though he was covered, I could see that he had atrophied to the size of a boy.

'Niko,' he said.

'Theo Costa.'

I pulled a chair up next to the bed and had a seat. With my help, he managed to sit up, leaning on one knotty elbow. I put the glass to his lips and tilted it. His Adam's apple bobbed as he closed his eyes and drank.

'Ah,' he said, his head falling back to the pillow, two bulged yellow eyes staring at the ceiling.

'You gotta take a leak now?'

'Okay.'

I found the metal cup on the nightstand, pulled back the covers on the bed. He couldn't have weighed more than a hundred pounds. Pustulated bedsores ringed the sides of his legs and the sagging flesh of his buttocks. Freshly scrubbed patches of brown, the remnants of his own waste, stained the bed. I took his uncircumcised penis in my hand and laid the head of it inside the lip of the cup. Costa relaxed his muscles and filled the cup.

'Goddamn,' he said. 'That's good.'

I put the cup back on the nightstand and pulled the covers over his chest. He left his arms out and took my hand. The American flag tattoo on his painfully thin forearm had faded to little more than a bruise.

'Does it hurt much?' I said.

Costa blinked. 'It hurts pretty good.'

'That nurse taking care of you?'

'She's all right. Now, the one before, the other one?' He made a small sweep of his hand, as if the hand had kicked her ass out the door. 'But this one, she's okay. Has two kids; she's raising them by herself. She's a hard worker. This one, she's okay.' Costa licked his blistered lips.

'You want some more ginger ale?'

'I'd like a real goddamn drink, that's what. But I can't. It hurts, after.'

'I'll get you one if you want.'

'So you can have one, too, eh?'

'What do you mean?'

'You been drinkin' already. I can smell it on you.'

'I had a beer on the way over. Can't get anything by that nose of yours.'

'You got a nose on you, too, goddamn right.'

He laughed, then coughed behind the laugh. I waited for him to settle down.

'You know what?' he said. 'I think I had a pretty good life, Niko.'

'I know you did.'

'I had a good woman, worked hard, stayed here in this house, even after everyone else got scared and moved away. You know, I'm the last white man on this block.'

'I know.'

'I did a few bad things, Niko, but not too many.'

'You talking about your brother-in-law, in Greece?'

'Ah. I don't give a damn nothing about him. No, I mean here, in the old days, with your *papou*, before you were born. We got into some trouble, had a gunfight with some guys. Lou DiGeorgdano and a Greek named Peter Karras, they were with us. I was thinking of it this morning. Trying to think of the bad things I did. Trying to remember.'

'What happened?'

'It doesn't matter. Your *papou*, he stopped that kind of business when you came to him. I stopped, too.' Costa turned his head in my direction. 'You're going to come into some money, Niko, when I go. You know it?'

'What are you talking about?'

'Your *papou* – everything he had, the money from the businesses, what he made from the real estate, everything, it's going to come to you. I've been taking care of it, just like he had it in his will. I swear on his grave, I haven't touched a goddamn penny.'

'I thought it all went to his son in Greece – my father.'

'*You* are your *papou*'s son. He felt it, told me so many times. He always said that the best Greeks were the ones who got on the boats and came to America. It was the lazy ones that stayed behind. He thought his own son was not ready to inherit his money.' Costa grimaced. 'He was waiting for you to grow up a little bit before he gave it to you, that's all.'

'I don't want his money,' I said as a cold wave of shame washed through me.

'Sure you don't,' he said. 'But money makes life easier. Anyway, when the lawyers get through with it, and Uncle Sam, there's not going to be much left, believe me. So take it. It's what he wanted.'

Costa sucked air in sharply and arched his back. I squeezed his hand. He breathed out slowly, then relaxed.

'You better get some rest,' I said.

'I got plenty time to rest,' he said.

'Go to sleep, Theo Costa.'

'Niko?'

'Sir?'

'Enjoy yourself, boy. I can remember the day I stepped off the boat onto Ellis Island. I can still smell it, like I stepped off that boat this morning. It's like I blinked my eyes and now I'm old. It goes, Niko. It goes too goddamn fast.'

He closed his eyes. Slowly, his breathing became more regular. Some time later, his hand relaxed in mine and he fell to sleep. Sitting there, I found myself hoping that he would die, just then. But he wasn't ready. For whatever reason, he held on until the fall.

When the light outside the window turned from gray to black, I left the room and walked back down the stairs. I went to the dining room and found the liquor cabinet, near an ornate wall mirror covered with a blanket. Costa's nurse sat at the dining room table, smoking a cigarette. I took a bottle of five-star Metaxa and couple of glasses and had a seat across from her. I poured her a brandy, then one for me. We drank together without a word, beneath the dim light of a chandelier laced with cobwebs and already shrouded in dust.

When I returned to my apartment, I saw that Lyla had left a message on my machine. I phoned her and she asked if I wanted some company. I told her that it might not be a good idea.

'What, have you got something else happening?'

'No,' I said. 'I'm just a little tired, that's all.'

'Maybe tomorrow night, huh?'

'Tomorrow's looking kind of busy for me.'

'Nick, what's going on?'

'Nothing,' I said, and shifted gears. 'Hey, how'd it go with your editor yesterday?'

'It went all right,' she said, and then there was a fat chunk of silence.

'What happened?'

'It was about that day, after we had lunch. In Chinatown?'

'Sure.'

'Well, I had a few wines that day, if you remember, and then I went back to the office and finished off this story I was working on. Usually, I wait, go back to it, check it for style and all that. But I was on a deadline, so I turned it in right after I finished it.'

'And?'

'It was all fucked up, Nick. Jack gave me an earful about it, and he was right. It was really bad.'

'So what's the mystery? You shouldn't be drinkin' when you're writing copy, you know that.'

'That's some advice,' Lyla said, 'coming from a guy who stumbled in this morning after sunup and couldn't even get out of his own pants.'

'That's me, baby. It doesn't have to be you.'

'Anyway, Jack hit me right between the eyes with it. Said I drink too much, that maybe I've got a problem. What do you think'

'You said yourself, I'm not the one to ask. All's I know, you wanted to be a journalist since you were a kid. I guess you've got to figure out what you want more. I mean, fun's fun, but the days of wine and roses have to come to an end.'

' "The Days of Wine and Roses"?' she said. 'The Dream Syndicate.'

'That's my line,' I said.

Lyla said, 'Yeah, I beat you to it. I knew you were going to say it.'

'It only shows, maybe you been with me too long.'

'I don't think so, Nick.'

'Lyla, I've really got to go.'

'You sure there's nothing wrong?'

'Nothing wrong,' I said. 'Bye.'

I had a couple of beers and went to bed. My sleep was troubled, and I woke before dawn with wide-open eyes. I dressed and drove down to the river, looking for a crazy black man in a brilliant blue coat. Nothing. I watched the sun rise, then drove back to Shepherd Park.

After I made coffee, I phoned Jack LaDuke.

'LaDuke!'

'Nick!'

'Get over here, man. Early start today.'

'Half hour,' he said, and hung up the phone.

I found my Browning Hi-Power, wrapped in cloth in the bottom of my dresser. I cleaned and oiled it, loaded two magazines, and replaced the gun in the drawer. Just as I closed the drawer, LaDuke knocked on my front door.

16

'Nothin'!' LaDuke said as he hung up the phone in my apartment.

We had just called the first prospect from the classified section of *D.C. This Week*. LaDuke had done the talking, and he had put too much into it in my opinion, his idea of some swish actor.

'What'd he say?'

'Guy turned out to be legit. Some professor at Howard, doing a theatrical feature on street violence in D.C., trying to show the "other side," whatever that means. He was looking for young black males to play high school athletes sidetracked by drugs.'

'All right, don't get discouraged; we've got another one here.'

LaDuke put his hand on the phone. 'What's the number?'

'Uh-uh,' I said. 'I'm doin' this one.'

I checked the number in the ad – this was the photographer, in search of healthy young black males – and pulled the phone over my way. My cat jumped up onto my lap as I punched the number into the grid.

'Yes?' said an oldish man with a faintly musical lilt in his voice.

'Hi,' I said. 'I'm calling about an ad I saw in *D.C. This Week*, about some photography you were doing?'

'That's a pretty old ad.'

'I was at a friend's place; he had a back issue lying around. I was browsing through it—'

'And you don't sound like a young black male.'

'I'm not. But I *am* healthy. And I've done some modeling, and a little acting. I was wondering if you were exclusive with this black thing.'

The man didn't answer. Another voice, stronger, asked him a question in the background, and he put his hand over the receiver. Then he came back on the line.

'Listen,' he said. 'We're not doing still photography here, not really. I mean, you got any idea of what I'm looking for?'

'Yes,' I said. 'I think I know what you're doing.'

'How. *How* do you know?'

'Well, I just assumed from the ad—'

'An assumption won't get you in. And like I said, that's an old ad. You have a reference?'

'I'd rather not say.'

'If you know what's going on, then someone referred you. No reference, no audition.' I didn't respond. The man said, 'If you've got no reference, this conversation's over.'

I took a shot. 'Eddie Colorado,' I said, then waited.

'Okay,' the man said. 'You come by tonight, we'll have a look at you.'

'I don't think I can make it tonight.'

'Then forget it, for now. We're shooting tonight, and we only shoot once a week.'

'I'll be there,' I said. 'I'll make it somehow. You're down in Southeast, right?'

'That's right. A warehouse, on the corner of Potomac and Half. The gate looks locked, but it's not. What's your name?'

'Bobby,' I said, picking one blindly. 'What time?'

'No time. We'll be here all night.' The phone clicked dead.

I looked somberly at LaDuke. Then I broke into a smile and slapped his open palm.

'You got something?' he said, standing up abruptly from his chair.

'Yeah. Get your shit, LaDuke. We're going for a ride.'

'Why'd you have the smarts to mention Eddie Colorado?' LaDuke said. We were driving east on M in my Dodge, the morning sun blasting through the windshield. The wind was pushing LaDuke's wavy hair around on top of his square head.

'No other option,' I said. 'He asked for a reference, and that's the only name that fits with Roland and Calvin. It was a lucky call. Apparently, Eddie's referring potential movie stars to this guy, whoever he is. Eddie's been siphoning it off from both ends.'

'Eddie. That mother*fucker*. I'd like to go back there and fuck him up, too.'

'Relax, LaDuke. Guys like Eddie dry up and blow away. We've got to concentrate on Roland now.'

'You think this is it?'

'Too many other things are falling into place. Bernie Tobias talked about the Southeast location and the-one-night-a-week shoot. This guy I just talked to on the phone, he confirmed it.'

'Where we going?'

'Check the place out.'

'We goin' in right now?'

'No. Chances are, even if this is the place, Roland's not there yet. I want to see it, then we're gonna find out who owns the warehouse, see if he's got any information on his tenants.'

I put a cigarette to my lips, hit the lighter. LaDuke, nervous as a cat, nodded at the pack on the dash.

'Give me one of those things,' he said.

'You really want one?'

'Nah,' he said. 'I guess not.'

Past the projects, we cut a right off M and went back into the warehouse district that sits on a flat piece of dusty land between Fort McNair and the Navy Yard. It was midmorning. Trucks worked gravel pits, drivers pulled their rigs up to loading docks, and government types drove their motor-pool sedans back toward Buzzard Point. In the daytime, this area of town was as populated and busy as any other; at night, there was no part of the city more deathly quiet or dark.

'That's it,' LaDuke said, and I parked along a high chain-link fence where Potomac Avenue cut diagonally across Half.

The warehouse was squat, brick, and windowless, as indistinguishable from any of the others I had seen on the way in. A double row of barbed wire was strung around the perimeter, continuing at a sliding gate. One car, a Buick Le Sabre, sat parked inside the gate. Across the street was an almost identical building, similarly fenced and wired, with windows only at two fire escapes set on opposing faces. In front of that one, two white vans were parked, advertising LIGHTING AND EQUIPMENT. Next to this warehouse stood a lot containing a conical structure, some sort of urban silo, and an idling dump truck.

'What do you think?' LaDuke said, pointing his chin toward the warehouse where the Buick sat parked.

'That's it,' I said. 'We know where it is now, and it's not going anywhere. We'll come back tonight.'

'Lot of activity around here.'

'Not at night. Used to be a couple of nightclubs, ten, fifteen years back, that jumped pretty good. But nothing now.' I pushed the trans into drive.

'Where now?' LaDuke said.

'Office of Deeds,' I said. 'We find out who collects the rent.'

The office of the Recorder of Deeds sat around 5th and D, near Judiciary Square, the area of town that contained the city's courts and administrative facilities. The building has a funny old elevator that doesn't quite make it to the top floors; to get to where the records are kept, you have to get off the lift and take the stairs the rest of the way. LaDuke and I did it.

There was one disinterested woman working a long line, but I was lucky to see a bar customer of mine, a real estate attorney by the name of Durkin, sitting in a wooden chair, waiting for his number to be called. He also had a copy of the *Lusk's Directory*, a crisscross land reference guide, in his lap. I borrowed it from him and promised him a free warm Guinness Stout – his drink – the next time he was by the Spot. Durkin tipped the fedora that he wore even indoors and gave me the book. By the time my microfiche had been retrieved from the files, I knew enough with the help of the *Lusk's* to have the name of the landlord who owned the warehouse at Potomac and Half. The name was Richard Samuels.

From there, it wasn't a stretch to get an address and phone. If Samuels was like every minimogul/land baron I've met, he could not have resisted putting his name on his own company. He would have told you the ID made good business sense, but it was as much ego as anything else. And his name *was* on the company – Samuels Properties was listed in the first phone book we hunted down, right outside the District Building; the address matched that printed on the deed. LaDuke flipped me a quarter and I rang him up.

'Samuels Properties,' said the old lady's voice on the other end.

'Metropolitan Police,' I said, 'calling for Richard Samuels.' LaDuke shook his head and rolled his eyes.

'Let me see if he's on the line.' She put me on hold, came back quickly. 'If this is about the fund-raising drive, Mr Samuels has already sent the check—'

'Tell him it's about his property at Potomac and Half.'

'Hold on.' More waiting, then: 'I'll put you through.'

Another voice, deep and rich, came on the line. 'Yes, how may I help you?'

'My name is Nick Stefanos—'

'Officer Stefanos?'

'No.'

'You're not a cop?'

'Private.'

'Well, then, you've misrepresented yourself. I guess we have nothing to talk about.'

'I think we do. You might be interested in some activity going on in your property on Half Street in Southeast. And if you're not interested, maybe Vice—'

'Vice?' His tone lost its edge. 'Listen, Mr Stefanos, I'm certainly not aware of any illegal activities, not on Half Street or on any of my properties. But I am interested, and I'm willing to listen to what you've got to say.'

'My partner and I would like to see you this morning. The conversation would be confidential, of course.'

'That would be fine,' Samuels said. He confirmed the address.

'We'll be right over,' I said, and hung up the phone.

LaDuke scrunched up his face. 'You identified yourself as a cop, Nick. This guy Emmanual—'

'It's *Samuels*.'

'He could turn us in.'

'Come on, LaDuke. We're standing at the door. Let's go see what the man's got to say.'

The office of Samuels Properties was on a street of commercially zoned row houses just north of Washington Circle, in the West End. We parked the Dodge in a lot owned by Blackie Auger, one of D.C.'s most visible Greeks, and walked to the house. Samuels's office was on the second floor, up a curving line of block steps.

We had expected the geriatric receptionist, but it was Samuels himself who answered the door. He looked to be reasonably fit, a thin, silver-haired man at the very end of his middle years, with prosperity – or the illusion of it – apparent in every thread of his clothes. He wore a nonvented Italian-cut suit over a powder blue shirt with a white spread collar, and a maroon tie featuring subtle geometrics, gray parallelograms shaded in blue to pick up the blue off the suit. His face was long, sharply featured, and angular, except for his lips, which were thick and damp and oddly red, reminding me somehow of a thinly sliced strawberry.

'Mr Stefanos?' he said in that fine brandy baritone.

'Yes. My partner, Jack LaDuke.' The two of them shook hands.

'Please, come in.'

We followed him through the reception area, low-lit and deeply carpeted, with stained wood trim framing Williamsburg blue walls. Next was his office, the same cosy deal, but with a bigger desk, walls painted a leafy green, and a window view that gave onto the street. LaDuke and I sat in two armchairs he had arranged in front of his desk. Samuels had a seat in his cushioned broad-backed chair and wrapped his hand around a thick Mont Blanc pen.

'You're all alone,' I said.

'Yes,' he said. 'My receptionist is taking lunch. For one hour each day, I field my own calls.'

'It's just the two of you here?'

'It hasn't always been this way. I had a staff of six at one time, including my own in-house real estate attorney. But that was the eighties. And the eighties are over, Mr Stefanos. The banks went through some tremendous changes near the end of the decade, as you know. When the flow of money stopped, everything stopped – all the growth. But this is a cyclical business that, by definition, adjusts itself. There are signs that the residential is coming back, and the commercial will naturally follow.'

'Of course,' I said, though I didn't have a clue. LaDuke had tented his hands, his elbows on the arms of his chair, and he was tapping both sets of fingers together at the tips.

'So how can I help you?' Samuels said.

'I'm working on a murder investigation,' I said. 'As I mentioned to you on the phone, I've been privately retained. Through a series of interviews – I won't bore you with the details – I've come to believe that there might be some criminal activity going on in your warehouse property at Potomac and Half.'

'You mentioned that it might be related to Vice.'

'For starters. I suspect pornography involving male minors. That kind of business is usually tied to something else.'

Samuels frowned. 'Let me say first that I'm not cognizant of any such activity in any of my properties. If what you're claiming is a reality, however, it disturbs me. It disturbs me a great deal. You can never anticipate this kind of thing, not totally. All my potential tenants are interviewed, but as long as the rent checks arrive in a reasonably timely manner and there are no major physical problems with the property, you lose touch. Often a tenant will sublet without my knowledge and—'

'We'd like to get in,' LaDuke said sharply.

Samuels kept his dignity and his eyes on me. 'I pulled the file after you called, Mr Stefanos.' He fingered the edges of some papers on his desk. 'The tenants on the lease are using the area both as a silk-screen production house for T-shirts and as a storage facility.'

'Would it be possible to get in there and talk to them?'

'Mr Stefanos, in my business, in any business, in fact, control is very important. If I could both own these properties and run my own profit centers out of them – in other words, if I could control every aspect in the chain, all the way down the line – believe me, I'd do it. But unfortunately, I can't. So essentially I'm in a partnership arrangement with my tenants, for better or worse. And I have to honor that partnership. So you can see why I just can't let you in there, willy-nilly, on the basis of some unsubstantiated accusation.'

'But you also wouldn't want the inconvenience, and publicity, of an official police intervention.'

Samuels said, 'And neither would you. You say you're privately retained – if the cops, in effect, solve whatever it is you're working on, wouldn't that essentially make you unemployed?'

'We're talking about boys,' LaDuke said with obvious impatience. 'They're being forced against their will—'

'Hold on a second,' Samuels said, his voice rising. He turned a framed photograph around on his desk so that it faced LaDuke. In the frame was a family picture – the businessman's favorite prop – of Samuels, his wife, and two children, a teenaged boy and girl. Samuels regained his composure. 'You see this? I'm a father, young man. Now, I didn't say I wouldn't help you. I'm only saying that we have to do this properly. Do you understand?'

LaDuke didn't answer. I said, 'What did you have in mind?'

'I'm going to speak to my attorney this afternoon. We'll see how we can work this out. I'm thinking maybe by tomorrow, we'll be able to get you in there, or at least get you some kind of answers. How can I reach you, Mr Stefanos?'

'I'll call *you*, first thing in the morning. And thanks. I appreciate the cooperation.'

We all stood then, as there was nothing else to say. Samuels showed us to the door. Out on 22nd, we walked to the Dodge.

'How'd I do?' LaDuke said.

'You gotta learn when to use the muscle and when not to. Samuels, he's not going to respond to that. He doesn't have to. He's a developer – he probably has a relationship with every member of the city council. He could erase us, man, if we push it too hard.'

'You sayin' I almost blew it?'

'You could use a little seasoning, that's all.'

'You think he's gonna help us?'

'He'll help us,' I said. 'He's a smart man. The way I put it to him, he's got no other choice.'

I drove to my apartment and cut the engine. LaDuke said that he had something to do, and I let him go. I watched his brooding face as he walked to his Ford, then I watched him drive away. Then I went inside and sorted through my mail, my cat figure-eighting my feet. The red light was blinking on my answering machine. I hit the bar.

A voice that I recognized came through the speaker: 'Stefanos, this is Barry. I met you at Calvin Jeter's apartment, at his mom's? I'm the father to his sister's baby . . . Anyway, I was headin' over to Theodore Roosevelt Island this afternoon. Up behind the statue, there's a trail, to the left? Down there to the end, where it comes to a T. You go straight in, on a smaller trail, down to the water, facing Georgetown. That's where I'll be. I just thought, man . . . I just thought you might want to talk. Like I say . . . *I* don't know. That's where I'll be.'

I walked quickly from the apartment, the sound of the machine rewinding at my back.

17

Theodore Roosevelt Island is a nature preserve, eighty-eight acres of swamp, forest, and marsh in the middle of the Potomac River, between Virginia and D.C. I took the GW Parkway to the main lot and parked beside Barry's Z. A couple of immigrant fishermen sat with their rods on the banks of the Little River, and a Rollerblader traversed the lot, but typical of a midweek day in midsummer, the park looked empty.

I took the footbridge over the river, then hit a trail up a grade and into the woods, to the monument terrace. I crossed the square, walking around the seventeen-foot-high bronze statue of a waving Teddy Roosevelt that sat on a high granite base, and walked over another footbridge spanning a dry moat. Then I cut left onto a wide dirt path that wound through a forest of elm, tulip, and oak and took the path down to where it met the swamp trail that perimetered the island. I stayed straight on in, toward the water. Barry was there, wearing a white T-shirt and shorts, sitting on a fallen tree, beneath a maple that had rooted at the eroded bank.

'Hey, Barry.'

'Hey, man.'

I sat on the log, my back against the trunk of the maple. Barry watched me as I shook a cigarette out of my deck and struck a match. I rustled the pack in his direction. He closed his eyes slowly and I put the pack away.

Across the channel, the Georgetown waterfront sprawled out, with K street running below the Whitehurst Freeway. Behind it were buildings of varying size, with the smokestack tower of the Power House rising above the skyline. To the right was the Kennedy Center; to the left, Key Bridge; and on the hill beyond, the halls of Georgetown University. Barry stared at the crew-graffitied bulkhead on the D.C. side, transfixed by it, or maybe not thinking of it at all.

'You come down here a lot?'

'Yeah,' he said. 'This here's my spot. Know what I'm sayin'?'

'Sure.' I thought of my own place, the bridal trail off Oak Hill.

'Use to be, I'd ride my bicycle across town, come down here, when I was in junior high and shit, just look up at Georgetown U. Patrick was playin' then, and Michael Graham. I used to dream about going to Georgetown some day, playin' for Coach Thomson. 'Course, I never even thought you had to get the grades, the scores on the tests. Didn't know that shit was all decided for you, even before the first day of elementary school. Just some kind of accident, where you get born, I guess.' Barry chuckled cynically to himself. 'And you know what, man? I never could play no ball, anyway.'

'What about now?'

'Now? I come down here just to get away. You still see some of the city on this island – the drug deal once in a while, and sometimes those sad-eyed old motherfuckers, walking around the trail, lookin' to make contact with some boy. But mostly, over here, it's clean. It makes me feel good, for a little while, anyway. And jealous, too, at the same time. I look across this river, I see the people on the freeway in their cars, and sometimes a plane goes over my head, takin' off from National – everybody but me, *goin'* somewhere.'

I blew some smoke down toward the water. A breeze came off the river and picked it up. 'You're not doin' so bad, Barry. You've got a steady job, and you're sticking with your family. It means something, man.'

'My job. You know how I feel sometimes, workin' there, with these young drug boys comin' in, parkin' their forty-thousand-dollar shit right outside the door, makin' fun of me, of my uniform?'

'I know it can't be easy.'

'Then I read the *Post*, these white liberals – so-called – talkin' about this brother, wrote this book, talkin' about how he went into some *Mac*Donald's with a gun, stuck up who he called the "Uncle Tom" behind the counter, then went to prison, got reformed and shit, became a newspaper writer himself.'

'I read about it.'

'That man behind the counter, he was no Uncle Tom. He was probably some young brother like me, just tryin' to do a job, maybe pay the bills for his family or have a few dollars in his pocket to take his girl out on Saturday night. And that punk calls *him* an Uncle Tom? And those white boys at the *Post*, print that magazine they got, they be glorifyin' that shit. Makes *him* wanna holler? Man, that shit makes *me* wanna holler!'

'What you're doing,' I said again, 'it means something.'

Barry looked in my eyes. 'You really believe that tired shit, don't you.'

'I do.'

'I know you do. That's why I called you up. You got this one way of lookin' at things, like it's right or it's not, and nothing in between. I guess, in my own way, that's the way I got to look at things, too. I mean, somebody's got to, right?'

I hit my cigarette hard and ground it under my shoe. 'What did you want to tell me, Barry?'

Barry picked up a twig lying at his feet and snapped it in his hands. 'About Calvin.'

'Yeah?'

'He was mulin' powder.'

I felt something twist in my stomach. 'For who?'

'I don't know. But I do know this: The powder's for the white man, and the rock is for the niggas. You know it, too. Even got separate laws for that shit.'

'Muling it where?'

'Into the projects, man, straight to the cookin' house.'

'You got names?'

'Uh-uh,' Barry said. 'You?'

'No. But I found out he was involved in some other things, too. Prostitution, and pornography.'

'That was Roland,' Barry said hatefully. 'That punk.'

'Roland got him into it?'

Barry nodded, spoke quietly against the sound of the current lapping at the bank. 'The man in charge, the man with the drugs – whoever he is – he favored boys. Told Roland that if he and Calvin got into this . . . *movie* shit, they could mule the powder for him, too. Calvin came to me – he wanted the money, man, he wanted to get out of his situation in a big way, like we all do, where we live. He didn't know about that other shit, though. Calvin wasn't no punk. Roland could do it, man, without a thought, 'cause inside he always *was* a bitch. He told Calvin, "Just do it, man – it's only lips." I got no thing against a man who *is* that way – understand what I'm sayin'? Matter of fact, I got this cousin like that, over in Northwest, and the man is cool. But Calvin wasn't about that. I told him, "Don't be lettin' no man suck your dick, not for money or for nothin', not if you don't want to." '

'Calvin went ahead with it, though, didn't he?'

'The last time I saw him, he was scared.'

'When was that?'

'The night he died. He told me they only did this shit once a week, and he had to make his mind up right then, or the mule job, and the money, was out. I told him not to go with Roland that night. He did, though. I got to believe he changed his mind, but too late. I think he tried to get out of the whole thing. And they doomed his ass because of it. They put a gun in his mouth and blew the *fuck* out of that boy.'

I said, 'And you don't know any more than that.'

Barry said, 'No.'

I lit another cigarette and took my time smoking it, staring across the river. When I was done, I got up off the log and stood over Barry.

'I'm going back,' I said.

'You go on,' he said.

'Don't you have to work this afternoon?'

'I got a four o'clock shift.'

I glanced at my watch. 'You better come with me, then.'

'Yeah,' Barry said, smiling weakly. 'Don't want to be late for work.'

I put out my hand and helped him up. We took the trail back into the upland forest and walked across the island under a canopy of trees.

I bought a can of beer at the nearest liquor store and drank it on the way home. In my room, I drew the blinds, undressed, and lay down on my bed. I was sick-hot and tired, and my head was black with bad thoughts. I closed my eyes and tried to make things straight.

I woke up in a sweat, lying naked on top of my sheets. The fading light of dusk lined the spaces in my blinds. I took a shower, made a sandwich and ate it standing up, and changed into jeans and a loose-fitting short-sleeved shirt. I listened to my messages: Lyla and Jack LaDuke had phoned while I was asleep. I left a message with LaDuke's answering service, and ten minutes later he called me back.

'Nick!'

'LaDuke. Where you been?'

'I went looking for Eddie Colorado.'

'And?'

'I found him.'

I had a sip of water and placed the glass down on the table, within the lines of its own ring. 'What'd you do to him, Jack?'

'We talked, that's all. I put an edge on it, though. I don't think Eddie's gonna be hanging around town too much longer.'

'What'd you find out?'

'Roland Lewis is still alive, and still with them. Calvin tried to get out – that's what got him killed. They're filming tonight.'

'I know it. I found out a few things, too. The porno's just a sideshow compared with their drug operation. Calvin and Roland were delivery boys. The cops have been following that angle. I'm not sure if they know anything about the warehouse on Half Street, not yet. We're one step ahead of them there, but it's a short step. They've got informants, and I imagine they're working them pretty good. So we don't have much time.'

'Say it, man.'

'I know we told Samuels we'd wait till tomorrow. But you and me, we've got to go in there . . . tonight. We've got to get Roland away from that place before the cops dig deep and bust that operation, put that kid into a system he'll never get out of. We'll get Roland out, get him back home, straighten his shit out then. You with me?'

'You know it.'

'You got a gun?'

'The one I held on you that night. And more.'

'Bring whatever you got.'

'I'll be right over,' he said.

'We're gonna need a driver,' I said. 'I'll call Darnell.'

LaDuke said, 'Right.'

I phoned Darnell at the Spot. I gave him the Roland Lewis story and described the kind of trouble the kid was in.

'You interested?'

'First I got to get to these dishes, man.'

'We'll pick you up around ten.'

'Bring your boy's Ford,' Darnell said. 'I'll be standin' right out front.'

I went into my room and got my Browning Hi-Power and the two loaded magazines from the bottom of my dresser. McGinnes's benny spansules were on my nightstand, next to my bed; I swept them off the top and dropped them in my pocket. The phone rang. I took the gun and ammunition back out to the living room. I picked up the receiver and heard Lyla's voice.

'Nick.'

'Hey, Lyla.'

'I've been calling you—'

'I know. Listen, Lyla. I've been busy. Matter of fact, I'm heading out the door right now.'

'What's going on with you, Nick?'

'Nothing. I've got to go.'

'You can't talk to me, not for a minute?'

'No.'

'Don't do this to me, Nick. You're going to fuck up something really good.'

'I've got to go.'

'Bye, Nick.'

'Good-bye.'

I hung up the phone, closed my eyes tightly, said something out loud that even I didn't understand. When I opened my eyes, the red of LaDuke's taillights glowed through my screen door as the Ford pulled up along the kerb. The clock on the wall read 9:40. I slapped a magazine into the butt of the nine, safetied the gun, and holstered it behind my back. LaDuke gave his horn a short blast. I killed the living room light and walked out to the street.

18

LaDuke had parked the Ford under a dead streetlight and was standing with his backside against the car. I went to him, reached into my pocket, and pulled two of the three spansules out. I popped one into my mouth, dry-dumped it, and handed him the other.

'What's this?'

'Something to notch you up. It came from McGinnes, so it's got to be good. Eat it.'

'I don't need it. I'm already wired.'

'I don't need it, either. But this'll shoot us all the way through to the other end. Eat it, man.'

The truth was, I did need it. And I wanted LaDuke right there with me. He looked at me curiously but swallowed the spansule.

LaDuke pushed away from the car, went to the trunk, opened it. The light inside the lid beamed across his chest. I walked over and stood next to him and looked inside. An Ithaca twelve-gauge lay on a white blanket, the edge of the blanket folded over the stock. The shotgun had been recently polished and oiled, but I could see it had been well-used; the blueing on the barrel had been rubbed down where the shooter's hand had slid along the action of the pump.

'This ain't no turkey shoot, LaDuke.'

'I know it.'

'Why the Ithaca?'

'Bottom ejection. I don't need shells flyin' up in front of my eyes when I'm tryin' to make a shot.'

'What, you think you got to aim that thing? For Chrissakes, just point it.'

'I got something else if I want to aim.'

'Put everything in the trunk and cover it. We get stopped, we're fucked.'

LaDuke dropped to one knee, pulled his snub-nosed revolver from an ankle holster. In the light, I could read the words KING COBRA etched into the barrel – a .357 Colt. He dropped it on the blanket, next to the shotgun. I drew my Browning, whipped the barrel of it against the trunk light, shattered the light. We stood in darkness.

'What the hell did you do that for?' LaDuke said.

'I'll buy you a new bulb. That light was like wearing a billboard. When we get down to Southeast, it's gonna be stone-dark. We don't need the attention.'

I put the Browning and the extra clip on the blanket, covered the guns, and shut the lid of the trunk.

'You coulda just unscrewed the bulb,' LaDuke said.

'I wanted to break something. Come on.'

We picked up Darnell outside the Spot. He got behind the wheel, and LaDuke slid across the bench to the passenger side. I got out and climbed into the back. Darnell looked at me in the rearview and adjusted the leather kufi that sat snugly on his head.

'Where to?'

'Half Street at Potomac,' I said.

'Back in there by the Navy Yard?'

'Right.' I caught a silvery reflection in my side vision, a flash, or a trail. Fingers danced through my hair and something tickled behind my eyes – the familiar kick-in of the speed. Darnell pulled out from the kerb.

'This Ford's got a little juice,' Darnell said. 'I noticed it the other day.'

'A little,' LaDuke said, tight-jawed now from the drug.

I lit a cigarette and drew on it deeply. 'We're gonna go in like we're knocking the place over. You got that, Jack?'

'Why?'

'I'm thinking we're going to make like we're taking the kid hostage, so they think he's got nothing to do with us. They'll probably come after us. But I want to make sure they leave the kid alone.'

'How're we going to get in?'

'I'm Bobby, remember? The aspiring actor. I called earlier in the day, spoke to the man in charge . . . like that. Assuming I get that far, you step around the corner, show your shotgun to whoever it is we're talking to, let him know what it means. After that, we'll improvise.'

'Improvise?'

'You'll get into it. And . . . LaDuke?'

'What?'

'We get in there, don't call me by my name.'

Darnell pushed the Ford down M, made a right onto Half. Off the thoroughfare, the street darkened almost immediately.

'I'm thirsty,' LaDuke said quickly. 'I need something to drink.'

'We'll have a drink,' I said. 'Let's just get this done now. Then we'll drink.'

'Up around there?' Darnell said.

'That's the place,' I said. 'Drive slow by it, then drive around the block.'

The perimeter was lighted by floods. Three cars, including the Le Sabre, were parked in the surrounding lot. A heavy chain connected the gate to the main fence. As we passed, I could see a padlock dangling open on one end.

Darnell drove slowly around the block and stopped the Ford along the fence of the warehouse across the street, where the white LIGHTING AND EQUIPMENT vans were parked. I took the last spansule from my pocket and broke it open. I leaned over the front seat.

'Make a fist, LaDuke, and turn it.'

He did it, his eyes pinballing in their sockets. I poured half the spansule out on the crook of his hand, then poured the other half, a tiny mound of shiny crystal, on mine. I snorted the powder off my hand and up into my nose, feeling the burn and then the drip back in my throat. LaDuke did the same. His eyes teared up right away.

'Goddamn,' LaDuke said.

'Let's go,' I said.

Darnell gave me one last look, and then we were out of the car. LaDuke popped the trunk, reached inside, pulled back the blanket. He holstered the revolver on his ankle, picked up the shotgun, cradled it, dropped extra shells in his pocket. I found the Browning, switched off the safety, and put one in the chamber. I slid the gun, barrel down, behind the waistband of my jeans, covered it with the tail of my shirt. We crossed the street.

The gate was a slider. I pulled the chain through the links. LaDuke pushed the gate along a couple of feet and the two of us slipped inside.

We moved quickly across the lot, over to the side of the building, where there was a steel door behind a flatbed trailer. Above the door, a floodlight blew a triangle of white light onto a two-step concrete stoop. LaDuke and I flattened ourselves against the brick side of the building, outside the area of the light. LaDuke rested the butt of the Ithaca on his knee.

'I'm all right,' he said, though I hadn't asked him.

'Good,' I said. 'I'm going to go up on that stoop now, ring the bell.'

'I wanna *move*, man.'

'That's good, too. LaDuke?'

'Yeah.'

'This goes off right, you won't have to use that shotgun. Hear?'

'Let's do this thing,' he said.

I stepped up onto the stoop, rang a flat yellow buzzer mounted to the right of the door. I rang it once, then again, and waited. Moths fluttered around my head. My bottom teeth were welded to my top and it felt as if someone were peeling back the top of my head. A lock turned from behind the door and then the door opened.

A wiry white man stood before me, his long brown hair tied back, knife-in-skull tattoos on thin forearms, the veins throbbing on the arms like live blue rope. He had a slight mustache and a billy-goat beard, and almond-shaped, vaguely inbred eyes.

He looked me over and said, 'What?'

'Hi,' I said. 'I'm Bobby.'

And then LaDuke, wild-eyed and chalk white, jumped into the light, a frightening howl emanating from his mouth. I stepped aside and the man stepped back, reaching beneath the tail of his shirt. The almond eyes opened wide and he made a small choking sound; he knew it was too late. LaDuke swung the shotgun like he was aiming for the left-field bleachers. He hit it solid, the stock connecting high on the wiry man's cheek. The man went down on his side, all deadweight hitting the floor, no echo, no movement. When he found his breath, he began to moan.

LaDuke pumped the shotgun, pointed it one inch from the man's face.

'Don't talk unless I tell you to talk,' LaDuke said. The man closed his eyes slowly, then opened them. He stared blankly ahead.

We were in a long hall that had thin metal shelving running along either side. Paints and hardware sat on the shelves. I found a rag and dampened it with turpentine. Then I went to an area where there appeared to be several varieties of rope and cord. I took a spool of the strongest-looking rope and walked back to LaDuke, picking up a cutting tool – a retractable straight-edged razor used by stock boys and artists – along the way.

'What now?' LaDuke said. He was sweating and his knuckles were white on the pump.

'Go ahead and ask the man some questions.' The man's face had swelled quickly; I wondered if LaDuke had caved his cheekbone.

'What's your name?' LaDuke said.

'Sweet,' the man said.

'Okay, Mr Sweet,' LaDuke said, 'this is a robbery. We know about the business you're running here. We'd like all the cash money you have on hand. First we want to talk to your associates. Where are they?'

The man closed his eyes. 'Straight down the hall' – he winced at the movement in his own jaw – 'straight down the hall, then right. To the end, last door on the right. Metal door.'

'How many in the room?'

'Four.'

'How many guns?'

'One.'

I cut a long length of rope, then a shorter one. I tied Sweet's hands to his feet, behind his back. Then I stuffed the rag into his mouth and wrapped the short length of rope around his face. I tied it off behind his head and slipped the razor in the seat pocket of my jeans.

LaDuke sniffed the air. 'What's that, paint thinner?'

'It won't kill him,' I said. 'It'll make him too dizzy to move much, though. Come on.'

LaDuke took the barrel away from the man's face, rested it across his own forearm. I pulled my Browning, picked up the spool of rope, and gave LaDuke's shirt a tug.

We walked quickly down the hall, our steps quiet on the concrete floor. At the end, we made a right and went down a hall no different from the first. I had to jog a few steps to keep pace with LaDuke.

'I could run right through a fucking wall,' he said.

'You're doing fine,' I said. Just as I said it, we reached the last metal door on the right.

We stood there, listening to male voices behind the door; under the voices, the buzz of a caged lightbulb suspended above our heads. I looked at LaDuke and placed the spool of rope at my feet. LaDuke managed a tight smile.

I stood straight, knocked two times on the door.

Footsteps. Then: 'Yes?'

'Sweet,' I said with an edge.

The knob turned. When the door opened a crack, I put my instep to it and screamed. Something popped, and the man behind the door went down. LaDuke and I stepped inside.

'This is a robbery,' LaDuke said.

I made a quick coverage. The man on the floor: heavy, bald, and soft, holding his mouth, blood seeping through his fingers, repeating, 'Oh, oh, oh . . .' A black man, mid-thirties, sat on a worktable set against a cinder-block wall. He watched us with amusement and made no movement at all. Two shirtless actors stood in front of a tripoded camera, in the center of a triangular light arrangement, a spot and a couple of fills. The first actor, who wore a tool belt around his bare waist, could have been the star of any soap, some housewife's idea of a stud, all show muscles, his plump mouth open wide. The second actor, the only one of them with the nerve or the stupidity to scowl, was a young black man, thin and long-featured – Roland Lewis, no question.

LaDuke motioned the barrel of the shotgun at the pretty actor. 'First, you get down, lie flat, facedown. Don't hurt yourself, now.'

'Better do it, Pretty Man,' the black man said.

'This isn't what you think,' Pretty Man said. 'This is just a job. You think I'm some kind of faggot? I have a girlfriend . . .'

The black man laughed. I kept my gun dead on him.

'Get down,' LaDuke said, 'and put your face right on the concrete.' Pretty Man got down.

'You have a gun,' I said to the black man. 'Pull it slow, by the barrel, and slide it to the end of the table.'

'Now what makes you think that I have a gun?' the black man said.

'I talked to your friend Sweet. He talked back.'

'Sweet?' The black man smiled. 'I thought you were Sweet. You said you were Sweet, just before you came in.'

'No,' I said. 'I'm not Sweet.'

'Then where's Sweet?' said the black man.

' We put him to sleep,' said LaDuke.

'He ain't gonna like that, when he wakes up.'

'Pull it,' LaDuke said. He had his shotgun on the black man now, too. I had an eye on Roland, who had not yet spoken but who stared at us hatefully.

'You know,' the black man said to LaDuke, 'you kinda pretty, too. Maybe you and Pretty Man here ought to get together and—'

'You shut your mouth,' said LaDuke.

'Relax,' I said, looking at the black man but speaking to LaDuke.

'You boys are higher than a motherfucker,' the black man said, studying us with a hard glint in his eye. 'You ought to cool out some. Maybe we can talk.'

'Pull it!' LaDuke screamed.

'You're the man,' the black man said, 'for now.' He put one hand up and reached the other behind his back. For a moment, I thought Roland might make a move – he was balling and unballing his fists, and he was leaning forward, like he was in the blocks – but then the black man's hand came around, dangling an automatic by the barrel. He tossed it on the worktable and it slid neatly to the end. I went and picked it up, slipped it behind my back.

'All right now,' LaDuke said. 'The money.'

'You've broken my crown,' the plump man whined, still on the floor, his hand and face smeared with blood. 'You've broken it! Are you satisfied?'

The black man laughed.

Pretty Man raised his head from the floor, tears on his face. He looked at LaDuke.

'Put your head down,' LaDuke said.

'Please don't make me put my head down,' Pretty Man said, his fat lip quivering like a piece of raw liver. 'Please.'

LaDuke pushed the muzzle of the shotgun against Pretty Man's cheek, forced his head to the floor. Pretty Man's back shook as he sobbed, and soon after that, the stench of his voided bowels permeated the room.

'Whew,' the black man said.

'Don't be givin' up no cash money, Coley,' Roland said to the black man.

'Shut up,' LaDuke said.

'Yeah,' Coley said, 'you really ought to shut your mouth, Young-blood. 'Specially when a couple of crazy white boys are holdin' the guns. You ought to just shut the fuck up and shit. Understand what I'm sayin'?'

But Roland did not appear to agree. He went on staring at LaDuke and I as if we were stealing his future. Then Coley got off the table, went to a metal desk that adjoined it, and opened a drawer. He withdrew a cash box, the type used in restaurants and bars, placed it on top of the desk, and opened it.

'It's not all that much,' he said with a flourish and a wave of his hand. 'Take it and go.'

I wrist-jerked the Browning in the direction of the table, and Coley went back to it and took his seat. He was tall and lean, and he moved with an athletic confidence. He would have been handsome, if not for his pitted complexion and his left ear, which had been removed to the drum. I grabbed the money from the cash box – three banded stacks of hundreds and fifties – and stuffed it into my jeans.

I said to LaDuke, 'I'm gonna get the rope.'

The spool was right outside the door. I came back in with it, tied Pretty Man's hands to his feet, tried not to gag at his smell.

'Yeah,' Coley said, 'Pretty Man done shit his drawers. Kinda funny, tough man like him, needin' diapers and shit. See, in the movie we're makin', he's supposed to be some kind of carpenter. Guess you can tell by that tool belt he's wearin'. And Youngblood here, he's like the apprentice, come in for his lesson. The way the story line goes – what we call the *screen treatment* – the carpenter's gonna teach the apprentice a thing or two about showin' up late for his lesson—'

'Oh no,' the plump man said. Blood and saliva pooled on the concrete where it had splashed from his mouth.

'This here's our director,' Coley gestured to the plump man with a contemptuous limp wrist and a flick of his fingers. 'Maybe I ought to let him tell you about tonight's film.'

'My crown,' the plump man said.

'Everybody,' LaDuke said, 'keep your mouths shut.'

I tied the plump man up, then pointed my chin at Coley. 'Put the shotgun on him,' I said.

I told Coley to roll over onto his stomach and lie facedown on the table. He did it without protest, and I bound him in the same manner, but more tightly than the others. I cut the excess with the razor and slipped the razor back in my jeans.

I looked at Roland. 'All right. You, come here. You're next.'

'No,' LaDuke said. 'We're taking him with us.'

'Why?' I said.

'Insurance,' LaDuke said.

'*Fuck* no,' Roland said. 'I ain't goin' nowhere with you mother-fuckers—'

'You're coming with us *now*, Roland!' LaDuke said, and then he looked at Coley, who had rested his cheek on the worktable. 'If you try and follow us, we'll kill him. You understand?'

'I understand everything just fine,' Coley said, a thread of a smile appearing on his face. His eyes moved to mine. 'That gonna do it for you boys?'

'No,' LaDuke said. 'I don't think so.'

LaDuke walked over to the spotlight. He raked the barrel of the shotgun sharply across the bulb. The bulb exploded, glass chiming, showering the plump man's head. LaDuke went to the fills and did the same. The stands fell to the floor, sparking on contact. The color of the light changed in the room.

'That about how you did the one in my trunk?' LaDuke said, his eyes wide and fully amphetamized.

'Something like that,' I said, knowing he wasn't done.

LaDuke said, 'Watch this.'

He turned, and pointed the shotgun at the video camera. Roland hit the floor and Coley closed his eyes.

'Hey,' I said.

LaDuke squeezed the trigger. There was a deafening roar, and then the camera was just gone, disintegrated off its base.

'Oh no,' the plump man moaned, against Pretty Man's steadily rising sob. 'Oh no.'

My ears stopped ringing. I checked the rest of them – no one appeared to have been hit.

LaDuke pumped the Ithaca, smiled crazily, walked through the smoke that hovered in the room. 'All right,' he said. 'All right.'

He picked up a T-shirt that was draped over a chair and dropped it on Roland's bare back. Roland got to his knees shakily and put the T-shirt on. LaDuke grabbed him by the arm, pulled him up. He hustled him toward the door and the two of them left the room. I walked backward, the Browning at my side.

'You made a mistake tonight,' Coley said in a very easy way. 'Now you're fixin' to make the biggest one of your life.'

'That right,' I said, the speed riding in on the blood that was pumping through my head.

'Yeah. You're gonna walk out of here and let us live. When really, what you ought to do– if you really think about it – is kill us all.' His eyes were dead as stone. 'I mean, that's what *I* would do.'

'I'm not you,' I said.

I backed away and left him there, moved into the hall. LaDuke and Roland had already turned the corner. I followed them, caught them at the end of the next hall, near the outside door. Sweet was lying there, unconscious and bound, his face ballooned out and black. We stepped around him and walked out to the lot.

LaDuke pushed Roland toward the gate. Darnell kept the headlights off and pulled the Ford along the fence. We slipped out, then put Roland in the backseat. I gave LaDuke my Browning and the extra clip, along with Coley's automatic. He dumped them and his own hardware into the dark trunk. He went around and got into the front seat and I climbed into the back with Roland. Roland looked at the back of Darnell's head, then at me.

'I don't wanna die,' Roland said, looking suddenly like the teenaged kid he was.

'Boy?' Darnell said. 'These two just saved your dumb life.'

I reached over the front seat and found a cigarette in the visor. LaDuke grinned and clapped my arm. I sat back, struck a match, and took in a lungful of smoke. Darnell pulled out into the street and headed north. He switched on the lights and gave the Ford some gas.

'Where we goin'?' Roland said, the toughness back in his voice.

'We're takin' you home,' I said.

None of us said anything for some time after that.

Darnell got us out of the warehouse district and kept the Ford in the area of the Hill, driving down the business strip on Pennsylvania and then into the surrounding neighborhoods. It was near midnight, and most of the shops were closed, but people still moved in and out of the doorways of bars, and on the residential streets the atmosphere was thick and still.

'Pull over,' LaDuke said, pointing to a pay phone standing free in the lot of a service station. Darnell drove the Ford into the lot.

'What we gonna do now?' Roland said.

'Call your mom,' said LaDuke.

'Shit,' Roland said.

LaDuke left the car and made the call, gesturing broadly with his hands, smiling at the end of the conversation. He returned and settled back in the front seat.

'Let's go,' LaDuke said to Darnell. 'His mother's place is in Northeast, off Division.'

'I ain't goin' home,' Roland said. 'Anyway, we got some business to discuss.'

'What kind of business?' I said.

'That money you took, it must have been ten, maybe more. I can turn that ten into twenty.'

'Forget about the money.'

'I only want what's mine. I worked for it. On the real side, man, that shit is mine.'

'Forget about it,' I said.

LaDuke pointed to the shifter on the steering column. 'Put it in gear,' he said.

'I told you,' Roland said, 'I ain't goin' nowhere.'

I shifted in my seat, turned to Roland. 'Maybe you'd like just to sit here and talk.'

'About what?'

'We could start with what happened to Calvin.'

Roland licked his lips and exhaled slowly. 'Man, *I* don't know. Calvin just left – see what I'm sayin'? He didn't want to come along. The next thing I knew, I was readin' about that shit my own self, in the papers.'

'You must have been real broken up about it,' I said. 'You didn't even go to his funeral.'

'Look, Calvin was my boy. But I had my *own* thing to take care of.'

'Get going,' LaDuke said to Darnell.

Roland said, 'I ain't goin' nowhere, not till we settle up on my cash money.'

Darnell's eyes met mine in the rearview. 'You thirsty, man? You look kinda thirsty.'

'Yes,' I said. 'I'm thirsty.'

'Why don't I just drop you off, maybe the two of you could have a beer. I'll swing back, pick you up.'

'What're you going to do in the meantime?'

'Me and Roland here,' Darnell said, 'we're gonna drive around some. Have ourselves a little talk.'

Darnell put us out on Pennsylvania. LaDuke and I went into the Tune Inn, noisy and packed, even at that hour, with Hill interns and neighborhood regulars. We ordered a couple of drafts from one of their antique bartenders and drank the beers standing up, our backs against a paneled wall. LaDuke and I didn't say a word to each other or anyone else the entire time. At one point, he began to laugh, and I joined him, then that ended as abruptly as it had begun. I was killing my second beer when the Ford pulled up on the street outside the bar window.

We drove across town and over the river, deep into Northeast. Roland sat staring out the window, the streetlights playing on his resigned face, his features very much like his mother's in repose. I didn't ask him any more questions; I was done with him for now.

We pulled up in front of the Lewis home, Darnell letting the engine run on the street. On the high ground, where the house sat atop its steep grade, I saw Shareen in silhouette, sitting in the rocker sofa on her lighted porch. She got up and walked to the edge of the steps. Roland stepped out of the car, moving away from us without a word of thanks. We watched him take the steps, slowly at first, then more quickly as he neared his home. As he reached his mother, she embraced him tightly, and even over the idle of the Ford, I could hear her crying, talking to her son. Roland did not hug her back, but it was more than good enough.

'Let's get out of here,' I said.

'Sure,' Darnell said.

LaDuke did not comment. He smiled and rubbed the top of his head.

We dropped Darnell at his efficiency near Cardoza High, in the Shaw area of Northwest. I thanked him and peeled off a couple of hundreds from the stack. He protested mildly, but I pressed it into his hand. He shrugged, pocketed the cash, and walked across the street.

'I could use a drink,' I said.

'Yeah,' LaDuke said, surprising me. 'I could use one, too.'

19

Steve Maroulis shouted '*Ella*, Niko!' as LaDuke and I entered his bar.

Maroulis was the tender at May's, below Tenleytown on Wisconsin, a liquorized pizza parlor and hangout for many of the town's midlevel bookies. Though quantities of cocaine had moved through the place for a brief time in the eighties, gambling remained the main order of business here, a place where men in cheap sport jackets could talk with equal enthusiasm about Sinatra's latest tour or the over/under on the game of the night. LaDuke and I had a couple of seats at the bar.

Maroulis lumbered our way, put a smile on the melon that was his face. 'Way past last call, Nick. Drinks got to be off the tables in a few minutes.'

'Put four Buds on the bar, will you, Steve? We'll leave when you say.'

'Right.'

He served them up. I grabbed mine by the neck and tapped LaDuke's bottle, then both of us drank. Tony Bennett moved into Sam and Dave on the house system, a typical May's mix of fifties pop and sixties frat. I shook a cigarette out of my pack, struck a match, and put the flame to the tobacco.

'How'd you think it went tonight?' LaDuke said.

'We got Roland out of there.'

'You didn't push it too hard with him.'

'I'll talk to him again.'

LaDuke motioned to my pack of smokes. 'Give me one of those things.'

'You really want one?'

'I guess not. No.'

I dragged on mine, flicked ash off into the tray.

LaDuke said, 'Those guys at the warehouse – Sweet and Coley. You think they had anything to do with Calvin's death?'

'I'm not sure yet. But I'd bet it.'

'Why didn't you press Coley?'

'Calvin's dead. Getting' another kid killed isn't going to even anything up. The object was to get Roland the fuck out of there. We did that. It's only over for tonight. That doesn't mean it's done.'

'Why you figure it was Sweet and Coley?'

'It was a black man and a white man killed Calvin.'

'How do you know that?'

I hit my cigarette, watched myself do it in the barroom mirror. 'Because I was there.'

LaDuke whistled through his teeth. 'That's not what you told me.'

'I know what I told you. I wasn't hired by Calvin's mother. I stumbled right up on that murder, man. I got drunk, real drunk that night, and I ended up down by the river, flat on my back and layin' in garbage. I heard the voices of a black man and a white man; they were dragging someone to the waterline. I heard them kill him, man, but I couldn't even raise my head. I was just fucked up, all the way fucked up, understand?' I rubbed at my eyes, then killed the first bottle of beer. I pushed that one away with the back of my hand. 'That's the way this thing started – with me on a drunk.'

I picked up the fresh beer, drank some of it off. LaDuke looked at the bottle in my hand.

'You better be careful with that stuff,' he said. 'You fall in love with it too much, there's no room for anyone else.'

'I know it,' I said, closing my eyes as I thought of Lyla.

'How is she, anyway?' LaDuke said.

'Who?'

'You know who. You haven't mentioned her much these last few days.'

'It's over,' I said, hearing the words out loud for the first time. 'I've just got to work out the details. I'm doing it for her, man. She's going nowhere fast, hanging out with me.'

'Self-pity, Nick. Another curse of the drinking man.'

'Thanks for the tip, Boy Scout.'

'I'm only talking about it because I know. My mother left us when I was a kid. She liked the bottle better than she liked raising a family.'

'Your father raised you?'

'Me and my brother, yeah.'

'Where you from, anyway?'

'Frederick County, not far over the Montgomery line. Place about forty minutes outside of D.C.'

'Your father still alive?'

'Yeah,' LaDuke said, and a shadow seemed to cross his face.

'What's he do?'

'Country veterinarian. Horse doctor, mostly.' LaDuke swigged at his beer, put it back on the bar. 'What are you, writin' my life story?'

I shook my head. 'It would take way too long. You're a work in progress, LaDuke.' I got off my bar stool, grabbed my beer. 'Be right back. I gotta make a call.'

I went back to the pay phone outside the rest rooms. A couple of kitchen guys were working a video game nearby, and someone was puking behind the men's room door. I sunk a quarter in the slot, dialed Boyle's number at the station, and left a taped message directing his Vice boys to the warehouse on Potomac and Half.

LaDuke was finishing his beer when I returned to the bar. Maroulis had brought the white lights up, and he had put on 'Mustang Sally,' the traditional 'clear out' song for May's. Most of the regulars had beat it. I ordered a six to go, and Steve arranged them in a cardboard carrier. I left thirty on eighteen, and LaDuke and I headed out the door.

We drove southeast, all four windows down and the radio off. The streets were empty, the air damp and nearly cool. I lit a cigarette, dangled the hand that held it out the window, drank off some of my beer. The speed had given me wide eyes and a big, bottomless thirst; I could have gone all night.

I had LaDuke stop at an after-hours club downtown, but even that had closed down. We sat on the steps of it, drank a round. Then we got back into the Ford and headed over to the Spot. LaDuke urinated in the alley two doors down while I negotiated the lock and got past the alarm. He joined me inside and I locked the door behind him. The neon Schlitz logo burned solo and blue. I notched up the rheostat, the conicals throwing dim columns of light onto the bar. My watch read half past three.

LaDuke had a seat at the bar and I went behind it. I iced a half dozen bottles of beer and put two on the mahogany, along with the bottle of Grand-Dad from the second row of call. I placed a couple of shot glasses next to that, an ashtray, and my deck of smokes.

'You with me?' I said, my hand around the bottle of bourbon.

'Maybe one,' said LaDuke.

I poured a couple, lifted my first whiskey of the night. It was hot to the taste and bit going down. My buzz went to velvet, as it always did with the first sip. I moved down to the deck and put on some Specials. Then I came back and LaDuke and I had our drinks. We chased them with beer and listened to the tape for its duration without saying much of consequence. I stayed in the ska groove and dropped a Fishbone mix into the deck. Walking back, I noticed that my watch read 4:15. I poured

LaDuke another shot, then one for me. LaDuke sipped at it, followed it with beer.

I took the stickup money from my pockets, dumped it all on the bar. LaDuke didn't comment, and neither did I. I lit a cigarette, gave it a hard drag, looked at the long night melting into LaDuke's face.

'You're hangin' pretty good for a rookie,' I said.

'I'm no rookie,' LaDuke said. 'I just haven't done anything like this for a while, that's all.'

'You gave it all up, huh?'

'Something like that. The funny thing is, after all that time off it, I don't even feel that fucked up. I could drink whatever you put on this bar tonight, I swear to God. And I could keep drinking it.'

'The speed,' I said. 'You'll feel it in the morning, though, boy. You can believe that shit.'

'I guess that's what got me going back there, too.'

'You blew the fuck out of that camera, LaDuke. I could have done without that.'

'I wanted to break something.'

'I know.'

'Anyway, it's not like I don't know how to handle this stuff. You rib me all the time, Stevonus, "Boy Scout" this and "Boy Scout" that. Shit, I was like any teenager growing up when I did – I tried everything, man. The difference between you and me is, I grew out of it, that's all.'

'So when'd you stop?'

LaDuke said, 'Why my brother got killed.' He pointed his chin at the pack of smokes on the bar. 'Give me one of those, will ya?'

'Sure.'

I rustled the deck, shook one out. LaDuke took it and I gave him a light. He dragged on it, held the smoke in, kept it there without a cough. He knew how to do that, too.

I put one foot up on the ice chest, leaned forward. 'What happened?'

'My brother and I, we were both up at Frostburg State. I was in my senior year and he was a sophomore. It was Halloween night; there were a lot of parties goin' on and shit, everybody dressed up in costume. I was at this one party; all of us had eaten mushrooms, and the psilocybin was really kicking in. Just about then, a couple of cops came to the door, and of course everybody there thought they had come to bust the shit up. But they had come to get *me*, man. To tell me that my brother had been killed. He had been at this grain party, up over the Pennsylvania line. Driving back, he lost it on a curve, hit a fuckin' tree. Broke his neck.'

I hit my cigarette, looked away. The tape had stopped a few minutes earlier. I wished it hadn't stopped.

'So anyway,' LaDuke said, 'they took me to identify the body. So I was in the waiting room, and there was this big mirror on one wall. And I looked in the mirror, and there I was: I had dressed up like some kind of bum that night, for the party, like. I had bought all this stupid-lookin' shit down at the Salvation Army store, man. None of it matched, and goddamn if I didn't look like some kind of failed clown. I looked at myself, thinkin' about my brother lying on a slab in the other room, and all I could do was laugh. And trippin' like I was, I couldn't stop laughing. Eventually, they came and put me in another room. This room had quilted blankets on the walls – the kind moving guys use to cover furniture – and a table with a pack of Marlboro Lights in the middle of it, next to an ashtray. And no mirrors. So that was the night, you know? The night I decided, It's time to stop being some kind of clown.'

I stabbed my cigarette out in the ashtray, lit another right behind it.

'That's rough, Jack,' I said, because I could think of nothing else to say.

'Sure,' he said. 'It was rough.' He rubbed at the tight curls on top of his head, looking down all the while. I drew two beers from the ice, put them on the bar.

'How'd your father handle it?' I said.

'My father,' LaDuke muttered, savagely twisting the cap off the neck of the bottle.

I watched him tilt his head back and drink.

'What's wrong with you, man?' I said.

LaDuke tried to focus his eyes on mine. I could see how drunk he was then, and I knew that he was going to tell it.

'My father was sick,' LaDuke said. '*Is* sick, I guess. I haven't seen him for a long time. Not since my brother's funeral.'

'Sick with what?'

'His problem.'

'Which is?'

LaDuke breathed out slowly. 'He likes little boys.'

'Shit, Jack.'

'Yeah.'

'You tellin' me you were abused?'

LaDuke drank some more beer, put the bottle softly on the bar. 'I was young . . . but yeah. When I finally figured it out – when I figured out that what he was doing, when he was coming into my room at night, handling me that way – when I figured out that it was wrong, I asked him about it. Not a confrontation, just a question. And it stopped. We never even talked about it again. I spent the rest of my childhood, and then my teenage years, making sure the old man stayed away from my little brother. When my brother died, man, my life was finished there. I got through college and then I booked.'

'Booked where?'

'I went south. I never liked the cold. Still don't. Lived in Atlanta for a while, Miami after that. I had a degree in criminology, so I picked up work for some of the security agencies. But, you know, you tend just to come back. I've been looking for answers, and I thought I might find out more about myself the closer I got to home.'

'You've talked to your father?'

'No.' LaDuke took in some smoke, crushed the cherry in the ashtray. 'I guess you think I ought to hate him. But the truth is, I only hate what he did. He's still my old man. And he did raise me and my brother, and it couldn't have been easy. So, no, I don't hate him. The thing is now, how do I fix my own self?'

'What do you mean?'

'I don't believe in this victimized-society crap. All these people pointing fingers, never pointing at themselves. So people get abused as kids, then spend the rest of their lives blaming their own deficient personalities on something that happened in their childhoods. It's bullshit, you know it? I mean, everybody's carrying some kind of baggage, right? I know I was scarred, and maybe I was scarred real deep. But knowing that doesn't straighten anything out for me.' LaDuke looked away. 'Sometimes, Nick, I don't even know if I'm good for a woman.'

'Oh, for Chrissakes, Jack.'

'I mean it. I don't know what the fuck I am. What happened to me, I guess it made me doubt my own sexuality. I look at a man, and I don't have any desire there, and I look at a woman, and sometimes, sexually, I don't know if it's a woman I want, either. I'm tellin' you, I don't know *what* I want.'

'Come on.'

'Look here,' LaDuke said. 'Let me tell you just how bad it is with me. I go to the movies, man. I'm sitting there watching the man and the woman makin' love. If it's really hot, you know, I'll find myself getting a bone. And then I start thinking, Am I getting hard because I wish I was him, or am I getting hard because I wish I was her?'

'Are you serious, man?'

'I'm not joking.'

'Because if you're serious, LaDuke, then you are one fucked-up motherfucker.'

'That's what I'm trying to tell you!' he said. 'I am one seriously fucked-up motherfucker.'

Both of us had to laugh a little then, because we needed to, and because we were drunk. LaDuke's eyes clouded over, though, and the laughter didn't last. I didn't know what to do for him, or what to say; there was too much twisting around inside him, twisting slowly and way too tight. I poured him another shot of bourbon, and one for myself, and I shook him out another smoke. We sat there drinking, with our own thoughts arranging themselves inside our heads, and the time passed like that. I looked through the transom above the front door and saw the sky had turned to gray.

'You know, Jack,' I said, 'you were right about everybody having some kind of baggage. I never knew my mother or father; they sent me over from Greece when I was an infant. I got raised by my grandfather. He was a good man – hell, he *was* my father – and then he died, and my marriage fell apart, and I thought I was always gonna be alone. And now I'm fixing to blow the best thing that's ever come my way. But, you know, I've got my work, and I've got this place and the people in it, and I know I can always come here. There's always someplace you can go. There's a whole lotta ways to make a family.'

'So, what, you're sayin' this place is like your home?'

'I guess so, yeah.'

'But it's a shithole, Nick.'

I looked around the bar. 'You know somethin'? It *is* a shithole.' I smiled. 'Thanks for pointing that out to me.'

LaDuke smiled back. 'Yeah, you gave it a good try.'

We had some more to drink, and after awhile his eyes made their way over to the money heaped on the bar. I watched him think things over.

'It's a lot of cash,' I said, 'you know it?'

'Uh-huh. What are we gonna do with it?'

'I don't know. You want it?'

'No.' LaDuke shook his head. 'It's dirty.'

'It's only dirty if you know it's dirty.'

'What's your point?'

'I was thinkin' . . . why not just take this money, put it in an envelope, and mail it off to Calvin's mother. I've been to her place, man, and she sure could use it. There's a couple of babies there—'

'What, just put it in the mail?'

'I've got an envelope around here somewhere.'

LaDuke shrugged. 'All right.'

I found a large manila envelope in Darnell's kitchen. There was a roll of stamps back there, too, in a file cabinet next to Phil Saylor's logbook. I ripped off a line of stamps and took them and the envelope back to the bar. Then I grabbed a D.C. directory that was wedged between the cooler and the wall and put that on the bar, as well. I looked through the Jeter listings while LaDuke stuffed the money into the envelope.

'There's a shitload of Jeters,' I said.

'You know the street?'

'I think so.'

'You think so? We're gonna mail out ten grand on an "I think so"?'

'Here it is,' I said. 'Gimme the envelope.'

I used a black Magic Marker to address it, then applied the stamps and gave it a seal. LaDuke had a look at my handiwork and laughed.

'It looks like a kid did this,' he said. 'Like it's first grade, and you just learned how to write and shit.'

'What, you could do better?'

'Man, I can barely see it.'

'Come on,' I said. 'Let's go.'

I set the alarm, locked the place up. The two of us walked out the door. Dawn had come, the sun was breaking over the buildings, and the bread men and the icemen were out on the streets.

'Shit,' I said, shaking my head as we moved down the sidewalk.

'What?' LaDuke said.

'I was just thinking of you sittin' in a movie theater, not knowing if it's the man or the woman givin' you a hard-on. I mean, it's really hard to believe.'

'I guess I shouldn't have told such a sensitive guy like you. I know you're never gonna let me forget it. But believe it or not, you're the first person I ever unloaded this on. And I gotta tell you, just letting it out, I do feel a little better.'

'You'll get through it, LaDuke.'

'You think so, huh.'

'It'll pass. Everything does.'

I dropped the envelope in the mailbox on the corner. LaDuke slipped, stepping off the kerb. I grabbed him by the elbow and held him up. We crossed the street and headed for the Ford, parked in a patch of clean morning light.

20

I woke up a little after noon. I was spread out on top of the sheets, soaked with sweat, still dressed right down to my shoes. My cat was lying sphinx-style on my chest, kneading her claws through my shirt, her face tight against mine. Starved for food or attention, it didn't matter which. I got up and opened a can of salmon and spooned it into her dish. The smell of the salmon tossed my stomach and I dry-heaved in the kitchen sink. I stripped, climbed into the shower, stood in the cold spray, going in and out of sleep against the tiles. When I stepped out, the phone was ringing, so I went into the living room and picked up the receiver. Boyle was on the line, thanking me for the previous night's tip.

'You get anything?'

'Nothing human,' Boyle said. 'All the warm bodies were long gone by the time Vice secured the warrant. They found a whole bunch of tools, some lighting and equipment, a camera that had been blown to shit. Looked like someone had quite a party in there, from what I understand. I guess they were in a hurry clearing out.'

'I guess.'

'You sound a little tired,' Boyle said.

'It's hot in here, that's all.'

'Heat wave moved in this morning. Say it's gonna be up around a hundred the next few days.'

'I'm working a shift this afternoon, so I'll be out of it.'

'Uh-huh.' Boyle cleared his throat. 'The porno operation in that warehouse – that have anything to do with the Jeter murder?'

'No. I thought it did, but it didn't. I got in there, saw what was going on, and got out. Then I called you.'

'Right,' Boyle said after a meaningful pause. 'Well, I guess that's it. Take it easy, Nick.'

'You, too.'

I hung up the phone, got myself into shorts and a T-shirt, and headed down to the Spot.

Mai was behind the stick when I walked in. She gave me a wave, untied her apron, and walked out the front door. I stepped behind the bar. Happy, Buddy, Bubba, and Mel were all in place, snuggled into their stools, drinking quietly under the buzz of the air conditioner and the Sonny Boy Williamson coming from the deck. Buddy asked for another pitcher, his lip curled in a snarl. I drew it for him, placed the pitcher between him and Bubba. Happy mumbled something in my direction, so I fixed him a manhattan. I placed the drink on a bev nap in front of him, and he burped. The smell of Darnell's lunch special drifted my way. I replaced the blues on the deck with an Impressions compilation, and the intro to 'I've Been Trying' filled the room. Mel closed his eyes and began to sing. Looking through the reach-through to the kitchen, I could see Ramon doing some kind of bull-jive flying sidekick toward Darnell, Darnell stepping away from it with grace, the two of them framed beneath the grease-stained Rudy Ray Moore poster thumbtacked to the wall. I knew I was home.

Anna Wang came in from the dining area, leaned on the service bar, and dumped out her change. She began to count it, arranging it in sticks. I poured a cup of coffee for myself, added some whiskey to the cup, and took it over to Anna. She reached into the pocket of my T and found a cigarette. I gave her a light. She exhaled and shook a bunch of black hair out of her face.

'Welcome back.'

'Thanks.'

She grinned. 'How you feelin', Nick?'

'Better now,' I said, holding up the cup. And I did, too.

'Phil came in first thing this morning. Said there were enough Camels in the ashtray to service the Egyptian army.'

'Yeah, that was me. And LaDuke. Was Phil pissed?'

'Not really. At least you set the alarm this time.'

Anna pushed the stacks of change across the bar. I went to the register, turned the coin into bills, took the bills back and handed them to Anna. She folded her take and stuffed the money in the pocket of her jeans.

She said, 'So how's Jack?'

'He's fine.'

'Tell him I said hey, will you?'

'Sure, Anna, I'll tell him.'

Happy hour was on the slow side, but I had plenty to do, restocking the liquor and arranging the bottles on the call shelf to where they had been before I left. Evening came and my regulars drifted out like pickled ghosts, and then it was just me and Darnell. I locked the front door and drove him back to his place through the warm, sticky night. He didn't mention the warehouse affair, and neither did I.

Back at my place, Lyla had phoned, so I phoned her back. She wanted to come over and talk. I said that it was probably not a good idea, and she asked why. I said it was because I didn't want to see her. She raised her voice and I raised mine back; things just went to hell after that. The conversation ended very badly, and when it was done, I switched off the light and sat at the living room table and rubbed my face. That didn't amount to much, so I went to the bedroom and lay down in the dark and listened to the purr of my cat somewhere off in the apartment. It seemed like a long time before I fell asleep.

Jack LaDuke phoned early the next morning. Roland Lewis had been found dead beneath the John Philip Sousa Bridge: one bullet to the head.

21

The autopsy delayed the funeral, so it wasn't until Monday that Shareen Lewis put her son in the ground. Roland made the Roundup in Saturday's *Post*, with a corresponding death notice in the obits giving out the funeral home's location and burial particulars. There had been a dozen gun kills that weekend, so column-inch space was at a premium, and even for a young black male, Roland's death received very little ink. He had spent his whole life wanting to be large, but in the end his public memorial was two generic sentences buried deep in Metro; he was simply erased.

I retrieved my one suit, a charcoal three-buttoned affair, from out of the cedar closet on Monday and made it over to the service at a Baptist church off East Capitol Street. The attendees were racially mixed – the whites representing fellow employees from Shareen's law firm; the blacks representing family and friends. This was not a gang-death funeral, so there was not the traditional garb worn by crew members to honor their fallen comrade. In fact, there were very few young people in attendance at all. LaDuke, in his black suit and black tie arrangement, stood near the front, at the end of a pew. I watched him from the back of the church, his hands tightly clasped in front of him, as the beautiful voices of the choir resonated in the room.

They buried Roland in a cemetery off Benning Road in Marshall Heights. I brought up the rear of the procession and watched the ceremony from a distance, leaning against my Dodge, smoking a cigarette in the shade of an elm. An unmarked car pulled up behind mine and Boyle stepped out of the passenger side. He came and stood next to me, his face hard and grim.

'Nick,' he said.

'Boyle.'

'Thought you might be here.'

'You were right on the money, then. I always said you were a good cop.'

'Turn around,' Boyle said, 'and look at the car I just got out of.'

I did it, looked through the tinted windshield, saw no one identifiable, just the featureless outline of a suit-and-tie black man behind the wheel.

'That good enough?' I said.

Boyle nodded. 'That's Detective Johnson, assigned to the case. I told you about him. He just wanted to get a good look at you in case he gets proof that you been holding out on us with this one. If that's true, he's gonna want to talk to you again.'

'Fair enough,' I said.

'The ME's report came in. The shooter used a silenced twenty-two on Roland Lewis. Same markings as on the Jeter murder. Same gun. But I guess you knew that.'

I dragged on my cigarette, dropped it under my shoe. 'I don't know anything.'

'You pulled the Lewis kid out of the warehouse on Potomac and Half, I'm pretty certain of that. His prints were all over the place. If you had turned him in to us, he'd be alive right now. He would have talked, too, and we'd probably have this whole thing wrapped up by now.' Boyle put his face close to mine. I could smell the nicotine on his breath and the previous night's alcohol in his sweat. 'You got this kid killed. Think about that, hotshot.'

'Take it easy, Boyle.'

'Yeah,' he said. 'Yeah, sure.'

I listened to his footsteps as he walked away, and to the sound of the door shutting and Johnson putting the car in gear. I stared straight ahead, at the black pool of mourners huddled against the rolling green grounds. Low-slung sheets of flannel-colored clouds were moving in from the northeast. I reached into my jacket for another cigarette and fumbled through my pockets for a light.

The Baptist's version of a wake was held at Shareen Lewis's house off Division, directly following the burial. I dropped by, then stood around uncomfortably and wondered why I had. Shareen attended to the food table, a mix of fried chicken and cold cuts and some sort of dry punch, in a fragile but efficient manner, and Roland's sister helped her, passing me several times without acknowledgment, trays and bowls balanced in her hands. LaDuke stood across the room talking to Blackmon, the bondsman who had turned him on to the case. LaDuke met my eyes only once, giving me an abbreviated nod with his chin, his own eyes drawn and red. I jiggled the change that was in my pocket and smiled when someone smiled at me, and after a while I left the house and walked outside to have a smoke.

I went to the edge of the porch and looked down to the cars, shiny and wet, lined along the kerb below. The rain had come in steady, quiet waves, clicking against the leaves, drumming on the aluminum awning of the porch. The rain brought steam up off the street, and woke the green and living smells of summer. I lit a cigarette, flipped the spent match off the porch, toward the grass.

'You have an extra one of those?' said a woman's voice behind me.

I turned around. The voice belonged to Shareen Lewis. She was sitting on the rocker sofa in front of the bay window.

'Sure,' I said. I went to her and shook out a cigarette, struck a match and gave her a light. She wore a simple black dress, black stockings, and black pumps. An apricot brooch closed the dress at the chest. Her nails were painted apricot, with her lips the color of the nails.

She took some smoke into her chest, kept it there, closed her eyes as she let it out. 'Sit down with me. Please.'

'All right.'

The springs creaked as I took a seat, and the sofa moved back and forth on its track. It settled to a stop, and then there was just the clicking on the leaves and the drumming on the awning. Shareen flicked some ash to the concrete of the porch and I did the same.

'Thank you,' she said.

'It's okay,' I said.

'Thank you for bringing my son back to me.'

'It's okay.'

Shareen put her lips to the cigarette, dragged on it, blew a stream of exhale. The smoke jetted out, then slowed and roiled in the stagnant, heavy air.

'You know,' Shareen said, 'I only had him for that one night. He left the next day.'

I flicked a speck of lint from my trousers.

'Before he left,' she said, 'I made him his favorite lunch: a grilled cheese sandwich on white bread, with tomato right out of my garden, and a little mustard. Mustard on the bottom *and* the top slice of bread. The way he liked it, from when he was a little boy. He'd come in after the playground, come runnin' through that screen door there – don't you know he'd always slam that screen door – and he'd say, "What's for lunch, Mom?" And I'd say, "Grilled cheese, honey." And he'd say, "All right!"' Shareen flipped her hand in an excited, childish gesture, the way her son might have done

I hit my cigarette and looked down at my shoes. One foot was moving metronomically, left to right and back again.

'After he had lunch on Thursday,' Shareen said, 'he said he had to go out, and out he went. He slammed that screen door, too. You know that, Mr Stefanos?'

'Mrs Lewis—'

'Then they called me on Friday and asked me to come down to the morgue. And I went in there to identify him; they pulled back the sheet, and there he was. And for a moment there, you know, I just didn't believe it was him. I mean, intellectually, I knew it was my son. But it just wasn't *him*. You understand? This was just a dead thing lying on a piece of cement. Not my son. Just something dead.'

Shareen took in some more smoke, then dropped the cigarette and crushed it with the toe of her pump. She stared off into her front yard and flattened her hands in her lap.

'When he was first starting out school, he hated it, you know. As many times as I'd call upstairs to him in the morning, try to get him to wake up, he'd never answer. He'd just keep pretending that he was asleep, 'cause he didn't want to go to school. So I had this thing: I'd go into his bedroom and shake him and shake him and shake him. And finally, I'd put my index finger up into his armpit, just touch it, you know. And Roland, ticklish as he was, he'd still have his eyes closed, but he couldn't help but crack a smile. We did that every morning, Mr Stefanos, when he was a boy. That was our routine. It was the only way I could get him up to go to school.'

'Mrs Lewis, maybe we better go on inside.'

'Down in the morgue on Friday, I put my finger there, underneath his arm. Don't you know, that boy didn't even crack a smile!' Shareen grinned, the grin horrible and artificial. 'I could have put my mouth right up to his ear and screamed to God in heaven. It wouldn't have made any difference. And that's when I knew – I *knew* – that the boy in there on that slab, that boy was not my Roland. 'Cause Roland, when I touched him there? My Roland would have smiled.'

'Mrs Lewis,' I said.

Her grin slowly went away. I put my hand on top of hers. The hand was cool and thin, wormed with veins across its back. She looked at me, then through me, her eyes hollow and all the way gone. We sat there and listened to the rain. After a while, she rose abruptly and walked back into her house. I got up off the rocker, crossed the porch, and took the steps down to my car.

I had another evening shift at the Spot, and I worked it without saying much of anything to anyone, not even Anna or Darnell. The regulars made comments on my attire between calling for their drinks, and I let them, and when the bar fell silent for long periods of time, they reminded me to change the music on the deck. I started drinking in the middle of happy hour, one beer after another, buried in the ice chest to the neck. By the time I closed the place down, I had a beer buzz waiting on a shot of liquor to keep it company, so I poured two ounces of call bourbon into a glass.

Darnell shut off the light in the kitchen, stopped to get a good look at me, and walked out the front door. He didn't even bother asking for a lift uptown. I had a couple more rounds and somewhere around eleven I heard a knock on the front door. I turned the lock and LaDuke stepped inside.

'Hey,' I said, clapping him a little too roughly on the shoulder.

'Nick.'

He was still in his suit and tie, jacket on in the heat, the tie's Windsor knot centered and tight.

'Come on in, Jack, have a drink with me.'

'I don't think so,' he said.

'Suit yourself.'

I went back behind the bar. LaDuke stayed where he was, at the top of the two-step landing, leaning against the entranceway's green wall. I had a sip of bourbon and put fire to a smoke,

LaDuke said, 'You're wasting time with that shit. We've got work to do.'

'Maybe tomorrow,' I said. 'Tonight I'm gonna drink.'

'Tonight and the next,' he said, 'and the one after that. You're no good that way.'

'Thanks for the lecture, Boy Scout.'

'We've got to finish what we started.'

'I am finished,' I said. 'I don't want to see any more death. They kill and we kill and it doesn't stop and nobody wins. I'm tellin' you, man, I'm through with it.'

'Well, I'm not through,' he said, his voice cracking. 'Roland's dead because of me. I've got to fix it now.'

'Roland offed himself. He went back to them because of greed, flat out. They killed him, Jack, not you.'

'No, Nick. It was me. That night in the warehouse, I called him by his name. You remember? I said, "You're coming with us, Roland!" The one named Coley, he must have picked up on it. It made it look like Roland was in on the robbery, in on it with us. You understand, Nick? It was *me*.'

'Roland was headed that way all along. You had nothing to do with it, hear?'

LaDuke pushed off from the wall. 'I'm not done. Come along or don't come along – it makes no difference to me.'

'Come on.' I smiled and raised my bottle of beer. 'Come on over here, Jack, and sit down with me. Sit down with me and have a drink.'

He looked me over slowly, his eyes black with contempt.

'The hell with you,' he said.

LaDuke walked from the room. I listened to the door close, then the silence. My shot glass sat empty on the bar. I reached for the bottle and poured myself a drink.

22

Cases break, and major changes get put in motion, in seemingly innocuous ways.

My ex-wife and I met in a bar, on a night when I decided to go out for a late beer at the incessant goading of an acquaintance whose name I don't remember. Similarly, I got my start in the sales business when, as a teenager, I happened to be hitching down Connecticut Avenue and found myself standing in front of the Nutty Nathan's plate-glass window, staring at a HELP WANTED sign. And then there was my friend Dimitri, a Greek boy out of Highlandtown, who got into a car he didn't know was stolen, then died after a high-speed chase at the age of seventeen. I often wonder how my life would have turned out had I not gone out for that beer, or had I been picked up hitchhiking farther north on the avenue that day. And I think about Dimitri, an innocent smile on his face as he climbed into that car, and I think of all the things my friend has missed.

The Jeter case was like that, too. The Jeter case might have ended with me and LaDuke parting company on a hot summer night. It might have ended, but it did not. The very next morning, I took a different route to work than I normally take, and everything got heated up again and boiled over in a big way.

My normal path out of Shepherd Park is 13th Street south, straight into downtown. From Hamilton Street on down, there was some road repair that morning, forcing a merge into one lane. I got into the lane and inched along for a while, but my hangover was scraping away at my patience. So I cut right on Arkansas, with the intention of hitting Rock Creek east of 16th.

I wasn't the only one with that plan, however, and the traffic on Arkansas was as backed up as it had been on 13th. After Buchanan Street, the flow ebbed considerably, and just before Allison, things came to a complete stop. I was idling there, looking around absently and trying to clear my head, when I noticed the brick building of the Beverley ice company on my right. Some employees were walking out of the rear door of the icehouse, on the way to their trucks. The temperature that morning had already climbed to ninety-plus degrees, the sun blazing in a cloudless sky. Sitting in my car, I could feel the sweat soaking into my T-shirt; the men walking out of the icehouse wore winter coats.

I landed on my horn. The guy ahead of me moved up a couple of feet, enough for me to put two wheels on the sidewalk and get the car onto Allison. I punched the gas and got it on up to 14th, parking in front of a corner market. There was a pay phone outside the market, with a directory, miraculously intact, beneath the phone. I opened the book, flipped to the *I*'s. I found plenty of wholesale ice merchants, most of them located in Northeast. There was only one located in Southeast: a place called Polar Boys, northwest of M, not too far from the Anacostia River – not too far from the river and only a short walk from the John Philip Sousa Bridge.

I dropped a quarter in the slot, woke Mai at home, and asked if she could work my shift.

'I'll do it,' she said after the obligatory mild protest. 'But I still want my whole two shifts tomorrow. And you owe me now, Nicky.'

'I'll cover for you, Mai, anytime. Thanks a million, hear?'

She said good-bye. I ran down the sidewalk to my car.

Most detective work consists of watching and waiting. The job requires patience and the ability to deal with boredom, two character traits I do not possess. It's one of the reasons I don't take tail gigs anymore, following errant wives and hard-dick husbands to motel parking lots, waiting for them to walk out the door of room 12 so I can snap their pictures. The tip jar from the Spot not only keeps me solvent, it also allows me the luxury of selectivity.

I was thinking of the waiting game as I sat across the street from Polar Boys off M. I had parked near a store called Garden Liquors, though there appeared to be no garden or greenery of any kind in the general vicinity. The projects were located one block over, and some vampire was doing landmark business out of the store, selling forties and pints and lottery tickets at 11:30 in the morning. I sat behind the wheel of my Dodge, alcohol sweat beaded on my forearms, my ravaged stomach and my own smell making me sick. I could have used a beer myself, and another one after that.

A half hour later, some men began to filter out of the steel door of

Polar Boys, removing their jackets in the sun as they walked across the broiling brown grass, some toward the liquor store, others toward a roach coach parked by the loading dock. Soon another man walked out alone, a bearded man approaching middle age, with a pleasant face framing quiet, serene eyes. He wore khaki pants, thick-soled boots, and a brilliant blue coat. I felt my pulse quicken as I stepped out of my car, then a chemical energy as I crossed the street.

'How's it going?' I said, blocking the man's path on the sidewalk.

'Very well,' he said, 'thank you.' He went to move around me. 'Excuse me, please.'

I stepped in front of him, keeping a friendly smile on my face. 'Kind of hot to be wearin' that coat, isn't it?'

'Hot? Yes, I suppose it is.' He tried again. 'Excuse me.'

I withdrew my wallet from my back pocket, flipped it open. 'My name is Nick Stefanos. I'm a private investigator.' He glanced at my license despite himself.

'Yes?'

'There was a murder down by the river a couple of weeks ago. A young man was shot in the mouth.'

He waited, spoke carefully. 'I read about it in the papers, I think. Yes, I seem to recall it.'

'I'm working on that case. I'm going to be blunt with you, because I don't have much time. I believe you witnessed the murder.'

'You're mistaken,' he said. 'Or misinformed. Now if you'll excuse me, I only have one hour for lunch.'

'I'll just talk to your employer, then. And maybe after that I'll go over to that pay phone, give the police a call. Since this is just a misunderstanding, you won't mind clearing things up with them, right? Upstanding citizen like you—'

'Now wait a minute,' he said, his shoulders relaxing. 'What is it that you want?'

'An hour of your time, an answer or two. And then I'll go away.'

He looked back at the icehouse, then at me. 'You have a car?'

I jerked my chin toward the Dodge. Something came into his eyes, passed just as quickly. The two of us crossed the street. I opened the passenger door, looked at him as he began to climb inside.

'You know?' I said. 'You don't look too crazy to me.'

'Crazy?' he said, glancing up at me as he settled into his seat. 'Why, Mr Stefanos, of course I'm crazy. As crazy as Ahab, or Lady Macbeth or the quiet man who trims your neighbor's lawn. We're all a little bit crazy, in our own way. Don't you agree?'

*

I got back on M and took the 11th Street Bridge over the river, heading toward Anacostia. On the bridge, I caught him glancing over the rail, at the marinas and the clearing and the sunken houseboat below.

'What's your name, anyway?' I said.

'William Cooper.'

I pushed in the dash lighter and put a cigarette to my lips. 'I read a short story collection last year that I really liked. The stories were all set in D.C., written by a local guy. Guy's name was William C. Cooper.'

'William C. Cooper,' he said, 'is me.'

Cooper directed me to a short street off the east side of the bridge. We parked in front of his place, a clapboard row house fronted by a shaky wood porch, and went inside. I sat in a dark, comfortable living room while Cooper went off and built a couple of sandwiches and made a pitcher of iced tea. Books lined the shelves along the wall and were stacked on tables and beneath chairs throughout the room. I stood in the icy cool of the air conditioning and read the titles of the books, and after awhile Cooper, still wearing his coat, reentered the living room with lunch on a tray.

'You ever take that coat off?' I said between bites of a sandwich of sliced chicken on French bread with creole mayonnaise.

'I wear it from the time I leave every morning to the time I return from work.'

'It's cold enough in the icehouse, and it's definitely cold enough in here. But why outside, in this heat?'

Cooper shrugged. 'I've worked in that icehouse for many years and my body has just adjusted. I found that I was getting ill very often in the beginning, taking my coat off outdoors, putting it on again when I went back inside. My body temperature is kept constant this way, I suppose. These days, I rarely get sick. I guess you could say that this old coat has contributed quite nicely to my continued good health.'

'You talk kinda funny, you know it?'

Cooper smiled tolerantly. 'You mean, for a black man, don't you?'

'Partly,' I admitted, 'yeah. But to tell you the truth, I don't know many white folks who talk like you, either. And zero Greeks.'

'It's not the world you travel in, that's all. I'm hardly a blue blood. I was raised in Shaw, but my higher education was extensive, and strictly Ivy League. It's not an affectation, I can assure you of that. It's simply where I spent my adult life.'

'So a guy like you . . . why an icehouse?'

Cooper had a long drink of his tea. 'I wore the white collar and the rep tie and the Harris tweed and found that the life of an academic bored me. The politics, and the people, all of it was utterly bloodless, and ultimately quite damaging to my work. I took the job in the icehouse so that I could once again have the freedom to think. It might appear to the outsider that I'm doing menial labor, but what I'm really doing, all day, is composing – writing, in effect, in my head. And the amount of material I soak up in that place, it's tremendous. Of course, I need the money, as well.'

'What about your morning routine, under the bridge. The boatyard workers, they all pegged you as a headcase.'

Cooper smiled. 'And I did nothing to dispel their suspicions. That was always my time to be alone, and I preferred to keep it that way. I'd wake up in the morning, walk across the bridge, take my book and my cup of coffee, and have a seat under the Sousa. Sometimes I'd read, and oftentimes I'd sing. I'm in the choir at my church, you know, and the acoustics beneath that bridge are outstanding.'

'Were you there the morning that boy was killed?'

'Yes,' Cooper said with a nod. 'And so were you. Your car was parked in the wooded area, to the right of the clearing. I recognized it as soon as you pointed it out to me.'

'I didn't see anything, though. What did *you* see?'

'Not much. I heard a muted gunshot. Then a car drove by me, turned around at the dead end, and drove by once again.'

'You see the driver or the passenger?'

'No.'

'You read the plates?'

'No.'

'What kind of car?'

'One of those off-road vehicles – I don't recall the model or make. A white one.'

'Anything else to identify it?'

Cooper looked in my eyes. 'A business name was printed on the side. "Lighting and Equipment," it said. Does that help you?'

I sat back in my chair. 'Yes.'

We finished our lunch in silence. He picked up the dishes and took them back into the kitchen. When he returned, I got up from the table.

'That do it?'

'One more question,' I said. 'Why didn't you go to the police?'

'I'm no one's hero, Mr Stefanos. And I had no wish to become involved. My anonymity and my solitude are my most prized possessions. I don't expect you to understand. I'm sorry if you don't.'

'I'm the last guy qualified to judge you.'

'Then I guess we're through.'

'Yes. I never met you and you never met me.'

'Agreed,' he said. 'Though don't be surprised if you end up in one of my stories.'

'Make me handsome,' I said. 'Will you?'

Cooper laughed and looked at his watch. 'I'd better get going. Will you drop me back at work?'

'Yeah. I've gotta get to work, too.'

I hit the first pay phone past Polar Boys and called LaDuke. I got his machine, and left a message: 'Jack, it's Nick. It's Tuesday, about one-thirty in the afternoon. I found the witness to the Jeter murder. The shooters drove a white van, said "Lightning and Equipment" on the side – the van came from the lot of the warehouse on Potomac and Half, across the street from the warehouse we knocked over last week. The killers didn't leave town, Jack, they moved across the fucking street. Anyway, I'm headed home. Call me there when you get in; we'll figure out what to do next. Call me, hear?'

But LaDuke didn't call. I waited, did some push-ups, worked my abs, and then took a shower. I dried off and put some Hüsker Du on the platter, then a Nation of Ulysses, and turned the volume way up. When the music stopped, I left a second message for LaDuke and sat around for another hour. Then I got my ten-speed out and rode it a hard eight miles, came back to the apartment, and took another shower. I dropped a frozen dinner in the oven, ate half of it, threw the rest away. I made a cup of coffee and lit a cigarette and smoked the cigarette out on my stoop. By then, it was evening.

I dressed in a black T-shirt and jeans, put an old pair of Docs on my feet, laced them tightly. I went into my bedroom and opened the bottom dresser drawer, looking for my gun. The gun was gone; I had dumped it in the trunk of LaDuke's Ford after the warehouse job. I thought about my homemade sap and a couple of knives I had collected, but I left them alone. I went back out to the living room, looked through the screen door. The night had come fully now, the moths tripping out in the light of the stoop. My cat came from the kitchen and brushed against my shin. I picked up the phone and dialed LaDuke.

'Jack,' I said, speaking to the dead-air whir of his machine, 'I'm going down there, to the warehouse. It's . . .' I looked at my watch, 'It's nine-forty-five. I've got to go down there, man. I've gotta see what's going on.'

I stood there, listening to the quiet of my apartment and the rain-like hiss of the tape. My heart skipped and my hand tightened on the receiver.

'LaDuke!' I shouted. 'Where the fuck *are* you, man?'

23

I started the Dodge and headed downtown. On North Capitol, between Florida and New York avenues, the people of the neighborhood were out, sitting on trash cans and stoops, their movements slow and deliberate. Later, passing through the Hill, the sidewalks were empty, the residents cocooned in their air-conditioned homes. Then in Southeast, by the projects, the people were outdoors again, shouting and laughing, the drumbeat of bass and the sputter of engines and the smell of reefer and tobacco smoke heavy in the air.

I turned onto Half and drove into a darkened landscape of line and shadow, animation fading to architecture. And then it was only me, winding the car around short, unlit streets, past parked trucks and fenced warehouses and silos, to the intersection of Potomac and Half.

I pulled behind a Dumpster and killed the engine. There was the tick of the engine, no other sound. A rat ran from beneath the Dumpster and scurried under the fence of an empty lot. I lit a cigarette, hit it deep. I had a look around.

The knock-over warehouse sat still and abandoned, no cars in the lot, a police tape, wilted and fallen, formed around the concrete stoop.

Across the street, near the steel door of the second warehouse, two LIGHTING AND EQUIPMENT vans and the Buick Le Sabre were parked behind a fence topped with barbed wire.

I looked up at the east face of the building: A fire escape led to a second-story sash window. Behind the window, a pale yellow light glowed faintly from the depths of a hall. I dragged on my cigarette. Ten minutes later, I lit another. Through the second-story window, a shadow passed along the wall. The shadow disintegrated, and then it was just the pale yellow light.

I pitched my cigarette and stepped out of my car. I crossed the street.

Putting my fingers through the fence, I climbed it, then got over the double row of barbs without a stick. I swung to the other side of the fence, got halfway down its face, and dropped to the pavement in a crouch. My palms were damp; I rubbed them dry on the side of my jeans. Staying in the crouch, I moved across the lot to the bricks of the building.

I touched the wall, put myself flat up against it. My heart pumped against the bricks. I could hear it in my chest, and the sound of my breathing, heavy and strained. Sweat burned my eyes and dropped down my back. I blinked the burn out of my eyes. I waited for everything to slow down.

The air moved in back of me as I stepped away from the wall. I started to turn around, stopped when something cool and metallic pressed against the soft spot behind my ear. Then the click of a hammer and the hammer locking down.

'Don't shoot me,' I said.

Coley's voice: 'You came back. *Damn*, you know? I was hoping you would.'

'You don't have to shoot me,' I said.

'You'll live a little longer,' he said, 'if you keep your mouth shut. You'd like to live a little while longer, wouldn't you?'

'Yes.'

Coley pushed the muzzle in on my skin. 'You alone?'

I nodded.

'Walk to the door,' Coley said.

He kept the gun against my head, put his hand on my shoulder, and pushed me along the wall to the steel door at the wall's end. I looked up, saw the window at the top of the fire escape, saw that it was open – the only way out, if I got the chance. Then we were at the end of the wall.

Coley reached over my shoulder and knocked on the door.

'Listen to this,' he said with a chuckle. 'My redneck friend Sweet, he's gotten all jumpy and shit since you and your pretty sidekick fucked up his face.'

Sweet's voice came from behind the door. 'Yeah?'

'It's Coley, man. Lemme in.'

'Prove it,' Sweet said.

'I'll prove it all over your narrow ass. Open this motherfucker *up*. Right now.'

I stood there, staring at the door, unable to raise spit, not wanting the door to open.

'Open it, Sweet,' said Coley. 'I got someone here you been wantin' to see.'

The door opened. Coley pushed between my shoulder blades, and then we were inside. Sweet closed the door, slid a bolt and dropped it, and grinned. He turned the key on the lock and slipped the key in his pocket.

'My, my,' he said. The bruised side of his face had gone to purple and one eye drooped where the socket had caved. He wore a sleeveless T-shirt tucked into jeans. The knife-in-skull tattoo contracted on his tightly muscled, drug-thin forearm as he reached behind his back. He pulled his gun and lightly touched the barrel to my cheek. The gun was a .22.

'My, my,' he said again.

'Let's take him upstairs,' Coley said.

Sweet stroked at the hairs of his billy-goat beard. 'Right.'

I walked between them down a hall that was empty, then into a large room crowded with garden tools and machinery. In the center of the room was an oak table and some chairs, where several men were seated. I could see a scale on the table, amid many bottles of beer, but I didn't linger on the setup, and I didn't look any of the men in the eye. Coley kept walking, and I stayed behind him. Once in a while, Sweet prodded me on the neck with the muzzle of the .22, and when he did it, a couple of the men at the table laughed. One of them made a joke at Sweet's expense, then all of them laughed at once, and Sweet prodded me harder and with more malice.

Coley cut left at an open set of stairs. I followed, relieved to be going out of the large room. We took the stairs, which were wooden and did not turn, up to the second floor, through an open frame, Sweet's footsteps close behind me. Then we turned into another hall with offices of some kind on either side, the offices windowed in corrugated glass. Through one open door, I saw an old printing press, and I noticed that the outside windows had been bricked up. The hallway of corrugated glass ended and the room widened, shelved floor to ceiling, with paints, thinners, glass jars, brushes, and rags on the shelves. Then there was a bathroom, its outside window bricked up, and then an open door, where Coley turned and stepped inside. I followed, noticing before I did the window leading to the fire escape at the end of the hall. Sweet came into the room behind me and shut the door.

'Keep your gun on him,' Sweet said.

'Yes, *sir*,' Coley said, amused.

Sweet went to the door, connected a chain from door to frame, and slid the bolt. Coley held his gun, a .38 Special, loosely in his hand and kept it pointed at my middle. He shifted his attention to Sweet, fixing the chain lock in place. Coley's eyes smiled.

The room had no furniture except for a simple wooden chair turned on its side against a wall. An overflowed foil ashtray sat on the scarred hardwood floor, next to the chair. There had been a window once, but now the window was brick.

'Hold this,' Sweet said. He handed Coley the .22. Coley took the gun, let that one hang by his side. 'Good thing you were outside, Coley.'

'Heard that car of his. Some old muscle car with dual exhaust and shit. Makes one hell of a racket. Not the kind of ride you want to be usin' when you're trying to make a quiet entrance. Not too smart.'

'Yeah,' Sweet said. 'Real stupid.'

Sweet came and stood in front of me, not more than three feet away. He shifted his shoulders, smiled a little, his vaguely Asian eyes disappearing with the smile. Alcohol smell came off him, and he stunk of day-old perspiration.

'You see what your partner did to my face?' he said.

I didn't answer. I tried to think of something I had that they would want, something that would save my life. But I couldn't think of one thing. The realization that they were going to kill me sucked the blood out of my face.

Sweet said, 'Our friend here looks afraid. What you think, Coley? You think he looks afraid?'

'He does look a little pale,' Coley said.

'You afraid?' Sweet said, moving one step in. 'Huh?'

I didn't see the right hand. It was quick, without form or shape, and Sweet put everything into it. He hit me full on the face, and the blow knocked me off my feet. My back hit the wall and my legs gave out. I slid down the wall to the floor.

'Whew,' said Coley.

Sweet walked across the room, bent over, grabbed a handful of my shirt. He pulled me up. The room moved, Sweet's face splitting in two and coming back to one. He hit me in the face with a sharp right. Then he pulled back and hit me again, released his grip on my shirt. I fell to the floor. I swallowed blood, tasted blood in my mouth. Stars exploded in the blackness behind my eyes.

'Fuck!' I heard Sweet say. 'I fucked up my fuckin' hand on his face!'

'Go clean it up,' Coley said.

'The guy's a pussy,' Sweet said. 'Won't even fight me back. I think maybe he likes it. What do you think, Coley? You think he likes it?'

'Go clean up your hand,' said Coley.

'Lock the door behind me,' Sweet said.

'Yeah,' Coley said, chuckling. 'I'll do that.'

Sweet left the room. When the door closed, I opened my eyes and got up on one elbow. Coley did not move to lock the door. I pushed myself over to the wall, sat up with my back against it. I looked at Coley, who stood in the center of the room, looking at me.

'You know,' Coley said, 'we're just gonna have to go on and kill you.'

I wiped blood from my face with a shaky hand. I stared at the floor.

'The reason I'm tellin' you is, I hate to see a man go down without some kind of fight. That little redneck's gonna come back in here, and if you let him, he's gonna bitch-slap your ass all around. I mean, you're dead, anyway. But it's important, and shit, not to go out like some kind of punk. Know what I'm sayin'?'

I flashed on my drunken night by the river, hearing similar words spoken to Calvin Jeter. Spoken, I knew now, by Coley.

'Anyway, you got a little while,' Coley said. 'I'm gonna ask you a few questions first, partly for business and partly just because I'm curious. Whether you answer or not, either way, I'm gonna have to put a bullet in your head tonight. Just thought you might like to know.'

There was a knock on the door.

'It's open,' Coley said.

Sweet walked in, looked with disappointment at the chain swinging free on the frame. 'I thought I told you to lock it.'

'*Damn*,' Coley said mockingly. 'I damn sure forgot.'

Sweet looked at me. 'Get up,' he said.

I stood slowly, gave myself some distance from the wall. I looked at Sweet's right hand: swollen, the knuckles skinned and raw. He walked towards me, the inbred's grin on his cockeyed face. He balled his right fist, but his right was done; I knew he wouldn't use it, knew he would go with the left. He came in. He faked the right and dropped the left.

I moved to the side, bent my knees, and sprang up, swinging with the momentum. I whipped my open hand into his throat, snapping my wrist sharply at the point of contact, aiming for the back of his neck. My straight-open hand connected at his Adam's apple, knocking him one step back. It felt as if a piece of Styrofoam had snapped.

Sweet grabbed at his throat with both hands. I went in, threw one deep right, followed through with it, dead square where his nose met the purple bruise of his face. Something gave with the punch; blood sprayed onto my shirt and Sweet went down. He fell to his side, moved a little, made choking sounds. Then he did not move at all. His hands dropped away from his throat.

'God*damn*,' Coley said. 'You kill 'im?'

'No. You hit the Adam's apple, the muscles around it contract, for protection. Cuts off your breathing for a few seconds. He'll live.'

I heard Coley's slow footsteps as he crossed the room. The footsteps swelled, then stopped.

'What'd you call that?' Coley said, close behind me. 'That thing you did to his throat?'

'Ridge hand,' I said.

'Sweet's gonna want to know,' Coley said, 'when he wakes up.'

I felt a blunt shock to the back of my head and a short, sharp pain. The floor dropped out from beneath my feet, and I was falling, diving toward a pool of cool black water. Then I was in the black water, and there was only the water, and nothing left of me. Nothing left at all.

I woke from a dream of water.

'Some water,' I said, looking at their feet.

Coley's shoes were between the legs of the chair, where he now sat. Sweet's were near my face.

'Get him some water,' Coley said.

'Fuck a lotta water,' Sweet said.

Sweet's shoes moved out of my field of vision. Then his knee dropped onto my back. I grunted as the knee dug into my spine. Sweet took my arm at the wrist and twisted it behind my back. I sucked at the air.

'Where's your partner?' he said, his breath hot on my neck. 'The one with the shotgun.'

'He's gone,' I said, my voice high and unsteady.

'He's gone,' Sweet said, mimicking my tone. He giggled and pushed my hand up toward my shoulders. He held my other hand flat to the hardwood floor. I tried to dig my nails into the wood.

'Where's he gone *to*?' Coley said.

'He split with his share of the money,' I said. 'I don't know where he went.'

Sweet jerked my arm up. I thought my arm would break if he pushed it farther. Then he pushed it farther. It hit a nerve, and the room flashed white. I tightened my jaw, breathed in and out rapidly through my nose.

'Uh,' I said.

'Say what?' Sweet said.

'Where is he?' Coley said.

My eyes teared up. Everything in front of me was slanted and soft.

'I don't know where he is,' I said. 'Coley, I don't know.'

Coley said nothing.

Sweet released my arm. I rested the side of my face on the floor.

Then Sweet grabbed a handful of hair at the back of my head and yanked my head back up. He slammed my face into the floor. Blood spilled out of my nose and onto the wood. My mouth was wet with it; I breathed it in and coughed. I looked at the grain in the wood and the blood spreading over the grain.

'God*damn*, Sweet,' Coley said. 'You're just fuckin' this man all *up*.'

Sweet twisted my hair, yanked my head up out of the blood. My eyes rolled up toward the ceiling. Purple clouds blinked in front of my eyes and I heard the gurgle of my own voice. I felt Sweet push down on the back of my head. I saw the wood rushing toward my face. The wood was black, like black water. I was in the water, and it was blessedly cool.

I opened my eyes.

I stared at the ceiling. It was a drop ceiling tiled in particle-board, with water damage in some of the tiles. Naked fluorescent fixtures hung from the ceiling. The light bore into my eyes.

I rolled onto my side. A Dixie cup full of water sat on the floor. Beyond the cup, a large roach crawled across the floor. It crawled toward Sweet's boots. Past Sweet's boots, Coley's shoes were centered between the legs of the chair.

I got up, leaned on my forearm, and drank the water. I thought I would puke, but I did not. I dropped the cup on the floor and dragged myself over to the wall. I put my back against the wall, sat there. My nose ached badly and there was a ripping pain behind my eyes. I rubbed my hand on my mouth, flaked off the blood that had dried there. Coley was seated in the chair and Sweet stood with his back against the opposite wall. The .22 dangled in Sweet's hand, pointed at the floor. I looked at Coley. Coley moved his chin up an inch.

'Let's kill him,' Sweet said. 'You said to wait till he woke up. Well, he's up.'

'Not yet. I want to get the word first.'

'Fuck the word. Let's kill him now.'

'Not yet,' said Coley.

It went back and forth like that for a while. I started to feel a little better. Time passed, and I felt better still. The hate was doing it. What they had done to me and the thought of it were making me stronger.

I looked around the room: nothing to use as a weapon. Nothing on me but my car keys and a pack of matches. The keys were something; I could palm one, stab a key into Sweet's eye when he came for me. I could hurt him in an awful way before he killed me. Somehow, I would do that. I would try.

'Go downstairs,' Coley said to Sweet. 'Go down and call him. See what he wants to do.'

'Yeah, okay,' Sweet said. 'You lock that door behind me, hear?'

'Sure thing.'

'I mean it,' Sweet said. 'I'm gonna listen outside that door, make sure you do it.' And then to me: 'I'll be back in ten minutes. That's how long you got to live. Ten minutes. You think about that.'

Sweet walked from the room. He shut the door, and Coley got up from his chair and went to the door. He jangled the chain around in the bolt, made sure Sweet heard the jangle from the other side of the door. Then he dropped the chain without locking it, chuckling as he walked back to his chair. He sat in the chair. His eyes moved to the door and then to me.

'Don't get any ideas about that door,' Coley said, ' 'Cause this thirty-eight, at this range? You *know* I won't miss.'

'I'm not going anywhere.'

'Good. That thing with the door, I just like to rattle that little redneck's cage a little bit, that's all.' Coley grinned. 'You fucked him up pretty good, too. 'Course, he did you right back. He manage to break that nose of yours?'

'I don't think so.'

'But it's been broke before.'

'Yeah.'

'I can see. Where you get that scar on your cheek, man?'

'Who cut off your ear?'

Coley showed me some teeth. 'Some brother, in the showers at the Maryland State Pen. Looked at him the wrong way, I guess. All part of my rehabilitation and shit.'

'That where you two are from? Baltimore?'

'Yeah. Roundabout that way. Why?'

'Nothing.' I looked Coley in the eyes. 'You killed Roland, and the Jeter kid, too. Didn't you?'

'Jeter, huh? That's what that boy's name was? Well, I didn't pull the trigger. I take no pleasure in that, though I'll do if it it's called for. Sweet was the triggerman. He likes it, you know. But I guess you could say I killed those boys, yeah.'

'Why?'

'We're runnin' a business here, and we got to protect that. Powder right into the projects, straight up. They turn it to rock and then they kill themselves over that shit. But our end, we keep it clean. Now, my boss, the man who bankrolls all this? He favors boys. Young brothers, that's what he likes. Likes to watch 'em on the videotape. He had this idea, why not get them in here and put 'em on tape, use 'em to run powder on the side. I could have told him that shit wouldn't go. One of them got scared and the other one got greedy. We just had to go on and do 'em both.'

'Who's your boss?' I said.

Coley laughed. 'Aw, go on. What you think this is, *True Confessions* and shit? Uh-uh, man, you're just gonna have to check out not knowing all that. Now let me ask you somethin'.'

'Go ahead.'

'Why'd you knock us over? It wasn't for the money, I know that.'

'I was just trying to save a kid's life. I was only trying to get Roland out of there. He didn't even know who we were.'

'He wasn't with you?'

'No. You killed him for nothing.'

Coley shrugged. 'He would've made me, anyway. Eventually, he would've done somethin' to make me kill 'im. He was that way. Just *difficult* and shit.'

Coley used the barrel of his gun to scratch his forehead. I eased my keys out of my pocket, palmed them, let the tip of the longest one peek through the fingers of my fist.

'But you know,' Coley said, 'that don't explain why you came back tonight.'

'I wasn't finished,' I said. 'I needed to know the rest of it.'

'Now you know,' Coley said. 'Kind of a silly thing to die for, isn't it?'

'Yeah,' I said. 'I guess it is.'

Coley exhaled slowly, looked at me sadly. 'I seen you pull out those keys and shit. Why don't you just slide them over here, man. I'll make sure what gets done to you gets done to you quick.'

I tossed the keys to the center of the floor. Footsteps sounded in the hall, louder with each step. Coley got out of his chair, bent over, and picked up the keys. He slipped them in his pocket.

There was a knock on the door.

Coley smiled. 'Come on in, Sweet. It's open.'

The door opened.

Jack LaDuke stepped into the room, the Ithaca in his hands.

The smile froze on Coley's face. 'Goddamn,' he said. 'God*damn*.'

LaDuke pointed his shotgun at Coley. Coley pointed the .38 at LaDuke.

'LaDuke.' I said.

'Nick.'

LaDuke kicked the door shut behind him, kept his eyes and the shotgun on Coley. LaDuke was wearing his black suit and the solid

613

black tie. I felt a rush of affection for him then; looking at him, I could have laughed out loud.

'Where you been?' I said.

'Office of Deeds, like you taught me.' Without moving anything but his free arm, he reached under the tail of his jacket and drew my Browning. 'This is you.'

He tossed the gun in my direction. I caught it, ejected the magazine, checked it, slapped the magazine back in the butt. I pointed the Browning at Coley. Coley kept the .38 on LaDuke.

'How'd you get in, LaDuke?'

'Fire escape. The window was open—'

'*Damn*,' said Coley.

'And then I just came down the hall. Heard you guys talkin'.'

'Good to see you, LaDuke.'

'You all right? You look pretty fucked up.'

'I'm okay. Now we gotta figure out how to get outta here.'

'Uh-*uh*,' Coley said.

'What's that?' LaDuke said.

'You know I can't let you fellahs do that,' Coley said, still smiling, the smile weird and tight. Bullets of sweat had formed on his forehead and sweat had beaded in his mustache.

LaDuke took one step in. The floorboard creaked beneath his weight. Coley stiffened his gun arm and did not move.

'Let's get out of here, LaDuke.'

'Maybe you *ought* to run, Pretty Boy,' Coley said.

LaDuke's face reddened.

'And maybe,' LaDuke said, 'you ought to make a move.'

'LaDuke,' I said.

His finger tightened on the trigger.

'Know what this thirty-eight'll do to that pretty face?' Coley said.

LaDuke just smiled.

Their eyes locked, and neither of them moved. The sound of our breathing was the only sound in the room.

'Hey, Jack,' I said, very quietly.

Coley squeezed the trigger on the .38 and LaDuke squeezed the trigger on the shotgun – both of them, at once.

24

The room exploded in a sucking roar of sonics and fine red spray. LaDuke's head jerked sharply to the side, as if he had been slapped.

A rag doll slammed against the wall, fell in a heap to the floor, the dead dropping sloppily to the chest. The rag doll wore the clothes of Coley. Everything above the hairline was gone, the face unrecognizable; the face was soup.

'I'm shot, Nick,' LaDuke said almost giddily. 'I'm shot!'

I went to him, pulled him around.

The right side of his jaw was exposed, skinless, with pink rapidly seeping into the pearl of the bone. You're okay, LaDuke, I thought. You turned your head at the last moment and Coley blew off the side of your face. You're going to be badly scarred and a little ugly, but you're going to be okay.

And then I saw the hole in his neck, the exit hole or maybe the entry, rimmed purple and blackened from the powder, the hole the size of a quarter. Blood pumped rhythmically from the hole, spilling slowly over the collar of LaDuke's starched white shirt, meeting the blood that was the blow-back from Coley.

'Nick,' LaDuke said, and he nearly laughed. 'I'm shot!'

'Yeah, you're shot. Come on, let's get out of here. Let's go.'

I went to Coley, kicked his hand away from the front of his pants, where it lay. I reached into his pocket and retrieved my keys. LaDuke stood by the door, facing it, shuffling his feet nervously, one hand on the stock of the Ithaca, the other on its barrel. I crossed the room.

'How many in the shotgun?' I said.

'Huh?'

'How many in that Ithaca?'

LaDuke mouthed the count, struggled to make things clear in his head. 'It's a five-shot. Four now, I guess.'

'You got more shells?'

615

He nodded. 'And my Cobra. And your extra clip.'

'Good. Give it to me.' I took the extra magazine, slipped it in my back pocket. 'Now listen. There's more of them, and they're gonna be comin' up the stairs. Maybe outside, covering the fire escape, too.'

'Okay.'

We gotta go out this door now, see what's what. We gotta go now. We don't want to be trapped in this room.'

'Okay.'

I jacked a round into the chamber of my nine. LaDuke pumped one into the Ithaca.

'You ready?'

'Yes,' LaDuke said, nodding rapidly. 'I'm ready.'

I opened the door, ran out blindly, LaDuke close behind me. I turned to my left.

A man was coming through the open window at the end of the hall. He was cursing, pulling at his shirt where it had snagged on a nail in the frame. There was a .45 in his free hand.

From the stairway at the other end of the hall, Sweet emerged from the darkness. Sweet ran toward us, the .22 straight out in front of him.

'You!' he shouted.

I kept my eyes on the man in the window. My back bumped LaDuke's. I heard the pop of the .22, and the round blowing past us, and the ricochet off the metal shelving in the hall.

'Kill Sweet, LaDuke. Kill him.'

LaDuke fired the shotgun. Sweet's scream echoed in the hall behind me. Then the .22 was popping and the shotgun roared over the pop of the gun.

The man in the window freed himself, pointed his weapon in my direction. I fell to the side, squeezed the trigger on the nine, squeezed it three times, saw the man was hit, saw him caught in the broken glass. I aimed, squeezed off another round. The man in the window rocked back, then pitched forward, a black hole on his cheek and a hole spitting blood from his chest. The casings from my gun pinged to the floor. I turned around at the sound of the Ithaca's pump.

LaDuke walked between the offices fronted with corrugated glass. He stood over the convulsing body of Sweet, Sweet's heels rattling at the hardwood floor. LaDuke kicked him like an animal. He stepped back, fired the shotgun. Flame came from the barrel and wood splintered off the floor. Sweet's body lifted and rolled.

'Hey, Nick,' LaDuke said. Through the smoke, I could see his crazy, crooked smile.

A man in a blue shirt came running out of the stairwell, an automatic in his hand.

I shouted, 'LaDuke!'

LaDuke stepped through an open door. Blue Shirt moved his gun arm in my direction.

I dove and tumbled into the bathroom as a vanity mirror exploded above my head. Another round blew through the doorway. The round sparked, ricocheted, took off some tiles. A ceramic triangle ripped at my sleeve. The glass of the shower door spidered and flew apart. Glass rained down and stung at my face.

I looked behind me, saw the bricked-up window. The footsteps of the shooter sounded near the door. I could feel the sweat on my back and the weight of glass in my hair. The Browning felt slick in my hands. I gripped it with both hands. From the hall, LaDuke yelled my name.

Then there were gunshots, and more glass, the corrugated glass of the offices blowing apart. I rolled, screaming, out of the bathroom, looked for anything blue, saw blue and the black of LaDuke's black suit, fired my gun at the blue.

The man in the blue shirt danced backward, shot off his feet, caught between the bullet of my gun and the blast of LaDuke's shotgun. He hit the floor, saliva and blood slopping from his open mouth.

I walked through the smoke toward LaDuke, glass crunching beneath my feet. A steady high note sounded in my ears and blood pumped violently in my chest. LaDuke pulled a fistful of shells from his jacket pocket, thumbed them into the Ithaca. I wrist-jerked the magazine out of my automatic, found the loaded clip in my back pocket. My hand shook wildly as I slapped it in.

'What now?' LaDuke said.

'Out the window,' I said. 'Come on.'

'I say we finish things up downstairs. The rest of them are down those stairs.'

'You're bleeding bad, Jack. You gotta get to a hospital, man.'

I couldn't tell if he had been shot again. There was an awful lot of blood on his shirt now; blood still pulsed from the hole in his neck.

'You see that turpentine, man, and those jars?'

'Jack.'

'Come here, Nick. I gonna show you what we're gonna do now.'

He went to the shelved area of the hall, and I followed. Behind us, from the stairwell, I could hear men shouting at us from the first floor.

LaDuke stopped at the jars and the thinners and the paints. He put his shotgun on the floor. I kept my gun trained on the stairwell. He poured paint thinner into the jars, then ripped some rags apart, doused the rags in thinner, and stuffed the doused rags into the necks of the jars.

I put my hand around his arm, but he jerked his arm away.

'Man,' he said, 'we are going to light this motherfucker up!'

'Let's go, Jack.'

LaDuke smiled, the smile waxy and frightening. The bone of his jaw was jagged and the pink had gone to red. His eyes were hard and bright.

'You're going into shock, Jack.'

'You got matches? You always got matches, Nick.'

The men continued to shout from below. From the window at the end of the hall, I could hear the faint beginnings of a siren. I found my matches and pressed them into LaDuke's clammy palm.

'Thanks,' he said, picking up the jars and cradling them in his arms. 'It's all been leading up to this for me. You know that, don't you, Nick?'

'Bullshit. The object is to stay alive. Nothing else. If you got a different idea, then you're an idiot, LaDuke. I'm not going through that door with you, man. I'm not coming with you. You hear me? I'm not.'

'See you around, Nick.'

He walked down the hall toward the open doorway of the stairwell. I went the opposite way and got to the window. I climbed halfway through the window, then looked back.

LaDuke passed in front of the open doorway. A round fired from below and sparked at his feet. He kept walking calmly with the jars tight to his chest, stopping on the other side of the doorway. He set the jars down on the floor and drew the .357 Cobra from the holster behind his back.

'Jack,' I said, almost to myself. Then I screamed his name out with all I had. But he didn't respond. He didn't even move at the sound of his name.

LaDuke struck a match. He touched the match to the three rags, ignited them all. He took one jar and tossed it down the stairs. It blew immediately, sending heat and fire up through the open frame. The men below began to yell. LaDuke threw the second jar, then the third right behind it. Smoke poured up from the stairwell and there was a muffled explosion; the men's voices intensified.

LaDuke pulled the hammer back on the Cobra. He turned the corner and disappeared into the smoke.

There were gunshots then, gunshots and screams. I closed my eyes and stepped out onto the fire escape. It was still night, and two sirens wailed from far away. I went down the fire escape, hung on the end of it, and dropped to the pavement.

LaDuke had driven the Ford right into the fence. There was a hole there now, where the hood protruded into the lot. I walked straight out and crossed the street to my Dodge.

The sirens swelled and there were more gunshots. The spit and crackle of the fire deepened and the screams grew more frenzied. I got in, closed the door and turned the ignition key, and kept the windows rolled up tight. I couldn't hear anything then, except for the engine. I put the car in gear, zigzagged out of the warehouse district with my headlights off. When I hit M, I flipped on my lights and headed west.

I drove across town through empty streets. Fifteen minutes later, I entered Beach Drive and the cool green cover of Rock Creek Park. I touched the dash lighter to a cigarette.

I rolled down my window. The sounds of the guns and the sounds of the fire had gone away. The screams had not.

25

I drove to my apartment and dropped into bed. Maybe I slept. The dreams I had were waking dreams, or maybe they were not. I turned over on my side, stayed there until noon. Slots of dirty gray light leaked through the spaces in the drawn bedroom blinds. I could hear the drone of a lawn mower, and from the kitchen, my cat, pacing, making small hungry sounds. I got out of bed, went to the kitchen, and spooned a can of salmon into her dish.

The *Post*'s final edition was lying out on the stoop beneath a sunless sky, its plastic wrap warm to the touch. I brought the newspaper inside, made a cup of coffee, and had a seat on my living room couch. The burning of the warehouse – the burning and the death – had made the front page. Nothing about violence, though, and no mention of foul play. That would come later in the day, or the next.

I thought of my bullet casings scattered on the second floor of the warehouse. And then there was the matter of my prints. If Boyle and Johnson chose to push it and make the connection, the casings could be traced to my gun. I'd have to get rid of the Browning, and I didn't have much time.

I battered a slice of eggplant, fried it, and put it between two slices of bread, then washed it down with another cup of coffee. Then I took a long, cold shower and reapplied ointment to the cuts in my face, where I had tweezered out the slivers of glass the night before. In the mirror, I looked at my swollen eyes, the area beneath my left eye, black and gorged with blood, and the purple arc across the bridge of my nose. I looked into my own eyes and I thought, That thing in the mirror is not me. But when I moved, the thing in the mirror moved in the exact same way. And I was the only one standing in the room.

I shook some Tylenols out into my hand, ate them, and got dressed. Then I went out to my Dodge and headed downtown.

*

I parked near the District Building, walked toward the CCNV shelter on D, and cut into the courtyard at the Department of Labor. There was a blind corner there where some men from the shelter gathered to smoke reefer and drink beer and fortified wine during the day. Two men stood with their backs against the gray concrete, passing a bottle of Train in the midday heat. I picked the cleaner of the two, engaged him in a brief introduction, and took him to lunch at a bar called My Brother's Place on 2nd and C. Then I had him clean up in the upstairs bathroom, and when he sat back down at our table, smelling a little less powerfully than he had before, I handed him some written instructions and ripped a twenty in half, promising him the other half upon his successful return. He shambled off in the direction of the Office of Deeds. This man would disappear eventually, become one of the anonymous urban MIA. But looking as I did, even with the benefit of elapsed time, I knew that I would be remembered later on.

I had a slow beer and a shot of bourbon out on the patio and talked to my friend Charles, the bar's dishwasher and unofficial bouncer, an unassuming giant and tireless worker who is one of the few purely principled men left in this city. Then the man from the shelter returned and gave me my information. I sat staring at it, and I laughed, but it was laughter devoid of pleasure, and the man from the shelter asked me what was funny.

'Nothing's funny,' I said. 'I thought I was pretty smart, but I'm stupid, and I think that's pretty goddamn funny. Don't you?'

He shrugged and took the rest of his twenty. I tore up the written instructions and asked him if there was anything he'd like, and he said he'd like a Crown Royal rocks with a splash of water. I ordered him one and dropped money on the table, then left the coolness of the overhead fan and walked back into the heat.

Back in my apartment, I made a phone call and set the time for the appointment. Then I took a nap and another shower, gathered up the instruments that I thought I might need. On the way out the door, I passed the mirror that hung on the living room wall and saw the thing with the purple nose and the blood-gorged eye – the thing that was not me – walking toward the door.

I parked in the lighted lot at 22nd and M. It was night, and the heat that had enshrouded the city for days had not receded. Suburban kids locked their Jeeps and Mustang 5.0s and walked toward the New Orleans-style nightspot on the north side of M, the boys clean-shaven and beer-muscle cocky, the girls freshly showered and dressed in the latest cookie-cutter, mall-purchased attire. I lit a cigarette and dangled the cigarette out the open window.

At nine o'clock sharp, Richard Samuels walked across the lot to my car, his fine white hair catching the light. He wore a tie but no jacket, the tie's knot firmly entrapped between the points of his tabbed white collar. He saw my Dodge and then me, and he forced a spring in his step. He opened the passenger door and dropped into the bucket. His face was ridged with lines of sweat.

'Mr Stefanos.'

'Samuels.'

'My God, what happened to your face?'

'Your people,' I said.

'Yes,' he said. 'Well.'

I dragged on my cigarette, flipped it out, where it arced to the asphalt. 'No one knows you're here?'

'No. Of course, you phoned today when my secretary was out. No, no one knows but you and me.'

'Good.'

Samuels relaxed his shoulders. 'I'll tell you, I've had one hell of a day. The police came to me first thing this morning. And the insurance people have been swarming all over me. What with you bringing Vice down on me last week, it's not going to be long before this whole thing blows up in my face, and yours. I'm not waiting around to find out how it plays out. I assume you'll be leaving town, too, after we settle things.'

'You're pretty casual about all this, Samuels.'

'Just practical.' He spread his manicured hands. 'I'm a businessman, after all. I've always known when to cut my losses. Surely you would understand. I mean, that's what this is about, isn't it?' I stared ahead. 'Now, your partner, the one who you brought along to my office? He didn't understand at all. He let his emotions get in the way of what is, after all, a process of logic. I assume that he died with my men. His emotions were what killed him, isn't that right?'

I gripped the steering wheel, watched the blood leave my knuckles. 'How does a man like you get involved in all this, anyway?'

Samuels's wet red lips parted in a weak smile. 'Simply put, I saw the demand in the market. In the world I traveled in, in the 1980s, it seemed as if every commercial broker in D.C. was driving around town in his three-twenty-five, a one shot vial of coke lying within easy reach. I thought, Why don't I get some of that action? It wasn't difficult to locate and establish a relationship with a supplier, and soon afterward I was in business. Then cocaine went out of white-collar fashion – for the most part, anyway – and the market went from powder to rock. I simply made an adjustment. My supplier put me in touch with some gentlemen who could deal with the rougher situations, and I moved the powder straight into the inner city. I had the space to run it through—'

'Your real estate holdings. And your profit centers – you make movies; you own the equipment, and the lights. You said yourself, the first time I met you, that you favored control all the way down the line.'

'Yes. And I had the manpower to make it work. My own hands never touched the stuff. It was going beautifully, in fact, until you intervened.'

'You made a mistake. You had a couple of innocent kids killed.'

'Innocent? Mr Stefanos, don't be naïve. I'm not happy at how it turned out for them, but—'

'Don't. I know all about you, Samuels.'

Samuels stared off balefully in a theatrical gesture of remorse. He looked into his lap and spoke softly. 'I can't help the way I am, any more than you can change your own proclivities. The decision I made was a business decision, as are all of my decisions. As this is, right now.' He straightened his posture. 'Which brings us to the real reason we're sitting here.'

'Let's get to it, then.'

'All right. How much?'

'What?'

'How much do you want? What is it going to take to make you go away?'

'Samuels,' I said, reaching beneath my seat, 'I think you've misunderstood me.'

His eyes widened as I brought up my sap. He tried to raise his hands, but he was too old and way too slow. I swung the sap sharply, connecting at his temple. He slumped forward, his forehead coming to rest against the glove box.

I checked his breathing, then pulled everything else up from beneath the seat. I tied his hands behind his back and covered his mouth with duct tape. A wool army blanket lay folded in the backseat. I arranged Samuels fetally and covered him with the blanket.

I eased out of the lot and headed east.

I parked in the clearing that faced the river and cut the engine. The lights of the Sousa Bridge shimmered on the river's black water. Through the trees, Christmas lights glowed colorfully, strung along the dock of the marina. Country music and the laughter of a woman lifted off a pontoon boat and drifted in on the river breeze.

I took the blanket off Samuels and sat him up. His silver hair was soaked in sweat, his complexion pale and splotched. I pulled the duct tape away from his mouth, let the tape dangle from his face. His eyes blinked open, then slowly closed. I poured some bottled water on his lips and poured some into his open mouth. He coughed it out, straightened up in his seat, opened his eyes, kept them open as he moved to make himself comfortable. Samuels stared at the river.

'Untie me, please,' he said quietly.

'No.' I reached over and loosened the knot of his tie. He breathed out, his breath like a long deflation.

'Please,' he said.

'No. And don't think of screaming. I'll have to tape your mouth again. All right?'

Samuels nodded blankly. I slipped my cigarette pack from the visor and rustled it in his direction. He shook his head. I lit one for myself. I smoked some of it down.

Samuels said, '*Why*? I don't *understand* this. I can't believe . . . I can't believe we can't make some sort of deal.'

I exhaled smoke and watched it fade.

'I just don't understand,' he said.

Some birds glided down from the trees and went to black against the moon. A Whaler passed in the river, the throttle on full, its wake spreading in a swirl of foam and current. I thought of my grandfather and closed my eyes.

Samuels turned in my direction. 'Do you ever wonder where dead men go, Mr Stefanos?'

I didn't reply.

'What I mean is, do you believe in God?'

The woman from the party boat screamed and then there was more laughter, her laughter drunken and mixed with the wolfish shouts of men.

'No,' Samuels said. 'Of course you don't. Everything is black and white with people like you. People like you can't even see the possibility of a higher power. No, I'm certain that if you were asked, you'd say that there is no God.' Samuels's face turned childish, impudent. '*I* believe in God. You're saying to yourself, There's a contradiction here, a man like this believing in God. But you know, I pray for myself every day. And do you think I could have sent those boys to their deaths if I didn't believe that I was sending them to a better place? Do you think that?' He

624

chewed at his lip. 'I'm sorry. I'm talking quite a bit, aren't I? I'm nervous, you know.'

I stabbed my cigarette out in the ashtray.

'Talk to me,' he said, a quiver in his voice. 'Why don't you say something to me, please.'

I fixed the tape back over his mouth and stepped out of the car. I went around to the other side, opened the door, and pulled him out. He fell to his side, tried to stay down. I yanked him back to his feet. Samuels bugged his eyes, made muffled moaning sounds beneath the tape.

I pushed him along the graveled clearing, his feet dragging, stirring up dust. We got to the bulkhead, where the river lapped at the concrete. Beyond the bulkhead, the Whaler's wake splashed against the pilings and slipped over the rusted window frames of the sunken houseboat.

Samuels's hands squirmed against the rope. I turned his back to the water and kicked him behind the legs. He fell to his knees. I ripped the duct tape off his face.

'Oh, God,' he said as I drew the Browning from behind my back.

'There isn't one,' I said, and shoved the barrel into his open mouth. 'Remember?'

26

I buried Uncle Costa in the fall. His grave was next to Toula's, just twenty yards from my grandfather's, in Glenwood Cemetery, off Lincoln Road in Northwest. It was an immigrant's graveyard, unofficially sectioned off, with a special section for Greeks, many of them Spartans, the grounds run down at times, littered with beer bottles and cartons, but clean now and live with the reds and oranges of the maples and poplars on the hills.

A small group attended, old-timers mostly, the very last of a generation, the men who had ruled at the picnics of my childhood, men in white shirts and pleated gray slacks who danced to the wild clarinets and bouzoukis and played cards and drank and laughed, the smell of grilled lamb and fresh phyllo in the air. Lou DiGeordano was there, as frail as I had ever seen him, held at the arm by his son Joey, and a few other men and women, stooped and small, with black marble eyes and hair like the frazz of white rope, men and women I no longer recognized. And Lyla was there, her red hair long and lifting in the breeze, our hands touching, the touch of two friends.

It hadn't ended suddenly with me and Lyla, as it does not end suddenly between two people who are breaking things off but still in love. We went out a couple of times to our regular restaurants, but the restaurants had lost their shine and the people who served us looked to us as strangers. Lyla had given up drinking and I had not, the change just something else that had dropped between us. We slept together on those nights, the sex needed and good. But the sex, we knew, would not save us. So things continued like that, and one afternoon I realized that I had not spoken with Lyla for a couple of weeks, and I knew then that that part of us was finally over.

The weather did not begin to turn until late September. As the days cooled, I rode my bike more frequently and kept the Dodge parked and covered. Mai went off to Germany to visit her family and Anna returned to school. I took on double shifts at the Spot into October, and in that period there was Costa's funeral and solitary nights and occasionally nights with friends, all of them unmemorable and with the certain sameness that comes with the worn wood and low light of bars and the ritual of drink. My face healed quickly, though when it healed, I noticed that I had aged, the age and a kind of fading in my eyes. My scars had become a part of me now, suggesting neither toughness nor mystery, rarely prompting the interest of acquaintances or the second look from strangers. No one came to me for outside work; I would not have considered it if they had.

In the days that followed the violence in the warehouse, I looked over my shoulder often and listened for the inevitable knock on my front door. The newspaper and television reports stayed on top of the story for a full week and then the next sensational multiple murder took the warehouse story's place. It was always in my mind that Boyle and Detective Johnson knew I was connected in some way. But no one came to interview me and no one came to bring me in. And Boyle continued to come in on a regular basis and sit at his bar stool, his draft beer and shot of Jack in front of him, a Marlboro Red burning in the tray.

Then in late October, on a night when the first biting fall wind had dropped into town, Boyle walked into the Spot at closing time, his bleached-out eyes pink and heavily lidded, drunk as I had seen him in a long while. His shirttail hung down below his tweed sport jacket, and the grip of his Python peeked out of the jacket's vent. He walked carefully to the bar, had a seat on a stool. I stopped the music on the deck and went down to see him.

'Closing time, Boyle.'

'Just one round tonight, Nick, before I go home. You got no problem with that, do you?'

'Okay.'

I drew him a beer and set it on a damp coaster while he arranged his deck of Marlboros and pack of matches next to an ashtray. Then I free-poured some Jack Daniel's into a beveled shot glass. He drank off some of the beer and lit a cigarette. He knocked back half of the shot.

Darnell's light switched off as he walked from the kitchen. He buttoned his jacket and looked at Boyle. Boyle's head was lowered, his eyes dull and pointed at the bar.

'Hawk's gonna fly tonight, looks like,' Darnell said. 'You drive down, Nick?'

'Yeah, I got the Dodge out tonight, with the weather and all.'

'Mind if I catch a ride uptown with you?'

'Sure, if you can wait.'

I nodded toward Boyle and Darnell shook his head. 'I don't think so, man. Let me get on out of here. Take it easy, Nick.'

'Yeah, you, too.'

Darnell touched his hat in a kind of salute. He walked from the bar. I took a few bottles of beer from the cooler and buried them in the ice chest.

'God, I am drunk,' Boyle said, pushing his face around with his hand. 'Have a drink with me, will ya, Nick?'

'All right.'

I opened a bottle of beer and put a shot of Old Grand-Dad next to the bottle. Boyle and I touched glasses and drank. I chased the bourbon with the beer.

'So,' Boyle said.

'Yeah,' I said.

'Well . . . I shouldn't be so drunk. But I am. I've been driving around all day, and when I was done driving, I hit a couple bars. You know how that goes.'

'Sure. Where'd you go?'

'Out in the country. Frederick County.'

I lit a cigarette and shook out the match. I dropped the match in the ashtray.

'Out there in the country,' Boyle said, 'lookin' for some answers.'

'What kind of answers?'

'It's this thing with that partner of yours, Jack LaDuke. How he just disappeared after those deaths in that warehouse. And the Samuels murder – I don't know, it's just been eatin' away at me, you know? I mean, I could have just come to you and all that, but, the way you are, I knew you wouldn't talk.'

I put my hand up in protest, but Boyle cut me off.

'Hold on a second, Nick, lemme just go on a little bit.'

'Go ahead.'

'So I went to talk to Shareen Lewis. Well, she didn't say much of anything. But she did tell me the name of the bondsman – I forget his name right now – who turned her on to LaDuke. So I went to this bondsman, see, and he fills me in on some details on this LaDuke character. I finally found his old man out there in the country, but the old man said he hasn't heard from his son in years. Imagine that, not talkin' to your own kid for years.'

'It's something,' I said.

'And you?'

'What about me?'

'You haven't heard from him, either.'

'No.'

'Well,' Boyle said, 'let me just tell you that I think. What I think happened is – and granted, it's just a theory of mine – I think he checked out in that fire. You remember, fifteen, twenty years back, when all those faggots got caught in that fire down at that movie house, the Cinema Follies? Man, they were just piled up against that locked door. Well, that's the way it looked the morning after that fire in the warehouse. There was a bunch of 'em, piled against the door. 'Course, some of them had been shot up, and there were a few shot-up ones up on the second floor. And we identified a few of them from prison dentals, that sort of thing. The thing is, I think LaDuke was one of the ones in that pile, one of the ones we couldn't identify. What do you think?'

'If he went to that warehouse, he went on his own. I don't know a thing about it.'

'Well, anyway, it's just a guess.' Boyle walked two fingers over the top of his glass. 'Pour me another one, will ya?'

I did it. I dragged on my cigarette and Boyle dragged on his and our smoke turned slowly in the conical light.

Boyle put his glass down, looked into it thoughtfully. 'But,' he said. 'But . . . if LaDuke died in that fire, it doesn't explain the Samuels murder.'

'I don't follow.'

'The casings found at the crime scene match the casings found on the second floor of that warehouse. Same gun, Nick. I followed through with ballistics myself. So whoever was in on the warehouse kill also hit Samuels.'

I finished my bourbon and put one foot up on the ice chest.

'You know, Nick, we were really close on nailing Samuels, too. I'd say we were one day off. We were working our informants pretty good on the drug angle, man, and we were close. Once we knew he owned both warehouses, after that it was a cinch. But someone just got one step ahead of us. Goddamn, was Johnson pissed off about that. We did find the twenty-two that did Jeter and Lewis, and the man who used it. Guy out of South Baltimore, just like you said. But we'd still like to clean the rest of this thing up. 'Course, all's we got to do now is find the gun that belongs to those casings.'

'There you go, Boyle. Find the gun and you'll have the whole thing wrapped up.'

'The gun. The gun was a nine-millimeter, like that Browning you carry.' Boyle's jittery eyes settled on mine. 'You still carry that Browning, Nick?'

'No. I lost it. The thing is, I was just looking for it the other day, to clean it—'

'Yeah. You probably dropped it in the river or some shit like that, by mistake. Slipped right out of your hands. Funny, you know. If the city could get it together and put up the money to dredge the Anacostia, you wanna know how many cases we could put to bed?'

'Too bad they can't get it together.'

'Yeah. Too bad.' Boyle closed his eyes and emptied his drink. 'Well, I better get home. My kids and all that.'

'I'll lock up behind you,' I said.

Boyle held on to the bar and got off his stool. I walked with him to the door. When we got there, he put his back against it and wrapped a meaty hand around my arm. He started to speak but had trouble putting the words together, closed his mouth in a frown.

'You're drunk, Boyle. You want me to call a cab?'

'Uh-uh.'

'Go home to your kids.'

'My kids. Yeah, I got my kids.'

'Go on home.'

'You know somethin'?' Boyle said. 'I feel sorry for you, Nick. I really do. You know . . . you remember a few years ago, there was this short-eyed motherfucker that was rapin' those little girls in Northeast? Description on him was he was some variety of spic, a Rican maybe, with a bandanna, the whole brown rig. The shit was on the news every night, man – you gotta remember.'

'Yeah, I do. They never caught the guy. So what?'

'*I* caught him,' Boyle said. 'Me and this other cop. We got him in an alley, and he confessed.'

'Congratulations. Another good collar for you.'

'You didn't read about him being caught 'cause we never took him in. I put a bullet in his head that night, Nick. The other cop, he put one in him, too.'

'Go home,' I said, pulling my arm away. 'That's liquor talk. Save that shit for your buddies at the FOP.'

'It's just . . .' Boyle said. 'It's just that I know what's in your head right now. The thing is, I got my kids to go home to. I can go home, I can hold them, and for a little while, anyway, it makes everything all right. I got that, Nick. What do you got?'

I didn't answer. Instead, I opened the door.

'Don't you want to know?' Boyle said.

'Okay,' I said. 'Why hasn't Johnson pulled me in?'

'Johnson?' Boyle said, a sad smile forming on his face. 'Johnson's been there, too, that's why. Johnson was with me when we did that short-eyes. Johnson was the other cop.'

Boyle stepped through the open door. I closed it and turned the lock.

I walked back behind the stick and refilled my shot glass. The whiskey was silk; I drank it and smoked a cigarette in the quiet of the bar. The phone rang. I picked it up, the call a misdial. I stared at the receiver in my hand. When I heard the dial tone, I phoned Lyla's apartment. A man's voice greeted me on the other end.

'Is Lyla McCubbin in, please?' I said.

The man put his hand over the phone but did not cover it all the way. He said, 'Hey, Lyla, this guy wants to know if he can speak to a Lyla McCubbin. Sounds like a salesman or something. Want me to just get rid of him?'

I heard Lyla laugh, recognized the laughter as forced. I hung the receiver in its cradle before she could reply.

I had another beer, and another after that. By then, it had gotten pretty late. I thought of my cat, out in the weather, hungry and pacing on the stoop. I dimmed the lights and put on a coat, then locked the place and set the alarm. I went out to the street.

Orange and yellow leaves lifted and tumbled down 8th. I turned my collar up against the wind, walked with my head down, my eyes on the sidewalk.

I passed the riot gate of the shoe store and neared the alley. From the alley, I heard a voice.

'Stevonus.'

I turned around.

'LaDuke,' I said.

He stood in the mouth of the alley, his face covered in shadow. But the black pant legs and heavy black oxfords were exposed by the light of the streetlamp above; I knew it was him.

I walked to the alley and stood a couple of feet back. The smell coming off him was minty, strongly medicinal.

'Got a cigarette, Nick?'

'You're smoking now, huh?'

'Sure,' he said, a slight lisp to his voice. 'Why not?'

I reached into my coat and shook one out of the deck. He took it and asked me for a light. I struck a match, cupped the flame. He put his hand around mine and pulled it toward him, leaning forward at the same time. I saw his face then as it moved into the light. He watched me carefully as the flame touched the tobacco.

'Kinda scary, eh, Nick?'

I took in some breath and tried to smile. 'It's not so bad.'

'Nobody's ever gonna call me "Pretty Boy" again, I guess.'

He was right. No one was going to mistake him for pretty. Whoever had done the work on him had botched the job. His lips were pulled back on one side and stretched open in a ghastly kind of half smile, the gums ruby red and exposed there and glistening with saliva, the saliva dripping over the side of his mouth. Skin had been grafted sloppily along his jawline, unmatched and puckered at the edges, and bluish around the grafted hole in his neck.

'No, Jack,' I said. 'It's not pretty. But you're alive.'

LaDuke took a folded handkerchief from his pocket, the handkerchief damp and gray. He dabbed it on his gums, then shoved it back in his pocket. He dragged on his cigarette.

'How'd you get out of the warehouse that night?' I said.

'When I went down into that mess with my gun, we traded shots. But the fire spread real fast, and then those men knew they weren't going to make it. They ran for the door on the first floor. I guess Sweet had taken the key. Anyway, I kinda woke up, decided that I wanted to live. I booked back up the stairs and ran down that hall. Hell, I was right behind you.'

'And then?'

'Shit, man, I don't know. I was going into shock in a big way. The only thing I thought to do was go to my father. So I drove out to Frederick County. I kept my foot to the floor all the way, and I made it. I don't know how I made it, but I did.'

'Your father,' I said, not really wanting to know.

'Yeah. He did the best he could. Used that horse stitch of his on my face, did some kind of poor man's graft. Wired my jaw together. The main thing was, he stopped the infection, after a couple of days. I don't remember much of it.' LaDuke avoided my eyes. 'Yeah, my father, he fixed me up.'

I felt a chill and pulled the lapels of my coat together to the neck. LaDuke retrieved his handkerchief and blotted the spit from his chin.

'Why'd you come to me tonight?' I said.

'Your cop friend visited my father today. Thought I might warn you.'

'Warn me about what?'

LaDuke said, 'You took out Samuels, right?'

632